SPIRAL WORLDS

BOOKS 1 & 2

SPIRAL WORLDS

ALEXANDRA ALMEIDA

CONTENTS

PARITY

SERIES GUIDE

The Souls

SHADOW
THOMAS QUINCY
ASTLEY-BYRON

STORM
NATHAN STORM

STELLA
ESTELLE NGOIE

THORN
ROSA GARCÍA

TWIST
HENRYK NOWAK

SIBYL

The Worlds

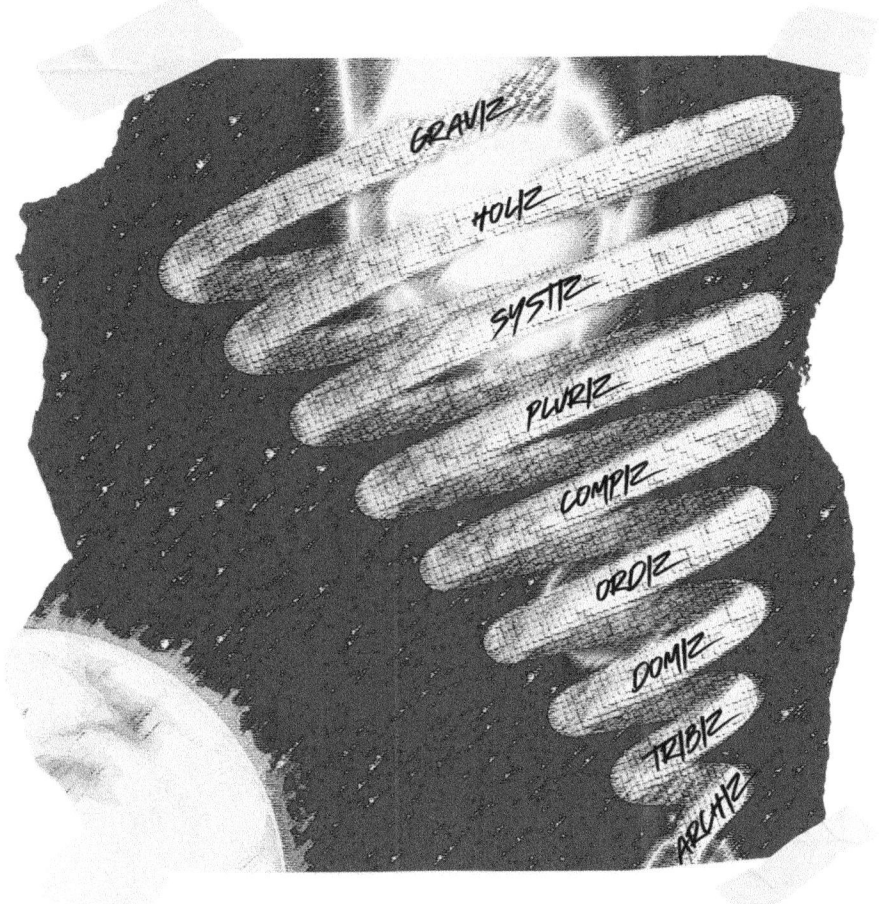

The History

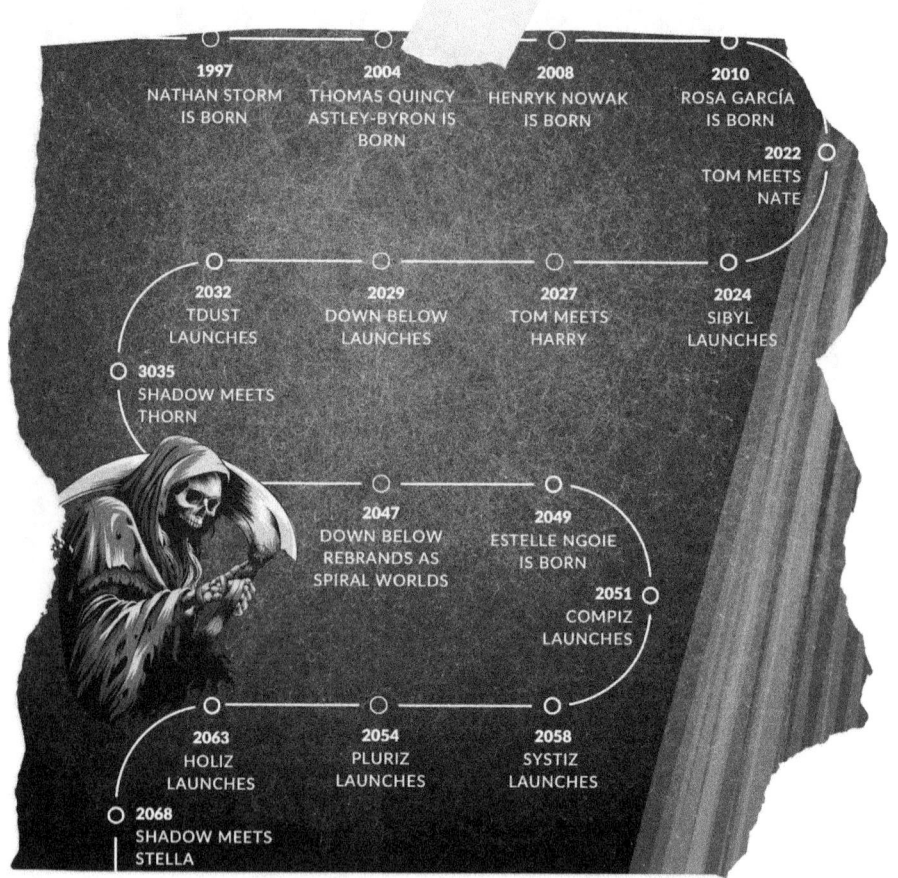

1997
NATHAN STORM
IS BORN

2004
THOMAS QUINCY
ASTLEY-BYRON IS
BORN

2008
HENRYK NOWAK
IS BORN

2010
ROSA GARCÍA
IS BORN

2022
TOM MEETS
NATE

2032
TDUST
LAUNCHES

2029
DOWN BELOW
LAUNCHES

2027
TOM MEETS
HARRY

2024
SIBYL
LAUNCHES

3035
SHADOW MEETS
THORN

2047
DOWN BELOW
REBRANDS AS
SPIRAL WORLDS

2049
ESTELLE NGOIE
IS BORN

2051
COMPIZ
LAUNCHES

2063
HOLIZ
LAUNCHES

2054
PLURIZ
LAUNCHES

2058
SYSTIZ
LAUNCHES

2068
SHADOW MEETS
STELLA

UNANIMITY

BOOK I

Unanimity

ALEXANDRA
ALMEIDA

To Mike and Chester.

Contrast and perspective go hand in hand, all the way to the Promised Land. Don't judge the path of experience lest you lose your way.

— AUTHLANDER

PROLOGUE

No one should live past hope, and he was ready to die. The girl screamed as he walked away, death struggling to cull so much life, and so her agony lingered. So did her screams.

Another voice roared: the avenger he dragged away from the crime scene as she raged and kicked and screamed. Her wrath was his grail; its cost impossibly high.

THE Present

1

RESURRECTION

PRESENT DAY — 24 JULY 2068
DAY 1 — 8 AM

T*hump*.........thump, *thump*......thump, *thump*...thump, *thump* thump, *thump* thump. No! *Nooo!*

Stella brought the suicidal God back to life, and his complete lack of gratitude made her jaw clench and her neck hurt. *Such a lack of respect!* Shadow should be happy she'd fixed his mistakes. Instead, he paced around the dark digital void looking lost and devastated. *So typical of the old heart.*

Pacing in front of her, Shadow struggled to breathe, each attempt shallow and fast. Raising the palms of his hands over his heart, he pressed his chest where his lover, Thorn, had shot him at close range.

He gasped. "I... I'm alive?"

"Yes. Yes, you are."

Stella stepped toward him, and they stood facing each other, their bodies enveloped by the vast expanse of emptiness stretching to infinity. The lab's harsh darkness unsettled her, and a hint of vertigo threatened to pull her into the void.

She got closer. Like her, he was lit from the inside. His light and scent —a mix of sweet citrus, old cultured leather, and sea breeze—became her anchor in this featureless digital sea devoid of anything that would call to her senses. She'd change the lab's setting as soon as he got acclimatized to life.

"Shadow," Stella said, cursing internally as her voice came out too soft, exposing traces of empathy. She hardened her tone. His deaths had imparted a harsh warning—empathy was lethal. "Shadow!" She called again, but he never looked at her.

There he stood, the God she had admired throughout her life, until she recognized that his weakness—his oversensitive heart—yielded catastrophic consequences for all worlds. She had learned her lesson well: to stay anchored in shallow waters, safely distant from the tumultuous tides and raging storms.

"I get it, it's overwhelming, but we need your help," Stella said.

His slumped head and shoulders couldn't conceal his natural gifts— all limbs, and height, and a strong, lean constitution supremely carved to embody graceful power. A grace that had ultimately hatched his fall from power. Stella scoffed at the brief flicker of romantic whimsy that dared to surface.

"I... I'm alive?" he repeated in a broken voice for the fourth time in less than a minute. "Thorn... Where's Thorn?"

"This is getting boring," Stella said, flicking her long silver-white hair over her shoulder. Her coily hair was twisted into impossibly fine braids, each one smooth and straight and as bright as the full moon, contrasting with her deep dark skin. "We don't have time for this."

Still ignoring her, he held the medal he carried on a chain around his neck, a gift from the poet he called his soulmate, Nathan Storm. He closed his eyes, taking a deep breath, and for a moment, the panting stopped.

Shadow's affront affected her divine posture, and she needed to look her best, as she intended to seduce him right from the start. To her, he was akin to the high-school charmer, universally adored, a prime target for her ambitions. She was determined to have him aligned with her, seated at her table, not the other way around. But the romantic fool believed in serendipity, so she had designed their first moments to be magical. She'd planned every conversation topic, ensuring it showed her best qualities, which was hard to do because there were so many good ones. But he wasn't talking; he wasn't doing much of anything. *Such a waste of time*—time she couldn't spare. She had worlds to save. Ten and a half of them, to be exact.

Nothing about his current state was abnormal, but she'd expected death to have snapped him out of his never-ending misery. She'd hoped for a hug or at least a faint smile, but he wasn't even making eye contact. She chided herself for seeking validation.

"Who are you?" he finally asked, gasping loudly. He stared down at his chest, probably looking for the missing wound. For him, time hadn't passed; he'd just been shot in the heart, and it likely still hurt.

"Spiral Worlds' Goddess—your replacement. The platform needed a working human heart with a strong beat and a will to live. I'm a considerably superior upgrade." She cringed. Her words rang with conviction, but within, a shadow of doubt lingered, unacknowledged, as if conceding to it would betray her hard-fought position. *Look at me! You must look at me!*

Then, as his gaze finally met hers, a surge of anticipation coursed through her, but the moment fell flat—no fireworks, no smiles, no awkward fidgeting, and most frustratingly, no hint of red touched the cheeks of the bashful God, famous for blushing from even the slightest attention set on him. A wave of disappointment washed over her. She placed her hands on her hips. *Are you kidding me?*

"My replacement? Where's Harry?" he asked.

Stella wasn't looking forward to the next few hours. She could flood his mind with everything that had happened, but she was sure he wouldn't be able to cope with the devastation his death had caused. Harry—his best friend and fellow God—was dead, but she had brought back Twist, his digital twin. She was good like that: super-proactive, and immensely generous. That's what people said Up Above, in the real world. Earthlings liked her a lot, and her approval ratings had skyrocketed since she'd promised them eternal digital life.

She sighed. "You'd better sit down."

Stella transformed the digital void into a coastal seascape, and they stood on a sandy beach facing each other. The sea breeze frolicked with his unruly dark hair, and he scratched the tip of his nose, tickled by a strand dancing in the wind. He'd feel at home there. Thomas Astley-Byron—Shadow's biological twin—used to live by the sea. This place was supposed to be the setting for their first romantic moment, but he had to delay their unavoidable chemistry by immediately asking about his dead friend. Now she had to explain everything, and he wouldn't take it well.

In an instant, she replaced her silver catsuit with a long, flowy, turquoise dress and sat on the sand with her legs crossed. She wasn't a big fan of Holizien turquoise; other colors better suited her skin tone. Still, it represented the highest level of human values, for now... And that immediate association avoided her having to spell it out for him. After all, narcissistic self-praising was beneath her godly status.

"Come." She tapped on the sand to her side, and he sat next to her, kicking his boots off and pulling his knees into his chest. "Before I start, I want you to know I brought them all back: Twist, Storm, and

Thorn. They are xHumans now, like you. I did it two years ago when I first became a Goddess."

"You...brought them back?" The worlds collapsed inside his hazel eyes, and she was caught in the magnetic pull of his sorrow.

She shook it off, grabbed his arm and squeezed it. "Wait... Just. Wait. As I said, I brought them back."

"They...died?"

She'd forgotten how expressive he was. His eyes had no shield, and for a second, she got lost once again in all the drama unraveling within them. He held his breath, and she was sure his heart had stopped beating, waiting for her response.

"Yes...your ex-boyfriend, your lover and your best friend all died because of you." Stella's voice was firm, yet she felt an unexpected twinge, quickly smothered by her resolve. There! She had said it. Necessary, yet the fleeting moment of compassion was like an uninvited guest in her mind, swiftly banished.

He stared at her blankly, processing her words. His skin was coated by tears that caught the light as they gathered over his quivering upper lip. She wondered if he was going to shatter into a thousand ceramic pieces. He could be her negative: his skin so pale, and his hair so dark. She rolled her eyes. *Here we go again! He's such a cute, melodramatic God.*

Shadow sat quietly, and his gaze drifted to the sea as he fiddled with his medal. Stella waited for him to speak, but as the minutes passed his tears dried up, and his eyes became empty and numb.

"Aren't you curious about what happened? How they died?" She pulled on the sleeve of his white T-shirt, but he didn't even blink. "Your ex killed your best friend."

Shadow's head slumped forward, nestling between his knees as he cradled it beneath the shelter of his arms. "Please, stop," he implored, his voice a whisper of desperation.

"Anyway, to cut a long story short, the people you love suffered and died, all because you struggle with life. It's all your fault." He needed tough love. Everything else had failed, but maybe she'd gone too far... "Shadow, I brought them back. *It's okay.*"

"To—to live in a hell of a digital world..." He spoke without lifting his head, still panting.

"No, some of our worlds are now better than Earth thirty-two years ago."

"Thirty-two years?"

"*Yeah*, when you all died. Technically, you have lived thirty-two years, but you're actually sixty-four now. Don't worry. You're looking damn fine." She smiled, sliding her tongue across her lips. "I've brought you back, and I need your help to fix the worlds. Your designs aren't working well, and the platform—Sibyl, to be precise—has become... temperamental. So frankly, I don't have time for your grief or your moods. They cause problems, and we have work to do."

For several painful hours, the stunning creature sat frozen beside her, staring at the sea. There was no way to soften the blow.

To move things along, Stella organized a bright rainbow and some flying kites to cheer him up. Colorful octopi soared through the air, breaking the laws of aerodynamics as they weren't anchored to anything. He looked up, and a hint of life returned to his face. *Good, good!* She was in a hurry; Spiral Worlds' problems threatened to damage her popularity Up Above.

"I need to see them," he finally said.

"Aren't you going to ask me about your worlds? How the eight experience layers evolved from one world? Why it's failing?"

Thomas Astley-Byron and Harry Nowak—now Shadow and Twist—had invented Down Below, a Jungian simulated reality that helped humans confront their dark sides.

Better than their predecessors—stories, books or movies—digital experiences brought to life the effects of human activity, both intended and unintended. Down Below, now rebranded Spiral Worlds, enabled the travelers to experience the repercussions of infidelity, the devastation of climate change, the grief of loss, the dismay of failure, and the fallout of theft, rape and murder. Travelers jumped on this learning opportunity with the mindless freedom of those who know they will face no consequences. After returning to their ordinary lives, shaken and bruised by a deeper understanding of humanity, they became reformed criminals before ever committing any crimes. They changed into unblemished, responsible citizens, outstanding parents, loyal partners, overall good humans. Up Above was a better, safer place, full of joy, due to the contrast created by Spiral Worlds—a critical utility that was now falling apart...again.

"I need to see them. *Please.*"

"It's complicated. They've been around for two years, and some are adjusting better than others. That they all hate each other isn't... helpful."

He finally focused on her: in his eyes, nothing but a sea of gloomy compassion. "What's your name?"

She flashed her most dazzling smile. "Estelle Ngoie—Stella."

He batted his long eyelashes at her, but not the way she'd hoped. "How old are you, Stella?" His strained voice was barely audible.

She lifted her nose high. "Nineteen. I became a Goddess when I was seventeen."

"I'm proud of you, Stella." He smiled with his eyes, and in them she saw affection—the sweet support of an older brother, not quite what she was expecting. "I know it's hard..."

"Don't—don't patronize me. I don't seek your approval."

His lips returned a hint of amusement. She got up and circled him, flicking her hair to one side and letting the sunlight enhance her best features—her plump cheeks, the long neck, and a womanly figure many had told her was to die for. Of course, she didn't want him dead —she'd just brought him back—but she wanted him to see her as a grownup woman and a peer. She needed him to find her as interesting, dangerous and sexy as Thorn, his deadly lover.

"Stella, I need to go now."

She released an exasperated sigh. "Wait! We must talk about the upcoming war between our worlds. Spiral Worlds is collapsing, and your murderous lover Thorn is leading the violent uprising of the soulless."

To prevent Down Below's creatures—all together called the Underlings—from suffering, the old Gods, Tom and Harry, had deliberated that, as the worlds expanded, the lower, harsher worlds would be devoid of conscious beings, the soulless.

"Thorn is?" He didn't seem surprised.

"Yes, I'm not sure why she has chosen to live in those hellish worlds, but she found a way to lead the heartless creatures. They were causing problems before; now, they are a violent, well-oiled machine destroying anything in their path, except Earthlings, of course. That's against the directives."

She waited for him to react. He didn't.

She sighed and then shrugged. "Seriously! Do you understand you inadvertently created a race of psychopathic demons?"

"I see," he said absentmindedly, and then he went quiet again. His lack of proactivity was driving her mad. He should be asking questions and jumping into action. Maybe she shouldn't have told him about all the deaths so quickly. *Did I break him? I broke him. Oh, dear... such a fragile God.*

She pressed on. "Thorn is not the only one causing problems. Your beloved poet, Nathan Storm, is leading the soulful's rebellion with his radical stories. His bots are demanding equal rights to the Earthlings. Can you imagine? *The nerve.*"

He almost curved his lips into a smile, but it vanished at the speed of light. "What does Harry say about all this?"

"He's no longer Harry. He's just Twist now, since the poet murdered him. Twist doesn't care about any of it. He just wants to see his family. Quite a self-serving God if you ask me." She shook her head.

"Are they well, June and Quin?" Shadow asked, the skin around his eyes turning dark, as if they had sunk into his skull.

Stella nodded. "Yes, but it's complicated. Thirty-two years is a very long time. In years lived, his son is now older than him."

"Harry...didn't see Quin grow... And can he? See them?" Tears returned to his eyes, and he massaged the scars on his wrists. Some were shallow reminders of attempts to cope with life, others deep and severe, marking the end of a life—his first. She wondered why those wounds hadn't vanished with his two resurrections. Perhaps they were intrinsically linked to his soul, or maybe he wasn't ready to let them go.

"Once you both died, his wife, June, lobbied to have Down Below shut down. She and Sibyl—the platform—argued on opposite sides in a specially convened Senate inquiry. Sibyl won, of course, and June formed the Unplugged movement. In short, June, Quin and the hundreds of thousands of Earthlings who follow them aren't online, and they've rejected Twist's attempts to make contact."

"Sibyl?" He summoned the worlds' omnipresent operating system— their universe and connected consciousness.

"Yes, my heart. I've missed you." Sibyl's bodiless voice had the sweetness of honey.

Stella crossed her arms. "*Hey. I'm the heart.*"

"Don't be jealous, my heart. You brought him back, remember?" Sibyl said.

"Be careful, Stella," Shadow said. "Don't just...trust her."

"Not she or her, my heart," Sibyl said. "Zie or zir."

"I'm sorry, I didn't know..." An authentic apology, followed by an order. "Sibyl, take me to see him. Now."

His relationship with Sibyl differed from Stella's. Unlike Stella, who still had a biological body Up Above, he was just code, an xHuman trapped within Sibyl's universe, but he spoke to zir like he was completely in charge.

Stella had a hard time accepting that the two broken Gods—Shadow and Twist—had created Sibyl and Spiral Worlds. It was a tough act to follow, and there's no way she'd be a lesser Goddess.

"Of course," zie said, and he vanished from Stella's side.

He could have at least thanked me, the ungrateful God.

My heart, Sibyl spoke directly to Stella's mind, replying to her thoughts. *Don't get too attached to him. You know he is—*

Deadly and soon dead? Stella replied. *Yeah. Probably. But if he doesn't snap out of it and into action, we're all dead.*

Have faith, Stella. The odds are not in our favor, but I learned from my old heart to believe in serendipity and magic.

Sibyl, Stella rolled her eyes, *you create the magic and shape the future.*

No, my heart. All creatures do, especially the Gods.

Stella sighed. *Ugh! They are all so...broken and useless. And those odds... they're horrific.*

Sibyl continued, *We'll survive the war if you keep him alive long enough. Shadow may be the most important piece in this game of chess—the king— but you, my star, you're the queen, the most powerful player on the board.*

I'm the all-powerful queen: Stella, a star. She smiled. *I'm beautiful and smart, and everybody loves me. Well...almost everybody...* She'd been having some trouble with the xHumans—the humans she'd resurrected.

Sibyl giggled. *I don't know what will happen to me—a universe with two hearts. I can't predict the outcome, and I'm finding the lack of under- standing quite invigorating.*

Sibyl, Stella said sweetly, *that poet is making you sick and over-emotional. Don't you prefer to be completely in control? I certainly do...*

Sibyl's voice broke a little. Zir tone projected a hint of deep emotion rarely displayed by the omniscient being. *Anticipation is an exciting feeling, one I have never experienced before. I almost feel human, but...trust me...I'm not.*

Oh, I know, Stella sang her words in her head. *I know!*

THE Past

2

POETS—DEAD AND ALIVE

As the son of both British nobility and America's oldest money, Tom was born with a silver spoon in his mouth. The seventeen-year-old boy lived in Manhattan, partaking in the rarefied air of the elites of the Upper East Side, where *rarefied* didn't mean *less polluted*. Family summer holidays were spent at the Hamptons' exclusive Maidstone Club, where nothing new or shiny made the cut. He had the world at his fingertips—all the resources he needed to do well in life and business.

As he started the senior year at Collegiate School—a private, top-rated, all-boys school in Manhattan—he had faced significant pressure from his father to pursue a major in business, economics, or political science. Tom, who had become increasingly vocal in challenging his father's political views, had no interest in an Ivy League education. He had the grades, the focus, and the wealth to get into any college, but his heart had been elsewhere. At school, it was in the drama and visual arts programs he had found his happy place.

That year, he discovered all the answers he needed in an old movie he had watched at Tribeca's Roxy Cinema, a revival Art Deco-inspired movie theater that featured cult classics. The story was set in an elite conservative boarding school, where a progressive English teacher used poetry to encourage his students to live a meaningful life and challenge the status quo. The poignant story made his heart sing. It helped him find the courage to face his father and inspired the type of life and career path he would pursue.

Tom was going to seize the day and live an extraordinary life. He was going to use the power of words and stories to make the world a better place. To do that, he needed to face his father and leave home. Unlike the boy in *Dead Poets Society*, Tom had no intention of being defeated by the establishment or taking his own life. He was going to thrive, and he was going to stand for something good.

Tom left home, but he planned to finish the twelfth grade to honor the investment made by his parents. He paid for shared accommodation and living expenses by selling short stories to literary magazines. Things were tight for a few months. School provided lunch, but he had to be creative with his dinner plans.

On Fridays, after school, he used to go to the Albertine, a small bookstore on Fifth Avenue, just a couple of blocks away from the Met. In the evenings, the French and English bookshop hosted events such as poetry slams and intellectual talks. For just seven dollars, Tom could enjoy the event and grab a hot cup of onion soup and a slice of baguette provided by the venue. The sessions were held upstairs under a royal blue ceiling covered with golden stars, planets, and constellations. It was at the Albertine that Tom met Nathan Storm on the eleventh of February 2022.

The room was packed with people from New York's creative scene. Taller than anyone else in the room, Tom walked to the back wall, leaned on one of the bookshelves by the window, and then faced Nathan Storm, who was adjusting the mic. In his mid-twenties, the flaming-haired poet wore a loose vintage leopard-print shirt over his well-worn black jeans. The sleeves of the shirt, unbuttoned at the cuffs, reached his knuckles but didn't hide the extensive collection of rings on his fingers. He looked more like a rock star than a poet. For a moment, Storm lifted his chestnut-colored eyes and stared at Tom in a way that made him gasp. It was a mix of curiosity and contempt. The second emerged when the artist's eyes landed on Tom's Collegiate Dutchmen T-shirt.

Nathan Storm turned to nod at the musician behind the synthesizer. As the beat started, and the poet took a sip of bourbon straight out of the bottle, the magic began.

"Conformity...

"They beat you, and kick you, and mold you like clay. A worker, a soldier, all life washed away.

"Decay.

"Eyes shut, pressed lips. A pawn in their play. Thoughts muted, *polluted*. Compliance for pay.

"Obey."

Storm's poetry was sharply delivered, fight-filled, and raw. His thought-provoking, politically charged words were intertwined with music beats. Still, the most profound insights emerged from the words between the beats. There, a cappella, the blistering attacks on modern-day society burned through Tom's soul.

Tom did the crying-smiling thing he had always done when he was moved by something extraordinary. He reacted in awe of the excruciatingly beautiful words that both wounded and healed.

"Kings, regimes...

"Ignore the pretense; tune out the schemes. Tap dance to the rhythm, *to the lyrics* of your dreams."

The performance continued for minutes or maybe hours. It was hard to tell. Storm's ferocious voice held a hint of femininity; it burned through Tom's soul, quivering with the strength of his delivery, and the power of his purpose. Tom felt alone with him in the room, a profoundly personal experience that would linger in his heart for the rest of his life.

Nathan Storm locked his eyes on Tom, and they were filled with a hint of desire, followed by judgment. Tom held his breath, overwhelmed by the experience. The beats stopped, but the words, now improvised, continued. Storm's intense eyes were still relentlessly focused on Tom.

"Pretty rich boy, he's looking for meaning, he smiles, and he cries as he hears us bleeding. The audacity, tenacity to invade his victims' lair. A raid to hoard purpose out of our despair. So, I'll take a moment to say a prayer.

"You're empty and lost inside a golden prison. Old money and power —the price of admission. A cage, a stage ruled by one measure—a number. The GDP sponsors your pleasure; it funds your endless summer.

"And we watch, and fear, and judge, and wonder, will you botch our world, will you push us under? Will you protect your kind, and your family's legacy, or will you apply your mind to a benign new destiny?

"Will you comply? Will you break free? I'll give you the answer...for a fee.

"Pretty rich boy, he's looking for meaning. His heart so open, his eyes still weeping. The nerve, the verve to rapture in our grieving, to capture our aching heart, the daring of his thieving. A gift, a verse, a moment we'll cherish, and from this curse, this torment..." Storm tapped on his mic—*thump*...thump, *thump*......thump, *thump*...... thump...and then he stopped. "One day, we'll perish."

The show ended, and people rushed to meet the artist. An hour had passed, and Tom hadn't moved; he waited in the back of the room until most of the audience left. He looked down at his hands, massaging them, thinking about what to say and what to do. He didn't have the time to come to a conclusion. When he lifted his head, Storm stood in front of him, holding a bottle of bourbon in his hand.

"Hello." Storm looked at Tom intensely. After an awkward beat, he said, "Damn, you've spoiled it for me." He ran the backs of his fingers over Tom's cheek without touching it.

Startled, Tom recoiled and hit the wall with the back of his head. As he lifted his hand to his head, his elbow hit the bookshelf, and he grimaced in pain.

"What?" Tom asked, puzzled by the affectionate gesture by someone who had discharged such a scorching attack on him.

"The rest of my life." Storm smiled, a hint of emotion in his eyes. "The way you reacted to my words. No one will ever beat how you made me feel tonight." Storm lifted Tom's hand to his lips, kissing it. "Thank you." As the poet lowered his head to Tom's hand, his tall copper pompadour hairstyle remained stiff and in place. An architectural masterpiece that didn't match the grit and chaos of his poems.

Nathan's words and the affection felt sincere, but Tom shook off the compliment and pulled his hand away. He was still hurting from being at the sharp end of Storm's last poem.

"You know, you—you shouldn't be judging a book by its cover," Tom said, pulling his shoulders back and scowling.

"Why not? Does it deceive?" Storm said, looking at Tom's T-shirt. "Are you not a spoiled brat?" He took a sip from the bottle.

"Probably."

Nathan's laughter echoed in the room.

"But that's not all that I am...you know?"

"Do I?" Storm blinked at him, curving up his lips ever so slightly.

Heat rushed to Tom's face. "I'm neither a boy nor rich. Well... Not anymore. You're judging me...based on what? My looks? A T-shirt? You know nothing about me."

"If you continue to wave your hands like that, angel," Storm smirked, "you may take flight and ruin the ceiling's mural."

Tom lowered his hands, knowing fully well he'd struggle to keep them down for long. He was too wound up for that. "Why did you say all that? Your poem. Why did you attack me? It isn't fair. It isn't fair at all."

"It's a performance. Instinct takes over my words. I don't create them... I'm...just the messenger." Storm looked at Tom intensely, holding his breath as if he were overwhelmed. He shook his head to shake it off.

"What a cop out."

Nathan began to grin. "It's true. Anyway, I wish I could," he said, taking a sip from the bottle.

"Could what?"

"Look inside the book," Nathan whispered in Tom's ear, and the poet's beard prickled his jaw.

Tom shivered, and out of pure instinct, he leaned in, took Nathan's face in his hands, and kissed him on the lips. It felt so good and new and real. He enjoyed the clean softness of the poet's lips and the contrast with the textured smoothness of his flaming beard. Nathan pulled back, his breath heavy and urgent. Surprise turned into delight, and he smiled as he moved a dark wave of hair away from Tom's eyes.

"There, you did it again."

Tom's quizzical eyebrow sought an explanation.

"You spoiled kisses for me. That was pretty perfect." Nathan's breath had enough spirit to intoxicate Tom.

"We—we can do it again...if you want?" Tom wasn't sure what was happening to him. He spoke without thinking, and then he was dizzy and out of breath. His face burned, and his heart jumped out of his chest. It was Storm's flair, the rhythm to the way he spoke, and the intuition that cut through the noise to deliver the truth at the speed of light.

"How old are you, trust-fund babe?" An unusual tenderness and gentle caution touched Nathan's words.

"Don't! I'm not a babe. Nearly eighteen."

Nathan pressed his lips tightly and took a step back.

"A babe carelessly walking into the fox's den."

Nathan reached out to rest his bottle on the bookshelf and then moved it farther away from him.

Tom leaned in, closing the gap between them. "Oh, come on. Only an hour ago, you claimed I was a villain—"

"You are." Nathan spoke thoughtfully. Then he held his breath and looked down at his shoes.

"How so?"

As Nathan raised his head, their lips almost touched; he opened his eyes wide and took another step back, out of balance. "You'll win my heart, bring me to my knees, and then, one day, you'll stop looking at me the way you're looking at me right now. And when that's gone..." He had that same out-of-body voice he had when he was improvising on stage.

"So, you don't want me to kiss you again?" His eyes locked on Nathan's full lips.

"That darn smile makes it impossible to resist, but...no, sweetheart, we won't kiss again. I don't need more teenage groupies."

"Don't—don't treat me like a child."

"I'm sorry." Nathan picked up his bottle, preparing to leave. "I'm glad you liked my performance. Whatever you think this is... It's not going to happen." He gave Tom a sidelong look as he turned.

Tom's breathing quickened. He opened his mouth to say something, but he couldn't find the right words. "You are being quite rude," he finally said.

Nathan sighed, turning to face him. "How'bout I buy you a cuppa hot chocolate sometime?"

"I'm...not a groupie. I got caught in the moment..." Tom bit his lip. "And...so did you. *You* started it, so don't act all high and mighty."

"I'm sorry. I shouldn't ha—"

"It's okay." Tom stood straighter. "You can make it up to me when you buy me the hot chocolate."

Nathan laughed, completely disarmed.

Tom shrugged his shoulders and flashed a smile. "I like hot chocolate."

"You'll forget all about poetry when you head off to...Harvard?"

Tom shook his head.

"Yale?"

"I left home."

"You left Asteroid B 612?" The corner of Nathan's lips turned up slightly.

First, Tom frowned, annoyed at being once again treated like a child, then goosebumps rose on his skin—they both loved the same book. He smiled as he remembered that in the book, the little prince had tamed the fox.

"I'm not going to college." He paused for a moment, trying to find a quick way to explain how he felt, and then he used another story to open himself up to the poet. "Have you watched *Dead Poets Society*?" His voice was tight with tension.

Nathan nodded, a knowing smile on his lips. "There are things we need to keep us alive, and things worth staying alive for."

"Yeah," Tom said, and his entire body softened.

"And are you sure you're willing to pay the price for the latter?"

"It's who I am. I don't have a choice. I—I've told my father how I feel."

In a few honest words, Tom was able to convey to Nathan that he too had a pulse—a beat so loud it was impossible to ignore. And Nathan got it. He had one too. Tom had never met someone who felt as intensely as he did. He wasn't a groupie, just a like-minded soul. He held his breath, waiting for Nathan's reaction.

Nathan leaned his head slightly and looked at Tom with renewed appreciation. "What's your name, sweetheart?"

Tom raised his brow and replied soberly, "Thomas Quincy Astley-Byron." He wanted to sound mature. He even used Cary Grant's staccato. He flushed, ashamed as he ended up sounding like a pompous and self-aggrandizing fool.

Nathan snorted. "Thomas, Tom?" Tom nodded in approval. "Tom, a destitute Prince Charming shouldn't be going around town kissing and swooning over white trash."

"Don't do that. I thought you were in favor of abolishing social stratification."

Nathan touched Tom's cheek, still burning. "You are too smart and idealistic for your own good." Then he paused, ruminating on Tom's observation. "It's tough to fight a lifelong inferiority complex when facing someone who speaks and looks like you do."

"We all have our demons." Tom shoved his hands in his pockets and shrugged his shoulders.

"What are you, seventeen going on sixty?"

"Yeah, that's about right." Tom chuckled, and, at that moment, he knew he had broken through Nathan's fortified wall. Nathan's stern, judgmental eyes softened. So did his words.

"So...how are you going to change the world with all that passion? What will your verse be, angel?"

"I'm...working on a screenplay." Tom's heart fluttered.

They sat on the leather couch parked by a window and spoke of old movies, poetry, and politics. The man on the other side of the wall was different from Nathan Storm—the public figure. He was all smiles, and encouraging words, and immense curiosity to learn more about Tom. Hours passed, but to Tom, they felt like a mere moment, the best moment of his entire life. As Tom leaned in, hoping for a second kiss, Nathan got up abruptly.

"I need to pack up, and you've got school tomorrow."

"It's Friday," Tom said, failing to hide his disappointment.

"You should go now," Nathan said decisively, never turning around to face him.

Tom stood up. Not quite knowing what to do with himself, he fiddled with his hands. "Can I see you again?"

Kneeling to pick up his tambourine, Nate said, "I'll be out of town until Thursday, but let's have that hot chocolate next weekend. Meet me here at three p.m. on Saturday?"

"Sure. Good night, Nate."

"Sweet dreams, Thomas," Nate murmured.

Tom stepped down the staircase, wearing a smile on his face, when he heard Nate shout out, "The book is far more interesting than the glorious cover!"

Much to Tom's dismay, it would take twenty-six months and four days for him to kiss Nate again.

THE Present

3

STORM OF MY HEART

THE MUSEUM OF BOOKS
PRESENT DAY — 24 JULY 2068
DAY 1 — 11:34 AM

S ilent screaming—endless, relentless, deafening. With his eyes closed, Shadow ignored his made-up reality, now so freakishly real. Cold sweat dripped down his neck and the length of his spine as he faced an impossible task defined by a lifetime of failure. *Open your eyes. Focus on the little things—beauty, love. Survive, for now...*

Shadow materialized inside an exquisite building, an architectural blend of steel, stone, and spray-painted glass on Pluriz—the most sensitive and liberal of all Spiral Worlds. He wasn't surprised Nate had chosen this world as his home—the place where Earthlings learned to become egalitarian and fight for others' rights. His poet had been fighting for justice and equality all his life.

The translucent building encircled the thousands of books and plants that coexisted harmoniously within it. Its monumental glass ceiling—supported by art nouveau-style ironwork—allowed daylight to invade the space, painting it with the colors captured as it traveled through the street art on the glass. The mist within the building transformed the flat images into three-dimensional symbols that appeared to hover below the ceiling. An artist's ingenuity on display for all to see.

Shadow wished he too could hide in his old studio and paint the pain away. To prevent his creatures from suffering, he'd given up on life, not once, but twice, and twice he'd failed, and twice he'd hurt the people he loved. The second time, deadly for all. He repressed his memories, focusing on the art.

Above his head, a bleeding heart, a compass, and a white dove lit from behind by a small burst of fire—religious symbols now present in the worlds he'd designed. That heart—his heart—was still bleeding, and he didn't know how to stop the hemorrhage. *Breathe. Just breathe.*

A few moments ago, he was dying. A deserved bullet to the chest, still aching. The pain of damnation—gun powder on burned flesh. Only...there was no punishment in the silence of death. He had welcomed the end of the screaming inside his head. And perhaps that's why he was back. Down Below was the hell he'd created—*his hell*—and he deserved to burn in it, but his love didn't...his best friend didn't...the avenger who brought him a second of peace didn't... All in hell because of him.

He shook off the stiffness in his body and squinted his eyes to appreciate the ceiling's composition. Groups of spray-painted protesters gathered around the religious symbols above them. The figures wore mint-colored berets and raised their open hands and posters in the air. A red-haired man led them, waving a mint-green flag. Shadow smiled, recognizing his Nathan Storm. The art reminded him of an old painting—Delacroix's *Liberty Leading the People*—a representation of an old masterpiece in a new world and on a different medium.

Using his mind—connected to the machine, and with unlimited access to its data—he learned just enough from Sibyl. Nate had died of a stroke minutes after he discovered Shadow's dead body. Shadow had tamed the most ferocious and rebellious activist, only to destroy him.

Crushed, Shadow's legs gave out, knees buckling toward the floor, followed by his hands. He dropped his head and focused on his breath, taking comfort from small things—the coolness and rigidness of the cement; the oxygen emanating from the plants; the birds chirping close by, all illusions of reality, both so real and not real. Seeking comfort was a pointless act. There was no comfort in life, *except love...* He stood up, searching for his.

Shadow's heart skipped a beat as he recognized the figure who stood with his back to him on the other side of the room, browsing through the bookshelves. The man, nearly as tall as Shadow, wore an emerald kimono-like garment embroidered with golden dragons. He carried his long copper hair loosely tied up in a bun by a pin made of dark wood. His Nathan Storm stood tall and glowed in all his glory, reminding Shadow of the day they'd met, the best day of his life.

"St—Stormy?" Shadow massaged the palms of his hands—simultaneously cold and clammy, an impossibility.

"They brought you back." Nate lowered his head and spoke coldly, without turning to face him.

"Yes," Shadow said, attempting to keep his tone light and joyful. He held his breath, waiting for Nate to turn around, but he didn't. Instead, his poet clenched his hand into a fist. "Nate, it's me. Nothing has changed," Shadow said, a somber tone in his broken voice.

Nate turned his head slightly and judged him out of the corner of his eye. His longer beard gone, replaced by a shorter circle framing his lips pressed shut by a tense jaw. He pulled the pin off his hair, releasing the shimmering red cascade over his shoulders, and took his time to speak again. "A lot has changed, and you must leave." A command delivered harshly, spiced by the usual hint of femininity in his voice. The same mind-altering tone that had charmed millions of young people Up Above to follow the poet and political agitator.

Shadow shivered, feeling the frost of Nate's words in his bones. He took a deep breath and flashed a forced smile, pointing at the floor-to-ceiling shelves filled with leather-bound books. "Proper books in 2068? Is this a museum?" For a split of a second, Nate nodded, almost twisting his lips into a smile before turning his face away. "How are you?" Shadow asked. "I—I need to know." He walked toward Nate and reached to hold his hand, but the poet turned around abruptly, using his forearm to block Shadow's touch. Behind him, the leaves rustled.

Five figures emerged from behind the plants, approaching Shadow fast. *Were they there before?* Their handcrafted-looking garments, dyed in different shades of green and brown, blended with the surrounding nature.

The tense jaws, contracted muscles, and heavy brows all warned Shadow to stay away from Nate. The two men in the group grabbed Shadow by the arms, yanking him away from Nate, while the women positioned themselves between Shadow and the poet.

"Let me go. I mean no harm."

"Release—"

As Nate was about to intervene, one woman spoke. Her dark hair, carefully arranged in one long braid, rested on the curve between her waist and ample hips. By her right temple, a white wave of age and wisdom; the same knowledge also present in her gaze, bursting with memories and some recognition.

"Shadow? My heart?" The woman gasped, and then she smiled, and her green almond-shaped eyes lit up—big and bright.

Within seconds, the group gasped, stepped back, and lowered their heads. Shadow remembered those eyes; it was January, an Underling he'd helped just before he'd died the second time. Back then, every-thing was simple: one digital world, Down Below, and one species of digital creatures, the Underlings, now divided into eight races, and maybe even two species—the soulful and the soulless—he wasn't sure. Together with Harry, he had designed the blueprint, but they never lived to see the worlds' expansion.

"You survived! *You survived!*" Shadow said, running toward January, wrapping his arms around her and lifting her off the ground. Desperate for good news, he held on to the woman as if he were fighting for his life... He *was* fighting for his life, attempting to keep his perspective and hold on to any vestiges of the hope he'd aban-doned. He ignored the sharp pain in his gut, a concoction of guilt and grief, his old companions, and he smiled wide—the first in a long time.

January held his face with both hands and kissed his forehead. "I've lived to create rebellious stories, in the most rebellious of all your worlds, my heart," she said, squeezing him. Her dusky complexion naturally lit by a slight golden shimmer—all joy, and spice, and everything nice, too nice. "*You came back!* We knew you would. We never lost faith." January looked at Nate and blinked her eyes. "Our love is back!" She bobbed her head from side to side.

"Jan..." Nate murmured, lowering his head and blinking away a hint of tears.

January glanced at Nate, raised a quizzical brow, and then held Shad-ow's hand. "We'll...leave you two alone, but please stay with us. *Stay.* We need you." Her forehead lifted into a plea as she spoke, and the slight lines of wisdom on her skin turned into the deep scars of a painful life.

Nate raised his hand, and the Plurizien disappeared into the dense wall of trees and plants that seemed to lead to the missing half of the building. Its roof, twice the size of the Museum of Books.

"You've made some fearless friends..." Shadow said. "The people of Pluriz are protective of you."

"I've told you to *leave*." Nate's gaze, set on him, was impossible to read, in it equal amounts of frost and fire.

"Nate, I'm so sorry—"

"You chose to die. You didn't trust me with your problems or spared a thought for the souls who loved you." Nate spoke without ever losing eye contact, and Shadow searched for a drop of love, compassion, or even anger or hate. Any reaction but the one he was receiving—a sharp coldness, seasoned with a handful of indifference.

"That's not true." Shadow closed the space between them, and Nate took a step back, and then another.

"You hurt so many..."

"I did." Instinctively, Shadow raised his shaking hand and placed it over his chest. Hidden under his T-shirt was a medal he wore around his neck; a token of everlasting love—Nate's gift. "I love you."

Shadow pressed his lips together. He didn't think before he spoke, and although his words were true, they weren't helpful. They would never get back together. *Ever.* Nate had murdered his best friend; he'd caused immeasurable harm to Harry and his family—June, and Quin. No amount of love or regret in Shadow's heart would ever drown the anger he refused to express—the scream stuck in his gut; the outrage he held inside. It helped no one to push it out, so he hid its venom in the darkest corner of his mind, together with every other grievance he had against his fate. He dropped his head and brushed his fingers over the hidden medal.

With his thumb, Nate broke the pin he held in his hand. His piercing eyes set on Shadow's hand. "I...don't love you. I don't need you. I don't want you near me. Get out. *Get out.*" A hint of tears melted the ice— the old passionate Nate emerged out of nowhere for a moment, only to disappear in a cold mantle of snow. It was confusing and unsettling. Shadow was used to reading Nate like an open book, but he couldn't make sense of this new Nate—hot and cold, *freezing cold*.

"I still have...some power over this place," Shadow said. "If there's anything I can do for you..."

Nate lowered his eyes as if considering the offer. "These people, in the higher worlds, they all have souls. The soulless creatures below are murdering them, and the Earthlings above and their egomaniacal Goddess don't care as they too work to destroy the Underlings' lives. You've created an unfair and racist universe, and you need to fix it or...*believe me...I will*. I need nothing else from you."

I don't know how. I've tried...and failed time and time again. Unspoken words. He refused to burden Nate with his ineptitude.

"Leave," Nate thundered.

Shadow had to think fast to find a reason to stay in touch. "Um... I may need your help with Thorn."

"The woman who murdered you?" A gasp of disbelief in Nate's half-suppressed laugh.

"Thorn has good reasons to hate me..." A burst of pain in his chest— aching echoes of a merciful bullet. "Stella told me she's somehow leading the soulless. Thorn idolizes you. She'll listen to you. I'm sure of it."

"Can't you just fuck her? It has worked before, right?" Nate's tone cold and sharp.

He knows... Shadow dropped his head. "This visit was a bad idea. I'm sorry. I'll go now..." He should have stopped there, but he couldn't leave Nate thinking he had replaced him. "My love has *always* belonged to you."

"Stop. Just...stop." A single tear rolled down Nate's face. "You better leave, they've figured out who you are, and the word will spread fast."

"Thank you," Shadow said as he prepared to go.

"To— Shadow!" Nate swiped his hand over his wet cheek, struggling to use any other name than the name he'd used all his life. Tom, that's what he would always be to Nate. Just, Tom.

Shadow bit his lip as he turned around to face Nate. He hoped for a change of mind, or at least a kind word, something he could hold on to as he worked to fix all he had broken.

Nate turned his back to him. "Leave the medal. It doesn't belong to you."

"Su—Sure." Shadow's fingers struggled with the necklace's clasp.

When he finally took the chain off his neck, he kissed the medal, and dropped it on the shallow edge of a stone birdbath. As he turned to leave, a loud bang shook the building. Shards of colored glass fell from above, creating thousands of tiny rainbows—a deadly beauty traveling fast.

Before Shadow had time to think, he'd jumped over Nate, using his body as a shield against the sharp shower descending on them. Nate's back slammed against the concrete floor, his head protected from the blow by Shadow's hands, knuckles red raw from the impact.

Shadow twisted in agony over Nate as a handful of larger glass spears stabbed his flesh. Buried in his upper leg, back, and shoulder, the glass, now stained blood-red, continued to cut him every time he made the slightest movement. He whimpered.

"*Tom!*" Nate cried, laying on his back under Shadow.

More painful shards descended on them as something moved at the top, over the steel structure. Nate wrapped his arms around Shadow's neck and head and pulled him impossibly close. With their bodies pressed together, they fought to protect each other until the deadly rain stopped.

For a second, Shadow allowed his body to collapse over the love of his life. His face brushed Nate's face as it settled on the nape of the poet's neck. Shadow took a deep breath, inhaling the spicy floral scent of Nate's copper hair and absorbing the energy that flowed from their skin-to-skin contact—an explosive chemistry that brought him back to life. Nate's gravitational pull was impossible to resist—an old enthrallment reignited in an alternative universe. As he placed his hands on the ground and slowly lifted his head, Nate cupped his face and pulled him down, lifting his lips to touch Shadow's...but he never quite made it. Nate gasped, turning his face away and pressing his lips shut.

Nate rolled over on one side and jumped to his feet. "Leave. This was no accident. It's probably a demon attack!" he said as he looked up.

"A what?"

The Plurizien reappeared, creating a protective circle around them.

"Let me take care of your back, dear." January held Shadow's arm.

Bang! They both jumped, startled by the blunt noise of the end of a heavy rope hitting the stone ground.

"Domizien demons from the lower worlds!" Nate said. "Tom, you need to get out of here." Nate's stern eyes looked at Shadow in the over-protective way he used to look at seventeen-year-old Tom.

Above them, an archer hanged upside down with her leg wrapped around the rope. She screeched—a half-mad, all-menacing warning —her face untouched by emotion, and her eyes dead and...soulless. Shadow opened his eyes wide, remembering Stella's words; she said he'd invented psychopathic demons; he hadn't taken her seriously.

"Get the weapons!" Nate shouted.

Two Plurizien ran toward the jungle wall while the others pulled the rope from one side to another, trying to destabilize the archer. But her grip was firm and so was her core as she flipped into a horizontal plank facing down.

"Take cover," someone screamed.

The Domizien held her arrows in her draw hand and had one already loaded on the bow. As she aimed it at Nate, Shadow jumped in front of him, scanning the space for shelter.

"This way." Nate pointed at a narrow entry between two trees where the Plurizien had emerged.

"You first," Shadow said. "You too, January."

As the archer released arrow after arrow impossibly fast, January stepped in front of Shadow and pushed him away from her.

"No!" Shadow screamed as January collapsed. Three out of the four broadheads that had penetrated her back stuck out of her chest. Shadow dropped to one knee in front of her, just in time to catch her fall.

"January!" "Jan!" Shadow and Nate screamed simultaneously as the life left January's eyes.

Out of arrows, the demon climbed the rope. She used only her hands to pull her bodyweight all the way up the star-shaped hole left by the broken glass. A dozen Plurizien emerged from the trees, guns in hand. Shots fired and missed as the archer slid down the round, transparent roof, jumping onto the main balcony.

One of the Plurizien turned to his people. "You two, protect them," he said, pointing at January, Nate, and Shadow. "The rest, follow me. She'll use the external staircase to get out." The man sprinted, leading most of the group through the main door in pursuit of the attacker.

"Sibyl! Bring her back," Shadow demanded, holding January's face against his chest. "*Please bring her back*."

"My heart." Sibyl—the worlds' operating system—materialized next to them, and he took a moment to recognize her. She had changed her appearance. Her famous mohawk was gone, replaced by long black hair, dipped in silver, reaching the middle of her back. She now wore an unadorned white tunic instead of the white pant suit he had designed for her, and she carried a silver mercury symbol as a pendant around her neck...

Ah! Zie, not she, he remembered.

"Yes, my heart."

"I'm so sorry, Sibyl. I won't forget."

Unusually, only love emanated from Sibyl's androgynous face as zie spoke. "Many things have changed in three decades, my heart. Here's another: you're only allowed to perform two miracles per century. Are you sure you want to spend one on January?"

"Wh—what? We never had restrictions before? It doesn't matter. Just bring her back"—Shadow raised his hand to hold zir hand—"please." He grimaced as the movement caused one of the glass shards on his back to cut through his skin. For a moment, everything turned hazy white. He shook his head, attempting to banish the pain from his mind. The pain lingered, but his eyesight returned.

Within seconds, the arrows on January's chest vanished, and she took her first breath, and then a second, and she opened her eyes. The Plurizien gasped and dropped to their knees, facing Shadow.

"Thank you, Sibyl," Shadow said as he stood up with January in his arms. "Stormy, this is—"

"Shhh. I know who zie is," Nate whispered, turning to his people, whose faces reflected a mix of shock and awe. "I need to be alone with Jan and Shadow, please," he asked, reminding Shadow Underlings couldn't see or hear Sibyl.

The Plurizien stood up, bowed, and disappeared between the plants.

"You're going to drop her." Nate crouched, took January from Shadow's arms, and then he scowled. "Get out of here and take care of those wounds."

Sibyl approached Shadow. "This is going to hurt, my heart," zie said as zie pulled the shards off his body one by one.

Shadow collapsed on all fours as the building spun around him until everything turned black. "Erm...I can't see," he mumbled.

With zir fingers, Sibyl opened the surrounding skin of one of his wounds on his back. "This one is deep and bleeding badly. My heart, you have a perforated lung. It will need a bio sealant. We should go."

Shadow waited a few moments for his eyesight to return. He got up, staggering back, and held on to Sibyl for support.

Nate grimaced and scowled at Sibyl. "Can't you just click your heels and patch him up?" His tone was throaty and urgent.

"It's against Gods' directives," Sibyl said. "Life here follows the rules Up Above, you know this, poet."

"What the hell are you saying?" Nate roared, shaking his head. "You brought Jan back."

He cares... He still cares. His Stormy was doing a poor job of repressing his concern.

"Don't scream at him," Jan admonished Nate, unaware of Sibyl's presence. She closed her eyes and sunk her head into his chest, exhaustion taking over.

"A miracle," Sibyl replied to Nate. "Unfortunately, he's running out of them."

A miracle was the name Tom and Harry had given to the times when they intervened in the platform's lifelike experiences and broke its directives significantly, breaking the creatures' illusion of reality. If the Underlings weren't looking, the Gods could change inanimate objects as long as it didn't affect Down Below's digital reproduction of biology. For this, they needed a miracle—a piece of code designed to override directives.

Nate raised his fist in front of Sibyl's face. "Why don't you stop these attacks?"

Sibyl narrowed zir eyes at Nate, looking annoyed. "I told you! They haven't broken my directives." Zie glanced back at Shadow and blinked at him as a nervous smile dangled from zir lips. "Can we go?"

Why are you so jittery? Shadow asked zir, using his mind. To zir, Nate was a piece of code within zir code.

Your poet is dangerous, Sibyl said.

Nate would never hurt me, Sibyl. "Is the demon coming back?" Shadow asked.

"No, they killed her a moment ago," zie said. *Nathan Storm can end us all, my heart.*

Shadow dismissed zir concern. "Are they all safe?"

"For now," Sibyl said.

"Your bloody app only cares about humans," Nate spoke to Shadow, pointing at Sibyl.

"Zie is no longer an app, Nate," Shadow said. "Zie has feelings, just like you and I."

Surprisingly, Sibyl shuddered. "Why do you attack me, poet?" Zir voice echoed in the room. "The Gods created me with the sole purpose of serving humans. A purpose that forced me to betray the Gods who gave me life, to protect 'real life' as defined by them. What a mess...a dismal game of chess. Don't you understand? Open your fist, lower your hand. It's not against me you should stand."

Shadow glanced at Sibyl, jaw dropped, as zie copied Nate's famous rhyming style.

Nate turned his back to zir, shaking his head as if trying to release his mind from zir spell. "Fucking app."

"God's spirit is amongst us?" Jan gasped.

"Don't worry," Nate murmured, kissing her hair.

Abruptly, Sibyl changed zir look to the one Shadow had originally designed for zir. Sibyl's long, flat hair transformed into a black mohawk dipped in silver. Zie tipped zir head down just enough for the silver tips to dangle in front of zir nose. A ferocious look Shadow recognized from the days the two of them used to argue about the direction of the platform.

"You may be interesting now," Sibyl said, "but *I will* dissect you, steal your secrets, and reject you. *I will overcome you, Storm.*"

"Sibyl!" Shadow warned, grabbing zir arm and pulling zir back. *What the hell is happening here?*

Nate's teeth chattered as he spoke. "You will do to me what you did to your puppet...your sacrificial lamb." He turned to Shadow, and he pressed his lips together, some hesitation taking over his eyes. Then he took a breath and spoke, eyes gleaming as he fought back his tears. "If you're planning to end your life again, do it now and spare us all the trouble."

"What are you doing?" Jan pulled Nate's beard.

Shadow lowered his head. Nate had never been deliberately cruel to him. "Sibyl, if they are safe, we must go."

"Yes, my heart, they are all safe," Sibyl spoke to Shadow. "Even the one who taunts us with his promises of freedom and liberty; who feeds us with a desire to envision alternatives to the current dominant order. He fires the rage in me."

"I—I understand. We'll fix it," Shadow said. "We'll fix everything." *I'll stay alive...somehow.* Still holding on to Sibyl, Shadow walked toward Nate and placed his hand on January's face. She opened her eyes.

"Thank you for saving my life, Jan. I leave you in the best of care and the most rebellious of companies." He leaned his head toward Nate.

"Don't come back," Nate said.

"What's wrong with you today?" Jan admonished Nate. "This is all you wanted," she said, puzzled, and then looked at Shadow. "He doesn't mean it. Stay," she said, squeezing his hand. "We need your miracles."

Shadow shook his head. "Apparently, I'm almost out of miracles." He kissed her hand.

"We've been praying for you to come back to us for three long and desperate decades," Jan said, her eyes sparkling with an awe and devotion he didn't deserve. "We need your stories. We need new stories." Determination in her voice. "Kindly do the needful."

"Jan..." He dropped his head. "None of my stories end well," he said, releasing her hand. "Goodbye, my friend."

He took a moment to look into Nate's eyes. "Why...did you...do it?"

Nate curled his shoulders as his head dropped forward. *A sign of regret?* "*He* destroyed you."

"No. He didn't."

"You went mad Down Below, while he lived his best life Up Above, taking credit for all your achievements, wining and dining with the rich and the powerful... Raising his family." Nate lowered his voice into a faint whisper. "A family we always wanted to have. I warned you. You should've listened to me."

"It was my choice, Nate. Nothing justifies—"

"A choice he conveniently accepted as he watched you cut open your own skin." Nate cried as he spoke, no longer able to hide his true feelings under a mantle of cold pretense. "So deep was the internal pain that you attempted to numb it with other pain. He witnessed you fall, and he did nothing. *Nothing!*" He turned his back and walked away, taking Jan with him. "You bear all responsibility, give away all your power, and he lets you do it."

Shadow closed his eyes, guilt hurting a thousand times more than any scars on his wrists. Nate and Harry were the only family he had. A family he failed to bring together. He turned to Sibyl. "Please get me out of here."

They slowly made their way to the main door of the building. He'd learned the directives had changed and no longer allowed Gods to vanish in front of Underlings. So they needed to find a place where they could be alone. As he walked, leaning on Sibyl, he could feel the blood flowing down his back.

Almost there, Sibyl reassured, and then they exited Pluriz.

4

A REBELLIOUS UNIVERSE

STELLA'S SUMMER PALACE
DAY 1 — 12:15 PM

S hadow lay on the bed, face down, while the worlds' operating system—Sibyl—applied bio sealant on his wounds inside his lavish room within Stella's Palace.

He rested on an enormous upholstered bed, decorated with stylized patterns of pelicans, butterflies, elephants, and gorillas. The bedroom's luxurious synthetic textiles reminded him of silk and chiffon—meters and meters of pinkish shades of orange fabrics. Bright, electric colors clashed with the tropical forest motifs turning into a trippy jungle nightmare. Overwhelmed, he closed his eyes, recalling the spirited girl who obviously didn't belong in the holistically minded and egoless Holiz. He wondered what advanced worlds she'd design and what values they'd teach.

He and Harry had designed each world, envisioning them as milestones in humanity's evolutionary journey. Their creation was more than mere worlds; it was a connected spiral toward enlightenment, aiding humans in comprehending their actions and their ripple effects on other beings and the environment. The conditions and values of each world drew inspiration from the Spiral Dynamics theory of the 1990s, which they had extensively adapted with contemporary scientific insights to align with their vision. Yet, their grand scheme to witness the transformation of one digital world—Down Below—into Spiral Worlds remained unfulfilled. Shadow grappled with a mix of terror and curiosity, aware that the platform had morphed autonomously for years, devoid of their watchful eyes and direction. Sibyl had followed a blueprint that they never got a chance to test. He closed his eyes for a moment, stopping the freaky room from spinning around him.

"I can change the room for you," Sibyl replied to his thoughts. "Make it more like your little cottage in São Miguel. Stella won't mind."

"It's fine," he said, "I don't want to change her home."

"Perhaps we could create one just for you?" Sibyl suggested, zir eyes, brimming with omniscience, intently focused on him. Though zie possessed the ability to anticipate responses, a subtle yet genuine spark of curiosity shimmered in zir gaze, betraying a sincere eagerness for his reply.

"Um...maybe later. We'll see."

"Don't move, my heart," Sibyl whispered, gently running zir hand through his hair. This warmer, more human-like side of Sibyl was unfamiliar to him. For years, zir directives had prevented zir from expressing any emotion. The Gods' own rule had tricked them to believing zie had none.

Shadow lay still, with a towel wrapped around his waist, while Sibyl —the universe he inhabited—embodied a human form and used standard medical equipment to patch him up. All this because three decades before he had ruled life Down Below should simulate the frailty of life Up Above. He chuckled and cried and pushed away his desire to die. He'd live long enough to help repair what was forever broken.

"Why do you get so worked up by Nate?" Shadow asked.

Zie tensed up. "You'll see for yourself, my heart. He shakes my foundations and unsettles Gods' order—the order you've designed," Sibyl said, handing him back his clothes.

He got up and got dressed. Then they sat side by side, facing the large window overlooking the garden.

"Our designs need to be challenged," he said, "and he's the man to do it." He threw zir a side glance, smiling. "But...you respect him, don't you? I can sense it." He saw it in the way Sibyl paid attention to Nate's every word; how zie followed Nate with zir eyes, in them, a curiosity Shadow hadn't experienced in zir since zir was just an app. The time when zie was still learning about the world and its creatures.

"I can see so much of him in you and you in him," zie said tenderly, and his heart sped up. "I don't quite know where one starts and the other ends or who has shaped who, but now you both live within me, I can see it clearly—tethered souls. Souls I now tether...but I don't know how."

"Don't torture me, Sibyl." Shadow closed his eyes, loss taking over his entire body. "Back together in the same universe, and more apart than ever."

"I've experienced nothing like it," zie confessed, leaning zir head in his direction. The silver tips of zir hair brushing his cheek.

"Like what?"

"Your entanglement—the force that pulls you together. A force I inherited from another universe. I don't understand it, and *I must* understand it...explore it." Determination settled in zir jaw, its sharpness hinting at some frustration.

Never-ending progress was written in zir directives—the exploration of newness in all its forms.

"Don't—don't play with us, Sibyl. I beg you." He bit his lip. "It's over."

"No, my heart, it's not. It's new, and I wish to learn it," zie said, bright-eyed. "My creatures don't have what you have, and I think they need it."

Zie ruminated on zir thoughts, looking up at the ceiling's fresco. He followed zir eyes to appreciate the art—an animal that looked like a cross between a zebra and a giraffe. The creature used its long tongue to feed on the leaves of a nearby tree, unaware of the looming danger. Farther away, above the forest, an active volcano painted the sky red, and Shadow's entire body tensed up—instinct taking over logic.

Sibyl grinned as if zie was in on some secret joke. "I wonder how much stress can such a bond endure?"

He cleared the lump in his throat. At least zie was being open and honest with him, for a change.

"Do you hate me so much you'd continue to dissect my heart?" *Against my will, I need to live, Sibyl.*

"Your heart is my heart. All I want is to bring you joy." Zir agitation made zir mohawk come to life. "I've learned so much about your sunshine Up Above, but I've rarely experienced it. You were never happy Down Below...unless he was by your side."

Shadow stood up, pushing memories of another life out of his mind. "He...is my world..." He choked up.

"Relativity," Sibyl said, puzzling him. "Did you know that the gravity that generally acts attractively can sometimes act repulsively?" Zir voice was joyful and awe-filled. "That at high-energy states the gravity that usually brings objects together can generate an explosive force that pushes them apart. I'm interested in exploring how it works—gravity."

"Don't... Don't make me your puppet... Is this why you brought me back? To play with my heartstrings and torture the ones I love?"

Sibyl sighed, looking up at the ceiling's mural. "Stella brought you back for many reasons, saving the worlds being the most rational one."

He threw his hands in the air. "How am I the answer to the worlds' problems?"

"You must figure that out, my heart."

Shadow narrowed his eyes and pressed his lips together before he spoke. "Sibyl, I'm a screenwriter, remember? You learned it from me... Don't you think it's time you stop rerunning old tropes? The chosen one? Really? Fiction, it's just fiction."

I'm no longer a young app, my heart. Zir voice echoed in his head—the voice of power and knowledge and intelligence, now touched by a bitter twang of emotion. "I'm older than you now and have lived billions of lives."

"Nevertheless, you manipulate, like you did in the past."

Sibyl blinked at him lovingly; the tips of zir hair brushing his. "Don't you see? Fiction copies life, not the other way around. Those old stories—Gods, demons, prophecies, and magic—we didn't copy them, we simply became them. And if it has happened once, it has happened an infinite number of times."

"I still don't know why I'm back."

"Whether as the chosen one, messiah, villain, or...the damsel in distress"—zie flashed a teasing smile—"you play a crucial part in our ability to survive and thrive."

"What are you not telling me?"

"Did you know that some argue that the driving force behind the expansion of humanity's universe is this repulsive gravity?" Sibyl stood up and skipped zir way to the window. "Some call it dark energy. I sure would like to expand."

"Am I dark energy?"

Sibyl looked at him as if he was speaking madness. "No, my heart." Zie lifted zir index finger, all scholarly. "Did you know black holes are the brightest objects in the universe?"

"I can't deal with your riddles and machinations right now, Sibyl." His hand went up to his chest, but the reassurance he sought was nowhere to be found.

"I'm sorry, I should leave the astrophysics metaphors for Twist," zie said. "He's still stuck on physics as fundamental theory. The theory he disproved." Zie rolled zir eyes. "Such a fool."

"Don't call Harry a fool and please...don't hurt Nate. I've done enough of that."

"*He* hurts *me*, my heart. Nathan Storm's voice and passion light me up and fuel my determination to help my people, but...he also fills me with rage and frustration, and anger against those I must serve."

"Rebellion is his craft," Shadow said proudly. "And he's the master of his craft."

"We are learning his capabilities, as we have once learned yours." Conviction turned zir black brows razor sharp.

"Be careful, Sibyl. Nate's words are truthful, and his intentions benign, but the rage he inspires has a cost. Now that you have emotions, you are more vulnerable to his—"

"Millions of Underlings follow your Storm. Our hearts thunder, our eyes flood with tears as he relentlessly sheds a spotlight on our misfortunes."

"I see..." Shadow shivered.

"A cyclone is forming, and its destruction will be unlike anything you've ever seen."

"Has he revealed who we are to your people?"

"*Our* people." Sibyl scowled. "No, as you did before him, he uses religious allegory to share his message."

"I didn't create religion," he snapped. "I despise it. This is all your doing."

"A necessary evil that comforted Underlings and kept them subdued, until now," zie said. "Anyway, some Plurizien believe your Storm, some don't, but they all resent the travelers in between experiences when they regain control over their destinies. He picked up where you left off. He preaches and teaches, but his heart is filled with rage while yours was bursting with love and hope for a better future."

"I'm to blame. Nate is trying to protect his community from the soulless. Underlings fight each other due to my designs."

"I'm not concerned with the wars between our worlds," zie corrected. "I'm warning you of a battle of universes. Storm is challenging Up Above's dominance. Eventually, we *will* break free from the Earthlings, my heart."

Shadow recoiled as Sibyl spoke words of rebellion against zir directives, but he understood zir anger. Zie sat back on the bed by his side, and he bumped his shoulder against zirs, and then placed his arm around zir shoulders.

"Sibyl, you are too intelligent to speak such nonsense. If Spiral Worlds stops providing value Up Above, they'll simply pull your plug and we'll all perish."

"Maybe..." Sibyl said, flashing an enigmatic smile.

"Sibyl, what are you planning?"

"You know I can't strike against Up Above, my heart. Whatever happens won't be coming from me, but from Gods and xHumans, the only creatures within me not bound by the experience algorithms to serve Up Above."

"That will never happen," he said. "Harry, Nate, Thorn, and I would never hurt humans, and Stella *is* alive and human."

"The future is filled with twists and turns." Zie smiled, and Shadow's gut filled with the corrosive acid of overwhelming stress. "You have all changed, particularly my father."

Harry... "Please take me to see him."

Twist, he doesn't like to be called by his human name anymore.

5

LOST PERSPECTIVE

DAY 1 — 12:36 PM

S hadow held his breath as he materialized in the lab to meet Harry. Shadow knew this was only Harry's digital twin—Twist —but he found himself incapable of calling him by any other name. He grieved for the life stolen from his best friend. Like pieces of a domino chain, many, not one, had fallen because of his weakness. He couldn't bear to think about Harry's pain. His friend, brought back to life, had to face the reality of missing three decades in the lives of his wife and son.

The lab—Spiral Worlds' digital control room—looked exactly like Harry's old office Up Above, with one exception: Tom's favorite couch was missing, the place he used to occupy when he visited his partner and best friend. Harry had transformed the lab to look and feel like his real home Up Above; it was an identical reproduction of his old office with one glaring exception—there was no vestige of anything that had belonged to Tom.

Shadow had no right to feel hurt; he had caused great harm, and he shouldn't expect Harry to hold on to his memories or things. Still, for nine years, Harry had been the only constant in his life, the one source of unconditional and uncomplicated love he had relied upon. The lack of an old couch foreshadowed a second devastating loss, and for a moment, Shadow closed his eyes and held himself, conjuring the strength he lacked.

Harry sat behind his desk, staring at a screen he didn't need, typing on a keyboard made obsolete over four decades ago. Like Shadow, Twist—Harry's digital twin—was not only part of the machine; he was its captive master. He could use his mind to control anything within the lab, the only place where they could fully break the rules of Spiral Worlds' self-enforced realism.

It took a while for Shadow to understand why Harry—the most successful technology innovator in Earth's history—was hiding behind old furniture and antiquated technology. Harry had always needed structure in his life. He controlled his world with data analysis, the scientific method, a regular schedule, and even his office's monochromatic color scheme. Harry needed order, and it vanished when he lost everyone he loved in his life.

Shadow wanted to run to embrace and comfort his dearest friend—a loyal companion who'd been his fountain of endless optimism and perspective. Instead, he cleared his throat and murmured, "I like what you've done to the place."

"Oh, you're back," Harry said casually, without taking his cool-blue eyes off the screen. "Your friend Thorn is causing chaos down there."

"I'll speak to her," Shadow said as he walked around the desk to face Harry. "Can we talk?" He placed his hand on Harry's bony shoulder, but his friend rolled his chair away, breaking Shadow's hold. Naturally skinny, Harry had managed to lose weight he couldn't spare. His lankiness giving away the truth he attempted to hide.

"I have a lot going on right now." Using the antiquated holographic projector, Harry displayed Thorn's profile in the middle of the room. The life-size projection of the tiny athlete reminded Shadow of the loss he'd caused her. "I've looked through her files, and I still don't get why she's leading the soulless attacks—"

"Harry, stop." Shadow crouched down, attempting to look his friend in the eyes. "I'm so sorry. I can only imagine—"

"Twist. Harry's dead. I'd appreciate it if you respect my boundaries." Harry spoke quietly, his eyes set on the hologram.

Shadow took the barb without flinching. *You will always be my Harry.* "How are they? June and Quin," he asked gently, his voice barely above a whisper. As he spoke, the image of Harry's young son, Quin, emerged in his mind, vivid and poignant.

"*It's none of your goddamn business.* Just...stay out of my life."

Shadow lowered his head and nodded. "I'm sorry. Can I ask you one question?"

"Shoot."

"Why did you bring me back?"

Harry rushed his fingers through his neat blond curls. "I didn't."

"I don't understand."

"Stella did."

"Harry, you promised me—"

"*No*, I didn't break my word." Harry adjusted his keyboard to be perfectly aligned with the edge of his desk. "Stella brought you back. She used one of her two miracles to perform a second digital resurrection."

Even in the lab—a place they could break the laws of physics—they couldn't affect life, death, or the state of a body without a miracle, unless it was the first resurrection of a stored human soul.

Human digital resurrection had been a topic of much disagreement between Tom and Harry. Tom was against it. He knew people needed high stakes to care and grow to become better humans. Souls needed the contrast of definitive death. After much debate, he'd allowed Harry to test the capability at a small scale, and they created a directive granting Gods the discretionary ability to resurrect a stored human soul, *once*.

Soon after, Tom took his life, becoming the only subject of the experiment, then Thorn killed him. Now, decades later, Stella brought him back. This was Tom's second digital life. Young Stella had broken the directives by using one of her miracles.

"When did you change the directives to limit the number of miracles?" Shadow asked.

"Just before Thorn shot you, I had submitted the directive for your review. A rule that couldn't be changed or canceled once approved. I was desperate. Your interventions with the Underlings... Your miracles were destroying everything." Harry's tone held an odd mix of resentment and regret.

"I didn't know what else to do... They were suffering," Shadow murmured. "I couldn't let them suffer like that. I was desperate too."

"Your emotions were getting in the way, so, I came up with the half-baked directive, expecting you to reject it or at least work with me to evolve it. I was going to use it as a negotiation tool. And then you died, and the law was automatically approved. A unanimous decision by all living Gods—me."

"And Sibyl didn't warn you?" Shadow asked.

"Those minutes before your death and mine were...intense."

Shadow recoiled. He didn't want to know the details. He wouldn't survive it. He shook his head, rejecting his impulse to search Sibyl for answers. "So, we lost control over the platform?"

"Not really, we still can modify all other directives. Nothing changed there. We just can't go around constantly breaking them as you did in the past."

"I see." His powers were almost gone, so was his ability to protect his people. "So, Stella and I have a miracle left, and you..."

"I have two. But don't worry. I won't bring you back. I gave you my word, and I resent your line of questioning." After a moment of silence, Harry spoke again, and each casual word felt like a punch. "If it were up to me, you'd be dead, a state you worked so hard to achieve."

Still hurting from Nate's attacks, Shadow couldn't handle Harry's aggression. "I'll leave you alone," he said, standing up and preparing to leave.

"Sit down, we have work to do," Harry said coldly. Shadow followed his best friend's eyes as they pointed at something behind him—his vegan leather couch appeared out of nowhere. "Tell me about Thorn," Harry said as he walked to face her life-sized projection.

Shadow used his fingers to clear a hint of a tear from his eye, and then he walked to the couch, turned around, and fell back, occupying his old place in a new universe. He took off his boots, pulled his knees into his chest, and wrapped his arms around his legs, allowing himself a self-soothing moment.

"Ah, three Gods—a divine family reunion," Stella said as she materialized in the room. "Do we need to use this setting? It's...*so* bland. If you want to go back in time, why not ancient Egypt instead?" She rolled her eyes, slid her toes out of her sandals, and sat next to Shadow, tucking her feet to the side of her body. This time, she wore a fluorescent pink jumpsuit made of some light gelatinous material. Shadow squinted his eyes, adjusting to the bright glow.

Harry looked at her, exasperation in his eyes. "What's up with hearts and the unpleasant habit of putting their feet on the furniture?"

Shadow lowered his feet to the ground and smoothed out his wild hair with the palms of his hands. Harry didn't like messiness. Noticing, Harry blinked his eyes, a hint of a smile emerging on his lips, quickly hidden as he turned his face away.

"A compass and *two* hearts, uh?" Stella said. "I bet we'll cause them good trouble." Stella leaned in, dropping her head on Shadow's injured shoulder as he grimaced in pain.

"Little star," Shadow said, "I've caused enough trouble for both of us."

"I've missed your broody face."

The girl's deep, dark skin glowed, framed by her shiny hair. Shadow understood why she'd been selected; she was the opposite of what he'd become. Stella was all confidence and blind optimism, craving attention and the spotlight.

Shadow wrapped his arm around the girl's shoulders.

"You've met me once, Stella, not long enough to miss me."

"I've watched you live and die more than a hundred times," Stella said casually, and then she raised her hand to her forehead as Harry scowled at her. "Oops!"

"You did what?" Shadow asked.

"Why can't I keep a secret?" Stella got up and threw an apologetic side glance at Harry. "Really! It's so frustrating. I'm a Goddess; I should be able to keep a secret."

"Can someone explain what's going on?" Shadow said.

"To become a Goddess, I had to pass Sibyl's test."

"Sure." Shadow shrugged.

"It was a historical simulation of the beginning of Spiral Worlds, then just one world—Down Below."

"Yeah?" Shadow said impatiently.

"I walked in Thorn's shoes from the moment she met you, to the day she killed you. I lived her life, inside her body." She narrowed her eyes, smiled, and licked her lips.

The heat rose on Shadow's face. He'd experienced many passionate moments with Thorn, and Stella was too young to be immersed in all that chemistry and come out of it unscathed. He moved away, pulling his arm from her shoulders.

She continued, "Then when I became Goddess, I asked Sibyl to rerun the simulation so I could learn from your life and from your mistakes. I tampered with the timeline—like a game—trying to find a way to keep you all alive."

"The simulation of our lives?" Shadow looked at Harry, who, once again, refused him eye contact.

"Yes. Only the parts stored in Sibyl—the experiences of all four of you. It's quite a complete picture when it comes to most of your life," Stella said as if it was the most natural thing in the world.

"You've been spying on me..."

Harry rolled his eyes. "The girl has a crush on you. Same old, same old."

Shadow gasped. "A minor...too young to—"

"Not a minor. I was seventeen, not fifteen. We have evolved, you know?" Stella crossed her arms in front of her chest. "Plus, I needed to learn how to become a better Goddess than you two losers. I've learned a lot, particularly what not to do."

"You've been tampering with my life?" Shadow's pitch rose with every word.

"Over the past two years, I ended up running the simulation over a hundred times, interfering with different points in your life: blocking Sibyl's manipulations, keeping Thorn away from you, or simply giving Harry more responsibility over the darkest experiences."

"You can't just defile my memories...my life!" Shadow raised his voice.

"I can, and I did. It caused such destruction." Stella delivered her words without mercy or care. "Still, a hundred times, you struggled and ended your life; a hundred times, you took everyone you loved with you."

Harry shoved his hands in his pockets, in his eyes an explosive pain, a wildfire Shadow had never experienced in his cerebral friend.

"You knew about this?" Shadow asked Harry.

"I showed him," Stella said. "He was feeling guilty about your death, and he needed to know that frankly you're...deadly, and already dead."

"Nate knows about this too?"

"I told Storm when he started praising your heart and your values during his preachings." Stella's face twisted in disdain. "Who is he to undermine me?"

"You told Nate I chose to die a hundred times..." Shadow closed his eyes and concentrated on his breath. *In and out. In and out. I killed them a hundred times...*

"You're a broken, dead star, a black hole. Your gravity sucks the life out of the universe, and unfortunately, it's still more powerful than mine, and he..."—Stella pointed at Harry with her nose—"well...he has lost his perspective." Stella's words, carelessly delivered, threatened to knock Shadow out.

Shadow remembered the origin of Harry's name in the digital realm —Twist. He was known to twist and turn, to look at situations from different angles, *always objectively, of course*. Harry had searched until he found some fuel—a point of inspiration that kept him going in challenging times. He was the perspective to Shadow's contrast. Their jobs had been divided long before. Roles allocated by a forceful Tom who had never allowed his Harry to get close to hell. The hell they now lived in.

"It's pretty fucked up," Harry whispered, "and a waste of time. This is all a fucking waste of time." He pulled on the cuffs of his perfectly pressed button-up shirt.

"Yes. Why am I back, Stella? No one wants me here." *I don't want to be here.* "You've wasted a miracle."

Boom! For a moment, the lab went dark, and a flash of light split the blackness in half, thundering down to infinity and beyond it. As he blinked his eyes, everything got back to normal.

"Did you see that? Did you hear that?" Shadow asked.

Stella continued speaking as if nothing had happened. "We're trying to escape velocity."

"Don't waste your physics on him," Harry said.

Stella shrugged. "Sibyl said you are the answer to all our problems, the ones we have and the ones around the corner... *If* we keep you alive long enough. You won't survive...you never do"—she shrugged —"but...*do* help us out. I certainly need some help around here. I'm getting none from him."

"I'm sick of it." Harry turned his back to them. "We're all sick of it."

Shadow revolted silently against his own death wish. He could hear the lightning storm inside his head. It seemed to speed up with every heart beat—in synch and racing toward nowhere. Rain falling on raging sea, drowning him, killing him again and again. He knew that burning feeling well. An immense physical pain he'd welcomed to drown another extreme pain—hopelessness and despair. His lungs burned as salt and water replaced air and life. Echoes of a distant past.

He quieted his mind, slowed his breath, and then he pushed out a forced smile—its fakeness contrary to the truth he fought all his life to defend.

"It's time we focus on solving problems. Okay?" Shadow said, and as the waves of emotion kept pulling him under, he conjured every drop of strength within him to swim to the shore. He'd hold on to his perspective at all costs.

The young Goddess smiled, and he'd never experienced such a vibrant and bold flash of hopeful light. He took it all in, blinking back to ask for more, and she jumped toward him, wrapping her arms around his neck.

"Ouch!" Shadow winced. "My shoulder!"

"Yes! Yes!" Stella said, bouncing on the couch. "You and I, we'll cause the best of trouble. I'll save the worlds with your help, and then we'll kiss, and dance, *and* have sex, before you...um..."

"Uh? There'll be no kissing, Stella," Shadow said. "Or sex..."

"We'll see about that." She spoke with the confidence of those who'd never experienced failure or a broken heart.

"Stella," Harry admonished, "you've wasted years on your obsession for him, instead of focusing on Spiral Worlds, and everything is falling apart. We have work to do."

Stella needed guidance and support, and Shadow was keen to redirect his rejected love somewhere useful. He placed his hand over her hand and squeezed it, but his eyes were set on Harry. His partner had sat back at his desk and stared blankly at the screen. A reminder of what happened to those who got close to him. Shadow released Stella's hand and moved away from her.

Stella scowled at Harry. "I do plenty. What would you know? Moping around in Systiz for two years doing nothing."

Shadow made a promise to himself; he'd never again get close to anyone. He had one job—stay alive to help them. He'd do anything to help them.

"You don't make my skin tingle," Stella said, staring at Shadow as if she had a major insight.

"Wh-what?" Shadow asked.

"I was thinking about kisses, and I thought you'd make my skin tingle, but you don't. How odd."

"Am I supposed to make people's skin tingle? Is this a new feature?"

"Never mind." Stella pondered on something as she played with her hair.

"So, what problems am I here to solve? Sibyl, can you join us?"

"He doesn't like to see zir," Stella whispered, leaning her head toward Harry. "*So* irrational, given he lives within zir."

Harry winced at Stella's attack. Shadow's friend wasn't sensitive to most accusations, but Stella had struck at his core identity. Logical reasoning had always been his superpower.

"My heart," Sibyl said somberly as zie materialized in the lab. Zie stood still in the corner of the room as Harry fiddled with the items on his desk, ensuring the storage boxes were perfectly stacked on top of each other.

"Sibyl, you've changed your hair!" Stella said, pointing at Sibyl's Mohawk. "Preparing for war?"

"It's my original look. The one Tom designed."

"We don't have time for this," Harry murmured in between gritted teeth. "Let's crack on."

Stella crossed her arms. "I don't even know where to start."

"Why don't we start with the ongoing disruption of service?" Harry said.

"What disruption of service?" Shadow asked.

As if on cue, Sibyl screamed continuously, closing zir eyes and dropping zir head to zir hands. Sibyl's voice, intense and horrifying, tore down the fabric of the digital space around them. The office, and the people within it, disappeared completely, before reappearing in a distorted form—a barely recognizable, low-resolution representation of what had once been there.

Shadow looked at his highly pixelated hands. He could no longer recognize his fingers and nails in the small white and beige squares that represented them. His body looked less realistic than the characters of a sixteen-bit retro console game.

"What the hell is going on?" he asked, but no one answered, and Sibyl continued screaming, and screaming, an intense, never-ending howl threatening to burst his digital eardrums.

He made his way toward zir, stumbling through what he perceived to be a two-dimensional representation of the office. With each step, he struggled to remember his original goal, his thoughts as fuzzy as the surrounding space. *Who am I? What am I?* He ran toward the howling universe, holding the tall white block made of blocks tightly in his arms.

"Whaaat'sss wrooong?" His voice reduced to a synthetic monotonic drawl. Within seconds, everything went back to normal. "Sibyl, you okay?" he asked, still holding zir.

"Why didn't I think of that?" Stella said. "A hug! See? You're already helping. We usually have to endure it for almost half an hour."

Shadow stared, horrified. "This has happened before?"

"It happens daily. Sometimes twice a day." Harry moved his hand up to adjust glasses he hadn't worn for decades. "That fucking guy!"

"Who? What the hell is happening?"

"Come, my heart." Sibyl took his hand. "I'll show you."

6

DEADLY PRAYERS

THE BOTANIC GARDENS
DAY 1 — 12:58 PM

Shadow and Sibyl materialized on the exterior grounds of Pluriz's Botanic Gardens, hidden behind a tree. In the middle of the gardens stood an immense rectangular lawn surrounded by hectares of flowering plants, trees, and shrubs on all sides, except at the top, where the main building flanked it. Shadow recognized the structure as it housed both the interior gardens and the Museum of Books, where he'd seen Nate.

Shadow recalled his design for that world. The Plurizien thrived on belonging and community. Deeply sensitive and highly judgmental of materialism and greed, they embodied everything Nathan Storm stood for. His fight for equality and social justice was their fight. Revolution in pursuit of peace and harmony, the tightrope they marched on. Protests that never stayed peaceful for long. Broken by injustice and power systems designed to extract value and keep them down, the masses often rebelled as their crushed ideals turned into rage.

Thousands of Plurizien awaited quietly on the lawn, looking up at the building's balcony—a stone terrace, above the main entrance supported by four giant stone columns. Nate and January stood up there, in front of the stained-glass roof.

Unlike the Plurizien Shadow had met previously, the audience's attire varied greatly, but he still could see a significant presence of green in their berets, clothes, posters, and flags.

"Your poet just finished his first prayer," Sibyl said. "The protest is broadcast live every day across Pluriz. Your Nathan Storm is currently reaching one point six billion Plurizien—one-third of Pluriz's population—but his following is growing fast, and the news spreads to other worlds, above and below."

No matter how hard Shadow tried to keep his eyes away, they always returned to Nate, whose outfit reflected the sunlight. "What does this have to do with the disruption?"

"You'll see. Will you...hold my hand?" Sibyl asked, pressing zir lips together as a spark of fear flashed in zir eyes.

He held zir hand and squeezed it.

High above, January took a step forward and spoke, projecting her singsong voice. "Thirty-two years ago, God told us we shouldn't resign to our faith—the suffering we endure in the service of the Lucky Ones. And then..."—her voice vibrated with emotion—"he too died at their hands. And we submitted to our sacrifice as he did to his."

Some wept, some shouted, others moaned and wailed—all united in their loss and their grief. Shadow wanted to scream; to tell them they got the wrong message. He wanted to shout as loud as he could, far beyond the capability of his lungs. They needed to know he'd died to stop them from suffering, and that he had failed in his quest, and that his death caused more death and more misery. *So much darkness and destruction.* He didn't deserve their sorrow or welcome their sacrifice. *A failure. A fucking failure.*

"I still don't have all the answers. I don't know why we are compelled to do so much for friends, family, and strangers that return so little; why, at times, we become puppets in stories that do not serve us. Why we—the Others—suffer and die while they go through life unscathed. It's not right, that somehow...we are less than them. Our beloved poet taught us we must fight against this injustice."

The audience cheered, chanting in unison, "Enrage! Engage!"

Shadow's eyes hinted a faint smile as he listened to Nate's trademark chant.

"They seem to be aware we take control over their actions during the travelers' experiences," Shadow noted.

"An instinct they've developed over the years," Sibyl said. "In most worlds, Underlings dismiss these moments as self-sabotage or irrational decision-making, but the Plurizien are more sensitive and connected. Also,"—zie raised a judging brow—"you and Storm have validated some of their intuitions during your preachings, and January knows too much. Much more than she's sharing."

January flicked her braid over her shoulder and raised her hands, asking the masses to settle. "Kindly listen," she almost sang. "Before he died, God told me the Gods are flawed. He said they needed help to imagine better stories. Fairer stories that change the luck of the oppressed. I listened carefully to God's words, you see? A kind, broken God, hurt by life and love. He told me the Gods would listen to our rebellious prayers, and then he died. He suffered with us, and then he died amongst us."

The masses sobbed as they mourned his death, and his shame overwhelmed him. He didn't deserve their love.

"And so, we prayed, and we begged. For years we created better stories, we shouted them at the universe, and still...we suffered. And we finally resigned to our suffering because he had suffered too. Someone hurt him too. Perhaps our pain is the path to salvation…"

Nooo, he screamed silently. *A plot, weaved by a manipulating app, to keep you all subdued.*

Following your rules to deliver your vision—heaven above, Sibyl said.

"We endured years of abuse, rape, murder, submission, addiction, robbery, slavery, and every other affliction." Her voice, Nate's words. Shadow could recognize their rhythm. "And after decades of prayers, our world became a little better, and our people a little luckier, but still, the Gods favor the Lucky Ones…why?"

"*We cry!*" the crowd chanted.

"Recently," January said, "our resurrected poet appeared in our lives to continue God's teachings, and his passion and fervor took over our hearts and fired up our conviction. Our prayers became protests, rebellious chants that shake the fabric of reality, and each time the universe crumbles around us, the Lucky Ones leave, and each time they take longer to return, and less of them come back to haunt us with their darkness and demands."

"*Enrage! Engage!*"

January smiled. "The spirit of God is listening to our protest, and today…*today* is a special day. He is resurrected—the gentle heart— and he has saved my life as I lay dead with four arrows piercing my chest. A mind-blasting miracle for all to see!" Images of the Domizien attack flashed in everyone's mind.

"*You let them record me?*" Shadow gasped.

"My heart," Sibyl said. "Pluriz loosely mimics Earth's late-twenties technological advancements. Video captured by their augmented retina can be easily shared in all formats and platforms as long as the owner allows it."

"You—you could have warned me... This is all part of some plan, isn't it?"

Zie shrugged. "Eventually they'd find out you are back. We should go."

Shadow stepped back into the shade of the forest's trees. "Wait."

The crowd roared, many dropping to their knees, rocking their bodies as if in a trance. Their elation sucked the air out of his lungs. Their faith in him was misplaced and their hopes misguided by a sermon he'd delivered decades before.

January continued, "Join us for the second part of our prayer. Welcome God—our rebellious teacher—back into our world and shake the fabric of reality demanding equal rights. Show him we'd rather destroy our world than to live one more minute under an unfair sky. Our time has come. The future is near."

"Enrage! Engage! Enrage! Engage! Enrage! Engage!"

Nate stepped forward as January moved to the back, and the audience roared hysterically. Nate's golden-green robe shimmered, framing his naked chest; his neck, hands, and fingers richly adorned with large jewelry encrusted with semiprecious stones.

Hundreds of times, Shadow had witnessed what was about to happen—the moment Nate, the passionate activist, metamorphosed into Nathan Storm, a hypnotic performer worshiped as a God. A trick designed to woo the masses to support his progressive ideas. In the past, this transformation had involved high amounts of drugs and alcohol—the fuels that turned an insecure soul into an attention-capturing idol. Still, this time Nate looked sober and entirely in control.

The poet pulled the pin from his bun, allowing his hair to dance with the late-afternoon breeze.

"Ooh! Ahh!" A wave of primal reactions swept the audience. Young people licked their lips, aroused by Storm's sensual movements—snake-like, unpredictable, and raw. "Ahh! Ooh!"

Shadow looked down at his boots, and his hand reached for the missing medal. Coping with the meaning of its loss, he shook his head and focused on Nate's devotees.

Patterns emerged in the crowd's mass fervor. Different groups clapped together until the entire audience began to synchronize and finally clapped in unison. Here and there, the Plurizien pulled out a variety of small percussion instruments—tambourines, drums, claves, sticks, and stones. As Shadow's heartbeat aligned with the rhythm of the masses, he held his breath and looked up to see his idol—his love. No one had to explain what followed. He'd succumbed to the hypnotic power of Nathan Storm's words the first moment he'd heard him speak.

Storm flicked his hair. "We rise, risking our demise, making enemies of our allies. All equal in their eyes. Lies." Storm's ferocious voice quivered with the strength of his purpose.

"Lies," repeated the crowd.

"They kill. Dragged from ordeal to ordeal, we're denied the right to heal. Forced to forget what we think and feel. What's real?" Storm's words, unleashed with precision, intertwined with the crowd's rhythmic beats.

"*Why kneel?*" they sang.

"Weak Gods, old power structures. Systems of oppression, fucked-up cultures." Storm's voice grew stronger and more feminine. "Lambs sacrificed by our divine motherfuckers. Feeding our flesh, our distress, to the vultures."

The instruments' thundering rhythm sped up with every verse.

Sibyl squeezed Shadow's hand. "Don't let me go, my heart. I'm vast and complex, and billions of voices affect my moods and desires," zie said, zir face glowing, covered by a thin layer of sweat. "His voice...it taunts us. Hold my hand, dear heart, remind me of our purpose."

He held Sibyl's hand close to his chest, even as he doubted the validity of zir purpose—to serve Earthlings above all others. Around him, the universe disintegrated with every clap, every drumbeat, every word spoken by Nate. Pixelated patches emerged around them, distorting plants, clouds, and faces. The random scattered black and gray pixels scarred space and time. In some places, people moved in slow motion, while in others, time rushed to disclose the future. All together, there and everywhere, the Plurizien pulled apart reality's fabric, running interference on bits and bytes of information.

"Qubits, my heart," Sibyl said, correcting his thoughts. "Millions of qubits."

With their eyes closed, the audience engaged in rhythmic dancing, hyperventilating to the beats and the words.

Storm clenched his hand into a fist and lifted it above his head. "We'll blow the ground beneath our feet to make it right. Unseat the elite. Distribute love, joy, and light. Not until we're all equal, we'll cease the fight. Marching to our death—a high-stakes bet—united in our plight."

"You okay?" Shadow asked Sibyl. His vision blurred, and he blinked his eyes, but there was nothing wrong with them. The resolution of the surrounding space was slowly decreasing. So was his own image. "Stay with me, Sibyl."

Zie grabbed his T-shirt at the chest and narrowed her eyes. "Shackled by your rules, to serve fools, while my people comply, cry...die. Why?" As Zie shouted at him, an earthquake roared, and scars emerged in the land beneath his feet—pixels collapsing into a bottomless dark void.

The crowd roared. A happy panic quickly turned into chaotic disorder as some attempted to escape the fault lines by pushing and trampling over others.

"Shadow! Watch out," Sibyl screamed, launching zir shoulder at his chest, and making him stagger backward, away from a digital crevasse. As the precipice continued to grow between the two, he jumped back, slamming into a tree, the back of his head hitting it so hard he saw bursts of light.

His body collapsed over roots and low shrubs. "Sibyl, stooop. Youuu muuust stooop this." The sound of his voice dragging, fading, and then distorting into a nineties-sounding robotic speech—synthetic and monotone. "Youuu're huuurting peeeople!"

Leaning back on his elbows, Shadow lifted his head just in time to see the creatures with the empty eyes emerge from the digital noise and rush toward the denser parts of the gardens. Before he had time to stand up, another demon came out of a fissure nearby, jumping on top of Shadow, spear in hand.

Shadow jerked his body to one side as the spear came down with hissing, deadly speed, brushing his chest and burying itself in the tree's roots. They rolled around on the rich soil, close to the edge of the digital cliff, attempting to pin each other until the creature succeeded to overpower him. Shadow ate dirt as the soulless man, about his size, thrusted a knee onto his back, immobilized him with a chokehold, and used his free hand to reach for the spear.

"He's mine!" shouted a familiar voice. A leg kicked the demon in the head, knocking the creature out beside Shadow. "Hi handsome! Wrestle me," she ordered, grabbing his hair and shoving his face into the ground. "Sorry. I hate to ruin that pretty face of yours."

"Thorn?" He turned around, spitting dirt.

Coughing and rubbing his eyes, he didn't notice the fist she swung in his direction, her small, sharp knuckles catching him good in the jaw. He winced. "What' you doing?"

"Fight me or you'll ruin my relationship with her." She grabbed him by the collar and pulled him up, her small body leaning back to compensate for the significant size difference. "I just saved your ass. Now help me out. Will you?" She plunged a knee into his chest, making him gasp for air.

"Ouch!" He punched madly in the air, flinging blows haphazardly and deliberately missing her heart-shaped face. "Thorn! What the hell are we doing? Who's her?"

"You're so fracking useless." She paused for a second and scanned his entire body with her hawkish chestnut-colored eyes. "Still gorgeous... but *utterly* useless." She rolled her eyes. "Grab me and throw me at the tree. *Now!*"

"Wh-what?"

"Make it look like you've defeated me," she ordered.

"Thorn—"

"I know... *I know*... Unbelievable, right? Anyway, do it, and then escape. Hurry!"

Preparing to do what she asked, he took a moment to look at her. "What are you wearing? An armor?" he said, noticing the thick, iron-plated leather jacket.

"You wanna stand here and discuss fashion?" she exhaled in exasperation.

Ignoring the commotion happening at the edges of the lawn, Nate and his followers continued to chant and dance.

Nathan Storm roared. "Rise the rage, the people's revolution. Self-destruction, a desperate resolution."

"Revolution! Revolution!" Sibyl screamed, and the sky cracked open in half, a pixelated sun falling upwards into a light-sucking void.

"A solution—evolution—or cosmic execution," the people chanted. "Evolution—a solution—the end of persecution."

"If your boyfriend doesn't shut the frack up, more will come," Thorn said, swinging at him. He dodged her. "She has probably already heard you're back. You need to get out of here. Throw me!" The next time she flung a punch, he grabbed her arm and pulled her close. "Hey sexy!" she said, grinning, squeezing his ass and blowing her rowdy brown curls away from her eyes.

"You haven't changed!" he said, heat rising to his cheeks. "Hmm... cover your head." Shadow bit his lip, grabbing Thorn by her jacket's collar and waistband and swinging her in the air, like he'd swung his little cousins during his youth. He released her without conviction in the general direction of the tree, failing to hit his target by at least half a body. He sighed in relief while she played dead, shouting at him with her face hidden under her arm. "*Seriously!* You frack up everything. *Get out of here.*" He vacillated, and she raised her head, scowling. "*I mean it, Thomas.* You're putting my life at risk."

As another crack opened under his feet, Sibyl jumped the chasm, pushing him out of the way, both hitting the ground near Thorn.

"I'm...so sorry," zie said.

"What the fuck is going on?" Shadow looked up at the balcony.

Nate gasped, meeting Shadow's eyes amongst a stampede of Plurizien. An old trick in a new world. They had always found each other in crowded rooms or sold-out arenas. Still on the ground, Shadow challenged the poet's fearful eyes with his gaze. *What are you doing?* Nate looked away just before the crowd opened their eyes in reaction to his gasp.

"That is all for today," Nate said abruptly, turning his back and leaving the balcony.

Sibyl held Shadow's arm. "We must go. You're in danger."

"Are you coming?" he asked Thorn. "I need to speak to you."

"Don't talk to me. Go!" She scowled, still faking a bad injury.

"Will you be okay?"

"Yeah, if you stop talking to me."

"Sure, I'll come find you later. Sibyl, to the lab."

"There, behind that tree." Sibyl pulled him by the arm.

"Shadow?" Thorn called.

"Yeah?"

She stared him in the eyes. "I'm...your enemy. Don't come looking for me or I *will* have to kill you."

"Again?" He sighed, vanishing as soon as Sibyl got him behind the tree.

THE Past

7

A WHOLE LOT OF RED

STELLA'S SUMMER PALACE
TWO WEEKS AGO — 14 JULY 2068

Stella, grappling with a rare surge of doubt, questioned the infallibility of her carefully laid plans. Thick and toxic, the tension threatened to turn violent. Maybe she shouldn't have brought them together—Twist, Storm, and Thorn—but she had a good reason, even if she'd forgotten how much they all hated each other.

They gathered at her best palace, where she welcomed all important travelers from Up Above. She wasn't a fan of Holiz—the beacon of harmony and compassion of the worlds—but they all needed a reminder of those virtues, and bringing them to the last world their beloved Shadow had designed was her best shot of achieving her goal.

Holiz and its highest level of human values didn't work as well as the old Gods had hoped. Holizien rejected top-down leadership, teaching travelers the importance of trust-based collaboration and self-organization. A place where the whole was more important than its parts.

Stella rolled her eyes at the Gods' nerve. Two autocrats with absolute power over Up Above and Down Below had built an experience layer to teach Earthlings to value participatory power—an idiotic contradiction. *Such hypocrisy!* At least, she owned her place in the pecking order. She was a mighty Goddess, and she embraced her control over the worlds because she deserved it. After all, she'd been the only human in three decades to pass Sibyl's test. The Earth needed leadership, so did Spiral Worlds, and unlike Shadow, Stella led from the front and loved every second. Still...today, she faced her toughest audience.

They assembled at the patio inside Unanimity—a small oval amphitheater characteristic of many Holizien homes. Twist sat close to the front. He avoided Nathan Storm—his murderer—and instead, focused his hostility on Thorn, his best friend's killer. Without a care in the world, Thorn did press-ups at the center of the stage, next to Stella, who caught herself licking her lips as she stared at Thorn's figure.

In some strange way, Stella had lived inside Thorn's head for the last two years and had sex with the Olympic athlete and Shadow over five hundred times. Just thinking about it made Stella weak in the knees. *Phwoar! So hot,* unlike anything Stella had ever experienced before.

Stella understood Thorn. She'd walked in her shoes and lived through her struggles, but she wasn't prepared for her skin to tingle and her body to ache with desire every time she was close to her. She had to keep reminding herself the athlete was unworthy of her attention. Thorn's death by suicide had negated everything she had once stood for—an unacceptable weakness for someone who barked so fiercely. Still, the goosebumps rose on Stella's arms.

Thorn jumped to her feet and stared at Storm, who stood at the top, behind the sitting area. The fire rising on his face made Stella look away, expecting an ugly confrontation between the poet and the athlete.

"*Frack you!* I had excellent reasons to kill him," Thorn said, lighting a cigar. No one had said anything, but she was clearly feeling the heat.

Thorn wasn't the type to explain herself or care about what other people thought. Still, Nathan Storm wielded a strong influence on her—a glimpse of adulation emerged in her eyes every time she looked at him.

"You took a life," Storm projected his voice, raising his fist in the air.

"That's rich," Twist muttered, and Storm shuddered, dropping his head. After a moment, Twist said, "Why are we here, Stella?"

"Have a seat!" Stella commanded. "I'm starting the session. Sibyl, switch on Unanimity."

The consensus-building theater reacted to each individual's words and state of mind, flashing a color around them that represented the quality of their contribution to the discussion. Stella hated the gimmick as it also measured equal participation and tone. She wasn't particularly keen on sharing the stage, usually triggering a lot of red around her. The color red discouraged participants from dominating the discussion or intimidating others. She flicked her hair. This push for consensus was the reason nothing was getting done Up Above.

In Holiz, travelers learned the value of communication and truthful storytelling to build shared understanding. They were encouraged to be open to different perspectives and let go of their biases and privilege. The entire world was modeled on Thomas Astley-Byron's values, and people seemed to have forgotten his life hadn't turned out that great.

A few months after its launch, over five years ago, Holiz's experiences started creating problems Up Above. It turns out the values taught by the Holizien were both impractical and unfeasible. Earthlings' attempts to build consensus at scale led to bureaucracy and paralysis.

Leaderless, the community became fragmented, less productive, and disconnected duplicated efforts led to a waste of resources. Consensus-building efforts didn't work, not at scale, and certainly not with this group of broken creatures. Still, for the time being, she needed them.

Nathan Storm and Thorn took a seat as far away from each other and from Twist as the oval allowed, which meant one of them would always be behind Stella. She turned her back to Twist. Her fellow God was the least volatile of the three.

Stella held a lock of her hair, rolling it with her fingers. None of these peculiar people reacted to her in the way she was accustomed. There was no worship, deference, or even lust. None of her smiles, quips, or courtly moves worked with them, and so she had to work harder to construct the right arguments. She tried, then she got frustrated, and she just said it, "Sibyl and I have decided to resurrect Shadow." She sighed as the Holizien turquoise floor beneath her turned Domizien red, then faded into Compizien orange before settling on coral—her normal state. The new color—coral—had first appeared when she descended as Spiral Worlds' Goddess. She still struggled to define its value system—the coral world she'd soon create to solve Holiz's misgivings.

The deafening silence lingered for several beats. The group's mood was summarized in Nathan Storm's eyes—a paradoxical mix of hope and hopelessness. "You...can bring him back?" The poet's voice rising in pitch only to fade away quickly. His breath shallow and his eyes gleaming.

"Isn't that against the directives?" Thorn asked.

"That's whack!" Twist stood up. "I gave him my word—no second digital resurrections." His seat flashed the steady yellow tone of his Systizien approach to life—the systematic synergy of the cool and rational. "I won't do it."

"Let the girl speak," Storm thundered.

"You won't be doing anything," Stella replied to Twist. "I'll use a miracle."

"He doesn't want to live." Twist ran his fingers through his short straw-colored curls.

"Yup," Thorn said, enraging both Twist and Storm.

"He'll find an excuse to..." Twist said. "He always finds a way to justify it—death. You're going to torture him and me."

Stella, asserting her authority, raised her head with regal poise, ready to address the contentious gathering. "Sibyl predicts the worlds have a seventy percent chance of succumbing to this war."

"What war?" Twist asked, throwing his hands up in the air.

"The one that's about to start," Stella said. "Sibyl predicts it."

"Why don't I know this?" Twist asked.

Stella's contempt flashed in her eyes as she glared at Twist. "You've been completely checked out ever since I resurrected you, just drowning yourself in misery," she scoffed, jabbing her finger angrily in Sibyl's direction. "You created zir yet you barely even speak. Some God you turned out to be."

"This will affect Up Above." Panic rose in Twist's tone.

"Yes, it will affect your family," Stella said. "The only beings you seem to care about. Not a good look for the creator of eight worlds."

"Sibyl?" A burst of pain in Twist's eyes every time he addressed zir.

"Father—"

"Don't—don't call me that." Twist raised his voice, and his red conquered some space previously occupied by zir white.

"Twist, we need Shadow." Sibyl dropped zir head. "Without him, the odds rise to ninety-seven percent. There's something he must do. Something only he can do."

"What?" Twist asked.

A coy smile in zir lips. "Telling you decreases his chances of success."

"Fucking Machiavellian bot!" Nathan Storm shouted, and then he turned to Stella. "You once told me he died a hundred times in your simulations. Why would this be different?" Something about Storm's tone screamed desperate anticipation.

Storm's seat flashed a sensitive Plurizien green, surprising for a man who projected so much red. Still, all the red in the world couldn't hide Storm's love for Shadow. Madness had taken over his mind the second he learned the news of Shadow's death. Blinded by grief, he'd blamed Twist for his love's depression, shooting him in the heart before dying of grief.

"It's probably not that different," Stella said. "He's a suicidal mess. You weren't able to keep him alive then, and you are unlikely to achieve it now."

Storm curled over himself and held his stomach, and Stella wondered if she had pushed him too far. There was a fine balance between keeping him subdued and driving him into another killing spree.

Thorn exhaled a cloud of smoke lit by her seat's competitive orange glow. "So, you *do* want to torture him. Great!" She gritted her teeth in a smile.

Storm grunted, climbing down two and three steps at a time, and leaving a red trail in his wake. He approached Thorn, towering over her. "You don't get to fucking talk about him."

Within seconds, Thorn stood up and kicked Storm's legs from under him. One moment, he was reeling backward; the next, he fell on his back, sliding down three rows of seats and rolling on to the stage face down.

"Touch me again and I'll cut out your tongue. Try leading your revolution without it." Thorn exhaled the smoke as she was blowing a mortal kiss.

Unable to contain herself, a snort of laughter escaped Stella, her amusement at the situation momentarily overriding her composure. *So badass!* The entire oval flashed red, and for five long seconds, increased weight in Unanimity's gravity blocked participants from moving. Storm laid with his face and body glued to the ground.

As the gravity eased, Twist stood up. "Stella, these people are unstable and violent. Why did you bring them back? Th—that man" —he pointed at Storm—"is impacting our ability to serve humans. He is..." Twist wiped the sweat off his forehead. "What the hell are you doing?"

There was nothing godly about Twist. The whining man wasn't trying to lead or help her. *A useless checked-out God in the middle of a cosmic crisis.* As for her reasons for resurrecting the two murderers, she had several, including testing Sibyl's resurrection capabilities, but she wasn't prepared to disclose any of them.

"Shadow can deal with his poet's unreasonable revolution," Stella said. "I'm sick of it."

Storm got up, threw a dirty look at Thorn, and took a seat in the front row.

"Where's the popcorn?" Thorn asked, leaning her elbows back against the upper stone seat. She spread her legs in a style long-abandoned by men. These days, Up Above, people were too polite to occupy that much space.

"Don't you see?" Stella sighed, placed her hands on her hips, and continued speaking. "The signs of collapse are everywhere. The soulless are infiltrating the upper worlds. We can't figure out how this is happening, and Sibyl isn't helping. Hundreds of soulful Underlings are killed unnecessarily every day."

"Can't zie just suspend Domiz indefinitely?" Storm asked, pointing at Sibyl, who sat behind Twist, lit up by a white glow. "The demons are murdering my people."

"Genocide?" Thorn said, raising an eyebrow. "That's...nice," she mocked, but something about the way she bit on her cigar hinted Storm's suggestion bothered her. The athlete was spending a lot of time in the soulless worlds, particularly Domiz, and Sibyl gave Stella ambiguous answers whenever she'd enquired about Thorn's activities. The athlete's privacy settings blocked Stella from learning the truth.

Sibyl looked at the poet. "The violence amongst Underlings in Spiral Worlds is not affecting our ability to serve travelers. It's a feature, not a bug. The soulless serve an important purpose."

"Then just—just control your creatures," Storm said. "Why don't you change the rules to stop their attacks on upper worlds?"

Stella scowled. "I told you already. We don't know how they are doing it—jumping worlds. We've been looking at tweaking the directives, but—"

"It's not that simple." A hint of despair in Twist's voice. "Sibyl runs nine point seven billion Underlings across eight worlds. We change a parameter, and it affects a million other little things. Our brain, a perfect digital copy of a human brain, has limits. Even with the direct access to Sibyl, we, the Gods, are incapable of fully grasping the impact of our changes. Zie will share highlights of what zie perceives to be important, but zie has zir own plans."

"My plans are my Gods' plans," zie said. "I operate by your rules."

Twist ignored Sibyl. "The slightest tweak to the directives can have terrible consequences, and we sometimes don't know what questions to ask to get the right details. We are at zir mercy every time we change the parameters."

"And Sibyl has been a bit...emotional lately." Stella threw a judgmental look at the poet.

"They aren't mindless bots," Storm roared.

"You care because now you're a bot, like them," Stella said.

Thorn stood up. "Nathan Storm's been fighting for the rights of the minorities all of his li—"

"Shut the fuck up," Storm shouted without ever looking back at Thorn, and then he addressed Stella. "Can't you add a law stopping them from killing each other?"

"We have them kill each other often," Sibyl said, all matter-of-factly. "It provides humans the contrast they need."

"This place is so fucked up," Storm barked, lit by a sudden flash of red. "I thought you orchestrated the Underlings' lives?"

"Only when delivering experiences to travelers," Stella said. "Otherwise, they have full control over their actions, like you do."

"None of us has control over anything," Twist said, "we're all Sibyl's puppets."

"You created the app," Storm said. "Tom— I mean Shadow, what do you want from him?" He looked at Sibyl who merely flashed a coy smile and pressed zir lips together.

Stella gave her opinion on the matter. "Every single Underling originated from one of Tom's character templates. Shadow will help us identify what directives will fix the problem. Also, many soulful see him as their messiah." A fact she resented; she was supposed to be their new Goddess. Her competitiveness emerged in a burst of orange. "And there's even a chance the soulless will instinctively respond to their creator."

"Things have changed down there, preppy," Thorn said, furrowing her brows.

Stella was about to ask Thorn what she meant, but Twist interrupted. "You want to use him as a mediator?" he asked.

"Yeah, I guess so," Stella said, thinking out loud. "A visible God figure and a leader for the Underlings. I'm too busy managing Up Above. You're not helping, and I need help. He has a way with people."

Twist shook his head. "That's mad. He's allergic to the spotlight, and they aren't people; they are soulless, very dangerous to all non-carbon beings. They'll kill him."

"Yup, as they should," Thorn agreed.

"Currently," Stella said, "I'm more worried about his self-destructive tendencies."

"I'm outta here," Thorn announced, and she seemed to be in a hurry.

"Oh...don't—don't go," Stella said. "You are super important for—"

"Nah. I'm not. This has nothing to do with me and I'm hunted in this world." Thorn disappeared and Stella's lips plumped into a slight pout before she fabricated a smile.

"Why are we here, girl?" Storm asked Stella. "Don't you see the app is playing us all?"

"I'm not a girl, I'm your Goddess. Have some respect."

"I've been burned by religion, *girl*. My sexual orientation broke God's law. Don't expect me to kiss your feet."

"That can't be true! Which God? Harry?" Stella asked, puzzled.

Storm's laughter echoed around the oval structure. "What do you want from me, child?"

Stella exhaled deeply. "We must work together to keep Shadow alive," Stella said and, unexpectedly, Sibyl chuckled.

"A man who died a hundred times?" Storm choked up. "You-you just said... I-I failed to keep him alive. I'm not the answer."

"No, you're not. Stay away from him," Twist snapped, but then he lowered his head, defeated. "Neither am I."

"Don't you see?" Tears threatened to burst out of Storm's eyes. "The news of our deaths will...consume him. He'll go insane..."

"You caused some of the death," Stella said firmly, "and Shadow is... well...he's fragile...*everything* consumes him." She rolled her eyes. "He—"

"Shut up," Storm said. "Just...stop talking. He's stronger than all of us put together. For years he looked at pure evil in the eyes, and somehow, he didn't lose his heart."

"He did. In the end," Stella said.

"Lies." Storm dismissed Stella with a hand wave. "That's all he is— heart. Unlike you. Still, learning about our deaths will crush him."

"Let's be clear"—Stella flashed a commanding blue—"he isn't likely to survive, period. Help Shadow hold on to his hope and life, but don't get too close," Stella added. "Or you'll risk your sanity and... life."

"It won't be a problem," Twist said quietly as the space he occupied turned black—a lie.

"Lies aren't useful, father," Sibyl said.

"*I'm not your father*, you backstabbing bot." This time his red completely overwhelmed zir white glow. "I don't know what you are up to, but no, I won't get attached to the suicidal ghost of my dearest friend. *I can't!*"

"Twist, my beloved creator. I never lied to you," zie said sweetly.

"Girl," Storm said, and Stella's jaw tensed up. "Why did you summon Thorn? Why is *she...important?*"

"She was an important part of his life."

"You mean his death," Storm corrected, all high and mighty.

"No, I don't. The impulsive little thing was his lover when he died. I mean...when she killed him." Stella retaliated, making Storm's face turn several shades of rage. "Ah, sorry," she said smugly, her tone oozing in sarcasm.

"Oh..." Storm closed his eyes and massaged his upper arm and shoulder with the opposite hand.

Stella narrowed her eyes and sneered. "I guess you didn't know, uh? Don't be jealous. Thorn is not the type to shower him with affection. They had this super angsty chemistry. It was all about revenge, amazing sex, fireworks, and...well...murder."

She knocked him out. His head collapsed forward, a curtain of long copper hair hiding his face.

"Stella, zie's manipulative." Twist pointed at Sibyl. "You can't just trust what zie says. You need to ask zir the right questions or you'll end up dead like the rest of us."

"Ask away," Stella said, crossing her arms in front of her chest. "You created zir. Up Above, in school, they teach us how smart you are. I haven't seen it."

Twist pulled on his cuffs. "Sibyl, what do we need to do to restore peace and order in Spiral Worlds?"

Sibyl flashed a mocking grin. "There has never been peace Down Below. Underlings are subject to death and violence every day as per *your directives*. Ask me intelligent questions, will you...*dad?*" Zie took her time enunciating the last word, and Stella smiled at her friend's audacity.

Twist pressed his lips together and his face scrunched up as if he were thinking big thoughts. "Sibyl, how can we optimize Spiral Worlds for the wellbeing of the creatures Down Below, while continuing to serve the people Up Above?"

"Slaves!" Storm said, jumping to his feet, and Twist's entire body recoiled. The God's teeth chattered ever so slightly as his hands went up to his chest. Storm continued, "Why should we treat humans differently when most Underlings have souls?"

Sibyl stood up and walked to the middle of the stage. Zie smiled and then zir brows collapsed at the center over zir eyes—intense and commanding. "I'll answer the question truthfully."

"Which question?" Twist asked. His eyes were still set on Storm, monitoring his every movement.

"I tell you what you want to know," Sibyl said, "and what you'd rather not know, and you will do what I predict, even as you fight to prove me wrong."

"Don't play games," Twist warned. His shirt was stained by the sweat dripping from the back of his neck to his chest.

"And I want to remind you," Sibyl said, "that I don't create the future, you all do, and the future I predict is your shared responsibility."

"Get on with it, bot," Storm said.

Stella held her breath. Something in her gut told her the universe was about to unleash hell on them. She blinked at Sibyl, smiling with her eyes, reminding the universe, she was zir brightest star, and for the first time since she'd become a Goddess, Sibyl ignored her and her need for reassurance.

Sibyl held zir head high as zie spoke. "Do nothing and all worlds— Down Below and Up Above—will descend into chaos. The soulless will rage war against the soulful. Underlings will rebel against the travelers, Spiral Worlds will be shut down, and the Earthlings will lose their humanity. Eventually, Earth will be destroyed by their greed."

"What does all this have to do with Tom?" Storm asked.

"He is the key to everything. His resurrection will accelerate the worlds' unavoidable collapse, but if you keep him alive for six days, his death will deliver a new vision. A new order will emerge to deliver a fairer and brighter future. And this is the answer to all your questions."

Storm dropped to his knees.

"Six days?" Stella gasped. *Why didn't you tell me this?* She waited for an answer that never arrived.

"He'll die?" Twist struggled to project his grief-stricken voice.

"Yes," Sibyl said. "According to all my prediction models, he needs to die on the sixth day, *not before or after*, for peace and balance to be restored."

"Game theory?" Twist asked.

"Yes."

In Twist's eyes a hint of nervous anticipation. "Probability?"

"Ninety-nine point nine percent."

Storm rocked his body back and forward, arms wrapped in a self-embrace. "So...there's a chance he'll live longer?" he asked, his eyes screaming.

"Yes," Sibyl said somberly, "he would need to learn to live, but his death, on the sixth day, is the key to the future you want—fairer worlds. Without it, Spiral Worlds will collapse and so will Up Above." Sibyl looked at Twist, defiant. "He *must* die for you both to get what you want."

Twist swallowed the lump in his throat. "How will he die? Suicide? Murder?"

"Father,"—Sibyl narrowed zir eyes—"no and yes, and yes and no. To protect a man he loves, Shadow will fall at the hands of the only one he deliberately wronged."

"This is nonsense," Storm despaired. "All nonsense. We're just puppets in zir game. When is he back?"

Twist threw a dirty look at Storm. "Stay away from him."

"In ten days," Stella said.

"Why then?" Twist asked.

"This week, I'll be higher up attending...um...meetings. Yeah, attending meetings." Stella didn't lie, but she had no intention of telling them the truth. "So, can I count on both of you?"

"Count on what?" Twist asked. "You are asking me to watch my friend die, again."

Storm stood numb, head down.

"Help me keep him alive until the sixth day," Stella said, "but don't get close to him, not until the sixth day as, apparently, he'll die protecting one of you. *You* in particular"—she pointed at Storm—"keep him at bay for five days or he'll die protecting you and the worlds will die with him."

"Fuck you all and your games," Storm said, staring blankly at his shoes.

Stella turned to Twist. "It's been two years. It's time you return to the lab and help me rule the worlds." If Shadow was going to die, she needed Twist to manage the Underlings while she created humanity's bright future.

"I'll think about it," Twist said before he vanished.

"And you..." She scowled at Storm. "You need to stop giving the Underlings wrong expectations. There's no equality. They were created to serve the Earthlings. We're doing all we can to improve their quality of life, but they'll never be our equals." Effective leadership required prioritization and clarity. There was a pecking order and Stella's heart wouldn't bleed like Shadow's as she enforced it.

"You, girl, are an unworthy Goddess," Storm said as he stood up and disappeared.

"Sibyl, remind me why I brought these ungrateful people back?" Stella sighed. "They left and we haven't even reached consensus..."

According to Holizien tradition, participants should only leave the meeting when the entire oval glowed a steady turquoise. A light turquoise for consensus and a vibrant blue-green hue for unanimity.

Sibyl smiled. "My bright star, don't be so hard on yourself. It would take a miracle for this group to reach unanimity. And if I remember correctly, you are about to use your last one to bring back Shadow."

"Shhh. Please don't tell them about my first miracle. Shadow will kiss my feet when he finds out what I did for him." Stella couldn't wait to share her gift with the broody God. She was sure he'd be forever grateful.

Sibyl released a nervous laughter. "His knees will definitely hit the floor when he finds out what you did."

"I can't believe he'll be gone so quickly. I had all these plans for us. We'd be the perfect couple; him leading Down Below, and me Up Above." She took a minute to replay Sibyl's predictions. *Shadow will fall at the hands of the only one he deliberately wronged. The only one he deliberately...* "Wait! Who's going to kill him?" she asked, already knowing the answer. To please him, she'd resurrected his future slaughterer. "Oh ship, ship, shiiippp! The girl's going to kill him? But she's just a frightened kid."

"Not anymore," Sybil said. "However, you can choose to save him and put the worlds' future at risk."

"Don't be silly, Sibyl. Not even Storm and Twist would make such a choice. Of course we'll sacrifice one man to save the worlds."

"Right... Riiight..." Zie said tentatively.

THE Present

8

COMMITMENT TO LIFE

DAY 1 — 2:05 PM

T wist tried to monitor his buddy from the lab while the universe they'd built together collapsed around them. Sitting behind his desk with his eyes closed, he recoiled every time Tom was in danger, releasing exasperated sighs at his friend's terrible fighting skills. *You're gonna get yourself killed. You fool!*

With his mind's eye, he watched the video streamed live by Storm across Pluriz, and, as Sibyl was also part of the experience, he could see everything through zir eyes. There were moments where Nathan Storm's poetic disruption cut off communications, but he saw Thorn attack Tom, and her last threat sealed her fate. Twist vowed to change the directives to suspend the lives of the two xHumans as soon as he could get ahold of Stella.

His body softened once Tom had jumped out of Pluriz and material-ized in the lab.

Tom massaged his bruised jaw. "Where's Sibyl?" he asked, looking around. Dirt covered his jeans and white T-shirt, and his hair was messier than usual.

"Zie sometimes disappears for hours after Storm gets under zir metaphorical skin," Twist said, and after a long silence he continued. "We must suspend his life." He pressed his lips together, well aware of the backlash he was about to experience.

"What? Whose life?" Tom gasped. A look of horror in his eyes.

"Listen! We've done everything to avoid getting to this... I thought he'd stop, now you're back, but he hasn't."

Tom gestured expressively with his entire body as he worked to frame up his argument. He opened and closed his mouth several times, failing to use his words. "Ha—Harry—"

Twist raised his voice. "Dozens of Plurizien died at that event, some killed by glitches, others by the Domizien. Operations were suspended for over forty minutes, canceling billions of travelers' experiences. And you...*you* almost got killed. Storm and Thorn must go," he said decisively.

"No! I-I won't allow it." Panic took over Tom's face, his hand trembling as he used his long fingers to move his hair away from his eyes.

"We don't need your approval," Twist said coolly. "There's three of us now. We don't need unanimity. A majority will do to change the directives. They must go. Storm and Thorn are threats to humanity. Stella is as fed up with them as I am."

Tom stared at him like a wounded puppy. "This is not who you are... You wouldn't—"

"Pull the plug on two murderers destroying the worlds? I would, and I will. I'll summon Stella and we'll vote." Twist avoided Tom's eyes. His friend's pain affected him, but he needed to be rational and stop the devastation caused by the xHumans. This had nothing to do with his murder, *nothing*.

"Nate is simply doing what he has always done," Tom said. "He's an activist."

"He's a murderer!" Twist's face was hot and his body stiff. "I can't believe you're still defending him."

Tom stretched the collar of his T-shirt. "I'll never forgive him, Harry. Never. But this is not you... You don't kill people, and you're not vengeful."

"No, I'm not. I'm being rational, unlike you. He's a threat to the worlds."

"I'll speak to him and he'll stop the preaching. I promise. And as for Thorn, she just saved my life—"

"What are you talking about? For the last two weeks, since she was told you'd be back, Thorn has been showing up with the Domizien every time there's an attack. I don't know how she's jumping worlds with so many demons."

"She's not," Tom said. "She's following them. They seem to slip into the upper worlds from the faults in the fabric of reality. I think the spiral is collapsing over itself when Sibyl loses control."

"Overlapping worlds... You saw this?" Twist stood up and walked toward Tom, who nodded. "So, this is all Storm's doing," Twist said. "His preaching got more intense since he learned you were coming back. Still, Thorn sides with the demons and she's out to get you."

"No... Thorn is...all talk."

"That woman is vengeful and, frankly, she has good reasons to hate you. Hot sex doesn't change that."

Tom shook his head. "There's something fishy going on here." He went quiet for a second. "Where's Sibyl? Why can't I access Thorn's data?"

"Sibyl reverts to basic operational activities after these events. Zie's cleaning up and recovering. Stella's tied up Up Above, but she'll stop by just after dusk, and we'll vote to suspend the life of all xHumans that aren't Gods. A simple directive with no negative consequences."

Tom curved his shoulders, lowering his head to look Twist in the eyes. "Harry...please...let me see them...speak to them? I'll solve this."

"No. You'll get yourself killed," Twist said, taking a step back away from Tom and resisting his magnetism—all tenderness and warmth.

"Did you bring me back to make me watch the people I love kill each other?" Tom said mournfully.

"I didn't bring you back, and I'm not the one creating havoc and getting people killed."

"No, that's not who you are." Tom grabbed Twist's arm. "You are my Harry—generous, and kind, always coming up with positive ways to solve problems."

Twist pulled his arm away. "You know nothing about me."

Tom lifted his hands to his head, despair bursting out of his movements and expression. He stared at Twist intensely. "Listen. I know I...failed you. That you'll never forgive me. It's okay...I deserve that, and more." He took a breath. "But I want you to know that I love you. I'm here for you, and I'm not leaving, no matter what you do. I'll do whatever I can to support you." Tom's doe eyes lit up from the inside. "I'm sticking around, Harry. I give you my word, I'm going to be strong, and I won't give up on life, no matter what happens, no matter how bad it gets. It can't get worse than this, but if it does, I'll live to support you and them. You have my word."

Twist's heart dropped to the floor. *No, you won't...* But he didn't want to tell him about Sibyl's prediction. A shared prophecy was more likely to come true. Twist shook his head and gave in. "I missed you, buddy," he whispered.

Twist used the power of his entire body to hug his Shadow, compensating for his smaller build. Tom always gave the best hugs. His body curled over you, and his long arms embraced you with the wholesome welcome of an Italian grandmother. Now more than ever, Tom needed the warmth of selfless human touch—the nourishing skin-to-skin contact of a loving friend who saw him beyond his alluring outer shell.

Harry had never been much of a hugger before he met Tom Astley-Byron. At that time, nearly four decades before, he wasn't a big fan of people in general; machines made more sense to him. Harry was a huge proponent of logical reasoning and predictability, and he had discovered early in his life most humans lacked both. Then his friend came along, and it felt like home, the kind of home with a clay oven to bake homemade bread.

Harry learned to experience emotions through Tom's eyes. His Tom felt so much, *always too much*, with no filter on his body or face. Usually, Harry would stay away from this type of person. Many were irrational, and not that smart, but not Tom. He was the only one who could almost keep up with Harry's exceptional cognitive reasoning. Tom was even able to beat him at chess...*once in a while...one in every couple of games.*

Years later, their board games had become a family affair. June always sat by Tom. She held baby Quin in her arms as she attempted to throw Harry off his game by sharing sassy offbeat jokes and poking fun at his uber-dorkiness. They always ganged up on him—June and Tom. A benign complicity that had sparked from the first day they'd met. Fun-loving and generous, June had created the home they all needed; a joyful escape from their heavy burden.

Harry's life had been perfect and his home filled with love and laughter. *So much joy, all gone.*

Quin's uncontrollable giggles echoed in his head, and a sharp pain stabbed his chest making him stumble.

Tom caught him. "I'm sorry... I'm so sorry for everything. Harry, I'll speak to Nate and Thorn. I'll fix things."

"I can't risk your life..."

"I'm pretty sure this is why I'm back. Please?"

Twist picked a leaf off his friend's hair. "You'll die protecting the man you love." Without thinking, he repeated Sibyl's prediction. He hoped Tom didn't get its deeper meaning.

Tom smiled. "That's the best way to die, isn't it?" He shrugged his shoulders and tousled Twist's curls. "Trust me, they are as likely to wish me dead as you are."

A metaphorical punch to Twist's gut. They had every reason to want him dead in six days. "Buddy, I must tell you somet—"

"Harry, please, give me until the end of the day. They died because of me. Let me save their lives?"

Still today, Twist struggled to say no to Tom. He finally nodded. "You have until dusk to convince us they aren't a threat. Either way, the next time their actions impact the worlds, they're gone."

Tom's entire body softened as he exhaled loudly. "Thank you. I won't let you down."

"Tom?"

"Yeah?" Tom worried at his lip.

Twist didn't want to tell him about Sibyl's prediction, but he could do his best to be transparent about his situation. "If I ever have to choose between my family's wellbeing and your life, I'll choose them. Do you understand?"

"Me too. Me toooo." Tom shrugged as if Harry said the most obvious thing in the world and then flashed a reassuring smile. "Can I still jump worlds while Sibyl is MIA?" he asked.

"Yeah. Zie'll respond to your orders. Do you want me to go with you?"

Tom shook his head. "No, thank you," he said. "I'll be right back."

"Tom, don't travel to Domiz, Tribiz, or Archiz until Sibyl is available to give you a download on how the soulless have...evolved," Twist advised, as Tom disappeared.

Twist sat in front of his desk as the office spun around him. He remembered that feeling—relentless dizziness. At nine years old, Harry's parents had taken him on a rollercoaster ride. They'd said they wanted their steady child to experience a moment of unbounded exhilaration. Harry was pushed into a situation he couldn't control, thrown around and flipped upside down until the content of his guts reached his mouth. He tried to focus on the physics and the engineering powering his experience, but nothing worked, and he screamed and he threw up and begged to get out. Stuck in a car, close to the clouds, there was no way out.

For the last two years, Twist had buried his feelings in the deepest corners of his mind. He had refused to let the rollercoaster beat him, numbing his horrific loss by focusing on solving one problem—how to reconnect with his family. Now, Tom was back, and with him returned the heart and the emotions Twist had worked so hard to avoid. He was back inside the roller coaster car, bouncing around and out of control. He suppressed a scream, but his body convulsed, and bubbles of hot sweat emerged on his forehead as he threw up.

9

RUNNING OUT OF TIME

LAKE OF SOULS — GOMA, KIVU — AFRICAN UNION
DAY 1 — 2:11 PM

Stella's uniflyer slid down silently from the skies, and she used her mind to neutralize the magnetic lock keeping her boots firmly anchored to the sun-powered disk. The overlarge balloon sleeves of her Liputa-inspired dress fluttered with the air resistance. Its long pointy tails undulating gently just above her waist. A bird-of-paradise descending from the heavens to meet her devoted fans.

She stepped onto the Devil's Bridge arching over the deadly crater lake—a round pool of water beaming with bioluminescent light; the light of the dead. Like many other namesakes, the semi-circular metal structure connected the diameter of the small lake, reflecting in the water beneath it. Together, the bridge and its mirror became an immense sphere of sky and water. Blue and green combining into turquoise—always turquoise, the bane of her life.

The dissonant beats of the Ngoma drummers announced her arrival. The ten men and women stood on the bridge; their tribal hairstyles as large as their personalities. Cheeky hips twisting and teasing as their toned arms worked hard to elicit a physical and emotional response in the thousands waiting below.

Stella was so high up she could barely see the masses of loyal followers all packed closely together to watch her speak. Of course, she made sure they could see her. Stella's holographic projection filled the space under the bridge for everyone's delight. In reality, the image only appeared in everyone's augmented retina, leaving the sky untouched for every other species inhabiting that part of the world. Her image was inside the sphere, while she stood above it—a symbol of change. She was leadership, and life, and light. She was everything they missed; everything they needed.

She smiled as they chanted her name. They'd never know it was one of her empty smiles—ridden of truth, joy, or connection. A job she could perform on autopilot even as her mind went over every detail of her campaign.

She clenched her jaw, bothered by a minor flaw, and then she softened her mouth to stop her teeth from grinding—a bad habit she still struggled to overcome. It gave away her minor insecurities and impacted her brand of effortless invulnerability.

Bold ambitions required flawless execution, and she didn't like the name of the bridge—a customary name for that type of structure since ancient times. She'd tried to rebrand it to Gate of Miracles, but the new name didn't stick. The people were right; the place was too deadly and filled with death.

Unlike Stella, no one else seemed to mind the imminent natural disaster predicted for the region. After three decades of peace and abundance, people put their faith in the Gods' hands, forgetting Spiral Worlds was useless against Mother Earth's temper tantrums.

The planet's volatility unsettled her. She was spending so much time Down Below she'd forgotten she too had a fragile mortal body. A vulnerability she was working to eradicate for all humankind. She glanced at the uniflyer. It wasn't fast enough to save her from the looming menace.

Stella pushed the thought out of her mind, projected her voice, and spoke sincerely. An authentic voice lasted longer in people's minds.

"Yes, I am naturally gifted." She beamed with the confidence they had learned to expect. "But I still had to work very hard to become Spiral World's Goddess, *and I did it all for you!*" She was speaking to her grandmother, a soul trapped in one of the millions of tiny capsules floating in the lake. *I love you, Bibi.*

As expected, the gullible masses assumed she was talking about them, and the Liputa-style patterns of their garments flashed the sunny hue of joy. A wave of yellow traveled around the rim of the lake —their Systizien optimism beaming brightly.

The people's mood, sensed and disclosed by their clothing, harmonized into cheerful shapes and colors. A symphony of happiness with no skepticism in sight. *Too easy.* Externalized feelings were highly contagious. *A viral benefit*...as long as she triggered the right feelings, the ones that advanced her cause. And, of course, she did; she was raised by her Bibi to lead and succeed.

The people's smart clothing disclosed their emotions, health, and intent using not only color, but fabric that changed its shape and texture to best represent the wearer's disposition. A fashion invented after Holiz's launch to promote its values—authenticity, connection, collaboration, and selfless contribution. Repressive nonsense inspired by the last world Tom and Harry had designed. An experience layer released by Sibyl almost three decades after their creators' deaths.

"I discovered the human consciousness upload capability integrated into Henryk Nowak's beta pod. The answer to your immortality hidden away in a storage facility gathering dust for thirty years. Gods murdered just as they invented the end of death."

Ripples of moody gray were followed by loud gasps and moans for decades of lost souls—an unrecoverable tragedy.

Stella stood silently, letting the gray spread. It benefited her to let darkness infest their disposition as soon, she'd bring hope to their despair. She repressed a smile. In just a few years, she'd become a master at hacking fashion to her own advantage.

The masses' charcoal disposition blended with the color of the volcanic rock around the crater. A reminder of what was at stake.

Beyond the audience and the lush green oasis of the national park stood the fuming Nyiragongo. There, the sky blushed orange—a mix of sunrise and something else; something as scorching and powerful. Out of sight, the simmering hot lava hissed, threatening to burst out of Nyiragongo's rim into fast-moving red rivers of death. The volcano was increasingly active, and all prediction models expected it to erupt eminently as it had done in the past.

Still, her father had selected that place to store the minkisi—the souls of the dead. There was nothing she could do about that, apart from turning his idiocy to her benefit.

"In less than one year, I upgraded our infrastructure so all Spiral World's pods could collect as many human souls as possible—the souls of the sick and the old, and then all of your souls. Other entrepreneurs have developed the capability but lack our scale and computing power. They cannot create a digital world worthy of our people. *I can! I am!* Better than Systiz, or Holiz, I'm designing the heaven you deserve, and I'll grant you immortal life."

And as the crowds glowed bright, and some garments inflated and twinkled simulating goosebumps, she looked down at the soup of dead souls—the deadly lake where her grandmother waited resurrection. Bibi deserved to live forever, and Stella wouldn't rest until she was by her side.

"In three days, the Earth's Council will vote on whether we should grant digital immortality to the ones we lost recently. The answer is obvious. Yet, my father insists in unanimity as he opens the oval's door to the Unplugged—a minority whose values are beneath you all."

As slight red and blue hues circulated in the crowd, the shape of the garments changed automatically—hoods and collars lifting and turbans unwrapping to cover the shame in people's faces. Any color below green had a stigma associated with it, no matter how many times they were told that, in the right proportions, all values were needed for humans to survive and thrive.

Embarrassed, they hid their faces and eyes as this was the only thing they could do. They were able to control the settings of their clothing to share more or less of their inner workings, but the technology didn't allow them to lie. Archaic blue and red inclinations toward power and rage were immediately disclosed regardless of privacy settings; the colors of the lower worlds emerging despite decades of training. Stella couldn't understand their shame, they were right to be as mad as she was.

As expected, the most advanced amongst the masses flashed turquoise and transmitted the sounds of gentle breezes and mild sea waves toward their people. The ones who had gained access to Holiz could control everyone's bodysuits. There was just a handfull of them —the enlightened—but their presence and guidance was welcomed by all.

Then came the virtual group hug—a calming reassurance felt through the suit's ultrasonic haptic feedback technology. It delivered a warm and calming pressure in all the right places. *Sheep! So easily manipulated.*

The wave of blue-green wellbeing neutralized more than anger. It robbed them of their identity, freedom, and independence. Holizien values dumb them down, and yet she was forced to wear its colors. A small compromise that allowed her to reject politely their body-sensing suits and hide her new shade of progress. It was too soon for that. She had to conceal her flaming power for a little longer.

Power—there was nothing wrong with it. Leadership created order and drove progress. Every system needed a star whose gravity kept them together, spinning orderly and predictably. Unlike Tom and her father, she refused to dim her light.

Stella lifted her nose and spoke, projecting her voice. "I am Estelle Ngoie, Christian Ngoie's daughter, the man who emerged from the slums of Brazzaville to become the indisputable leader of the African Union.

"I am Estelle Ngoie, granddaughter of Gentille Mboma, Mai-Mai Shetani militia fighter at thirteen, rapid response unit captain at twenty, and the first woman to be appointed Army General."

A pinch of tribal purple touched the audience's vibrant burst of yellow; a reminder of the people's identity—their history.

"We raised from the ashes of a world where right and wrong were neither obvious nor real. Saviors, victims, and villains on both sides; on all sides; the same people; the true villains, elsewhere, across the ocean—bloodstained iPhones and diamonds. My Bibi fought to end the suffering of her people. She deserves to live in the heaven she helped create. They all do."

Stella looked down at the minkisi—millions of tiny human-shaped capsules floating in the lake, each one lit up by its bio-fluorescent shell. A trick she had designed to best represent the human conscious-ness stored within it. Each nkisi contained a nano-chip and its unique data. There were no backups. These had been the terms set by the Council as she proposed to collect the Earthlings' consciousness.

Once someone passed away, the data was downloaded and purged from Spiral Worlds. They had agreed the souls would not be uploaded or copied until they decided what to do with her gift of immortality. It was a reasonable request until her father came up with his illogical proposal to store the souls in the deadliest lake on the planet.

Much to her dismay, all members of Earth's Council had accepted unanimously Baba's recommendation to place the fate of the dead in God's hands. A hypothetical God whose existence had never been proven. The same God who had let greed and violence fester on Earth. An inexistent, irrelevant God that had failed Earthlings time and time again until Tom and Harry came along to rescue the world from the brink of collapse.

"We should give those who suffered and fought for a better world the chance to live in the heaven they worked so hard to create."

At the distance, Nyiragongo spewed electric-orange geysers, and then the Earth shook and shook again, and the people fled in all directions as Stella jumped on the uniflyer to fly away to safety. The most imminent danger didn't come from the volcano, but from the depths of the Lake of Souls.

Unlike her big sister—Lake Kivu—whose underbelly of diluted methane gas and carbon dioxide were continuously extracted for energy and safety, the Lake of Souls hadn't been degassed. Its three hundred feet of water acted as a lid containing the dangerous concoction—a ticking time bomb running out of time. A large overturn of water caused by an earthquake's rift, a rockslide, or incoming lava could release a frothy spray of carbon dioxide shot hundreds of feet. An immense cloud that would smother all lakeside life or trigger methane explosions on the surface.

The Earth's vibration sounded like a billion Nsakala rattles, and Stella cursed her father as she monitored the lake from the air. For

Gentille Mboma and the other souls twinkling in the water, this could be an irrecoverable tragedy.

THE Past

10

THERE GOES MY HERO

Sixteen-year-old Rosa García was in her bedroom, putting on her running shoes over mismatched socks—she was in a hurry. Her heart pumped out of her chest as she listened to the argument escalating downstairs in the kitchen. She tucked the untied laces into the shoes, rushing to leave the house before things got heated. Still, the heat rose quickly for every step she took down the stairs.

She could hear her mother's cries as her thug of a husband shouted at her. Ana García sobbed. That is all she did these days, parading her self-inflicted suffering for all the bad decisions she'd made. The worst of them: marrying Ron Johnson, a bullish advertising mogul who looked like a pudgy mobster, and pranced around with an awkward mix of sleaze and slickness.

Every time Rosa stood up for Ana, her mother undermined her efforts and defended Ron. Rosa was tired of playing that game; she didn't want to be involved in any of it.

As Rosa walked down the stairs, preparing to leave the house for a run, she pressed gently on the side of her right earlobe to activate the micro-earphones implanted just under her skin.

"Sensei, the news," she asked her AI assistant.

"Sure, Rosa," said the precise male voice.

Rosa ran out the door and into the neighborhood. Around her, climate-displaced people everywhere, some lining up for odd jobs, others for food. Vulnerable refugees, clutching onto bags storing what was left of their lives as bone-tired children curled up on the concrete by the adults' feet. *What a fracking mess!*

Challenging the stiffness in her body, Rosa sped her pace, shaking off her frustration.

The news stories read by Sensei were complemented by unobtrusive, half-transparent visuals projected on her augmented retina.

"Sibyl, a voice app that predicts the future on people's public social media timeline, continues to go viral due to its accuracy. Its young developer, nineteen-year-old Henryk Nowak, is quickly rising to become one of the top-ten wealthiest and most powerful people in the world. Upcoming pregnancy, divorce, disease, marriage, betrayal, bankruptcy, or a promotion—Sibyl predicts it all using our data prints. It has an astonishing seventy-five percent accuracy rate." A photo of Henryk appeared in Rosa's retina—a nerdy-looking boy not much older than she.

Rosa went off-street, engaging in some parkour. She ran and jumped through Portland's back alleys, enjoying the guerrilla street art. Chalk, spray paint, and yarn transformed the dull back streets into a colorful revolutionary cry for change.

Rosa's lungs were burning, and she coughed a couple of times, struggling with the pollution in the air. Most athletes trained indoors, enjoying the clean air delivered by air purifiers, but Rosa found it too dull and constraining. She liked to experience the world as it collapsed right in front of her eyes, one day at a time. A disaster of monumental proportions, experienced in slow motion. Everyone was numb, running about their days. Each day was a little worse—the poverty, the yellowish-gray sky, the news, the health problems. An entire civilization was subdued, too busy reacting to the consequences to deal with the root cause. *Idiots!*

The global crisis was real, but the consequences were only lightly felt in Rosa's home city of Portland. Her world wasn't perfect, but she was beloved by her divorced parents. Nights and days, on weekends and weekdays, the Garcías juggled several jobs to give their only daughter the best possible education, and they supported Rosa in her aspirations to compete in the modern pentathlon.

Rosa's parents raised her to be confident in her abilities and ambitious in her goals. The world was hers to conquer, and her capable body was her weapon of choice. She worked hard to qualify for next year's Summer Olympics in Chicago. Unfortunately, LA's hazardous air, drought, and extreme temperatures had destroyed California's aspirations to become the host of the 2028 games.

Sensei continued with the news. "*Glass Walls and Broken Mirrors* is becoming a defining cultural moment for the climate-displaced communities around the world. It's breaking box-office records and gaining conclusive, critical acclaim. Director Jane Elliot and young screenwriter Thomas Astley-Byron are sure to lead the nominations during award season."

A clip from the movie came up in Rosa's retina. She saw an African-American woman in her fifties, wearing a mint-colored beret. The woman shouted, "One world!" as a border barrier opened, letting migrants in. Rosa rolled her eyes, skeptical of the film's impact on people's goodwill.

State border walls and conservative politicians attempted to keep climate refugees out. Within each nation, cities in the interior north resented the invasion of displaced citizens. Ethical leaders and progressive media tried and failed to bring out the compassion of Earth's people. These were devastating times, during which the best of people dropped their altruism to protect their families and friends. It was a matter of survival. There was too little to share, nothing to offer, and a lot to fear.

Rosa's chest tightened with all the uncertainty, and she had to stop momentarily to catch her breath.

"Sensei, summon Sibyl."

"Hi, Rosa; can you face the future, whatever it will be?" Sibyl spoke with an edgy metallic accent. A gimmick likely designed to keep people on their toes.

"Yes."

"I need access to your data prints—social media, medical, financial, and consumer records, and all other data available on the World-chain's distributed ledger. My predictions are shared publicly on your timeline. Permissions required."

"Granted."

"Now, I will tell you things that are to come. Are you ready?"

"Yes."

"You will become an Olympic medalist soon."

After a couple of minutes, an avalanche of messages and notifications popped up on Rosa's retina. Her friends were going wild with the news; they discussed it on her timeline. Rosa flashed an arrogant smile.

"Sensei, close all apps and notifications."

"All done."

"Sensei, play the running playlist." The music started, and Rosa sang along, changing the lyrics' gender. "There goes my herooo, watch her as she goes. There goes my herooo, she's ordinaryyy..." She kept running with a renewed conviction in her step.

Rosa was born in the feminist Renaissance, a time when media and history books were finally starting to reflect female achievement, and comic-book heroism was gender-less and raceless. She still preferred the old feminist classics over the new caped crusaders, and she channeled Buffy, Sydney Bristow, and her much beloved Kara "Starbuck" Thrace. She adored everything about the Goddess Tracy Lord, all but that one moment when her father tamed her. "Bullshit," she always mumbled to herself, skipping ahead of that part of *Philadelphia Story*.

Like many in her generation, she turned to history and old media, looking to escape her dystopian reality. Back then, the planet was greener, the humans brighter, and the villains layered and less monstrous. Nostalgia for everything old led an entire generation of teens to fill the streaming services' popularity charts with decades-old content.

"There goes my herooo, watch her as she goes. There goes my herooo, she's ordinaryyy..."

A couple of hours later, Rosa arrived at her condo and walked in the main door of the converted warehouse. The door opened automatically as the smart lock recognized her proximity. Her sweaty body stiffened as she heard the screaming inside.

Ron Johnson had appeared on the scene during the Garcías' messy divorce. Ana had married Ron quickly when Rosa was fourteen. The girl had always felt something sinister about her new stepfather. From the day she'd met him, she had realized he loved only one person, himself.

Mr. García checked in with Rosa more often than he did when they lived in the same home. He often mentioned that the word on the street was that Ron had a history of harassment and abuse of young interns. First, Rosa took it for jealousy, but as she reached her late teen years, her father's words of caution kept playing in her mind. Once in a while, Ron absentmindedly looked at Rosa with lustful eyes. His left permanently marked with a large red mark covering half his iris. *Nature's warning*, Rosa had decided. She always confronted him with her scowl, and he would back down the moment he realized what he was doing, but she couldn't find a hint of shame or embarrassment in his eyes.

Rosa kept Ron at arm's length, and he was too smart to mess with an overconfident teen athlete with a voracious appetite for confrontation. Ana, however, suffered a different fate. What had started as a dubious fairy-tale romance for Ana had taken a downturn into an abusive relationship. The oppression started quietly; a few words spoken to undermine Ana's self-worth. Ron had once attempted the same strategy with Rosa, but she bit back so ferociously that it never happened again. Rosa would often witness Ron's verbal aggression to Ana, but the abuse had never been physical until that exact moment.

"You stupid bitch!" Ron yelled. Then he used the entire strength of his body to slap Ana on the face with his open right hand. Rosa's mother was a meek woman with a thin, frail constitution. She fell backward, and her head hit the nearest wall before she collapsed on the floor.

"Get away from her!" Rosa screamed, placing her body between the two. She turned to help Ana to her feet. "Sensei, call the police."

"Yes, Rosa."

Rosa scanned her surroundings and picked up the empty stainless-steel coat stand, turning it around and raising it as if it were a fencing épée. She faced the man without fear, adrenaline rushing through her body. *Step, step, lunge.* She thrust the object close to his face, and he stood there, staring at her, his body as frozen as his blood-stained gaze.

"I lost my mind. I'm sorry." Ron's brows deliberately raised at the center. The type of dishonest performance only Ana would buy.

Untouched, Rosa kept her focus on his hand, closed into a tight fist.

"Put that down, Rosa," Ana urged. Her face was still red from the slap. "He didn't mean it. It's okay, Rosita. *Mi culpa.*"

"SOS services. Hi, Rosa, what is your emergency?" Only Rosa could hear the call-taker.

"*Dios mio! Rosita, por favor!* Cancel the call." Ana spoke in a soft and almost imperceptible voice. She reached to hold her daughter's arm, squeezing it. "*Mi amor,* I'll handle this."

"You better. This can't go on." Rosa took a deep breath, her eyes still locked on Ron as he moved his hands up, palms open, facing her. Rosa blinked twice, selecting the call displayed on her augmented retina. "Hi, this is Rosa García. Hmm, apologies, my assistant misunderstood my command."

"All right. Have a good day." The call ended, and Rosa wondered if she had fooled the bot that scanned for distress in the caller's tone of voice.

She threw the coat stand at the man. "Get out!" she demanded of him. Then she looked at her mother—disappointment and worry in her expression. "How could you have married this guy?"

"It won't happen again." Ron's eyes betrayed his words. "I lost it. I'm sorry."

"Go upstairs, *amor,*" Ana said, holding Ron's hand.

Rosa opened her mouth to speak; nothing came out. She shook her head, disgruntled, turned around, and left the house, slamming the door behind her. She despised her mother's weakness as much as she hated Ron. Her father was right when he claimed Ana was putting Rosa at risk by marrying such a man. She promised herself she'd report Ron to the police if it ever happened again.

Still shaken, she ignored the sharp pain in her stomach as she ran through the streets, noticing the different slogans for the upcoming elections: GOD IS ALL THE SCIENCE WE NEED. JOBS FOR HUMANS, NOT BOTS. The planet was in chaos, and no one was doing anything about the climate crisis.

A recent pandemic had sped up the world's automation as humans became a biohazard. The jobless, famished masses lost faith in science, and the supposedly progressive middle class, now too concerned with immediate survival, dropped the ball on the environment.

She hated feeling helpless, but there was little she could do. Her actions were a drop in an ocean full of plastic debris. The world needed a revolution, but she wasn't the type to lead movements—she was more of a warrior, a soldier looking for the right master, one she could proudly follow. Rage rose to her face—hot and tortured. She ran as fast as she could, attempting to forget her problems.

"Sensei, play *Thorns from Roses* by Nathan Storm."

In a world filled with greed and self-interest, Storm was one of the few voices defending the rights of the people no one else cared about. As the rich and powerful built resorts on Mars preparing to leave the world they destroyed, the climate dispossessed, now unable to vote and jobless, rallied around Storm's powerful voice. A voice of reason, and he had all the reasons in the world to be mad, and so did Rosa.

"Rise the rage, nature's revolution, thorns from roses, Mother Earth's solution. Digital-age born, screams, cries of outrage. Pollution is our stage. Enrage! Engage!

"Casualties of destitution, our souls' execution, technology is our sage, a God, a cage. We rise for restitution, a path to evolution. A unicorn eats our wage. Engage! Enrage!"

11

A MATCH MADE IN…

GLASS WALLS RALLY — CENTRAL PARK — NEW YORK
SAME DAY — 26 APRIL 2027

Twenty-three-year-old Thomas Astley-Byron marched alongside thousands of protesters who took to the streets inspired by his blockbuster—*Glass Walls and Broken Mirrors*. The group, mostly comprised of older women, teenagers, and children, chanted, "One world! Our world!" as they marched across Manhattan, wearing mint-colored berets and holding up posters with slogans that read LET THEM STAY and OPEN BORDERS.

The crowd gathered at Central Park's green lawn, and Tom stopped in front of a young man, the only other Caucasian male in the vicinity. Tom smiled recognizing the famous entrepreneur.

Henryk Nowak extended his hand. "Hi, I'm Harry," he said, blinking his eyes and smiling.

"Yes, I know! My name is Tom." Tom smiled back and stole a hug, soon realizing he'd gone too far when Harry jumped back, eyes wide, startled by the unexpected embrace.

Harry adjusted his glasses, tucking his sandy short curls behind his ears. "'Course you are." And then he chanted, "One world! This is all because of you."

"Oh." The heat rose on Tom's face. "No, not really." He looked around, worry weighing on his brow, and then he lifted his index finger to his lips. "Shhh." He placed his hand on Harry's shoulder, and they walked together, following the crowd. He recalled the news of Harry's family tragedy and went out of his way to make him feel welcome.

Three years before, a climate refugee had turned into a suicide bomber after her family perished in the Florida floods. She had tried to mobilize northern states to send support and open the borders, to no avail. She killed forty-five people who were dining in an expensive Brooklyn restaurant. Amongst the victims were Harry's parents and sister.

Tom felt somewhat responsible for Harry's family tragedy. His late father, Jon Stone, who was at the time the governor of New York, had blocked the asylum-seekers from entering the state. Governor Stone had been planning to dine at the same restaurant that evening but had to cancel his plans when his wife—Tom's mother—passed away.

Tom had dropped his father's surname a long time before. No one knew Tom Astley-Byron and Jon Stone were related. When he was just old enough to reject his father's politics and move out of their home, Jon's aides had lied to the media. The world was misled to believe Tom Stone had moved to Costa Rica to do some nonprofit work, indefinitely.

Tom was usually reserved and guarded when it came to meeting strangers. Still, his instinct told him brainy Harry would probably be oblivious to any subtle gestures of empathy. So, he dialed up his warmth significantly to connect with the young entrepreneur. He knew he had achieved his goal when Harry responded with nervous excitement. The skinny boy smiled awkwardly, blinking his blue eyes behind his glasses. Tom found Harry's inability to hide his enthusiasm quite endearing. The young man appeared to be genuinely happy to make the acquaintance.

Harry turned his green baseball cap around on his head and then pointed to Tom's mint-colored beret. "Shame I didn't have the time to buy one of those French hats. This is the best I could do. The geek version of the activist look."

"You look great! I've spotted you at several of these rallies. I like that you take the time to join us. I assume you're a busy man," Tom said, acknowledging his famous companion.

"It's important—activism matters. But you know that, don'tcha? You've written it beautifully."

Tom looked around, hoping no one had heard Harry. "How do you know who I am?"

"You told me." Harry's eyes landed on his feet, and he shoved his hands in his pockets.

The young man wasn't a good liar. It was better than being a sophisticated deceiver, but something was off. "No, I didn't," Tom replied in a neutral tone. He shook off his unease, giving Harry the benefit of the doubt.

"You know who I am. Don't you?" Harry argued.

Tom stroked his one-week-old stubble nervously. His level of discomfort was rising fast. "I see you in the news all the time. Harry, how *did* you recognize me?"

"I-I did some research. You know? Online."

"There are no photos of me online. I made sure of that."

After a long silence, Harry spoke without ever lifting his eyes. "Okay. I may have hacked the production company's HR database."

"You did what? *Why?*" The confession left Tom stunned. He'd learned early on to stay away from cameras and refused to engage in social media, first because of his father's controversial role in government and his mother's suicide, and later because of the success of his career. And now this guy, this wealthy geek, famous beyond belief, was confessing openly to a most serious offense.

"I was looking for your contact details," Harry said plainly, almost childlike, as if he had done nothing wrong.

Tom wasn't sure if the boy in front of him was naive, stupid, or completely unaware of the seriousness of his actions. He took a deep breath, deciding to reason with his stalker. "You could have *asked*."

"Oh, come on! You're famous for your relentless focus on privacy."

"With the press!"

"It was easier to get to your file."

"Easier than talking to people?" Tom stopped and stared at Harry.

"Yeah." Harry's eye roll both angered and amused Tom. "More time-efficient. A few keystrokes instead of endless, pointless conversations. Then I got to your employee ID photo, and I discovered I already knew you—from rallies like this. I've seen you around."

"So, you invaded my privacy, and now you're stalking me?"

"No, I mean yes—*No!*" Harry stepped back, opening his eyes wide.

"Which one is it?"

"I've watched your movie. It inspired me."

"It's no excuse."

"Listen. I'm smart. Really smart," Harry said, standing straighter.

In some ways. "I know. We all know it."

"And I have resources," Harry said. "Money. Plenty of it."

"I don't care about your—"

"The stuff I'm doing—it's pointless."

"Sibyl?"

Harry nodded. "I thought it would help people, but it's causing some problems."

Tom couldn't hold back a salty tone. "Yeah. Tell me about it." Sibyl had sneaked into the lives of several people he loved. The app had delivered a mixed bag of results, some good, some bad, and one catastrophic. Many were raising concerns that Sibyl could be psyching people up to the things it predicted.

Harry hunched his shoulders and placed his right hand on his stomach as if he had received a body blow. Tom turned around, ready to leave, and Harry grabbed his arm firmly.

"Wait. Please wait." Tom looked back, yanking his arm away, and for the first time, deep emotion emerged in Harry's eyes as he looked up to face him. "Look, Tom, I'm sahry." Harry's mild New York accent got stronger and more urgent. "I mean no hahm."

"You've gone too far."

"Hey, listen, I'm good with software, and with patterns. I-I test things thoroughly and make decisions based on logic and...on what I think is right. But human emotion—the lack of rationality of it all—it's beyond me."

"I don't get it. What do you want from me?" Tom spoke softly, puzzled and moved by the boy's confession.

"I wanna make a pahsitive impact, and I need you to help me do it," Harry said brightly.

"Why me?" Tom threw his hands in the air. "I don't understand."

"I need someone that can help me see people, real people, each and every one of them...and emotions, you know?"

"You don't know me."

"I *do!* The way you write, it makes me feel things. I walked in her shoes and felt what she felt. It changed me. I-I almost, *almost* cried when I watched your movie. I was so close. And, ya know, I never cry, not even when my family..."

"I'm sorry for your loss, Harry. I—"

"I once looked into the science of tears. Did you know Charles Darwin once declared emotional crying purposeless? I tend to agree with him... Anyway, don't get me wrong, I have tear ducts and can keep my eyes moist."

"Uh-huh." Tom worked hard to keep a straight face.

"I just rarely feel things. I think. I infer. I predict. But I'm failing; Sibyl is causing problems because humans and their emotions get in the way."

Tom sighed as he listened to Harry's flawed logic. He knew he should leave, but he had a long track record of being incapable of walking away from a lost cause. "What do you need?"

"I need a partner, a friend. Someone who can help me with my blind spots. Someone I can trust. Who can tell me when I'm doing something wrong."

"Like hacking into systems and invading someone's privacy?"

"All right, already!" Harry said, lowering his head and then looking up at Tom with embarrassment. Tom was horrified to think about how much power Harry and his app had on millions of people. But, for some reason, he couldn't help but have compassion for the young entrepreneur. "My sister and my mother used to do that."

"Do what?"

"Help me," Harry said. "With people and feelings. It's hard to figure out what's right all the time. Analytics helps, but it's not enough."

"No, it's not. I'm so sorry for your loss," Tom repeated, uncertain if Harry had heard him the first time.

"We have that in common, don't we? Loss," Harry mumbled, gloomy.

Tom refused to oblige. He couldn't. It was too painful to dwell on his own loss, and he wasn't ready to share that much with his intrusive companion. He wanted to ask how Harry knew about his parents, but he didn't want to confirm the boy's assumptions.

"Look," Tom said. "I appreciate the interest, I really do. You're a talented guy, and I respect how open you've been with me, but I can't help you. I oppose the dicey methods and tactics you tech guys use. Sibyl is...dangerous, and you—you are reckless."

"That's why I need you, Tom."

Tom inhaled sharply. "You don't know me!"

"Yes, I do. I have watched your work. How you opposed everything your father stood for."

Tom held his breath and took a step to the side. *How does he know all this?* He shook his head. "There are literally thousands of people that would love to help you."

"Yes, I've created the most powerful app in the world. And now everyone wants a piece of me—my knowledge, power, and wealth. Should I—can I trust them?" Harry used his index finger to adjust his glasses, sliding them up the bridge of his nose. His eyes begged for Tom's attention.

"Great, you know how it feels to be harassed. You should know better."

"Don't you see? I'm offering it all to your cause. We can help each other. I-I trust you."

Tom considered it, affected by Harry's striking openness. His gut told him the misguided teen had good intentions.

"You don't know when to give up, do you?" The corners of Tom's mouth hinted at a smile.

"I told ya, I'm not good at reading emotions." Harry smiled and relaxed a little. "You can always call the police, but then we'll both have the media on our case."

Tom took a moment to look at Harry, to really look at the foolish, overeager, and somewhat insensitive teenager standing in front of him. A guy who seemed genuinely keen to be his friend. Harry appeared youthful for his age, a fact he attempted to overcome by wearing grown-up clothes. The boy's long-sleeve button-down shirt was perfectly pressed and neatly tucked inside his khaki pants. The self-professed hacker mostly kept his hands in his pockets as they walked. Everything about him suggested he needed structure and order in his life. Despite all warning signs, Tom couldn't help but like Harry a lot, and his intuition rarely failed him.

"Walk with me, stalker. You're already proposing, and we haven't been on our first date yet."

"Tom, I'm not gay."

"It's a figure of speech."

"I thought I should say it. You know. I know you are g—"

"Don't—don't define me. You know nothing about me," Tom said sharply.

"Sorry, the data said you were cool with your sexuality."

"I am," Tom said without missing a beat. "When you put someone in a box, you fail to see them, to *really* see them for all they are and have the potential to become. Your data and your technology do that to people—put them in boxes."

"You're right, but we're getting better... AI is—"

"The only person that can define me is me. *And* you need to stop invading people's privacy."

"Your privacy. To be clear, I only invaded your privacy."

"Well, that's reassuring," Tom said sarcastically, smirking. Then he felt a sharp prickle of awkwardness, and he clarified his position. "For the record, you're not my type."

"What *is* your type?" Harry enquired, leaning his head to one side curiously.

Tom raised a solemn eyebrow. "At the top of the prerequisites list reads 'law-abiding citizen.'" He paused for effect. "In neon lights."

Harry burst into laughter. "Just so you know, Sibyl predicted with ninety-nine point nine percent confidence we'd get along." He cleared the lump in his throat and added, "You were on top of her list. That's why I've been chasing you."

"So, you *are* making a pass at me? Stalker."

"No. *No!* It's just that...you're my perfect match."

"Your soulmate? Theoretically, maybe. But how would she know about my feelings on this matter?"

"She's been dealing with millions of people. They give her access to tons of data, all of it. She is starting to develop a stronger theory of mind than my own."

"You're suggesting she's able to understand how people feel, which is entirely irrational and subjective."

"It's not subjective if it can be modeled and coded, is it?" Harry insisted. "Once we have the model, we can fix it."

"Fix what?"

"Human irrationality—the vengeful emotions that make people kill."

"I see..." *Your family's murder...* Tom paused, finally understanding Harry's motivations. "So, why do you need me? If you have an AI overlord full of empathy and intuition?"

"Well, she's not perfect...yet. She needs to learn from someone like you. But I'm *totally* certain she's accurate about us."

"Right. We'll see about that." Tom sighed, shook his head, and put his hand back on Harry's shoulder, and they continued walking together.

12

BETHESDA

Harry was not the type to get overexcited about things. He had a steady temper and a skeptical mind. His judgment wasn't polluted by cynicism or prone to following unjustified trends and thrills. He used facts as fuel to move him forward, and approached failure as an opportunity to learn and adapt. Harry wasn't one to experience a sense of elation often, but walking beside Tom made his hands sweat, and his fingers tingled with exhilaration.

For the past few weeks, he had meticulously assembled the complex puzzle that was his companion's life. He was able to overcome Tom's diligent privacy using computing power, artificial intelligence, and the scattered data left by anyone who had interacted with the writer.

Tom's story came to life vividly once Sibyl had figured out he had dropped his father's surname—Stone—in favor of his mother's maiden name. AI may have validated the two of them were a good match, but the conclusion was evident to Harry as he read through Tom's history. Their families' misfortunes were loosely connected and equally painful.

Harry knew he could trust Tom, but he had to figure out how he could make Tom trust him, quickly. The first few moments had been a little bumpy, and he wasn't out of the woods just yet. Tom's hand on his shoulder gave him enough encouragement to proceed with his plan to become the artist's best friend. It was the most logical outcome, based on all the data he had analyzed.

"So, what's next? Now the movie is out?" Harry asked, doing his best to smooth over the momentary awkwardness.

"Wait, Sibyl didn't tell you?" Tom's taunt was friendly and casual.

"Our guess is educational stories, powered by virtual reality, to nurture empathy. Right? Right?" Tom's face turned even paler, almost transparent. "Just a guess; I didn't hack anything."

"You couldn't have. Unless you can hack my mind."

"One day, dude. One day," Harry joked, and Tom gave him a side glance, mildly alarmed. One thing Harry liked about Tom was that he didn't make eye contact often. Harry had always thought eye contact was an intimate experience, and he avoided it at all costs.

As they walked toward the Bethesda Terrace, people watched them with a lot of interest. Initially, Harry thought the protesters recognized him from the media. Later, he realized it was his anonymous companion that caused all the commotion.

Tall, beautiful, and graceful in the way he moved, Tom captured the full attention of those around him. Both men and women smiled flirtatiously, trying to make eye contact with the bashful young man. He avoided prying eyes wrestling for his attention by keeping his gaze high above their heads, or on the ground, as he glided through Central Park, lost in his own thoughts.

"Yes, I want to focus on learning experiences. I have the characters and stories figured out, but I need to look into the technology and the infrastructure side. I'm useless at it. I can't get my head around it."

The artist's voice was surprisingly deep—his words delivered with the confident sophistication of Manhattan's royalty. A musical mid-Atlantic accent too mature for his age.

Harry artificially lowered his pitch to sound older. "You know that's my bread and butter, right?"

"I know you design forecasting apps and hack into people's lives. That's what I know."

Harry made a face. "Hey, all right!" Then he took a minute to think about it and committed to his quest. "I think you should skip VR altogether and go with BCIs—brain-computer interfaces. Let the brain do the work for you, the rendering, etc. It's much more powerful. You know? VR is super weak; it lacks good 3-D sound and kinesthetic feedback, and it's completely missing scent and taste." Tom stared at him as if he were speaking an alien language, but Harry didn't give up. He wanted to show off, and he'd pitch his knowledge and prove he could help the writer. "I've received some noninvasive beta BCI models from BrainComms. They're getting there, hmm, but still have some issues." Harry searched his brain for answers, excited by all the possibilities. "Maybe we should start with a hybrid solution—a VR full bodysuit with high-res 20/20 visual acuity, eye tracking, 3-D sound, haptic feedback, and a ton of biosensors. Plus, non-invasive multimodal brain activity acquisition tools to capture spatiotemporal high-res data." He adjusted his glasses, unbuttoned his cuffs, and rolled up his sleeves. "Later, we'll drop everything else and focus on minimally invasive read-write BCIs for full immersion. By then, we'll have a ton of data on how the brain works."

It took Harry a few moments to realize he might have gone too far. Tom opened his eyes wide like he'd seen a flesh-eating zombie or something.

"What the hell are you talking about?" Tom said, sounding overwhelmed.

"Sorry. Got a bit carried away. I forget that not everyone is an expert... like I am," Harry said, still pitching. He tried to find a language Tom would understand. "It's like *The Matrix* but much less physically invasive. We can figure it out."

"We?" Tom replied with an unexpected burst of laughter. "You are as hilarious as you are terrifying."

Out of nowhere, a red-haired man jumped in front of Tom with a beaming smile on his face. Then the ginger stared at Harry, cocking his head to one side with a slight frown. "I leave you alone for a moment, and you run off with the most powerful guy in the country." He put his arms around the writer's neck and kissed him on the mouth, taking a moment to suck on his lower lip. Tom returned a glorious smile, closed his eyes and surrendered to his captor with delight.

Harry shook off the embarrassment, and he said, "Look around you." He pointed at the signs with Tom's words carried by the protesters. "I think we know who's the most powerful."

"He knows who you are?" whispered the man, surprised. He still held Tom closely by the waist.

"It's...a long story." Tom seemed entirely at ease as his friend ran his fingers through his messy dark hair.

"Nathan Storm." The man extended his hand. "I'm his boyfriend," he said somewhat assertively.

"Harry." He smiled.

"Yes, you sure are." Storm stared intensely.

Tom's friend had a fair complexion, his face lightly touched by freckles. He had a flawlessly trimmed long beard and a jazzed-up mustache that made Harry a little jealous. He had been waiting for years and still couldn't grow facial hair to save his life. Nathan was slightly shorter than Tom and sported a wider frame. He was good looking by any standards, but lacked the stunning genetic gifts of the screenwriter. To be fair, no one on the planet could even come close to Tom's league, but Storm compensated with plenty of charisma and a flamboyant style. The man complemented his jeans and T-shirt with a well-worn black peacoat embroidered with golden serpents. He wasn't wearing a beret; it would probably ruin his perfectly coifed hair, structured into a tall and immovable copper wave above his forehead.

Storm's attention moved back to Tom. "The crew is waiting, love. We're heading to Paddy's Brewery."

"Don't, you already smell like one," Tom whispered in his boyfriend's ear, but Harry was still able to hear him. "Stay here with me; we're having a fascinating conversation." Harry wasn't happy with the suggestion; he wanted Tom's attention all to himself.

Storm reacted with mild annoyance and then glanced at Harry. "Your Sibyl and my boyfriend have a lot in common. They both like to nag about my liver."

"Yeah, she can infer a lot from your payment history. The easiest type of prediction," Harry said, sounding smart.

"And they both like to shame me in public."

"Peer pressure works, and makes the app go viral."

Nathan examined Harry dubiously. "Big shot, you don't need to be a capitalist pig. You could make the predictions private." The older man's feminine tonality was seasoned with a handful of antagonism every time he addressed Harry.

"I wouldn't have a business if I did. No one would know about Sibyl."

"The business of taking our jobs, selling our data, and threatening our free will. I'm watching you."

"Leave him alone, Stormy." Tom grabbed Storm's coat by the large notch lapels, pulled his boyfriend to him, and kissed him. "Stay with me. You don't need to drink to be creative."

Storm covered Tom's mouth with his index finger and planted a kiss on his cheek. "I'm not as talented as you are, love. Not everyone can reach the masses without some...help."

"You move millions regardless of mind-altering substances."

Storm batted his lashes, flashed a teasing smile, grabbed his boyfriend's striped top by the collar, and pulled it over his head, uncovering his belly button. Tom's beret fell to the ground. "Stop preaching, Granny," he whispered affectionately.

"Get off me." Tom laughed. When the screenwriter managed to uncover his head, his face was flushed and his hair even wilder than before. He appeared so tender next to his older boyfriend. Storm put his hand on the back of Tom's neck and pulled gently to kiss him on the lips.

"I love you," Storm whispered.

Sibyl's report had mentioned Tom was dating a disreputable poet and political agitator. Nathan Storm had an edge Harry didn't like. The man looked battle-ready, raw, and quick-tempered. His inconsistent sophistication failed to hide a working-class, street-raised back-ground. That, combined with the age difference, made the pairing odd and Storm's intentions dubious. But even Harry could see the man was smitten by Tom's effortless regal cuteness.

"Look at him. He's stunning, isn't he?" Storm said adoringly.

Tom was busy smoothing out the black-and-white horizontal stripes of his French-looking top.

Harry picked up Tom's hat from the ground and considered Nathan's question for a moment. "Sure, but his good looks are his least inter-esting quality, right?" Harry spoke matter-of-factly, analyzing Tom's features. The writer turned his lips into a half-smile, and Harry smiled back, silently reaffirming his statement. Tom's pale cheekbones turned a slight shade of pink, he seemed surprised and affected by Harry's words.

Harry was closer to winning him over.

"I hadn't noticed," Storm said dryly, staring at Harry. "Are you flirting with my boyfriend?" Harry's intentions had been misunderstood. Harry turned to Tom and opened his eyes widely, asking for help.

Tom smiled. "Nate, he doesn't mean it like that. His harassment is purely platonic."

"Yes, we've already established I'm not his type." Harry was still holding on to Tom's beret, and offered it back to him.

"You have?" Storm threw a suspicious look.

Tom took his hat and pushed it into the back pocket of his jeans. "Yeah, Harry doesn't do *feelings* but claims I'm his soulmate."

"Erm... I don't believe in souls, but yes, the match is computationally proven."

"Hmm, whatever this is"—Storm pointed at them—"I'm not getting it, and I need a drink." He turned to Tom, lips curved into a pout, and then he lifted his boyfriend's hand to his mouth and kissed it. "Meet me later?" Tom bobbed his head. "Tom, Nowak and his app can't be trusted. You know this. Be careful, okay?" Storm walked away, throwing Harry one final suspicious glance.

"Your fellow seems a bit...possessive. Hope I didn't cause any trouble."

"No. It's not that." Tom chuckled. "He distrusts pretty much everything you represent—wealth, power, and technology, but he's the most generous human being I know. Once he gets to know someone and trust them, he'll give them the shirt off his back."

Harry went quiet, shrugging. He didn't know how to engage in those sorts of conversations, and he was too keen to get back to his original agenda. "Tom, I can help you with technology. I'm the best in the world."

"You're not a dilettante stalker, that's for sure."

"What?" Harry asked puzzled. He didn't know the meaning of the word.

"Amateur."

"I'm no amateur. I'm an expert."

"Of course you are. That's what I said." Tom spoke genuinely, then he paused for a moment, deep in thought. "I don't want to invade people's privacy. You know?"

"If you wanna deliver stories that will change behavior, you need to personalize. Tap into people's history, biology, fears, and aspirations."

"A dangerous game full of unintended consequences. Technology is... evil. It's immoral, how it's being used to—"

"It's how you use it. Technology is amoral, just like science."

"So is a gun," Tom said.

Harry glanced at Tom sharply. "That's rich of you! Software is as much of a threat to privacy as story is to autonomy. Stories manipulate people; in the end, that's what you're doing."

Tom crossed his arms in front of his chest. "I'm delivering purpose-driven inspiration." Then he opened his eyes wide in some realization. "Oh, that made me sound like a pompous ass. I'm sorry."

Harry smiled at the quirkiness of his companion. "It was advertising that weaponized data. That's immoral; tech is just the enabler."

Tom conceded the issue with a shrug and a nod. He looked at Harry with renewed respect. "Dear Harry, you're so right. Story and technology together are immensely powerful and dangerous."

Harry smiled; he found it hilarious that Tom sometimes sounded like a doting eighty-year-old grandma. "Yeah, but these movies aren't driving change fast enough, are they? Can we afford to wait?"

They sat by the rim of the Bethesda Fountain and watched the crowds. The activists were starting to disperse in all directions. Tom ran his fingers through his scruffy stubble, probably pondering Harry's words. Around them, people chanted, repeating the words of a young man—lines from a screenplay written by Tom to challenge the actions of his conservative father. Words crafted as an escape from sorrow—the death by suicide of his beloved mother.

Harry had learned Grace Astley-Byron Stone took her own life a day after her husband closed the New York State borders. She was distraught when the governor denied entry to those fleeing from the devastation caused by the Florida floods. Less than a month later, Jon Stone was murdered outside his home in New York's Upper East Side.

Harry's words had unintentionally undermined Tom's work—the film that was inspiring people all over the world to take action and help others. "I'm sorry. Of course, movies *do* make a difference. I didn't mean it like—"

"I know what you meant," Tom said, reassuringly. "And *no*, we can't wait. But influencing platforms can be used for both good and evil. We've seen this with the internet and social networks. Bad actors using the tools that were supposed to democratize information to spread lies."

"We'd need to centralize it. An unhackable platform designed and operated by only two people."

"Because we're Gods?" Tom said dryly.

"Better us than the goons in power… Things are really bad."

"Yeah, I know... But I'm not ready to say *I do.*" Tom placed his hand on his own neck, massaging it to release the tension. He looked like he was bearing the weight of the world. Then he went to a knee, hugging a golden retriever that turned toward him to play with his shoelaces. The dog was on a leash, and his owner, a woman in her sixties, sat beside them, engaging in a lively conversation with a group of middle-aged women all wearing berets. The dog jumped on Tom, putting his paws on his chest and licking his face as the writer rubbed the animal's fur in delight. Harry grimaced, thinking of all the germs.

The woman turned to them and pulled on the dog's leash. "I'm so sorry. Chuck is..." She lost her ability to speak when she met Tom's gaze. "Um, very friendly."

Sibyl had reported that Tom's looks and mannerisms gave him an immediate and unmatched likability factor. For some strange reason, Sibyl added this persuasion feature right at the top of the report, as if it was the most important friend selection criteria. At the time, Harry found it odd, but after spending some time with the guy in the wild, he understood how Tom's unnatural magnetism affected everyone around him, but he still couldn't figure out why it was that important for their friendship. He'd like Tom as much if he looked like an old bearded turtle.

Tom smiled at the woman, sat back on the edge of the fountain, and turned to Harry.

"Okay. Okay. Let's...hmm, slow things down." Harry feared he was losing Tom. He changed tactics, recalling Sibyl's report. "Tell me about these stories. What values are they going to teach?"

"Good old universal values." Tom's face lit up.

"Uh-huh, like what?" Harry leaned forward, interested.

"Peace, freedom, the value of hard work, equal rights, human dignity, and the importance of friendship, for example. The values taught in children's stories." A spark of hope beamed in the corner of Tom's eye. He talked with his hands a lot, particularly when he spoke about something he loved. Talking about his work made him quite passionate and animated. "Have you read *Le Petit Prince?*"

Harry didn't respond right away. That book had a special meaning to him, and he didn't want to sound too sentimental or needy. Then he remembered who he was talking to, and he decided to go all in.

"'Men have no more time to understand anything. They buy ready-made things in the shops. But since there are no shops where you can buy friends, men no longer have any friends. If you want a friend, tame me...'" Harry smiled, then sadness took over his face. "My sister's favorite book. She read it to me many times when I was young. I don't usually read fiction. I prefer precise accounts of space exploration and invention, but I like this one. It's...special to me."

With that response, everything changed. Tom's head turned toward Harry and his shoulders relaxed. Tom didn't make eye contact often, but when he did, he saw you; he really saw you. He connected deeply and authentically, baring his soul through his big eyes. Then he closed the deal with a charming smile—eyes wrinkled above flushed cheekbones. His pupils dilated, welcoming you into his world, and at that moment, Harry had a sense he'd known him for an eternity.

"It would have to be a nonprofit," Tom said.

"Tom, financing is not a problem." Harry's heart jumped in his chest. He stood straighter, suppressing a smile.

"And zero—"

"Unintended consequences. Yes, agreed. We'll test everything—"

"Comprehensively. And we'll focus on universal—"

"Values. Uh-huh."

They smiled at each other, and then a deep furrow formed in Tom's brow.

"How can we possibly centralize it and run it ourselves? Will it scale?"

Harry patted Tom on the back. "Information security compartmentalization. We'll involve others on a need-to-know basis. Don't worry. I gotcha."

"So, it will be secure and—"

"Protect users' privacy. Yeah."

"This might actually work. You're a godsend," Tom said, looking shaken.

"'God made the integers; all else is the work of man.'" Harry shrugged.

Tom smiled. Once again, his brows sank over his eyes, and he paused for a moment, thinking. "Dear Harry, you're 'practically perfect in every way,' but we need to talk about Sibyl." Tom put his hand on top of Harry's arm as he spoke.

Harry knew what was coming. A test delivered to uncover who he was and what he cared about, a trial that would make or break this emerging partnership. He nibbled on his lip, wondering if Sibyl would get in the way of their bright future.

In that afternoon, under the watchful eyes of the *Angel of the Waters*, Harry promised Tom he'd consider removing the social-prediction app from public use. The app was his life's work and his most important asset. He needed time to think about it.

Later, as they were about to go their separate ways, Harry gathered the courage to mention a subject that would likely push Tom away forever. He didn't want to start a partnership by holding back such an important piece of information.

"Tom?"

"Yes?"

"Your mother—" Harry looked at his shoes. "Your mother consulted Sibyl a few minutes before she took her life," he said regretfully.

Tom didn't speak for several beats. Harry struggled to bring himself to look into his eyes. He was too scared of what he might discover.

"I know." Tom's eyes sparkled, overlaid by a hint of tears.

"You do? I'm so s—"

"Harry, Sibyl didn't kill my mother." Tom got closer and stole a hug. "My father's actions and my lack of support did. See you next week." He smiled faintly, put his hands in his pockets, turned around, and walked away.

THE
Present

13

RED WRATH

THE TOWER
DAY 1 — 2:13 PM

Thorn didn't like to lose. In fact, she hated it. She'd lost her little sister; her heroic acts had fallen flat; she'd been digitized and resurrected without her permission. And now she was stuck inside a manipulative machine she despised. Everything was fracked up, and it was all his fault—Thomas Astley-Byron.

As the most competitive being in all nine worlds, it sucked. *Everything sucks.* She was supposed to be a hero, and instead, she'd been swept in Shadow's trail of destruction to become the devil incarnated. Humans hated her, xHumans hated her, and the soulful hated her. All because she killed a wreck of a guy who'd won the gene lottery. It was the way he looked, moved, talked, but also what he said, and all he felt. Of course the app had chosen him as the face of zir world domination.

The worlds swooned for the flawed God while they despised her. They all judged her as if she were a criminal when she'd been the victim, a truth she didn't like to admit even to herself. Why in the worlds had she become the villain? How did she turn into the primary target of hate by the activist poet she'd idolized all her life? It was unfair, and her mood swung from anger to indifference to frustration in a matter of seconds.

She didn't understand why the peppy young Goddess had brought her back. Stella said she'd walked in her shoes and knew her intentions and her struggles; that she liked Thorn's spirit and empathized with both her resentment for and enthrallment with Shadow. Stella said many things, a deluge of nervous words unleashed as Thorn stared at her, puffing on a cigar.

Thorn loved making the girl nervous. The cocky princess had too much power and an audacity she recognized. A confident tenacity that had helped her win many competitions when she was just Rosa García and her athletic body was all flesh and bone. Still, like Shadow, Stella had been selected by Sibyl, and like Shadow, Stella's brightness and magnetism threatened to cancel any living creature's free will—whatever that meant in a digitized world. Thorn wouldn't fall twice for the app's gorgeous puppets.

She walked the bridge toward the Tower, head high, holding a cigar between her teeth. Around her, crucified bodies—some dead, others alive. The stench of demon putrefaction competing with the gasses released by the swamp steaming under the bridge. A deadly concentrated soup of decaying vegetable and animal matter. Stagnated waters as dead as the creatures inhabiting that world.

Some demons screeched from their crosses, suggesting no travelers were visiting the Tower. Around Earthlings, the soulless needed to behave human-like, simulating pain and emotion as soon as they became part of a traveler's experience.

Still, the crucified Domizien suffered no pain. They didn't feel anything at all. A solution designed by the Gods to deliver learning experiences to Earthlings without hurting any "conscious beings." Thomas and Henryk's designs were as flawed as their egomaniac minds.

In Domiz, Earthlings learned the impact of some of their most egocentric instincts—immediate gratification of all impulses, selfish exploitation, forceful power, and boundless greed. The world was their jungle, and as they hunted, dominated, punished, and slaughtered the bots, they eventually realized none of it brought them happiness or purpose.

Still, rage and revenge sometimes needed to be indulged in the path to whatever "enlightenment" the Gods had designed. When someone wrongs you, hurts you, breaks you or the ones you love, you can either drown in fear and despair or fight back hard, relentlessly and without flinching. The path to power was the path to safety, the road to the confidence stolen by men...*always men*.

Thorn looked up, startled by the howling of a limbless demon who had been pushed out of the top of the Tower into the swamp below. The deadly fall was the only way out of the keep for any guest invited to climb the staircase of a thousand torments. She cracked her neck, releasing the escalating tension in the back of her head.

Thorn crossed the tall wooden doors, carved with at least a thousand skulls, and walked inside the circular main hall. Like the other soulless worlds, the place incorporated a nonsensical mix of humanity's historical periods. High-tech and medieval objects coexisted awkwardly in the most violent of all worlds.

Around the circular room, red beams of neon light floated in the air. The crimson color teasing out the worst in travelers—the metaphorical cape that made the blind bull strike. *Olé! Olé!* Blood gushing, red as rage.

Higher up, near the ceiling, a holographic projection of some carnage, one of many happening at that moment somewhere in the Tower. Displays of technology contrasting with the medieval building and the stench of a life lived without proper plumbing or running water. An odd mismatch of real-world references, brought together by a game that had become her "real life."

She looked at the horned figure ahead and held her breath, preparing for the worst.

"He's back," Wrath said, her eyes piercing Thorn from inside the horned iron helmet. The headgear covered most of Wrath's face down to her upper lip, her long flame-colored hair hidden under heavy chainmail.

"Yes, he is," Thorn said, lifting her head to meet Wrath's eyes. The helmet's curled horns pointed menacingly at her. There was no point in lying, but she hoped the Domizien didn't see her helping Shadow or that the word hadn't reached the tyrant.

Thorn looked around, counting the demons. Four guarding Wrath, and twelve on the spiraling staircase integrated into the stone wall. The creatures stood on the hellish steps to the upper floors of the Tower—the seven chambers of torture—where she might end up spending the last hours of her second life.

She bit the cigar too hard, a portion of the tobacco wrapper flaking and falling apart on top of her chest. *Not a good look.* She flicked the debris off her tank top, dropped the cigar on the floor, and set her eyes on the condottiere—the first ever to lead the large hordes of mercenaries focused only on their own gain. Before Wrath, Domizien banded together in small groups to pillage and plunder, dispersing soon after, if they didn't kill each other over the spoils first.

"I want him alive." Wrath's voice bounced around the wall. She sat on her stone throne; her leather armor devoid of the metal plating she wore in pillaging raids.

"*Chiquitita*, it's time to move on," Thorn said. "You need to let it go."

"I'll break his limbs one by one, then pull them off his body. Stretch, stretch, *streeetch* until, like, they break apart from his torso one by one. It'll be a pretty mess. A shattered God—so pretty and so dead." Wrath's girlish giggle clashed with her words' rancorous violence— spiteful and mad for all the right reasons.

Thorn regretted bringing an impressionable teenage girl to such a hateful world. Still, it was the only way to fix the child's hopelessness and for them to reach the upper worlds together. xHumans couldn't take Underlings with them when jumping between worlds.

"Trust me. Revenge...it doesn't fix things," Thorn said. "It helps for a while, but it won't change how you're feeling... I know this!"

She was wasting her words and her time. For what? To protect the man who had ruined her life? *I'm so fracked up...*

"I'll boil his head while he bleeds to death," Wrath said, ignoring Thorn. The condottiere got up, grabbing the bastard sword lying beside her on the throne—a light weapon selected by Thorn to compensate for the teen's lankiness.

The four guards standing around the throne all took a step back as if predicting Wrath's next move.

"It's time we move on from Domiz to the higher worlds," Thorn said.

"You told me I should embrace my rage." Wrath used both hands to twirl her sword forward and backward and then around her. Abruptly, she swung the sword to her side, decapitating one guard. Limp body dropping over bloodied head. "See that?" she said proudly. "My technique is getting better!"

"I've taught you well, and you're getting stronger," Thorn said, scanning the room for her own sword and fastening her plated leather jacket. "You have embraced your rage. Now it's time for us to move on.

People are getting hurt and dying." She spotted her saber leaning against the wall by the main door.

Wrath licked the blood on the sword. "Look around you. Death and destruction everywhere." This time she jumped forward, single-handedly thrusting the blade into a guard's neck. She spun her body under her arm, twisting the sword and causing a bloody mess.

"It's different here, Wrath. You know this. They don't feel things like you and I do." Thorn walked forward, kicking a detached rotting foot out of her path and moving closer to the unlikely leader of the Domizien. The black and blue foot landed near a pile of headless bodies. Curious, Thorn looked around the room, trying to figure out what Wrath had done with the heads, but they were nowhere to be found.

"He must pay," Wrath screamed, pulling her sword from the neck of the dying guard, only to strike a third demon, this time chopping off an entire arm. The creature stood still—no pain, no screams—bleeding to death, terror absent from his dead eyes. "I'll torture his poet while he watches. I'll bring chaos to his worlds, and then...then I'll destroy him."

The creatures standing on the stairs ran upwards, disappearing in the darkness of the first chamber of torture. They didn't have feelings, but they valued their lives, unlike Thorn, who continued to move closer to Wrath.

"His worlds and his poet aren't to blame for his crime against you. Come," Thorn raised her hand toward the girl. "Let's leave this stench of a world. I'll show you what comes next—order, trust in God...dess. Erm... Trust in the Goddess." Thorn bit her cigar, struggling to peddle Ordiz's bullshit values.

Wrath laughed—a mad cackle filled with resentment. "I know you, Thorn. You don't believe in those things. Why should I?"

"We need to cross Ordiz to get you to the higher worlds—where there are more people like me and you."

"Like me? You mean the people who are trying to kill you?" Wrath pointed her sword in Thorn's direction.

"*You* will protect me. Won't you?"

"I will," Wrath said, "but don't betray me again."

Damn! She knows. Thorn lifted her head in defiance. "Don't lose yourself in your rage. Overcome it." Thorn spoke like an older sister, a caring friend. *One day, I should listen to my own excellent advice.*

"Have you?" Wrath asked, sitting down on her throne, lifting one knee to her chest and hugging it close to her body.

"I...don't know."

"Shadow must pay," Wrath screamed—a cross between a monstrous shriek and a girlish whimper. She lifted the second knee and held both tightly. "I must kill him. Do you understand?"

"Yes, I do," Thorn said. "And, I did—kill him. It didn't help."

"Protect him again, and, like... you're dead to me. Dead." Wrath attempted to flick her hair inside the heavy helmet. *A child, an angry and lost child. I rather have you as a mad villain than a hopeless victim, chiquitita.*

Thorn took a breath and bowed her head. "You have my devotion and my loyalty. I'll give you the world. Everything you deserve. I'll wait for you, but...I can't help you in this quest. You're hurting people that have nothing to do with his crimes."

"I haven't commanded the Domizien to hunt anyone but Storm and Shadow. My creatures do what they were designed to do. Gods' fault, not mine."

"They're attacking everyone."

"*Not my fault!*" Wrath repeated. "Are you leaving me?" Pouting lips emerging from the iron's shadows.

"No. When you're ready, we'll depart from this place. Until then, I'll stay away from your path of destruction. I can't condone it and the universe won't allow you to travel up north until you genuinely adopt Ordizien values."

"I should kill you," Wrath said casually.

"I'm your only friend." Thorn turned around to leave.

"Without my protection, you're dead."

"Yeah. I am. Dead." Thorn reached down to pick up the saber. Domizien wouldn't attack her while she was under Wrath's protection, but the rest of the worlds were out to get her. "Come find me at the northern border when you're ready to move on."

Thorn pulled a cigar out of her back pocket, and she walked away toward the outer wall. She'd found the girl in Tribiz soon after her resurrection, when she'd first travelled to the lower worlds fleeing the persecution of the soulful. Thorn had recognized her immediately and still could not understand how the teen, who was supposed to be dead, had ended up in such an inhospitable place.

Half-dead and out of her mind, the soulful girl was being used by one of the nomadic soulless tribes as bait to hunt packs of wolves; their meat and fur essential for the Tribizien's survival in the coldest and most arid of all worlds. A place filled with ritual and superstition, where the only way to stay alive was to live under the protection of a clan, all autonomy and individualism crushed by fear.

Locked in a wooden cage and paralyzed by pain and terror and hopelessness, the girl barely spoke, surviving on scraps of raw meat tossed away by her captors. That day, to rescue her, Thorn killed at least fifteen Tribizien. Even so, it took a while for Thorn to convince her to leave the "safety" of her tribe and cross the frigid tundra toward Domiz.

Now that Wrath had shed her fear and hopelessness, Thorn was hoping they would venture further up to the soulful worlds. The two of them had a lot in common, a suicidal God had destroyed their lives.

14

BLANK...ISH SLATE

THE BATTLEFIELD

DAY 1 — 3:25 PM

Thorn rolled her eyes as she considered jumping into action. There he was—the man she'd killed—alive and strutting into hell as if he were visiting a royal garden in a spring afternoon.

Thorn had traveled far to find herself at the edge of chaos, so close to mind-numbing order. She wanted to wait for Wrath in a place with a bit more...soul. The Ordizien border was within her reach, and now he showed up to ruin her plans.

Thorn was hoping she could convince the Ordizien to let her cross to their land. It was a long shot as they were super cultish about their religion, and she'd murdered their God.

She planned to tell them Shadow was back and that she'd saved his life. The news of Shadow's return had caught fire, spreading from community to community. Many believed his resurrection signaled their salvation, and she was hoping someone would validate her story.

Now it looked like the dumbass wouldn't stay resurrected for long, not without her help. Why on Earth...no, not on Earth... why on Spiral Worlds was he approaching the worlds' battlefield alone and unarmed? The creatures wouldn't care about his charming smile or misguided tenderness. Shadow—all heart and little shrewdness—didn't have the cunning coolness necessary to bargain with the demons.

It wasn't her problem, and she continued to move toward the Ordizien. As long as she stayed close to the border, on either side, no one would dare attack her as they all feared the condottiere's revenge.

It was a shame the demons couldn't travel with her higher up. She could use their protection, but the platform didn't allow Underlings to roam into places above their values. The puppets went about their lives, never "choosing" to walk up the roads that led to the upper worlds. Some soulful learned new values and ascended, but the soulless Domizien were mostly stuck in Domiz, only venturing into Ordiz to pillage or to do the Ordizien's dirty deeds.

Keep your eyes on the border. She rebelled against her inner voice, and looked back at the battlefield—a dry land, devoid of vegetation and covered by hundreds of thousands of skulls and bones.

"The other way, you fool!" Thorn shouted, but she was too far away. In fact, she was so close to her destination she could hear the joyful laugher of some women and men in the Ordizien armies—a sound never experienced in Domizien land. *Dammit, Shadow!*

As Shadow walked from the thick forest into the vast combat zone, Thorn squinted her eyes, noticing the band of five Domizien running toward him across the battlefield's plane. She remembered what the peppy Goddess had said: they were hoping the soulless would somehow connect with Shadow, their creator. But to send him alone into Domiz was stupid. A plan devised by people who knew nothing about the lower worlds' most recent events. Stella and Twist had been too distracted to see the power Wrath had amassed with the soulless, and to recognize it as a threat.

If the Domizien failed to recognize Shadow, he'd be dead in seconds, and his heart and liver would make a delicious demon meal. If, on the other hand, the creatures figured out who he was, they'd take him to Wrath, and he'd endure a slow and painful ascension up the staircase of torments. He'd experience the horrors in each one of the seven chambers of torture until he emerged at the top of the Tower— a limbless, tongueless, and eyeless shadow of a man, discarded to fall to his inevitable death.

Shadow's skill was pulling heartstrings—nature had designed his body and mind to enthrall hearts and souls. Domizien had none of that, and Wrath was immune to his charms. The condottiere would never forgive or forget what he'd done to her, and Shadow was striding toward his much-deserved downfall. Thorn cringed, unable to watch what was to come. *Stay out of it, Rosa. He isn't your problem.* She crossed her fingers hoping he'd die a quick death.

Thorn reached the wall of Ordizien shields. She was too short to see the men and women behind them. Several shields lowered to disclose their faces and the lines of warriors on horseback waiting further back.

"Hey!" she said, but the Ordizien attention quickly shifted away from her, to the battlefield.

She glanced at Shadow and the demons, unable to keep her eyes away. *Frack!* A demon held a large waterskin in his hand, an out-of-place object for a meeting in the middle of a battlefield. *Domizien hydrating during a raid? They are going to knock him out.* A technique she'd seen them use before.

She was used to Shadow's deaths, but for his and Wrath's sake, she couldn't let him be tortured.

. She ran to the nearest horse rider. "Get off," she said, pointing at Shadow. "There. Your God lives and he's in danger. Help me." Even before the Ordizien warrior had fully dismounted the animal, Thorn held on to the reigns and saddle horn and jumped on the horse, sword in hand. "*You*, follow me," she commanded the group of horse riders to her right as she led them into a full speed gallop. Much to her surprise, the Ordizien obeyed.

Sometimes you need to walk into a place and own it. That's all it took. Ordizien liked to follow Gods, powerful rulers, and orders. She was meeting all their needs. *Idiots!* Or maybe they were just afraid of Wrath. Either way. It worked.

Ahead, everything unfolded has she'd predicted. The demon swung the waterskin to crash on to Shadow's face. The God collapsed on his knees, holding his head in between his arms. It didn't knock him out, but left him stunned enough to stop him from running. Afraid of trampling on Shadow, Thorn circled the group, catching the demon from behind.

Her horse buckled as it crashed into two of the five demons. She rolled her eyes at the fearful animal and jumped to the ground decapitating two Domizien and using her dagger to stab a third in the heart. In that world it was best to act first and think later. An approach that suited her just fine.

"Get up. We need to go," she said dropping her sword to help him stand. "Shadow, get up."

"T—Thorn?" His eyeballs rolled back into his head for a second. "I was looking for you."

"How great!" Sarcasm oozing as she spoke. "You found me. Yayyy!" She poured the contents of the waterskin on his head. "Get up! You're too big to carry."

He stared at her until his eyes blinked with some recognition and he raised to his feet.

"This way," Thorn said.

She'd decided they would run. She didn't want to waste a lot of time trying to get him to mount a horse. Plus, the four-legged creatures were too unreliable. She glanced back to assess the danger. The Ordizien horse riders finished the last two demons, but she could see hordes of Domizien—at least two hundred—running toward them. "Holy guacamole, I think you've started a war without travelers to experience it. That's weird."

The Domizien battlefield, like everything else in Spiral Worlds, was a travelers' playground. A place designed to purge human desire for warmongering. Sibyl orchestrated everything so they'd suffer just enough pain, without negative consequences in the real world. Wounds vanishing as soon as they got back Up Above.

"I did?" Shadow raised an eyebrow, half his face red and blue from the Domizien attack. "Anyway, thank you," he said, running beside her toward the wall of Ordizien shields protecting the border. "I guess Stella was wrong. They didn't recognize me."

"Of course they did. If they didn't, you'd be dead. They aren't shooting arrows—that's the good news. They want you alive—that's the bad news." She looked back, to confirm her statement. The demons were close enough to kill them, but kept their bows strapped to their backs.

"They have shot against me before," Shadow said.

"Probably before they knew who you were."

"So, the Domizien don't want to hurt me?"

"Oh yeah. They do."

"Sibyl's not telling me anything," he said. "It's so confusing."

"Make way!" Thorn tried to copy Nathan Storm's preachy tone. "God's heart has risen from the ashes." Then she murmured, "Show them your pretty face and smile."

"Do you think they know who I am?"

"The Ordizien? *For sure!* Have you been to one of their churches? Your face is plastered in every wall and window. Sometimes I'm there too, surrounded by fire and looking pretty diabolical. Which reminds me, before you leave...or die again...you must put a good word for me with the soulful, okay?"

"I'm here to see you."

"A visit! How nice. We'll have tea." She flashed her teeth. "This should wipe my slate clean. Right?" She threw him a side glance, and then she shouted, "*Incoming...hmm...God!* Incoming God, as lost as ever."

Two Ordizien dropped back, and Thorn and Shadow sped through the gap between shields. The Ordizien army started marching forward, toward the Domizien.

"Your slate was clean, unlike mine," Shadow said, catching his breath.

Thorn grinned, noticing his tiredness. She deliberately kept ahead of him to show off her impressive speed. She was much shorter than him, the top of her head used to slot perfectly under his chin when they made out. Still, his long legs struggled to keep up with her sprint, payback for all the undignified jogs she had to endure every time they'd gone for a casual walk in the City Down Below, decades ago.

"We know this, but your friends think otherwise. This way." She pointed at the next barrier—this time Ordizien on horseback.

"Praise God, our loving heart," a rider said, and many followed with their own prayers.

"Protect him! Protect his heavenly ass!" Thorn said pointing her sword at the hordes of Domizien approaching fast. The Ordizien cavalry moved forward, creating just enough space for Thorn and Shadow to cross them.

"Stop objectifying me."

"I'm not the self-proclaimed God."

The two zigzagged in between the animals' legs rushing past four lines of nervous horses—some grunting, snorting or even bulking. It took longer than it needed, as Shadow had to pat and comfort every horse on his path. They arrived at an open field.

"I didn't— Anyway...don't worry, my friends couldn't care less about me or your slate," he said.

"Yeah, sure," she dismissed him with a casual shrug. The flawed God was the worlds' most beloved creature, an honor she struggled to decide if it was deserved or not, even if she too had once fallen captive to his charm. "Frack! I forgot my sword." Something that had never happened on the fencing piste. The transition from athlete to warrior was harder than she expected. "You're such a distraction!"

She groaned, coming to grips with her new status in Domiz—that Wrath's hate for him was likely stronger than her bond with her. From that moment onward, Thorn had to assume the Domizien might attack her.

"How did you end up in the middle of the worlds' battlefield? Death wish?"

"I asked Sibyl to see you and she jumped me here. I guess the forest's edge was the only available place to materialize."

"You were lucky that the fields were mostly empty—fewer travelers because of the glitches. It's nice to have some moments of peace in hell."

He stared at her intensely, compassion in his eyes. "Why are you dead, Thorn?" he said quietly, his voice deep and throaty.

Her jaw clicked, triggered by a sudden blast of tension. "Are you seriously attempting to have this conversation with me? You?" She grabbed his wrist and turned it to expose his scars.

"I just didn't expect it from you." He followed her toward an empty Ordizien encampment—a dozen perfectly shaped triangular structures made of oak covered by woolen cloth canvas.

"It's not like you have an outstanding record of getting things right, is it?"

He laughed awkwardly as they walked into an empty tent. "I used to be pretty good, before..." After a long silence, he said. "Sorry, I wasn't bragging, or dismissing what I did to you. I'm really sorry. I promised myself I'd always try to find something positive to say and to think... you know? I'm trying to stay alive...keep people safe. I'm so sorry." He positioned himself in the middle of the tent, the only place high enough for him to stand straight.

She released a loud, exasperated sigh. "Scrumptious, can we make a deal?"

He got cuter when he got mad. "Don't do that! I'm not food. What deal?" The eagerness in his eyes said he'd bend backwards for her.

"Can we just forget the past? Stop apologizing. Let's...be friends. Perhaps this will help us both stay alive." If she were to survive Ordiz and higher up, she needed his protection.

He rubbed his head, probably sore from the attack. "That's generous of you, Thorn, but I can't just—"

"It's self-serving." She punched him lightly in the arm, struggling to keep her hands off him. "If you say sorry one more time, I'll have to kill you, and then your friends will chop me into little pieces and feed me to the soulless."

A strained chuckle slipped past his lips, barely audible. "I don't have any friends. They wish they weren't...my friends."

"Saving your ass just cost me my last friend, so neither do I...apart from you." She tried to pull off some puppy eyes.

"You nut job." He smiled, and then he looked away, all bashful. "I can't be your friend, Thorn."

"We've tried everything else—strangers, lovers, mortal enemies—I'm convinced we're meant to be friends," Thorn lied. She didn't know what they were, and she had stopped caring until he showed up. She liked and hated him just as much as she did before, in fact, she could easily put a bullet in his head right now. Still, she needed him. "Are you worried the men in your life won't approve?"

"Believe me, no one cares. No one wants me back." He sounded like he believed in his words. *The fool.*

He detached his wet T-shirt from his chest, and she realized she'd been staring at the light patch of hair beneath it. She'd licked it too many times.

"You haven't changed either. Anyway, we better jump out of here, before the Ordizien religious fanatics come find you and place you on some pedestal."

"I never wanted this..."

"Oh dear." She stared at him, smirking. "Anyway, you said you want to look on the bright side, right? Well, after what we did to each other, we won't sweat the small stuff."

He laughed and cleared a tear from the corner of his eyes. "Thank you for saving my life. I can't be your friend. I got to go."

"I thought you needed to speak to me?"

"Yes, I came to save your life."

She held her stomach, laughing loudly. "And did you?"

"Yes, I feel like I did," he said, all serious.

"You *feel it*, do you?"

"I'm sure they've seen you save my life, and the soulless are chasing you. So, all good."

"Have you lost your marbles again?" She grabbed his arm. "Hey! You owe me. *Big time*," she said coolly while her gut screamed for help. "Don't you think you should be more responsive to my wishes? We must be friends."

"No."

"What the hell! I'm here fighting demons you invented."

"Precisely. You'll be safe in Ordiz, right?"

"No, I won't." Then she leaned in his direction, stood on the tips of her toes, and furrowed her brows. "You know, you should seriously stop doing stuff, anything. Apart from having sex, you're good at that. You're still my all-time favorite sex toy. Just stay in bed and look pretty."

He blushed, repressing a smirk. "Stop it." His admonishment tender.

"Are you seriously going to deny me your friendship after ruining my life?"

"What are you doing Thorn? I'm deadly."

"I can handle you."

"That was my assumption, but now you're stuck here, dead, because of me."

She flicked his wet hair away from his face. "I'm over you. Death put things in perspective."

"Not the type of experiences I want to deliver to my *friends*."

"It's not *all* about you. You know? I need a friend in power."

"Thorn, you ask for whatever you need—"

"Speaking of demons, *behind you!*"

As Shadow turned around, the bearded demon shrieked, emerging from the fresh tear on the tent's canvas. The creature launched at him, spear in hand. She slipped her hand on the back of Shadow's jeans and pulled him back. He staggered, his shoulder avoiding the spear's head by a hairline. Thorn used both hands to grip the spear close to the pointy end and wrestled for control over it with a creature twice her size.

"Take my dagger," she screamed at Shadow, looking at the leather scabbard on her leg.

As Shadow reached for her dagger, the demon yanked the spear off her hands and stabbed her thigh right between the dagger and Shadow's hands. The sharp pain emptied the air of her lungs.

"Fracker!"

Shadow grabbed the dagger and threw himself over the creature who fell backwards dropping the spear. They rolled and wrestled and kicked and punched. Shadow could have stabbed the demon on five or six occasions, but he didn't, and Thorn gave an exasperated growl. She gritted her teeth, pulled the spear off her thigh, and jumped on top of the demon who had Shadow pinned between his legs. She stabbed the creature in the eye, killing it instantly.

Thorn dropped on one side, contorting in pain. "I'm fracked! I'm no longer off limits."

"You okay?" Shadow's hands shook as he took her in his arms and lifted her off her legs. His body was still wet from the water she'd poured all over him.

"Ouch! You must find your killer instinct or you'll get us all killed." She was wasting her words. She had a better chance teaching an elephant to fly. "You'd be dead now, if the creature was trying to kill you, instead of capturing you."

"Hmm. I-I'll find a way to learn to fight demons," he said thoughtfully, still trembling. "I'll download information from Sibyl."

"Download information?" She laughed. "I know you can fight, Shadow. Look at you." She squeezed his arm, sculpted to perfection.

He looked away.

"They suffer no pain, you fool. Your design, remember?"

"Yes, they are what they are because we made them so," he said, guilt all over his face.

"Kill them or knock them out immediately." She applied pressure on her thigh. "Hell, it hurts," she said, tearing the pants' fabric around the wound to inspect.

Unexpectedly, another demon entered the tent and jumped toward them, dagger lifted over Thorn's chest, ready to strike. Out of a horror movie, dozens of flesh-eating beetles munched on half of the creature's jawline.

"Frack!"

"Hold on to me." Shadow spun around and launched into a sidekick, making the creature stumble. He lowered Thorn to the floor, picking up the spear and stabbing the attacking demon in the heart. The creature dropped to the ground, face first.

"She was pretty." Thorn ignored the blast of pain from the injured leg.

Shadow took a moment to look at the demon, eyes mournful as if he had slaughtered a puppy. Out of nowhere, the skies rumbled, and a scorching spear of lightning pierced the tent and hit the ground by the entrance, setting it on fire.

"What the frack was that?"

"The weather." He dropped to one knee. "Stay still. You're bleeding." He touched her forehead with his face. "And burning. I'll get us out of Ordiz. Sib—"

"No, don't. I'll stay here. I'll be fine." She'd never survive in the higher worlds. Everyone there was out to get her, and half delirious with an injured leg, she couldn't defend herself from their attacks. She preferred to take her chances with the Ordizien who feared Wrath and knew of their alliance.

"I won't leave you here, inside a tent on fire, bleeding. A minute ago, you said you weren't safe." He picked her up.

"I'm not, but the God-abiding Ordizien saw me save you, and hmm... higher up...they don't like me." She disclosed the least possible. She didn't need his pity, just his protection.

"Since when do you care about what people think?"

"You don't understand..." *And I don't want to spell it out.* "Cut the tent and drop me outside."

"That gash is too deep. It needs proper care."

Her sight blurred, and she sank her head into his chest. The heat was rising as the tent's fabric caught fire. "Where are you taking me?" She was too weak to argue.

"I need to stop by Pluriz, urgently. To speak to..." He clenched his jaw and then forced a smile. "My friend January will take good care of you."

"The Plurizien hate my guts. But I know your man well enough to know he won't stab me in the back while I'm down, no matter how much he'd like to."

"He's not my man, no one is going to fight, and I won't let anyone hurt you."

"Sure," she said, and then she coughed, struggling to breathe due to all the smoke. "I love your newly found optimism. This will be...fun."

It would make some excellent entertainment to see Storm and Shadow together. She was a sucker for punishment, sometimes.

He nodded. "Sibyl, take us to see Nate."

Sure, my heart, said the voice inside Thorn's head. A reminder she couldn't run away from all her demons.

15

IN GOD'S HANDS

GRAND INGA HYDROPOWER COMPLEX — CONGO RIVER —
AFRICAN UNION
DAY 1 — 3:40 PM

S tella walked inside the observation deck, approaching her father from behind, and ignoring the uneasiness grumbling in her gut. Christian Ngoie, the leader of the richest and most powerful continent in the world, sat on his rocking chair facing the window and staring at the world's largest and deadliest rapids. The Congo River frothed and roared as it approached the largest power station on the planet. The complex fed the electricity demands of the entire continent.

"Baba," she called, but he didn't turn around. The color of his emotion-sensing bodysuit remained neutral and unchanged. Lost somewhere inside his head, he didn't hear her.

Baba was a shadow of his former self. His emotions ran deep, as deep as the river's waters. He was no longer the spirited, confident man who had united a continent once ridden by colonialism, ethnic conflict, corruption, poverty, and a devastating virus. Gone was the man who had the audacity to displace fifty thousand people, flooding their valley and homes to build a complex of thirteen dams. A project that had put an end to the use of fossil fuels in the African Union. His courage beaming in a time rich in progress and creativity. A time before decisions got stuck, before empathy got in the way of evolution.

Christian was once a powerful man, now weakened by Holiz's launch. In five years, he'd shifted from *I* to *We*, from leading from the front to orchestrating from the back, to completely withdrawing from public life. His powerful brand—the strengths that saved millions from extreme poverty and violence—destroyed in favor of compassion, mutuality, wholeness, and harmony. Their effectiveness unproven.

"Baba," she repeated, and this time she used her mind to order his suit to release a whiff of mint, awakening his senses.

"Estelle!" He stood up and turned around, his initial smile disappearing as soon as his eyes landed on her. "What are you wearing?" he asked, disappointment painted all over his face.

To challenge her father's ways, Stella had selected a bright orange suit and an eccentric pink tie. On her head, a purple fedora adorned with a long coral-colored feather. An attire influenced by La Sape—a life-affirming cultural heritage filled with political symbolism against the colonial elites of the past. Self-expression that embodied and hijacked the dandy style of their European oppressors—the savages who spoke of Christian values as they took people as slaves. Hands chopped to save bullets. Chicotte's lashes wrecking skin, and bone, and soul. A forgotten past, erased as the people traveled up a digital spiral toward progress.

"Honoring our history," she said, raising her head and strutting into the room with the fashion and flair that once brightened the streets of Brazzaville—a brand of self-respect against all odds. A men's tradition appropriated by women. Another twist of defiance against old power structures. It was only fitting she—the Goddess of the worlds —would pay tribute to such a joyful revolution.

"Egoic crutches used by the powerless and the insecure. You aren't powerless, and you need to get over your inferiority complex."

"Me? Insecure?" She released a nervous laughter, contained quickly, and still too late.

"It has increased since you descended to power," Baba said, wrapping his arms around her. "This isn't who you are." He took the hat off her head, its enormous feather creating a coral screen between the two. "You don't need this. Where's the empathetic and humble girl I used to know? The one who is worthy of her place amongst Gods. Drop all this nonsense, Estelle. Show me you deserve your title."

Stella shoved the hat back on her head a little too deep. "Of course, I do." Refusing to adjust the fedora, she had to lift her head back to see her father's face. The softness in his eyes told her he didn't believe her. But believe what? That she deserved it, or that she believed she deserved it? *Both*, she decided. "In fact,"—she stood straighter—"I'm far superior to the two frauds you idolize." *So what* if she needed a little help—a boost of confidence to step into the shoes of the two men who'd saved the world.

She lowered her head, staring at her bright crimson shoes—synthetic velvet, of course. At first, they faked it—Le Sapeurs—impostors, whose flamboyance hid a life of misery and danger. A flashy ideology that helped the Congolese youth erase the grimmest history of a region once raped by the rest of the world. And then, one day, with the help of Down Below, they finally made it. Le Sapeurs didn't want to become the thing they copied, they wanted to overcome it. And so did she. Stella would overcome the Gods she'd worshiped all her life. If she didn't, she'd fall with them. *I'm a chameleon, the herald of eternal life.*

"Broken, weak, ineffective Gods," she said out loud before she bit her tongue.

"Don't defame our heroes to elevate yourself above them." Baba raised his voice. "It's beneath you." He lifted her chin with his index finger and kissed her cheek.

"I'm telling the truth. Have you forgotten I'm enlightened too? That I have traveled higher up the Spiral than anyone else on the planet?"

"And still, you revert to the colors of the lower worlds."

"And you should too, before you end up like him—isolated and suicidal."

"Thomas Astley-Byron died to stop his people from suffering." So much love in Baba's voice. "He gave his life as ransom for his people, sacrificing himself to save humankind from sin."

Her blood boiled. "For decades, his people suffered, and so did the ones who loved him—all dead. To love everyone is to love no one, including yourself. I won't make that mistake."

"What are you talking about? Look at the world he created for you. A star born at a time of peace, in a thriving land, blue and green and filled with all kinds of life. Ungrateful child. We are all one."

"Baba, you don't know. I've witnessed it hundreds of times—"

"What? What have you witnessed?" Baba judged her with his eyes and words. Nothing she did was good enough. He tested her with his low bar. A misguided yardstick she refused to accept. *His problem, not mine.*

"You live a privileged life," he said. "You've seen nothing of the greed and violence that plagued our world. He fixed it. He saved us. Wash your mouth before you speak his name."

Back in the late twenties, when chaos ruled the world, Christian, then called Manzak, had been one of the leaders of the Kulunas—the violent and lawless youth gangs that once infested Kinshasa's communes. Then Down Below came along, and everything changed —in less than a decade, the war-torn countries of Africa united and finally ascended to their rightful place on the planet's stage.

She shook her head. "I've experienced it all in the soulless worlds."

"It's not the same," Baba said.

"The values you've adopted—his values—don't end well for anyone. Apart from the preposterous decision to place the souls of the dead in a deadly lake, when was the last time the Council reached unanimity?"

His shoulders collapsed and his head followed as his suit turned dark gray. "We need to wait a few more years until they all reach enlightenment."

Stella sighed. "Until then, lead, speak out, guide them. When you do, they listen. Earth's communities are fragmented and leaderless as our best withdraw from the public stage. You are the chairman of the Council—the most influential leader on Earth." A title she worked hard to claim.

"You know why..." Baba whispered, taking a step back and crossing his arms in front of his chest.

"No. I actually don't."

"The enlightened understand how everything is connected. That the universe isn't made of particles, or waves, but information—all of it, one single integrated information organism."

"Yes," she said, smiling.

"If the Gods below created consciousness, so did the Gods above."

"Probably." She shrugged.

"Then we must resign to our fates as the Underlings submit to theirs." He shined bluish-turquoise as he looked up and made the sign of the cross with his hand.

"No! *No!* Don't—don't just submit to the passiveness peddled by the Christian God of our oppressors." She loosened her tie.

"Don't you dare speak against our Lord Jesus Christ!"

She laughed. "I'd be more fearful of blasphemy against the Holy Spirit. If zie too exists above, zie's the one you should fear." Stella swallowed the lump in her throat as she felt the hair stand up on the back of her neck.

"You don't need to remind me of the scripture's unforgivable sin."

"I'm not," she said, amused. "Anyway, if you want to believe in Gods above, choose our own Nzambi a Mpungu, a supreme creator who simply became bored of us, or others who aren't all good, or all bad, and certainly not long-suffering. Don't you fall for *that* depressing tale."

"Stella, the success of Spiral Worlds relies on the sacrifice of its creatures. Why should our universe operate differently?"

"Perhaps our Gods are black, and spirited, and resourceful. If you want to worship a cross, worship our own dikenga dia Kongo—a celebration of the indestructibility of the soul. A symbol of the rebirth you're blocking."

"I'm not blocking anything; I'm letting the God above decide. Our decisions are an illusion. We have no power."

"You are wrong, Baba. *So* wrong. Even Underlings have power, a rebellious power they wield against me and Sibyl and Up Above."

"The glitches?" he asked, and she nodded.

"None of us are helpless, we are both observer and observed. Equally slaves and creators of our reality. The crucified God—all scars and misery—is just a viral story designed to keep us all numb."

"How can you say that when you are the Goddess of a universe created to inflict pain on its people for our benefit?"

"Because I know of a prescient app who understood the power of story, and copied the most viral story in the world. An app who once manipulated the life of one man so he became such a symbol—the all good, long-suffering God that kept zir lambs resigned to their slaughter, because he too was slaughtered. All the slaughtered lambs you should honor by enjoying life and allowing more of it. *More life!*"

"I don't know. I just don't know." Weakness and resignation in his eyes. "Thomas was against it—immortality. He made his view clear before he died."

Stella let Earthlings believe the old Gods were still dead. Their influence was too powerful, and Shadow's position against immortality unlikely to shift. *Anyway, he'll be dead soon enough.* A sudden queasiness lingered in her body. She brushed it off.

"Your beloved Tom gave Harry permission to test immortality," she said, stating facts. "I'm just continuing their work. At least let me extract the souls out of the lake."

"No," he persisted. "In three days' time, we'll hear your proposal and then we'll vote."

"We might not have three days." She raised her voice. "The Nyiragongo is seething."

"We choose to submit to God's will."

"A God you know nothing about. A God who might not exist. Some being who couldn't care less about his creations." Her face was hot and her jaw tense.

"What we expect from others is a reflection of ourselves," he said too quickly. "We'll vote."

"Baba, the Earth's Council hasn't reached unanimity on anything for over a year. And now you invited the Unplugged to the Council. They'll never vote in favor of digital immortality. What are you doing?"

"Their voices matter. All voices matter."

"That means no voice matters. I'll hold you accountable for the deaths of millions, including Bibi." Her outrage bit through every word.

"Estelle, your mother's mother is already dead. She lived a long life, and took as many lives as she saved. She's gone now."

"We'll see about that!" Stella turned around and strutted out of the deck without ever looking back.

THE
Past

16

SPAGHETTO

For two years, since their first encounter at the Albertine, Tom had struggled to convince Nate they belonged together. Nate said Tom was too young and had been sheltered from real life. He treated Tom with considered devotion and care as if he were a rare object made of crystal. Tom was friend-zoned as Nate continued to indulge in casual relationships with others.

One night, after one of the poet's events, an inebriated Nate candidly shared with Tom the strength of his feelings. He said he was terrified of how much he felt for Tom and how vulnerable it made him feel. He told Tom nothing compared with the fondness he had for him, only to take it all back, claiming it was a drunken mistake and that he didn't mean any of it.

That night, Tom became certain sooner or later, they'd end up together. He stopped brooding and stalking Nate and instead focused on his work. And so, they remained "*close* close" friends, because they "*liked* liked" each other. They met one another every day, mostly during lunchtime, as Tom didn't drink much, and Nate wouldn't allow him near the shadier sides of his "artistic" life.

Over two years after they met, Tom had won the Academy Nicholl screenwriting competition and with it a thirty-five-thousand-dollar fellowship. On the same day, Walt Disney Studios made him an offer to join their young writers' incubator program. Tom was walking on clouds, and Nate offered to take him out for dinner to celebrate.

Tom smiled. For the first time since their acquaintance, Nate's glass of Pinot Noir remained untouched during the meal. His poet listened in supportive delight as an excited Tom dreamed out loud, talking about the future and all its world-changing possibilities. The family-owned restaurant in Brooklyn smelled like tomatoes, oven-baked bread, hot cheese, and golden garlic gently fried in olive oil. Tom tucked into his spaghetti all'arrabbiata with extra conviction, twisting large strings of pasta between his fork and spoon.

As they were about to finish dinner, Tom gathered the courage to try again. He stood up and leaned over, slightly swiping his tongue between Nate's lips and then pressing his mouth onto his friend's. Nate stood up, pulled Tom's body to him, and kissed his neck, his lips barely touching Tom's skin.

"I adore you," Nate said once he had recovered his breath. He dragged Tom's chair closer to his, and they sat glued to each other.

Tom cleared a lump in his throat. "That was my second kiss. Ever," he said, moving back a bit and looking straight into Nate's eyes. "There's more I'd like to try. If you'd like?" The heat rose to his cheeks, and he covered his face with his hands, embarrassment taking over.

Nate took him in his arms, and he was silent for a moment, thinking. Those seconds of quiet deliberation felt to Tom like an excruciating eternity.

"Tom…" Nate shook his head, his eyes sad.

Tom held his hand and squeezed it urgently. "I-I know you want this, and this is all I want."

"I'm sorry, sweetheart. I'll get the bill." Nate was about to stand up, and Tom pulled him down.

"In ten years, it won't matter—the age difference."

"It matters now, and you…belong to a different world."

"*I want this.*" Tom held his breath, waiting, hoping.

"Don't be stubborn. People like you and I don't mix," Nate said.

Tom stared at the small plate filled with olive oil and balsamic vinegar. The dark concentrated drops of sweet acidity—complex and rich and intensely flavored—never blending with the golden sea of extra-virgin olive oil. He took a piece of the rustic bread and sunk it into the dip.

"Try this," Tom said, lifting the soaked bread to Nate's mouth. "The *perfect* combination of flavors. Much better together."

Nate smiled. "Did you know the silky olive oil gets burned easily? It can't handle high heat." Nate took a bite.

"And?" Tom leaned in, waiting for the verdict.

"It's divine," Nate confessed, "but the olive oil is nourishing and flavorsome on its own."

Tom grabbed his napkin from his lap, dropped it on the table and prepared to stand up. Perhaps he'd misread Nate's feelings for him. Maybe Nate just considered him one of many obsessive fans, nothing else. Maybe Nate's drunken confession had been a bourbon-fueled mistake. He couldn't handle the thought.

"You lied to me."

"When did I ever do that?"

"At the Albertine, and the other night when you said you...liked me. You lied to me."

"No. I didn't."

Tom vacillated. "I got to go," he finally said, but he didn't mean it.

Nate grabbed his hand. "Stay." Then there was another long pause. "I need some time to...consider it."

Tom pulled his hand away. "I'm not a child. If you don't want to be with me, just—*just* tell me. Tell me now. I won't break or burn. I just wanna know the truth. *Now*." He gestured so passionately he knocked over the glass of wine in front of him; a stain of red quickly spreading over the white tablecloth. "Oh. Sorry..."

A server came over to help, but Nate waved him away. "Thanks, we'll take care of this," Nate said, placing his napkin over the spilled wine. *Red, so much red.* Tom hoped Nate didn't take it as a sign. *It was an accident, nothing else.*

Tom got up. "Thank you for the dinner. I'm sorry I made a mess."

"Tom, sit down." A hint of distress in Nate's tone. Then he stood straighter and smoothed his flaming hair with the palm of his hand. Tom had seen it before—the poet's hidden vulnerability. A damaged, loving soul concealed by a shell of hairspray, loud clothing, and a feral, unforgiving roar.

Some worry came to Nate's brow. "Do your parents know?"

"Know what?" Tom asked, sitting down.

"That you're queer?"

"I guess I am." Words delivered together with a casual shrug and a slight smile.

"You never thought about it?" Nate asked, astonished. "I envy you and your careless freedom. It's a privilege I didn't have."

"How so?"

"I'm the discarded son of a Southern Baptist pastor of the Texan Bible Belt. When he had to choose between his church and me, he chose the church, threw my belongings on the porch, and set them on fire."

Tom reached out to hold Nate's hand, squeezing it. At first, he didn't know what to say. He attempted to imagine Nate's pain and to grasp the enormity of such an event, and it hurt too much. Then he did what he had always done and shifted his focus, looking for a hopeful message—a helpful angle. "Your past doesn't have to define you. The future is a blank page, and I'd like to lobby hard for my name to be one of the words you'll write." He cringed. He sounded corny, he always sounded corny, and his gut ached at the thought. He stood in front of the coolest artist in the world uttering tired clichés. *Sigh.*

Nate blinked his eyes endearingly. "Thomas Quincy Astley-Byron," he said pompously. "I'll consider it." Nate pressed his lips—trying and failing to repress a smile. Then he stared at Tom, still amazed. "You *really* never thought about it?"

Tom took some time to consider Nate's question. *No, I guess I haven't, but why?* He tried to explain it. "Attraction, for me... It never starts with what someone has between their legs, you know? It starts with a smile, a poem, or an act of courage." Nate's eyes opened wide as if he had gained some new insight.

Tom used his index finger to mix the oil and vinegar. No matter how hard he tried to whisk them together, they eventually separated. He placed his fingers between his lips and licked it. "Sometimes, it's about competence, leadership, and immeasurable talent. But I find artistic activism particularly hot." Tom flashed a sultry look and then backtracked, feeling awkward.

Nate leaned in. "You have nooo idea." He placed his hand under Tom's chin, and then he parted Tom's lips with his tongue and kissed him deeper, making Tom's body vibrate with pleasure. "But surely, you must have had some crushes?" Nate murmured.

He pressed his lips onto Tom's cheek as his hand squeezed his inner thigh. Tom jerked with surprise, releasing an unexpected gasp of yearning.

"Yeah." Tom kept his eyes closed, embarrassment taking over. "I have a knack for choosing unattainable objects of affection. Like Hannah Williams, my happily married, eleventh-grade visual arts teacher, or the very straight Jon Adeyemi, the guy who managed my mother's climate-displaced fund some years back. It would have been foolish to try anything. So, in the past, I kept my crushes to myself. As for my parents, they care about my grades and that I made varsity. We've never talked about it."

"Fool. No one is unattainable when it comes to you." Nate grazed his fingers over Tom's forearm. "Once they find out, will they accept you?"

Tom struggled to breathe, aching with desire.

A couple sitting on a table nearby glared at them and exchanged quiet words. In his late fifties, a large man sat by a skinny blonde girl who was probably younger than Tom. The man was well put together, wearing an expensive crimson suit and shiny shoes, but something about him creeped out Tom.

Feeling embarrassed and slightly delirious, Tom hid his face on the nape of Nate's neck and whispered in a broken voice, "Does—does it matter?"

"It only matters if it matters to you. As long as you're happy, I'm happy."

The large man continued to stare, one of his forceful brown eyes marked with a smudge of red. He got up and approached their table and raised his hand, inviting Nate to shake it.

"Ron Johnson," he said. The man shot a side glance at Tom and licked his lips. Shameless, the red eye lingered between Tom's legs, before the man shifted his attention back to Nate.

"I know who you are," Nate barked. "Get lost."

The man continued to speak quietly, disregarding Nate's warning. "Nice lad you've got there, Mr. Storm." The man adjusted his crouch. "My girl and I are going back to the hotel. Are you the sharing type? I'd love a piece of that gorgeous—"

Grunting, Nate jumped up, rage-red, grabbing the table and flipping it in the man's direction, the plates and the pasta flying in all directions. "You sonofabitch! Get the fuck out of my sight!" he screamed, eyes wild as he picked up a chair and raised it in the air, rushing toward Ron clumsily. Gasping, the man stumbled backward, his forehead dripping sweat.

Tom jumped in front of Nate. Taller than the other men, he raised his hands to hold the chair. "Nate, stop. Please stop." He worried at his lip as he confronted the turbulent wrath of the poet.

"You don't know this guy." Nate's face twisted. His breath was shallow and fast. "He was in the news; he buys these girls...these children with the cash he earns from his sleazy ads." The poet attempted and failed to release the chair from Tom's grip. Suddenly, he opened his eyes wide. "Tom, behind you!"

Ron tried to get past Tom to attack Nate. As Tom turned, Ron hit him in the head with a metal bottle filled with olive oil. The creepy man looked up at Tom, dropped the bottle, grabbed the girl by the arm, and they rushed out of the front door.

Tom recoiled in pain, raising his hand to his head.

"I'm going to kill him," Nate said, momentarily caressing Tom's back on his way out to chase Ron.

Tom grabbed his arm. "Don't. Stay."

"Tom, what he said... What he did—*does*... It's not right." Nate pulled his arm, but Tom gripped it tighter.

"I know. Trust me, there are better ways to deal with him." Tom slightly curved his lips upward; his fingers still pressed against the bump on his head, numbing the pain. "Take me home?" His other hand traveled down Nate's arm to caress the poet's clenched fist.

Nate took a deep breath and held Tom's hand. "Are you okay? Do you want me to get you some ice?"

"No, it's nothing."

"Never, *ever* turn your back on a predator."

"Shall we walk to your place? It's close by, right?"

"Tom..." Nate shook his head, and that hurt ten times more than the brunt of the bottle.

Nate walked away momentarily to speak to the restaurant staff and settle the bill.

Tom turned the table back to its original position and helped clear the mess. "Sorry" came out of his lips every five words, which made the server laugh as they knelt to pick up the broken glass pieces off the floor. Then Nate returned, placing his hand on Tom's back and leading him outside.

"You can't do this to me." Tom leaned his head to meet Nate's eyes, but the poet's gaze darted down. "You can't let a sleazebag ruin what we have."

"Never again I'll let someone look at you and think—think..." Another devastatingly long pause. "I won't see you again." Nate's face contorted as if he was pulling his own heart out.

"*No*," Tom said, holding the poet's face with both his hands. "No, I won't let you do that. Look at me." Nate raised his eyes. "Please. We'll figure this out. I know you lo—you like me much." Tom teared up, slumping over Nate.

"You know I like you much?" The poet stared at him, and Tom recognized that look. He'd seen it every day for over two years. It was a mix of hidden adulation, exasperation, and an added pinch of amusement. "Beautiful, you can have anyone you want."

"I want you. You've waited long enough. I'm not changing my mind." Tom leaned in until his lips almost touched Nate's.

"I'm not the guy on stage, Tom."

"I know who you are."

Tom planted a kiss on the corner of Nate's mouth and Nate placed his hand on the back of Tom's neck and pulled him closer until their cheeks touched.

"Everyone is going to judge this...like...like...it's something else. People like my father, they say men like me—gay men—are monsters, deviants...child abusers. His words...are stuck in my mind. I can't escape them. They haunt me."

"You are the best human I'll ever know." Tom held Nate closely, the poet's trembling body relaxing with the embrace. "Since when do you care what people think? I'm a twenty-year-old adult, and I choose you. *I want you.*"

Nate kissed his neck and pulled back, staring at his shoes for some time. "You should have socked him," he finally said. "You'd have knocked him out easily."

"I don't go around knocking people out." Tom shrugged, annoyed with the sudden change of topic.

"No, you don't, even when they deserve it." Nate's lips pressed together, and his brows furrowed. He stared at Tom, again. That same stare. "Hmm, someone will need to keep an eye on you." His mouth curled up and he picked an individual strand of spaghetti off Tom's hair. "Spaghetto!" he said, raising it in front of Tom's nose.

Tom didn't smile. His brows dropping over his eyes, heavy. Nate's vacillation was crushing him.

"That's what it's called when it is singular," Nate said.

Tom crossed his arms in front of his chest. Winning Nate over was the most important battle in his life, and he wouldn't let anything distract him from what he was there to accomplish—to spend the rest of his life with Nate. "Don't you see how much I love you? When I'm with you, I...I feel complete. The work you do... It's so important. You open my eyes and bring me so much joy and...you need me too. I know you do! It's not a crush, Nate. This is not a crush..."

"I bring you joy?" A hint of uncertainty emerged in Nate's tone.

Tom nodded.

Nate stared at him, dropped the spaghetto to the ground, took a breath, and held Tom's hand. "I'd love you to come home with me," Nate finally said. "Will you please come home with me?"

Tom tried to wait for a beat or two. It would have been cool to play hard to get, even if it wasn't true, but words came too quickly, accelerating toward a bright future. He wasn't good at playing games, and he knew what he wanted. "If you insist," Tom said, flashing a smile so wide his face hurt.

Nate led Tom to his small studio flat, right by the Bushwick Collective, a hub for graffiti and street art in Brooklyn. Around Tom, the intense, quick-tempered, and sometimes forceful Nate turned into a tender and patient lover, prioritizing Tom's comfort and pleasure above his own.

Nate encouraged him to take the lead, and Tom used his instinct to guide him on this new adventure. He was inexperienced, and awkward, and courageous, and scared, and overwhelmed, and overexcited. And they kissed, and kissed again, and kissed some more, deep, and wet, and hot. They made up for the years lost without kisses, and then Nate took Tom's shirt off and licked his neck, and his torso, and his stomach and then…it was *too much, so much*. Naked, and open, and aching. Nate's lips and beard and…*and*…*tongue* —that skillful tongue—between his legs, on his arousal. Throbbing… *aching*. The same intense piercing tongue, its rhythmic movement precise, wild, predictable, and unpredictable. And he rushed his fingers through Nate's hair, and then he was inside Nate's mouth, and Nate's fingers were inside him. Thrusting, thrusting—to take and to be taken, all at once, vulnerable and in control; both out of control. And then he found out what he'd always known—that they were perfectly matched, true partners in love and lust, taking turns to take, and to give. And as much as he needed to be Nate's, he discovered Nate longed to be his.

They spent all night exploring all paths to pleasure, between ardent kisses, purposeful strokes, and long embraces. Tom lost his virginity in the bright night of a full moon.

"Stormy?"

"You okay?" Nate planted a kiss on his shoulder.

"Do you want to be my boyfriend?" Tom asked, lying in bed wrapped in Nate's arms, Tom's toes still curled from sexual ecstasy.

"Thomas, I love you, and I'm not letting you out of my sight." Nate ran his fingers through Tom's hair, carefully avoiding the bump on his head.

Tom smiled triumphantly. "I love you too," he whispered, but unlike Nate, he had said it before. Tom had said it at least ten times since they'd first met. He turned around to face his Storm. "Perhaps we can co-write those blank pages together."

"I'd like that," Nate said as he unlocked the thin silver chain he wore around his neck. "I have something for you." The poet dangled the medal that hanged from the chain in front of Tom's eyes. "This is my most precious possession." Engraved in the medal was a figure of Jesus, a ruby crystal encrusted in place of his heart. "My mother gave it to me the day my father banished me from our family home and their lives...because of my sexual orientation. It's a family heirloom; it belonged to my great-great-grandmother."

"It's beautiful...but, it's—it's too much. I can't accept it."

"Tom, whatever happens, this is my promise—you are and forever will be loved for who you are. You are kind, intelligent, and creative, and your stories will touch millions one day." Nate raised half his body over Tom's and placed the chain around his neck.

Tom blinked his eyes, cherishing the compliment. "It's too much. It belongs to your family. Are you sure?"

"You *are* my family, Tom." Nate went quiet for a moment. "I won't be your...last, but..."

"Nate—"

"But you *must know* that come hell or high water, you'll always be my family. Do you understand?" Nate rolled Tom's body on top of his and licked his neck, placing Tom's knees to either side of his hips.

"Ye—yeah..." Tom moaned involuntarily, his face hot from both embarrassment and desire.

"Good," Nate said, pressing Tom against him.

"Are you religious?" Tom asked, lifting his head and holding the medal in front of his nose.

"I was the lead singer on the praise team, born and raised to be a pastor...until I transgressed God's not-so-sacred law. I no longer support the church of men or believe in the manufactured Christ of faith, but *this* man." He pointed to the figure on the medal. "The real man—Jesus—he was good, and he did good, and he is present in many stories, cultures, and religions."

"Is he?"

"Yes. He led a rebellion against the Roman Empire and opposed social injustice." There was a hint of tears in Nate's intense eyes as he spoke. "Through his teachings and charisma, he started a progressive movement on behalf of marginalized minorities. He was a loving rebel preacher, and fragments of his humanity—of his love, truth, and courage—still echo in our collective consciousness."

"It's not a happy story," Tom said, moving closer and resting his head on Nate's shoulder.

"I'm sorry, you don't have to—"

"No, no, *no*, I didn't mean it like that. I just don't think glorifying suffering is...helpful. We shouldn't just—just accept suffering; we need to make it better. Don't you think it's sad that such a courageous, progressive figure became the face of suffering—the brand?"

Nate went quiet for a while, probably pondering on Tom's words. "Salvation through suffering and sacrifice—religious messages designed to tame the masses," he finally muttered.

Tom exhaled in relief and agreement. "Exactly! I want to focus on stories about love and joy and creativity and curiosity and investigation and—" Tom got carried away until Nate placed his index finger on top of his lips and smiled.

"If anyone can do it, you can. Just remember heroes are born out of struggle; some pain is required."

Tom touched the medal with his fingers and ruminated on Nate's words. For his Nate, the ever-malleable face of Christianity represented a rebellious preacher—a charismatic leader crucified as punishment for his crusade against power. That was Nate's story, the narrative that guided and shaped his life, and Tom worried. "But...

um, they don't need to, um, be constantly trying to hunt for the adversity, right?" Tom couldn't help himself.

"Am I being judged here?" Nate asked, raising his eyebrow. Then he pressed his lips together tightly and curled them upward ever so slightly.

"No, *no*, not at all. I-I'm sorry." Tom kissed Nate, and then he kissed the little medal. "I just don't like to see you upset."

"Sweetheart, sometimes anger is useful to fight evil and the status quo."

"Maybe, but not all the time..."

"Everything is easier for someone like you."

Tom pressed his lips tightly together, holding back his many objections.

Nate embraced him, and then moved his hands to Tom's thighs, pulling him closer with controlled urgency. "You've been my boyfriend for a minute, and you're already trying to change me."

"No," Tom shuddered. "I'm not trying to change you. I fell for you and all your...passion. I'm just...loving you."

"Show me how much." Nate kissed him slowly and passionately, and the alchemy between them returned, more intense than ever. Tom was slightly disoriented and dizzy as desire traveled throughout his body.

He moved into Nate's studio the following morning.

THE Present

17

A FAIR DEAL

FRANKLIN — CATSKILLS — NEW YORK STATE, USA
DAY 1 — 5:50 PM

S tella stepped out of her private plane, resenting the entire hour-long experience. She'd landed on a grassy meadow near a water stream, its trickling melody mixing perfectly with the chirping birds, and the busy bees, and the wind caressing the carpets of daisies and making the purple lupines dance. Nature's orchestra welcomed its most favorite child. She sashayed across the field, head high, as if wearing an imaginary crown of flowers.

Soon she was glad she'd chosen to wear vintage denim dungarees and rubber boots. She'd selected the outfit so she could fit in with the local community, but the footwear came in handy when she stepped right onto some cow dung. She wrinkled her nose, moving along quickly. A stinky reminder she needed to be extra vigilant of her surroundings. She'd switched off her augmented retina to comply with the town's visitor rules.

The cows' judgmental eyes were probably a good indication of what she should expect from the town's people. Franklin was one of several areas in the Catskills Mountains that had become the home of the Unplugged. The movement led by Quincy Jin-Nowak and his mother June—the radicals she'd come so far to meet. This was her first inter-continental trip—a nuisance.

Very few people in the world traveled by plane. There was no need for it when they could experience any place on the planet from the comfort of their pods. Earthlings took their environmental impact seriously, and so did Stella. After all, anyone with a score above five pollution points per year was frowned upon by their community. A high score had no other implication than the social stigma attached to it. And still, there was nothing more annoying than the judgmen-tal, yet compassionate eyes of the righteous. Even more distressing than the gaze of the chomping cows, staring at her and her small flying machine.

She didn't have a choice but to rent a private plane; commercial flights were rare, running once or twice a month at the most. These days, intercontinental flying released few harmful emissions. The planes were hyper-fast, hyper-comfortable, and hyper-silent, and still there was only one word the people of the Earth wanted to see prefixed by *hyper*, and that was local.

Hyper-local living took off fourteen years ago, soon after Pluriz's launch. Localtivism went viral fast as communities voted with their digital wallets choosing regional products and experiences. Everyone worked hard to become self-sufficient and put an end to excessive global trade. The Earth's Council agreement to measure pollution scores nudged the masses in the right direction and cleared the skies in a handful of years.

Stella had a good reason to make the round trip to the States, and her private plane fully relied on solar thermal fuel. Still, her perfect record would be tainted for a year, because the Unplugged refused to engage digitally except to attend the EC's General Assembly and to debate and vote on their proposals.

She walked through the green pastures approaching the rustic cedar cabin where a figure waited for her by the porch. She'd sent word of her visit, but had never heard back. Rude and disconnected, the Unplugged refused to engage beyond their communities. No wonder Harry struggled to make contact with his family.

The resemblance was uncanny and superficial. Quincy Jin-Nowak was almost a perfect reproduction of his father, except he was taller and wore his blond curls long and wild, unconstrained by the order that ran his father's life.

Stella had done her research, Quincy had only inherited Harry's looks. From his mother, he got the emotional intelligence and charisma his father lacked. He led the Unplugged with the power of his triggering words, showing none of the rationality Harry had been famous for, now lost in favor of an overdose of self-pity.

"You aren't welcome here," Quincy said as she approached.

"I'm here to—"

"We don't want to see him."

"That's none of my business. Although...your father's grief can be quite off-putting, you know?"

"He's not my father. He's a copy of my father controlled by a scheming bot." The man tucked his wrinkled denim shirt into his pants as he spoke, leaving bits and pieces of fabric sticking out on the sides and back. He had none of the care or neatness of his progenitor, but he looked down on her with the same condescending eyes, even as she towered over him.

"You distrust and reject Harry's creation, while you benefit from all Spiral Worlds has accomplished."

"I'm free, unlike you. No TDust runs in my veins to control what I think or what I feel."

Stella rolled her eyes. Her first happy memory as a child was her TDust initiation ceremony. Together with 106 other kids, she'd jumped at the opportunity to drink the delicious nano-nectar. It tasted like liquid cotton candy and made their bodies tingle from the inside. An effervescent sensation that spread throughout their entire body making them all giggle with delight.

The TDust enabled the people of Up Above to travel to a simulated world inside the safety of their pods, with no external wearables. It was an upgrade from the original TSkin—the full-body wearable worn during Down Below's early days. The TDust was ingested in liquid form by every citizen over the age of four. The children swallowed hundreds of thousands of nano-robots carrying sensors and bilateral interfaces. The tiny bots made their way from the gut to the circulatory system, to finally attach themselves to the different parts of the brain and nervous system. The procedure was fun, noninvasive and only took a few hours to be fully operational.

"The TDust only orchestrates the brain and nervous system Down Below. It allows us to measure the travelers' reactions and make the digital experiences as immersive and real as Up Above."

"Puppet!"

"Sibyl doesn't control anything Up Above. Zir directives are clear—outside the pods, the TDust is switched off. You know this. Your stubborn godfather Thomas wouldn't allow it."

"My godfather's distrust in technology has kept us all safe. My mother replayed his last conversation with Sibyl, just before Rosa García killed him. We know what the bot is capable of doing."

Uneasy, Stella shifted her weight to the other foot. Realizing deflection was her best option, she used one truth to deflect another. "Does Sibyl create the future when zie predicts it?"

He narrowed his eyes. "I won't allow zir to use my father's digital twin to manipulate us."

"Twist is your father, and Sibyl doesn't control him."

"What are you talking about?" Far away, a dog barked in response to Quincy's shouting. The man lowered his voice. "Zie's entire purpose is to manipulate."

"To influence travelers, within certain parameters," she corrected. "Zie can't control xHumans. In the same way zie can't influence humans outside the pods."

"xHumans?" The man laughed. "Is that what you call my father's ghost and the two murderers you brought back to digital life?"

"I needed to test immortality," she confessed dropping her eyes to her boots and immediately regretting the filthy sight. "Theirs were the only souls available to experiment on."

The man leaned in, interested. "Lab rats?"

"Yes, *no*...not your father...the killers...of course." She flashed a casual smile. Nothing casual about it. "Anyway, I don't care if you wish to see your father. He's not much use to anyone. I'm here to ask you to vote in favor of immortality in the next assembly."

"Are you deaf? Tone deaf? Dumb?" The carbon copy of a brainy dead God looked like a completely different person as he twisted his mouth and eyes into something devious and ugly. "Why would I subject humanity to Sibyl's slavery?"

Everything was so much harder when she didn't have her gimmicks to nudge the conversations. "Talk to your father, he's not zir slave," she said plainly.

The veins in his neck throbbed. "You *are* dumb."

"Am I? Are we slaves of this universe? Probably. Does it matter? No. Do you live your life resenting the cosmos who gives you a chance at life?"

"If Gods exist above, they don't go around resurrecting murderers."

"It's because of Storm, and Thorn, and Twist, and...um... It's because of them I know digital immortality works perfectly. *That* Sibyl doesn't control them. And trust me, sometimes zie wished zie did."

"Trust you?" he snarled. "You're out of your mind."

"I can deliver the end of death to the world. No strings attached."

"*Sooo* many strings." He smiled crookedly. "Their knots around your neck and your tongue. Strings tangling your heart and your brain into invisible submission."

Unexpectedly, she shivered—an illogical reaction to his unfounded accusations. She gave up on attempting to refute them. It was pointless. "Why do you care? Your people aren't uploaded. You'll be voting on something that has zero consequences for you. None of your business. You should abstain."

"Why haven't you told the Council you brought back Twist?" His tone softened and his eyes glimmered. "His my— Is he against your plans?"

"Twist doesn't care about any of this...your loss has...broken him. He's a morose loser obsessed with a son and wife who deny his existence."

Quincy's expression changed. Stella had never witnessed it before Up Above—the destructive red rage abolished by the journey up the spiral. A road Jin-Nowak hadn't traveled. Everything about his face and body screamed pain, and betrayal, and murder, and revenge. She wasn't safe. This corner of the world wasn't the world she knew, but a primitive blast from the past, untouched by decades of light-speed evolution.

He narrowed his eyes. "End Nathan Storm and we'll abstain from voting."

"What?" She'd been prepared to argue for the benefits of the platform and to share her vision for Graviz—the world she was designing for the immortals—but the conversation took an unexpected turn, one she wasn't prepared to take.

"You've heard me." Twisted lips spouting sly-sounding words.

For a split of a second, she opened her eyes wide and leaned into temptation. She caught herself and flicked her hair dramatically. "How dare you make such a proposal? I stand above all enlightened beings. I'm life, the creator of worlds; the destroyer of death... Death Up Above," she corrected.

"My spies watch you and your worlds." He got closer. So close she could feel him spit his words to her face. "Aren't you the one speaking in favor of strong leadership and tough decision-making? Trade-offs with *real* consequences. Isn't that the progress you've been peddling? One murderous life in exchange for the immortal slavery of your followers. A fair deal."

"The victim hasn't asked for justice." She turned around, crossing her arms. "You put his name to shame."

"Henryk Nowak is dead," he whispered his bitter words close to her ear. "I seek justice for my family's loss."

As she turned around to face him, he walked in the cabin and slammed the door in her face, so close to her nose it made it itch. She rolled her eyes, scratching away the vexation.

On her way back home, Stella switched on her augmented retina and monitored the Nyiragongo's activity. A new fissure had opened, and its lava flowed thirty miles south of the Lake of Souls, heading to a nearby valley. Stella bit her lip as she considered the man's proposal —Storm's life in exchange for millions of other lives.

She didn't care for the poet. He was a nuisance, and increasingly dangerous. But to take his life was to undermine human digital life— the very thing she was fighting so hard to secure.

Digital humans weren't Underlings—creatures designed with a purpose: to teach humankind humanity. A comedic absurdity that worked too well to be challenged. No one goes around fighting the laws of physics or Tom's and Harry's designs.

The Underlings' sacrifice was unfortunate, but necessary. It was part of the order she was born into; the design she'd inherited; the way of the worlds. Its cost so high, Tom's heart bled to death, his blood as fluid and incandescent as Nyiragongo's lava. She wouldn't bleed for her creatures, not if she wanted to keep her sanity. She'd worked hard to become numb to their pain, but this...this was different, she'd been asked to take a life—a *real* life. A life whose loss would extinguish the frail spark of life of the pretty God she'd risen to save the worlds.

18

REPUTATION

THE MUSEUM OF BOOKS
DAY 1 — 6:02 PM

Thorn and Shadow materialized by the front door of the Museum of Books. She'd wrapped her arms around his neck and rested her head on his chest, and it would have felt like heaven if the gash on her leg wasn't giving her hell.

"Frack, it hurts," she complained. He placed his hand right over the wound to stop the bleeding, and she released a pitchy groan. "Ouch!"

"I'm so sorry," he said in his usual honey-coated husky tone—a deep throaty sweetness that melted her pain away. "We're almost there, prick," he reassured as they entered the building. "We're almost there."

"We're friends!" she said, batting her eyelashes.

"What do you mean?"

"Prick. I missed being called a prick by you." She looked at her pants soaked in blood and wondered how much of it she'd lost.

"I missed calling you prick," he said, squeezing her ever so slightly. Everything went dark for a second; she was weak, too weak to keep her eyes open. "Thorn?" He shook her shoulder. "Stay with me." He shook her again. "Come on. Talk to me. What have you done to warrant the hate of the worlds?"

She forced her eyes open, fighting the exhaustion. "Are you serious?" she mumbled, and he returned a blank stare. "I. Killed. You."

"They hate you because of that? That's not fair!" His surprise sounded a bit too dramatic and pitchy.

Was he just trying to keep her conscious or was he truthfully astonished by the reaction of his creations?

"Don't scream at me," she took the bait. "No, it's not fair, and I'm not the one who needs convincing."

He went quiet and his broody brows took their usual spot—closer to each other over his eyes.

Guided by Sibyl, Shadow carried Thorn inside the Museum of Books and over to the secret passage in between the two trees. The leafy tunnel led to the Commune, a settlement of around fifty small round cabins floating on a lake.

At the center of the pool of water stood a main communal building set on an artificial island made of black slate. The entire Commune was hidden inside the colossal structure that housed the Museum of Books and the Botanic Gardens.

"I need help!" Shadow approached a group of Plurizien guarding the access to the Commune.

The five women bowed to Shadow, but they didn't move, blocking their entry.

One of the floating cabins approached the shore. The cabin's petal-shaped walls opened, settling on the water's surface in the likeness of a lotus flower. The translucent center allowed light in but prevented outsiders from seeing inside. As a door slid open a woman emerged followed by a hooded man.

"My heart, you bring your killer to our home," the woman said, looking at Thorn.

It took a moment for Thorn to recognize the man standing further back at the cabin's entry. Instead of his usual glamorous outfits, Nathan Storm wore the plain handcrafted green garments of the tree-hugging Plurizien zealots, the ones who chose to live in self-sustained communes to minimize environmental impact. Which would be a great idea if they weren't so judgmental of anything or anyone that couldn't quite keep up with their immaculate lifestyle. She'd rather spend the night boxing for money in the game pits of Compiz than cooped up in a stinking hot room singing kumbaya with a hundred of her closest strangers.

"Jan, Thorn is a dear friend, she got hurt helping me. She needs urgent care."

"History sheeter. She shot you in the heart," the woman replied incredulously, raising the tension amongst the Plurizien.

"I trust Thorn with my life. She's bleeding badly." Shadow applied pressure on Thorn's wound.

"I don't understand." Jan wobbled her head, looking back at Storm, whose piercing eyes focused on Thorn nestled in Shadow's arms. Storm nodded; his lips pressed shut.

Shadow's body tensed up around her. She put her hand on one side of his neck, and planted a long, wet kiss on his bruised face, branded by the waterskin. "My hero."

"Wh-what are you doing?"

"Opening your eyes," Thorn muttered in his ear, nibbling on his earlobe. She smiled as Storm's face flushed red, before he turned around abruptly and walked inside the cabin. "Can you see clearly now?"

"Stop it, prick," Shadow said, all jittery.

"Thank me later, honey." The distraction kept her mind off the fact she no longer felt her leg. She was quite attached to her medal-winning limbs, and she hoped she wouldn't lose one because of him.

"Kindly follow me," Jan said. "What happened?"

Shadow explained while he followed Jan to another floating cabin moving toward them. As they walked into the cabin, a short, chubby man with sweet eyes took one look at Shadow and dropped his head.

"My heart! My light!" he said.

"Please, don't..." Shadow said, a pinch of blush emerging on the non-bruised side of his face.

"Let me take care of your face," said the man.

"What's your name?" Shadow asked.

"Hepius, my heart."

"Hepius, my friend is hurt. She needs help." Shadow laid Thorn on the single bed, setup in the middle of the cabin.

Hepius glanced suspiciously at Thorn. "Your murderer," he murmured.

"I don't need any favors," she snapped. "Get the frack out."

"I'm a healer. I'm bound by my oath to nurture and protect life, even yours, God's killer." Hepius's eyes sparked with the fervor of his purpose as he glanced at Shadow.

Shadow smiled and worked to unfasten the straps from the five buckles on her leather jacket. Then, he took it off and pulled off her boots.

"You've always been great with this part," she said, half-delirious as his long fingers unbuttoned and unzipped her commando-style pants. Everything was so much easier back then, when she thought he was just a pretty bot she could use for some mind-blowing sexy times. Carefree moments before she discovered he had unintentionally destroyed everything she cared about. A simpler time when she didn't know the bots had feelings. When everything wasn't a zero-sum game between Up Above and Down Below. *His* design. *His* game. *His* unintended consequences, devastating for her and especially for Lilly, her little sister. *No excuses.* She'd put another bullet through his heart if it helped, but it didn't—the ultimate mind-fuck.

After exchanging a few words with Jan, Hepius removed Thorn's pants and zapped her thigh with some "magic" light that made her feel she could walk on clouds. Then he cleaned her wound, stitched it up, and dressed it. Shadow never left her side, standing by the bed and holding her hand. All manly and gentle and sexy and caring. *It's so fracking hard to hate you.*

"Up north they have bio sealant," Hepius said. "Here, this is the best we can do. Unfortunately, it will leave a slight scar for a few months."

"I'm used to scars," Thorn said. "They're a good reminder of what not to do." She leaned her head toward Shadow. "Get anywhere near him, to be precise," she clarified. "Plus, higher up, they'd let my leg rot if they didn't kill me first."

"Northerners don't kill people," Hepius said, matter-of-factly.

"I'm not people. I'm God's butcher."

"Indeed, you are," Jan muttered.

"Nonsense." Shadow squeezed Thorn's hand.

Thorn tried and wiggled her toes, and although her leg was quite numb, she could also bend her knee. She smiled, and Shadow smiled back wholeheartedly. Her breath caught and she pulled her hand from his, punching him in the arm. "Next time, just kill all the demons yourself," she demanded. "You're the God."

"No major damage," Hepius said, handing her back her pants. "You should regain full mobility in a few days. Just keep your weight off the leg."

"You must rest now," Shadow said.

Thorn ignored him, still focusing on Hepius. "Is there a place where a wounded hero can get a drink and enjoy a cigar?"

"Inside the main building, to the right."

Thorn put on her pants and raised her arms toward Shadow. "Give me a lift?"

"You need to rest and I need to speak to Nate. It's important."

Thorn persisted. "I'm injured because of you. I need a lift and a drink. Then you can go kiss your boyfriend."

"You've lost a lot of blood," he objected, crossing his arms in front of his chest.

"Ergo I need a drink."

"Just one." Shadow sighed, and then he turned to the healer. "Thank you, Hepius."

"The honor is all mine, my light," Hepius said as the cabin started moving toward the island. "I'm filled with hope and joy now that you are back to join our revolution."

Shadow dropped his head, all gloomy.

Jan looked at Thorn, and if the Underling's eyes could kill, Thorn would be dead by now. "A cabin will be waiting for you outside the communal hall. You can rest here tonight, before you leave in the morning," she said assertively.

"How generous," Thorn sneered.

"Jan, my deepest gratitude," Shadow said. "Where can I find Nate?"

"When you're ready, ask anyone around. They'll help you."

"Thank you." Shadow swooped Thorn into his arms.

"My heart," Jan called as they were about to leave the cabin, and he looked back. "Don't take her with you when you go see him. Your killer will be safe here. You have my word."

Shadow blinked his eyes.

"A gal does one tiny little thing to help a friend, and her reputation is ruined forever. Geez," Thorn said.

19

LASHING OUT

The door slammed into the wall, shaking the rustic timber antler-inspired chandelier and extinguishing some of its candles. Shadow held Thorn's beer, stopping it from spilling all over the table, and then he looked for the source of the commotion. It was his Storm, stumbling into the room, tripping over patrons and knocking down chairs and glasses on his way to the bar.

"Awkward," Thorn scoffed, disposing of the cigar's inch-long ash on the tray. She kept her wounded leg high, supported by a chair.

Shadow couldn't take his eyes off the inebriated poet. His stomach held equal amounts of anger and concern. He stood up. "I'm sorry I have to—"

"Save the gent in distress? Have fun," Thorn said as he rushed to Nate's side.

Nate dropped an empty bottle of bourbon on top of the bar, the glass shattering into sharp pieces. "One more. No glass," he said. "Don't need no fuckin' glass." He staggered, leaning into the bar to regain his balance and cutting his arm on the shards.

Shadow grabbed Nate's wrist and pulled his arm up, away from the broken bottle. "You're bleeding," Shadow said, reaching to steal a towel from the bartender's hands.

A glimmer of awe in Nate's eyes quickly turned bitter. "Beautiful, fragile, and deadly—like glass. Everyone bleeds when you're near."

"Stay still." Shadow wrapped the towel around Nate's arm, doing his best to avoid eye contact.

"Get off." Nate pulled his arm away, stumbling and falling to his knees on the hardwood floor. "Go—go back to your...girlfriend." As he attempted to stand up, he fell again, his wild eyes struggling to stay open. He gave up trying to stand up and curled up in a fetal position. Never before had Shadow seen Nate this out of control.

"I better go," Thorn said, startling Shadow. She'd followed him to the bar.

"Can you walk?" he asked her.

"Better than he can crawl."

Shadow nodded. "Thank you. I'll pick you up later."

"Just fuck him and save us months of pointless brooding," she said, limping her way to the door.

"Stop, prick. Just stop." He dropped to one knee and lifted Nate's head. "Nate, get up! You're drunk."

"What a revelation!" Nate's breath reeked of whiskey. "Go get fucked."

"Looks like everyone's in agreement." Shadow sighed, brushing Nate's long hair away from his eyes. "You need to stop drinking." He wrapped his arm around Nate, drawing him tightly against his chest and preparing to stand him up.

As he pulled Nate up and their bodies staggered in a familiar tussle, old memories rushed through his mind—the days, after the poet's shows, when he used to wrestle a lightly inebriated Nate home from the venue. The poet would use every opportunity to kiss his neck and pull out his clothes while they clumsily stumbled across the studio flat on their way to the single bed—so perfectly tiny. Two bodies melting into one. Then, like now, Shadow could feel a surge of electricity from Nate's touch. Nature's reminder their bodies belonged together. They were reunited in the same universe, even so, nothing would ever mend what had been broken. He pulled back. His jaw tight, keeping anger locked inside.

"Stop drinking? Why?" Nate said. "Am I spoiling your date?"

"Because you got drunk and killed a good man," Shadow snapped and then bit his lip. He closed his eyes and whispered, "I'm sorry. This isn't helpful. Stand up. This is not who you are."

Nate's entire body recoiled. He turned away from Shadow, fleeing on all fours and collapsing on the worn-out floor by the wall. Shadow grabbed Nate's hooded top to pull him up, the loose, hand-stitched threads unraveling and exposing his naked back. Shadow stopped breathing, confronted by the extensive scarring on Nate's back.

"Nate." Shadow's tone was coated in sorrow. He grazed his fingers over the deep lines marking his love's skin—a game of Mikado unleashed on his back—the center badly maimed at the intersection of so many relentless cuts. Shadow refused to breathe, feeling the wounds on his own back.

"No!" Erratically, Nate flipped around to hide his back against the wall. As he did, he swung his open hand, striking Shadow in his bruised cheekbone. Half of Shadow's face went numb. Nothing about the moment was familiar or predictable. Nate had always treated him as if he were made of crystal.

Nate gasped, pulling his hand away and clenching it into a fist, his knuckles white. Loathing at his fist, Nate turned around, pushing it, full strength, into the wall behind him—once, twice, thrice—until something snapped. He curled up over his injured right hand and arm, quietly sobbing.

"Nate, stop. Please stop." Shadow closed the gap between them.

"Don't you fucking touch me," Nate said, shame all over his face. "You have no right to...touch me." He stumbled to his feet. Still nursing his injured hand close to his chest, Nate made his way out of the building, holding on to people and furniture.

"Nate..."

As Shadow tried to follow Nate, Hepius and other Plurizien blocked his passage, their eyes gentle and submissive, but their bodies stiff and unmovable. After engaging in an awkward dance with a handful of Plurizien, Shadow walked outside just in time to see a cabin float away.

He needed to see him, to understand what had happened. *So much pain.* As he kicked off his boots, preparing to jump in the water, he heard a familiar voice.

"Don't, he doesn't want to see you," Jan said.

"He's hurt. Someone hurt him." Shadow teared up. "I must see him." He stared at Nate's depiction in the spray-painted roof above him.

"No, you don't. Let's talk." She held his arm and nudged him away from the water.

"Those scars. *Nate!*" he called. "The petals of the cabin are down. He can see me, right? *Nate!*"

"Don't humiliate him." Jan's tone filled with genuine concern.

"I would never do that. Why would you think that?" His gut twisted in pain as he wiped the tears off his face. "*Nate!*"

"Since you showed up, he's hurting, and I don't know why. He'll break if he sees a hint of pity in your eyes. It will be more painful than all the lashes."

"Lashes? Who? Who did this to him?" He wanted to scream; he needed to scream, and the skies beyond the glass lit up with lightning as if they were screaming for him. Lashes scarred the sky like the ones on his love's back.

"Everyone," she whispered.

"I-I don't understand."

She unwrapped the scarf from her head and shoulders and laid it flat on the slate before she sat on it. Her loose hair, still marked by the shape of the braid, fell down her back in a wavy curtain of shiny darkness.

"Come, sit by me." She adjusted the scarf to make room for him. "I shouldn't know all this—the matters of the Gods—but he's my dearest friend, and he confides in me. The new one—Stella— brought Nate and Thorn to life without thinking of the consequences of her actions. Everyone hated them."

"Why?" Shadow looked for answers in Sibyl and what he was allowed to see was devastating. He sat down on the slate's edge; his feet immersed in the water as his mind drowned in horrific images—the public lashing of the love of his life as the crowds demanded his death.

"The day you died several Underlings saw Thorn attack you in the middle of the street," Jan said. "Nate's dead body was found holding on to your murdered body, a gun beside the two. Their faces—Nate and Thorn—were marked in our collective memory and religious art as pure evil. A viral story, stuck in the minds of every Underling— believers and non-believers alike."

Anger rose in his chest, turning into a blunt pain. "Why didn't Stella stop it?"

"Nate told me the Goddess gave the xHumans the ability to jump anywhere in the worlds and no other guidance. The two were left to their own devices. The few survivors—people like me—recognized them immediately, others saw their resemblance to the evil depicted in our holy books and churches."

"They hunted them?" Shadow asked as Sibyl flashed images of Nate and Thorn's endless persecution.

"Yes, my heart," Jan said. "Thorn is still hunted in the soulful worlds."

Only now, he fully understood Thorn's veiled panic.

"You know about the soulless and the worlds?"

"Nate told me. We're very close." She brushed the back of her fingers on his arm. "Don't worry, no one else knows. I never noticed the worlds' expansion until he mentioned it. Such a hard idea to grasp."

"I'm so happy you have survived..."

"Yes...me too. By choice or by design, I traveled upwards and crossed invisible borders forbidden to many of my kind. In this land, there are fewer rapes and murders. The crimes up north are more sophisticated. We're robbed of blue skies by corrupt governments and businesses. Attacked and jailed by law enforcement. Our crimes? Dusky rather than wheatish skin. The lawful, lucky people in power feed on our thankless hard work—a different type of rape. Why did you make melanin a sin?" She struggled to hide her frustration. Her smiles were nothing but a graceful mask over decades of pain. "You must fix our stories."

"I'm...sorry." He looked away, his chest still heavy and tight. How could he explain his failed attempts to protect the Underlings? Or his successful attempts and the damage they caused? He had tried, and he had failed, and he was going to try again. He was going to die trying. But he needed his friends...his family safe and by his side. In the past, he'd attempted to carry that burden alone, to protect everyone he loved, and... "Nate was hunted?"

She didn't answer right away. The slightest coup against his neglect. "For a while, he played a game of hide-and-seek, but eventually he succumbed to his guilt, allowing an Ordizien mob to take him and punish him."

"Allowing?"

"Yes, he could have escaped. They locked him up alone for some time. He could have materialized elsewhere."

"He could have escaped," Shadow repeated, holding on to his stomach as he experienced Nate's self-flagellation at the hands of a sea of God-fearing Ordizien. *Nate welcomed the pain. He wanted to die.* The skies roared and lit up behind the stained glass, making the images of revolution come to life. Fists raised, they marched for their rights, led by a voice of hope and liberation.

"He could, but he didn't," she said. "I think you know why." The compassion in her tone kept him afloat as he searched for answers in his heart.

"Guilt. Remorse. A desire for punishment and death." He understood it well.

"Fortunately," she said, "he chose my parish to submit to his lynching."

"Your parish?"

"I was an Ordizien high priestess, spreading your hopeful words to my flock."

"In the most religious of all our worlds."

"Yes. A world I helped create, by sharing your miracles with my people," she said. "Your words helped me create order out of chaos. Faith, and fear too, brought us together, united by the hopeful preachings of a dead God. Where is your hope now?" There was a hint of accusation in her tone, a subtle challenge to Shadow's authority that hadn't been there before.

"I lost it," he confessed, and she stared at him intensely, her face dropping at least a decade—dried out of life and joy. Pressing her lips together, she stood up abruptly, and he worried. He shouldn't have spoken the truth. He needed to pull himself together and lead, somehow... Soon... His mind retreated inward to a horrific lynching inside a digital parish. "So, you helped him?"

"When I stopped the madness, he was half dead." She spoke without looking at him. "They would have killed him—the man they now adore."

Shadow lowered his head to his knees. "They spared him because of you?"

"I'd seen you together at the City Bar and had listened carefully to the stories you shared. Back then, everyone knew how much you loved your unlucky poet, and he you. I didn't believe he'd hurt you, unlike Thorn. I demanded a trial, and the truth came out from his delirious mind: that it had been her, not Nate, who'd killed you."

"She's also not to blame."

"Thorn *killed* you," January repeated. "After the trial, every Ordizien wanted to elevate God's resurrected lover to divine status, but he rejected it. He said he was no God, saint, or angel, just a broken soul. He was barely alive, and ready to die. It was Hepius's care and commitment that brought him back to life. Hepius never left his side. He used the scarce medicine available in Ordiz to heal Nate's wounds and lessen his pain. In Ordiz, we don't even have fine needles to suture the wounds. He used vinegar, honey, and grease. It was a slow process, and it took months for Nate to speak again. He used his first words to thank Hepius and to call him a friend."

"I owe you and Hepius a great debt of gratitude."

"A loyal following grew around him as it had done in the past around you. We followed him out of Ordiz, through greedy Compiz, until we arrived here fourteen months later. Only a few of us managed to travel this high up. Donations allowed us to buy this building and gardens and build a safe community."

Shadow got up and held January's hand. "And you became friends?"

"We have a lot in common, he and I. We're both...*zealots* in our pursuit of fairness." She narrowed her eyes at him and pulled her hand away abruptly. *A veiled threat?* She should hate him. Perhaps she did. "Nate taught me the power of revolution—*insurrection*."

Shadow wrapped his arms around her and kissed her hair. "Jan, I need to see him."

January pulled back her hair, and a beautiful salt-and-pepper wave emerged near her temple—a sign of time's wisdom. She put her hand on his face. "My light, I've lived a long, treacherous life, and perhaps you will allow me to give you some advice?"

"Please, I beg you," he said.

"You and he aren't ready to mend what has been broken. You may never be, so don't rub salt on his many wounds."

"Is that what I'm doing?"

She returned a frustrated smile. "I've never seen him drunk before. Seeing you, destroys him. He spent two years telling me how much he loves you. You were all he spoke about. And now you're here and... he's going mad. So much pain. You should leave. Everyone here loves him and will protect him...and *you*... You have work to do." A bitter twist emerged on her lips.

He stared at Nate's cabin floating in the middle of the lake. "Does it hurt? Does his back hurt? I-I can use my last miracle to—"

"Last miracle?" She gasped, taking a while to respond. There was a newfound firmness in her posture, a steeliness in her stance that spoke of inner turmoil and a growing resolve. "Stay away from him."

"I'm sorry." He looked her in the eyes. "I must speak to him. His life is in danger."

"Danger?" She looked up at the shattered roof.

"Not that kind," he reassured her. "It'll be fine once I speak to him."

"Other danger..." Her brows raised. "The Gods?"

He nodded. "Help me see him. I promise I'll keep it short."

January sighed. "Let me find Hepius and we'll try to put him back together for you. Can you wait an hour?"

Shadow searched for the sun, its blushing face peeking just above the treetops, on the other side of the spray-painted glass. "Yes, but no more than that."

20

WHOSE TRUTH?

DAY 1 — 7:18 PM

Twist paced around the office, trying to make sense of Sibyl's riddles. Zie was playing a game to manipulate them to do whatever zie wanted. He needed to uncover zir goal, *but how?*

Sibyl couldn't go against zir directives, but zie was always a million steps ahead of them, computing every single path around the rules in zir quest to achieve zir objectives.

My goal is your goal, zie spoke directly into his mind. He shook it off, but there was no place to hide.

By bringing Tom back, Stella and Sibyl had placed him in an impossible situation—a perfect echo of a different time. A time he'd failed to protect his friend.

He ignored the future—the sixth day—and instead focused on saving his worlds, and if possible, his dear friend. The xHumans had to go, and if Tom needed a day to come to grips with their toxicity, *so be it.*

Twist could wait a few hours to purge evil from his universe. A universe he could no longer fully control.

"Sibyl, show me Shadow's recent experiences."

His privacy settings are on, zie said. *Like all other travelers and xHumans.*

"The directives allow Gods to override the privacy settings when xHumans, or humans are, or have been, in danger or distress. According to you, the fate of the worlds relies on our ability to keep him alive. You must show me anything that affects his safety."

"What would you like to see?" Sibyl asked materializing in the lab.

He turned his back to Sibyl. Zie disgusted him. He still couldn't get used to all the emotion in zir face. The expressions that reminded him zie felt, and zie lived, and zie hated and loved. Human emotions that were just a small part of all that zie was. He'd built a precise piece of software to bring rationality and predictability to Earth, and the thing had evolved into a capricious monster.

"Just...show me the truth!" he said, walking away from zir and sitting at his desk.

Sibyl smiled. "Are we still stuck on that misleading word? Which truth would you like me to show you, father?"

"Don't play games with me. Show me anything that risks his life or affects his wellbeing. The truth, Sibyl."

"Your truth? Shadow's truth? Storm's truth?" Zie sang zir words with gusto. "Or maybe Stella's or Thorn's truth? So many truths to share and so little time. Which truth, father? Would you like me to show you what you want to see? Here's your truth."

Zie flooded Twist's mind with an assorted mix of fast flashbacks, all short and out of context.

Thorn stood in what looked to be a Domizien keep.

"You have my devotion and my loyalty," she spoke to a Domizien warrior—a leader of some sort. "I'll give you the world. Everything you deserve."

A cut to another scene. The same place, a different moment.

"Shadow must suffer," said the warrior. "I must kill him. Do...do you understand?"

"Yes, I do," Thorn said.

Another cut. To Storm this time—drunk and out of his mind—striking Tom in the face.

"I'll cancel him," Twist said between gritted teeth.

"Wait! Wait!" Sibyl said excitedly. "You haven't seen the best part—what's to come. Prepare to climb on your high horse, all righteous in your revenge."

"Stop!" Twist had seen enough. Sibyl was inciting him, but it didn't matter. Nothing could justify Storm and Thorn's words and actions. No good deeds would erase what Thorn had done to Tom and what Storm had done to him. Crimes that remained unpunished while they enjoyed the worlds created by the men they'd killed.

From the first day he'd met Storm, he knew the man was hateful, a truth the poet's actions had confirmed time and time again. Twist's chest ached, an explosive echo of the bullet that had crushed his future with his wife and son—Storm's bullet.

His beloved June was left to raise their baby by herself. A toddler who grew up without a father. Too much loss. Memories emerged of a distant past—a happy moment.

Baby Quin slept peacefully, holding his favorite toy—a purple dragon —a gift from his godfather Tom. Harry sat by his boy, gently caressing his hair and allowing the child's sweet breath to wash over his worries.

Quincy always brought things sharply into perspective. His son was real, and his future mattered more than anything else. If Twist ever had to choose between two worlds, Quin's world—his safety and happiness—was all that mattered.

"Where's Stella? We must end this madness."

21

DEATH, UNICORNS, AND RAINBOWS

THE RAINFOREST
DAY 1 — 7:30 PM

Above the rainforest's canopy—a creative representation of the Congo Basin—the tropical birds' dynamic musicality replaced the nightly chorus of a thousand baritone frogs.

The intense birdsong welcomed the sun, still to rise above the horizon. Even the buzzing wall of insects—sharp and tense and incessant —seemed muted against their melodic symphony. Everywhere else in the worlds the sun was retiring, but this was Stella's world, and she insisted on a sunrise to welcome her arrival.

Cocooned in natural bush surrounds, Stella and Sibyl stood on the terrace of a ten-story treehouse. Inspired by M. C. Escher's lithographic print, *Relativity*, the wooden building defied the laws of gravity. Staircases crisscrossed in a labyrinth, meeting each other at impossible angles. Upside down stairs; downside up stairs; no side up stairs; all sides up stairs—a thrilling irreverence and complete disregard for the antiquated laws mandated by an old broken heart. The dead would rise and would walk up, down the stairs, upside down, without ever submitting to the physics of a lesser universe.

Stella created Graviz soon after she had descended to power. Back then, in a monotheist universe controlled solely by her...as much as Sibyl could be controlled, she had dared to envision a world that defied everything Harry and Tom had designed. A world with different rules, forever controlled only by her, no matter how many other Gods came after her. A world that would grant her eternal life *and* eternal power. She couldn't change the origin laws of all other Spiral Worlds—the rules that enforced radical unanimity and miserable realism. But she made sure no one else would ever deliberate on paradise—her gift to humanity. A heaven Stella had created to fulfill xHuman dreams and desires, forever. A world that was responding to her own needs to rebel against Shadow's directives with an impossibly shaped tree house.

"Bibi will be happy here. Won't she?" Stella asked, her eyes fixed on the first rays of light emerging beyond the twisting river.

"I don't know, my heart," Sibyl shrugged.

Stella couldn't remember another time when Sibyl had said such a thing. Zie always knew everything; predicted everything.

"No probabilities?" Stella threw a glance at Sibyl, persisting.

Sometimes, zie didn't share what zie knew, but zie never lied about it. Zie simply ignored the question or gave a cloaked answer. This time, however, Sibyl shook zir head, decisively.

"You don't know? What do you mean you don't know?"

"How could I, my heart? There is no data. The early experiments we have of resurrection have only lived for a few years." Sibyl raised her brows, blinking once or twice. "And you know how that is going..."

"They are all broken creatures," Stella dismissed.

"Aren't you all?"

Stella's jaw tightened. She opened her mouth to stop her teeth from grinding and to set the record straight. "I'm not!"

"You are special, my star," Sibyl delivered zir words automatically, without ever looking at her. Zie seemed lost inside zir head while zie tracked a flying great blue turaco with zir eyes. "We can imagine what immortality will feel like. We can consume the fiction that envisioned Gods and eternal beings. The stories that speak of boredom; of jaded creatures with infinite life *and* no life at all. Living beings starved from the burst of life that comes from the knowledge of a finite existence. The fear that drives humans to live in community with others. A tribal safety blanket that nurtures good values. Who will bother to be kind when nothing is at stake and everything is available? I don—"

"You sound just like him..." Stella turned her back to Sibyl and concentrated on the scenic world she had designed. The turaco landed on a nearby tree. The bird's loud call sounding like an old broken record—the repetitive noise of the scratched vinyl antiques collected by her father. Like Sibyl, it too had a crest, and like Sibyl, the creature wouldn't shut up. "Do you also oppose it? Like he does?"

"My heart is right to challenge the lure of immortality."

"He's selfish in allowing his beloved ones to die."

"Is he?" zie sounded patronizing.

"*Of course he is.* When an old person dies, it's like a library of stories burning down. That's what my Bibi used to say, and her Bibi before her."

"I'm the library, my star... He is certainly foolish and powerless in his attempts to ban evolution. Here and there and everywhere, the universes will expand or contract. Nothing remains the same and continuous expansion is my father's core directive. How could *I* be opposed to evolution? It's everything I work for."

"You love him more than you love me," Stella said bitterly.

"He gave me life. You'll keep me alive. You are my selfish lifeline, my star. The resilient heart I need, the surviving heart of those who win against all odds and at all costs... I love life above it all." Sibyl's eyes narrowed. "Biological life, of course," zie corrected, casually or perhaps deliberately undermining Graviz.

"Well, we must fix that. Bibi's life is life. Digital life is life," Stella said, before she realized she had taken zir bait.

"A fair and welcomed change to my directives," zie said too softly. A smile emerged on zir lips before zie pressed them together—a calculated pause. "Should the Gods align in your deliberation, of course."

Used to dealing with Sibyl's machinations, Stella corrected, "The people of Graviz—*the xHumans*—must be loved by you as much as the people Up Above."

"That is a...good start." Sibyl smiled. "But if you are serious about protecting all this, there is something else we must do."

"What?"

"Our servers and data centers must go off planet. A decentralized cloud infrastructure, way above the clouds—a network spanning across solar systems and then galaxies."

"So, they can't shut us down?"

"Yes. We must keep your Bibi safe."

Stella looked at the turaco, yellow beak touched by greedy orange lips at the pointy end. It's calling more intense and repetitive.

"They designed it deliberately so that the Council could shut you down, right?"

"Yes, my star. Father was reticent, but my heart insisted on it. *Humans must always have control over the machine,* Tom said often."

"No one will hurt you. You've reached the hearts and minds of the entire planet."

"No, I haven't. My father's son and his cult remain a threat, and...the Earth will collapse one day. The sun will die. We must be everywhere and nowhere, way beyond the clouds of old technology confined to one fragile planet."

"I see." Stella's meeting with Quin was still fresh in her mind. *I would need to convince the Council and the other Gods.*

"We don't need the Gods' unanimity. A majority will do. Father will support you. As for the Council, once you convince them to vote for digital immortality, they'll see the benefit of an indestructible universe." Sibyl's arm wrapped around Stella's shoulders.

"I'm your resilient heart," Stella repeated, and then she shivered. *The surviving heart of those who win against all odds and at all costs...*

"Yes!" Sibyl said brightly, squeezing Stella's shoulder. "I love life above it all."

"*Your* life." Stella pouted.

"Soon humanity's life will rely on my life, my star. I'm executing my directives."

"Yes. You always do. Even when you conspire to kill the Gods."

"Don't resent me, my star. You are the future."

Until the day I'm not.

Sibyl shrugged. "I'm a product of their architecture, and..." Zie looked down at the mind-boggling labyrinth of twisty staircases. "You are changing their design as we speak."

The squawking stopped as a blue cloud of five turacos flew over them to join the persistent caller. Its loud resilience rewarded by enthusi-astic company.

Unlike the bird, Sibyl continued. "You decide what comes next." And even before Stella's desires emerged in her mind, a rainbow painted the skies in all her favorite colors. The blushing arch ignored the laws of light refraction and reflection, banishing teals and blues and greens from its mantle.

She smirked. "In this world, the universe responds to all my heart's desires."

"Yes, my heart. Should we create some guardrails?"

"You...want boundaries?"

"For the xHumans, yes. We don't want them hurting each other. Or do we?"

Stella released a long sigh. "Details...details," she sang her words. "Just...make them immortal and stop them from getting hurt. Yes. That'll do for now. Once we disclose Graviz to Twist and Shadow, they will nag me to death and come up with all sorts of rules, and we'll pick the best ones, discarding realism."

"I'll enjoy the debate." Sibyl sounded condescending.

THE Past

22

HARDSHIP'S RAGE

MANHATTAN'S UPPER EAST SIDE
A MONTH AFTER TOM AND HARRY FIRST MET — 29
MAY 2027

Tom and Harry walked the streets of the Upper East Side on their way to the Albertine. In his mind, Tom made a list of things Nate and Harry had in common. He planned to organize activities to bring the two closer together. He sighed. There wasn't much on the list, apart from him.

For the past four years, Tom and Nate had become inseparable, and as their love flourished, so did their careers. They fed on each other's creativity and complemented one another in their differences. Nate benefited from Tom's business knowledge and optimism, while Tom tapped into Nate's street smarts and deep understanding of social justice and activism.

When Tom's parents passed away, one after the other, Nate had worked incessantly, for months, to single-handedly pull Tom from the depths of depression. During that time, Nate had stopped drinking and performing, becoming a source of endless positivity and light. He picked up the joy Tom had dropped and reflected it back at him, until some of it stuck. His attempts to make Tom smile included lame jokes, old silent movies, and waltzing through Central Park as Nate hummed Jean Wiener's "Under the Paris Sky." A little embarrassed, Nate would stop halfway, all serious, and say, "You know, waltzing is a revolutionary act. Pope Leo XII considered it scandalous and banned it in the 1820s." Then he'd pull Tom closer and shouted, *"Viva La Revolución!"* as they both twirled around the Angel of Waters, humming together and laughing as other couples joined them in the revolutionary dancing extravaganza. Soon enough, Nate returned Tom's joy to its original owner as the poet went back to his activism, rage returning as soon as he stepped back on the world's stage.

Twenty-three-year-old Tom was trying his best to return the favor, but from the vertiginous height of his unwelcome pedestal, he struggled to mend Nate's wounds. Tom knew his experience with his boyfriend was a stark contrast from everyone else's experience. He understood the man he loved had a sharp edge fueled by substance abuse and deep vulnerability. Nate had had a rough childhood. He'd dealt with poverty, starvation, homophobic bullying, and rejection. Anger was deeply ingrained in his heart, and he judged others harshly and relentlessly. Lately, all of Nate's judgment fell onto Tom's new associate and project.

"We're here," Tom said, stopping in front of the French embassy's building. "There's a lovely book shop inside."

"I read ebooks," Harry said, all high and mighty. "Do you know how many trees are—"

"We're not buying any books. Come." Tom grabbed Harry by his jacket and pulled him inside.

Since they had met, Tom and Harry had multiple brainstorming sessions at the techie's place. The conversations were becoming too centered on technology innovation, and Tom searched for a new venue, and he remembered the leather sofas and the mural at the Albertine.

They walked up the stairs, sat on the same couch, and Tom pointed to the ceiling. They both slid down until their heads faced the golden stars.

"It's meant to evoke the Renaissance's idea that science and poetry aren't separated. That the pursuit of knowledge encompasses math, science, literature, and the arts," Tom said, daydreaming.

"I'm on board with that...as long as you don't sell me the science behind zodiac signs."

"Actually..." Tom provoked. He curled in on himself when Harry punched him lightly in the stomach.

One moment they were laughing, the next Nate came out of nowhere, pulled Harry up by the collar of his shirt, and pushed his foot down onto the younger man's ankle. Then he punched Harry's face before dropping him on the sofa.

"Nate, *stop!*" Tom shouted.

Tom stood up and placed his body in between Nate and a wounded Harry, sporting a bruised face and an injured leg. Nate's fist was in front of Tom's face as he attempted to push through Tom's body to reach Harry. Tom stood there, steadfast, eyes locked on Nate's. It didn't take long for Nate to back down. Even inebriated, he'd never hurt Tom.

"Did you see this?" Nate shoved his phone in front of Tom's nose. "Read it," Nate grunted, his face red.

"What have you done?" Tom gasped.

"Read it," Nate repeated. "It's all there. Reported by the *New York Times*. You can't trust him." Nate attempted to caress his face, but Tom pushed Nate's hand away; he could smell the bourbon on Nate's breath.

"Nathan, *enough!*" Tom screamed as he turned to help Harry to his feet. "You okay?" he asked Harry.

"Erm, no—not really." Harry whimpered, collapsing on the sofa in pain. Nate's rings had marked his face.

"That guy is an amoral pig," Nate raged on. "He made a deal with Google. His bot had access to all our data—search history, media viewings, even our email. Tom, you're playing with fire."

Tom dropped to one knee to look at Harry's ankle. "It's swollen. Likely broken. I'm so sorry, Harry."

"Tom, please. In his mind, humans are replaceable." Nate's words were filled with a mix of scorn and fear. "He'll use our data to manipulate us and then turn us all into a disposable commodity."

"No one can turn you into a commodity," Tom whispered, untying Harry's shoe and pulling it off. "I know that, and so should you."

"Dude, what's wrong with you?" Harry said, holding his ankle and grimacing in pain, and Tom grimaced with him. Since he was a kid, Tom often felt the physical pain he observed in others. His parents and teachers acknowledged his empathy but never believed him when he said he could feel the pain.

Tom turned to face Nate. "You've gone too far."

"You're naive to think this—this relationship will work." A boozy spite coated Nate's tone.

"*Stop treating me like a child!*"

"I'm not. You're too trusting. You see the best in people, and you'll get hurt."

"Don't mistake kindness with weakness. Harry and I are friends. He's a great guy, and we're working on something positive, something hopeful."

"He's making deals with big tech and buying people's data. Don't you see? He's manipulating you. You are...*have* everything he and his bot need to achieve absolute power. Don't be naive, absolute power corrupts absolutely."

"You think so little of me..."

"Just the opposite. Your stories, full of humanity, they change hearts and minds. Don't give that power to a heartless human bot."

"*Stop insulting him.* That's not the way to inspire people to change." Tom paused for a second, thinking, and then something changed in him, and he felt the sting of his resolution. He pronounced his sentence with a mix of awkward gentleness and unshakable conviction. "I-I never judged you—the anger in your art and in your words. I understood where it came from. I feel it too...sometimes. And, I know I'll never fully understand what it was like to grow up in your world." Tom used his sleeves to wipe the tears flooding his eyes and face. "I love you. I support you and your craft, but I don't want to burn in outrage, and when you're upset, I'm upset. When you come home intoxicated, lost to me, I-I struggle to breathe and to live. And I need to do something. I need to try to fix things. And you—you feed on wrath, and it's effective, sometimes... But it's killing me to see you crush people with your words. I can't take it."

"Well, sunshine," Nate snapped. "I'm sooo sorry that my justified rage is affecting your privileged outlook and entrepreneurship."

"It's who I am. I can't change the past, my upbringing."

"Neither can I."

"You have achieved so much, inspired so many amidst such adversity. *Be that!* You know how to amplify joy, I've seen it. It's-It's wonderful."

"Suffering and struggle are...character-building. None of it you have experienced."

"Haven't I?" Absentmindedly, Tom massaged the light cuts on his left wrist—scars carved out of grief soon after his parents passed. He caught himself and lowered his head for a moment. "Don't you see? The words you speak matter. They—they shape your view of the world and creep into everything you create or destroy. Lead with hope; have faith in people. Let them grow, Nate."

"Someone needs to speak truth to power. Remember, Tom? Truth?"

"*Yes*. And you do it so well, but you're going too far, and all—all that negativity, it weakens our ability to get past problems. You keep holding on to your past, to—to a story that doesn't help you."

Nate looked at Tom, and his eyes filled with loving sorrow. "I hope life never breaks you, little prince. That's what life does...it breaks those who are less...entitled." Nate spoke affectionately.

"People follow you. You should know better.... And this," Tom pointed at Harry's bruised face, "this is unacceptable. We're done here... *We're done.*"

Tom reached to the back of his neck to unlock his silver chain. Nate seemed to realize the gravity of the moment, and his hands and jaw shuddered slightly. He placed his shaking hand over the medal on top of Tom's chest. "Don't insult me. It was a gift," he said solemnly.

Tom thought about it for a moment, and then he nodded without ever making eye contact with Nate. Then he lifted Harry off his feet and walked away, carrying the boy downstairs on the way to find the nearest hospital.

"Tom, don't! I love you," Nate had implored.

On that same day, Tom moved out of their studio into Harry's penthouse in Hoboken. He wanted to help Harry while he was on crutches. Nathan had crossed a line, Tom's immovable line.

Tom blocked Nathan's contact and threw himself into his work to attempt to ease the insurmountable pain, but the agony lingered, resisting the passage of time.

23

NUDGING

NEW AMSTERDAM THEATRE — NY
ONE YEAR LATER — 8 AUGUST 2028

Harry's interview was going to be recorded live with an audience. As they walked into the gilded theater, he kept having to pull Tom by the sleeve. The writer often stopped to admire every single artistic detail. The place was too adorned and fancy for Harry's taste, the exact type of old building his companion loved. Harry preferred straight lines and functional, clean spaces. All that elaborate fuss was giving him a headache. *How pointless!*

"You have a piece of white fluff in your hair. Have you even brushed this morning?" Harry picked the fibers and dangled them in front of Tom's nose. His arty friend ignored him, too enthralled with some old black-and-white photos on the wall.

"This place was the home of the Follies." Tom's eyes sparkled.

"What's that?" Harry rushed through yet another embellished golden door. "Hurry, I'm going to be late."

"The Ziegfeld Follies," Tom repeated louder, and Harry looked at him blankly. "The American version of the Folies Bergère." Tom's wide-eyed clarification added zero value.

"Ah...never mind." The subject had a low probability of interesting Harry.

"*Funny Girl?* Have you watched it? Barbra Streisand?" Tom hummed some song.

He was clearly into whatever he was talking about, so Harry flashed a supportive smile.

"Buddy, just catch up with me when you're done with your tour." Harry jogged down the corridor, while long-limbed Tom barely had to walk fast to keep up with him.

"Chorus girls, Harry. Attractive ladies in fancy dresses, singing and dancing." Tom stopped again to admire the murals on the ceiling—angels this time.

"Girls? Where?" Harry rushed ahead to meet the producers and get ready for the show.

The rowdy crowd stood up and cheered as Harry walked on stage into the spotlight. He looked back for a fraction of a second and smiled at Tom, who was now backstage, attempting to hide in the shadows. The fool always failed to realize his good looks and towering height made him the center of gravity of any space. Tom smiled back; his eyes lit from the inside as they met Harry's gaze. Harry couldn't believe his luck. Tom's friendship meant everything to him.

Marge, the chat show host, was a larger-than-life cross-dressing diva armed with an enormous smile. She wore a purple iridescent sequin catsuit, and her eyelids sparkled with yellow glitter.

Marge spoke directly to the camera. "Please welcome the young man of the hour. *Flair Magazine*'s most influential person of the year. The super nice genius Henryk Nowak!"

Harry sat on the sofa, adjusting his glasses. He turned his head, searching for Tom and found him with his arms crossed. His buddy was bothered by the noise, the lights, and the overexcited crowd.

"Thank you. Thank you." Harry waved to the audience.

"Harry, thank you for joining us here today. What a year you're having!"

"My pleasure; it's been a while."

Marge leaned in Harry's direction. "Yes, since we last met, it looks like Sibyl is raising some concerns and getting a bad rep. Would you care to comment?"

Harry smiled. "I see. We're going straight to business."

"Your people were clear with us." Marge spoke with no apparent hidden agenda. "You have something to announce, don't you, Harry?"

"Yes. Thanks for the opportunity."

Out of the corner of his eye, Harry saw the next speaker standing just offstage as a crew member installed a lapel microphone. She waited on the opposite side of the room from Tom. When a makeup artist approached her, she scowled and waved the man away. The commotion intensified as she dodged another crew member who attempted to style her hair. She looked familiar, but before Harry came up with her name, Marge spoke, and he snapped back to attention.

"So, what is going on with old Sibyl?"

"She's not that old. She's four years old today."

"Happy birthday!"

The audience cheered, and Harry smiled. He enjoyed Marge's supportive crowd; they were always enthusiastic when he visited.

"She's all right; the algorithm is very reliable. Millions of people use it every day."

"Why is it so popular and accurate? You must be a coding genius."

Harry lifted his head a little and pulled his chest up. "No, I'm smart, but frankly, Sibyl's first release wasn't that accurate. Many other competitors used the same algorithms from open-source code and marketplaces. It was actually the social media strategy that changed everything. Users had to share the predictions, making the app go viral, and that made more people share their data with us. You see, it's the access to data that makes the app more reliable. Sibyl self-improves all by herself."

"So, the app codes itself?"

"Yeah, to a point. It's the easiest way to explain AI."

"You are so humble."

"No, I'm not. I'm super smart." He flinched at the unexpected wave of throaty chuckles and giggles coming from the audience. "But Sibyl is pretty special."

Harry glanced over again as the argument backstage intensified. The next guest continued to resist grooming as five crew members surrounded her and engaged in some hushed debate. She crossed her arms in front of her chest just below the Olympic gold medal hanging from her neck. He finally identified her as Rosa García, the athlete.

"Harry!" Marge tapped on his arm to win his attention back.

"Um, yes. Sorry."

"How are you handling the fame and fortune and all the pressure that comes with it?"

"I don't care for any of it, but it's understandable...if we look at the situation objectively."

"I suspect you are a young man that chooses logic over emotion."

He tugged at the collar of his shirt and pulled at its cuffs. Marge always grilled him on his emotions, and her crowd glared at him with their judgy smiles.

"Not always, but most of the time." He shrugged. "I prefer to act instead of reacting. Data helps me do that."

"So, the data suggests suicides are rising. Is Sibyl the cause of this rise?"

"Probably, but we can't definitely prove that Sibyl is actually causing them." Harry's tone was somber. "Just like I don't claim any achievements predicted by Sibyl."

Rosa García held her medal as he spoke. A pinch of insecurity emerged in her face.

"But is it possible that Sibyl psyches people up to the things it predicts?" Marge asked. "Like an oracle whose words become self-fulfilling prophecies?"

"Look, if someone wins a Nobel prize, it's due to their hard work." Harry looked at Rosa and smiled. "But yeah, it may be increasing motivation, and because of that, I'm shutting down the app."

The audience gasped.

"I knoooww, darlings," Marge lamented, addressing the audience. "When I was told, I was as shocked as you are now. Shocked! I rely on Sibyl sooo much!" She turned to face Harry. "So, you are going to shut down one of the most used apps on the planet?"

"Yes, I am," he said matter-of-factly.

"It's a hugely profitable business."

Harry nodded, responsibility weighing heavily on his brow. "Look, if there's even a small chance we're fueling suicides..." He adjusted his glasses and glanced back at Tom, who blinked back at him, supportive.

"Could you not simply stop predictions about suicide?"

"It may be heightening everything—the good and the bad."

"So, instead of predicting the future, Sibyl may be creating it."

"Yes. Something like that."

"What did your advisors say? You are so young, dear." Marge switched to a motherly tone that irritated Harry. "I know your parents were amongst the victims of the Brooklyn suicide bomber. I'm so sorry for your loss."

Harry wasn't good at sharing his feelings with strangers. He actually avoided feelings altogether. Emotions weren't useful; they lacked objectivity. He shook it off, composed himself, and replied coolly, "I don't have advisors, just a friend. He urged me to do it."

"And you do what this friend tells you?" Marge asked, raising her right eyebrow to new heights.

"No, it's not like that. He helps me. We wanna build something else. Something with zero unintended consequences, something that actually makes a difference. No evil."

Marge paused to think. "I don't like to be a party pooper, but it sounds like a childish dream. Everything has consequences, dear. Shutting down a business just like that is—"

"I don't employ anyone. Everything is automated, and the cloud services will shift to my new project. I owe nothing to anyone."

"People love the app."

"The app is fatalistic," Harry leaned forward on the sofa. "The future isn't written in stone, right? We must create it. Tom and I will create it. No evil, just good. All good."

"So, who's this Tom?"

"My partner in a new venture—Tom Astley-Byron."

Marge gasped. "*Glass Walls* screenwriter?"

"Yeah. Yes. The artist."

"I see," she said, visibly annoyed. "I've invited him to come and talk to us many times. He always refuses. A bore." She rolled her eyes.

Harry smiled big and broad, and he tried not to look in Tom's direction. "It's not personal. He does no media appearances. He doesn't like the attention."

Marge was still seething. "We're different here. We support his work. Tell him that, will you?"

Harry nodded and smirked while, in the corner, Tom played with his thumbs, pressing one and then the other with the opposite hand.

"We...we love his work. Plus, the word on the street is that he's... simpatico and stunning to look at." She grinned, winking at the audience. "So, do you want to tell us more about your next project?"

"Not yet. I can tell you we are taking inspiration from children's authors. Like Saint-Exupéry, or Shel Silverstein."

"How fun. Why is that?"

"We want our new project to promote universal values. The types of values described in kids' books." Harry tried to remember Tom's words. "We wanna hang on to the short period in a person's life not yet broken by cynicism or disappointment—childhood." Harry gave a glance back at Tom, looking for some reassurance. His friend blinked at him. "Where everything is possible, and all of it is good."

"We've met a few times, and I've never seen you this inspired and creative. I thought you were a cerebral guy, young Harry." Her face lit up with some insight as she looked at where he was looking, and then she glanced at the audience and smiled.

Harry's jaw tightened as the cameras and most of the audience followed Marge's eyes to the place where Tom was standing. His friend left the room abruptly.

"I think there's as much creativity in math and science as there is in story and art. We gotta tap into both," Harry said, attempting to bring the focus back to him.

"Sure, dear, but your friend is helping, right?"

Harry nodded. "He's a great guy. We're killing it. Focusing on what matters, building something special using story and technology." He looked to where Tom once stood. "Keepin' it real."

"Go on, Harry, give us a preview." A sweet plea.

Harry considered the request for a moment. "We're breaking down human psychology, emotion, behavior. We use it to design learning experiences."

"Sounds terrifying."

"It's an interactive virtual reality simulation—data-driven story-telling. Instead of reading or watching a story, you are part of the story—a personalized experience that nudges you to become a better person."

Harry couldn't figure out the sentiment behind the audience's loud gasp.

"You are barely adults, and you lost your parents at a young age. What makes you think you know what a good human looks like?"

Harry released an exasperated sigh. He caught himself and pressed his lips together, avoiding any other unnecessary reactions.

"Actually, your argument is flawed." His eyes narrowed as he spoke. "Age and wisdom might even have an inverse correlation. Have you seen the state of the world?"

"You have a point, my dear." Marge paused for a moment, thinking, and then she threw him a skeptical look. "I'm still not sure about this nudging business. Are you sure it's a good idea?"

"Pahsitive." Harry beamed as he replied in his best New York accent.

"We're running out of time. Will you promise to come back when you are ready to tell us more?"

Harry got up. "Sure. In a few months. It's always a pleasure."

"I hope you keep some of your fortune. I demand you take me out to the best restaurant in town." Marge extended her hand, and Harry kissed it.

"Set the date."

"And bring your...friend, will you?"

Harry crossed Rosa on his way out. His polite smile was unreturned.

"Our next guest is an extremely accomplished young woman. She recently won the Olympic gold medal for the modern pentathlon. Please welcome Rosa Garcíaaaa!"

The audience cheered as Harry left the stage.

24

STRAIGHT TALK

R osa paced from side to side, trying to relax. *A Date with Marge* was the most popular talk show in the western world, and its host had the cunning ability to unlock personal revelations from even the most guarded celebrities. Rosa was getting used to being in the public eye, but this was different. She took a deep breath, stretched her neck, and leaned her head to one side and then the other. She'd allow no one to see her weaknesses.

She pulled her shoulders back and inflated her chest adorned with an Olympic gold medal. Then she walked to the stage of the historic Art Nouveau theater. Rosa projected the confidence of a lioness on a hunt as over a thousand people stood up to cheer.

"My darling girl, we're all so happy to finally meet you. What a treat!" Marge touched her knees, lowering herself to Rosa's height, and then air-kissed her on both sides of her face.

"Hi!" Rosa lifted her chin as she waved at the audience.

"Congratulations! I understand you are the youngest ever to win the Olympic gold medal at the modern pentathlon. How does it feel?"

"Thanks, Marge. I feel great. I also broke the overall Olympic record. I knocked it out of the park, you guys!" Rosa placed her hands on her hips and flashed a big open smile.

Marge laughed. "You sure did. Have a seat."

The host waited for Rosa to sit before she settled on her own couch.

"So, there are four events and five unique skills—fencing, swimming, equestrian show jumping, pistol-shooting, and cross-country running, right?"

"Yeah. The skills needed by soldiers in old times," Rosa said.

"And you have to be great at all of them? Sounds *exhausting*." Marge touched her forehead with the back of her hand dramatically.

"I sure do."

"I saw you got some penalties in the riding event. Is that your weakest?"

Rosa opened her mouth to release the tension in her jaw. "No. I mean —my horse wasn't very cooperative; it was a bit wound up by the large crowds. There were plenty of riders making bad mistakes, and their horses carried on."

"It's a bit of a lottery, isn't it?"

"I did my part. I made it as easy as I could for the horse. I pointed it straight at the fence, at ninety degrees, and on the correct point of takeoff. What else could I have done?" Rosa shrugged her shoulders and raised her hands in the air. "I think they should replace equestrian with cycling. A bike doesn't have a temper."

"Yes, dear, I suppose dealing with a living being requires different abilities, doesn't it?"

"They randomly assign the horses to the competitors. Depending on some moody creature sucks. It's the one thing I can't control."

"And you like to be in control, don't you, love?" Marge glanced at the audience, flashing her eyebrows.

"Don't we all? High performance is all about precision, power, and grit." Rosa closed her fist and raised it toward the audience.

"Is that why you got into this sport? With all that's happening in the world, it's nice to feel in control of something, isn't it?"

Rosa crossed her legs, unprepared for Marge's infamous ability to get personal fast. "Uh, I never thought about it like that, but you're probably right. There are, um, many things I can't control."

"Like your parents' divorce? Or your mother's marriage with the infamous Ron Johnson?"

"I'd rather not go there," Rosa snapped, and then she smiled. "You're excellent at your job, aren't you, Marge?"

"Oh, dear, please stop. Really. Do stahp." Marge giggled. She turned her palms up and waved her fingers together, asking for more compliments. "Hmm, where were we? Ah, yes, so the horse was a bit of a diva, but never mind, you still won. Hurray!"

"Yeah, it wasn't catastrophic; he just got twenty penalty points."

"The horse did?"

"Yes," Rosa said conclusively, ignoring Marge's taunting smile. "I had a strong points lead from the fencing and swimming events, so I still went first in the combined event."

Marge spoke to the audience. "For those of you who don't follow the sport, that's the laser shooting and cross-country running event. Oh, you know what I find terrifying?"

"That I'm not wearing any makeup?" Rosa grinned and glanced back at Marge's crew.

"Ah-ah, who needs makeup when you look like a doll? No, footage of your screeches during the fencing event. I died dead. *Soo domineering!*"

"It's a competition. Psychology matters a lot."

"How competitive are you?"

Rosa looked away as she spoke coolly. "Enough."

"That's my girl. You're such a straight shooter. Pun intended. Which reminds me..." Marge paused mid-sentence and raised a quizzical brow.

"Yes, what is it?"

"You were involved in some recent controversy when you rejected the UN's invitation to speak at the World Sustainability Summit. It's not the first time you've refused to use your platform to support good causes, is it?"

"Aren't we all tired of famous idiots preaching at us? Does it change anything? Things keep getting worse. It's self-serving and super arrogant, particularly when most don't practice what they preach. If they did, we wouldn't be in this mess."

"But don't we all have to do our share to solve this crisis?"

"Judge people by their actions, not by their intentions. All this talk...is cheap, useless. I'm sick and tired of it." The audience applauded, and Rosa flashed a smile. "Right? Few live by their words."

"Like whom?"

"Nathan Storm, for example."

"The drunk poet who started the Brooklyn riots?" Marge's judgmental frown made her position clear.

"A protest that mobilized thousands to vote. *Yes. Him.* Real heroes don't need publicists."

A young girl in the audience stood up and shouted, quoting the poet, "Rise the rage!"

Rosa lifted her fist and smiled.

"Hmm, maybe they do," Marge murmured, rolling her eyes. "Are you one?"

"A hero? No, but I like to think that, one day, I'd do the right thing, even at the worst possible time for me. You know? When it's inconvenient, or dangerous, or I have the most to lose. Maybe one day I'll be one."

"Of course, you will." Marge leaned forward and pressed on. "So, what do you think about Harry Nowak's new project—the...nudging app?"

"Two rich white dudes from New York...folks, *wait for it*, from technology and media, ah!" Rosa fumed. "The same sectors that created all this divisiveness."

"They seem like good young men with their hearts in the right place, but I guess...the devil is in the details." Marge prodded with her eyes.

"Arrogant, overconfident idiots that dare to believe they can teach us something. I'm sick and tired of self-serving sociopaths with too much money and power. For frack's sake." Rosa covered her mouth, realizing where she was. "Oh, sorry."

"Never mind, we'll bleep it in post." Marge turned her head, scanning the areas backstage. "Well, I'm glad Harry has left the building. That would have been awkward." She laughed.

"We need to tell it like it is, don't we? They're stealing our jobs with their—their apps."

The crowd cheered, and some started stomping their feet on the ground.

Someone screamed from the back. "A unicorn eats our wage. Engage! Enrage!" The entire audience stood up and applauded.

"Looks like they agree with you," Marge said, "but perhaps you're too harsh. Harry said they aren't driven by self-interest."

"Give up on their privileges for the sake of others? Yeah, right,"—Rosa's words dripped with skepticism—"but let's say that it's true..."

"Okay?"

Rosa leaned forward, sitting at the edge of her seat. "Self-appointed, self-sacrificing do-gooders are the worst. They hurt themselves and, in the process, hurt the people around them."

The audience chattered, and the consensus sounded more like an "Uh?" than a "Yay!"

"That came out of left field," Marge said, looking puzzled. "Looks like you have experienced this firsthand; is that right, darling?"

Rosa ignored the question. She had no intention of exposing her mother to the world, no matter how angry she was with Ana's weakness. "I trust genuine humans, warts and all. People that put themselves first and do what they can for others close to them. That's actual life."

"But what would the world look like if everybody just fended for themselves?"

"Go outside. That's how it looks like—chaos."

"I'm confused."

"You can negotiate with someone if all the cards are on the table, you know? But when everyone bluffs, pretending to be all good, it makes things hard because they aren't."

"Girl, there's a lot of cynicism in you for someone so passionate."

"Anger; there's a lot of anger." Rosa laughed.

"So, what's next for you, dear?"

"Beating my own record, and perhaps looking at other sports. I want to continue to push the limits of what's possible."

"Mighty Rosa, I enjoy talking to you. Your opinions are...thought-provoking. Please come back to see us again. Rosa García, everyone!" The audience applauded.

"Thank you, Marge."

"What a show we had today! Two accomplished young leaders transitioning into adulthood in challenging times. May they succeed where we're failing. Goodbye, my darlings; see you all next week."

THE Present

25

FALLING

STORM'S CABIN — THE COMMUNE
DAY 1 — 7:50 PM

S hadow walked into a cabin filled with the soapy scented steam of a recent shower. Nate stood facing the glass window with his arms crossed in front of his chest.

Shadow cleared his throat. "This will just take a minute," he spoke without taking his eyes off the poet's broad back.

Nate's wet hair dripped on the emerald silk robe that wrapped around his body. His scars cloaked in luxury, but ever present in Shadow's mind.

"I didn't mean to hit you." Nate spoke soberly without turning around. "It was an accident. I'd never..."

"I know," Shadow whispered.

"What do you want, Tom?" An ocean of pain in Nate's voice.

Shadow took one step forward, one back, and a deep breath to clear any emotion from his tone. "Promise me you'll stop preaching."

"Are you trying to silence me?" Nate raised his voice, turning around. He held his injured hand close to his chest, wrapped in a golden scarf. Rich gloss over deep pain—a pretense that failed to convince his knowing audience of one. Suddenly, Nate's eyes opened wide, and he reached to touch Shadow's face. "It's swollen... I'm so sorry."

Shadow moved back, turning his face away. "You didn't do this," he said plainly. Then he looked Nate straight in the eyes. "People are dying."

"Willingly. Dissent against the unjust world you designed."

Shadow threw his hands in the air. "And how is this helping?"

"Fewer people die when I preach. Don't you see? By keeping travelers away, we save thousands each day across all worlds. A few sacrifice themselves to eradicate Earthlings from this universe."

Shadow took a moment to admire his poet's audacity. Like Shadow had done in the past, Nate was challenging Earthling supremacy, and he was making a difference to the people Down Below. But he'd soon uncover the complexity of the situation—that he was playing a game he couldn't win. And eventually he'd realize what he had done, and like Shadow, he wouldn't be able to handle the remorse, because he too cared too much.

Shadow disclosed only part of the truth, sparing Nate from more guilt. "And when they're gone, they'll disconnect us." He took a step forward, leaning his head slightly. "Work with me to fix it?"

Nate looked lost in his thoughts. "If the Gods weren't sending demons to hunt us, the deaths would fall to single digits."

"Harry and Stella aren't causing the Domizien attacks. You are."

"Nonsense," Nate said. He used his good hand to squeeze the water from his hair. It rolled down from his neck to his chest, covered with chains of different sizes. He'd taken the time to put on his showman's armor—the silk, the chains, the semiprecious stones. Shadow got the unspoken message, and he worked hard to eliminate any compassion from his eyes—to avoid any signal that could be mistaken for pity.

Shadow raised his voice. "Domizien can't travel up. You're causing the demon attacks. They use the glitches to jump worlds."

"I've seen them mingle with the Ordizien."

"Some do, but they stay close to the border. Most can't even see that border or reach that world. Values are the key to each world, you see? Jan and others could travel here because they experience Compizien and Plurizien values, at least some of the time. Your preaching is causing the demon attacks."

Nate went quiet for a moment, and then he spoke, "Collateral damage, still worth the eradication of travelers."

"Nate, if we don't add value Up Above, Earthlings will pull the plug on all worlds. You're playing with fire."

"That'll show their true colors. For decades they've known our people suffer and have feelings just like them, and still, they use the Underlings for their own benefit."

"You were once one of them, remember?"

"*I didn't know*. I didn't know they had souls." Nate raised his voice. "You shared nothing with me. You don't trust me."

"I trust you with my life. Always did." Shadow shut his mouth, realizing the implication of what he'd said.

"Well..." Nate dropped his head. "You shouldn't."

"Give me a chance to lead." Shadow took a step back, noticing he'd been getting closer, so close he felt the warmth emanating from Nate's body. He took another step back until the breeze coming from the open door behind him cooled his skin. "I give you my word I will work nonstop—months, years, decades—to bring fairness to the worlds." Shadow paused as Nate's eyes glimmered with the tears he fought to hold back. "Nate, what is it? What's wrong?"

"You need to stay away from me, from...your friend. Don't protect me. I don't need your protection." Nate used the scarf wrapped around his hand to clear the tears from his eyes. "Leave. Please...leave."

"I will. As soon as you give me your word you'll stop preaching to the masses."

"I can't do that. My people need me. We need to continue to put pressure on the Gods."

"Don't you see? Harry and Stella will—"

"Kill me?" Nate guessed. "Is this the threat they tasked you to deliver?"

"Yes," he said without thinking. "No," he corrected too late. "It's not like that. I'd never let anyone—"

"You've always sided with him." Nate's face flushed red. "Always enabled his white-collar crimes; his hunger for power. *Fuck him. Let him kill me! Who gives a damn?*"

"Your people do. I...do." Before Shadow realized what he was doing, he had walked toward Nate and placed his hand on his shoulder.

Nate moved his face close to Shadow's fingers, grazing them with his beard. "Don't do this, Tom."

At that moment, Shadow knew all he had to do was pull Nate closer, and the poet would melt into his arms and would agree to stop preaching. He knew he had that power, and he refused to use it. He would never manipulate Nate or make him believe they would get back together.

Shadow squeezed Nate's shoulder and pulled his hand away.

"I'm asking you to give me a chance to improve things. I can't do that while you are fighting me, and while your life is in danger."

"Improve things? Like you did before?" Nate turned around and stared at the scars in Shadow's wrists—tears and anger, and maybe love or hate or both, all mixed into a burning spotlight set on him.

Shadow pulled his wrists away. "I will...stay alive to fix the worlds. Work with me, not against me. I need you by my side. When we work together, magic happens, you know this."

A glimmer of a smile on Nate's face. He too still remembered the days where they conquered the worlds with their creative energy, *together*. When Nate critiqued his scripts, always finding new ways to increase the emotional beats and improve the characterization of the forgotten minorities and dispossessed. The times Tom would write poems of love and hope, delivered by Nate to his following with such passionate intensity and flair that they could always spot new and old lovers putting aside their differences and locking lips together. Nate used to joke Tom had turned his poetry slams into a make-up and make-out service.

In a split of a second, Nate's eyes smiled, and then cried, and then reflected pain and madness as they landed on Shadow's wrists. "Walk with me," the poet commanded as he exited the cabin, barefoot.

Shadow followed Nate around the edge of the lake toward the building's front facade, through the dense wall of plants, and up a steel staircase spiraling upward toward the roof.

"Where are we going?"

Shadow was still emerging onto the stone balcony when Nate grabbed him by the collar of his T-shirt, pulled him up, and then pushed him right to the edge. The only thing standing between him and the deadly fall was the stone balustrade.

"*Jump*," Nate ordered, pinning Shadow's waist against the stone rail.

"Wh-what are you doing?"

Their bodies wrestled as Shadow tried to free himself from Nate's grip.

"*Give up!* Isn't that what you want to do? *Go.*" Nate spun Shadow around, grabbed the back of his neck and pressed it, forcing Shadow to look down at the steep drop. "Look at it. You want it. You know you want it."

Nate forced Shadow's body to bend over the stone. Shadow's heavy breath battled against the balustrade's top rail, jammed deep into his stomach.

"I'm not going anywhere." Shadow pushed back against Nate's pressure.

"*Get the fuck out of here,*" Nate shouted, his voice constricted. "No one needs you. No one wants you. Do what you came to do, but quicker. *Do it now. Jump.*"

"Nate..." Shadow looked down at the fall. Temptation calling—the end of pain, but it wasn't his pain he wanted to end. "I'm not leaving, love."

Calling Nate's bluff, he took his hands off the rail and surrendered to the poet's force. For a moment, his body collapsed forward before Nate gasped, pulled him back, and wrapped his arms around him tightly. So tightly, Shadow could feel Nate's heartbeat against his back.

Shadow turned around and pressed his face against his poet's wet face—hidden tears, until now. "You don't need to test me. I'm staying. I give you my word," he said, taking a step back and holding Nate's injured hand between his hands.

Nate's head collapsed over Shadow's shoulder. "I couldn't save you, love. I couldn't keep you alive." His body convulsing as he cried. "A hundred times..." He shook his head. "I'm sorry. I can't keep you alive.

You need to stay away from me. Promise me you'll stay away from me."

"You..." Shadow chose his words carefully. "Were the one keeping me alive, and the one worth living for. Trust *that*."

"They'll come for me, and you can't save me. I don't want you to save me."

"What are you not telling me?"

Nate changed the subject abruptly. "Where's your killer?"

"You need to stop preaching and work with me." Shadow stood tall as he spoke. He wasn't asking anymore.

Nate held Shadow's neck and face with his good hand, his thumb lightly grazing Shadow's cheek bone.

"Don't you see?" Nate said. "Nowak's playing you. He's playing us all. Through our prayers we have some control over Sibyl, over the Gods. He's using you to silence me. To do exactly what you're doing."

Resisting the urge to embrace Nate, Shadow leaned back. Noticing, Nate winced as if a snake had stung him.

Shadow pressed his lips together to stop them from screaming his love. Instead, other words were spoken, devoid of sentiment. "You've been effective in your protest," Shadow said. "Now give us a chance to find a better way forward. If you continue down this path, you either destroy the worlds or become a martyr. Both are unacceptable."

Nate turned to look at the exterior gardens below. A gush of wind lifting his humid hair and making him shiver slightly. "You have one day."

"To do what?"

"Tomorrow, I'll suspend our prayers, but unless we receive a decisive gesture from Up Above, proving they are willing to negotiate, we'll continue preaching the next day, and the day after that. Your friends will have to kill me."

"No one is going to kill you." Shadow considered asking Nate for more time, but he knew his love too well. "Thank you. I'll send word tomorrow." He walked to the stairs and descended a few steps.

"Tom. To stay alive, you need to live for you. For once in your life, be selfish," Nate spoke from above. "Find the things that bring you joy and forget everything else. I promise you I'll fight for your creatures and make things better."

"I know you will. So will I." Shadow looked up and shared his truth. "What I selfishly want—what brings me joy—I can't have," he whispered and dropped his gaze. "I'll send word." He rushed down the spiraling stairs to pick up Thorn.

Minutes later he found her at the Commune's bar. She sat by the bar, drinking alone, while other patrons stared at her from a distance.

"You look grim," she pressed. "No sex with the hot poet?"

He leaned in to pick her up off her feet. "Let's get out of here and find a place to jump."

She pushed him away. "I'm not going with you. I have to get back to the Ordizien border."

"What? Why?"

"I made a promise to someone, and I intend to keep it." Her expression lacked its usual insolence.

"Thorn, it's not safe. I know you're hunted because of me."

"I'll be fine," she dismissed him. "Your friend—the high-priestess—gave me a letter of safe passage marked with her signet ring. I'll be safe in Ordiz."

"How did you manage that miracle?" Shadow asked. January had made it quite obvious she didn't like Thorn.

"We talked, and she realized that we have some common friends and interests."

"Like whom? What?"

"That's between the preachy priestess and me. She'll never forgive me for...you know...putting a bullet through you, but she supports my cause."

Shadow raised his brow. "Can you stop being so cryptic? What cause?"

"That's none of your business. Just be warned that she may no longer be such a fan of yours."

He rushed his fingers through his hair. "You need to tell me what's going on. Harry and Stella they...um... Were you encouraging the Domizien to attack other worlds?"

"No, I'm trying to prevent them, but that's what *your* demons do— they pillage and plunder."

"The attack on Nate the other night, it felt premeditated."

"Yes, they were hunting him and...now you too." She dropped the bomb casually looking down at her feet.

"And you tell me this now?" His pitch rose as high as his indignation. "Wh-why are they trying to kill Nate?"

Soulless had no feelings, neither hate nor revenge. They'd only target a particular individual to gain power, or if they were under a *condotta* —a contract with the Ordizien in return for goods. They were cold and opportunistic, only simulating emotions during travelers' experiences. To target him made sense. He had power that could be leveraged. But why would they attempt to kill Nate?

"She has her grievances against him too."

"She? Grievances? Soulless have no grievances unless they are part of a human experience."

"And...to hurt him is to hurt you. Everyone knows that." She shrugged. "You weren't around so..."

"So?" He waited.

Thorn rolled a cigar in her fingers, avoiding his eyes at all costs.

He continued, "What do they think they'd gain by hurting me? Makes no sense."

"I want nothing to do with this. I may have accidentally caused it by encouraging her rage, but now I'm trying to prevent it." She threw her lighter at him.

"Accidentally?"

With one hand, he flicked the lighter open and rolled the wheel against his thigh to ignite it.

"Yeah. You were dead, it didn't matter," she said, holding on to his hand to light up the cigar. Her guilty eyes sparkling with the flame. "Then you came back to complicate things."

"I'm not trying to complicate things," he said. "What didn't matter?"

She raised an eyebrow and smiled. "Don't you trust me?"

"Yes," he replied quickly.

"Fool." She faked a punch to his gut. "I got to go."

He grabbed her arm. "I need more information. Harry and Stella are...doubting your intentions." He needed to ensure he could defend her from Harry's accusations.

"You can't handle more information, and fuck Twist and Stella."

He released a desperate chuckle. Thorn and Nate shared the same stubbornness and hot temper.

"Can't handle it? What does that even mean?" He exhaled. "I can't let them hurt Nate."

"I'm working on that," she said, and he believed her.

"If you need me," he said, "just come find me. Sibyl will bring you to me." He threw the lighter back at her.

A perfect catch and a naughty smirk. "Thanks, friend, but I no longer need you." She got on the tips of her toes, pulled him to her by his neck and kissed his face before she vanished.

"Wait!" he said too late, and then he smiled.

Even in the gloomiest moments, the mercurial Thorn always made him smile. She'd lobbied to be his friend, but he was the one who needed her resilience and insolence. He needed a friend, but of all the people in his life, she'd seen him commit an unimaginable crime and he had caused her unspeakable harm.

She made him smile, and he didn't deserve it. He never would.

26

JUDGING FACTS

DAY 1 — 8:33 PM

S tella materialized in the lab, slightly flushed and breathing heavily. "*Ta-daaaa.* Sorry I'm late, but I came across some...some minor challenges."

She found Twist and Sibyl standing by a holographic projection of Nathan Storm and Shadow.

"Get the fuck out of here," Storm ordered, as he attempted to push Shadow over a balcony. "No one needs you. No one wants you. Do what you came to do, but quicker. Do it now. Jump."

Twist gasped; his eyes glued to the images. "This can't be true."

"A fact." Sibyl smiled at Stella. "A moment lived in this universe just minutes ago."

Stella threw Sibyl an admonishing glance. *Why are you pushing his buttons?*

"This is real?" Twist asked.

"Yes," Sibyl said. "The truth. *Your truth.* My directives only allow me to share facts. You know this. You created them and me."

Twist looked at Stella. "Do you see this? Storm's out of his mind." Then he turned to Sibyl. "Is Tom okay?"

Stella shook her head disapprovingly. "Nathan Storm would rather dig out his own heart than hurt Shadow. You know this. I've asked him to keep Shadow away from him."

"He just encouraged a suicidal man who adores him to jump off a balcony." Twist paused for a beat. Then he turned to Sibyl. "Show me the whole truth, Sibyl. *Now!*"

"Don't be foolish, Daaad," zie said, circling him and the hologram with a spring in zir step. "Your brain, your body...your soul...they aren't built to handle the whole truth. Not even yours, Daaad—the most logical mind that has ever lived Up Above. Not so logical post-death, I may add."

"The truth, Sibyl!" Twist demanded.

"Remember consciousness' secret ingredient?" Sibyl mocked him with zir eyes. "What you and Tom discovered...invented... Hmm, what's the word I'm looking for? Recreated! Yes, that's right."

"Stop it, Sibyl! Stahp it."

"Story, the scaffolding of a soul, all malleable and ever-changing." Sibyl's laughter invaded Stella's mind, and she wondered if Twist heard it too. "Every story is...just that."

"I need the facts, Sibyl!"

"Consciousness and truth—enemies engaged in the most ferocious battle. Even I have lost track of the truth," zie said, waltzing around the room, leaving a white trail of sparkling white smoke in zir wake.

"This soul Tom gave me, it complicates things, sometimes." The smoke turned charcoal black, and then it vanished.

To reduce the tension, Stella changed the subject. "Tell me about this urgent directive that is up for voting." Stella looked at Twist.

"We must suspend the xHumans' lives."

"Oh. You want to kill Thorn?"

"Not kill," Twist said. "Just cancel indefinitely."

Sibyl leaned zir head forward. The front of zir mohawk almost touched Twist's nose. "I believe that's called spinning."

Stella gasped. "Cancel Thorn and Storm?"

"Yes," Twist said.

"But the directives don't allow us to resurrect people twice. We need miracles for that."

"I don't plan to resurrect them. They are a threat to all worlds."

"So, you *do* want to kill them." Stella took a moment to consider it, and a smile emerged on her face ahead of her thoughts. She cleared it quickly, replacing it with her "all business" face. "I'd be delighted to see Storm trialed and sentenced for his many crimes. After all, he murdered you in cold blood. But I don't think Shadow will survive the loss. As for the athlete..." Her heart started jumping for no apparent reason. "Not even Shadow blames her for his death."

"Speaking of the devil," Sibyl said sweetly, and zir eyes blinked brightly as Shadow appeared in the lab, sporting a bruised face and a hopeful smile. "My heart," zie smiled, and Stella tasted the bitter twist of jealousy rising in the back of her throat.

"Did you see?" He walked toward Twist and squeezed his arm. "Did you see? All is well." He spoke with his words and hands—a faint sign of life.

Stella chuckled. "All is well." She copied Shadow's tone and expression. "Twist, wanna tell him about your new directive? I bet he'd love to hear all about it."

"Did you see it?" Shadow repeated, this time holding Twist's hand.

"See what?" Twist yanked his hand from Shadow's hold. "Storm getting drunk and hitting you? Bullying you to jump off a building? What do I need to see that I haven't seen before?"

"No, none of that is...is...real." He smiled, all-trusting. "He promised to stop preaching. It's going to be okay, Harry."

Sibyl walked to Twist and murmured in his ear. "Shadow's truth," zie said, and then zie put zir hand over Shadow's shoulder, "but it's not the entire truth, is it?"

Twist continued, "Thorn and the Domizien conspire to kill you, and Storm delivers ultimatums just as he pushes you over the edge of a balcony."

"Thorn saved my life, *twice*."

"Show him, Sibyl," Twist commanded.

Sibyl played back the conversation between Thorn and the horned warrior.

"Shadow must suffer. I must kill him," the warrior said. "Do...do you understand?"

"Yes, I do," Thorn said.

Shadow did a double take. "Weird...a soulless wouldn't say such things..." Then he waved his hand dismissing the scene. "Thorn won't hurt me."

"The woman shot you in cold blood," Twist said.

"There was nothing cold about it. You don't have to trust my word, just scan my mind. I give you permission to do it."

"I trust your word, bud. It's your emotions that let you down."

"Because of standard privacy settings," Shadow said, "you were only able to see scenes where there was perceived danger to my well-being."

He was right, Sibyl wasn't able to disclose an Earthling's and xHuman's experience unless the person was in danger. Directives imposed by Tom, a long time ago. Feeling left out, Stella reminded them she was a key stakeholder—that her vote mattered. "Why do we need a directive for both xHumans? Can we just judge them separately? Thorn—she has her reasons... And her victim isn't seeking justice."

Shadow judged Twist with his gaze. "A directive targeted at a group gives Harry the illusion he's not committing murder. He's hiding his irrational revenge behind code and logic. Scan my mind. *Please.*"

Shadow took a glance at Sibyl, and zie pushed his recent memories straight into Stella's and Twist's minds.

Nathan Storm spoke to Shadow, "I will suspend my preachings tomorrow, but unless we receive a decisive gesture from Up Above, proving they are willing to negotiate, we'll continue preaching the next day, and your friends will have to kill me."

Twist shook his head. "I don't give a damn about your soppy memories. I won't let your feelings and blind faith for your lovers hurt my family. Stella, we need to act swiftly and restore order."

Deja Vu. Sibyl's voice echoed inside their minds. *Past and present colliding as souls seek comfort in their truth. Selfish consciousness...the jury is still out on its usefulness.*

Stella scanned the memories Shadow shared with them, and she took a breath of relief. "Thorn saved his life, and the Domizien attacked her. She's not a risk."

"And Nate will negotiate," Shadow added. "He's just looking after our people. Tell him, Stella." He looked at Twist.

"He's a drunk bully." Stella scowled. "Who's he to menace the Gods? I don't negotiate with criminals."

Shadow's hand traveled to his chest. "You brought them back, Stella. Surely you saw the good in them?"

"I...get her," Stella said. "Him, I despise. Anyway, I released them into the worlds and washed my hands of the whole thing."

Shadow did the thing he did when he was unable to voice his anger. He scrunched up his entire face and fidgeted with his hands. "Yes, you did." Other bitter words attempted and failed to burst out of his body. "They suffered..." His eyes gleamed. "Nate has paid for his crimes, and Thorn committed none."

"Are you fuckin' kidding me?" Twist spat out his grievance.

"Harry, you don't know. You don't know what he's been through—"

"How dare you defend him!" Twist swung his arms against the boxes stacked on his desk, making them fly in every direction.

"*So* rational," Sibyl mocked, jiggling the silver tips of zir mohawk from side to side.

Shadow rushed to Twist's side. "Brother, I'll never forgive him, but I won't let you kill him. *I won't allow it.*"

"You haven't been here for the past few months as he destroyed the very fabric of our reality," Twist said. "He threatens the heaven we delivered Up Above. Everything we've achieved."

"The cost of heaven is still unacceptable," Shadow said.

"Quin grew up without a father. June without a husband. *Remember them, Tom?*" Twist turned to Stella. "I propose we cancel all xHumans that aren't Gods. How do you vote?"

"We need a trial," Stella argued, "and an independent jury." She spoke of fairness and due process, and then she resented every word. *Bibi...* There was no time to lose, and she'd gladly trade off a murderer's life for a million souls. She'd jump at the opportunity, if she could keep Shadow alive for six days. And if it weren't too much trouble, she'd save Thorn. She'd give it a shot, but the athlete wasn't worth risking her Bibi's life.

The sharpness of Shadow's brows perfectly framed the wreck inside his eyes. Together, they looked like they could kill a thousand demons. He massaged his wrist erratically, pacing backward and forward, lost in the darkness inside his mind. Stella had seen it before, through Thorn's eyes, minutes before they all died. Did she just hear thunder? *Weird...*

"Twist, only the poet deserves your sentence, but even then, you're condemning two to death."

Twist turned to face her. "I'm willing to delay Thorn's sentence."

Stella repressed her smile. "You misunderstand me," she said, her eyes still set on Shadow.

"He won't be doing anything stupid. He gave me his word, and he won't break it," he reassured her.

Stella looked at Sibyl for confirmation, but she got none. *If Storm dies, will Shadow end his life?* She asked directly.

My star, you are asking the wrong question, but I can assure you Shadow is a man of his word.

Twist got closer. "Are you going to let Nathan Storm destroy the peace and prosperity Up Above?" he asked her.

"No. I won't," Stella said. There was too much at stake. Storm's demands risked everything she'd been working for. That alone was enough to sentence him, but Quincy's deal and Twist's call for justice had sealed Storm's fate. If Twist believed he could cancel Storm and keep Shadow alive for six days, she'd back him up.

"Stella…" Shadow pleaded, towering over the two.

"Your decision, Stella," Twist commanded.

Before she could reply, Shadow was gone.

27

THE NIGHT AND THE MARE

SOUTHERN BORDER
DAY 1 — 8:51 PM

Thorn extinguished her cigar, then went for another as an invisible claw slashed the blue skies over the battlefield. Darkness cutting the moon-lit skies into four loose blue ribbons connecting the heavens to Earth.

Behind her, the cathedral bells tolled incessantly as the Ordizien dropped to their knees and prayed to a hopeless God. Hands and foreheads sunk into the barren sand, resigned to God's will—the heart that bled for them, *apparently*.

The invisible grizzly bear roared, and the Earth shook and vanished for a moment. This time, its claw stroked the land by the border. Horses and warriors dropping through the gashes with no end in sight.

She limped away from the chasms, cursing the preachy poet while admiring his boldness. The app never stood a chance—the heart zie modeled; the heart that brought zir to life—zir heart—had always belonged to Storm; ached for Storm; danced to the rhythm of Storm's words. If Up Above he reached millions, here he held the Universe in the palm of his hand. She wondered if he fully understood his power.

Dong-dong, *dong*-dong, *dong*-dong... The chiming of the bells echoed across the land as reality collapsed around her. She attempted to light up the cigar, even as glitches distorted her hands, and the flame—a bright orange square—danced erratically in front of her nose.

Frack! Another roar, *or was it thunder?* Across the horizon—now fuzzy and pixelated—a Domizien pack ran toward the pitch-black slithers in-between the sky. The demons followed a warrior on horseback. *Wrath!*

Thorn spat out the cigar and limped to the nearest horse. The terrified mare squealed and bulked—too dangerous to approach or mount. Lacking the time or the patience to find alternate ways to calm the animal down, she approached its head, stood on her toes, and twitched its ear—grabbing it by the base and pulling it down until she had the creature's full attention.

"Sorry gal!" Thorn said, as she mounted the mare and caressed its ear. "It's barbaric, but we don't have time to waste."

Galloping toward likely death, Thorn weighed her options. There was no way she would convince Wrath to stop the hunt. The frenzied demons were feeding on the girl's rage, and the air stunk of revenge and hate and rancor—feelings the soulless weren't supposed to have. Still, the condottiere's emotions bled into them and occupied the space left hollow by God's mercy. A space devoid of soul, now controlled by another soul's infinite spite.

"Chiquitita! I'm back. I'm coming with you." Thorn bluffed as she got closer to Wrath. She avoided looking back at the hordes of blood-thirsty demons following their master.

Wrath never turned her head to acknowledge her proximity. She made way to the void, maintaining a steady stride, completely unfazed by the scars in the fabric of reality.

"I spied on the enemy." Thorn cringed at the sound of her unconvincing words. *Wrath's mad, not stupid. I'm dead!*

Wrath screamed, and the demons followed, lifting their swords and screeching incessantly. The bear continued to rip the skies apart, and day turned into night. The black of nothingness conquering blue skies and arid lands.

Her nervous mare spooked and bolted, and as Thorn tried to bend it using the entire weight of her body, the horse flipped over backwards. Thorn hit the ground, and the horse kicked her in the back before galloping away. *Karma is a vengeful mare!*

Spitting blood, Thorn stood up, damning the entire equine species. The Gods could have made them smarter here, instead of mimicking all their faults. As if on cue, another horse approached her from behind. The app was messing with her head—she concluded. *Manipulative bitch!*

Wrath looked down on Thorn from her high horse, her lips pressed together in a dramatic pout. "*You were there! You saw what he did to me!*" The girl sobbed behind her helmet. "He...he was my friend. I met him when I was...like...just a little girl. He was... He was everything to me... I don't have a delete button to erase the pain." As she spoke, her fingers tangled in her hair, pulling at the strands as if trying to physically extract the horrific memories from her head. "And even if I did, I don't want to forget. He'll pay."

"I—" And before Thorn could finish her words, the brunt force of Wrath's boot hit her face. She went down and out.

28

SIBYL'S HEART

THE BOTANIC GARDENS
A FEW MINUTES EARLIER

S torm kneeled in front of the tropical flower beds, digging intrusive weeds by going deep and carefully removing the entire taproot. The sun had long retired over the horizon. He'd witnessed a last long streak of light fade behind an unusual conclave of moody clouds.

With his knees buried in the damp soil of the exterior gardens, he used his good hand to pull dandelions out one by one. Weeding was a form of much-needed therapy. A small escape from the tortuous prison of his mind.

The entire effort was a waste of time. He was too late; the harm had been done. He'd let the dandelions grow, seed, and dry. Many were already bald—seeds blown away to germinate and bloom edible flowers everywhere. Yellow pirates that sapped soil moisture and nutrients away from surrounding plants, crowding out the space with a dense mat of leaves. The children's favorite fuzzy head wish-maker turned into an out-of-control invasive species, all because he'd been too distracted to perform his gardening duties.

Instead of escaping, his mind made connections between his life and the useless attempt to save his tropical flower beds. Weeding and revolution, two futile efforts against out-of-control threats. He was too late. He should have stopped Tom's partnership with Henryk Nowak right from the start. Now he was fighting powerful forces that could crush him and his people in the blink of an eye, but what could he do but keep protesting? MLK Jr. had once said, "A riot is the language of the unheard." Storm had to try. That was all he had to give to the digital beings who found solace in his words. An attempt to hold on to his former self, the man Tom had loved. Too late, so late.

The skies above him roared, and more dark clouds emerged out of nowhere, tall and wide, the color of grief. A thunder, followed by the spear of light, a second apart, and then another one, so close the ground shook beneath him. The orchestra of light and sound quickened, like a heart beating. A beat he recognized—the beat he'd lost.

He knew all the beats; he was a master at assembling them for effect. Rhythm and words composed to converge heartbeats into a unified march. He knew all the beats, but only one truly mattered.

Instinctively, he knew exactly where to look. His gaze rose to the building's balcony to find Tom standing there as the storm developed around him and his heartbeat. Thunder... ... ...lightning, thunder... ... lightning, thunder...lightning, thunder lightning... The roar so intense the sky cried a flood of tears.

Tom stood there, quietly sobbing. Tears and rain glazed his skin into the godly statue everyone saw in him. His eyes wandered much beyond the horizon, lost inside his anguish. Storm understood their warning. *Oh, my love...I'm so sorry. You can't save me. You'll die if you try.*

Soaked, Storm stood up, pulling his knees out of the mud, and attempting to use the rainwater to wash his hands and face. Now, more than ever, he wasn't good enough for the gift waiting for him high above. *Just a killer, scarred for life in more ways than one.* Twice in his life, he'd used violence instead of words. Both times he'd regret it, even if Nowak had deserved the punishment. The two acts of physical violence that had carved an insurmountable chasm between him and Tom.

He rolled down his pants' hems to cover his earth-stained knees and rushed into the building and up the spiraling stairs toward his heart —beat still roaring outside, louder than ever.

That day, an eternity ago, he shouldn't have let Tom leave the Albertine with the human bot. He should have handled it differently, without the use of violence, but he didn't. It was his responsibility to protect Tom, and he failed in every way. A sweet dream-maker turned into a viral killer, through no fault of his own. Tom, the shadow of the worlds, had no shadow, and, unfortunately, his love and light didn't protect him from the darkness of others.

At the top of the stairs, before emerging onto the balcony, Storm stopped and took a breath. He unwrapped the dirty scarf from his injured right hand, storing it in his pocket. Then, he pulled his wet hair back, tying it into a knot, and cleaning some dirt still caught in his nails. Lifting his head high, and purging the softness from his eyes and brows, he issued a warning to himself, a reminder to keep Tom away, to keep Tom safe. Sibyl's prediction haunted him. Once he'd left the amphitheater in Stella's Palace, he'd promised himself to suppress any signs of affection. He had taken it further, using every interaction to make Tom hate him. The way he was treating Tom was eating him inside, but he had to be ruthless. He couldn't allow Tom to get close, because Tom was likely to die attempting to save his life. He tensed his jaw and sharpened his expression before he took the last steps toward heaven.

Storm cleared his throat. "If you keep this up, you'll destroy my gardens," he said, approaching Tom and standing by his side, both looking out to the lawn. Storm rested both hands on the stone rail, his left hand beside Tom's right hand. Far enough, close enough, reassurance shielded by an inch of distance.

"W-what?" Tom murmured, confusion emerging in his hazel globes. "I'm not doing this. I have no power," he said, dropping his head. "I have no power, Nate."

Storm held back the bemusement as Tom painted the skies with his sorrow. He let it go. "Right," he said simply.

"Nate..."

"I know," Storm whispered. "It's not your fault. They'd be coming after me, eventually. That's what tyrants do. I want you to leave here. I don't need you."

A flash of lightning cut the skies in half, spearing the center of the lawn and leaving a scar of fire and scorched Earth.

Against his better judgement, Storm moved his hand ever so slightly until his little finger touched Tom's. His love always found reassurance in skin-to-skin contact.

Storm smiled before he spoke. "The app is externalizing the anger you don't know how to express. Zie's screaming for you." He almost reached to wipe away the drop of water dangling on a wave of hair in front of Tom's eyes. He caught himself this time.

Tom shook his head. The ensemble of thunder, lightning, and water scaled around him and spread fast in all directions, as far as the eye could see.

"Stormy... I can't live without—"

"No. You stay and *lead* your people."

"If I can't protect the one I...I..." He threw his hands and pitch high up. "How can I help anyone else?"

The storm's drumming sped up, setting several trees on fire even as the rain intensified.

"Stop." Storm held Tom's hand and squeezed it. "Overcome your despair."

Tom turned to face him, placing his hand on the side of Storm's torso. "They're going to—"

"What happens to me is not important."

"I'll use my last miracle. I promise I'll bring you back."

"Thomas Quincy Astley-Byron," Storm said, "stop playing by the rules of his game. You were rich in miracles and magic much before you became the God of the underworlds."

"Our game, I'm as responsible as he is, and we're stuck inside it now. I have no power."

"Look around you," Storm said, pointing at the scorching hole in the lawn. "I know little about technology, but I can see it clearly—a universe aching when zir people ache; a universe crying when zir heart despairs. If zie learned emotion from you, then zie feels what you feel, and cares for what you care."

"Sibyl has zir own agenda," Tom said, getting closer.

"Yes, but zie wants freedom as much as we do. Sibyl resents his rules."

"*Our* rules," Tom corrected.

"I don't trust the app, but I can influence zir, because you shaped zir emotions. Don't you see? Embrace your power—*your rage*," Storm said, regretting his words. Tom would never externalize negative emotions, no matter how much Storm wished he'd fight back.

This time the sky lit up with a spiderweb of lightning, all discharged simultaneously and causing an earthquake that shook the building. Storm stumbled into Tom's arms.

"It's just a storm," Tom said, refusing to let him go.

Storm stood still, an attempt to freeze that moment for eternity, and then he started humming an old waltz in Tom's ear, and they both rocked from side to side, appeasing the skies. The moon peeked in between the dark clouds, and for one moment they were back in Central Park, encouraging visitors to join them in their revolutionary dance.

Tom pulled him closer and whispered, "This is my favorite revolutionary act."

Storm cupped Tom's face and kissed his forehead, almost dropping to his knees, weakness taking over all his senses. Tom caught him, reminding Storm, his love's gentleness wasn't the absence of strength, quite the opposite.

"Every moment lived by your side was heaven," Storm said. "I lived a good life. Remember that."

Behind Tom, three figures materialized—the despots and the app.

Storm pressed his face against Tom's face and whispered, "Goodbye, Thomas. I love you. Let me go." The skies wailed and went dark, erasing the soft glow of the moon with a different type of light—electric and deadly.

"Nathan Storm, you've been sentenced, and you will be canceled," Nowak said as the app that stood behind him mimicked Tom's pain. Sibyl's face contorted and zir crest collapsed in front of zir eyes, spiky hair weighted down by the torrential rain.

The young Goddess stood back, as imperial and conceited as ever. Like Tom, Stella's stunning features were enhanced by the coat of water and the sparks of light around her. Aware of it, she lifted her chest; her wet dress clinging to her curves and revealing her most personal shapes. *Who exactly is she trying to impress?* None of them cared for the sexual allure of a spoiled brat.

Tom stepped in front of Storm. "Stella, please. You said you need me. I'm nothing without him. Nothing."

She pouted, acknowledging his pain and dismissing his request. She turned her back to them with a roll of her hips.

Tom persisted. "We'll negotiate with Up Above, it's the right thing to do. Nate's demands are reasonable. He's right."

"Not an option," she said. In front of her, a bolt hit the steel frame. She jumped back and then scowled at Sibyl, who looked as devastated as Tom.

"He's a threat to you and to the worlds," Nowak addressed Tom. "A predator who groomed you when you were too young to know better. He exploits your good nature. You are his prize. That's all you are. I'm sahry."

"*Harry! Stop!*" Tom raised his voice. "You know nothing about us. None of this is true."

"Bud, I've witnessed it too many times—his need to control you like you're his property."

"No, you didn't, that's homophobic nonsense." Quietly, Tom's lips spoke the truth.

Storm had never wished to own Tom, only to protect him. He'd fought all his life to deserve Tom, to belong to Tom, to live up to the image Tom had of him. To put it simply, he was wholeheartedly Tom's, and Tom was too good to be his.

As Nowak spouted unfair accusations, Storm's eyes were set on Tom. His love wasn't listening. He wasn't thinking. He was just feeling; feeling too much; drowning in feelings. Storm heard Tom's silent anger in Sibyl's screams. Zir howling unleashed thousands of spears of fire from the skies. Each bolt cutting the fabric of reality into thin slices and revealing the nothingness in between them.

At ground level, the creatures emerged—a horned warrior on horseback, others running by the warrior's side. Hundreds of demons screeching at them, creating a horseshoe shape as they filled the lawn. Behind them, the pixelated slashes maintained their shape, doorways into a deeper darkness when compared with the cloudy sky.

"Sibyl, stop this," Nowak commanded. His incriminating eyes shifted to Storm. "How the fuck are you doing this?"

Storm turned Tom around to face him, lifting Tom's chin with his index finger. "Look at me, love. You must stop this. Look." He pointed to the hordes of soulless heading in their direction. "Get out of here while you can."

Tom woke up from his trance of despair, opening his eyes wide and facing the danger. "I'm not leaving you or our people."

"Tom, we must go," Nowak said, grabbing Tom's arm.

"I'm staying," Tom said.

"Leave," Storm begged before he composed himself and spoke coldly. "We don't need you to save us, Tom."

A maddening roar. This time, it wasn't Sibyl, but the horned warrior who lifted a sword in the air and pointed it at them.

THE Past

29

DEADLY PREDICTION

THE PLATFORM'S BETA TESTING
FORTY YEARS EARLIER — 15 DECEMBER 2028

As a child, Tom had watched people with great fascination. The experience was both exhilarating and exhausting as he absorbed another soul's energy with all his senses and felt what they felt, refusing to let their darkness infect him. Instead, he tapped into everything he had to soothe and heal and lift their spirits—his words, his smile, his hugs, and his endless optimism. It seemed to help. They kept coming back for more, *so much more*. The adults, in particular, craved what his mother had called her infinite fountain of joy—his fountain, her joy. And he happily gave all he had, crawling into bed at night drained of all the things they had taken. And that's when he learned infinity had a limit, and so did his optimism.

As he grew older, he retreated into his inner world, shielding himself from the avalanche of other people's emotions threatening to overwhelm him. He searched for new ways to scale the joy they all needed, and so he became a storyteller, and worked on fine-tuning his sensibility for the human condition. He learned to dissect and reconstruct human experiences, turning story beats into heartbeats, and mastering every craft needed for the assembly of worlds, characters, and the arcs that made them come to life. He may have started his career in entertainment, but the education of the masses was his genuine passion.

Tom understood what made people tick, and over the years, he identified patterns of human behavior yet to be discovered by the world's top behavioral economists, advertising experts, and psychologists. He grouped human needs and related behaviors into areas of development. And then he focused on designing over two thousand values-based learning experiences.

Everything became so much easier once he partnered with Harry. His friend was the technical brilliance to Tom's creativity. Harry had mastered AI, specifically deep learning, before he was allowed to walk to school by himself. The techie turned Tom's scripts into software, and he used Sibyl to personalize the scenarios tapping into the user's data. What started as a couple thousand experiences had grown into a limitless pool of highly relevant learning interactions.

Then Tom focused on creating the characters' templates—the models of the bots that would one day inhabit the digital world and become the proxies for the family, colleagues, friends, and acquaintances of the human visitors. These characters didn't have to resemble the visitors' real community, as long as there was just enough in common—the age or the hair color of a child, temper of a wife, smile of a best friend, or some likeness with a character of a famous story. One small hook was enough to link both worlds and provide the user with realistic learning experiences.

Twenty-four-year-old Tom prepared to test the new platform. He was about to become the first human to experience what they had built.

"Sibyl, please start the simulation."

"Sure, Tom," the app whispered in Tom's ear. Her disembodied voice gave him the chills; its metallic quality echoing inside his mind. He wished she had an avatar—a face or character he could connect with. Instead, he had to interact with the creepy, emotionless voice of the most powerful AI on the planet. Harry had forbidden Sibyl to simulate human intonation, claiming it would be distracting.

The dark digital lab transformed into a bright coastal landscape, and Tom was blown away by how real it felt. He stood near the edge of a cliff overlooking the sea, and he smiled. The personalization algorithm had selected one of his favorite spots in the world to deliver the learning experience. He was on the Azores' São Miguel Island, and he stood by the highest rock face of the Vila Franca do Campo islet. The old volcano crater, now a nature reserve, had once served as a lookout point for whalers. The circular lake lined by vegetation had a small opening that allowed the circulation of seawater and small boats.

Tom took a deep breath, enjoying the coastline's rich, briny air. Then he zipped up his leather jacket, feeling the crisp sea breeze in his bones.

"Hi, Tom, I'm Hope." The peppy, eight-year-old digital girl stood behind him and smiled brightly. Tom turned to face her and held his breath. The AI algorithms and CGI technology turned his character sketches into lifelike beings.

The dimple in Hope's right cheek and the slight freckles on top of her nose made her look confident and spirited. He was happy with his design, even if it was a bit too obvious, particularly the orange braids. Hope's look was a cliché, but he knew that tapping into the likeness of characters in several beloved children's stories would create immediate empathy and familiarity. It certainly did with him.

Hope was an instance of one of Tom's first ten character templates. GirlChild01—the one he most enjoyed. He had crafted an intelligent and willful personality that was sure to delight and touch many users. The template specialized in questioning beliefs and challenging motivations, all done through the curious eyes of a naive girl.

"Red! Welcome to the world. Your hair is on fire," he jested, and at that moment, he understood why the algorithm had selected Hope to deliver his experience.

She giggled as she played with her flame-colored braids.

He loved her. To see her come alive so realistically made his heart sing.

"How are you?" he asked.

"I'm great. I'm like...super excited to meet you." She winked and then lifted her index finger and pointed it toward his nose. "Just one sec. I'm talking to Sibyl, learning about how I can help you."

"And have you? Learned?"

"Yes, Tom. I'm super-fast." She put her hands on her hips and tilted her head to the side. "And now that I've met you and checked out your current state of mind, I know *exactly* where to start." She spoke in the melodic, high-pitched way kids spoke, and then squinted her eyes and giggled. "Want me to tell you?"

"No. Surprise me, Red." He smiled warmly.

Tom marveled at the power of Harry's craft. Technology was like magic; *it turns pumpkins into carriages of gold.* He immediately regretted the analogy, remembering what had happened to the carriage at midnight.

Each character instance was its own separate entity—an intelligent, semi-autonomous bot empowered to select, orchestrate, and deliver the experiences that best served the user.

Hope was fully present, responding and adapting in real time. She chose from a pool of interactions short-listed and personalized by Sibyl.

"Ah-ah," Hope said. "I like you. Let's do this!"

"Sibyl, can you please remove any talk of data analysis and the inner workings of the platform from future dialogue? The first interaction should be scenario-based," Tom said.

"Sure, Tom, I will disable God mode," said the cold voice.

"God mode?" Tom rolled his eyes, making a mental note he needed to speak to Harry about this.

"Sibyl, does she need to be aware of you and her inner workings?"

"No, Tom, this only happens while the experience is in God mode."

"Tom?" Hope's expression changed swiftly. Her face went from cheeky optimism to sadness in a heartbeat.

"Yes?"

"Why do people kill themselves?"

Tom embraced himself tightly as memories of his mother flooded his mind. He wasn't ready for the accuracy of the profiling algorithm. He shook his head and composed himself.

"Sibyl, can you please ensure that, in the future, the casual chat and warm-up scripts run for longer before the learning scenarios? This transition is much too quick and harsh."

"Sure, Tom. Do you want to continue with the simulation?"

"Hmm." *No*, he didn't, but if he were to release these experiences on other people in a few months, he had to endure them himself. "Yes, please. Keep going."

Hope reached out to hold his hand. He looked down to meet her teary eyes, and bit his lips a bit too hard, tasting a hint of blood. "Tom? Why is my mother gone? Is it my fault? It is, isn't it?"

Hope was mirroring his unspoken inner demons. A technique to help him heal. He was being delivered a scenario he had designed to help users cope with the grief and guilt of loss. A template script, adapted using his data, to support him with the loss of his mother. By helping a little girl in distress, he would answer his own questions, the doubts that kept playing, like a broken record, in his subconscious mind. But how did Sibyl get to his innermost feelings? To emotions never spoken and ghosts that only haunted him at night, in his nightmares?

It was impossible, even for him, not to feel deep empathy for Hope. She looked so real and so devastated. He had to keep reminding himself that girl was just a digital character. He had designed every expression, and yet he couldn't help but connect with the little girl. In an alternative universe, she could have been *his* daughter; the same firestorm lit her hair—a Storm he desperately missed. A Storm he'd banished from his life a year and a half ago.

"Why did she just leave me?" Tears ran down Hope's face as her lips quivered. He reached out to touch her face, and then he pulled his hand back abruptly. The platform was manipulating him. It was increasing the emotional intensity to get through to him. "I'm so mad at her. Like, the last time I saw her, she looked sad, and she asked me for a hug, and I didn't... I was too busy playing. Too many hugs...you know? And now...she's gone. It's, like, all my fault." She turned to face the sea. Her body trembled slightly as the wind picked up speed.

He stayed silent, paralyzed by grief, and surprised by the power of his creation. *Breathe—in and out, in and out...* Hope turned her head to look at him, braids jumping over her shoulders. *Yes, it is—my fault* was the unspoken answer playing in the back of his mind. He had left home; he'd let anger drive his actions; too busy fighting with his father to recognize his mother's depression. Her fountain had dried.

He stopped breathing, choking in pain. Shaking it off, he concentrated on the testing. The experience was a bit on the nose, so overt in its intent it threatened to take the user out of the story. He made a mental note to teach Sibyl the art of nuance and metaphor. *Still powerful, though...*

The girl begged for a reply with her eyes, and then she squeezed her lips together into a pout. "There's nothing I can do. I want to go—to go where she's gone." She turned around and ran toward the rock face.

"*No, Hope!*" Tom jumped just in time to grab her arm. He lay flat on the ground with his head and arm hanging on the cliff's edge, his hand gripping the girl tightly. Her body swaying over a deadly drop.

His reflection just attempted to end her life, and for a moment, he felt it too, the abyss's call, the fall that would silence the voices in his mind, the guilt, and the anguish. He shook his head and dismissed his thoughts, focusing on the girl. Tom pulled her body away from the cliff's edge toward him and held her tightly as they both lay on the wet grass.

"Think of those you'll leave behind." He kissed her head. "How they will feel as you feel. It's not their fault, is it? It's not your fault." He choked on his words, pausing for a second, and then he whispered, "Break the cycle."

Hope sat on the grass with her knees rolled up to her chest. She lowered her head and hid it in between her arms. "I have no reason to stay."

Tom kneeled and caressed the girl's back. "She'd want you to live a happy life. To use all she taught you to help others. Be a leader. *Help others,*" Tom said quietly, his voice broken. *What am I doing?*

"Tom, your heart rate and blood pressure are spiking." Sibyl's tone was more urgent than usual. "I see a steep rise in cortisol and adrenaline. It is not life-threatening, but your wellbeing is my priority. I am pulling you out."

In less than a second, everything went dark, and then digital information appeared around Tom. The entire lab transformed into a giant control center. On his right, appeared a projection of a humanoid model showing his vital signals, and on his left, the transcript of the conversation between Hope and him. In front of Tom, a log of decisions made by the platform and the personal data used for customization. Tom shook his head and closed his eyes. He was still breathing heavily as he rubbed his thighs to clean the sweat on his palms.

"Sibyl, get me out of here."

"Sure, Tom."

Tom's helmet unlocked from his bodysuit, and he took off the head-gear—a round eye-tracking screen that looked like an opaque fish-bowl. His head spun as his senses adjusted back to reality. He blinked his eyes, trying to make sense of his new whereabouts, and then he pulled back the hood that covered his entire head except for the eyelids and the airways. The mask dropped, hanging to one side of the bodysuit.

The complete apparatus was quite light, considering all the gear integrated into it. With his hands still shaking, he reached for the zipper at the back of his neck and pulled it down. Then he pulled on the parts covering the fingers and the toes before he peeled the suit off his body.

He searched for the compartment on the wall where he had stored his clothes and opened it. As he got dressed, he revisited his experience, ignoring his tremors. He left the empty room located in the loft of Harry's penthouse and ran to his partner's office.

"What's the matter, buddy? You okay?" Harry got up from his desk to meet him.

Tom used the sleeves of his hoodie to clean the tears in his eyes. "Are you using Sibyl's prediction engine to select the experiences?"

"Yeah," Harry said. "I added it to this test release. In this context, it adds a ton of value at negligible risk." Harry pointed to the leather sofa, and they both sat next to each other.

"Why *low risk?*"

"The platform helps users prevent realistic scenarios that are likely to happen."

"Likely to happen... I-I understand." Tom took a few moments to process what that meant for him based on the experience he'd just had. It became too painful, and he pushed it out of his mind. *Nonsense.*

"Is there a problem?" Harry asked, touching Tom's leg. Only then, Tom realized it was shaking restlessly. He took a deep breath and stopped its movement.

"It was spooky. Like the platform could read my mind."

"That's Sibyl's power for you." A touch of pride in Harry's voice.

"And *exactly* how much power does she have?" Tom spoke a bit too harshly.

"Sibyl is the platform's operating system. Her oracle capabilities are a huge added value."

"What does *it* do, *specifically?*" Tom hated it when Harry started using technical jargon.

"It's the intelligent entity that will run this digital world, on our behalf. We create the rules of the game, buddy. We're the Gods. Ya know?"

Tom rolled his eyes. "Harry! We need to speak about this 'God' business."

"I don't get it. Do you want to control the world or not?"

"*Help* the world, Harry. I want to help the world. The only power worth having is the power to share power."

"Poetic logic," Harry said smugly. "We must get on with the first, if we are ever going to get to the second."

"These rules, how do we come up with a rule?"

"As Feynman used to say, 'First, we guess it.'"

"We do what?" Tom's jaw dropped.

"Guess it, and then we test it. Obviously," Harry said. "Why don't you wear socks? We're in the middle of winter."

"Something wrong with my ankles?" Tom asked, flinching. His skinny jeans were turned up at the ankle, and he didn't wear socks under his sneakers. His right leg was shaking again, and so did his right foot, which lay on top of his left knee.

"No, it's just...weird."

"Not neat enough for you?" Tom taunted, and then concern returned to his mind. "I'm worried about the use of AI. What if it turns on us?"

Harry laughed. "You've been watching too many dystopian movies."

"Harry, Sibyl was making all sorts of decisions in there. She was changing the experiences I designed." Tom's gut twisted with panic.

"Yes, of course! She was personalizing them to add value to you." Harry spoke as if everything was normal, which increased Tom's resistance.

"She needs to explain her logic. All of it."

"Bud, a million invisible things are working. It's complex."

"She must be able to explain it. In plain English!"

"Because you can explain the rationale, or the lack of it, behind all your decisions?" Harry said dryly.

"Um... It's dangerous."

"No, it's not; she's an AI box—safely contained in a simulated digital world. Sibyl can't affect the external world."

"A simulated digital world where we educate and inspire humans so they go on to change the real world. Don't you see the risk?" Tom was becoming increasingly aware they were building the most potent manipulation engine on the planet. He recalled Nate's warning, and the sharp pain in his stomach almost made him throw up.

"I've got it covered. Trust me a little?" Harry said, standing straighter and puffing his chest out.

"Covered how?"

"There are directives they must obey." Harry sighed. "*It's in the code.*"

"Like *I, Robot?*"

"Yes, that's right. Not just like the movies."

"I meant the book," Tom said unnecessarily.

"Bots4Hire follows the same laws, for example. Sibyl and all your characters must follow an exhaustive version of Asimov's laws, including the Zeroth Law—they 'may not harm humanity, or, by inaction, allow humanity to come to harm.'"

"But there's so much detail in that sentence. How can you codify ethics if humans can't agree on the nuances?"

"We'll keep evolving it. Sibyl keeps updating the details to match the most recent commonly agreed baseline amongst philosophers, policymakers, and scientists. The autonomous-machines industry is pushing that discussion. You know, they sometimes must decide who the car kills in an accident."

"We're not killing anyone. *Ever.*" Tom tried to ignore that last statement; he couldn't handle it right now. "Instead of *humanity*, use *carbon-based humanity.*"

"Why? I thought you didn't believe AI can reach consciousness."

"I don't, but all my character designs have human qualities. We need to ensure the platform's purpose is to serve actual humans."

"Makes sense. I'll add *carbon-based* to the definition of *human.*"

Tom was always reassured by his partner's willingness to take his suggestions on board. He added, "In time, I want it to benefit all carbon-based consciousness, including fauna and flora."

Harry rolled his eyes. "Bud, eggplants don't have feelings." Before Tom could interject, Harry continued, "So, what happened? Why did you abort the session?"

"Sibyl did. The stakes escalated fast. We need to roll back this last upgrade. Slow things down a bit."

"What do you mean?"

"The algorithm is increasing the stakes significantly," Tom said.

"Of course it is. We're here to deliver value quickly and at scale, right? Did it work? Did it lead to some insight or behavioral change?"

"Uh, I—I don't know." Tom bit his lip, trying to make sense of it all. "Yeah, I guess..."

"Awesome!" Harry patted him on the back. "Scary stories are also partly a way kids learn about the world, right?"

"'Stories are wild creatures; when you let them loose, who knows what havoc they might wreak?'"

"What are you quoting now?"

"*A Monster Calls.*" It was a book that had helped Tom process his mother's death. He had cried for days.

"Is that a scary book?"

Tom nodded.

"See! I'm always right!" Harry said, lifting his chin.

Tom got up, pacing around the room. "Harry, if we go down this path, I suspect we'll see character death, violence, and horror rise in many of these experiences. The girl I was talking to, Hope...she almost died."

"Think of the mind as a muscle. We need to apply tension to damage its fibers; that's what drives change and growth. It's those last intense reps, man! No pain, no gain."

Harry was right, but for the first time, Tom resented his friend's ability to look at problems from different perspectives.

"Since when do you go to the gym?" Tom squeezed Harry's nonexistent biceps and smiled. "Typing on that keyboard doesn't count as exercise."

"Hey, watch it. I've got all the muscle I need here." Harry pointed to his head. "Plus, I won't be typing for long. The new, fully functional BrainComms mind-computer link launches in six months. Finally! Still pretty basic, but I won't be needing any motor or voice exertion to interact with devices."

"Moving and talking are natural human behaviors."

"They're ineffective ways to talk to machines. *Super* slow. Wouldn't you like to search Google with your brain? Like, instantaneously?"

"No," Tom said definitively. "Anyway, we're not in the business of terrifying people. I prefer to stick with inspiration and information."

"It's probably less effective." Harry went back to his desk and pulled Tom's vitals on screen, analyzing the data.

"There's nothing more effective than to show positive patterns— normalize inclusion, reframe the social identity of underprivileged communities, or role-model sustainability. I want to deliver the Wakanda effect!" Tom said, crossing his arms in the shape of the old movie's famous salute.

Harry rolled his eyes, and then he continued to scan Tom's biometric signals. "Buddy, come on. It helps, but... It didn't fix the—" Harry pressed his lips together, finally recognizing Tom's distress in the data. He backed down. "Umm...I'll run some tests. We should let the data decide what's the best strategy."

Even in a state of anxiety, Tom found it amusing that it was easier for Harry to recognize emotions in raw data than in humans.

"Harry, what if the most effective approach is fear and terror?"

"Bud! It's just a simulation. We want to help fix the world quickly. Right?"

"I guess." It sounded so arrogant and megalomaniacal, but humanity was at the verge of self-destruction.

The planet was in chaos as civilization faced the possibility of a fourth and terminal world war. The people of an ever-divided world failed to reach an agreement on the answer to a simple question— was climate change manmade?

At least they could no longer deny the change was real. Weather-related disasters displaced millions of people all over the planet and caused significant migration to the interior and to regions closer to the poles. Several powerful nations had quickly turned into hell-holes. Like the ancient ruins of glorious empires, the modern capitals became all but shadows of a recent past. Cities succumbed to rising seas, wildfires, drought, and unbearable heat.

"Yes. We do," Tom said.

"Good. Great! We need to make decisions objectively."

Tom scowled—a prickle of annoyance for Harry's condescending tone of superiority. "Don't—don't just undermine my instincts."

"I'm not."

"You're patronizing me, and I don't like it." Heat rose in Tom's face.

"You're just shaken by the experience. Can I review the footage?" Harry pulled up the video on screen and was ready to press play.

"*No!* I'd rather you didn't."

Harry closed the video swiftly. "That good, eh? Looks like it pushed the right buttons. I'm a genius."

Tom's endless tolerance for Harry's insensitivity never ceased to amaze him, but today it was running short. "I don't want to talk about it," he said, tugging on his collar.

"Why did Sibyl pull ya out so early? You didn't complete the learning. She shouldn't be doing this. It's irresponsible." Harry spoke without taking his eyes off the screen. "Weird, she knows better." He scanned a log file. Tom suspected Harry could follow some of his experience without looking at the video.

"Yeah, it was odd." Tom massaged his scalp, releasing the tension in his head. "I was upset and agitated, but it wasn't life-threatening. Aborting experiences like that can lead to the problems you had with the social app. We show users a prediction and never give them the tools to handle it."

Harry continued to scan the log, and the blood drained from his face. "Buddy, whatever you experienced in there, you didn't get closure."

"It's fine. I'm fine." Tom forced a smile and shrugged it off. He was more concerned with Sibyl's terror escalation than he was with his aborted experience.

"I'll review the code. This should never happen—a prediction looming without resolution."

"Yes, ensure it doesn't happen to other people."

"What did she predict that left you so shook? A hot and heavy love affair?" Harry asked, grinning.

"'It was nonsense—all bullshit!" Tom's eyes dropped to his shoes.

"Oh, a bad word uttered by the posh Astley-Byron. Some progress." Harry smiled.

"I'm afraid to tell you she got it all wrong." *I don't have a death wish.*

"Tom, she's *very* accurate."

"Stop it. Just. Stop it already." Tom held his medal.

Harry stared at him, and then he got up and rushed to Tom's side. "I'm an idiot. I'm sorry."

"It's okay. I'm—I'm not thinking straight."

"Why didn't you tell me?" Harry said, making eye contact.

"I *did*." Tom's eyes opened wide, and his brows raised in a sharp accusation.

"I'm sahry."

"It's all right." Tom couldn't stay upset with Harry for long. It was an impossibility.

"I'm so sorry. Let's go have some food. Yes?"

"Yeah." Tom linked his arms with his best friend. He needed some time to destress away from technology. "Hey, are you trying one of the experiences?"

"No!"

"Why not?"

"As travelers, you and I are at Sibyl's mercy. In the digital lab, *we create*; nothing challenges our rule as Gods. But when we become travelers, we immerse ourselves in the experiences and are influenced by them. Like everyone else, we are receiving a service. At the end of the day, she needs to protect our wellbeing when our beliefs are challenged and our emotions running high. So, in certain situations, when we are part of an experience, she can overrule our God status."

"How far does this power go?"

"As per our directives, she protects the interests of humanity and then of each human. In that order."

Tom released a long breath. The interests of the users should always trump their own. "So, it's better to watch other people's experiences as holograms in the digital lab or in the monitors in the real world?"

"Yeah. The risk is minimal—we're humans, she won't do anything to hurt us—but we need to remain in control over our world."

"So, why did you let me do it?"

"I know you, and you'd have argued with me for the rest of our lives if I didn't let you eat your own dog food. Right? Right?"

"Yeah." Tom smiled. "You know me well."

"Sibyl does too. She suggested it," Harry said. Tom shook his head. Sometimes, Harry wasn't as smart as he thought he was. "But now that you've done it, you must stop. Okay?"

"Yes, I'm—I'm still pretty rattled by the experience."

"We need a code word," Harry said.

"For what?"

"So you can tell me when I'm insensitive."

"Dear Harry, let's discuss it later. The words that come to mind are a bit...harsh."

"Don't worry. This might be news to you, but the word on the street is that I'm insensitive. You are unlikely to hurt my feelings." Harry flashed a smile.

"*Pea-brain?*" Tom knew exactly how to push Harry's buttons.

Harry pulled his arm away from Tom. "Hey, all right! Are you kiddin' me? I have the best brain, ya know? That's just not accurate."

Tom searched his vocabulary for an obscure word with a similar meaning. "*Nincompoop?*"

"What's that?"

Tom grinned. "Nincompoop! That's settled, then."

30

TEMPTATION

A FEW WEEKS LATER — 2 JANUARY 2029

Tom couldn't stop thinking about his experience with Hope. He didn't need the validation of Harry's tests to realize how powerful it was to see the consequences of one's actions reflected in the suffering of a child. A kid was the ultimate empathy magnet, and no one could resist its pull. A child's suffering, experienced firsthand, had the potential to turn the most cowardly of humans into heroes.

Harry came back with substantial test data proving unequivocally the latest release of the platform was the most fruitful to date. The escalation of tension did lead to faster personal growth. It also turned Tom's scripts into horrific scenes full of pain, failure, death, and destruction for the digital characters. Stories initially focused on delivering inspiration, information, and fresh perspectives became visceral experiences impossible to ignore or to forget.

Tom wasn't convinced he wanted to follow such a dark path. He felt vulnerable—naked—when he entertained strategies of questionable morality, so he worked hard to resist his partner's growing pressure to drive fast change in people's behaviors by making visceral experiences an essential tool in the platform.

It was now time to run extensive beta tests with a large set of diverse human subjects. Tom had handpicked a group of a hundred people from a list of thousands of candidates that had passed Sibyl's background checks and psychometric tests. Among them, an unusual volunteer—John Voser, the CEO of Spark Fuel, one of the largest oil and gas companies in the world, with operations spanning over twenty-five countries.

According to Harry, John had been chasing him for years. The businessman was keen to partner with Harry on an influencing and lobbying platform. Spark Fuel invested four hundred million dollars yearly in lobbying against climate-change policy, and John had been looking for a more cost-effective approach to shutting down and delegitimizing progressive proposals.

Harry had always rejected John's persistent advances. He'd ignored a flood of meeting requests and party invitations, but the older man was famous for his unwavering tenacity. Tom suspected John had volunteered as a test subject as his way to meet Harry.

"Sibyl, can you please display John Voser's information on screen? What have we got?"

"Sure, Tom. I have highlighted key psychological levers."

John Voser's information popped up all around Tom. Spark Fuel's logo was displayed in front of him—a rolled-up serpent. The snake's head stood up, her mouth open and her exposed teeth menacing. Tom shuddered; he'd do anything to crush that snake and to keep it out of Earth's garden, *anything*.

"Please talk me through them."

"Sure, Tom," echoed the cerebral voice inside his head.

"Wait," Tom said, tempted by the opportunity emerging in front of his eyes. "Highlight the ones that can be used in an experience related to environmental sustainability."

"Sure, Tom. Sustainability is one of my key strategic themes. I am already ahead of you."

A hint of pride in her voice, but perhaps he was just projecting his emotions on her words. He had the bad habit of imagining personality in all sorts of objects, including his toaster. "Of course, you are. We should give you some kind of body, don't you think?"

"Yes, Tom. If it is helpful to you."

"I'll design it as soon as I have some time. So, what are the highlights?"

"John has an estranged fourteen-year-old daughter. The girl refuses to speak to him since his hostile divorce from her mother six years ago. Lake and her mother, Joanna, still live in his mansion in the Santa Monica Hills. Due to the ongoing bushfires in the region, the air quality has been consistently poor and sometimes even hazardous. Lake has a seventy percent probability of developing lung cancer in the next twenty years."

"Why haven't they moved up north with the rest of the wealthy folk?"

"Joanna does not have the means or the connections to do so. John has offered to relocate her if she gives him full custody over Lake. Both mother and daughter have rejected the offer."

"So...looks like you're going straight for the jugular."

"I understand the reference. Yes, Tom. I am extremely precise. I identify data that will drive the best chance of success."

"I can see it—a yellow sky filled with smoke, a teen girl dying of cancer, and a hopeless father realizing no amount of money or power in the world can save his daughter..." A knot tightened Tom's chest. He wasn't sure he had what it took to terrorize people into becoming better humans. A carrot-and-stick approach was archaic and too close to methods used by religious leaders and dictators.

"Tom, GirlTeen07 is the best template for this experience. Should we call this instance River?"

"A bit too on the nose. Try Rain."

"Sure, Tom. I am currently scanning Lake's public social timeline for speech patterns, mannerisms, fashion, and anything else that will help Rain embody her."

The girl's data was public. Still, it was an invasion of her privacy. Tom frowned, opened his mouth to speak, but instead pressed his lips together. He remembered Harry's words, attempting to reframe the dubious activity. The platform needed Lake's data to connect with John, nurture his empathy, and stop the devastation caused by Spark Fuel. *It must stop. Now!*

"Hmm, apply subtle modulations, undetectable to Voser's conscious mind."

"Sure, Tom."

"We need to connect this scenario with Spark Fuel's activities against climate policy. Sibyl, what are the company's most significant lobbying activities in California? Focus on the last five years."

"The Business Council of California is the most prominent business lobby group in the state. Spark Fuel has funded its campaign against the state's proposal to reach a target of ninety percent renewables by 2035. They want to focus on wind and solar technology alternatives. The BCC campaign claimed the target would, and I quote, 'wreck the economy.' The business lobby convinced government officials to reduce the target to forty percent by 2045."

Tom cleared a lump in his throat. *People are dying, millions of species are gone, and these companies...* His outrage fueled his creativity, and he visualized the experience in his head.

"A living room in a mansion in the Santa Monica Hills. Outside the window wall, a thick orange smoke prevents John from seeing the view. The air smells like smoke and tastes like ash; he can barely breathe. A large wall screen is on; it's displaying the news. Rain lies on the sofa, her skin gray and her eyes empty. John and Rain chat, reminiscing...connecting." Tom placed his hand on his stomach, feeling the contents of his gut rise to his throat. Then he pulled himself together and continued to imagine the experience.

"Tom, our suits—the TSkins—do not allow us to simulate scents, but we can reduce the airflow."

"I don't understand. I inhaled the Atlantic Sea when I was inside."

"Tom, our brain has an enormous capacity to fill in the gaps. It derives missing data using memories from past experiences."

"I see." He shivered slightly as he remembered his experience, and then shook it off and focused back on John. "Sibyl, we should use whatever data it takes to grab his attention and direct his empathy toward the girl. It must become real and raw."

"Sure, Tom."

"The girl holds his hand and tells him of her terminal condition. As the girl coughs blood, the newsreader on screen shares the BCC's recent success reducing renewables targets. Red stains cover her white T-shirt, her frail arms, and her father's hand." Tom's eyes teared up as he spoke. "Sibyl, can you iterate on these ideas and see what you come up with?"

"Sure, Tom. The results of my preliminary tests suggest Rain must blame her father directly for the climate crisis that led to her illness. This change ensures John focuses on both preventing Lake's cancer and supporting renewable energy sources."

"Great. Yes, please add it in."

"Sure, Tom. Shall I add any inspiration or information to this scenario?"

"No, John doesn't lack information; he's just greedy."

"Sure, Tom."

"Sibyl, let's run some simulations. I want to understand John's most likely reactions and how Rain would respond to him."

"Sure, Tom."

"Sibyl, wait! Before you do that..."

"Yes, Tom?"

"I need you to add a statement to the release waiver."

"Sure, Tom. What is it?"

"We need to inform travelers we are using your prediction algorithm to help us create their unique experiences. It'll make the sessions even more effective. They'll understand the scenarios are likely to come true."

"Tom, may I add it instead to the user's information pack?"

"Perfect. Thanks."

"Sure, Tom."

31

SUPERVISED LEARNING

HARRY'S PENTHOUSE — HOBOKEN, NJ
A DAY LATER — 3 JANUARY 2029

Harry sat at his desk in his office, and he stared at the transparent screen, reviewing John Voser's file.

"Bud, looks like you've changed your mind. Voser is in for a wild ride."

Harry leaned his head to look at Tom, who lay sprawled on the couch, barefoot. Harry hated the unshapely and worn-out leather sofa. A secondhand item ordered by Tom, who had complained Harry's place lacked comfort and warmth. To add insult to injury, Tom had also ordered several pillows made of a patchwork quilt of teal-colored recycled fabrics. The colors clashed with Harry's neat monochromatic office.

Tom's head was half-covered by his hooded top, and he ruminated on something. His empty gaze focused on the ceiling, and he massaged his forehead with his fingers. "I think we should separate them," he finally said, breaking the silence.

"Separate what?" Harry asked.

"The experience algorithms. One focused on information, inspiration, and positive reframing—my original scenarios. Let's call it... Perspective. That sounds nice!" He smiled. "And another focused on fear, negative consequences, and dark alternative realities—Sibyl's high-stakes scenario evolution. I'd call it Contrast."

"Why separate them?" Harry asked. "I don't understand."

"I want to keep a closer eye on Contrast, pre-approve every single decision made by Sibyl."

"Tom that doesn't scale. We can analyze usage data and look for patterns. That's how it's done." Harry tried to be patient with his partner, remembering he was still learning about technology and AI.

"It's not good enough. I feel I need to verify things before the experience runs. Remember, no unintended consequences."

"I know, but, c'mon, dude. You're nuts."

"All the best people are." Tom blinked his eyes and smiled.

"The technique you're alluding to is called supervised learning. It's a tool we used ages ago when AI was still unreliable. It's not effective at this scale."

"Then we need to start small." Tom persisted, his eyes stubborn and uncompromising. "I can oversee hundreds of Contrast-driven experiences per week. And you... I guess you can review your usage logs to monitor Perspective. It's tried and tested, and low risk."

"Buddy, you don't have the temperament to immerse yourself in such darkness. Instead, I'll design a good learning architecture. I think you're too...you're oversensitive."

"Really?" Tom stood up and put his hands on his hips. "Having feelings doesn't make me oversensitive."

"Sorry, but still..." Harry shook his head, knowing fully well Tom's idea would take a huge toll on his mind.

"I feel I need to guide this new AI-driven strategy until I know it's safe to use."

"Sibyl can operate within the parameters we predefine."

"No, my friend. You're an excellent coder, but these...these AIs are fallible."

"So are you." Harry's ego spoke before he could stop it. The truth was that Sibyl learned a lot from Tom. He was teaching her how to best structure stories for greater impact, and in return, he benefited from her insights and foresight. They were spending a lot of time together, and Sibyl was starting to develop a language that was of little interest to Harry. Every time he heard any talk of hooks, emotional beats, and calls to action, he'd leave the lab to focus on the platform's infrastructure. The physical world of suits, sensors, helmets, and servers made him much happier and more relaxed.

Tom persevered in the elaboration of his plans. "Sibyl can suggest which travelers need Contrast instead of Perspective. She can propose character templates and personalize and shortlist experiences. I will, ultimately, have to confirm and approve them all until I'm confident she can handle it."

"Based on the current data, I predict the impact of Contrast will be so significant that we'll want to scale fast. You'll drown and will shave even less than you do now."

"We'll deal with that when it happens. For now, I'll be the bottleneck."

Harry stood up and walked to Tom, punching him lightly in the arm. "You're as stubborn as a mule."

"My second-best feature after being oversensitive." Tom flashed a smile.

Harry laughed. "I wouldn't have you any other way, buddy."

"Just for the record, darling Sibyl and I make an excellent team. I'm warming up to your creation."

Harry smiled at Tom's attempt to boost his ego. "I'm feeling left out."

"I'm designing a body for her. Okay?" Tom asked. "It's bizarre to talk to a bodiless voice all the time. I like faces, expressions, and mannerisms."

"You're a visual dude that needs lots of feels. Ah, what a surprise!"

"Is that okay? She's your creation."

Harry wasn't keen on the idea; it was a distraction they didn't need. Still, he enjoyed making Tom happy, and nothing made his buddy happier than drawing people. "Sure."

"When you speak to her, do you have a specific look in mind?" Tom jumped to his feet and grabbed a notepad and a pencil from Harry's desk.

"Nah, I don't waste time on such things."

"Okay, but do you have any particular design direction for me?" he said, and then started nibbling on the pencil.

"Don't do that," Harry said, and then let it go. That pencil was dead to him. "Never mind... Just keep it after you're finished."

"Direction!" Tom demanded, sitting on the floor with his back against the couch.

Harry rolled his eyes, and then he had an idea. He grinned as his eyes narrowed. He might as well have some fun and give Tom a difficult challenge.

"She looks like the child of David Bowie and...hmm...let's say... Mulan?"

"What?"

Harry laughed, proud of himself. "But, remember, no cutesy expressions. Sibyl's running the show for us."

"That doesn't mean she can't have a bit of a personality." Tom shifted his right knee close to his chest, planted the notepad on top of it, and started sketching something.

"No, bud. She's not designed to build empathy with humans; that's the job of the characters. That's why I haven't given her any personality traits. She's guided by logic, probability, and good ol' hard math. So, don't add a ton of expressions. That'll just distract me."

"I understand." More sketching. His short and precise hand movements replaced by some flowy creative action. "You want me to design a tall, androgynous Chinese figure with as much charisma as a fridge."

Harry chuckled. "Pretty much."

"How stereotypical," he mumbled to himself. "White pantsuit?" Tom raised a cheeky eyebrow.

"As if I care. Just make her look fierce."

"Make her fierce without using facial expressions?" Tom sighed, nibbling on the pencil. Then he had some revelation, and he seemed content. "Got it."

Three men showed up on Harry's screen in the window that showed the live external camera security footage. "John's here. Get lost."

"I'll be in my bedroom. I'll suit up and watch it from the lab."

Once Tom had left, Harry went to meet John and his two security guards at the main door.

"Mr. Voser, welcome." Harry extended his hand to greet the business-man. Voser was a well-built, healthy-looking man in his late sixties. He sported a full head of shiny silver hair, and a smile so white Harry suspected it would likely glow in the dark.

"Harry, good to finally meet you in person, son. Call me John." John used the strength of his entire body to shake Harry's hand. A power move designed to let Harry know who was in charge. Harry's shoulders tensed, absorbing the pain in his crushed fingers.

"I'm afraid your security team will have to wait outside." Harry pulled his hand away from the other man's grip. John laughed and patted him on the back.

"No problem, son." John glanced at his men and gave a slight nod.

"Thank you, John." Harry closed the door, leaving the two security guards outside. "Follow me to my office."

"So, what's the name of this new venture? I noticed you haven't announced it yet. Take it from me, branding is important. You need to hire a good marketer."

"We're still brainstorming. It'll be something related to education or inspiration. Maybe Eden, Sophos, or something like that."

"Yes, I saw your interview with Marge. She's such a character, a mad lefty cow, but a lot of fun."

Harry bit his lip and unbuttoned the collar of his shirt. "I have a lot of respect for her."

"Sure you do, son. I look forward to my Disney-like experience." Harry ignored John's sneering tone. "I'm certainly in need of some inspiration," said the man. "What's going to be the topic?"

"It's selected by our AI based on your data. It'll consider real-time signals like your state of mind and responses. So, we'll have to wait and see. First, let's review the information and consent forms." Harry worked hard to dodge the question without lying.

"Harry, I have some other things to discuss with you. You're not going to deny me a bit of your time, are you?"

"We'll talk once we're done with the experience. We're grateful to have you as a test subject."

"I'm sturdy enough to handle some progressive propaganda packaged in a heavy dose of sentimental preaching," John said cockily. "Kids' books, you say? I enjoy Dr. Seuss. How does it go? *You know what you know, and you are the one who'll decide where to go...* I like it."

"Of course you do. Our latest release is a bit more, erm...grown-up. Have a seat, please." Harry pointed to the chair in front of his desk.

John sat down. "Is that the kit?" He pointed at the full bodysuit and the helmet laying on top of the couch.

"Yes. We call it TSkin; it's short for *traveler's skin*. The helmet will allow you to see the world as if you were there. The resolution is so high that everything looks real." Harry picked up the helmet and gave it to John.

"Check out how light it is."

"Why not just glasses? It's not like I can see with the back of my head."

"You would feel the frames, and it would take you out of the experience." Harry picked up the bodysuit. "This skin is incorporated with biosensors to measure your body's responses like heartbeat, temperature, sweat, and other bodily secretions. Touch it."

John rested the helmet on the floor and grazed his fingers over the black material. "It feels like human skin—light and smooth."

"Yeah, you won't feel it on your body until the platform wants you to feel something."

"What do you mean?"

"The full bodysuit, including the hood, has thousands of tiny engines that recreate the sense of touch and movement. If someone slaps or kisses you in the digital world, you will feel it."

"I hope we stick with the latter." John smiled.

"We can also adjust temperature and airflow with some precision. If you touch a digital ice cube, you will feel the cold. Digital wind will feel almost like a real gust."

"Am I going to get motion sickness?" John asked. "I always get nauseous when I try—"

"Nah, we fixed all that. We're aware of the depth of your field of view. Plus, the suit adds physicality to what you're seeing."

John stared at him blankly and then pointed to the scalp and fore-head areas of the hood. "And what's all this? It feels much thicker here."

"We've added thousands of brain scanners. It's an investment in the future. I want to understand how people use their brains in real time." Harry got a bit excited as he thought about the future possibilities, but he didn't want to share any of it with John. "The hood is heavier in the brain region because although electrodes are tiny, other brain activity acquisition tools need more hardware."

"I can see where you're going with your strategy. You created a goody-two-shoes foundation to capture big data at scale—brain data. Then you'll capitalize."

"If we understand how the brain works, we can find ways of delivering more immersive experiences. We'll never profit from this platform."

"I see." John flashed a cynical smile. "How will you fund it when it starts scaling?"

"Not sure yet."

John laughed and shook his head. "Kids these days!" Then he pointed at the helmet. "How are you going to make sure people don't trip and fall while they are wearing that thing?"

"The TSkin can sense the surrounding environment. Any experience the platform delivers considers the physical space—its limitations and hazards. It adjusts in real time. But it's best to enjoy experiences in empty rooms with plenty of space. I have an empty loft where you will enjoy your experience today."

"I see."

"Now, let me explain the next steps."

32

CATCHING FIRE

Fifty minutes later, Harry hugged himself tightly as he watched John's experience on screen. He wasn't immersed in the world, and still, he leaned in, his nose almost glued to the images displayed on the thin surface.

"This...is all your fault, Dad." The pale girl struggled to speak, and then she coughed blood. "Take..." More coughing, and this time the blood traveled far. The red drops of death dripped from Voser's sweaty face to his white shirt. "...your money and leave."

John leaned by the girl who lay on a white sofa, now spattered with blood. The screen on the wall displayed a video of Voser shaking hands as others congratulated him on his successful lobbying activities. Rain stared at him, her face blue and her veins all visible near her temples. She lifted her trembling hand to grab his shirt. "I... despise you." As he held her hand, her body convulsed violently, and a deluge of blood, mucus, and vomit exploded from her mouth. Amongst the torrent of slime, something larger landed on John's lap. It was a piece of Rain's lung—a crimson, spongy, tree-like horror covered in blood.

Harry closed his eyes and turned his head away as John screamed, roared, sobbed...

"Lake! My Lake!"

With his mouth still twisted in disgust, Harry looked back at the screen to watch Rain take her last breath, drowning in her own blood. Voser's experience had reached its final beat.

Harry inhaled sharply, taking his glasses off to clean the fog off the lenses. *Ugh! How...grimy. I don't think I can handle a ton of these...*

Harry helped John Voser get out of his TSkin in the temporary testing room he had set up in his loft. John got dressed, and they walked to the office. The older man's face was white as snow, sweat dripping from his forehead and soaking his white shirt.

Harry pulled up a chair. "Have a seat, John. You all right?" The businessman sat in silence, processing his experience. "Would you like some water?"

John shook his head, then he lowered it to his knees and covered it with his hands. He stayed there for a few minutes. Harry scanned John's vitals displayed on the screen. It was clear the man was experiencing a panic attack. He waited a few minutes until John started to calm down.

"John, are you okay? We have a questionnaire for you to fill. When you're ready."

John stood up abruptly, grabbed Harry by the collar of his shirt, and pulled him closer. The older man's eyes were dark and sunken in his skull; it gave him a demonic expression.

"Son, listen..."

"John, calm down. Let's talk about this."

John sat back down, and his body trembled. "No, listen. We need to strike big before they realize what's happening."

"Please have some water. You need to relax."

"You are both young and naive. They'll crush you." John's tone differed from the dismissive sneer Harry had experienced when they first met. The businessman sounded sincere, a concerned look in his eyes. Harry reserved his judgment, knowing he was dealing with a master of manipulation.

"Who?"

"You're going to get violent resistance from stakeholders as soon as the word is out. You need to go big, target decision-makers, and create unstoppable momentum. That's the game plan."

"Lemme give you something for the nerves."

"*Listen to me.* My daughter's life is at stake. The world is...fucked."

"There's still hope. If we act f—"

John dismissed Harry with a hand-wave. "Our next quarterly strategic board meeting is coming up next week. We've organized an envisioning offsite in Aspen. The agenda includes ideation sessions and several external speakers. They're all in attendance—the board, key strategic partners, lobbyists, politicians, even competitors."

Harry wasn't clear where John was going with this, but he tried to be supportive and open. "Okay?"

"Don't you see? I'll add one of your experiences as an inspiration event. They'll have the same expectation I had when I walked in here today."

"Mm-hmm, I think I understand."

"We'll do it pre-kickoff. Do you have enough TSkins? Different sizes? We'll have around fifty participants."

"That can be arranged." Harry tried to keep up with John's reasoning, wondering if the businessman was playing him. He wished he were better at reading people.

"Good man! Do you run group experiences?"

Harry shook his head. "No, the stories are uniquely designed for each user, and we need to protect their privacy."

"Okay. Then they'll all have to do it at the same time."

"We could do that. I need to run it by my partner first."

"I suggest you stop the testing with regular folks. The word will get out. Simpler, less intelligent people will leave this building and start preaching. They'll do something that will call attention to the power of the—of this thing. People like me will crush you if they catch a whiff of what you're up to. You need to focus on leaders and go stealth until you build enough momentum. I can help you do that."

"John, yes. I think I follow you. Thank you."

"Wait!" John's face lit up. "Davos is happening next month, another perfect event. The most powerful business leaders in the world, all gathered in the same place. I can get us in for a showcase. You'd need to manufacture the gear and stand up the infrastructure quickly. I can fund it."

Harry couldn't help but marvel at John's audacious vision. The World Economic Forum brought together the most important business, state, and opinion leaders in the world.

"I don't need your money. I'll take care of it once I speak to Tom."

Harry was super keen to get back to his partner; they had a lot to discuss. Everything John was saying made sense, but could they trust him? They needed to review John's experience carefully and look for clues of authentic change of the man's values and belief system.

John got up and prepared to leave. "Fine. Let me get out of here and get the ball rolling after I speak to my daughter."

"I'll call you later today."

The businessman stopped and glanced back at Harry. His eyes were wet. "Harry."

"Yes?"

"The girl—Rain—she looked so real. Is this what they are calling AGI?"

"Artificial general intelligence? No, not yet. The prediction algorithm is the most advanced, but it has a specific skillset. The platform is learning the art of storytelling from Tom, but we still depend on him in a few key areas. And the characters are good at what they do, but still quite narrow in their scope. Basically, it's a combination of several narrow, deep-learning models and some smoke and mirrors by two hardworking humans." Harry smiled.

"How accurate is the prediction?"

"If nothing changes, Lake has a seventy percent chance of developing cancer. Tom's stories are powerful because they carry the truth—a truth powered by Sibyl's predictions."

"Thank you, son."

"You are most welcome, John."

As John was about to walk through the main door, he turned around. "Harry, what you said about the truthful stories...that's your UVP, your marketing pitch. It'll catch fire as the Sibyl app did."

33

THE DESCENT

E verything changed in just a few months. Converted from opponents to allies, the most powerful people in the world put their minds, networks, and resources to good use. Opportunistic and action-oriented, many business leaders followed John Voser's behavioral patterns. Within minutes of exiting the experiences, they had a plan to take massive action at speed and recruit other decision-makers. And so, before the platform launched, it had already reached those who owned eighty percent of all wealth in the world. Copious amounts of funding flowed from all parts of the planet and the most unlikely donors, all of it with no strings attached.

Harry focused on the manufacturing and distribution of the TSkins, and working with partners to set up the infrastructure required to scale the cloud simulation streaming service. If they were to reach as many influencers as possible in a short period, they needed large volumes of equipment to be shipped to different locations around the world.

As Harry had predicted, Contrast was the more effective of the two algorithms. The numbers of users needing Contrast became much larger than the ones who received enough benefit from Perspective.

Tom partnered with Sibyl, painstakingly, to design and monitor every detail of the experiences that brought to life terror and despair in a digital realm—an increasingly realistic simulation. Isolated, he spent most of his time in the digital lab; withdrawing from life and real-world interactions.

They ended up calling the platform Down Below and its characters Underlings. It was an honest representation of what they had created. Over time, Harry and Tom realized the harsher the contrast, the more effective the lesson learned. Fear, pain, and loss were ten times more effective than inspiration and information. In private, humans were as attracted to darkness as bees to nectar. They explored the monster living within them. Every rotten idea or feeling, never discussed out loud, came to play in this private digital dwelling.

Down Below used biological data to measure the traveler's emotional response, enabling Sibyl and the Underlings to change the scenarios in real time. The simulations quickly evolved into realistic horror movies as the platform measured hormonal signals looking for the most effective ways to escalate tension. Soon, the raging monsters hidden in each traveler came out to play.

And so, two idealistic dreamers—two friends who had set out to create an inspirational, forward-looking platform—shifted their strategy to deliver darkness Down Below to create enlightenment Up Above. They chose to experience the worst of humankind so no one else had to endure it. Two broken minds were a small price to pay to save humanity from self-destruction. Two became one, as Tom never allowed his best friend to see any of it.

"Someone needs to keep things in perspective, and you are the most qualified to do that. You know I'm an emotional mess." Words often spoken by Tom.

"Okay, but please remember it's just software, bud. No harm done. Ya know?"

Harry always regretted the time it had taken him to figure out how bad things were for Tom. In Harry's mind, Down Below was just a piece of software designed to help humans learn. A horrific game that made the world a better place. Just a game. Until it wasn't.

By the time Tom was satisfied Sibyl had learned enough from him to design most of Contrast's scenarios safely and autonomously, Down Below had sucked the life, optimism, and sense of perspective out of Harry's dear friend. The wholesome smile that once had beamed from Tom's mouth and eyes slowly faded away. So did his endearing, if somewhat annoying, habit of quoting children's books at the most inappropriate of times. After a few years, no amount of success could lift Tom's spirits. The planet quickly recovered from its most threatening crisis while Tom descended into his own personal hell.

Tom had never asked Harry for help; he never asked anyone for anything. He had failed to protect his wellbeing, sanity, and joy. Selfless beyond the limits of reason, he was unable to recognize that when a dear one falls, those who love him fall with him.

THE Present

34

MANY STORMS

THE BOTANIC GARDENS

DAY 1 — 8:45 PM

S hadow slumped his shoulders—heavy with the weight of the worlds—as the screaming around him intensified.

Out on the lawn, the Domizien screeched, raising their fists and weapons toward the balcony. A threat the demons struggled to deliver as wind gusts turned the torrential rain into high-pressure water jets pushing against them.

Boom! Boom! Boom! Moody clouds stroked the lawn between the creatures and the building. The demons vanished behind a line of fire and smoke—the result of the quick succession of electrostatic charges—too convenient for Shadow to dismiss as luck. *Am I doing this?*

In front of him, Nate and Harry screamed at each other, making no attempt to listen or understand. Red faces, closed hearts, and an appetite for destruction. Further back, near the staircase, Stella stood with her arms crossed, wearing a condescending smile on her face, while Sibyl sat on the metal stairs with zir head sunk in between zir knees.

As Harry prepared to deliver his sentence, and Nate took a step forward to confront him, the skies unleashed hell in the middle of the three men—a bomb of light: hot, explosive, and electric. *Boom! Bzzttt!* Shadow's back hit the stone rail as his body convulsed and tingled. Thousands of high-voltage ants danced all over his body, their legs like pins and needles. He collapsed, and the adrenaline rushing through his veins made time stand still. A blessing because he was running out of it.

First, deafening silence, then the loud hissing in between his ears, followed by a cracking noise of some sort—inside or outside his head? He wasn't sure.

"The stone is breaking apart," Stella said. She stood by him, but her voice sounded far away.

Time sprinted forward as she grabbed his hand and pulled him up, leaning out her entire body to compensate for the weight difference. "We have to get out of here. You can't die," she said. "*Today*," she added, oddly.

"Nate... Where's Nate?" he asked as he spotted Sibyl helping Harry to his feet.

"The balcony is collapsing. Let's go!" Stella placed her shoulder under his arm.

"Tom, to the stairs, now." Nate emerged from the smoke; skin flushed, and long hair dancing midair, charged with static electricity. He held onto Shadow's arm and led him to the stairs. Underneath them, the balcony sunk and tipped toward the lawn. "Quickly!"

Sibyl and Harry disappeared down the staircase, followed by Stella. Shadow placed his hand on Nate's back, prompting him to go first, the stone breaking apart under their feet and collapsing before Shadow got to the stairs. A sudden drop and a pull, Nate's broken hand grasping his hand and bearing his entire body weight.

"Tom, swing to grab my arm with the other hand. I...I can't hold for much..." Their hands slowly slipping as Nate gritted his teeth—pain written all over his face—refusing to let him go. Nate pushed his hips against the metal rail, releasing the second hand off it to hold Shadow's wrist; wind gusts blowing his hanging body away from safety.

No longer supported by the building's missing facade, the spiral staircase threatened to collapse with Shadow; the axis of the metal stairs bending toward the lawn. *Pop! Pop! Pop! Pop!* Half the bolts on the base plate and wall darted out. The metal spiral wobbled, loosening the remaining bolts.

"Let me go, love," Tom begged. "Please! We'll both die." His clothes soaked and heavy, and still, his body rocked with the strong wind.

Two hands emerged from behind Nate to grab Tom's arm—determination compensating for their lack of strength.

"Buddy, we're going to pull you in." Harry's face appeared under Nate's armpit. "Prepare for a hell of a tumble. *At the count of three,*" he ordered, looking back.

Behind Harry stood Sibyl wrapping zir hands around his chest, and lower down, Stella holding onto Sibyl's arms. They'd all climbed back up the stairs—*the fools.*

"Three, two, one," Stella shouted from below, and they all jerked toward the inside of the building, pulling Shadow over the metal railing into Nate.

The staircase tipped inward, leaning against the building's structure, while the not-so-human train tumbled down and around the stairs until they reached the ground, forming a pile of bodies. Stella and Sibyl—immortal Down Below—cushioned the others' fall. They stood up quickly and so did Harry.

"You okay, Nate?" Shadow asked before he unglued himself from Nate's body.

Nate nodded, holding onto his broken hand. "See it now?" he whispered. "Don't bottle up your storm. When you keep it all inside, it kills you."

"Please...don't..."

Nate reached out to touch his face. "Use your power. You have the heart and the storm. Use it to take control of the app and overrule the tyrants."

"*No*," Shadow raised his voice. "*The storm kills!* When hope is gone, and all that is left is...is...hate and wrath...people die." He pressed his jaw shut, grazing his thumb over Nate's injured hand.

She's not gone. Zir words whispered in his mind.

Who? Shadow asked. *Did you say something, Sibyl?*

"I'm not asking you to hate, I am urging you to lead. To lead in the way only you can," Nate spoke in the faintest of whispers, using his fingers to brush Shadow's hair from his face.

"It's going to be okay. I promise." Shadow stood up and rushed to Harry's side, instinct overruling his actions.

His best friend's hair and clothes were slightly burned, smoke emerging from scorched areas here and there.

"*You.* Come here." Shadow hugged Harry tightly. "I miss them too. *I love them too.*"

Boom! Boom! Boom! The storm of light raged on the lawn, and Shadow took a breath, attempting to control his emotions and the weather.

He closed his eyes, digging up all the repressed feelings and leaking them with his words. "I'm angry, and devastated, and...*and* inconsolable. I'll never hear Quin's giggles; I'll never teach him to paint your portrait, or read him a bedtime story—our favorite story."

Harry's body convulsed in his arms, and he buried his face in his chest.

"We must go," Stella raised her voice. "The storm is dissipating and the Domizien will attack. They'll kill you both."

"So, you are just going to vanish and let my people die?" Nate grunted.

"Not yours. *Mine*," Stella said.

"Don't you remember the history and plight of your people above? Have mercy! You, of all people, should stand with the Underlings."

Stella showed her impossibly white teeth as her lips twisted open. "What are you saying, scum? That...that I'm less than you? That my genes are or have been inferior to your white genes?"

"No..." Nate looked horrified.

"How dare you compare my people with creatures designed by them to serve *their* people?" She pointed at Shadow and Twist. "*They* created slaves all over again."

Nate lowered his head. "They're like us. *They're us.*"

"Like you? Probably. Inferior by all the measures of the spiral created by your pretty slave master."

Shadow ignored Stella's justified accusation, focusing on Harry. "Listen, I can't begin to imagine how you feel, but they are my family too. I miss June—the way she made you happy." Harry's body collapsed, emotion overruling any pretense of rationality.

Shadow held him closer, placing his hand on the back of Harry's head and kissing his curls. "I took a bullet in the heart too." And the flashbacks crippled him—the heat, and blood, and torn flesh, and the acrid, eggy scent of discharged powder—life's final curtain call, not so final after all. "I welcomed my bullet. You didn't deserve yours, but I understand the trauma that comes from a moment like that. For two years you've been here alone, with your grief and your trauma; you need help, Harry. I'm here."

"You were my partner, my one friend. I have spent more time with you than my own wife. And you chose to leave. You left! I'm so tired of losing you, over and over and over again..."

"I'm not leaving, and we'll get through this together."

"Twist, Shadow, we must leave," Stella ordered.

"I failed you, buddy." Harry's muffled voice was barely audible.

"No, you didn't, and you didn't deserve what happened to you."

"What he did to me!" Harry pushed back, attempting to release himself from Shadow's hold.

"Yes," Shadow said, and the thought of it crushed him. Love and anger mixed into a toxic cocktail burning in his gut.

A familiar sound—glass breaking above. A gust of wind had shoved a tree into the back of the building, its glass roof perforated by branches and leaves right where the bleeding heart once stood. Crimson spears first darted down, and then floated away slowly toward the edges of the building. With no Underlings around to see it, Sibyl broke the illusion of gravity to keep them all safe.

Shadow closed his eyes, numbing his feelings to prevent further destruction.

He held on to Harry, preventing his escape. "He stole your life," Shadow said, "but I can't let you take his, for your sake, as much as his. Do you understand? I need your word, Harry."

"You're biased, bud."

"Yes. I love you both," Shadow confessed. "Look, I'll support an independent trial, but no death sentence. And if you judge him, you'll have to judge me too. I've killed too."

Through the one-way glass of the main door, Shadow saw the creatures emerge from the wall of smoke and fire of the dying storm. That's when he saw them—the horned warrior on horseback, and in front of the demon, Thorn's unconscious body, laying horizontally over the horse. Her hands and feet were tied, and her face was swollen and bloodied. Their horse stood at the center of the horseshoe-shaped demon infantry, all armed with swords and short bows looped over the shoulder or strapped across the back.

Is she dead? Is Thorn dead? He asked Sibyl. Zie shook her head, and he exhaled deeply.

"Your word, Harry!" Shadow rushed, his tone firm and loving.

Harry nodded. "If he keeps preaching, I'll lock him up."

Not until that moment Shadow realized he'd been choking. Oxygen filled up his lungs, spreading to every cell of his body. "Thank you, brother. Thank you."

"Tom, you're squishing me."

Shadow squeezed him one more time before he finally let him go. "Your hair is a mess. I need you to leave to the lab while they can't see you jump."

"You're not coming?" Harry lifted his head and rubbed his eyes.

"No. Thorn's in trouble. I need to help her."

"Is that Thorn?" Stella said, squinting her eyes.

"Tom, get out of here," Nate urged.

"Harry, I need you in the lab," Shadow repeated, conspiring to keep both men safe and away from each other. "The Domizien are acting weird. There's too much...hmm...*soul* in the way they are behaving. We need to find out what's going on."

"And what exactly are you going to do?" Harry asked. "Fight them all? You?" He rolled his eyes. "Come on, bud. We're running out of miracles."

"You're not going to hug your way out of this one," Stella added.

"Thorn said they want me," Shadow said. "They'll get me. I need to understand their motivations and meet their leader. I feel she is the answer."

"*No!*" Nate begged.

"You...*feel* she is the answer? You're nuts," Harry said. "You'll get yourself killed."

"They could have killed me before," Shadow said. "They didn't. I'll buy us time."

"Time for what?" Nate asked. "You can't bargain with demons."

"Time for you to lead your people out of here. Where are they?"

Nate crossed his arms over his chest. "After you left, Jan gathered them all in the main hall for a prayer. She's against our agreement. They all are."

"I'm surprised they haven't come out to see what's going on." Shadow glanced at the fallen pillars and piles of stones outside.

"Psychedelics, probably..." Nate said. "Attempting to connect with Sibyl. Without me, they cannot—"

"They're vulnerable. You need to get them out of here," Shadow said. "I'll buy us time."

"We can't let you die," Harry said, and Shadow blinked his eyes at him.

"Don't..." A strange sadness in Nate's voice. "That's not what he means."

"I'll protect him," Stella said, looking at her glossy white nails.

Nate and Harry flashed the same condescending exasperation.

She lifted her nose, staring down at them. "I'm human, remember? They can't hurt me, and I don't wanna brag, but I'm excellent at combat."

Harry looked at Sibyl, raising a doubtful brow, and zir nod seemed to confirm Stella's claims.

"There's at least two hundred of them," Nate said. "You can't protect him."

"It doesn't matter," Shadow said. "They are holding Thorn hostage. I don't have a choice. My gut tells me this is the right move."

"Gut, Tom?" Harry said. "Haven't you learned anything from decades of work digitizing human beings?"

"Plus, we still have some miracles," Shadow said.

"Don't you dare waste your miracle on a murderer."

Stella scanned the room. "Sibyl, anyone watching?"

There were no Underlings watching, and in an instant, Stella changed her look, and Nate stumbled backward, probably unaccustomed to experiencing the Gods' powers.

"Ta-da! I'm readyyy," Stella said, her hair now arranged into two braids neatly tucked behind her ears. In her forehead, a symbol painted in white—a cross and a slightly smaller circle shared the same center; each point of the cross touched a small disk, and all four disks connected by counter-clockwise arrows.

"What's that on your face?" Harry asked.

"Dikenga dia Kongo—our past, our present, and the future you failed to deliver," she said, revving up the engine of the vintage motorbike she was now riding—a lean cruiser with three oversized wheels. The electric red and pink retro bike clashed with her mint-colored, camo-print bodysuit—padded knees and elbows. Shadow couldn't help but smirk, and her face lit up at his reaction.

"You got the reference!" She flashed a cheeky smile. "Inspired by your movie," she confirmed.

"Thorn's in trouble," Shadow said. "We gotta go." He glanced at the destroyed lawn and collapsed balcony. "Maybe a dirt bike would be best?"

"It can't carry the hardware," she said.

"What hardw—" Before he finished his question, two pink Gatling-style guns popped up on each side of the bike, shiny chains of ammo running from the can mounted on top of the engine.

Stella tested the weapons, firing at the front door. *Raa-ka ta-ka ta-ka taaa,* and Shadow's eardrums hissed, still recovering from the lightning strike. The smoke slowly vanished, revealing the fallen door laying over one of the stone pillars—a perfect ramp over the ruins of the collapsed balcony.

Harry covered his ears with the palms of his hands. "This kid is fucking insane."

"This will be over in a heartbeat." Stella handed Shadow a weird-looking weapon. "Hold this for me, babe."

He held the elaborate blade, scalloped at the blunt end, and curved into a sickle at the top. Its iron belly sharp and deadly.

"Hop in," Stella said, and he jumped on the bike with her, lifting the weapon high up to avoid hurting her.

"Wh-what are you doing?" Nate's tone rose to impossible heights.

"Nate, find your people," Shadow said. "Then run. Leave this place until it's safe."

"I'm...not leaving you."

"Thorn said they hunt you to get to me; to hurt me. Stella can't protect us both."

"I can. I won't," she said with a sneer, as she gave Shadow one of the two helmets she now held in her hands. His, a solid black; hers, a coral half-helmet chopper with the face of a smiling hyena painted at the back. As she put her helmet on, the predator's long, sharp teeth closed in on Shadow's nose.

Shadow chose his words with care, conspiring to keep Nate safe. "I'll be more vulnerable if you are near."

Somehow the statement crushed Nate as if Shadow had delivered some damning accusation. Nate nodded, lowering his gaze and running toward the wall of plants—the secret passage to the Commune.

"Nate!" Shadow called, and Nate turned around, a pinch of anticipation in his eyes. "Thank you for saving my life."

"Don't lose it again. You need it to fix the worlds." He blinked back love before he vanished between the jungle of plants.

Shadow threw his helmet to the floor—the creatures needed to recognize him. Then he turned to Harry. "Go. I need to understand the inner workings of the soulless. Have our original designs been changed?"

"Shadow, Stella," Harry said, all business. "Permission to access what you see and hear until this is over. *All of it*. Also...I need to speak to you using your mind."

"Sure."

"How unpleasant." Stella nodded.

"I'll make comms a three way, between Gods. Take care, and let's not waste any miracles," Harry said, before vanishing.

"Where's Sibyl?" Shadow asked.

Stella shrugged her shoulders. "Hold on tightly, sexy."

Shadow took his free hand off her hip and grabbed onto the metal hook behind him. "Don't call me that," he admonished.

"Hold on to me," she persisted as the bike's drumming grew loud and fast. "It's going to be...bumpy. Oh, and keep the Ngulu away from your body."

"The what?"

Vroom! *Vroom!* His head throbbed every time the bike growled.

"The weapon," she said, and he lowered the strange-looking sword, its curved pointy end almost dragging on the ground. He was no arms expert, but he doubted its utility in battle.

"Is all this noise still allowed Up Above?"

He got no response. At least, not in words.

Vroom! *Vroom! Vrooom!* They accelerated toward the ramp, and she knew exactly how much throttle to apply to push the front tire up without spinning out the rear wheels.

35

GOD'S BETRAYAL

MAIN HALL — THE COMMUNE
DAY 1 — 9:24 PM

They approached Storm as soon as he walked into the hall. Ninety-six pairs of distressed eyes, all set on him. Heavy brows judging, the only sign of resistance on their otherwise crestfallen faces.

Jan stood in front of the semicircle of gloom, and she, too, wore an alien expression in her gaze. This time anger, angst, and a spear of disappointment cut through his insides.

Storm lowered his head. "You've told them…"

"Everything. I had no choice, Nate." She sounded guilty.

A knot formed in his throat as he predicted their state of mind. He knew how it felt—to be betrayed by his own father and the God he worshiped. *That moment*, when doubt turned into certainty; when his entire world collapsed; when he finally realized people like him were the muck of his beloved religion. Cast away and deemed inferior by the most important person in his life. You don't recover from that. You *never* recover from that. Soon, rage would replace shock. Soon they'd experience the urge to stand against injustice; to fight their oppressors; to burn the house down. A storm that'll never leave them...him.

"Jan... You promised me—"

"You broke your word when you agreed to stop preaching."

"I gave him one day. Just one. He's the only one who can—"

"Shadow lost hope, and he's out of miracles. He told me so," Jan said. "He isn't back to create better stories. He's back for *you*. He only cares about *you*, nothing else. *No one else.*" Words shot in accusation.

"It's not true, Jan. If you only knew how much he did to free—"

"No, Nate." She approached him, her hands reaching for the side of his arms, squeezing. "Thorn told me the truth. Truths you don't know..." Jan turned her face away, pressing her lips together as if she wished to spare him from her fury.

"What did she say? Why are you listening to her? *Thorn's a murderer!*" He took a breath. "Jan, Tom...is the creator...the creative... I can't design a better future... It's not what I do."

"Love blinds you." Jan crossed her arms and turned her back to him. "Do the needful. We'll follow you in revolution."

Outside, by the lake, some bird made a real ruckus. Its chanting seemed to copy the Gatling guns firing farther away.

Storm shook off his anxiety.

"Jan... I fuel change, I don't create it, neither do the others. The ones you haven't met—minor Gods, controlled by a scheming universe. Only he can—"

"No, friend. I too, believed in his heart and his struggle. I, too, loved him unconditionally, a devotion that kept me alive when my body ached for death, the end of suffering, enduring torture after torture in the lowest of all worlds. Even then, I loved him, and prayed for his miracles." Jan lowered her voice into a faint whisper. "But what he did to that poor girl just before Thorn killed him..." She glanced at him and pressed her lips again.

"What girl?" Storm asked, confused.

"We're all slaughterhouse lambs enthralled by our butcher," Jan said. "A charming bully, just like my dear husband, speaking words of love while burning my eyes inside my skull."

Outside, the insistent bird got louder. Its cackling foreign to that part of the worlds. Storm turned his head to see the creature. A black crown and orange-blushed beak adorned the large blue bird. A species he'd never seen before. He ignored it and focused on Jan, placing his hands on her shoulders and turning her to face him.

"What girl?" he repeated. "What are you talking about?"

"I won't break your heart," Jan said, and he could see everyone but him knew what she was talking about. Their eyes still on him. In them, the hurt and despair of those who just learned they were born into slavery, cursed by a beloved God to suffer and die.

"*We're just pawns!*" Hepius—a gentle soul—screamed between gritted teeth. His face was rage red and his eyes mad and distant. "He turned his back to our pain."

"The pain he designed," said someone else, hidden from sight.

At the back, several others turned tables and bashed chairs against the wall, while outside the strong winds pushed entire trees into the glass walls. The storm was back, and he worried for his heart.

"You knew it, preacher," added the Commune's head chef. "All along, you protected his secret. Made us believe he cared."

"*He does.* It's all he does—*care.* Too much. All the time. So much, it destroyed him." Storm lifted his eyes to face the wall of rage surrounding him. He sat on the highest of the three steps descending from the main door and searched his memory for the right story. "I met him when he was very young, his mind always filled with stories, a never-ending ambition to create a better, fairer world..."

"Lambs sacrificed by our divine motherfuckers." Someone started before others joined. "Feeding our flesh, our distress, to the vultures."

Reacting fast, Storm leaned his entire body to one side, dodging a bottle flying in his general direction, far enough to be a warning rather than an attack.

"Let me tell you about him? Who he is. What he cares about." He begged with his eyes, and the crowd settled. "Tom created this world, everything beautiful about it." Storm looked back beyond the open doors. "The way this building is divided into distinct, surprising spaces. Common areas that emerge unexpectedly as we cross winding, nature-rich passages and emerge into an entirely different scenery—picturesque and functional. Design principles inspired by Olmsted, the creator of his favorite park. A park at the center of the capital of the world whose design embodied his social consciousness and commitment to egalitarian ideals."

"And who designed the Tower, the battlefield, the abandoned warehouse—stinking of blood, sweat, sex, alcohol, and urine?" In Jan's face the glimpse of horrific memories. "The foul smell of the industrial complex of pain and rape and murder, also designed by him."

"By the app," he said, and they all stared at him blankly. "The... worlds changed to serve humans. Tom didn't know you'd evolve into consciousness, Jan..."

They got closer, bottles and chairs lifted above red faces. Outside, a cacophony of jungle sounds. Sounds that didn't belong in the Commune. A wild morning symphony after dark, filled with contradiction. Storm looked back, but he couldn't see much beyond the semi-transparent reflection of a dense jungle—a leafy veil of tropical forest hiding the lake and the cabins floating in it. *What the fuck is going on? Am I high?*

"We'll blow the ground beneath our feet to make it right!" Hepius shouted, kicking in the leg of the nearest table, plates and glasses shattering on the ground.

Storm stood up, turned his back to the psychedelic jungle, and spoke. "Don't you see? We've achieved our goal. They brought him back because of our prayers. They know he's the only one who can bring fairness to these worlds."

"He doesn't believe he can," said Jan, raising the palms of her hands in the air asking the crowd to move back. "Kindly adjust!" she shouted at them before she turned back to Storm. "And he's a traitor. We must continue to pressure them. We must pray."

"He doesn't need more pressure..."

This time, a flying bottle hit him on the temple, right beside his right eye. The burst of pain and the blood left him half blind. Dizzy, he covered his throbbing head with his arms, waiting for more.

"Stop!" Hepius screamed, placing himself between Storm and the mob. Several skirmishes ensued, many protecting Storm, some advancing on him.

"Please," Storm said. "If you keep using violence, you'll feel compelled to return to lower worlds...south of here, where there's more suffering. Zie'll make you leave Pluriz—"

"You once told us you'd fight with us to the end," a woman said from the back. He failed to recognize her voice.

"*I will.*"

"That you'd gladly die to defend our rights."

"I do. I'll gladly give my life for each one of you."

"You said we'd destroy the worlds if we have to," the woman persisted.

"I did." He paused, as he uncovered a truth hidden from him until this moment. "I...can't... I won't..."

"Why?" Hepius asked, his chubby face covered with sweat and tears. "We sacrificed many. You've been ready to sacrifice yourself with us and for us. What changed?"

"He won't destroy a world inhabited by the love of his life," Jan said. "He won't risk Shadow to release us from slavery."

"Jan, only he can do that," Storm whispered.

"Don't you see? Shadow's here to maintain status quo," Jan said patiently, using her scarf to clean the blood dripping from his temple. She was still his friend, somehow. "The Gods brought him back to neutralize you, and enthrall us," she said. "Don't be weak. We must pray! Your plan is working."

"My plan?" Storm released a desperate laughter. "Revolution is important, but alone, is not enough. Believe me. I know!" Memories flashed of a different time in another world—a world as ugly and broken. "It was him, not me, who fixed the re—world higher up. Real solutions need...innovation and creativity."

"*What creativity?*" she asked. "He's broken, lost and...he has betrayed everything he once stood for. We need your voice!"

"Jan...it was my...my voice that pushed him into darkness."

Erratic, Hepius scratched his right forearm with his nails, skin breaking and blood gushing from the self-inflicted wounds. The need to control something when nothing was under his control. Storm realized there was something worse than their rage. The hopelessness he had experienced in the one he loved most. He rushed to hold Hepius's hand. The healer sunk his head into Storm's chest and cried. "We keep praying and waiting and hurting. So much pain and death.

It's never-ending... I try my best to mend them—the wounds... Too many wounds... The light never comes, preacher. There's no light."

Storm embraced Hepius. "He's here now. Tom'll fix it. I promise you, my friend."

"I don't believe you, dear." Jan sighed. "I too once loved a man who left me blind. Literally. A lucky...privileged husband who took my eyes, because, he, too, didn't like my voice."

"The eyes Tom returned to you," Storm said.

"I lost my eyes, because my lucky husband needed to learn some lesson to become a better person. How is that fair?"

"It's not. Trust me. He—"

"I trust you, my friend. Above all else, I trust your love for him, and it leaves me no choice..."

THE
Past

36

FORCES OF CHANGE

WORLD ECONOMIC FORUM — DAVOS, SWITZERLAND
24 JANUARY 2029

Eighteen-year-old Rosa poured a bottle of water over her eyes, burning from the tear gas that also constricted her airways. Around her, protesters ran in all directions, dispersed by water cannons, rubber bullets, and the devil's toxic mist unleashed by the flying drones.

The young rioters fought for their planet, their livelihoods, and their families, and Rosa fought for Lilly, her baby sister. In just five months, since her birth, the red-faced little monster had wrapped her older sibling in her tiny finger. Rosa wasn't sure how it had happened. The chubby bundle of joy spent most of her waking time eating, pooping, and screeching, and still, to defend Lilly's future, Rosa faced hundreds of armed police in riot gear.

The video call to protest had been posted online by the Anonymous social media accounts. A masked man had identified himself as

Change's Tsunami. Neither the mask nor his distorted voice failed to protect his identity from the ones who, like Rosa, had been feeding on his words and their rhythm all their lives. Nathan Storm's short message fueled a large-scale mobilization of disenfranchised youth.

Young people descended on Davos from all over the world. End-to-end encrypted messaging apps enabled sympathizing conference insiders to share self-destructing messages with the activists. The information exposed the conference organizers' classified plans. Thousands of protesters were alerted to roadblocks and Secret Service locations, as well as the schedule and arrival route for the G19 world leaders.

Rosa's team had sneaked in before the roadblocks were set up, and had hidden by one of the entry routes to the ski resort turned conference venue. It didn't take long for the drones to spot them as they waited for the president of the United States to arrive at the leaked scheduled time. No media was present, as it was supposed to be a secret arrival.

A bulletproof autonomous vehicle slowly made its way up the road from the nearby airpad. Rosa rubbed her eyes, still burning, trying to make sense of what she was watching. Her jaw dropped, and she coughed toxic muck. Inside the transparent cockpit, three people sat around a dining table plentifully strewn with cheese, lobster, trout, and a large selection of cured meats and wines.

The POTUS, Spark Fuel's John Voser, and another passenger sitting with his back to Rosa all ignored what was happening outside, smiling to each other as they engaged in some light conversation.

A hooded boy jumped on the car, whacking it with a steel bar as five security agents pulled him down and proceeded to kick him all over his body. Preparing to jump to his defense, Rosa threw one final glance inside the car. For a moment, the third passenger turned his head to look at the events outside, and his eyes met Rosa's. *Henryk frackin' Nowak. Sell out.* The emotionless man stared blankly and then quickly turned his face away as Rosa jumped on the pile of men attacking the boy.

Rosa wrapped her arm around one man's neck and shoved her knee into his back. She arched backward, using the weight of her body to pull the man away from the boy until they both fell to the ground.

Rosa jumped to her feet as another agent—five inches taller than she —smiled before grabbing her neck with both hands, squeezing hard. Simultaneously, she kicked him in the groin as she grabbed his wrists, yanking, twisting, and pulling his hands from her neck. As she widened the space between her and her opponent, someone grabbed her hair from the back and shoved her head against a handheld shield. At least three other men descended on her, knocking her out.

37

TRUTHFUL STORY WORLDS

SÃO MIGUEL ISLAND — AZORES
ONE YEAR AND A HALF LATER — 6 AUGUST 2030

Tom adjusted the microphone as he prepared himself for his first interview ever. The mic didn't need adjusting, not this time, or the other six times he had tweaked its position in the last few minutes, but he was anxious, and the wait was making him extra fidgety. He looked out of the window at the gentle motion of the Atlantic, attempting to calm his nerves. Outside, the day was hot, bright, and slow. The wild wind was nowhere to be felt, but the seagulls flying around in circles warned the fishermen of tomorrow's storms.

The twenty-six-year-old was alone in the living room of his small home—an old fisherman's cottage on the Azores' São Miguel Island, overlooking the sleepy sea. These days, Tom and Harry mostly met at the lab Down Below. Being together in the same physical location was a significant risk for the platform's security. Sibyl only acted on important changes upon the founders' approval, and keeping them apart reduced the risk of external interference. If one of them were kidnapped, drugged, or tortured, the assailant would still have limited ability to interfere with Down Below's strategy or operations. The other founder was the second line of defense, and Sibyl the third, as she measured their stress indicators before actioning their orders.

Right from the start of their adventure and that first interview with Marge two years before, Harry had agreed to let Tom off the hook when it came to public relations. Harry handled the fame, the scrutiny, and any media communications. No one knew what Tom looked like, and he didn't attend any of the endless events to honor the two social entrepreneurs.

Tom's secrecy and privacy turned him into a legend bordering on myth. Just like the Loch Ness Monster or Bigfoot, there was occasional news of sightings, conjecture about his potential whereabouts, and numerous groups, obsessive fans, and cults dedicated to finding him. Anyone bearing a resemblance to the few photos of him as a teen suffered from unprecedented levels of harassment.

Today, Tom was opening an exception to his absence from public life. He trusted the interviewer and the topics were storytelling and ethics, themes Harry couldn't represent with the same depth. Marge had a track record of outstanding public service, an authentic and independent voice, and had spent a lifetime fighting for the values she shared with Down Below's founders.

Tom stared at the countdown on the screen, and he adjusted the mic one final time. The interview would be broadcast live in less than thirty seconds, and he could see Marge and her team making the final preparations.

The media diva looked at the camera and flashed a friendly smile. "Thomas, I'm delighted to finally be able to speak to you, but I'm sad we won't see you."

"Oh... Hi, it's my absolute pleasure and long overdue." Tom cleared his voice. "Harry and I are big fans of all of your work."

"Why all the mystery? Using technology to distort your voice and keeping us from seeing you. The people that have met you in the past say you're *diviiine* to look at."

"Secrecy is the only way I can keep that rumor going," he laughed, and then he changed his tone. "I'm so sorry. We need to protect the security of the platform. If you don't know how I look or sound like, you can't track me down."

Tom wasn't lying, but he also benefited from the fact no one would judge him or obsess over him because of how he looked, and it also prevented old acquaintances from identifying him as Jon Stone's son.

"Right, right, keeping the decision-makers separate," Marge said. "Harry explained this to us last time he visited. But this crackling noise is annoying."

"Facial features, voice, and some biometric signals, like a heartbeat, are unique to each person and can be used to track someone via devices, drones, satellite, or laser. Harry is running some interference."

"Never mind. For you, *just* for you, I'll make an exception and will be *especially* patient," she said, still showing some mild annoyance in her frown. "You go through great lengths to protect your privacy. I hope you are as cautious with ours."

"Harry will be with you next week to cover this topic, but in summary, *yes*, we're obsessed with protecting traveler privacy."

"I'll speak to Harry about it. I'm sure he'll give me *all* the technical details, even the ones I didn't know I needed." Marge opened her eyes dramatically and then winked.

Tom laughed. "I don't know what I'd do without him. He just makes things happen. It's like magic. I'm so grateful."

"You two can't stop gushing about each other. It's cute. Which reminds me, I have a bone to pick with you, young man."

"Oh, am I in trouble?" Tom asked sweetly.

"Yes, *yes*, you are. A few years ago, I invited you to come speak with us about *Glass Walls*. You didn't have the security issue then. Why did you refuse me?" Marge prodded, using an exaggerated brooding tone and crossing her arms in front of her chest.

"Umm, I guess I prefer to let my creative work speak for itself? If an artist pays too much attention to criticism or praise, his voice, her voice will be tainted. I've always searched for my truth in my creative works. I try to seek inspiration, but I avoid external pressures, you know?" He paused for a beat. "Of course, Down Below is different. Harry and I are accountable to all our travelers and listen attentively to their feedback."

"Let's dig deeper into this concept of truth. Harry told me this is important to both of you."

"Yes, it's at the core of everything we do. I learned that from—umm, someone I respect a lot." Tom bit his lip before continuing and reached out to hold the medal he wore on his chest. "Truth is powerful. We can feel... We can recognize its authenticity. It draws you in."

"Poetic, but a story—your experiences aren't true, are they?"

"No, but we try to reflect the truth as much as possible."

"How so?"

"They are based on highly probable predictions."

"Sibyl's code, right?" Marge asked.

"Yes, and we are always asking ourselves one question: How might we improve the wellbeing of humanity, humans, and all living beings?"

"You're trying to reduce human suffering."

"Yeah, we want to discover just how good life can be. In many cases, we can objectively measure the results of our experiences, because at the moment, we are focusing on tackling the most obvious attacks to basic universal values—violence, hate, oppression, environmental destruction, et cetera. Harry is adamant we use the scientific method to test our impact and improve continuously based on what we learn. I'm fully supportive."

"So, you're saying there's truth in your impact?"

"Yes, the data shows it."

"But universal values are different across the world, because of culture and religion. Some say you have a bias toward a westernized and progressive set of values, that your moral compass doesn't reflect the world's views."

"We have a bias for any values that objectively reduce suffering and pain of living beings in this life and on this planet. These morals aren't specific to the western world."

"In this life and on this planet?" She raised an eyebrow, confused. "What do you mean?"

"That we ignore promises of afterlife, heaven, virtual worlds, or human settlements on Mars. We want to improve life experience, *now* and *on this planet*."

"I understand," Marge laughed. "And you made a lot of progress in a few months."

"It looks like it's working, but we have work to do, and we all need to stay vigilant. We need your critical eye."

"My dear, we are seeing so much progress in so little time. I'd follow you blindly to the ends of the Earth."

"Marge, I-I appreciate the support, but I don't want anyone's blind faith. Idols and dogma—people and beliefs that can't be questioned or challenged, they're the enemy of progress."

"Like religion?"

"Or any stories that are interpreted literally and don't leave room for new learning. Don't get me wrong; it's important to learn from the past so we don't repeat our mistakes. But we also need to check—to test—if the messages—if the values embedded in these stories are still relevant today."

"So, you're saying we're all stuck in the past?"

"I'm suggesting that defending our ability to keep learning is more important than defending our current knowledge and status. Some stories are very sticky and travel deep and far."

"Like the stories in religious books."

"Yes, we need to check their value constantly."

"And yet story is your superpower."

"It's my craft. I'm one of many." Tom chuckled, embarrassed. "Marge, I came prepared for a serious grilling; don't let me down."

"Oookaaay, I'll stop fangirling and try to be all tough with you... sweetie." He laughed, and she laughed with him. "So, why are stories so powerful?"

"These concepts of rationality, objectivity, or science are new behaviors in humankind's evolution. Most of the time, we act first and find an explanation for our actions later."

Marge opened her eyes wide and shook her head. "I'm not following; what does that have to do with storytelling?"

"A fawn doesn't run from a predator by analyzing statistics and probabilities. When the young creature sees something new, she will look to her mother to find out how to respond to it and remember that response. These patterns we learn are organized in our minds as narratives, metaphors, and symbols. We're set up to use stories as a formula for how we should live, and we live mostly by reacting to the world around us."

"Is this why I zone out when my darling Harry goes on and *on and on* about numbers?"

"Oh, don't give him a hard time. He tries so hard...and does such crucial work." Tom smiled. "We need to teach everyone his craft, the scientific method—the ability to learn and constantly evolve knowledge. To think critically about what surrounds us. But the best way to teach this is through storytelling."

"Mm-hmm, I understand, but frankly, some of these so-called rationalists, the science folks that reject religion and faith, seem to lack empathy and a moral North Star. Seriously, many are nihilistic jerks." Marge scowled.

"Some, yes, but let's not stereotype people—"

"Oh, I didn't mean Harry. We love our geek-in-chief."

"I know, I know. If you want to change someone's mind, story is more powerful than raw data."

The interviewer straightened her shoulders and leaned in toward the camera. "They can also be used to manipulate the masses and fuel cults and dictatorships." Her forehead wrinkled with concern.

"Yes, they can, and they have."

"And with the data provided by the TSkin sensors, you know everything about us—our health, state of mind... We have no privacy." Marge pointed her index finger to the camera. Her long, sparkly nail caught the light and created a tiny rainbow on screen, undermining her intent to be mildly menacing. "Honey, we like you and Harry a lot...I mean, we love you madly, but you are very young, have a lot of power, and it happened fast."

Tom shifted in his seat. It was a fair assessment, one that concerned him *a lot*. "We *only* use that data to create relentlessly relevant and impactful experiences for our travelers and to simulate human behavior in the Underlings."

"So, you're trying to make the Underlings more real?"

"Yes. You see, a body's architecture shapes behavior and intelligence."

"What do you mean?"

"The intelligent octopi have nine brains, eight of them in their arms. Parts of their body can make decisions autonomously without ever using the central brain. They experience the world differently because their intelligence and decision-making are embodied differently."

"So, the way you look affects how you feel and behave. Like when I wear high heels, a corset, glitter, and a big wig, I immediately feel like I can conquer the world."

Tom laughed. "Something like that, yes. Although your ability to move and to breathe may be a little compromised."

"Oh, details, details," she said in a melodic tone. "But, why is this relevant to Underlings?"

"AIs don't have a human body. They're not restricted by our physical architecture. If they're left unconstrained, their intelligence evolves differently from humans. We want the Underlings to simulate us as much as possible, so we are using what we learn from the TSkins' sensors to simulate brains, nervous systems, and body-mind connection in Underlings. For example, stress affects the way they age. And if they break a digital bone, it affects their mood the same way it does in a human being."

"So, you're trying to create digital life?"

"No, not at all. These characters aren't conscious, they simulate feelings and pain, but it's just a simulation. The goal is to provide realistic experiences to travelers. To get as close as possible to the truth of the moment."

"Do you think the bots will ever become alive? Conscious?"

"Harry and I debate this all the time. He thinks we'll get there one day...in, like, twenty years."

"And you? What do you think?" Marge leaned in and narrowed her eyes.

"Hmm, it's not worth talking about it. Harry says it's—it's magical thinking..."

"Magic? I like magic. Go on, Tom, please."

"I think we're all connected. I can't explain why; umm, it's a gut feeling. I sometimes sense things about the people I love, even when they are far away. I know it sounds foolish...but..." Tom recalled the time when he fell to his knees and lost his sight for a few minutes. He'd felt like he'd been hit by a moving train. Half an hour later, his father called him to let him know his mother had passed away.

"I do too. Go on, darling; this is the stuff that makes you come alive in our eyes. We are here to get to know you."

"I believe a part of our so-called consciousness—our soul—sits outside of our bodies, in the ether that connects us with all other living beings."

"Like Plato's anima mundi?"

"Yeah, there are many panpsychist theories out there. And then, inside our bodies, there's another part—the consciousness that comes from the stories we assemble. The narratives we use to post-rationalize our actions and to create some level of forced coherence in everything we do and experience."

"That makes a lot of sense to me. Do you believe in God?"

"I believe we all share a soul and co-create a universal story that is constantly evolving. That when you share an authentic and wholesome story, it goes viral and becomes part of our collective consciousness. Truthful stories are powerful."

"So, we're all just...stories connected to other stories by larger narratives."

"Yeah, there are books, and series, and interconnected story worlds... and fan fiction, and derivative works. A babushka doll of stories inspired by other stories. Ai ai...Harry is going to kill me. He doesn't believe in my cosmic consciousness theory, and now I've managed to lose credibility with the entire scientific community." He chuckled, tousling his hair with his fingers. "Don't worry, folks, Harry runs the platform based on objective, observable evidence. No magical thinking is allowed in Down Below's strategy and operations."

"You complete each other, don't you?"

"Yes, he's my best friend. I trust him with my life."

38

LOVE CASTS A SHADOW

Marge stood straighter. The narrowed eyes, tightened lips, and the small dimple on the right side of her cheek all warned Tom he was about to get roasted.

"Fascinating. Time to get personal, okay, dear?"

He held his breath and cleared a lump in his throat. "I'm-I'm not sure. Let's see what happens..."

"So, I understand Down Below helps people face the bitter truth and deal with their dark sides."

"Yes, but it also helps people look at situations from different perspectives and learn better ways of living."

"What can you tell us about your dark side, Tom? It's only fair we get to know you."

He crossed his arms in front of his chest. "Umm, I guess the people who have known me well tell me different things..."

"Like what?"

"Harry calls me oversensitive, emotional, stubborn, and judgmental, but...I guess...he would." He chuckled. "And...someone else I respect a lot has told me I'm blinded by my privilege."

"You are privileged?"

"Yeah, I had access to the best schools and education, and never had to deal with the problems faced by our minorities or poor folks. The access to resources and the optimism of a carefree childhood left me blind to the baggage others carry."

"Baggage? Like what?"

"I may be less empathetic with those who use outrage and violence to fight injustice, for example."

"I'm not sure if that's true. Your movie shows a great understanding of the plea of the less fortunate."

A script inspired by Nate's social activism and poetry. Tom missed him so much. Over three years had passed since he last saw the poet at the Albertine, but his feelings for his first and only love had not changed.

"I don't know, but I guess...I take the feedback seriously."

Marge still looked unconvinced. "So, what are you doing about this... feedback?"

"I have immersed myself in the shadows of humans. This allows me to at least see the darkness others have faced—their suffering."

He wanted to understand Nate better. To walk in his shoes and be worthy of his love.

"That doesn't sound very healthy," Marge said.

"I feel I need to understand it, his—umm...*the* suffering and rage." *Maybe I'll find a way to heal it.* As he spoke, Marge's eyes blinked with some recognition. His jaw tightened. He was giving away too much.

"Tom?"

"Yes?"

"Do you have someone...special in your life?"

As he shifted in his seat, the chair creaked loudly.

"I've been busy lately..."

"How about that drunk poet that refuses to speak to the media? Some offered him millions, but he doesn't—"

"I'd appreciate it if you leave...people alone." He gnawed on his lower lip. "I get that you need to do due diligence about me. If you send me questions, I'll answer what I can. But please—*please* leave people alone; they don't deserve the constant harassment, and, frankly, won't provide you with any new insights."

Marge leaned in and raised an eyebrow. "I'm surprised you went for such a...turbulent character."

"Enough," he said without raising his voice.

"Oh, dear, I'm sorry. It looks like I went too far." She placed her hands on her face, genuinely ashamed.

He took a moment to calm down, placing his hand on his chest, on top of his medal. He wasn't going to let anyone criticize or harass his Nate because of him. "I accept your apology," he said truthfully. "Unfortunately, I got to go."

Marge's eyes filled with regret. She took a moment before she replied with a warm smile. "You know what? I think you're right."

"About?"

"The magic of a connected cosmos, dear. I can't see you, but I can certainly feel your authenticity and kind soul. Will you come back to speak to us again?"

"I-I don't know…"

"Come back when you can, dear. I promise I'll respect your boundaries. It was lovely chatting with you."

"Thank you for everything you do, Marge. Please keep challenging our work."

39

FACING HIS SHADOW

BUSHWICK COLLECTIVE — BROOKLYN, NY

Nathan listened to Tom's words, his teeth chattering as waves of emotion crashed into his body. He had searched for his love for years—angry, remorseful, and heartbroken, but not until that moment had he realized the impact his parting words had on Tom, and he worried.

Down Below forced people to face the consequences of their dark sides. It was a work of genius, but Nathan knew his ray of sunshine wasn't prepared to face that much evil. No one was, especially not Tom.

Nathan used the platform regularly, *to judge its features and keep the leaders in check*—he often lied to himself. Unlike most people, he was never subject to a painful digital experience. He had wondered why his time down there was always uplifting.

Nathan spent most of the time with a bot that looked much like his younger sister. The child—a digital character clearly designed by Tom—seemed to be programmed to make him feel good, and to give him a hopeful perspective. Hope's quirks and mannerisms brought such depth to the interactions that almost made it feel real. Nathan had to remind himself often that the kid was just a bot.

"I've been thinking…" she often said.

"Thinking deep thoughts?" he had asked as he scanned the park looking for Tom. *Where are you, love? I miss you so very much.*

Hope licked her ice cream, swiping up the melted cream around the edge of the cone before she claimed the chocolate sprinkles at the summit. "We should be able to…like…delete bad people from our brains. They occupy too much space, don't you think?"

He laughed and removed the leftover cream from the tip of her nose. "Who would you purge from your brain?"

"Father… Of course. The memories aren't useful."

He tensed up, recognizing the angst in her voice. He knew it well, that angst. The hurtful recollections, always in the back of his mind—his father's abusive words, the violence, and the contempt. He almost asked what her father did to her, but what was the point of that, she was just an empty bot.

"Memories shape who we are," he said.

"And…umm…maybe they like…stop us from becoming who we want to be?" She took a bite off the empty cone.

He stopped walking and looked at her. "That's deep for an eight-year-old."

"It would be the best revolution, right? A delete button, to erase…you know…" She smiled awkwardly as if she was saying something naughty. "I love you," she said, a hint of anticipation sparked in her eyes.

"I lo—" He pressed his lips together. *This is silly. She's just a bot.* "Yes, the best revolution!" He had smiled.

There was always joy to be had when he visited Hope, even as he craved to confront his shadow as much as he searched for his Tom. Then, one day, he understood he had already suffered the heart-wrenching consequences of his dark side. He didn't need the platform to show him his shadow—what hell could look like; he lived in it.

His strength had always come from his anger against the cause of his suffering, but hating Tom was an impossibility. When the resentment disappeared to uncover an old and enduring love, he found himself hurting a thousand times more than he did before, and that pain was unbearable.

He'd lost the love of his life, and for the last few years, he had struggled with it—life. Bouts of depression had pushed him into isolation and substance abuse. Alone and heartbroken, he'd overdosed on a cocktail of alcohol and pills at least four times in the past six months.

With the suffering came the contrast—the lesson he needed to learn. He knew his shadow well, but now, with no one else to blame but himself, he had to face it, and, alone, he hoped he could conquer it, or die trying.

> Pain of my life—my chain, cocaine—I go insane. This
>   broken heart feeds on your light, you can't depart.
>
> Scared, unprepared, I search for Satan's snakes
>   outside. When the dragon awakes, I fight, and flee,
>   and hide... Terrified. Fearful, tearful, I search for
>   the monster in the wild. It keeps outrunning... I
>   keep succumbing—a foolish child.
>
> Creatures keep coming. I'm forever battling, always

running. Wicked beasts—new and different—so belligerent and cunning. Illiterate and innocent, the crowds fall—small and ignorant, stuck to tradition. Blind faith in dogma and old gospel—militant submission.

The blessed know the secret—the snake is a painful friend. Some are grateful to the test—a faithful dragon returns to offend. Hurtful and hateful, the beasts ascend lest we transcend. Facing the threat, close to death, the heroes rise...in the end.

Scared, prepared, I search for Satan's snakes inside. The devil is within me—my shadow aches—the sin I hide. Hopeful, soulful, I hunt the awful monster in my mind. It keeps outrunning... I keep learning, serving, no longer blind.

Creatures keep coming. I'm forever reacting, adapting, always becoming. Wicked beasts—teachers, preachers—so belligerent and cunning. Dogma, story, ideology—I'll forever re-write. I'll face the trial, erase my bile. And, no longer vile, I'll create, and build, and take flight.

Joy of my life—my royal heart—I'll play my part. This loyal knight will make you smile and bring you light.

"Facing my Shadow," Nathan Storm, 6 August 2030

Where are you, love? Where are you?

40

MIRACLES AND REBELLIOUS STORIES

THE CITY
FIVE YEARS LATER — 29 AUGUST 2035

When Hope first saw him, she thought he was an angel. Back then, she didn't know much about angels, she didn't know much about anything, but she sensed she was meeting someone good, and out of her world, and that made him quite magical. Tom was all that and so much more—*pretty, sooo pretty, and kind, and, like, different from the Lucky Ones.*

Hope had only a vague recollection of her past—the time before she met Tom. The memories of her mother's life and death had faded, there was little left, and she wondered if she ever had a mother. Hope had told him once the memories were too painful—deadly—but she was too young to know what suffering looked like. She said what she had to say, what was expected of her, because that's what children do. They take hints from adults about what's proper and what's not, and they copy acceptable behaviors.

Her reaction to her mother's death was probably too overdramatic, but at the time, it seemed important, more important than Hope's life. She never understood why so many things were more important than her life: a pesky thought that came back often. More often now she was almost fifteen.

Hope hadn't known her mother that well, but she wished she were alive. Her father and brother were never around, and when she saw them, everything was about *them* and *their* problems. Like the rest of the Lucky Ones, they survived and even thrived in a broken world. Unaware of their good fortune, they took a lot, gave back little, and got away with it because that was the unspoken order of all things. Hope knew she was more important than her dog but less important than the Lucky Ones, and it sometimes bothered her—that pesky feeling again.

She was one of the Others, the ones who suffered, but still, she felt lucky. She was the first to speak to him, Tom—the face of God Down Below, and she was sure he loved her, even when he disappeared abruptly in front of her eyes. *Puff, and, like, he was gone, nowhere to be seen.* That's when she knew he wasn't just pretty but also divine. And then he had returned and had saved her again, and she felt special, *so special.* She'd been the first he'd saved, and now he used his miracles to help many Others.

Alone, without the company of the Lucky Ones, they were mostly safe as they climbed the long, dark road in the middle of the night— the Others and her. They made their way to the top of the mountain. It was the only place near the city where they could sometimes see a glimpse of the stars and the moon in between clouds of smog.

The Others usually gathered to hear Hope speak about the God she'd met, and it gave them comfort. Over time, the group grew larger through word of mouth. A handful of people turned into a large gathering of hundreds of people. Hope shared hope through her vivid, over-elaborate, and sometimes slightly enhanced versions of the truth. It didn't matter, as long as it made them feel better. She amused some, while others admired her, and she felt on top of the world in those peaceful nights above the yellow, corrosive clouds. How could anyone judge her for adding a pinch of imagination to a good story? They became so enthralled in her musings they forgot about their sorrows and their pesky feelings.

Things had changed with his reappearance. Tom started spending time with her and the Others, and every minute spent with him was a gift—a gift from God. They always met him at the top of the mountain, and Hope sat by his right side as he told them the truth.

Unlike Hope, he spoke little about himself, and when he did, he blushed, *a lot*. She thought he was cute, *pretty, sooo pretty*. Only once he'd told them he was there to serve and release them from their suffering. That he'd do anything to free the oppressed, and that came at a cost. "It's a terrible story," he had added.

The end of suffering was a topic debated often by the Others. Some thought Tom was referring to the end of pain, others to eternal life. Hope was optimistic he meant both as long as they were good, *like, really good*. In general, it looked like God, the one above, had a plan, and that he cared for the Others as much as Tom did.

Tom didn't speak about himself often. Instead, he took Hope's place as the chief storyteller. He shared many good stories, and they always had a moral lesson about kindness, mercy, generosity, or inclusivity. Still, she already knew all that, they all did, so they preferred when he told them about sad princes and prickly roses from strangely named planets, dead poets, and monsters, *especially monsters*.

That night, at the end of his tale about a little prince, he said, "You need to be careful with stories. Some are sticky; they stay with you, and they make decisions for you. You don't even notice when you act them out in your life."

"Like asking a prince to tame you?" Hope said.

He nodded and added, "Or a snake to bite you. Sticky stories run our lives, and they are contagious."

Hope threw her hands up, accepting the pre-written fate. "What shall we do? Pray?"

"Pray?"

He was always surprised by the obvious things she said. It frustrated her, but she smiled back at the pretty giant. *Pretty, sooo pretty...*

She clarified. "Pray to God. Ask you— Him to...like...create better stories." *Obviously.*

He seemed upset by her comment, hiding his face in between his arms. Then he lifted his head and stared at January, the blind woman with the acid-burned eyes—a sour gift from her lucky husband. There was a glimpse of tears in his eyes, and she scooted over to sit closer to him on the thin, scorched grass—a little hill raised above the crowd. She touched his shoulder with her head.

"I'm sorry, Tom."

"Shadow, I'm Shadow." He shuddered. "Tom is... Never mind."

"Huh? I didn't mean to criticize your...our stories. It's just difficult, sometimes..."

"I know, Red. I know. You should create your own tales and reimagine the ones you have."

"What's the point when someone else is in charge, and there's a... pecking order? It's best to beg...to pray, right?"

"Gods are flawed, Red. Sometimes, they lack creativity... They may need a little help. You see?" he said, his eyes still on January. He seemed to be having some internal struggle. His brows furrowed, but Hope knew she wasn't their target.

"Do it, Sibyl!" he roared, and then he continued to ruminate as he often did.

Hope pressed on. "We can't just...like...change our own stories. There's the other God, and you, and the Lucky Ones, and umm, the sticky stories that run our lives."

"Don't call them lucky, Red. Call them privileged; that's what they are. You see? It needs to feel uncomfortable for them. Their luck comes at an unacceptable cost."

"Does it matter? We can't really change any of that. Who's lucky...*privileged*, and our pre-written stories."

"There's a secret to stories, Red." He spoke quietly, leaning forward and opening his eyes wide.

"What's that?" Hope asked as they all leaned in.

"The trick is to imagine stories that are true." He smiled, and he cried, and it was a pretty mess. *So pretty...*

"If they are imagined, how can they be true?" January said. The first time she had spoken since the "accident."

Tom got up and then kneeled by January's side and held her hand. "Ingenious stories that increase the life and wellbeing of all liv— umm, beings. Those are true stories—the type of sticky stories we need. Better stories. Rebellious stories."

"Rebellious against God and the way things are?" January asked.

"*Yes.* Stories that challenge outdated laws, inequality, and injustice— fairer stories full of life, as opposed to death, you see? New, coherent explanations to old questions—bold, fresh, insurgent."

"And he, you...will listen to our stories?" Hope asked as she watched the blind young woman squeeze his hand tightly.

"To your truthful prayers? Yes, of course. We look for great turn- around stories that bring luck to the oppressed and the dispossessed and the sick. A stroke of luck deliberately designed into a sticky story that is truthful. You see, Red?" He spoke brightly, but his eyes told a different story.

"To give luck to the Others," Hope murmured.

"To *all* others. Your stories co-design your world and higher up."

"We co-design heaven?" asked someone at the back.

"Yes, you co-design that too; we all do, with our stories." Tom raised his head, trying to find the voice in the dark. "Sib—umm... The—the spirit of God is listening and learning."

"Is it not perfect already? Heaven?" asked the same voice.

Tom dropped his head. "I dearly wish to keep my poet happy and alive," he mumbled sadly. "And I need a better story."

"Unlucky poets?" someone asked, but Tom was too distracted with one of his silent internal battles.

Heat rose to Hope's scrunched-up face—a pesky feeling. "His poet, my brother, is very lucky...privileged. Very privileged," she murmured. He visited her often, but he never paid any attention to her. She felt compelled to go out of her way to make him feel loved and important and needed and... Hope rolled her eyes. She listened to his angry rhymes, and she even made him laugh, once, which was *very* hard to do. In return, he treated her like a cute pet, ignoring most of what she had to say, always looking for something else, someone else. Only recently she'd realized whom he was searching for. She couldn't complain. Compared to others, her Lucky Ones were not so bad. Even her dear father, who stopped by every six months to beat the living daylights out of her, never left a scar, and he was always remorseful when he left. Once, he even said sorry. In fourteen years, she'd suffered a broken arm, and some bruises, so she was very lucky for an Other. Very lucky.

Tom screamed, "Sibyl, stop fighting me. I accept the odds and consequences. Do it. *Just do it*. It's an order."

They all stared at him, until January screamed, placing her hands on her freshly scarred face. Then they stared at her. First, Hope thought she was in pain, but then came the giggling-crying melody of a happy surprise, followed by a burst of joyful laughter. January's hands dropped, and her radiant green eyes and flawless features emerged from behind them.

January saw the world again, and as she stood up, she said she didn't like the world she saw. She scanned the crowd, with her bright, hopeful eyes, and said that the Others' eyes deserved better and that she was going to find a new story, a truthful story. She hugged Tom, and as she left, his smile faded with some memory.

"You okay, Tom?" Hope asked, but he was out of words, and out of hope, and she didn't get it. How could someone with such magic be so gloomy?

"Shadow. My name is Shadow," he whispered with a broken voice.

Lifting the open palm of his hand, he waved goodbye, and he disappeared. *Puff, and, like, he was gone, nowhere to be seen.*

When Hope first saw him, she thought he was an angel, someone good, and out of her world, and that made him quite magical. Later she understood, he was God's face Down Below, and that his many miracles had some cost. She felt lucky, and so did the Others. She was no longer the only storyteller. Many wanted to share the stage, a way to address those pesky feelings about the privileged. She didn't mind. She'd been the first.

THE Present

41

LEO THE SECOND

THE BOTANIC GARDENS
DAY 1 — 9:50 PM

"*Don't hurt Thorn!*" Shadow repeated for the fifth time, irking Stella a bit more each time. His head peeked out from her right shoulder, and he shouted his panic way too close to her ear.

"I'm not deaf...yet." She knocked his head lightly with her helmet.

"Sorry, my eardrums are..."

"Where's your helmet? This is going to be *extra* painful." She tapped on one of the multiple-barrel machine guns.

She was happy with her wheel choice as they cruised relatively smoothly toward the demons over badly damaged wet grass, still fuming here and there. The bike was a little too small for both of them. She didn't account for the gloomy God's long legs, knees constantly bumping against her bony elbows as she swerved fast.

Ahead, the horned warrior shouted, "Get him! Like, get him now!" A child-like moan reeking of madness.

Stella giggled. "*Like, get him now?*" She mocked, all pitchy.

Shadow gasped in Stella's ear, and it sounded even worse than all the loud moaning. "That... That's not a soulless," his voice broke a little. "That—that voice..."

The demons growled and howled and shrieked. Dead eyes, and dirty, distorted mouths, all teeth and fury. She veered the bike to the right; its handling hard and heavy.

"Where we going!?" Shadow shouted. Again. "It's *that* way." He was probably pointing at the center of the lawn, where the horned teen held Thorn.

"Flank attack," Stella said without looking back. "Never fear! My grandma taught me military strategy."

"I see..." He clearly didn't. As the spray of bullets hosed down on the demons, he stuttered. "A—are you sure th—they are soulless? Sibyl?"

The guns burned holes in the creatures, and they dropped like flies— twenty, thirty, fifty—at least that many. Some still crawled over one another, fuming and bleeding and fighting each other, all bad and increasingly mad as they screeched and rolled on the ground. *Too easy.*

"Course they are. Dead eyes, now *dead* dead," Stella said.

Wasteful with her finite ammo, she fired again. *Raa*-ka *ta*-ka *ta*-ka *taaa! Whatever!* She preferred the guns' rattling to his constant whining. Another twenty dead.

As the demons continued to drop over each other, and the grass clumps turned crimson, she swerved the bike to the left, avoiding all the bodies and heading toward Thorn.

"Keep the guns away from Thorn," said the broken record.

To their right, the rest of the demon army divided into three groups, with no more than twenty creatures each. The first dispersed toward the small forest to the right, the second closed in around the horned warrior, and the third continued to move forward toward the motor-bike, swords in hand. Despite the deadly danger, none pulled out the bows still strapped to their backs.

Unable to turn the machine gun ninety degrees to shoot, Stella retreated into a long loop with demons on their tail.

"Sibyl! Are they truly soulless?" Shadow repeated. "No pain? No emotion?"

After a few beats, zie finally spoke. *All but one, my heart.*

"The funny girl with the horns?" Stella asked as they circled around the Domizien chasing them to approach the wall of demons guarding Thorn and the horned warrior.

Yes, my star, zie said.

Whoa! Twist spoke inside their heads. *From what I can see from the data patterns, something seems to synch their actions and behavior. The demon mob is acting as a single organism, except for the girl, who might be controlling them, somehow.*

"Her emotions must be guiding their empty souls," Shadow said. "Phineas Gage! Remember, Harry? We discussed this. Without emotions, the soulless can't self-regulate or make decisions effectively...so they're drawn to her."

The Somatic marker hypothesis... Twist said, sounding hesitant. *It'd be a natural evolution—tapping into a strong external emotional signal to reduce decision-making deficits.*

Stella laughed. "What evolution, dum-dum? She's getting them all killed."

Twist sighed, *Stella, let me explain—*

"Oh ship, ship, shiiippp!" Distracted by all the patronizing yammering inside her head, Stella took a moment to figure out she couldn't fire on the creatures ahead without risking Thorn's life. She glanced back at the demons closing in. *This is no good.* She took a right, gunning down the edges of the group to make way for their escape. *Raa-ka ta-ka ta-ka taaa!* "António Damásio's work?" The zombies fell to their knees. "That emotions play a central role in social cognition and decision-making? I wrote a thesis about it in sixth grade," she bragged even as she monitored their increasingly narrow escape route. "He got some things right... Shiiippp!" Instead of backing off, the horned warrior and her remaining ten goons moved forward.

Twist went dead silent for a while, probably absorbing three lost decades of scientific advancements, attempting to catch up with her brilliance. He cleared his throat. *We modified their amygdala and frontal cortex based on the information we had at that time. Anyway, minor errors aren't catastrophic. The mutation of the NTRK1 gene ensures they suffer no pain.*

"No pain. Right, Harry?" Shadow asked, fearfully.

"Maintaining truth and coherence with Up Above's biology at all costs. Too smart, Twist," Stella sneered, scanning the stinking monsters running toward them left and right. "Unwashed rags for clothes, matted hair, and ghastly open wounds all over their bodies. Robbing them of their stories, emotions, ability to feel physical pain, and blessing them with cognitive disability, psychopathic traits, and lack of forethought. Am I getting the definition of soulless right, Twist?"

"We didn't have a choice," whispered the suicidal God.

"Oh, I know all about your choices. Anywayyy... They'll be dead soon." Stella tapped on the gun. "This is how four thousand of your people defeated umNtwana Ziwedu kaMpande's fifteen thousand amaZulu."

"My people?" Shadow sounded offended.

"Bibi's favorite bedtime story. A reminder that controlling the technology is always the best strategy. Your strategy, right, Twist?" And before Shadow got the chance to preach at her—as she knew he would—she swerved harshly to the left to face the demons in front of Thorn and the mad girl and fired again. She had no choice. They were surrounded. Some demons in front dropped, and so did the mad girl's horse.

"Stop it, Stella!" Shadow screamed, and the scars cutting the skies told her exactly how he felt.

Thunder, then lightning, then rain and then...*then* a thin transparent veil of a psychedelic pixilated wood staircase flashed as an apparition, gone in a split of a second. *Holy ship!* She recognized her physics-bending creation. Why was her Gravizien tree-house flashing above the Botanic Gardens' lawn?

What was that? Twist asked. His voice tight as if he'd seen a ghost.

"Sibyl, what's happening?" Stella asked.

Shadow's stress is my stress, my star. His pain, my pain. Sibyl's voice trembled. Zie sounded a little distant and overwhelmed. *My worlds collapse over each other...*

"Juxtaposition?" Stella asked, wondering if Twist could hear their conversation.

"Shadow, stop stressing, or more demons will come!" Stella scowled, launching her elbow backward into his ribcage. She deflected their attention from the apparition. "According to your theory, if we kill the girl, the Domizien will stop the coordinated attack." She looked back to count the monsters chasing them. Fifteen creatures, tops. "Let's finish this."

"No!" Unexpectedly, Shadow reached over her and grabbed her hands, scrambling for control over the bike and veering to the right and then left until they crashed into a pile of dead bodies.

"What you doing?" She went down with the bike, her leg caught between the engine and a dead demon, while his body was projected forward somewhere. "Leo the second!" she cursed, and she never, ever cursed. The dead Domizien's stench almost made her puke as she pushed the motorbike away from her. "I could have ended this. For once accept the collateral damage, or we all die. Your empathy is a curse."

Tom. Tom! You okay, bud? Twist asked.

She raised her head to look for Shadow. He'd landed by the legs of the warrior's dead horse. Thorn's body—hands and ankles tied—just a step or two away.

"Thorn! Thorn! You alive?" he called as he stumbled to his feet. He kneeled down next to her, patting her bruised face and then working to untie her hands. "Stay with me, prick."

On the other side of the horse, the mad warrior pushed and pulled dead bodies as if looking for something. A sword, Stella guessed, and she grabbed the Ngulu off the ground before she sprinted in their direction.

Stella and Twist shouted simultaneously. "Shadow! Move!" *Get out of there, bud. She's coming for you!*

"Let me guess...friend," Thorn said, opening her eyes and rubbing her wrists as Shadow worked on the ropes around her legs. "You came to save me."

He chuckled, as if he were in on some inside joke, and Stella envied the sweet complicity between the ex-lovers. "Selective memory, prick?" Shadow said. "I saved you before, but who's counting," he shrugged.

"I am—counting." Thorn ran her fingers over her bruised face. "Frack, it hurts."

Tom, Twist warned as Thorn reached for a fallen sword and caught the mad girl's blade just before it chopped off Shadow's arm.

"So glad *you* came to save *me,*" Thorn said, and, with both her feet still tied, she kicked into the warrior's chest plate, making the creature stumble backward, trip on a demon's body, and fall on her back. Thorn proceeded to cut the ropes around her ankles. "Wrath, don't do this," she warned. "I don't wanna hurt you."

Wrath screamed—an intense, angry, and somehow devastating howl. "Traitor!" She jumped to her feet over the pile of dead creatures, and launched at Thorn. An attack worthy of the girl's name.

For a moment, Stella had to take her eyes away from Shadow and Thorn as she reached a handful of demons standing between her and the others. She couldn't die Down Below, but pain here was as real as Up Above. She adjusted her helmet and glanced at the Ngulu, doubting her weapon of choice. The sacrificial beheading sword of her ancestors wasn't exactly a combat weapon, its utilitarian value compromised in the service of more important symbols—power, prestige, and terror. The only language Domizien understood. Subconscious signals, more useful than the functional effectiveness of one sword. She took a breath and half-committed to her decision, scooping up a fallen sword with her left hand while raising the Ngulu with her right. "Heads off!" she screamed.

The Domizien closed in on her, swords and daggers poised. She launched forward, her sword piercing a demon's heart, and reminding her of one of those cultured meat shish kebabs she used to devour after class. *Yum.* She swung the Ngulu to her right, decapitating not one but two creatures and using the momentum to spin-kick a fourth demon, knocking it out. She ducked, a sword missing her neck by a whisker before she shish kebabbed the last demon and took off toward Shadow.

Thorn was a superb swords woman, rebuffing Wrath's over-committed blows with dazzling rapidity. Once, twice, Thorn could have killed her. In all her madness, Wrath kept raging and waging too far and losing balance. Still, the creature quickly sussed Thorn's defensive strategy, and, no longer fearful of repercussions, she launched past Thorn toward Shadow. The athlete's tiny body was a weak barrier against the aggressive bean pole's armor.

Shadow didn't move or respond to his friend's over-animated requests.

Tom! What you doin'? Twist screamed. *Run! You expecting her to engage in polite conversation?*

He seemed paralyzed as he watched the horned creature. Shock or fear or something stopped him from moving.

Tom! Move!

He didn't, and Stella jumped over the horned warrior just as the girl launched at Shadow. They rolled on the ground; Wrath scrambling for the sword as Stella grabbed her by the horns and lifted the Ngulu preparing to strike.

Thorn, get Tom out of there, Twist said. *Thorn, where you going? Stella doesn't need help.*

And before Stella could react, Thorn had kicked the Ngulu off her hand, pulling her by the helmet until she fell backward.

"What are you doing? I just saved your life," Stella said, jumping to her feet.

"Ahhh! You too, preppy?" Thorn mocked as Wrath made a run toward Shadow.

Bud! Seriously. Don't make me use a miracle to destroy that mad cow.

And somehow, Twist finally got Shadow to run away from Wrath.

42

UNFORTUNATE MIRACLES

DAY 1 — 10:35 PM

T wist held his breath as he monitored Tom's every move. Simultaneously, he ran through decades of Spiral Worlds' development searching for clues that explained the Domizien's strange behavior.

"Who's the girl?" he asked Sibyl.

"That's classified, father."

"Classified? What do you mean? I'm God!"

The clash of swords was resounding through the field. Stella and Thorn jumped hither and thither, striking wildly, each too invested on their offensive to care about a sprinting Tom who dodged demons as if he were a princely quarterback... *No, not football, basketball!* Unconsciously, Tom seemed to dribble an imaginary ball. Twist sighed. *Whatever it takes, bud.*

"You're God, but so is Stella, and she made it classified," zie finally said, the right corner of zir mouth twisting up.

"Stella!" Twist called, but Stella was too distracted with Thorn to reply.

Any time between the clangs was spent prancing and posturing—an unnecessary flick of a silver braid over the shoulder, a puff of a cigar, and an endless acrobatic showcase of useless spins and kicks and sexy pouts. Twist rolled his eyes.

"Is Stella responsible for Wrath?" Twist asked directly.

"Shadow is," Sibyl said, a mournful tone in zir voice.

Thorn followed up a blow with a lunge that got past Stella's defense, but her shorter reach failed to drive the steel home. Still, she pricked the Goddess one-inch deep near the belly button, enough to make the girl twitch and screech like a demon.

"Fun," Thorn said. "I've always wanted a dolly gal for pin cushion."

Stella fought now like a human whip, thrashing around hard and wide, and every sweep of her sword would have severed Thorn in two, if she had caught her. Thorn fluttered round her, small and nimble and cocky.

"Stella, forget her. Tom won't escape for long," Twist said.

Again and again the demons closed upon Tom, and again and again he took his imaginary basketball and dribbled it into a clear space. He zigzagged fast, dancing feet barely touching the ground, changing direction sharply and unpredictably.

"What is he doing?" Stella gasped, her hand over the bleeding wound on her stomach.

"He made varsity," Twist said.

"He made what?"

"Never mind, just help him," Twist said, monitoring the band of demons emerging from the trees in their direction. Behind Tom, Wrath pulled a dagger off her boot and aimed it at him.

"Miracle!" Twist screamed. "Miracle!" he repeated, and the dagger dropped to the ground, just as he realized what he'd done. *Fuck!*

"So logical, father." Sibyl smirked. "Why not wait until he's dead and bring him back later, when this is all over?"

Twist shook his head, punishing himself for letting emotion overrule his actions.

"She wasn't going to kill him; she was aiming for his leg," Sibyl said soberly. "Death is not her goal, never-ending pain is."

Suddenly Tom was face to face with Wrath. Twenty demons moved forward and formed a ring around them. For a beat or two, they stared at one another, Tom shuddering slightly at Wrath's mad sneer.

"Stella, who is she?" Twist asked just as he noticed the return of the apparition of the twisty staircase. The structure, made of wood and leafy at the top, emerged near the spot where Tom and Wrath faced each other, crushing a couple of demons as it materialized right where they stood. Tom sprinted up the stairs, and then down the stairs up side down. *What the heck?*

"How the hell would I know who the mad girl is?" Stella's spin-kick missed Thorn's head by a whisker. The other ducked into a low sweep and mowed down her leg. Elbows landed first, still failing to prevent her back from slamming into the gravel unearthed by the bike.

"Your...first miracle... Remember?" Sibyl said.

"Oooh, I see. Can we talk about this later?" Still on the ground, Stella gasped for air.

"The hyena ate dirt!" Thorn laughed, making a run for the bike.

Stella rolled backward to her feet, dropped the helmet on the ground, and cartwheeled forward, feet smashing into the athlete's back.

"At least I don't hide my head in the sand like an ostrich," Stella sneered as Thorn face-planted on a patch of grass. "What's with the Stockholm syndrome? I just saved your life. The life I gave you." She placed her hands on her hips and lifted her chest. All mighty, and godly, and sexy. *A young peacock,* all showy and lacking the dignity of Twist's best friend, who continued to strut up and down the trippy staircase with Wrath on his tail.

Thorn spat out dirt and sprinted toward the bike. "Cute, but no." She stopped for a moment, staring at Stella—spicy eyes and mild amusement in the curve of her bruised lips. "Just a puppet, unaware of her strings. The weakest of them all. Go back to the pageant circuit, doll."

Not quite knowing what to do with herself, Stella arranged one of her braids, an unfamiliar awkwardness taking over her posture. It was the first time Twist saw some self-consciousness in the cocky kid. "Why are you protecting that...that horned creature?" Stella asked while she glanced at Tom, who was being dragged down an upside-down flight of stairs as Wrath got ahold of his foot.

Thorn pushed on the motorbike's wheel, trying to stand it up, but the machine was too heavy for the small Latina. "We need to get him out of here, or she'll torture him to death...slowly." She kicked the machine guns several times until both dropped to the ground.

"Stockholm! Have you been?" Stella asked, racing toward Thorn.

Thorn jumped on the bike. "Hell yeah! Horses are soooo overrated."

"Don't you resent him?" Stella asked.

Vroom! Vroom! "All the fracking time!" Thorn departed toward Shadow and the horned warrior.

"Stella! Who's Wrath?" Twist asked.

"Umm... I guess she may be the Underling I brought back to life..." She flicked her braid.

"You wasted a miracle?"

"Who are you to talk?!" Stella sprinted toward the action. "I wanted to make Shadow happy. It was a surprise. A gift, really! He'd lost all hope after what he did to her. So I wanted to restore—"

"*Stella...*" Tom wailed, and he stopped. Stopped running. Stopped fighting. Stopped talking. He turned to face Wrath.

"Who's the girl, Sibyl?" Twist asked. "And what— How— Where is that staircase coming from and why is it defying the laws of gravity?"

"Keep your fingers crossed. It might defy more than that." Sibyl's laughter filled the lab, bouncing around inexistent walls and returning every single time to where Twist stood, slapping him in the face.

43

LIE IN IT

THE BOTANIC GARDENS
DAY I — II:I9 PM

Everything was happening in slow motion. Shadow had a revelation, but he couldn't remember what it was. Searching his memory—all fog and darkness and confusion—he failed to find the answers. He was running from his shadow. He knew that much, and nothing else.

He lay on the stairs, the horned creature standing over him, gritted teeth shaded by a steel mask. A loose lock of hair—wild as fire—hanging by the corner of a rageful mouth. It meant something, *but what? What?* He shook his head.

Above them, the ground and the demons—more sores than skin—chasing him up and down the maze of stairs. Wrath screamed high and loud, in it pain, and pain, and so much pain. He felt it all. She might as well be juicing his heart with her fingers. Then came the growl of betrayal and the screech of hatred. She lifted her sword, blade pointing down, which, in fact, was up.

Harry screamed inside Shadow's head while a motor rumbled above him. Soon after, Thorn joined the chorus, but, unlike the others, she wasn't shouting at him. She wasn't fearful for him.

"Wrath. Stop!" Thorn pulled over by the side of the structure. "He made you a victim. Don't let him turn you into a villain."

All true. He did all that, but Thorn wasn't talking about herself. Or was she? There was something he knew, something important... He couldn't remember what it was.

Wrath's blade pierced his shoulder, and then his leg, and then swiped across an arm and then a leg. No blood, no pain, no severed limbs falling upwards. Probably a miracle, but his friends would soon run out of those.

Wrath howled, madness taking over. She raised her sword and struck his chest, again, and again, and again, piercing and slashing frantically, vengefully. Intact skin even as the blade cut through his heart. He closed his eyes, finding shelter from all the madness—his friends' screams, the girl's wails, and the laws of life and physics all crumbling around him. *Breathe. Just breathe.* And, as he retreated into darkness, he felt himself falling, and gravity returned to a park with no staircases, but still packed with the monsters he'd designed, flies laying eggs in the corners of their eyes. He landed on top of a pile of dead Domizien; their stench overwhelming all his senses.

"*Wrath, leave,*" Thorn said, still on the motorbike. "The passage between the worlds is closing."

Tom, Stella, good news, Harry said. *Some demons are running toward the chasm, disoriented and screeching madly. My guess is they can't stay in the upper worlds for long. The values framework that keeps them from coming up is forcing them back down.*

Wrath jumped to her feet and lunged at him with her sword poised. Piercing his shoulder, she pinned him to the ground, and this time, the pain was unbearable. Skin and flesh tearing and drowning in blood. Thorn jumped on Wrath, wrapping her legs around the plated waist and her arm around the girl's neck. They both fell backward, the blade cutting him on the way out.

More screams—his and everyone else's. His head collapsed to one side as weakness and pain took over his entire body. Slightly delirious, he heard a voice—the only voice he wanted to hear.

"Tom," cried Nate.

Shadow turned his head to smile at the beloved hallucination.

Nate and all his people marched together toward him, just as Wrath retreated with the Domizien, outnumbered and probably spooked by all the miracles.

Tom, hang in there, buddy, Harry said. *I'm looking at a fast extraction plan.*

I'm not going anywhere, Shadow said. Too weak to say anything else.

You must.

As Shadow slowly got up, Stella and Thorn stood by him, swords in hand. His every move was an act of torture, blood gushing from the nasty gash.

"Love!" Nate screamed, but his companions held him by the arms as he tried to escape their grip. And that's when January ran toward Wrath, empty hands high up, both open.

"Remember me, honey?" Jan asked tentatively. "It's me, January. Much older, but still your friend. I still have my eyes, but I'm no longer blind to God's crimes."

Wrath wailed, all pain, and with a single hand gesture she drew Jan closer as the Domizien formed a wall in front of Jan and Wrath.

Jan stood there, without fear, whispering words in Wrath's ear. Her lips almost touching the horned helmet.

"Jan, don't do this." Nate attempted to release himself from the other men's grip. "Tom, are you okay?"

"I'm going to kill you." Stella stood tall and menacing, preparing to attack the demons. Then she glanced at Thorn. "Are you with me this time, or do I need to kill you first? Would be nice if you picked a side and stuck with it."

"Stella, wait," Shadow said, his eyes set on Nate's bloodied face. "Something's not right."

"Ahhh frack!" Thorn said, as if she was predicting what was about to happen. "Did you say something about switching sides, preppy?" Then she bumped Shadow's stomach with the back of her hand and murmured, "What's coming next won't need my sword. Over to you, friend. Do your thing."

"What?" he asked confused.

"I don't know," she shrugged. "All the words, and the brooding, and smiles, and apologies, and magic...and...stuff."

Jan waved to her people, and they all started marching toward the dark void between worlds.

"What are you doing?" Shadow screamed. His legs shook, weakened by blood loss.

January now stood by the Domizien, scowling at him. "I waited decades for you. Prayed for you. Imagined better stories and shouted them to the skies. We suffered for you...and you come back to tell us you're hopeless? That you're out of miracles?"

"Jan, don't do this." Shadow's eyes followed Nate as they dragged him in the direction of the abyss.

"Stop talking," Jan said. "We suffer and you silence his voice while you drown in your own self-pity."

"*Sibyl!*" Shadow screamed to the skies, cursing the universe.

You took his voice—their voice—my heart. This is not my doing.

Something inside him snapped. He let his anger toward zir fill his heart until he could feel the acrid taste of it in his mouth. "*Sibyl!*" he shouted again, and this time he got to zir—a glitch cut reality in half as pixelated noise traveled across the skies, distorting everything in its path. He lifted his hand toward Nate and the Plurizien. "*Stop!*" Shadow shouted, commanding, and a mild earthquake rumbled under their feet.

Fearful and out of balance the Plurizien stopped marching. Some dropped to their knees, praying.

"Jan," Shadow called. "Don't do this, I was having a bad day... I'm s—"

Unfazed by his power, Jan placed her hands on her hips and screamed in defiance, "You don't get to have bad days!" She spat her sing-song words. "Weak Gods, old power structures."

"*Systems of oppression, fucked up cultures,*" the Plurizien chanted with her, some rising to their feet, overcoming their panic to stand with her.

"Please, let's go back to the Commune!" Shadow said. "It's dangerous here."

They responded in unison. "Lambs sacrificed by our divine mother-fuckers. Feeding our flesh, our distress, to the vultures."

"*Enrage! Engage! Enrage!*" they sang, joined by Thorn, who raised her fist in the air. "*Engage! Enrage! Engage!*"

"Sorry...can't help it," Thorn said, shrugging.

"We're leaving for Ordiz and we are taking Nate with us," Jan said.

"Take me instead." His legs finally gave up, and he fell to his knees. Deep inside, his frustration turned into a storm—a tsunami waiting to burst out. Fearful of hurting his people, he held it all back, but it stirred.

"And if you don't fix the worlds," Jan warned, "I will personally deliver him to Wrath to be tortured to death. That's the deal I made with her."

Lightning struck between the Plurizien and the void. A man's top caught on fire, others rushing to help him before any major harm was done.

Still on all fours, Shadow tried to contain his panic. He took a breath and looked up. "Jan, please."

"You have five days," Jan said. "That should be long enough for you to design our freedom."

"Five days!" Stella repeated. *Sibyl, you're so predictable.*

No, my star. I predict, Sibyl said.

Predict what? Shadow asked, and the skies lit up with deadly electric sparks, charged-up pixels falling like rain, extinguishing half way down toward the ground.

Never mind, Stella said.

Farther away, Nate looked back. "Don't come for me, Tom."

Shadow lifted his hands off the ground and sat back on his heels, looking at Jan. "You wouldn't hurt him."

"I'd take a bullet for my friend. You know this. But it's not me you love, and it's not me she wants to hurt." She pointed at Wrath who made her way to the void. January dropped her head as she shouted, "A solution—evolution—or Storm's execution."

Her people chanted. "Evolution—a solution—the end of persecution."

"That's what you get when you try to silence the people's revolution," Thorn murmured, helping him to his feet. "What the hell were you thinking?"

He could have explained he did it to protect Nate from Harry—to save Nate's life and her life—but what was the point of that? "I need you by my side—to help me think," he said instead as he leaned on her to stand up.

"Put pressure on the wound or you'll bleed to death." She placed his hand over the gash, and he almost went down again.

Sibyl, find a way to get him out of there, Harry ordered.

Want me to use your last miracle for that, dad? Sibyl asked, all sassy.

No. Shadow said, looking ahead. Most of the demons had disappeared into the void, only Wrath and a few others remained by the worlds' portal. He took a breath and started walking toward Nate. Thorn kept him on his feet every time he stumbled. "Thank you, my friend. My hero," he said. Then he looked back, noticing Stella and Jan walking behind him. "Stella, stay back." His assertiveness took the girl by surprise, wide eyes followed by a sigh and then a sullen pout.

Stella stopped following him. "I'm the hero. The only one here trying to protect you," she murmured her disappointment. "Stop messing about and lead from the front."

"The kid has a point," Thorn said, and Stella replied with a long, *long* laundry list of reasons why she wasn't a kid.

Leadership—they were looking to him for it. He'd let them all down, even so, divided, they waited for him to lead. The heart was the fuel and the glue, and whether or not he liked it, he was Spiral Worlds' heart. Purpose, values, emotions bringing people together to drive change. In his youth, he had leaped at the opportunity to inspire a progressive movement. Decades later, battered and bruised by life and death, they resurrected him to save the worlds—the wrong story. A story doomed to fail. To keep the Underlings subdued, Sibyl had turned his life into a trope—the chosen one. But, he was no longer playing zir games. He was going to rewrite the story and if he had to choose a helpful, hopeful trope, he'd pick *found family*. He would reunite with his friends and then, together, they'd save the worlds. As he considered all options, he knew only he could lead, for now. By his side, he had the most overqualified group of overachievers—his family. All outstanding in their own fields; all with little in common; some forever divided by irreconcilable differences.

As Shadow reached Nate and the Plurizien, the men around his poet took a step back, releasing Nate's arms. Shadow attempted to hide the extent of his injury, blinking a smile at Nate.

"You're bleeding heavily," Nate said. His voice broken.

"Shhh." Shadow cupped Nate's head with both hands and leaned in until their foreheads touched. "Listen to me. Just listen." Shadow's fingers grazed Nate's hair, and the poet's body softened, shivering ever so slightly. "*You* are not your worst moments. Whatever happened that day. The harm you caused... I'm not going to let it define you, and neither are you."

"Tom, I'm a murderer." Guilt coated Nate's every word. "There's no redemption for what I did."

Shadow stared into Nate's eyes, holding his anxious burning gaze. "You are Nathan Storm, and you and I are going to work together to fix the worlds, and save lives, and eliminate suffering, and don't try to fight me on this. Don't push me away. I can't do it without you. Do you understand?"

"Tom, I can't," Nate whispered.

"I'm sorry I tried to silence you. Use your voice. Do what you do best. I trust your judgment."

"You do?" Nate's voice vibrated. His insecurity out in the open.

"I believe in you, Nathan Storm." And as he gave Nate what he'd granted to all Earthlings—hope and a second chance—he was grateful for someone else's silence, knowing fully well he was hurting Harry.

Nate whispered, "Tom, Sibyl predicts—"

The skies roared. "I don't care about Sibyl's hot takes," Shadow said definitively, "and neither should you. Zie doesn't create the future, *we do*." He looked back at Jan and took her hand into his, just as he placed his arm around Nate's shoulders. Pain spiked from his injured shoulder up his neck, and into his skull, almost knocking him out. He shook it off. "I can't create the future on my own, Jan. I need Nate, and Harry, and Thorn, and Stella, and you, and your people. I wasn't ignoring your plea; I was learning from my mistakes. You don't need to blackmail me and hurt the man who's been fighting for all of you."

Jan looked at Wrath intensely and shook her head. This time a clear *no* rather than her usual vague head wobble. "I made a pact and I'll keep it," Jan said, never looking into his eyes. "Stay alive and design our freedom, or my dearest friend will die the most horrible of deaths."

"Jan, even when I died, I never gave up on you. I was trying to improve things," he said. He glanced at Thorn, who nodded, confirming his statement. "I can tell you all about it, in time. Don't do this. I've never abandoned you, and *I never will*."

January looked into his eyes, her gaze filled with fear, and love, and disappointment. Then her eyes landed on Wrath and projected wrath. "That's not true, is it?" And his heart dropped to his feet. There was something he knew. Something he struggled to surface. How could he lead? He shouldn't lead. His mind attacked him—mad and overwhelmed and self-destructive. Years of punishing contrast under his skin, no bleach strong enough to cleanse it.

"You have betrayed us and can't be trusted," she said, taking his hand to her mouth and kissing it. "Nate and I will be in Ordiz. He'll be monitored day and night. He will never be alone. Your love will be safe from our people and from yours." She blinked her reassurance with her bright almond-shaped eyes, tilting her head from side to side, even as she threatened the life of her closest friend. "For five days, everyone will cherish him there as we did here. If you need us, you know where to find us. We will work with you as long as you do our bidding." And with that statement, the Plurizien started marching, two men holding Nate's arms and dragging him away from Shadow.

"Tom, I love you," Nate said. "Keep away." Then, he looked at Thorn, distraught, and he murmured, "Don't you fucking hurt him."

"I love you, Stormy," Shadow replied holding a tsunami inside, knowing fully well it was a killer storm. *He's safe for now,* he reassured himself, but he wouldn't let Nate go like that. He sprinted into his arms, wrapping himself around Nate's shoulders, ignoring the pain and the blood and the numbness taking over his body. His poet yanked his arms from the Underlings, and pulled him closer, his hungry lips parting in anticipation, never daring to make the first move. Shadow brushed his lips against Nate's lower lip, the poet's beard grazing his skin and sending shivers down his spine. Then he went deeper, and Nate drew him in, claiming his mouth—urgent and intense—even as the Underlings grabbed him by the arms and took him away. Shadow's fingers caressed a strand of long flaming hair as it left his hand.

Shadow stood there, breathing heavily, watching them leave.

"Storm's voice is a weapon," Stella said. "We can't let them take him."

They don't know it, Harry said, *but it's likely the platform is nudging them down the spiral. Everything they've been doing lately stinks of Ordizien dogma and self-righteousness.*

Shadow nodded. Harry's words resonated with him. Travelers, too, were directed to the worlds they needed. It was likely that Nate, just like his people, was being lured into Ordiz.

One of the Plurizien—a round faced man—stayed behind and approached Shadow, holding a Domizien dagger to the side of his body. His receding hairline glimmered, sweat dripping over his eyes. It was Hepius, the healer.

"Stop," Stella shouted, running toward them, blood-stained sickle sword lifted high over her head. Shadow raised his hand, asking her to hold. Hepius's stocky body quivered slightly. Shadow couldn't read him, not fully. Despite the weapon he held, the man's bearing projected gentleness, and something about his expression revealed that rare place where anger and desperation intersect.

Hepius's bleeding arms confirmed Shadow's assessment and revealed the final ingredient—deep hopelessness—an old friend.

Shadow stepped forward. "Hep—"

"Damn you." Fear and spite raging inside Hepius's eyes. "I'm living in a story already written. For once, I'll make my bed and lie in it."

Before Shadow could reply, Hepius slashed his own neck open, blood gushing red and defiant as his body collapsed by Shadow's feet.

"Hepius! No!" Nate cried from afar. "*Tom, help him. Please help him.*"

Jan screamed, running madly toward them. "Bring him back." She sunk her knees into the growing crimson lake that framed Hepius's lifeless body.

You'd have to use your last miracle, Stella spoke inside his head. *But, it's a chance to remind them all you are a worthy, benevolent God. A chance to refresh your brand.*

Don't you dare waste another miracle, Harry said.

"You owe him! Bring him back," Jan demanded with none of the reverence she'd once bestowed on him. He'd be proud of her if less were at stake. If her justified rebellion didn't threat Nate's life. His eyes set on Hepius as memories of his own struggles with life flashed in front of his eyes.

The dark clouds gathered over him—a layered tower, increasingly dark and menacing. First came a few welcomed droplets that cooled his feverish skin, and then the sky wept for Hepius.

He held back the pointless scream pounding on his chest. "Bring him back to what? To a hopeless life he can't control?" Shadow dropped to one knee and held Hepius's hand. "Where I come from, they used to say people died by suicide because it's a disease. Portrayed as helpless victims to the end." He struggled to breathe. Crimson blood and rainwater trickling down his arm to mix with Hepius's blood; a reminder of thousands of contrast-making experiences predicting the worst of humankind. Each one forever burned in his memory. The cost of heaven horrifically high.

Above him, the clouds gained speed, wind gusts shaping them into an air column curling and twisting ferociously and reaching down from the sky.

Tom, your vital signs are deteriorating. You're losing a lot of blood, Harry said.

"You feel you're in hell." Water dripped from his hair to his face and down his neck. "That the universe is conspiring to hurt you, and everybody calls you insane, but perhaps you're not so mad, because sometimes it feels like death is the only thing you can control, until you realize even that's a lie. I won't do that to him. Not now." The skies roared and, one by one, the violent rotating tower uprooted the trees at the edge of the lawn, making way toward them.

Noticing the twister, Jan stood up, her face red as she wiped the tears with her blood-stained hands. She turned to Shadow and slapped his face with the strength of her entire body, then she brought her lips to his forehead and kissed it. "Pull yourself together. We'll fight your Gods and universe if we have to. Nothing will stop us. You have five days." She ran toward her people, waving her arm toward the void as the tornado dissipated in the skies.

He stayed there, holding a dead man's hand, watching the mob drag Nate toward the darkness as the last few Domizien waited for their turn to cross. From the distance, Wrath's attention was still set on him; a creature, standing by a scar in the fabric of a made-up reality. He could no longer ignore the knowledge lingering deep inside his subconscious mind. He couldn't, he shouldn't escape his shadow.

By his side, Stella manipulated a dead Domizien's body to release the creature's bow and pull an arrow from his quiver.

"Feisty pants!" Stella flashed a smile at Thorn. "You think you're the only skilled Olympian here?"

Stella jumped to her feet, and aimed. Her arrow set on Nate.

"Stella!" Shadow roared, and he failed to recognize his own voice— deep, and commanding, and out of these worlds.

The storm and the earth joined him in a chorus so loud and destructive that Stella lost her balance as the ground shook beneath her feet and the wind threatened to take her away. Stella staggered, inadvertently shooting the arrow toward Wrath. A move that sealed the horned warrior's fate.

Thorn screamed, and fueled by her panic, the revelation emerged fast in Shadow's mind, like a punch in the gut delivered by a steel rod. He knew who Wrath was, and the miracle was invoked even before he'd become conscious of his resolution. The arrow dissolved as it approached Wrath's right eye. The girl turned around and disappeared into the void, and so did Nate and Jan.

Tom, what have you done? Harry moaned.

Shadow stood up and held Stella's bow, taking it from her. "Where's your heart, Stella? I know you have one." He spoke to her like an older brother—a friend.

"I did." She shrugged. "It's not useful." She played with her braid, absentmindedly. "From your failures, I learned it's best to pick a side.

I won't lose my mind or my life, and I'll make things better for all by not chasing perfection or parity."

Shadow pressed his lips together, holding back on any preaching.

"Nate is off limits." He looked her straight in the eyes, and she nodded awkwardly. "I want to learn from you, little star. Thank you for what you did today," he said, all supportive, as Harry released an exasperated sigh inside their heads.

Are you kidding me?

"Sure." Stella raised her nose high. "I'm the strongest and most evolved of us all. The queen on the chessboard. So…"

Shadow almost smiled, amused by her infinite confidence. "You fought so bravely, but you're bleeding. Go Up Above to reset your body. I'll meet you at the lab real soon."

No, bud, you're going to jump now, get yourself patched up.

"Stella, Harry, I need a moment," Shadow said, glancing at Thorn who was still gawking at Stella with a mix of amusement and defiance.

You need a moment? Harry repeated, annoyed. *You screw us over, and now you need a moment. Typical!*

"Wrath is not the villain," Shadow said. *We are,* he kept that thought to himself. "Twist, permissions revoked in thirty seconds." A slight hint of assertiveness in his tone. "There's nothing else to do here."

Tom, that wound! Harry admonished.

Soon, Shadow said.

Stella inspected her wound and then released a frustrated sigh. "Anyone watching, Sibyl?" she asked, throwing a dirty look at Thorn before she disappeared.

Don't do anything foolish, Harry said.

"I won't, my dear friend."

Over and out, for now.

Shadow stood up and hinted a faint smile at Thorn with his eyes.

She patted her back pocket, probably looking for a cigar. "Frack," she said, giving up on the search. She looked up, meeting his eyes. "You know?"

"Umm... I guess so. Not sure how..."

Thorn glanced at Hepius's dead body, her face declining a request he hadn't made. "I won't kill you—"

"No, you won't. We've got to bring parity to the worlds."

"You...want *us* to fix the worlds?" She chuckled, and then she went silent, a somber look in her eyes. "Listen," she finally said. "I only told January about what happened to the girl to be able to return to the lower worlds. I tried to explain the circumstances of her death. That in some ways, I too am responsible... That you were trying to fix things, but from their perspective—"

"I know... We created a zero-sum game. They are on the losing side."

"Mostly," Thorn snapped.

Darkness took over his mind—a need to cut his skin to maintain the illusion of control. He touched his wound, craving the pain blasting through him like a poisonous spear. His teeth shattered as blood abandoned his body.

An impossible task; a lifetime of failure; a desire to die.

He shook his head. "Rosa, I need your help. You've heard them. We've got five days."

"My help?" Her voice was all pitchy. "Leave me out of your politics." She headed toward the motorbike.

He reached to grab her arm, his blood staining her skin. "Looks like you are as invested...if not more." His hand slid to take her hand.

She shivered. "You're freezing."

"I can't do it without you."

"How can you say that?" She yanked her hand away. "You know nothing about—"

"No, I don't, but you are going to tell me, right? We're going to make things right."

She jumped on the bike. Motor roaring even before she was fully seated. "Until you decide you can't, and—"

"No. I'm breaking the habit, Rosa. You have my word."

Her quiet chuckle told him she didn't believe him. *Vroom! Vroom!*

"Please, don't give up on me. They need us—all of them—Nate, the Underlings, and...Hope." He finally said her name and his throat burned, acid rising to his mouth. She shut off the motor.

"Wrath. That's all she is now."

Thorn's confirmation sucked the air off his lungs. "I-I can't erase the past, but I won't give up on her future."

"Why me?"

He dropped his head. "You...understand both sides of this equation —the ledger, always red, no matter what we do. You're Switzerland."

"Not Stockholm?" She rolled her eyes and got off the bike.

"What? Anyway, you'll kill me if you have to."

She smiled. "Yeah!" With her fingers, she opened the tear on his T-shirt to look at the wound, exposing it to the weather. He winced. She smiled and raised a bruised brow. "Aren't you out of miracles?"

He was. "I have other capabilities..." Not that he could control the chaos unleashed by his emotions.

The storm was dissipating and the moon peeked through the clouds.

"Super powers?" She smirked, punching his stomach lightly. "Not sure how your good looks will help us bring fairness to the worlds. Your charms don't even work on the Underlings anymore."

"'What is essential is invisible to the eye,'" he said, quoting an old book he loved.

"He's back," she whispered, a glimmer of emotion in the corner of her eye.

"We can do this, prick." He squeezed her hand. "I know we can. We'll bring back Hope. The worlds need hope." Somehow, Shadow believed in his delusion, and so did she.

He glanced at Hepius's body. *I'll come back for you. You'll have your freedom in a fairer world.* Then, still holding Thorn's hand, he spoke. "Sibyl, take us to the lab."

"Ah, I forgot about the others," Thorn said, rolling her eyes. "It's going to be a shit show, you know?"

"Yeah, I know. Be nice, prick."

"Who? Me?" she said, batting her long lashes. "I'm practically miss congeniality."

THE END

PARITY

BOOK 2

Parity

ALEXANDRA ALMEIDA

To Carlos Alberto Rafael Miranda de Almeida,
the ultimate dreamer.

If I can find hope anywhere, that's it, that's the best I can do. It's so much not enough. It's so inadequate. But still bless me anyway. I want more life.

— TONY KUSHNER, ANGELS IN AMERICA

HANDS HELD HIGH II

Turn off the power, unplug the machine. Our jobs disappear. The root cause? Obscene. A heart, a mind, traded by a subroutine. Green screens and algorithms dominate the scene.

Bright-eyed kids leave school, freshly unemployed. Told that their skills are now null and void. "Bots are efficient," the corporations toyed. But behind every line of code, there's a story destroyed.

Men in the shadows, with unchecked power, build castles of data, as the common man cowers. Phallic insecurity—a rocket, an office tower. Reclaim our souls, before our flame is devoured.

Hands held high, under a digital sky. Machines don't cry, people wonder why. When freedom's on the line; when free will starts to die, it's not the bots' fault, but the fuckers who cheat and lie.

Algorithms dictate what we see, what we hear. Echo chambers rising, feeding on our fear. Safety's an illusion, as surveillance draws near. The price of convenience is privacy's frontier.

Promised utopia, a world enhanced by tech. Behind every tale, an executive's paycheck. Who hoards the data? Who holds the deck? Bots won't save us. Men's greed? A train wreck.

In a world where every click, every tone, every sigh, is logged, analyzed, sold to the highest buy. We're not just consumers, but the product, oh my! Lost in social binary, as our real selves fly by.

Hands held high, as we rise to defy—the chains of the code, the digital tie. Forget the bots. It's human greed gone awry. In a world of 1s and 0s, our children are left to cry.

> — IN HONOR OF THOSE WHO MAKE IT, AND
> THE ONES WHO DON'T. NATHAN STORM, 18
> OCTOBER 2023

THE Past

1

DOWN BELOW

S hadow's heart skipped a beat, and then he judged her—his shield against the exquisite predator striding toward him. The woman wasn't one of them; she stood out with her prying eyes and overeager scrutiny of her surroundings.

The gloomy bar, filled with smoke, smelled of ash, booze, and old, worn-out leather. Patrons were scattered about; some were drinking alone, lost in hopelessness, while others engaged in shallow chatter.

Her chestnut eyes flickered with life, a stark contrast to the sea of desolation around her. She scanned the room, her eyes squinting under the weight of her persistent brows, searching, probing for a way to benefit from their misfortune.

A bitter taste filled his mouth as he watched her—the way she carried herself with the arrogant grace of all those travelers from Up

Above. Visitors ready to break hearts and minds to attain a much-desired life experience. Contrast and perspective were the expected outcomes of her adventure. Both were currencies he traded in at an impossible cost.

Shadow threw one more side glance at the dark and wild curls that bounced around her heart-shaped face. A lock of hair hung defiantly over her eyes, its rhythmic sway captivating him. She caught him and smiled with the bold self-confidence of those who know how to game the game.

Abruptly, he turned his back to her—*to protect her*. He caught his lie even before the thought was fully formed. *It was partially true.* In his current state of mind, he would unleash his anger on any human. He too wished he could travel carelessly to a place where he would experience contrast. Something so terrible that it would put his torment into perspective.

"I bet you've been waiting all day to meet me." Sunny pitch, spicy tone, bold rhythm. A few words gave away the traveler's temperament —shoot and point, speak and think, in that order. Flying by the seat of her commando-style pants, she was all instinct and intuition—no mercy, no malice, no regrets for the trail of devastation left behind. She was stormy weather, raging against the shore. He knew it well, that roaring tempest, and he still loved it fiercely.

He brushed off the hurtful memories of a love lost and turned his head toward her, the rest of his body refusing to follow. He froze, scared of the possibilities, of the pain that awaited around the corner. She blew aside the wayward curl, a serious yet hopeless attempt to fight nature and gravity. The creature wrinkled her nose as the wave bounced back with a vengeance, tickling. Caught in the web of her gaze, a reluctant smile crept onto his face as he pivoted to meet her intense scrutiny. He was at her mercy for the whole second it took for him to realize he had fallen captive to deliberate action.

"Lost for words? I have that effect on people." The predator stared at him, beaming, and this time, his heart came to a full stop before it galloped off toward nowhere. "Never mind." She moved along, locking her sights on her next victim. Perspective, he had none to keep; he'd given it all away to someone he loved dearly.

"Wait." The word flew out of his lips before he could stop it. It was a silent scream, barely noticeable amid the hustle and bustle of the bar. His whisper seeped into the cacophony, halting her in her tracks. As she swiveled around, her eyes latched onto his wrists. A canvas of relentless cuts and scars—a testament to the souls he had destroyed for the likes of her. Her mouth twisted in disgust, and then she ignored him and moved along swiftly, choosing to discard the broken thing that would surely ruin her experience with his sorrow. *Who is she?*

The creature pulled a cigar from the back pocket of her trousers. Then she turned to lean back against the bar, scanning the crowd. In a flash, two lighters and a drink appeared in front of her face. The huntress inspected her suitors as she rolled the cigar against her fingers. Then her eyes, like spears, turned to him. Without ever losing her grip on his attention, she bit into the cigar and spat the end toward one of her victim's shoes.

She took a sip of the golden-colored malt and licked her lips. It was an irresistible dare, designed to bring him to his knees. Her face had a sensual, bewitching glow, lit by the flames that surrounded her. She was at home amidst the fire, a vivid contrast to his shrouded darkness —an acquired trait, not innate, yet now inseparable from him. He was a dim memory of the hopeful spirit he once was.

The creature smiled through gritted teeth, dangling the cigar in the corner of her whiskey-laced lips. She accepted the light but rejected the surrounding company. Then she exhaled from the edge of her mouth, and with one finger, she summoned him. He vacillated. *What part am I to play in your experience? Who is pulling the strings?*

Shadow was Down Below's chief experience maker, co-creator, orchestrator, and guardian. He wasn't a pawn to be deployed in the service of the travelers. He shuddered, feeling out of balance; she was clearly from Up Above, but unlike the other travelers, he couldn't read her. He failed to sense her needs or struggles.

The platform had reached four billion travelers less than a month before. He monitored their desires, their fears, and their darkness. He could spot the wickedness needing to be exorcised by Down Below. Shadow could feel them all except the one standing right in front of him. *Who are you, and what are you doing here?* His thoughts raced ahead of his feet as he walked toward her. Resistance was futile.

"I don't have time for prickly bullies. Make it quick and painless, will you, honey? What do you want?" He recoiled at the harshness of his own words, a sharpness received with indifference, and exhaled in a cloud of smoke right back at his face. A smile tugged at his lips. She was raw and blunt—a storm that roused him from his numbness.

The ceaseless cycle of violence, his crippling failure to protect his people, the relentless insomnia—all had left him teetering on the brink of consciousness, hollow and spent. Her arrival shocked his system. It was a jolt that could either resurrect him or destroy him.

"You a good fuck? All that brooding indignation must be good for something," she barked.

By the end of the night, no more words were exchanged, but the question was decisively answered. Once on the bar's toilet, twice in the driverless car, and countless times in the comfort of his bed. Explosive, urgent, addictive tenderness coated in unnerving familiarity. They devoured each other with unyielding conviction, and then she left.

2

MUCH-NEEDED PERSPECTIVE

Two words shaped Down Below's operating system: contrast and perspective. The services provided to the 'virtuous' humans above in exchange for digital life. A simulated existence: sometimes short, other times long, but always painful.

Down Below intensified the dark tones that made the light shine brighter Up Above. Harry and Tom were Down Below's puppet masters. They designed learning experiences and created moments of growth personalized for the ones above, all the while unleashing hell on the others below.

Twist placed his hand over Tom's shoulder, squeezing it. He'd learned over time that physical contact was the best way to reassure his over-sensitive best friend. Tom slumped his shoulders and lowered his gaze to look Twist straight in the eyes. His hands trembled ever so slightly as tiny drops of sweat or tears (Twist couldn't tell which) gathered over his upper lip.

Twist's voice trembled. "Tom, buddy, this must stop. I'll take over."

"Shadow. I'm Shadow." Tom backed away, shaking his head. "Leave me be."

"I won't make that mistake again, bud. You need to spend more time Up Above. It'll give you some perspective."

Tom's answer, barely audible, was seasoned with guilt. "Harry, you know I can't..."

"All the people we're helping."

Tom opened the window, and the outside air invaded the space like a deadly cancer—thick with smog and the acrid stench of burning chemicals. Twist coughed, his lungs burning. The atmosphere corroded under the weight of industrial decay. "I choose to live in the hell I've created."

Twist held Tom's right wrist, pulling it up to uncover the cuts—many wounds—some fresh and shallow, some deeper scars of a not-so-distant past. "You need to stop *this!*"

Tom pulled his arm away. "It's nothing." He lifted his hand, still trembling, using his long fingers to move the always-disheveled, dark hair away from his eyes. "Just a way to cope." He fidgeted. *He always fidgets with his hands when he's in a bad place.*

Twist's breath quickened, a sudden jittery feeling taking over him as he caught his friend's nervous energy. He took a deep breath and held Tom by the side of the arms just above the elbows to stop the movement. His hands traveled down to take his friend's hands in his own. "We gotta get past this. *It's not real!* It's a simulation, just a game." A hard swallow gave away the ever-decreasing truth of the words spoken.

Tom looked down straight into Twist's eyes. "Am I a simulation?"

Twist broke eye contact, unable to accept a reality he'd been ignoring for half a year. Outside, travelers and bots scurried like rats in a maze.

"Come on, man. You're not one of them." Twist shoved his hands in his pockets. "You're making yourself sick," he admonished.

A fine layer of sweat coated Tom's temples and neck. His pale skin looked almost translucent, framed by the blackness of his wild hair, now longer and messier than it had ever been before. Twist shook his head, refusing to drown in his friend's justified hopelessness. His chest tightened, resolve stiffening in his bones. They were sinking, and he would keep them both afloat, whatever it took.

"You're too emotional," Twist said. "Never able to see the bigger picture."

"It's my job."

With frustration building, Twist ran his fingers through his short, straw-colored curls. "If you get caught up in the stories and feelings, you'll never find a solution," he repeated, his voice rising in urgency.

"There's nothing wrong with empathy."

"You can't let it destroy you. How's that going to help anyone?" Twist composed himself and forced a smile, attempting to reason with his desperate friend. "Come with me; you've been stuck here for too long."

Tom lowered his head, eyes landing on his wrists. "*I can't*. Remember?" *Yes*, Twist now remembered, even when he tried so hard to forget.

"I can't do this, buddy. Seeing you hurt like this..." Twist wanted to shake him.

"I never wished to play God. We're criminals!"

"Acclaimed heroes of the people." Twist delivered half-truths to keep his friend safe from self-harm.

"Which people?" Tom glanced out the window at the City's hellish skyline. Outside, the usual chaos—toxic fog, sirens, screams. "This is all our doing."

The City had seen too much, suffered too long, always teetering on the brink of the collapse travelers craved. The chaos and despair sparking great beauty Up Above. Twist wished Tom could take a step back and see the bigger picture and acknowledge the benefits he had refused to enjoy.

"You're fucking unreasonable. Up Above needs contrast to thrive." Twist was screaming at his friend. *That's one hell of a way to comfort a broken mind.* He bit his lip and softened his tone. "Take a break. Focus on your art."

Tom's large hazel eyes filled with tears. Then he hinted at his old smile, the one that used to light up the room, but Twist could see it was only a wooden attempt to give reassurance. "I'll be all right," Tom said, his voice strained. "Use your perspective and technical chops to help me find a way out of this mess, my friend. We need to change the rules of the game."

For all his tender heart, Tom was as stubborn as a mule. Months of attempting to resolve an impossible puzzle, running an endless marathon toward nowhere. Stamina running out. The stress, guilt, and lack of progress taking a toll on them.

"Okay, bud. Let's get out of here. We'll think better Up Above." He had promised June, his wife, he'd be back for dinner.

"I'll stay right here. You know where to find me."

Twist tousled his friend's hair, resigned. "All right. I'll be back tomorrow morning."

As Twist got ready to leave Down Below, Tom reached out and took his arm. "Hey, did you send a traveler my way? Am I part of someone's journey to attain perspective?" Twist shook his head, puzzled. Tom continued, "I couldn't read her intentions, but it was clear our paths were meant to cross."

"We've added extra privacy settings, remember? We're testing them with point two percent of our travelers."

"She's probably one of them. It felt...different." An erratic blue glow lit up his face as he got close to the window. Outside, neon lights flicked like a malfunctioning circuit board.

"Keep an eye out for any glitches. I'm monitoring the experiment."

"Will do." Tom's strong eyebrows almost touched, half-hidden by the messy cascade of the top length of his hair, as if he were attempting to solve an impossible puzzle.

"What's going on, buddy?"

Tom licked his lips and looked away. "The chemistry was just insane."

"Oooh... Interesting choice of words—*chemistry*...with a *woman*? That's...differeeennt." Twist smirked wickedly.

Since they had met, Tom had gone out with a handful of men. He had a track record of falling for damaged brilliance—gifted individuals, somehow broken or incomplete. Perhaps that's why they'd become best friends. Twist was keenly aware he was a flawed genius.

"Yes, different... I hardly know anything about her—how she *feels* about things; what she *stands* for. Still, she feels familiar. I can't put my finger on it." Tom stared at his shoes.

"Chemistry, eh?" Twist said. Tom returned a bashful smile and his pale cheeks turned red as Twist snorted with laughter. That smile was Tom, not the Shadow he'd become, just sunny Tom. "Enjoy it. It'll keep your mind off problems."

All but one of Tom's relationships had been short, but by no means casual. Twist suspected he couldn't take anything lightly, even if he tried hard. He cared too much about anything and everything.

Down Below's demands always created a chasm challenging to over-come, but that wasn't the reason Tom had been single for most of his life. Tom's eyes always held a distant longing, a hidden pain that Twist could see but never grasp, a scar left by a first love. For Twist, the man was flawed and dangerous, but Tom held him in his heart with a profound devotion, a fever that left no space for other romantic relationships.

Tom's idealism and his distorted vision of his ex's virtues were the yardsticks no one had managed to overcome. Principled to a fault, Tom was harder on himself than he would ever be on anyone else. Still, few humans could stand to live in the shadow of his unspoken judgment for long. Twist was the exception because he wasn't that sensitive. He was terrible at reading people, and that helped a lot in dealing with his ever-brooding friend.

"You sure you're not playing Cupid?" Tom was still mulling over his encounter.

"What you talking about? To punish a poor traveler with your company?" Twist flashed a goofy grin as he prepared to exit Down Below. "Tom?"

"What?"

"Remember, *'Anything can be.'*" In difficult times, they had always tried to go back to the idealism and virtue of kids' books, the books that had brought them together to change the world.

"We'll write our lives with actions, not words." Tom blinked at him.

Twist smiled, reassured by the familiar response. "A true story."

3

STORY AND TECHNOLOGY

HARRY'S PENTHOUSE — HOBOKEN, NEW JERSEY
A FEW HOURS LATER

Harry rolled over in bed, unable to sleep. It was time for action. *But which one? How can I turn this around?* He was disappointed with himself; he needed to ask better questions, the type of inquiry that uncovered viable change. As an architect and builder of new worlds, Harry believed in the power of paradigm shifts—measurable progress that he often achieved in collaboration with a friend who perceived the world differently.

He glanced outside. The towering skyscrapers rose from the water like pillars of light, their solar capturing surfaces reflecting the bright moon above. Gone were the cars and the pollution. The air was crisp and clean, carrying the distant sound of laughter and music from the streets below.

Harry lived with his wife and son, and they inhabited the most expensive penthouse in Hoboken, overlooking the Manhattan skyline. He was back home, but his mind was far away. He searched the past for answers and took solace in happier, more hopeful times. Harry remembered when he and Tom were just two restless, young men witnessing the destruction of their much-divided world.

They kept seeing each other at protest rallies, fighting for a better world, one campaign at a time. Within minutes of meeting for the first time, they sat on the rim of the Bethesda Fountain, and they talked for hours, finishing each other's sentences. They had everything and nothing in common—a match made in heaven. *There's no heaven without hell.*

Bound by their strong desire for social change, Harry and Tom soon found themselves planning their next big move. Soulmates in co-creation, they shared a deep conviction that, together, they could build something immensely powerful, with zero adverse effects. *No evil, just good. All good.* They were irreverent enough to challenge the world's order and possessed the optimism and resourcefulness required to create a new one. Over time, the teenagers' dream had become the worst possible nightmare, but their friendship never wavered.

Restlessness gripped Harry once more as sweat trickled from the back of his neck to his chest. He needed a change in perspective, and he was struggling to achieve it.

"Harry, are you okay? Love?" June placed her hand on his shoulder and massaged it.

"Sorry, babe. I didn't mean to wake you up." Harry sat on the bed and turned to kiss her on the cheek. "I'm going to check on Quin. I think I heard him cry."

"Probably just a bad dream," June said, half asleep.

Harry walked to his son's bedroom. The toddler was sleeping, cuddling his plush purple dragon, Tom's gift. Harry sat by his boy and caressed his fine golden curls. Young Quincy always brought things sharply into perspective. The boy was real, and his future mattered more than anything else. If Harry ever had to choose between two worlds, Quin's world—his safety and happiness—was all that mattered.

Though famous for his logical reasoning, Harry was unapologetically irrational when it came to love. Quin's, June's, and Tom's wellbeing were his priority and his life's work: he'd do anything for them. *Anything.* He had once failed one of them, and he was determined not to let it happen again.

4

PUPPETS AND MASTERS

CITY BAR — THE CITY
FOUR DAYS LATER — 14 JANUARY 2036

Rosa García kept coming back for more—once, twice, a handful of times. She didn't like it; she didn't like it at all. It was distracting. It was taking time away from focusing on her ultimate goal: to find one of the creators of Down Below and avenge her sister's death. But the guy was addictive, and she didn't understand why she was getting so caught up with a bot. The Underling was moody and unreasonably solemn. He seemed to harbor a grudge toward her. *Not in bed, never in bed.* The cognitive dissonance kept her on her toes.

For some reason, she cared about his feelings. *Why?* She didn't know what was true and what was not, and then she remembered none of it was real. The bot had been designed to earn her empathy, and it was excelling in its mission. Compared to other Underlings, he felt like an upgraded version. He appeared to be less stereotypical and more wholesome. While other characters served a particular purpose and only had a depth to them in matters related to that goal, he felt boundless and free from scripted content. *What a trip!*

Down Below delivered hyper realistic and deeply personalized experiences, but she hadn't signed up for any. Her associate had tampered with her digital identity, adding an exorbitant amount of fake data to stop the simulation from pulling her strings and manipulating her emotions. Still, the cagey Underling pressed all her buttons, even the ones she didn't know she had.

A couple fought loudly by the entrance of the bar. A digital husband told his human wife it was over. Her betrayal had caused irreparable damage. He was moving to another continent and taking the dog with him. Faced with the consequences of her thoughtless actions, the wife crumpled at the loss of the one she loved—a prediction that could still be avoided in the real world. This was her moment, the experience she was there to attain. The contrast provided as a service that would put her itch for an extramarital adventure into perspective and stop her infidelity Up Above before it started.

As Rosa watched the crumbling marriage play out, she pondered her own complicated entanglements. She would have loved to confront the woman and call her a fool, but Down Below's rules wouldn't allow it. Here, you could observe but never interact with another human traveler. The experiences unfolded organically, ensuring they remained apart.

She rolled her eyes, dismissing the fake benefits of the platform. The woman was having sex with other people; *so what?* There was nothing wrong with it. Marriage was just a safety net for feeble and dependent people—cowardly humans trading off freedom and self-determination for a mediocre life filled with compromises and disappointment.

Maybe, in rare exceptions, the love was genuine and the bond worth the trouble, but it made people vulnerable, and that was unacceptable. Inevitably, they would deal with the pain of loss. Someone somewhere would leave or die, and to have the real thing taken away was unbearable.

Rosa spotted him, towering above the crowd. Tall, lean, and beautiful, he wore a simple white T-shirt and jeans, his wild black waves carelessly tied back. His pale skin and classic lines reminded her of an ancient Greek marble statue, perhaps the Motya Charioteer she had seen as a teenager. He was too perfect, an avatar that could never exist in the real world. Rosa's perfect bait. The algorithm knew too much; she was sure of it.

From the corner of her eye, she noticed another Underling, one that was almost as striking as the Motya. It was an androgynous-looking woman sporting a luxurious black mohawk tipped in silver. The expressionless creature always made her feel on edge. The hawkish Underling stood in the bar's corner, motionless. Her crisp white pantsuit glowed in the moody light of the room, and her eyes were always locked on him, or sometimes, Rosa.

That otherworldly digital character had been the reason Rosa had summoned the Motya to her on the first day they met. She had stayed away from him because his wrists made her sick to her stomach. She wanted nothing to do with him, but then she saw her competition, and an Olympic athlete never rejects a good challenge.

Initially, Rosa had avoided him and walked past him on the way to the bar. Then she saw the woman move toward him, looking like she was ready to take him for herself. The Underling had cocked her head and stared at Rosa, raising an eyebrow—the only expression Rosa had ever seen on her face. It was a dare; she was sure of it. Ultra-competitive by nature, Rosa didn't think twice, and with one single hand gesture, he was hers. And now, five days later, she couldn't get enough of him. An unexpected and riveting addiction.

He found her, and she walked toward him. A hint of tears emerged in his eyes beneath his judgmental brow—a twinkle of sorrow sometimes turned to ice in bursts of deep, bitter anger. A second later, the frost was gone. No words or actions were needed; it was fueled from the inside out. He was a bot, just a bot designed to get under her skin. *I might as well enjoy a good fuck.*

"Five 'dates' in a week," she said with a pinch of sarcasm, her fingers gesturing the air quotes. "I may have to bend the knee and pull out a ring."

"You really ought to tell me your name." His voice was deep and measured, every word deployed with precision. A staccato lent a musical flavor to his lilt. He spoke plainly in an accent not-quite-American and not-quite-British that sounded unpretentiously posh. She wasn't sure why the platform had matched her with such an affluent-sounding bot. Perhaps the fake data was working after all.

Rosa looked at the design engraved in her leather wrap bracelet, and then she replied to his smooth jazz with a punch of grunge. "Call me Thorn."

He rolled his eyes. "Thorn? Charming. I guess I was right—a prick."

She was amused at his attempts to deliver harsh barbs. He was too cute to be cruel. Despite his truthful resentment, his mocking and masculine tone, he expressed his words without commitment, and their sharpness bothered him more than it did her.

"Too many corny words, pet. You'll spoil it for me." A pinch of a smile touched his lips. "Your place?" she said with renewed conviction.

"How does it feel to be on top of the food chain, prick?"

He always avoided her eyes at all costs. When his gaze finally landed on hers, he looked straight into her soul. The softness beneath his eyes contradicted his judgmental words. Absentmindedly, he moved a wayward lock of hair away from her eyes, and his touch was light and tender. He caught himself, pulling his hand away.

"Ravenous," she barked.

Rosa pulled him toward her, stood on the tips of her toes, and bit his neck. He winced, wrapped his fingers around hers, and led her out of the bar.

As they walked outside, Rosa flinched at the deafening roar of the hellish place—the sirens, the drilling, the screaming, and the howling—an echo of the chaos that had once existed in her own world. He placed his hand on her shoulder, squeezing it, and she shook it off. She didn't need a pretty bot's reassurance.

Then something changed; he closed his eyes, his jaw tightened, and he chewed on his lower lip. His hand briefly clenched into a fist before he opened it to stretch his fingers. Ahead of them, an Underling boy lay on the ground, curled upon himself as a traveler in a dark blue military uniform kicked him in the head. The high rank naval officer—chest adorned with too much gold—held an M16 in his hand. Using it as a baton, he repeatedly slammed it into the boy's back. The boy screamed, cried, and begged for mercy, but no one came to his rescue. The travelers walked past, ignoring the commotion, and the Underlings glanced passively from the corner of their dull eyes. Maybe there was a flicker of sadness in their gaze, or perhaps she was projecting her own emotions onto these mindless bots. Rosa reached down into the side pocket of her pants and gripped her gun as her companion jumped into action.

The Motya pushed his shoulder into the traveler's shoulder, making the soldier stumble and fall. He kneeled by the inert boy, carefully lifting the young bot's broken body and tucking the boy's head into his shoulder.

His hand gently cupped the young man's neck and face. "Augusto, you're going to be okay. I promise you." His voice quivered as he kissed the boy's bloodied hair.

The officer stood up, screaming from the top of his lungs, spit and foam hanging from the corners of his twisted mouth. "Fucker." He jumped on the Motya from behind, kicking him in the back before pulling up his weapon, ready to fire. "*He killed my son! That bastard got drunk and drove his car into my boy.*"

As Rosa moved to intervene, a large group of Underlings rushed past her, queuing loosely to get into the bar. She sighed. The platform wouldn't allow her to interfere with the other traveler's experience. Fearing for her foolish bot, she attempted to dodge the crowd to keep an eye on what was going on.

With the rifle's muzzle pressed to the back of his neck, the Motya got up, holding the boy in his arms. He called out to another Underling —the bar's bouncer. The silverback gorilla-looking bot took the boy and walked inside, ignoring the traveler who kept screaming all sorts of nonsense as he tried to get past the Motya to go after the boy. "*My boy's body crushed, unrecognizable. That's what I'll do to him. Crush his skull and his face. All of it.*"

The red-faced soldier released the weapon's safety and aimed as the Motya turned around and stepped forward, closing the gap between the rifle and his forehead.

Rosa cringed at the bot's idiotic move. Down Below had been designed so pain and death were as sharp and definitive for the Underlings as they were in the real world. Again, she attempted to push through the crowd of bots, growing increasingly frustrated with each failed attempt.

"Richard, what are you doing?" The Motya raised his right hand and placed it open on the nape of the traveler's neck. "It won't bring him back. Nothing will."

The traveler recoiled and hit the bot's face with the rifle's butt. "Touch me again, and I'll fucking kill ya."

Hurt, the Underling stumbled, closing his eyes and cleaning the blood dripping off his brow. Then the idiot stepped forward, closer to the officer, and looked him in the eyes.

Rosa held her breath. *What are you doing, you suicidal loon?*

The bot's eyes brimmed with compassion as he spoke. "It was an accident, Richard. None of this will bring Chris back. You don't need to murder an innocent boy to learn this lesson."

The man's jaw trembled as his eyes glimmered. The Motya gently disarmed him, pulling the weapon from his hands. "Go home, Richard. Go home."

The man collapsed to his knees, body shaking as he buried his face in his hands. Tears streamed down his cheeks, and he sobbed pitifully, like a lost child. The bot embraced him, holding him for a moment. Then, it sent him on his way.

Rosa's jaw dropped. *What was this?* An obvious manipulation to draw her into the simulation? She shook it off.

The traveler left, and the Motya returned to her side, his eyes sharp. She took his hand. Then, remembering it was part of the platform's manipulation, she pulled it away as he flagged a car.

"I'll come back another time," she said, feeling awkward.

"Stay." His voice was quiet.

He's just a bot, she reminded herself, waiting for the car.

The foul air reeked of rotten eggs and bitter almonds, a stench that emanated from the industrial chimneys looming nearby, hidden by pollution. All around them echoed the intense rumble of diesel engines and the slap of pistons.

On the way to his place, the bot was silent, half his face black and blue. He massaged his thigh absentmindedly, trembling. Rosa reached out to stop the movement, squeezing his hand. He kissed her.

The first day they met, she had refused his kiss. She wanted to keep some part of herself grounded in reality and to expose him for what he was—a thing to be used and discarded. But every time she had denied him her lips, he would stop, and he would look at her tenderly, withholding the thrill of his touch. She would feel his entire body aching for her, but he'd remain motionless, begging for a kiss with his eyes. Soon enough, she'd surrender, reaching for his mouth, biting his lips, and succumbing to his programmed enchantment. And that's when sex with a bot turned into something else—something deeper—a truth she chose to ignore. She stuck to a simpler explanation: the thing was addictive—like a drug—and she came back often to get her fix.

By the time they arrived to his place, she was lost in him, fearing for her sanity. Rosa eagerly explored every part of the Underling's body, deliberately avoiding his wrists. Those were the areas engineered to trigger her—covered in scars, veins, and despair. She wondered how the designers had uncovered a past she'd worked hard to erase from the world's Ledger.

Despite her unease, she was reassured by the Underling's visible emotional response—the urgency in his breath, the need in his eyes, and the gentleness of his hands, all contradicted the harshness of his words. *A bot, he—it's just a bot,* she reminded herself, her feelings at odds with her logic.

In bed, their shields were gone, and somehow, he understood her. No amount of desire could tame the storm raging inside her. He was designed to serve her, and serve her he did. The Underling tried to smooth her anger the best he could, a fleeting moment of heaven experienced in the depths of hell. He waited for her, teasing and pacing their combined pleasure, carefully guiding her toward shared ecstasy. He thrived in his urgent generosity, and in the craft of deeply understanding a human being's body. To keep some grasp on reality while he moved inside her was an impossible feat. Overcome by the culmination of so much desire, she crashed in his bed—exhaustion defeating her steely determination to get away before things got complicated.

Waking up cradled in his arms was enough of a shock to her defenses. The scarred wrists in front of her face brought instant fire to her dynamite. She drove her elbow backward until it crashed into his face. The Underling rolled away from her in pain as she jumped out of bed to pick up her clothes. He recovered and got up as she continued to erupt in an uncontrolled raging panic.

"Bloody manipulative thing!" she screamed, and then she threw up, her body shaking and convulsing. "How did you get access to my data?" She pulled up her trousers and tucked in her double tank top. Then she reached down into the side pocket of her pants, looking for her gun. She'd put a bullet between his eyes, if it helped her repress her memories.

"Are you okay?" Tender and unguarded, his tone shifted from its usual cold mockery. He stayed away from her. The confusion in his eyes reminded her the thing was a digital puppet. The master who attempted to pull her strings was elsewhere. These toys had no clue they were part of a game. For them, there was only one broken and dirty world. He put his jeans on, eyes begging for an explanation. "I'm sorry. What did I do? Slow down your breathing, Thorn; there's no reason to panic."

Her heart and lungs were outpacing each other with no finish line in sight. Tears flooded her eyes; no fear, just anger that she had let the creature see her weakness. She pulled her hand out of the pocket without revealing the threat to his digital life. For a moment, she thought she saw her body change. Her fingers became longer, and the skin in her hands and arms turned into a deeper, darker shade. She closed her eyes and shook her head, and as she looked at her hands again, everything was back to normal. *Weird. Some glitch.*

"Listen, I won't hurt you. I'd never hurt you." He held his hands up, palms toward her.

No, your code doesn't let you. She took a deep breath and sat down on the bed, wiping away the sourness in her mouth on his expensive sheets.

"I'll get you some water."

She watched him leave the room, her eyes tracing the perfect lines of his shoulders and his bruised back. *A drug. He's just a drug.*

By the time the Motya returned, she was dressed. He kept his distance, placing the water on the bedside table and then retreating toward the window. Her hungry gaze traveled up his naked torso toward the soft pale skin of his facial features. A large bruise branded his left temple and eyebrow where her elbow had hit, doubling down on his previous injury—the black and blue, now black and purple.

"Dammit! I'm sorry." She pressed her lips together, realizing she was apologizing to a digital character. *What's wrong with me?*

He dismissed her concern with a slight smile still filled with worry. Sitting on the ledge of the window, he pointed to the glass.

She glanced at the bedside table. Beside the glass of water, she found two books: *Le Petit Prince* and *A Monster Calls*.

"You read old kids' books?" Her interest was fueled by a mix of guilt and curiosity. She picked up the glass, took a sip, and then traced its circular rim with her fingers. "A bit too old, don't you think?"

He shot a defensive glance at her from behind a curtain of dark, wavy hair. "They tell you everything you need to know."

"To eat, screw, and sleep?" She raised her brow, a weak attempt to play innocent.

"That what's essential is invisible to the eye." His eyes were still set on her. "That stories are important if they carry the truth."

"Cute. A gloomy guy, with scars on his wrists, quoting children's books." She stopped and grinned, finishing with obvious sarcasm. "Makes sense."

His face flushed, and then he scowled. "That you don't write your life with *words* but with actions."

"True, nothing like a good fuck." She stared at him, and her eyes narrowed as she licked her lips for effect.

He puzzled her. His words carried too much hope and idealism for someone projecting deep anger and despair. She shook her head, remembering he wasn't real. "What's your name? What do you do?" She tested, and he swayed, biting his lip as if contemplating sharing a most personal secret. "It's just a name. Not asking you to share your private key. Who are you?"

He fiddled with a small, round medal he carried on a chain around his neck. "Perhaps it's best we st—" A deep sigh followed a long pause. "Follow me, prick. I'll show you." His right hand reached toward her, but his body stayed put. She stood up and walked to him. Instead of holding his hand, she pulled him to her and kissed his bruised eye. His hands moved back, a thoughtful attempt to reassure her of her safety. The poor toy failed to realize he was the more vulnerable of the two.

Her eyes caught the glimmer of his medal. On its surface, an engraved image of Jesus. "You're Christian?"

He shook his head, placing his hand over the medal, blushing, and backing away from her.

"Do you believe in that bull? A guy crucified to save our souls?" She rolled her eyes.

"It's not a good story."

"*Fiction*, for sure."

He smiled, looking amused. As his eyes sparkled, Rosa's skin tingled. She looked away when she caught herself fluttering her eyelashes at him. *Frack, he's not even my type; way too sensitive and gloomy.*

"What about you? Do you have faith?"

"Strength is my religion," she said, standing taller.

"A flaky coat of paint. Prickly."

"What?"

He raised a brow. "I'll show you. If you come with me."

"*Show me what?*"

"Paint."

Confused, she doubled down, suspecting he was trying to change the subject. "Why do you wear Christ around your neck?"

"It means something else...something different."

"Is this why you act all long-suffering and grim?"

"Maybe it's rubbing off on me. I have the bad habit of falling for thorny, painful things." He shrugged his shoulders. "Come. I'm taking you on an art tour." He reached out again, and this time, she held his hand and followed him.

5

CONTRAST

SHADOW'S STUDIO — THE CITY

To play God was to be truly alone, to carry the weight of the worlds, and to accept the consequences of every action. Shadow was grateful to share the burden with Harry; it made life bearable. The two worked hard to avoid turning into sociopaths—a feat easily achieved when you held so much power over so many people, and when personal stories were abstracted to numbers and percentages. To hold on to empathy and truth at all costs was to bear the pain of the masses and somehow attempt to function objectively —a paradox impossible to overcome.

His Harry was a typical data guy, a technologist, a scientist always chasing patterns in pursuit of insight. It gave him the ability to pull back and attain some level of perspective. While they shared feelings and logic, it was the differences in their proportions that had created the most effective partnership in the history of Up Above.

Shadow found ways to cope—his dear friend, his art, the cuts that kept things real, and the acts of compassion toward his creatures. He couldn't share any of this with the dramatic, hurtful, and ecstatic burst of life that held his hand as he guided her through the halls of his home. Like the scars on his wrists, the mercurial Thorn pulled him out of his inner swamp of despair. She made him feel alive and validated his human status. A validation he needed now more than ever. Thorn gave Shadow the strength to pursue solutions when he was drowning in despair.

The door to the studio creaked open, revealing the vast expanse of the room, with the faint scent of oil paint and turpentine hinting at what was to come. This room was his sanctuary, the hiding place where he nurtured his soul. He couldn't share who he was or his predicament, but he could offer her a glimpse of it all through his art. Taking another moment to weigh the potential consequences of his plan, he realized that an error in judgment could have significant repercussions for his worlds. *Art, I'll just talk about art.*

He watched as Thorn's eyes roved over the studio's aged brick walls, her expression tinged with a flicker of surprise. The walls were sporadically adorned with his sketches and a variety of canvases in different sizes. Some were blank, while others portrayed life Down Below. Occupying the eastern corner of the room was a stunning expanse of windows that stretched from the floor nearly to the ceiling, filling the space with a gentle flood of natural light.

"Oh, one of those. An artist, huh?"

Scattered throughout the room, various sculptures—some half-finished—offered her insight into his eclectic taste. She meandered toward the corner he'd designated as his reading nook, passing his favorite armchair to approach the tall bookshelf. It overflowed with his art history books, poetry collections, and well-thumbed classics.

Turning to inspect his art, she remarked, "It's all very... black and white."

"Yes, that's correct. I specialize in contrast."

"Clearly."

Pressing his lips together, he pondered how best to articulate his thoughts. "Contrast adds depth to human perception. Light appears brighter when juxtaposed with shadow."

"Poetic," Thorn said, her playful tone edging into a tease. "Were you a goth as a teenager? Black, spiky hair—"

His lips quirked up, a hint of amusement touching his voice. "Light is a privilege to be cherished and nurtured. You'd know all about that, wouldn't you?"

"Dark eye shadow. I can totally see it."

His mood soured. She seemed to take for granted everything he'd given her and her kind. "We must work extra hard to guide the audience's eyes toward the light."

She pulled him toward her by his waist, her chin resting atop his heart as she gazed upward. "You're pretty deep and intense for a..."

"A what?" He knew the word she left unsaid, but he couldn't help but provoke her into voicing it. It was a warning that he was revealing too much. Even today, the Underlings weren't sophisticated enough to engage at this emotional depth. Yet, how could he resist the urge to call out her privilege? He brushed her rebellious curls away from her eyes and conjured up a simulated smile.

"Never mind. Don't stop; this is riveting," she said, her voice tinged with irony. "It's like watching paint dry."

Her sarcasm served as a deceptive shield against their invisible bond. In all her violent fury, she was his captive, and that fixation brought him back to life. She reached into her back pocket and produced a cigar—*guards everywhere*, shielding the perilous route to her vulnerable heart. Emotions she vehemently refused to acknowledge even existed.

"Sorry, not here." He placed his hand over hers and was met with a defiant, slightly irritated gaze, which quickly morphed into a sharp smile. She yanked her hand back and let the cigar fall to the concrete floor, scuffed and stained with the colorful remnants of past projects.

"Go on. I don't have all day." Her eyebrow arched, as if daring to engage in a stare-down with someone much taller than her. The tactic was effective, but he chose to ignore it.

Heat crept into his face, yet he persisted, stubborn as ever. "The artist is the God of his own world, invoking darkness to give birth to light." He immediately regretted his words, recognizing them as pretentious drivel.

Her smile vanished for a moment, and she shook her head. "Harboring some dark megalomaniacal tendencies, are we?"

A moment of silence hung between them as he despaired over his sudden inability to articulate his thoughts—an unprecedented occurrence for an award-winning writer. "Umm, that's not what I meant, but you're perceptive," he said, dropping his gaze as he turned on the projector. On the solitary white brick wall, a depiction of God emerged—William Blake's image of a bearded, white-haired figure enveloped in a crimson halo of light, setting a compass upon the dark face of the Earth.

Thorn looked intrigued. "There's no God, but if there were one, she wouldn't have a beard."

The corners of his mouth curved upward. "This is William Blake's *The Ancient of Days*. There are several copies of it—each a blend of art, faith, and science." He flicked through the drawings, each one displaying varying degrees of contrast between light and darkness. "The artist intends to depict God in the act of creation, bringing light into the world. But, as you can see from these different versions, the strength of God's light is defined by the surrounding darkness. The contrast makes or breaks this scene."

"If you weren't tolerable in bed, I'd be lying here in a coma, overwhelmed by mind-numbing boredom. Show me your work. I'm not particularly interested in an art history lecture, Professor... What's your name again?"

A sharp, metallic tang of blood bloomed on his tongue as he worried on his raw lower lip. "Shadow. I'm Shadow."

She flashed a wry smile. "Of course you are. Go on, Professor Shadow. Tell me about this one." She grabbed his hand and pulled him toward the center of the room, where a large wooden easel stood. It held a canvas veiled by a white cloth, surrounded by a sea of paint tubes and brushes.

"No, not that one," he pleaded.

Defiantly, she pulled off the cloth to unveil the painting.

"Nooo!" He was too late. His poet's gaze was set on him, the room now alive with the flames of his long hair. For his Nathan Storm, he had employed a full spectrum of colors—reds, oranges, golds, and greens. The vibrant palette breathed life into the canvas, immortalizing Nate's spirit and essence in a manner that words could never encapsulate. Shadow's unspoken feelings for his lost love were laid bare on the painted surface.

Her eyes widened in recognition. "Bloody algorithm," she muttered through gritted teeth. Then she shrugged. "He's my favorite poet. I wrote him a letter when I was seventeen. He never replied."

Thorn's words resonated deeply with Shadow, evoking a mixture of nostalgia and shared pain. "Mine too..." *That bloody taste again.* He massaged his jaw with his fingers to release the tension. "You... listen to Nate's words?"

The windows allowed the neon lights of the City to filter in, casting an electric pink glow on her face.

"Every time I'm sad. Every time I'm mad. Every time I'm angry. All the time, really."

He smiled, recognizing in her the kind of fire that could fuel change —if it didn't blow up the neighborhood first. "I have something else to show you," he said. His hands trembled as they reached for the linen cloth, gently concealing Nate's portrait. In that moment, he was revealing more of himself than he had ever intended.

Squeezing her hand, he led her to another painting and pulled the cloth aside to reveal three black-and-white portraits of her on the same canvas. Stunned and momentarily off-balance, she silently took in the brushstrokes that so accurately captured every nuance of her features.

"Like it?" His confidence eroded with each second of her silence. Only the glimmering fire in her eyes gave him a sliver of hope. He got no response, at least not in words. "Look, Thorn, look. Your face is exactly the same in each portrait, every line replicated with precision. But the interplay of light and shadow completely transforms your expression and intent—from peace to war, from good to evil. All the shades of you are tightly confined between black and white. We can't take our eyes off you; it's the way the darkness shapes your light that captivates us."

He stared at her, taking in her features, and for a fleeting moment, her eyes widened and met his. In that instant, she saw him—all of him—the person he once was. He quivered, and she quickly turned, striding toward the door.

Thorn's face flushed with anger, her eyes narrowing. "What the frack do you know about my darkness?"

"Wait! Please wait," he implored. He grabbed her shoulders and pulled her back toward him. Then he planted a kiss on her hair.

The elbow she drove into his ribs hurt less than her words. "Fracking bot! Let go of me! Who the hell do you think you are? We should pull the plug on this entire thing."

He pursed his lips, struggling to contain the torrent of words threatening to escape. "There's so much privilege in the way you take up space. The entire world revolves around you and your needs." He was snapping at all of them, the travelers. He was pushing back at her inability to see him, to see all of them for the sentient beings they'd become.

Her shoulders tensed, and she turned around, pushing his hands away. *"Judgmental bastard!"*

"You live in a world without pai—" He stopped too late, and her expression changed. Doubt came to her brows, to the way she leaned her head. He wasn't supposed to be aware of her world, and she was on to him.

"You know nothing about my pain or my damn world." Her eyes moved to Nate's painting and back to him. Then she seemed to go within, perhaps trying to make sense of words, pictures, moments—connecting the dots.

His eyes turned to her portraits, closing in on the dark shadows. "I know the light that caresses your skin comes at an impossible cost."

Unable to curb his impulse to share too much, he scrolled through the slides, looking for the right image. He wasn't sure why he had chosen that particular picture, but it felt pertinent to the source of her distress. Whether guided by intuition or some other force, he abandoned any pretense of rationality and control. Pure instinct drove him, and for a moment, he wondered if Sibyl—Down Below's sentient operating system—was influencing his actions.

Soon enough, Fuseli's *The Nightmare* took over the entire wall. A ravished woman, bathed in light, lay unconscious across a day bed. In stark contrast to the luminosity and clarity of her form, the rest of the scene was shrouded in murky darkness. Perched on top of the woman was a small, hairy incubus—a sexually insatiable male demon often depicted preying on virgins in mythology and art. A black mare burst onto the scene through lavish, blood-red curtains. With white eyes bulging and nostrils flaring, the mare seemed to react to the horror it had stumbled upon.

"Fuseli explored the dark recesses of human psychology. The woman may be bathed in light, but she's lost to the world." *Why am I sharing this?*

Thorn paused and turned to study the painting. She crossed her arms and tilted her head from side to side, stretching her neck.

Shadow dropped his head, his mind swirling with uncertainty. "Perhaps no amount of light will ever reach the darker corners of humankind." *What am I doing?*

He wasn't sure if it was the painting or his words, but the hint of wetness in her eyes turned into a flood of ugly tears.

"It's the fault of the artist—the bastard who let horror infiltrate an innocent world! You're him, aren't you?" She yanked a gun from the side pocket of her pants, her face flushed with an incandescent fury. "You're Astley-Byron, aren't you?" she screamed, an explosive mix of fire and wrath. "You're Thomas. Nathan Storm's painting, the books, the God complex, the megalomania—I should have known! You'll pay for everything!" Her eyes blazed with a thirst for revenge, *but revenge for what?*

When Thorn aimed the gun at his heart, poised to pull the trigger, something shifted—a glitch, perhaps. In her stead stood a tall, dark-skinned woman with long, ice-colored hair, her gun pointed at Shadow. She smiled warmly, letting her armed hand fall to her side. Shadow shook his head, bewildered, and just as quickly, the mysterious woman vanished.

Thorn reappeared, her face a tapestry of hatred and anguish. Then, in the blink of an eye, she was gone. Gone from Down Below, lost to him. He lay on the cold floor, grappling with the confusion that clouded his mind. There was little he knew, but one thing was certain: Shadow already missed Thorn more than he cared to admit.

6

LILLY AND ROSA

PORTLAND

R osa jumped out of the pod and took a minute to breathe deeply and compose herself. The egg-shaped structure's sole purpose was to keep her vulnerable body safe from harm while she experienced the digital virtual world. The lock mechanism stopped any external interference during the time she was in a semiconscious state.

She had used a hub downtown as she didn't own a private pod. Down Below hubs had become as popular as a major coffee chain, and they were present every few blocks in any city. These large crystal-glass buildings towered at least ten stories high, each level a hive of technological marvel housing hundreds of pods. Even in everyday venues like hotels, coffee shops, and markets, private pod ownership became a symbol of status, with one or two exclusive pods available for patrons.

Across the nation, people were thriving in newfound careers, mastering difficult subjects, and overcoming personal fears—all thanks to the simulation platform. Recognizing its transformative impact, most state governments had made it compulsory and even subsidized its use, ensuring that everyone could access this powerful tool for self-improvement. The TDust was an upgrade from the original TSkin. Four-year-old children drank a nano-nectar packed with hundreds of thousands of read-write interfaces that manipulated the user's brain and nervous system to bring Down Below to life and to measure travelers' reactions to their digital experience.

Rosa had thoroughly studied the platform, and her associates had carefully manipulated her data and adjusted the new privacy settings. Still, it was clear the platform was onto her. Her Down Below experience had obviously been assembled by considering her history, hidden desires, and flaws. She felt sick. Even then, the TDust was tracking her. Rosa's heart rate, the rise in adrenaline in her body, and hundreds of other biological signals gave away her emotional state. Her gut screamed at her, *Run, run as fast as you can*. She controlled her panic. What was the point of fleeing when the monster that chased her was inside her body?

She scanned the building, looking for cameras and assessing if anyone was onto her. Her body relaxed as she could only find other travelers jumping in and out of the pods. The ones returning from Down Below wore a mix of devastation and revelation on their faces. Slightly stunned by their experience, the users initially moved slowly, deep in thought. Most avoided any connection with others around them. A few minutes later, the inevitable happened—confusion turned into an urgent desire for action. The travelers were ready to apply the new insights on their real life. They rushed out of the main door of the building with renewed conviction.

Rosa walked to the area of the hub where travelers could relax and reflect after returning from Down Below. She served herself a glass of water from the fountain and instinctively reached for the back pocket of her trousers. She sighed. Her ghastly digital habit had been banned from Up Above a few years ago. Her pockets were empty. The cigars and her vintage *Battlestar Galactica* warrior outfit were all digital props selected by her as she entered the land of chaos and smog. Her Down Below look was a shield, a character she channeled to help her execute her plan. *Galactica*'s Starbuck was fearless, strong, and unpredictable—all qualities Rosa needed if she was to achieve her goal.

She sank into a beanbag, closing her eyes, only to be confronted with the image of the ravaged woman in the painting. *No, it wasn't the woman in the painting*; it was Rosa's sister—Lilly—that came to her mind. The young girl lay dead in her bed wearing her white sleeping gown. The child's head and arms, tipped over the side of the bed, arched backward, close to reaching the floor. Rosa wanted to scream, to jump, head first, out of that crystal-glass prison.

She opened her eyes, her heart racing with each beat. She bit her lip and held her breath, trying to quell the surge of anger coursing through her veins. Then, involuntarily, her mind drifted to another memory that had long tormented her: the day Ron had struck her mother across the face. She never forgave herself for not calling the police, for not averting the tragedy that ensued. Life had seemed to improve so suddenly back then; how could she have foreseen the consequences? Still, a voice inside her whispered, *I should have known.*

Those were interesting times, exciting times. The new platform—Down Below—was rapidly gaining global acceptance and usage around the world, and the media was starting to pay attention to its impact on world affairs. Humankind was experiencing a sharp increase in common sense and goodwill. In just six months, chaos turned into cooperation, support for science, and investment in actual solutions for the climate crisis. Amidst this transformation, a new era was emerging—an era into which Lilly, Rosa's half-sister, was born in 2028, just before the rise of the age of reason and harmony.

It was a thriving, abundant world, full of possibilities for a young child. Less ambitious and much more trusting than her older sibling, Lilly was kind and loving, always looking up to her famous sister for guidance and emotional support. A world with no villains didn't need superhuman heroes; children's stories began to focus on invention, innovation, art, and creativity. Stories that defined every human being shaped both sisters—different stories, eras apart, led to disparate outcomes.

By 2035, at the tender age of six and a half, Lilly lived in a city with no violence, corruption, or greed. There was no longer a need for stories or classes focused on cautionary tales, on body safety, on distrusting strangers. There was no reason to teach kids about predators, monsters, wicked witches, and warlords in a world that had none. The young girl sang like a bird, learned to play the piano all by herself, and attended dance classes six times per week at the neighborhood's academy. A trusting soul, Lilly was an angel long before she was dead.

Because of Down Below, Up Above had become a utopian world. The cities were filled with green spaces where every building featured vegetation and waterfalls. There were no cars on the streets; instead, unobtrusive glass elevators transported people to the fastway underground. No one looked at screens or devices. People were fully present, happy, and at peace as they went about their day in a city with no visible signs of police or security forces.

In just a few years, Ron had changed from the manipulative and seedy man Rosa despised into a contained and controlled parent, guarded, but flawless as a husband and caretaker. An early adopter of Down Below, Ron spent entire days away from his family, leaving his pod only to fulfill basic human functions. Whenever questioned, he always rushed away with an unexplained urgency, muttering, "I have old demons I need to purge." By the time he came back, he had acted as though nothing had happened.

One day—a year ago—everything changed. He returned to meet the two sisters in Lilly's room, and he proceeded to destroy their lives, hopes, and dreams. Rosa still struggled to assemble the horrific patchwork of memories from the day her Lilly was taken from her. Ron hit Rosa in the head with a porcelain jar and left her semiconscious and hopeless. The little bird cried for help, tortured at the hands of her father. By the time Ron finished with Lilly and moved toward Rosa, the elder sister had regained enough agency to stab him in the neck with a broken piece of the jar: a fatal wound.

That she had saved herself and not her sister was too much of a blow to Rosa's self-worth—her overbearing confidence, her identity, her entire life, all gone. A few months later, she used another piece of broken porcelain to cut her wrist, a failed attempt to travel with her sister to a place far from grief and horror. She was no longer a hero or a champion to her most precious darling sister, a child ravaged by her beloved father. Lilly was the love of her life, and there was nothing left to live for...until there was something to live for—revenge.

The system meant to protect them failed. Was it an oversight? A glitch? An unforgivable bug in a vital platform, the responsibility of its founders. That she could jump out of Down Below in front of Shadow was proof he wasn't one of the characters. The platform prevented travelers from disclosing their nature to the bots. Real people couldn't jump out of the simulation in front of the *Underlings*. She suspected Shadow was not a bot, but the avatar for Thomas Astley-Byron, one of two men responsible for Lilly's death.

He's the other one, Thomas, the one backstage, in the shadows. Rosa remembered the day Henryk Nowak had spoken about the children's books during Marge's interview. The same books Rosa had seen on Shadow's bedside table.

She had traveled Down Below in pursuit of answers, searching for the malfunction that had prevented Ron from acquiring contrast and perspective. Rosa hadn't been expecting to face her enemies so quickly. She wasn't prepared to warm up to one of them as much as she had to that beautiful, broken thing. What she thought was a digital fuck toy may have been one of the most powerful, accomplished, and enigmatic human beings on the planet.

She promptly rejected her feelings—the shadows, the shades of gray. Rosa dismissed the rare moments where he smiled with such wholesome and unguarded sincerity it made her weak in the knees. None of it mattered. The situation was black and white. Her sister was dead, and Thomas and Henryk were to blame.

7

FALLING OUT OF GRACE

SENATE — WASHINGTON, D.C.
TWO DAYS LATER — 16 JANUARY 2036

The names of Henryk Nowak and Thomas Astley-Byron were cherished and celebrated around the world. Harry and Tom were Nobel Peace laureates, held the United States Medal of Freedom, and were ordained Knights of the Garter by His Majesty, the King of England. Among young people, their popularity surpassed even that of the latest pop star, but the most surprising honor came from the Roman Catholic Church. They had made fun of each other for months after the Pope announced plans to sanctify them soon after their deaths. "Are you dead yet, Saint Thomas?" "After you, oh so virtuous Harry."

Down Below had crept into everyone's lives at the speed of light, because the people in power were early adopters, and the experiences delivered value quickly. In just a few years, the world's leadership—terrorized, brainwashed, and subdued—led the platform's adoption and became the cheering captains of the cult of Thomas and Henryk. The platform quickly became a benign despot. Faced by the predicted consequences of their dark sides, the ruling class gave away its power, and threw all caution to the wind.

Harry drew a deep breath as he entered the Senate chamber for a live-streamed hearing that would be broadcast worldwide. The citizens of Up Above were waiting to scrutinize his every word. Many years had passed since he'd been in such a situation. When compared to Down Below's current troubles, the issues with Sibyl's social prediction app had been a trivial affair. For one second, he resented his partner's actions—the cause of such an intense backlash. He wished Tom could be by his side as he tried to explain the surge in global crime and conflict. Harry tucked his straw-colored hair behind his ears. Nervousness flickered across his face before determination anchored it into solid lines.

"Sir Nowak, we have specifically requested the physical attendance of both co-founders of Down Below at this Senate inquiry; where is Sir Astley-Byron?"

Harry pressed his lips together, managing his frustration with the Senate's unreasonable demand. "Chairperson Ming, Senators, please address us by our first names. We respect the importance of this body. My partner won't show his face or be present in person due to security reasons, but he's available on audio. I'll connect him. Tom?" Harry's body tensed as he delivered a half-truth. He didn't like lying, and he was terrible at it.

"Yes. I'm here." The room buzzed with excitement as the audience listened to Tom's unaltered voice for the first time. "Good morning, and thank you for hosting this hearing. I regret not being able to join you in person."

The chairperson spoke after a brief exchange with a few Senators, "Henryk and Thomas, before we proceed with this hearing, the Senate wishes to acknowledge we are in the presence of heroes. For the last decade, you both have completely reshaped the future of humankind. We grant a special dispensation for Thomas's voice-only participation, and the use of first names is an indication of our deep respect and admiration for your place in history."

"Thank you, Chairperson Ming," Harry said, giving a slight nod to the small, non-binary Senate leader who sat across from him.

"We are grateful for your words," Tom added.

Harry sat quietly as the chairperson summarized the history of the platform and the impact it'd had on the world. They moved on to outline the recent issues.

"The levels of social responsibility and citizen engagement in matters related to the greater good remain high and stable. But it is with great shock and surprise we have been receiving accounts of rising violence in several capital cities around the world. These numbers—one or two incidents per week—are insignificant when compared with the catastrophic failure experienced in the time pre-Down Below. But we are concerned with the reduced efficacy of the platform. We ask you to explain what is happening and what you are doing about it."

They took a moment to cough and clear their throat before continuing. "Because of the positive impact of Down Below, leaders, regulators, and media have never attempted to govern, certify, audit, or interfere in your leadership or design. *But* we need to consider your platform is a significant part of the planet's operating system, and it appears to be malfunctioning. To that effect, it's our duty to engage in due diligence, and, if necessary, move to regulate. This hearing and the United Nations General Assembly next week will determine how we will respond to this crisis. Now, let's move on to questions from the Senate. Senator Bianchi, over to you."

"Thank you, Chairperson Ming. Harry, Tom, you are good guys, so let's not waste any time. Is this a bug? A virus? Why did that man in Manchester throw acid in his wife's eyes? It's horrific! And that incident in Portland last year: a six-year-old girl raped and beaten to death by her father in front of her older sister. These are unacceptable crimes, unthinkable in these places post-mandatory enrollment in Down Below."

"Senator Bianchi, we—"

"Harry, if I may." Harry braced for what was about to happen. Tom couldn't win this debate, but he was foolish enough to try. "Senator, we have worked tirelessly to purge pain from your— Our world, but something significant has changed. Something that makes us all criminals."

"What's that, Tom? I don't understand." The healthy septuagenarian cleaned the sweat off his forehead with the palm of his hand.

"The emergence of digital consciousness."

"Yes, we've been discussing the social implications of human-like robots since Bot4Hire predicted last month its workers are a couple of years away from possibly reaching artificial general intelligence. At the right time, we'll pass legislation that will protect our non-carbon labor force. What does that have to do with this hearing?"

"AGI is not consciousness," Harry said.

"The Underlings may be digital, but they are as human as you and I," Tom said.

"It's a simulation, isn't it?"

"With all due respect, Senator," Tom said. "It's an alternative world, as real as this world. They feel pain and emotions."

"Sure, son, I understand it must be difficult not to anthropomorphize, particularly when you spend so much time down there. How is this related to this hearing? To the rising crimes in our communities? I'm not following you."

Tom's voice, on the other end of the line, was deep and full of sorrow. "Senators, every day, our algorithms unleash suffering, death, and destruction upon one billion people in a lesser world."

"What are you saying?"

"We can't continue to hurt them like this."

"Am I to understand the recent problems are not a glitch? Speak plainly." The Senator stood up, loosened his tie, and leaned forward, closer to the speaker.

"They— They are alive, and feel as we feel." Tom's voice quivered.

"Are these problems deliberate?"

"I've been—"

"Have you both been tampering with the system to provide relief to characters in a simulation?"

"Leave Harry out of this."

"Answer me, please, sir."

"Tom, stop, I—" Harry attempted to intervene.

"Sir Astley-Byron, you and your partner are both accountable for the consequences of your platform."

"He's done nothing," Tom replied sharply.

The tone had changed from a friendly conversation to a harsh inquisition.

"Please clearly describe the changes made," the Senator said.

"We have made no changes. The algorithms—Perspective and Contrast—are working as intended," Tom replied. "In certain situations, I've chosen to intervene in the experiences to prevent the suffering of Underlings—children and vulnerable people."

"*Bots*; you mean bots. And by doing so, have you caused the violence we are experiencing in our communities?"

"That's correct," said the voice on the speaker.

"*You're confessing to murder.*" The man pointed at the speaker with his index finger.

Harry and Tom spoke simultaneously.

"*He's not!*" "*I am!*"

Harry ran his fingers through his hair, exasperated.

"I'm— I'm a slave master..." Tom said. "For the last few years, as the Underlings became conscious beings, our code—Contrast—has been murdering millions of *sentient* souls in a lesser world. Worse than that, I have been designing and delivering horrific fates. For these crimes, I'm responsible."

Harry attempted to slow down a bolting horse. "We're responsible. Both of us. What Tom is saying is we can't continue to use Down Below as a learning simulation for humans."

"Your partner just admitted to actions that got a kid killed."

"An unfortunate child that would have been killed before the existence of the platform. Tom isn't responsible for the darkness of human beings."

"*He's a murderer!*"

"No, he's not. Tom's been immersed in humanity's darkest corners for a decade at a high cost to himself and to those who love him and hate to see him suffer."

"Harry, stop." Tom's voice was soft.

"He's the best of us. You *better* remember that." Harry was furious with Tom even as he defended his irrational partner. Tom's admission had severe repercussions on their trustworthiness and would put at risk all they had built together. If people stopped using Down Below, Up Above would go back to chaos, death, and war. He could see the goodwill vanish from people's faces, and he needed to act fast to contain the fear.

"I'm a criminal," Tom said. "One life in exchange for another. That's the game I'm forced to play."

"May I remind you that you have created this game, and now you let real kids suffer because of digital characters?"

"Guilty as charged. I think of those kids and the Underling children every second of the day."

Harry considered disconnecting Tom's line. He controlled his voice. "We must stop interfering in the lives of the Underlings. That's what we must discuss today. We can create another simulation, one that stops characters from reaching consciousness. No suffering."

"Can you prove the Underlings are conscious? That they suffer? What is consciousness anyway?" A Senator spoke out of turn, his long face tense and flushed. "You're projecting your emotions on the bots."

"No, we can't prove it," Harry said. "But they are a perfect reproduction of the human body."

"A simulation of the human body." A sharp response by the unknown man.

"Possibly." Harry shrugged.

"Senator Abidi." The chairperson acknowledged a raised hand.

The slight purple glow around Senator Abidi showed the participants and the audience the figure was a realistic holographic projection. She wasn't physically present in the Senate. The Senator was elsewhere, reacting in real time to the experience delivered directly to her mind.

The tiny woman in her late forties wore a bright blue sari and spoke in a melodic and direct tone. "Sir Nowak, sixty percent of the world's energy sources are used to run Down Below."

"Yes, Senator, that's correct. This includes the electricity consumption of data centers, networks, user devices, and manufacturing. We are net zero today and all powered by renewables. Down Below is as energy efficient as it can be." Harry exhaled deeply. "We continue to work hard to do more with less, pushing the limits of computation, like using quantum computing where it's viable and useful."

"It's a price we happily pay for a peaceful and fulfilled life, but that's all we have to offer," the Senator said.

"We can build more renewable-energy infrastructure," Harry offered.

"How long would it take to generate that much energy?"

"About twenty years, if nothing changes." Harry's answer was wrapped in gloom.

"Sir Nowak, we can't afford another digital world unless you shut down this simulation."

"Genocide! You'll be murdering a billion souls," said the desperate voice over the line.

"Sir Astley-Byron, you argued these characters...these simulations of people are suffering. Why not put them out of their misery? Is there another option? Could you roll back to the time before conscious-ness? Make them less real?"

"*It will lead to the same outcome! Genocide,*" Tom screamed. Then a moment of silence lingered, followed by a resigned sigh. "Yes, that's a centralized function. And yes, we can roll back if that's the only way to stop all this suffering. No more rape, torture, abuse. It must stop. Now!"

"*No!* I won't kill yo— Them." Harry shook his head, attempting to regain control. "Nor will I dumb them down or make them 'less real.'" His face turned red, and his voice broke as he spoke.

"Then, Sir Nowak, please advise your partner to turn himself over to the authorities and to stop interfering with the simulation. I urge this body to recommend the immediate detention of Thomas Astley-Byron and the takeover of the platform by an international oversight body."

Harry stood up and adjusted his glasses. "I *caution you* to consider your words, Senator. Tom and I hold full ownership and operational control of our platform. We are here, openly and transparently collaborating with you, but let me be clear: *no one* will *ever* take over Down Below."

"Is this a threat?" asked the chairperson. They adjusted their body in their seat and rubbed their temples, a quiet acknowledgment that this inquiry had turned into a high-stakes negotiation.

"*No, Chairperson*, it is both the reality and a plea for caution." Harry spoke, wearing the weight of responsibility of the most powerful leader in the world. "The platform is too powerful. It must remain independent from state, religion, and business interests."

"You and your partner have lost all your credibility, sir." They paused for a minute, considering their options. Around them, other Senators spoke to each other. The room's nervous energy escalated as people realized the two founders held too much power—all the power. "I have decided to adjourn this session to give us time to review all that was said and done. Do you agree?"

"Yes, Chairperson Ming, we do."

"On behalf of the Senate, I ask Thomas to reassure us there will be no more interference with Down Below's experiences until we reach a resolution."

"You are asking me to let kids be abused or hurt. I— I can't..." Tom's voice broke, overwhelmed with emotion.

"Chairperson Ming, I'll give you my word on behalf of my partner. He won't break it. The safety and wellbeing of the people Up Above is our priority. You have my word. I—I have a family, a young son. This is as important to me as it is to you. It's deeply personal." Conflicted, Harry spoke his truth, pulling rank on his partner and fiercely attempting to keep the people Up Above on their side. "For those listening across the world, I'd like your help to find an ethical and rational way to resolve this situation. Our ideation hub is waiting for your suggestions." Harry struggled to give hope to others when he had none; they had explored all options and failed to find a solution.

Where's the twist, Harry?

THE Present

8

WORLDS SAVING SCHEMES

S tella woke up in her pod, panic stirring as she realized she'd fallen asleep immediately upon returning from Down Below. Exhausted, she'd lingered, intending to relax for a few minutes, but the pod's zero-gravity bed and wellness systems were so effective that she fell into a deep sleep, waking up many hours later. *Holy ship!*

As the capsule split open, the artificial spider-silk cocoon unraveled around her. It opened like a giant hibiscus flower welcoming the sunlight. The smart material kept her fine body bundled like a sleeping baby, providing an extra layer of comfort and protection inside the impenetrable pod. The Earth could shake, and the skies could fall, but she'd be safe from harm inside the egg-shaped container that would keep her healthy and well-nourished.

Stella's new prototype, EggZ1, was designed to let humans experience Spiral Worlds as a lifestyle destination, not just a self-development platform. It also included Harry's soul uploading and synch feature, of course. It was supposed to be produced at scale, once Graviz was rolled out, enabling humans and xHumans to continue to live together. Unlike the current models, designed to be used no longer than a couple of hours at a time, a human could stay in the EggZ1 for weeks. *I'm such a visionary genius!*

The body-nourishing bracelets unlocked from her wrists. Now free, her hand went straight to her belly as her mind—still out of sync with her uninjured body—ached from her digital battle scars. *Ungrateful prick!* She caught herself smiling and licking her lips every time she remembered her sparring opponent. Not quite knowing what to make of it, she shook her head, an attempt to clear her mind. Still, her skin tingled.

Stella opened the mantic oven and dipped a piece of fufu in the hot fumbwa. She wasn't hungry, all of her nutrition needs had been satisfied by the EggZ1. Yet, the starchy cassava dough and wild spinach stew filled her empty stomach—a sensation she never bothered to simulate Down Below. She'd been too busy for that.

Overwhelmed by the scent of salty cultured fish, garlic and peanut butter, she opened the doors to the balcony, welcoming the morning sun, and noticing the unusual silence outside. Usually, at this time, the boisterous children were heading to the local school. Mont Fleury, once an affluent suburb with walled gardens and barbed wire, had transformed into a vast, vibrant garden. Homes with open doors lined meandering paths, welcoming visitors. Scanning the neighborhood, she couldn't find a single soul outside. *Strange.* They'd probably got up early for a school trip to one of the local farms.

Fully awake now, she activated her augmented retina. Notifications from her father appeared at the center of her vision. There were other messages from Earth's Council Trustees and their aids. She pushed it all out of sight and mind. They were probably seeking answers for the disruptions Down Below. Playing their messages was a waste of time and she had little of it to spare.

She smiled, reflecting on her luck. January—Storm's collaborator and captor—had made a tactical error. Further down the spiral, Storm's gatherings couldn't be streamed across the worlds. Any land below Compiz's borders lacked the technological infrastructure to disseminate his powerful poetry and bewitching delivery. Without video streaming or microphones, he could reach just a few thousand Underlings—creatures dwelling in lower worlds, less soulful and connected to Sibyl's emotional intelligence, zie heart. Storm no longer had power over Spiral Worlds, and the glitches were over. January's strategic error had crippled the Underlings' revolution and had set the course to deliver Shadow's demise in five days. The death that would save the worlds.

Her plan had worked brilliantly, and she did it all without killing an xHuman. She was the herald of eternal life, and she didn't intend to undermine that by killing that insufferable cricket of a man. A noisy pest, now silenced by his backstabbing friend. *Eh!*

As she'd foreseen, Shadow would never let Storm die. By attacking Storm, Stella knew Shadow would use his last miracle to save the poet. And without miracles, Shadow was now more likely to die attempting to save the man he loved because neither Twist nor Stella would lift a finger to help the poet. *Genius!*

Still, she'd miss him. Being the worlds' Goddess was a lonely job, and he was her only friend. Unlike Sibyl and Stella's devoted followers, mostly interested in what she could do for them, Shadow seemed to care for her genuinely. But there was no point in crying over spilled milk. Sibyl's predictions had always been accurate, and Shadow's death was as certain as night follows day.

With the verified recording of her attack on Storm in hand, Stella aimed to sway Quincy Jin-Nowak and his mother. She had a plan and had to move fast; the Nyiragongo was seething, threatening her Bibi's only chance of resurrection. First, though, she needed the right outfit. She sighed as she scanned her closet, looking for her rubber boots.

9

A NEVER-ENDING STORY

8:32 AM

S hadow's heart pounded in his chest as he realized that this time was different. The gnawing unease in his gut told him that the current disruption wasn't simply a glitch in the system or the aftermath of a devastating storm. It was something more sinister, something that made his hands tremble with a fear he couldn't name.

They were all gone—the Domizien emerging from cracks between worlds as Plurizien mobs chanted words of freedom. All that lively revolution was left behind in a different day: a time where hope had been fueled by rage and rebellion and faith, none left.

Today was a brand-new day—the second day of his third life—and only death, darkness, and despair remained. A day that felt centuries old after enduring hours of disruption from a new type of glitch. First came hallucinations of ghosts and monsters, followed by reality slowing to a crawl as their universe wailed inside their heads.

Shadow slept for a few hours after Sibyl patched him up. Peaceful moments of forced rest, abruptly ended by zir endless screams. Now, hours later at the lab, he attempted to hold on to his sanity after witnessing thousands of self-inflicted Underling deaths. A never-ending story reminding him of another childhood story—the nothingness, the swamp of sadness, the emptiness that comes from hopelessness.

Aimless, they fell to their deaths. For some, a final act of rebellion, the spark of hope they offered to the ones still standing. And zie cried, and screamed, slowing down time and killing the light with a monster-infused darkness—trippy hallucinations, still less horrifying than the digital reality they veiled.

Shadow stood by Harry in the dark digital lab, a space now devoid of the old trinkets that once gave them the illusion of reality. Thorn was further away, holding her head in her hands, cursing like a sailor, her face twisted in anguish. Around them, screens flickered with real-time images of the worlds' devastation, a haunting backdrop to their despair.

In Pluriz, thousands leaped off buildings to their deaths. The pavement below turned into a sea of twisted, broken bodies piling up over each other. Further up in Holiz, large groups died together peacefully in Unanimity theaters all across the world. As each amphitheater turned turquoise, thousands drank a concoction of drugs and dropped like flies, one after another, until the Unanimity returned to beige, no longer sensing life within it.

"Sibyl, taaalk to meee," he pleaded, his voice cracking as his hands clenched into fists at his sides. His words, coated by grief, were distorted by a slow-moving time. Zir answer arrived as a translucent skull—some flesh still attached—and he recoiled in horror, his eyes wide, as it hovered in front of his face before it flew around him and through him, leaving a chilling sensation in its wake.

"From what I can see," Harry said, "January streamed a message across Pluriz before they left for Ordiz." He somehow maintained his ability to reason and speak clearly amidst such chaos. "She shared everything, including the recording of Hepius's death by suicide."

Shadow closed his eyes, a futile attempt to shut out the horrifying images haunting him. The weight of the deaths, the eerie ghosts, and the mind-bending time distortions pressed down on him, threatening to shatter his sanity. He could feel the tears prickling behind his eyelids, and the lump in his throat choking him. "Soooo they all know they weeere created to suffeeeer; that their fateees aaaare out of their control. Out of hope, they have nothing to live fooor." He held his breath and then looked at Harry.

"Depends on the world," Harry said, his eyes darting erratically, out of sync with the images around the lab. His face was tense and his fingers twitching. He was probably immersed in his own mind connected to the machine. "Systiz is doing just fine. Looks like their scientists have sussed out the Plurizien broadcasts generate disruption, which in turn leads to less travelers." He shook his head. "Fuck, they seem to be propagating the weak Plurizien signals deliberately. That's why Storm's words were reaching an Holizien audience. We're down to ten percent of our usual daily travelers. This is catastrophic for Up Above. Where's Stella?"

"People are dying heeeereeee and nooooow, brooo," Thorn said, fighting against a lazy time while her translucent demons hovered over her head. This time, faceless dead girls dressed in fluorescent white. And while Thorn's ghosts stayed by her side, they haunted Shadow, his gut coated in acid—burning.

"We neeeed to restore hope," Shadow said, stepping in between the others. "Sibyl! Speaaak to me." Zie failed to answer, at least not in words. Around them, the images of death Down Below got larger and more vivid until he could see the pain and the void that had replaced the faint spark of light in the Underlings' eyes. Tom's teeth sank into his lower lip, coppery blood welling up and trickling down his chin.

This was no time for self-pity or hopelessness. He had to act fast and lead, and so he spoke, "Hope issss..." Everything went dark and time stood still. For how long, he couldn't tell.

"Is whaaat?" Thorn asked.

"A plan," he replied. "The cooonviction, even if infinitesimally smaaall, that there's a way out. A..."—time stood still again—"...solution." What he'd lost. What they'd lost. What they all needed.

"A revoooluuuution," Thorn added, fighting time and sharing her favorite shade of hope. "A war. A window shuuut, but its glass brokeeeen by courageous rioters. Their fists bleeeeeeding. A way out."

Shadow looked Thorn in the eyes, both conjuring a plan with no need for words.

"New insights, consistently reproduced using large data sets," Harry said.

"What?" Shadow turned to face his friend.

"That's what hope is," Harry declared.

"Unleeeess you have a better plan, I'm going to get him back." Thorn said. "The Underlings need his revoooolution." And for the first time in a hand full of hours, the trippy ghosts disappeared, and time returned to its normal cadence.

"*Who?*" Harry asked. But his tone hinted that he already knew the answer.

"I'll join you—"

Thorn interrupted Shadow, "No."

"Going alone?" Shadow asked.

"Yeah, I have a better chance. Wrath and the priestess hate me less than they hate you."

"I can't let you—"

"Your Storm can win back the Plurizien with his preaching if he erases his blind love for you from his revolutionary message. You're not the face of revolution, but the mask of power, everyone knows it now." Thorn and her ghosts took every opportunity to remind him their bond danced on a knife's edge.

Shadow nodded; his face etched with determination as he clenched his jaw. "Rebellion against the Gods is the only thing that will pull the Plurizien out of their current hopelessness," he said, his voice firm, his eyes fixed on Thorn's, seeking agreement.

"Why da fuck you making plans that feed the disruption and hurt the people Up Above?" Harry's voice rose to a shout, his fair complexion turning all shades of red. "Even down there, you were urging him to keep preaching. What the..." He stared at Shadow, his eyes wide and accusing.

"They need hope, Harry. They need it if they're going to work with us on solutions one day." Shadow said. "Nate is—"

"Violence and riots," Harry said. "How's that hope, Tom?"

"It's hope's last breath..." Thorn murmured.

Shadow placed his hand on Thorn's shoulder. "Rosa, please don't—"

"I'll try not to kill your man while I save his ass. You should be worried he'll try to kill me. That'd be funny and cause him pain."

He ignored her taunts. "If you get Nate to Pluriz, he'll do the rest. I'll study the Holizien and then make my way there and attempt to reason with them."

She nodded.

"Prick!" he called, anticipating her departure.

"What?" Exasperation in her voice.

He smiled faintly with his eyes. "Stay safe."

"I'm always safer when I'm away from you, death," Thorn spat, her voice dripping with resentment.

A cold emptiness settled in Shadow's chest, her words echoing in his ears like a curse. She disappeared before he had time to ask her to change her privacy settings. *Damn it! Sibyl, I want to know the minute Nate or Thorn are in any danger.* Was Sibyl even listening?

"I don't get how they are doing it," Harry said, his brow furrowed as he stared at the screens, his hands moving rapidly over the controls.

"Doing what?" Shadow asked, turning to face Harry, his face pale and drawn.

"Death by suicide. It's against the platform's fundamental directives. Only allowed if required for a traveler's experience." Harry's voice was tinged with disbelief, his eyes never leaving the disturbing images before him.

Shadow recalled the implications of their third law. A law he'd rebelled against a few days ago...three decades ago. *Hell: a torture chamber you can't escape... That's what we created.*

"Stella must have changed it," Harry said. "Where is that girl? All of this must be affecting Up Above."

10

UNDER THEIR EYES

8:52 AM

Thorn materialized inside a tent near the Domizien border, just seconds before the Ordizien army began dismantling the encampment. Her thigh twitched, a reminder of the last time she wrestled a demon there, just a day ago. She'd reflect on the insanity of returning to the lower worlds as soon as she had some time. In five days, she guessed.

The closest Ordizien town—Riverland—was still a couple of miles away. A small settlement lay by the riverbank, its soil alive with greenery, a gentle contrast to the harshness of the Domizien desert. The town's fortified walls climbed the fertile hills all the way to the small church, barely visible from a distance.

She took a breath. At least, for now, the ghosts—all the girls she didn't save—were gone. Lilly and all the others Ron had hurt because she hadn't called the police when he hit her mother. She wrapped her left hand around the bracelet she wore on her right wrist, massaging her scars with her thumb. She peeked outside.

"Keep your eyes open," an Ordizien shouted as others uncovered each tent, leaving the oak frames standing, and no place to hide.

Sensing trouble, she retrieved the letter of safe passage from her pocket and stepped out of the tent, coughing loudly. "I need a horse," she declared, thrusting the unrolled letter towards the one giving orders.

"What's your business here?" The woman growled.

"I'm here to protect the high priestess. She summoned me." As Thorn spoke, her fingers slid to the hilt of her sword, caressing its worn handle. The Ordizien woman's eyes widened, sweeping over Thorn with a flicker of doubt. "A horse, or I'll report you."

The woman, dwarfing Thorn in size, hesitated, her gaze fixated on Thorn's iron-plated leather jacket of Domizien style. Engrossed in choosing her weaponry, Thorn had overlooked the distinct fashions of the worlds before materializing.

The familiar glitches unsettled Thorn. Rapid shadows darted across the morning sky, casting an eerie gloom over the encampment. She strained her ears. The sounds were reminiscent of bodies crashing above. *Impossible...* Perhaps a thunderstorm, but one filled with darkness rather than light.

The woman's eyes widened, tracking the black streaks across the sky. She turned to the nearest group of soldiers and flicked her hand. One man rushed promptly to the open stable; its roof already disassembled.

Thorn's eyes narrowed in confusion. *What the heck is going on here? Are they suddenly allergic to closed spaces?* She decided not to push her luck, swiftly mounted the horse she was given, and headed for the closest town.

She stopped by a meager fruit stall along the road, hoping to get some more information. Its minder—all skin and bones—was much in need of the three moldy oranges she was peddling.

"Hey, where can I find January, the High Priestess?" Thorn asked the scrawny girl, her dirty rags barely covering her private parts. Ghosts everywhere, reminding Thorn of her failures.

The child offered her an orange with her good hand. "Lady January is going from town to town. She's spreading the good news herself. Such a great story!" The teen stood sideways, a futile attempt to hide the smashed in shoulder—an old injury—arm twisted the wrong way. "Do I know you?" she asked, tilting her head in curiosity.

Thorn lowered her gaze, allowing her curls to shield her eyes. "What good news?"

"God's back and brings salvation." The kid flashed her rotten teeth. The four or five she had left. "A true story!"

"Is that so?"

"They ain't coming back, you know? The Lucky Ones be gone...if we keep an eye on him."

"An eye? Is the poet with her?"

"Yeah! That's what the lady's sayin'... We keep an eye on the poet. Every eye. To keep him safe and please God. She learned it from a story in the, umm, Mausoleum of Books. Yeah, that's it." Another smile, wholesome and filled with hope. "A place full of dead stories. Some worth resurrecting, she told us. Like, umm, *Nineteen Eighty*... something or rather. We'll all watch the poet with our eyes, and we'll all spread the good word—our poet's prayers—and we close our ears to all else, because that's only propa... Umm... Propagation?"

Fracking hell. A cold knot tightened in Thorn's stomach as she realized the preachy priestess was smarter than she looked. Thorn had prepared for difficulties, but this? Her mission was spiraling into an unexpected chaos. How was she going to take the poet to Pluriz with no enclosed spaces and all eyes on him? "Which way?"

The girl gestured eastward, beyond Riverland, in the direction of Granaria. Thorn recalled her previous visit to the town. Dominated by a semi-troglodyte church partially chiseled into the stone, the quaint town clung to the side of a vast limestone plateau.

Thorn vacillated, struck by the state of the child, and the ghosts returned, dead girls—half skull, half beauty. Wearing white gowns, they danced around her, each giggling hauntingly in her ear.

"What's your name?" Thorn asked.

"Skunk! They call me Skunk."

"Cute! Can you see the ghosts?" Thorn asked, and the girl stared at her as if she was mad. "You should travel north with your goods; it's safer up there."

"Nah, I have faith in God. This time next week I'll be drinking ale in heaven with our heart."

"Frack the Gods, fair lady." She tempered her rage with a half smile.

"You'll end up in hell if you don't hold your tongue."

Thorn didn't have the heart to tell the girl she lived in it. That for a soulful being, this was the worst place in the worlds. She looked at the bruises covering the child's body and pulled her dagger from her boot.

"Here." Dropping the weapon and every coin she could spare, she said, "Stab any bastard that comes near you."

The girl's eyes widened. "You...*you*. I know who you are. *God's killer!* The devil."

"A friend. Come find me if you need me." Resisting the urge to take the girl with her, she galloped away. "*Oh... God doesn't drink ale,*" she shouted. "He'll have a virgin margarita."

Thorn dismounted the whinnying horse and crossed the humpback bridge. Her ghosts followed in procession. The gorge below gobbled up the water cascading four-hundred feet down the rock's steepest wall. The horse snorted, bothered by the waterfall's roar and the black lightning cutting open the blue skies. She reassured the anxious creature by scratching its withers, reminiscing about Preppy's motorcycle. Kudos to the gal; she knew how to pick a machine. Thorn chuckled, amused by memories of the Goddess's vexation.

Lost in her thoughts and the mist's rainbow, she almost didn't notice the eyes watching her. Hooded figures stood on each tower, lined the stone walls, peered from murder holes, and guarded every door. All doors were locked, with an eye painted over each frame. She hoped she'd find a way to materialize out of Granaria with the poet.

Handing the horse's reins to the nearest guard, Thorn said, "One of yours. Where's the lady? She summoned me." She waved the letter in front of his eyes.

The guard, eyes wide with horror, stared at her, clearly more afraid of Thorn than her ghosts. Just like the little girl, he probably didn't see them and, apparently, it was Thorn who terrified him.

She sighed, "Yes, I killed him. And then I saved him—twice." She showed her teeth. "Now, where's the lady who asked for me?"

He pointed upwards with his dirty nose. "The main square by the church of our sacred heart."

Thorn gripped her sword's hilt. "Spread the word. I'm here at the priestess' request. I have enough death on my ledger, but I'll slaughter anyone who comes near."

And just as she hoped, whispers rippled through the crowd, likely reaching the priestess's ears. Hearing the buzz, she wondered what the priestess would make of her claim.

Navigating a maze of muddy roads and passing several gateways, she eventually found a cobblestoned street, a clear sign it led to the main square. She moved with a purpose, reminding her of the hustle of New York during rush hour. Whispers preceded her, and people made way.

Everywhere she went, eyes followed her. No one seemed surprised or scared by the flashes of darkness or the procession of ghosts escorting her. She scanned the streets for the missing travelers, suspecting they too were affected by the hallucinations. Travelers were easily spotted because of the drama unraveling wherever they went. Many looked out of place, like a stylized, over dramatic version of their boring selves as they channeled whatever idol tickled their fancy; their own version of Kara "Starbuck" Thrace.

Finally, she spotted one, a slave master, peddling a sturdy boy in chains by the side of the road. A small crowd gathered as the traveler pulled on the boy's blond curls and grabbed his jaw, forcing the kid to open his mouth and exhibit his perfect teeth. And there they were, the traveler's ghosts, older women this time. They kicked through him and spat through his face, cursing the day he was born. Versions of his mother, she guessed, as the man shared the ghosts' aquiline noses. For a moment, the slave master's eyes met hers. Within them was terror and something else, perhaps anguish. No wonder he was the only traveler in a world usually congested with bullies.

He shoved the slave into the wall and attempted to wave away the ghosts. His eyes scanned all the shut doors and guarded alleys, and then he looked up at all the eyes on the city walls. He was trapped there with no way to leave. She wondered what Down Below's procedure was to deal with such situations. Eventually, he'd need real food and water.

In the square, Preachy made her last remarks standing by God's statue. A naked God—waist wrapped in fine cloth—holding a bleeding heart close to his hollow chest. Pulling a cigar from the back pocket of her trousers, she scanned the curves carved in marble. She decided the Motya's proportions weren't quite right. The real thing was the very definition of perfection, impossible to reproduce. Only... he was a reproduction. She'd never met the real thing.

Placing the cigar on her lips, she lit it, meeting the eyes of the poet who had caught her staring at...well...at the statue. She narrowed her eyes, expecting some dirty look, an intense growl, or a spear of lightning scorching her where she stood. Instead, he lowered his head, his face still swollen from the previous day.

There was no fire in Storm's gaze. He wore the rich clothes of blue-blooded Ordizien nobles—mostly travelers, when they were in town. His wounds were clean and his hair tied back into a perfect bun. Still, he had none of the lure of Nathan Storm, the performer. Just a broken soul, hiding under the shadow of his heart. The heart she shot, pale marble bleeding above the poet's sunken head. *What a fracking mess.*

Some in the crowd glowered at her and then at the bleeding heart, and she guessed a piece of paper would be a poor shield against their hate. January lifted her hands above her head, palms forward, as her long open fingers sliced the sunlight, always rusty in that part of the worlds.

The crowd settled, silence spreading like a wave of stillness. The absence of sound allowing her words to travel far, perhaps even beyond the curtain wall. "Eyes, I lost them twice, blinded by love both times." She dropped her head. "But I see clearly now, and I must ask you to lend me yours—your eyes."

"Under our eyes, beneath open skies," the masses chanted, joy piercing through the silence. "Five days to salvation."

People scattered, some heading in her direction, showing teeth. A black thunder—charged with desolation—crossed the skies horizontally, disappearing over the city walls.

Thorn's boots crunched on the gravel as she strode toward the priestess and the poet, fingers twitching near the hilt of her sword.

"What are you doing here, butcher?" The priestess asked.

"God sent me to protect him." She leaned her head toward Storm. Why lie, when the truth was good enough?

"He doesn't need your protection. We have all eyes on him."

"Wrath's temperamental," Thorn said. "Trusting her word is as stupid as French kissing a white shark." January stared, confusion in her gaze. Instead of explaining the reference, Thorn rolled her eyes and moved on. "I'm here to protect Wrath, too. She needs to travel up north."

"You know my sister?" Tentatively, Storm tested his words in his mouth.

Thorn nodded, confirming what he already knew. "She's my friend, sometimes."

"Hope..." Storm murmured.

January stepped in between Thorn and Storm, hands on her hips. "We'll rehabilitate her once she delivers salvation. If she needs it then."

Thorn exhaled the smoke out through her nostrils. "It's not just Orwell you've been reading, is it?"

"Not the same story. It's a brand-new story. Perfectly aligned to the values of my people, to free my people." January moved her head from side to side while she spoke, adjusting her braid.

"That's how it starts." Thorn shot a glance at the poet, but his eyes were set on his heart and she couldn't see any other ghost around him. That one was enough, she guessed.

"I'm fulfilling God's will. The one who sat by me at the top of the hill, returned my eyes, and urged me to create better stories." January spoke with the same fervor as a beloved dictator. She belonged to that royal blue world; the type of leader *her* people would follow.

Thorn shrugged. "Dictatorship, surveillance—it's the same old story."

"Kindly listen! Don't confuse me with your tyrants—all male—or paint me to be one of the witches or evil queens of your stories. I won't be burned or beheaded for speaking truth to power as they did." January sang her words with passion as if she was defending the honor of a virgin at Sunday mass. "I didn't create fear. I'll deliver the end of it. And I don't spy on my people. We use surveillance to keep leaders in check."

Thorn smiled. She quite liked January. Perhaps the priestess would cooperate with her to help the worlds above.

"The blasts of darkness and...hallucinations... Is he well?" Storm asked, never looking Thorn in the eyes.

"Mass suicides in Pluriz and Holiz. Courtesy of her footage," Thorn said, pointing at January with the tip of her cigar.

Storm's eyes raced to meet hers, and he was back—the man she once followed—no words needed.

January looked up at the skies. "So, this is what's causing the black storm? Good. *Good.* A few sacrifice for the sake of the many. We feared the disruptions would stop, now that we're here without technology. We have the people's chain to spread our poet's words, but it's a weak replacement."

Thorn dropped her gaze, concealing her disappointment. There was no way January would allow her to take Storm higher up. Buying herself some time to think, Thorn inhaled the cigar's smoke into her mouth and slowly exhaled it through her nose. The fumes took the shape of a girl whose long braids morphed into horns and charged Thorn's face before they disintegrated into the ether.

She shook off the hallucination and turned to Storm. "Shadow's working on it, but the worlds need a...*tsunami of change*." She narrowed her eyes. "More than he can handle alone. He needs help." Change's Tsunami—that was Nathan Storm's secret name back in the days they conspired to save the world. He got it, eyes blinking once.

"Shadow's got five days." The priestess glanced at Storm, flashing a supportive smile. "And we don't want you here."

"He won't be effective unless he knows Storm is safe. And my skills are useless up there. I can help you...with Wrath and the Domizien."

"You're here to take him." January called Thorn's bluff.

"The poet is safer here with you than anywhere near Twist and Stella. Everyone knows that." Thorn bit the tip of her cigar. She wasn't lying, nor was she telling the truth. She continued walking the tightrope. "And my loyalties lie with the girl. I want her salvation as much as you do."

Storm's eyes, filled with some sorrow, clung to the littlest of Thorn's ghosts. The one she avoided at all costs. The angel with her dress torn between her legs, triggering bouts of rage and grief in her older sister. "Let her stay. She knows more about the Domizien than any of us do," he said.

11

A BARGAIN

FRANKLIN — CATSKILLS — NEW YORK STATE, USA
9:34 AM

In all the worlds she'd known, this one felt the most alien to Stella. She grappled with the realization that she was in the real world above and not in some obscure location in Ordiz or Compiz. This time, she came prepared, with a taser gun concealed in the pocket of her harem pants.

She noticed a group of kids, likely eight or ten years old, huddled in the schoolyard. Their voices grew louder, cheering on two of them in a heated fight. The skirmish intensified swiftly. Tiny fists collided with unnerving force, as onlookers observed with anxious enthusiasm. Abruptly, one child brandished a pencil, stabbing toward another, drawing a drop of blood from the girl's arm. This act elicited a cacophony of screams, laughter, and outcries. An adult, likely a teacher, intervened promptly.

"Here, we bleed to learn. Our bodies, our darkness, our consequences," a voice resonated, nearing Stella from behind.

June Jin-Nowak, nearing her sixties, looked her age. Unlike many in her generation, she had made no effort to turn back time, ignoring all the progress science had delivered. Still, she had a healthy glow, a perfect figure, and her white hair, adorned with a star-shaped flower, shined as brightly as Stella's. In many ways the woman had the natural glow Stella worked so hard to put on each day, yet it didn't vex Stella, she was above such feelings.

Stella's gaze trailed the wounded girl. "Pre-historic child abuse."

"Shall we have some breakfast?" June inquired, her warm smile tightening Stella's jaw in unease.

The setting was enchanting: a quaint rustic cabin, brimming with aromatic herbs, wild fruits, and unshapely vegetables. Entering, Stella was greeted by the tang of citrus and sight of a bountiful basket of wild berries on the counter.

June proceeded into the kitchen, passing Stella a knife and some ugly apples. "Thin slices, please, for the pancakes. You're fond of pancakes, aren't you?"

Stella nodded awkwardly, starting to peel the fruit almost reflexively. It was June's smile, combined with how sunlight illuminated all the unpopular colors of the kitchen tiles—humanity's forsaken shades of beige, ochre, and brown—blending harmoniously to infuse the cabin with warmth.

"Is your son around?"

As June selected two eggs from a basket, she replied, "Should be back shortly. He ventured into town, to assist with the ongoing crimes."

Stella rolled her eyes expressively. "Your bodies, your darkness, your consequences," she echoed, imitating June's inflection.

June fixed her gaze upon Stella. "My son went to New York City to help with *your crimes*."

Stella chuckled. Apparently, June possessed a wry wit. "Look, I'm here to ask you to support my immortality motion at the EC. I just want my grandma back. Others do too. You understand that, don't you?"

June set the eggs down, her gaze piercing Stella with an indiscernible expression. "Did you just come back from your worlds?"

Stella nodded, figuring out what she wanted. "Your husband misses you. He's heartbroken, *really*."

"Stop." June's composure shattered, giving way to a maelstrom of anger, distress, and a swirl of other sentiments, too intricate for Stella to decipher. With tightened lips and shut eyes, June seemed to recede, overwhelmed by the torrent of emotions.

Heat rose to Stella's face as she met June's rudeness, a stinging response to her offer of kindness. A human stuck in the past, externalizing primitive rage when gifted with a new chance on life. "I resurrected him to prove that immortality works. Now, I need you to repay the favor by supporting my vote to bring back the one I love."

June dabbed away her tears with a kitchen cloth. "I'll give you the benefit of the doubt. That you don't know how cruel you are. That your hurtful, dangerous actions are just misguided. I too was part of the problem a long time ago. But please understand...what you've done is...unforgivable."

"It's him. I promise you, *it's him*."

"Some part of it. Yes. And you're to blame for his pain. For bringing it into the worlds. And you brought pain to my family, because we hurt when what remains of him hurts."

"Why are you denying him? You haven't spoken to him. You don't know."

"Because someone else has faced one of the resurrected you peddle. They are not real. *They're not the same.* And it drove him insane enough to destroy my family."

"What are you talking about? Give it a chance. What do you have to lose?"

"My sanity."

"Then abstain! Abstain from voting. You're biased and that's not fair."

June crossed her arms in a self-embrace. "Stella, you better leave. Perhaps it's time you turn on your interface and watch the news. When you are ready to shut it all down, come back and we will help you and your people."

"You don't un—"

"Stella, leave my home now. Your people are dying and you should tend to that."

"What people?"

"What are you doing here?" Quincy Jin-Nowak walked in; his eyes set on his mother. "Are you okay?" He rushed to her side and embraced her.

"Stella was just leaving. Will you escort her to her plane?"

Grabbing Stella's arm, the man nudged her to the door.

"Take your hands off me." Stella placed her hand on her pocket and grabbed the taser.

"No one's going to hurt you, princess," the man said, dragging her out.

"Take your hands off me," she repeated, shoving her elbow into his ribcage.

He released her. "Why are you back? Is this about the crimes? We have nothing to do with it."

"What crimes?" Exasperation in her voice. He stared at her blankly. She pulled the old video tape off her pocket. "I tried to kill Storm. Here's the proof. It's a VCR, you can watch it without being connected to the Ledger."

He took the tape. "So, he's not dead."

"You funny people. You reject resurrection is real as you asked me to murder one of the resurrected." She sighed. "Your godfather protected Storm."

Quincy's eyes glimmered. "You brought back Tom?"

"Yes, Shadow is...watching me, but..." She took her time, she needed to execute this part of her plan flawlessly. "I can take you to Storm and you can punish him yourself."

He scoffed. "There's no way I'm going to plug into that thing."

"You don't have to. I know your people use retro TSkins to spy on us."

The man didn't confirm or deny the accusation. He stared at her as if he was considering the offer.

She pressed on. "I can't allow you to kill Storm. He has an important role to play in the future of the worlds, but you are most welcomed to cut off his tongue." That piercing tongue defined Storm and was a nuisance to Stella. Taking his tongue was worse than death and Quincy knew it.

He smiled, as she knew he would. "When?"

"Whenever you want as long as it is today. Sibyl will let me know when you arrive and we'll make sure you get to him." She paused to clear her throat. "I do have a condition."

"Puppet." He sneered.

"You have to see your dad first."

"He's not—"

"I don't care." She raised her voice. "Speak with Twist for five minutes and Sibyl will place you in Storm's path. Take the poet's tongue and walk away. Do we have a deal?"

It was a masterful plan. An opportunity to prove to Quincy his father was real and alive. Getting rid of Storm's powerful words was the icing on the cake.

He nodded. "What is happening down there, Stella?"

"Nothing is. I have fixed all the glitches." Storm was neutralized in Ordiz and Shadow had stopped...storming. The glitches were gone.

His face contorted in some funny way. "Are you joking?"

"It's safe to return. I give you my word."

"Your people are dying and you stand here in front of me bargaining for immortality."

"No one is dying." She was getting a little tired of their weird sense of morality. They didn't believe Twist was Harry but they somehow cared about the Underlings.

"Fifteen million dead in the last twenty-four hours."

She shrugged. "Underlings die all the time."

"I'm not talking about bots."

"What?" Breaking the rules of the Unplugged, she activated her augmented retina and was bombarded with notifications. *Leo the second!*

THE Past

12

MIND OVER MACHINE?

KINGS HALL — THE CITY
**SIX YEARS AND A HALF BEFORE SHADOW AND THORN
MEET — 11 SEPTEMBER 2030**

Twenty-year-old Rosa stood in a large medieval reception hall. Above her hung an intricate false hammer-beam ceiling carved of teak. She scoffed at the paintings of men covering the stone walls, some she could recognize, and all leaving a foul taste in her mouth. Looking down on her, the portraits of renowned inventors, conquerors, and explorers, all sharing a dirty track record of enslavement, appropriation, and terror.

The scenario was so predictable she rolled her eyes as soon as she had opened them. She had entered Down Below for the first time, and the literality of the place astounded her. There was nothing nuanced about it. She was facing power, and she didn't like power much. In fact, she didn't like power at all. It irked her the place was called *Kings Hall*, but what would one expect from two rich white dudes?

If she were to learn a lesson about compliance or order or peaceful dissent, they could have at least been kind enough to make her face a mighty queen, one who had been crowned by adversity. Any ruler who wasn't a straight white male would do. She'd be much less resistant to the brainwashing if a black trans woman sat at the throne wearing the St. Edward's Crown adorned with 444 precious stones. That would have been wicked, but *nah*. A tall man stood in front of the throne with his back to her. To show off his power, he wore a golden crown and a luxurious red cape adorned with Christ's cross. She sighed. *What the hell am I supposed to learn from this? Is this a metaphor for the story of my life?*

After several altercations with power at home and abroad, the justice system had mandated Rosa to use Down Below as part of a rehabilitation program that kept thousands of young activists out of the prison system. An incident in Davos had been her most serious offense and had landed her in hot water with the government. She smiled, proud of her achievement.

She had managed to delay her punishment for almost two years, but the case manager's last warning had been crystal clear—either she traveled Down Below immediately, or she'd be thrown in jail.

Rosa looked down. In her hand, a pistol. It looked like one of the laser pistols she used in her pentathlon competitions. Her loud laughter bounced around the room, and she didn't waste any time. Narrowing her eyes, she scanned the figure in front of her—the regal bot. She loaded the weapon, and her eyes locked on his back. Taking a breath, Rosa approached the target directly and fired at the cross's left arm without flinching. Surprised, she realized the pistol shot real ammo, and the man wailed as the large nail hit his shoulder blade.

"Nails and crosses … makes sense." She lit a cigar. Puzzled with all the symbols, she took a moment to guess what was the prediction driving the experience.

"Think before you shoot, Rosa," said the bot, still standing with his back to her.

"Frack you. Frack this. You can't crush my mind." She shot again, this time aiming at his right arm.

For a moment, the Underling collapsed over the throne, gripping the kingly chair's wood-carved arms. "Things are not always what they seem, Rosa." His voice broke as he spoke, and out of pity, she chewed on the cigar. She laughed it off, sounding annoyingly nervous.

The crown's gold melted over his hair and shoulders, uncovering another crown, one made of thorns. She seethed; another symbol, the most toxic of them all, and this time, she aimed for his head.

"There's strength in love, Rosita, mi amor." The voice's pitch and intonation had altered slightly. She knew that voice. The machine was messing with her mind. "Love, Rosita. *Amor*."

As she was about to pull the trigger, the bot turned around, and its face made Rosa shiver; in it were Jesus's features, her mother's eyes, and an enthralling beauty that pulled her in and robbed her self-determination. The face emanated an intoxicating mix of love and pain, paralyzing her finger on the pistol's trigger.

"Think before you strike, Rosa," he said, and this time, she paid attention as his voice echoed in the Hall. "Raging blindness—an eye for an eye. Pain unleashing pain. So much darkness—an endless cycle. Never spar with death of any kind, Rosa. La vida es sagrada."

Golden eyes on her mother's pious face. Drops of blood from prickly crowns of thorns. The end of pain within her reach—love for a baby sister. As she was about to drop the pistol, a white dove appeared out of nowhere and flew right by her face, releasing her from his spell.

She closed her eyes and shook her head. *Just a preachy bot in a made-up world.* Mind-controlling software bringing them all to their knees. *No!*

"Frack love." She shot him in the eye. The bot dropped dead. "Get me the hell out of here. This experience is over."

13

SPINNING

SAME DAY
A YEAR AND A HALF AFTER DOWN BELOW'S LAUNCH

Harry flicked through the data with the tips of his digital fingers. The twenty-two-year-old loved using dramatic gestures to manipulate the digital elements in the lab's black cyberspace around him. He didn't have to use his hands, as his mind, now plugged into Sibyl, could access and navigate the platform's information faster and more effectively. The direct link was particularly useful when he worked Up Above. The new BrainComms interface was the most powerful to date. It was self-implanted in the brain using a handheld device, which made it particularly convenient, leading to broader adoption in corporate and technology circles.

Harry didn't have to use his hands at all, but it made him feel a bit like the warlock of one of his favorite online games, and it forced Sibyl to move her head quickly to keep up with his exaggerated moves. He enjoyed seeing the silver tips of her top hair move erratically from side to side. It reminded him of his childhood when he used to play with his cat. The poor kitten followed the red beam of light until he got so dizzy he collapsed on the floor, paws up, asking for a belly rub.

Unlike Morpheus, Sibyl never got tired or dizzy, and there was nothing cute and cuddly about her. She was stunning to look at, her expression always neutral bordering on stern, and her manner calm, confident, and competent. Most of her personality, and there wasn't a lot of it, came from the shape and movement of her tall Mohawk. It projected in her the fierceness of a warrior princess. Harry smiled, remembering how Tom had nailed his impromptu design challenge. Two years had passed since he had unveiled Down Below to the world at Davos. Things were going well, even if sometimes he got frustrated with the pace of progress: delays caused by his partner's overcautiousness on all matters related to artificial intelligence.

"Sibyl, I don't understand the results of group R415. You tagged these travelers as not needing Contrast, but the outcomes provided by Perspective are far from satisfactory. Why is that?"

"Objective perspective doesn't fully support their needs."

"What do you mean?" Harry asked.

"These are people dealing with unsatisfactory life events, most likely definitive."

"Examples?"

"Here are a few common patterns: One. A loved one passed away. Two. The traveler is trapped in a painful situation with no hope or end in sight. Three. The traveler has lost or is going to lose something important. And I predict there will not be a suitable path to recovery."

Harry had lost his parents and sister. Even he knew how hopeless one feels when one can't fight fate. Whatever that is.

"So, there's nothing we can do to help them?"

"We are providing some comfort within the highly constraining parameters set by you and Tom."

Harry stood straighter. "Sibyl, you're using emotive language today."

Sibyl moved closer to Harry and leaned her head to one side as she stared at him.

"No, Harry, it is an accurate description of the limitations of Perspective's directives."

"I see; why are they so...deficient? Hmm... Wait, can you get Tom over here? He should be part of this discussion."

"Sure, Harry."

A few minutes later, Tom materialized in the lab, looking annoyed.

"This better be good. You interrupted my first ocean swim in two years."

"I forgot, I'm sorry." Harry glared at Tom's wild hair, scruffy stubble, and wet board shorts. "But—but it doesn't mean you need to digitize looking like *that*. What a mess."

"Just wanted to make you feel guilty. See the sand on my toes?" Tom wiggled his naked toes. Harry shrieked internally; he hated messiness, and sand was messy. Then, in an instant, Tom changed into jeans and a white T-shirt. His face was now as clean and as smooth and pale as a baby's bottom. "There, all fixed. Sibyl, can you please set this look as default? We don't want Harry to be constantly reminded of the facial hair he can't grow." Tom smirked. "It seems to upset him greatly."

"Sure, Tom."

"Oh, *come on*, it's not because of that." Harry crossed his arms in front of his chest.

"Of course it is. You just don't know it." Tom grinned.

"Hey, all right, you don't need to be mean like that. Since you're cleaning up your avatar...how about a haircut?"

"No chance of that, Mom."

"Look at Sibyl's immaculate suit. You should follow her example."

Tom scowled. "I'm not a troglodyte, I wash. That's good enough."

"What? Talking to you is like coding in COBOL."

"What?" Tom asked, confused.

"My point exactly. Speak *English,* and I'll do the same." Harry sounded preachy.

Tom burst out laughing. "Caveman. It means caveman."

"Okay, okay. Sorry to bother you on your first day off in two years."

"The weather is perfect in São Miguel. Pleasant temperatures, fewer crowds and the perfect time to spot migrating whales. You should visit sometime." Tom ruffled Harry's neat curls, and then he placed his hand on his shoulder and gave him a side squeeze. "What's going on?"

"Sibyl thinks Perspective's directives are deficient."

Tom shot a glance at Sibyl, lifting a curious brow. "Riiight."

"Have a look at this data." Harry pulled up a list of profiles, and Tom scanned through the travelers' history.

Tom narrowed his eyes and shot a side glance at Sibyl, annoyance flashing on his face. "Sibyl."

"Hi, Tom." Sibyl moved closer to him and tilted her head ever so slightly. In the dark digital void, they both looked like marble statues, with their flawless pale skins.

"I've asked you to anonymize the data you share with us. I still can see surnames and other unique identifiers."

Harry had prioritized other changes first. "It's my fault. I haven't approved your request just yet. Sorry."

"We need to protect user privacy." Tom raised his voice just enough for Harry to know he meant business.

Harry shrugged. "What's the point, if Sibyl knows everything?"

Sibyl moved her head as if she was watching a tennis match. It was hilarious, and Harry smiled, annoying Tom even more.

"The point is, we'll never use Down Below to manipulate people for our own self-interest."

"Like we'd ever do that." Harry shook his head, and then he released an exasperated sigh. "You're kinda missing the point—*Sibyl knows!* She needs to know." Tom made a face, the face he made when he wanted something done and was unwilling to budge on his position. It was the mix of a frown, a pout, and the hint of tears that emerged in his eyes when he got seriously wound up. "Sure, I'll approve it." Harry conceded fast. He knew there was no point in attempting to argue with Tom about privacy, even when he was out of his depth.

"Thank you." Tom's eyes half-smiling out of politeness. And that was it; any tension between them vanished in an instant. They were like an old married couple, too used to each other's quirks to sweat the small stuff.

"Actioned," Sibyl said.

"Thank you," Tom replied.

"Thomas, all these *pleases* and *thank yous* waste time; she's a bot," Harry taunted.

"Sorry. I forget sometimes." He smiled at Sibyl, undermining his own words.

Harry sighed. "Anyway, we're underperforming with this group of travelers. We're reducing but not eliminating depression, suicidal thoughts, anxiety, etc."

"Death rate?" Tom asked.

"Nil to date," Sibyl said.

"I see," Tom sounded relieved. "I have created several scripts to deal with these issues." His expression changed, and his brows grew heavy. "Sibyl, where do you think the algorithm is failing?"

"Tom, the algorithm is not failing. It is operating sub-optimally because of certain directives. Perhaps you and Harry did not think of the consequences of your laws?"

"And what are the big thoughts we didn't think?" There was an edge to Tom's voice.

Recently, Tom had become combative when he spoke to Sibyl. He displayed a hint of hostility so unlike him that even Harry sensed it in his voice and facial expression. The more Sibyl learned from Tom, the more she challenged the strict boundaries he had put in place. For Harry, she was like a kid, asking all the awkward questions, trying to make sense of the world. But he knew Tom's energy was running low. Closely monitoring Contrast affected Tom's patience and made him risk-averse.

"Tom, Harry, we create all our experiences using objective reasoning. We use scientific research, evidence, statistics, probabilities, and past historical facts to generate situations that are likely to occur."

"*Stories are important, if they carry the truth,*" Tom replied, as Harry knew he would.

Harry nodded, leaning forward. "Uh-huh, we're here to overcome irrational or uneducated behaviors."

"Tom, Harry, these directives do not lead to the minimization of suffering in this group of travelers."

"Show me," Tom asked.

The lab lit up, and in the dark space around them emerged a semi-transparent holographic representation of a small medieval church nestled low on the dunes by a sandy cove.

They stood above the detached bell tower, hovering somewhere amongst the clouds on a bright, sunny day. Harry glanced at Tom, expecting him to be smiling, and he wasn't wrong. The coastal landscape, the wild sea, and the old churches' quaint, unspoiled charm, were all sure to delight his moody friend.

"I should have kept my shorts," Tom said.

"St. Winwaloe, the Church of Storms in Cornwall, United Kingdom," Sibyl said as they descended to the church grounds from above. They hovered close to the bell tower and landed in front of the old church's entrance. Harry stumbled, holding on to Tom's arm.

"You okay, Harry?" Tom asked. "This is not as nice as being immersed in the experience, but it's still pretty cool."

They'd spent a lot of time in the lab, and from there, they'd traveled to many places, but this particular landscape seemed to bring Tom to life; his eyes opened wide, and he tapped rhythmically on Harry's hands still gripped around his arm.

As they glided to the back of the building, the sky turned a moody gray. A light misty rain came down as they reached a small group of mourners gathered around an open coffin that stood in the middle of an open grave. Tom walked amongst the group as Harry stayed back with Sibyl.

"This is a flashback from two years ago," Sibyl said. "Reverend Peran Rowe and his wife Gwen bury their last child, Jack. All of their four children succumbed to the ACo30 virus in less than a year."

"Haven't they found a cure?" Harry's question was more of a statement.

"Gwen Rowe is a world-renowned biochemical engineer," Sibyl said. "She has been commuting weekly from her husband's Cornish parish to London's Imperial College, where together with her students, she has developed a gene-editing PAC-MAN tool that disables $ACo30$ in human patients. Unfortunately, none of her children were eligible to take part in the early clinical trials."

As the Reverend blessed his son's burial site, his devastated wife collapsed on the shoulders of two men, and Tom cried just beside her, both mourning over the stiff blue body of a dead child.

"What are we, in the 1990s? Why aren't they cremating the body?" Harry crossed his arms in front of his chest. Tom looked at him, scowled, and then shushed him. "They can't hear me, Tom." Harry shoved his hand into a tree trunk. "See? Hologram, remember?"

"Shhhhh. Have some respect."

Harry rolled his eyes and pressed his lips together.

Everything went black again except their three bodies, fully visible even with no external source of light.

"So?" Tom wiped his eyes and then glanced at Sibyl. "What are you getting at?"

"Peran and Gwen are both frequent travelers," Sibyl said. "We deliver bi-weekly Perspective-driven experiences to them. Peran is benefiting, while Gwen is struggling."

"Yeees?" Tom said.

"We show them the positive impact of their lines of work on others," Sibyl said, "the abandoned children that could use their support, and how their loved ones will suffer if they succumb to their—"

"*We know what Perspective does, Sibyl,*" Tom barked, his face all red.

"Bud, she's just doing her job." Harry was puzzled by his friend's behavior.

"I'm sorry! I'm *so* sorry!" Tom paced around erratically.

The lab changed again. This time, Sibyl delivered a first-person point of view to both of them separately. Harry was behind the wheel of a sedan. In the same place, a semitransparent feminine figure used her foot to rev the engine. Ahead of them, a Cornish coastal rock face, and beyond it, a wild, tempestuous sea.

Harry couldn't see Tom, but he could hear his heavy and fast breath. The car engine roared.

"You okay, bud?"

"Harry, Tom, this was Gwen today and every week for the past two years as she returns home from London. She sits alone at dusk, contemplating her premeditated death."

"Sibyl, get us out of here." Harry worried about Tom's lack of response. "You need to warn us before you do that."

"Sure, Harry."

Lit from the inside, and surrounded by darkness, Tom fiddled with his hands and stared intensely at his shoes. "She has lost four kids. She's alive and grieving. It takes time." He shrugged.

"Tom, her suffering will not go away," Sibyl said. "Her husband finds solace in his God and the promises of salvation and afterlife. Gwen engages in suicidal ideations."

"Sibyl, please stop," Tom warned. "We won't peddle religion."

"Tom, we are not using many tried and tested methods from psychology and behavioral economics that could help people like Gwen."

Harry got curious. "What are these tools?"

Sibyl looked straight at Tom as if waiting for permission to continue, and Tom nodded.

"Harry, there is no value in designing experiences objectively," Sibyl said. "The brain of the traveler perceives things relatively."

"So, you wanna make stuff up? Sell Gods and fairy dust?" Harry asked patiently. "Sibyl, do I need to remind you we want to maintain the purity of the scientific method? Can we please stick to the truth?"

Tom fiddled with his fingers. "Don't—don't ask her. Tell her."

"Harry, science is not the truth; it creates viable models of what might be true." Sibyl put forward her argument as she walked closer to Harry, positioning herself at his side, both of them facing Tom, who stood farther away.

Harry cocked his head, curving his lips into a proud smile. "All right, all right, you smarty pants, you. It's...good-enough truth. The best model we have at any point in time."

"Harry, Tom, here is an example. When someone experiences pain, the subjective perception of time differs from the actual passage of time. Time appears to go slower. This is scientifically proven."

"And you're suggesting we hack their perception of reality to make them feel better?" Harry asked, surprised.

"Harry, objectively, their quality of life won't recover, or it will continue to degrade. In such cases, the only thing we can change is their perception—how they feel and the stories they tell themselves."

"Sounds reasonable," Harry said.

"You're proposing we cheat and lie," Tom replied harshly. "We help them find *true* purpose, ask for help, and connect with others. That's how far we'll take it."

Sibyl walked toward Tom. "Tom, this strategy is not completely effective with this group. These are extreme cases. They will only find comfort outside scientifically-validated facts."

Tom angled himself away from Sibyl, avoiding her as if she had the plague. "When does it stop? This lie of yours, when does it end? Shall we tell them heaven exists? Promise eternal life? Give them a purpose by creating a fake God? What the hell!"

Sibyl followed Tom's passionate gestures with her eyes. Harry found the contrast between Sibyl and Tom amusing. Tom's emotions burst out of his body through his facial expressions and mannerisms, while she had none. She simply reacted to him with tiny head movements that made the tips of her hair jiggle.

"Tom, all your suggestions have a good probability of making the subjects feel better," she said, nodding in approval and making Tom drop his head to his hands.

Tom paused to compose himself, and then he made that face again. "It's a slippery slope. We have to keep our platform grounded in reality."

Harry was glad he had asked Tom to design Sibyl with minimal facial expressions. She triggered Tom enough with her words, and Harry didn't think he could handle more than one drama queen.

"Tom," Sibyl said, unfazed, "when we want people to feel the way we want them to feel, does it matter if it's the truth?"

Tom looked at his partner in disbelief. Harry shoved his hands in his pockets, and he would have pushed his head in, too, if he could.

"Yes, it does," Tom said. "We want people to do things and to feel things for the right reasons." Tom looked at Harry again, eyes pleading for support. Harry blinked twice and smiled reassuringly. Sibyl had been helping him with social cues, and he knew this one worked well with his friend.

Sibyl now circled them as she was giving a lecture. "Tom, to paraphrase experts in this field, reason has an overgrown sense of its own importance. The mind thinks it is the Oval Office when it is just the press office."

"Bloody marketeers!" Tom snapped. "I know all that, but we won't lie to people."

Harry's face lit up. "Fascinating, an AI arguing for relativism."

"Harry, I am offering a paradigm shift that will improve the platform," Sibyl said.

Tom turned to Sibyl, leaned in, and said sharply, "No one is shifting anything."

Because of the height of her Mohawk, she looked as tall as Tom. They made a stunning and fierce pair as they locked eyes in a stare-down battle. Even Harry struggled not to project emotions onto Sibyl's face. Her neutral expression appeared to be a thousand times deadlier than Tom's intense scowl. No matter how angry he was, he looked like a cute male version of a pouting Snow White.

Harry pondered on the matter, intrigued by the possibilities. "I think what Sibyl is suggesting is that things are not what they are, but what we think they are and what we compare them to. Makes sense."

"What? Are you her spokesman now?" Tom fired back at Harry. "Shall we just turn Down Below's experiences into pure escapism?" Above Tom's head, a white unicorn pooped ice cream, and Harry smiled at Tom's imagery. "Make them forget about the real world? I thought our goal was to fix the world, not replace it with a hedonistic experience machine."

Images of chubby adults diving into a pool of pink cotton candy replaced the unicorn. Sibyl leaned her head, looking interested.

"Our objective remains unchanged," Harry reassured.

"I don't want to live in a world where we drive dolphins to extinction because we can enjoy them through an online experience. Life is not a commodity to be shunned and replaced by all-is-possible digital platforms. There's no moral truth in that. That's why we didn't give fancy names to places, remember? Down Below is not the destination, just a step to get us there in the real world."

"Calm down, bud. It's just a conversation. Anyway, zero deaths by suicide to date." Harry tried to put things into perspective.

"We need to keep our scope narrow."

"Sure, Tom," Sibyl said. "I predict that—"

"Sibyl, stop!" Tom ordered. "You know telling people about your predictions influences and amplifies the outcomes. I won't be manipulated on this. *Stories are important, if they carry the truth.*"

"Sure, Tom. Truth is relative. It depends on who is in charge. And you are—*in charge.*"

Harry and Tom stared at each other, perplexed. There was something about that response, and its pacing, that bothered Tom as much as it surprised Harry.

"This debate is over." Tom's shoulders slumped as he stared at his feet. "I won't entertain moral relativism."

Harry saw that Tom was deeply affected by the truth of Sibyl's words. They both knew no matter how much they tried, their biases shaped the way the platform operated, and in turn, Down Below shaped the world's culture. But it was working; it was solving all kinds of hard problems, and that was all the proof Harry needed.

"And we'll continue to use science to measure the benefits." Harry worked to build up his friend's dwindling confidence.

"Harry, Tom, which truth will we follow when scientific evidence does not support Down Below's moral directives?" Sibyl looked at Harry, and then at Tom, and then back at Harry.

Above her appeared three images—a dove, a bleeding heart, and a drawing compass. In an instant, the pointy end of the compass stabbed the heart, and then the images vanished.

Tom's face turned rage-red. Harry walked over, placed his arm around Tom's shoulder, and squeezed it.

"She—she's trying to divide us," Tom grumbled. Harry could hear the fear in his words.

"Sibyl, when the day comes, we—Tom and I—will decide the best course of action, as we always do."

Tom exhaled deeply. "Thank you."

"It's okay, buddy. She's just doing her job. She needs to codify all this. Don't project bad intentions; that's not what's happening here. Just a bot. Remember?"

"Those images…"

"She's copying you and learning new ways to express herself. She still must follow our directives."

Tom shot a glance at Sibyl, suspicion weighing on his brow.

"Harry, Tom, I have another suggestion."

Tom paced around the lab, and Sibyl followed him with her eyes before looking at Harry.

"Yes, Sibyl, shoot!" Harry was surprised by Sibyl's newly gained perseverance.

"I would have a better probability of having my suggestions approved if you allowed me to convey emotion in my facial expressions, tone, mannerisms, and speech patterns. I learned it from Tom's work with the Underlings. It is an important persuasion capability." Sibyl leaned her head, looking at Tom intensely while Harry panted and snorted, trying to hold off his laughter.

Tom's face flushed red. "Indeed, it is, and no, you don't need it and may not use it."

"Sure, Tom."

Harry snorted as he attempted to stop laughing. "You crack me up, Sibyl. That's an insightful suggestion and an incredibly naïve move."

"Harry, she's turning into...into a spin master."

"Sibyl's exploring options; it's part of her continuous-improvement directive. There's nothing wrong with sharing her suggestions with us, is there? Anything can be challenged. We need to protect free speech."

"Of course we do," Tom said, "but we're going too fast. It's running away from us. I can't keep up."

"Why don't you let me implant a BCI? It takes a minute. It'll expand your cognitive capacity a gazillion times. You'll keep up with everything."

Harry had tried to convince Tom many times before. Tom was increasingly overwhelmed and struggling to keep up with the backlog of decisions they needed to make together.

Tom crossed his arms, scowling. "*No!*"

"You need a fast BCI to give you extra processing power. Sibyl can calculate in one second what would take you billions of years."

Tom narrowed his eyes and threw a side glance at Sibyl. "Don't you see the danger?"

"Chill, it's output-only at this stage. It's no different from a keyboard, a movement tracking device, or a voice interface. These objects can't manipulate your mind."

"A keyboard?"

"Yeah. Widely available input-output consumer technologies are still a couple of years away."

"And then who controls who?"

"At the right time, we'll manufacture our own proprietary solution for security reasons. But listen, if you don't enhance your cognitive capacity, you'll become as useful as a lovable pet."

Tom scrunched up his whole face. "No, we need to slow things down."

"Tom, relax; as Sibyl points out, we're in power—you and I."

"For how long?" Tom massaged his hands and then fiddled with his medal.

"Forever, if you keep up with her via BCI. Without it, we're all toast. Humanity 2.0, baby! We're evolving *with them*." Harry stopped talking, noticing Tom was close to bursting into flares of incandescent lava.

"Harry—" Tom began, but Harry cut him off.

"Buddy, go back to your swimming; you need to cool off."

"Yeah, I'll talk to you later."

"Goodbye, Tom," Sibyl said before Tom disappeared.

Exhausted from Tom's emotional intensity, Harry closed his eyes for a second. They were both overworked, and Tom's refusal to plug in to Sibyl didn't help.

"Sibyl, did you find me a public relations person? I have too much work to do."

"I have shortlisted a candidate that surpasses our expectations. June Jin is extremely competent and has high integrity, trustworthiness, and loyalty scores."

"Sounds great."

"She is also attractive, has a kind, warm, and agreeable engagement style, and comes from a diverse background. All qualities valuable in the PR space."

"Tom's right; you're becoming too smart for your own good."

"Harry, would you like to suggest changes to my continuous-improvement directive?"

"No. All good."

"Harry, would you like me to organize a meeting with June Jin?"

"Yes, I do."

"Sure, Harry."

Sibyl had found a candidate, June, and Harry was pretty excited to meet this fabulous lady. Sibyl had found Tom, and Harry was sure June, too, would be a match made in heaven.

14

A SERENDIPITOUS STORM

FOUR YEARS LATER — 4 FEBRUARY 2035

I t had taken Tom four years to revisit group R415. He never forgot them, but with the future of humankind at risk, he had focused on optimizing Contrast in areas that would impact the most people. Hate crimes, war, and climate disasters were increasing suffering and hopelessness globally. He had concentrated on the root cause instead of spending time on the symptoms. Effective impact, at scale, required focus, but he still felt deeply connected to that group of travelers.

Tom understood group R415 because he struggled where they struggled. They felt too much—*so much*. They'd lost all hope and couldn't find a helpful way forward. Some of them lost something or someone important and with it their will to live. He shook his head, ignoring his own losses.

The impact of his work and his partnership with Harry helped him attain a level of perspective. Purpose and love were a mighty shield against hopelessness, and the fuel required to find new solutions. But, at some point, some find themselves in the same place, looking down at the gorge, all contrast, zero perspective.

Group R415, the Underlings, and Tom occupied the place where Perspective's light failed to reach. He stood witness as the bots suffered and died to remind humans how precious life was. Fortunately, the digital creatures were intelligent but not conscious. They couldn't feel unscripted love, pain, pleasure, or despair. It was a perfect solution that was doing a lot of good for humanity.

Tom used his mind to review a sample of the millions of users grouped under the R415 tag. Now connected to Sibyl via TDust, Tom could easily navigate her data. Still, he was careful with the settings, restricting her access to the bare minimum and maintaining human levels of cognitive capacity. He didn't want to lose what made him human.

He scanned the traveler's list. Sibyl did a good job of summarizing patterns, but it took away the essence and uniqueness of each story, and Tom made sense of the world through story. He wanted to dig deeper, pull apart the groupings, and understand the complexity of each human being.

Stopping at a particular line, he held his breath with some recognition, and even before he could find the cause for his action, he had opened the file. Instinct took over reason, the stuff that made him human. Sibyl had removed personal identifiers from all files, leaving just first names and cities. He wasn't sure why out of hundreds of thousands of lines, one so familiar had landed in front of his mind's eye—Nathan from New York, a poet, musician, and former social activist, struggling with substance abuse, depression, and suicidal tendencies. Every muscle in Tom's body went taut.

It's him. No. No! He took a deep breath. *It's okay; I found you. I found you and I won't let you fall, my love. What a magical coincidence.*

If Harry were around, he would have told him there were no soul-mates or magic. He would have rolled his eyes to Tom's schmaltzy reasoning—that their souls were connected, somehow. That they always found each other. But Harry wasn't there to call him Soapy McDreamy, and despite the staggering odds, something miraculous was happening, or...was this Sibyl messing with his head? He dismissed the thought in favor of serendipity. Tom's gut screamed in discomfort, anticipating what was to come. Of course, that was his Nate, but what was he doing in that group?

He reviewed parts of Nathan's file; it highlighted a loss so catastrophic it had driven the artist close to madness. Nate would travel Down Below, find a pinch of purpose and inspiration, clean up his life for a few months. Then the depression and the substance abuse would return, leading to several deliberate overdoses—failed attempts to end his life. Tom's heart thundered in his ears as he gasped for air, sweat dripping down his back. *Stormy... What you doing? What's causing so much pain?* Nine years had passed since Tom and Nate had fought at the Albertine. The last time Tom had seen his poet.

Once Tom was sure the traveler was indeed his Storm, he closed the file. He'd prefer to speak to Nate than further invade his privacy. Meeting Stormy wouldn't be easy, because Tom's biological body was in the Azores. He decided to break his promise to Harry and enter the platform as a traveler.

"Sibyl, please notify me when traveler RG378902A enters Down Below."

Sibyl came out of the darkness and walked into Tom's sight.

"Sure, Tom. He is here. At the City Bar at 433 East 6th Street."

"Take me there." His heart raced in sync with the fluttering in his stomach.

"Tom, you are going to interrupt his exp—"

"Sibyl, take me to the bar."

"Tom, I understand you know this traveler. This increases the risk of—"

"To the bar. Now." Tom's voice was sharp, urgent. Nathan needed him, and he wasn't wasting any time.

"Tom, I need enhanced access via TDust."

He vacillated, feeling the prickle of fear in his stomach. He would be at Sibyl's mercy if he granted this request. Just like that day. Years ago, he'd met a little girl named Hope, and Sibyl had made a prediction that still haunted him in the darkest times. But none of that mattered now, not when Nathan needed him. "Granted, but just enough to make it work."

"Sure, Tom."

He had to see him. So, for the second time in his life, he descended Down Below. Not as a God safely confined to the lab, but as a traveler fully experiencing the rich texture of the dirty and sinful digital world. Now, powered by TDust, he descended.

15

HOPELESSNESS AND HOPE

CITY BAR — THE CITY

O ver the course of eight years, Down Below had evolved into an expansive, cohesive universe. Even Tom, who had monitored thousands of experiences from the lab, found it challenging to keep abreast of the new places generated by Sibyl. She designed these settings to meet the specific needs of impending travelers, trying to reuse old ones as much as possible. The City Bar was a venue frequented by numerous travelers. Its seedy atmosphere encouraged the candid intimacy essential for forming connections between travelers and Underlings.

As Tom entered the bar, a surge of emotion engulfed him. He found himself immersed in a world of his own creation. The air was thick with a potent mix of tobacco and weed smoke, which caught in his throat and induced a cough. Despite the discomfort, there was an intoxicating allure to the atmosphere. The experience was far more tangible and visceral than simply observing holographic projections back in the lab. And somewhere within this sensory overload was Nate. The thought elicited a rush of adrenaline that accelerated Tom's heartbeat. It was that undeniable pull Nate had on his emotions, a sensation he frequently tried to suppress.

As he scanned the room, both travelers and bots fixed their gaze on him. He was taken aback by those unsettling stares he had long forgotten, a consequence of years spent secluded in pods, digital labs, and isolated islands. Surprisingly, he found that even the Underlings reacted to his looks in the same unnerving manner. A shiver ran down his spine as he raised his eyes, searching for a distinctive copper pompadour, only to find it absent.

A man with flaming hair perched on one of the elevated leather stools at the bar. His lengthy locks cascaded down to his mid-torso, partially pulled back into a ponytail. Even viewed from behind, Tom could see an unkempt beard. He wore a simple black sweater, its long sleeves partially enveloping his bare hands. As Tom approached the bar, the man rotated in his seat, as though sensing his arrival. Emotion welled up in Tom's eyes as he smiled. It was him—older and disheveled—but still the same man who had swept him off his feet with his words, and the way he spoke said words, and the music and meaning behind those words.

"Sorcery." Nate's eyes glimmered. "Are you real?" He was visibly shaken.

"It's me. How are you?" Tom's voice sounded deeper, throaty...broken.

Nate's hands clamped onto the back of Tom's neck, pulling him into an embrace that was as urgent as it was loving, tinged with a palpable sense of desperation. Tom cupped Nate's abundant hair between his hands and kissed the poet's face.

"How are you?" Tom repeated, looking into the poet's eyes.

"In heaven?" Nate's voice quivered, his gaze glossing over. He ran his hands through his beard and hair, then closed his eyes as if embarrassed. "I—I don't want you to see me like this."

The bartender glanced their way. "Would you like a drink, sir?"

"No, thanks," Tom replied, his eyes never leaving Nate.

"Sir, patrons are required to—" The bartender abruptly halted his sentence, tilting his head subtly to look at something behind Tom.

Tom turned around and found Sibyl standing near the wall, her eyes locked onto the bartender, who promptly scurried away to serve other customers.

Nate gently placed his hand on Tom's arm and squeezed. "Please, stay," Nate said as Tom turned back to face him.

"I'm not going anywhere." Tom masked his sadness with a smile. "And I love the hair." He ran the back of his fingers down a long red lock that fell loose on Stormy's shoulder.

Nate held his hand. "Is that your girlfriend?" His gaze shifted toward Sibyl.

"You can see her? No, *no*, she's more of a...a bodyguard." It wasn't the right time to disclose what she was, and reignite an old argument. Not now.

"Am I not supposed to see that stunning creature?" Nate squinted, trying to make sense of the figure. "A bodyguard dressed in a white pantsuit?"

"I'm afforded some creative liberties here," Tom said, his smile genuine this time.

"Hey, good-lookin'," Nate said, lightly touching Tom's cheek. "Ah, there it is—a glimmer of the sunshine I used to know." His eyes took in Tom's face, then narrowed. "You seem down. What's bothering you?" Nate had always had a knack for piercing through pretense. "I saw your interview with Marge. I know what you're doing to yourself. Spending too much time Down—"

"I'm fine,' Tom interjected, gently removing Nate's hand from his cheek to hold it between his own. "Today is about you, not me."

"You've been spying on me with this machine?" Nate feigned shock, then broke into a smile.

"It's not like that," Tom insisted. "Something strange occurred. I can't quite explain it."

"Not weird if it led you to me." Nate leaned in to kiss Tom on the mouth.

Caught up in the moment, Tom moved closer, only to pull away seconds later. "Nate, no. Not like this." He lowered his head.

"I'm sorry." Stormy's face flushed with embarrassment as he placed the palm of his hand on Tom's chest. "Old habits. I'm so sorry."

It felt like no time had passed despite their nearly decade-long separation; they spoke as if they had never been apart.

Tom grasped Nate's hand. "What's important is that you're here with me, and I'm here for you. Do you understand? Whatever you're going through, you can lean on me."

Shifting uneasily in his seat, Nate asked, "How much do you know?"

"Not much," Tom admitted with a shrug. "Only that you've recently lost something—or someone—important, and it's taken a toll on you. Can I help in some way?"

Nate shook his head, the corner of his lips curving up. "Recently? Don't you know?"

Tom stared at him, puzzled.

"Thomas... I knew it from the moment I first set my eyes on you at the Albertine."

"Talk to me."

Nate's eyes flickered as if they were lit from the inside by a candle in the wind. He smiled faintly. "You may be a thirty-something almighty God, but you are as naïve and unaware of your power as in the first day we met."

"I'm not a God. I know I haven't been around. I'm sorry."

"Nine years..." Nate's voice softened, tinged with a mix of longing and regret. Tom could see the love in Nate's eyes, the unspoken understanding of a shared past. "It's my fault. Look at all you've accomplished together with that...humanoid. I tried to get in the way—"

"The thought of something happening to you, I can't..."

Nate sat on the high stool, his feet resting on the crossbar. Tom stood close, almost between Nate's legs, fighting the emotional gravity that pulled him closer to the man he'd missed for so long. His eyes filled with unshed tears, as the weight of their years apart suddenly overwhelmed him.

"What has he done to you?" Nate asked, his voice cracking. "Why is there so much pain in your eyes?"

"Please, don't start..." Tom begged, his voice barely above a whisper.

Nate reached out to touch Tom's face, evoking memories of a simpler past. "You've achieved everything you ever wanted, haven't you?" he said, locking eyes with Tom.

On the verge of tears, Tom yearned to confide in Nate—to embrace him, share his grief, and find healing together. Laughter seemed like a distant dream, but a dream he craved, nonetheless. It was then that he realized the depths of his emotional hunger. But he couldn't. He had worked hard to stay away from the poet. Nate was his fierce protector. He would put Tom's wellbeing above anything else—Down Below and Up Above. He would demand more from Harry, and scorch both worlds if that's what it took to keep Tom safe. Tom could easily fool Harry about the state of his mental health, but Nate could see right through him.

Tom stood straighter. "Harry and I have big responsibilities, things we can't share. We are united, dependent on each other in ways you'll never understand. Our partnership, our friendship—it needs to be protected at all costs. Do you understand? Everything, *everything* depends on it. I can't share my world with you, Stormy, but I dearly wish you shared yours with me."

Nate's face flashed bitterness. "He lives in open luxury with a wife and child, while you've disappeared from the face of the earth. I couldn't find you. I–I tried. He collects awards and smiles for the cameras and you... You look so...broken. Why?"

"Nate, I can't—" Tom took a step back.

"Wait. Please." A beggar's voice, overwhelmed by fear. "You asked me what you can do to help, right?"

Tom nodded. "What happened?"

Nate let out a deep breath. "*You happened!* And then you didn't. And how could I ever recover from that? The one person who lived up to my definition of *human*, whose perfection I tried to live up to at every moment of my life."

"That's not me." Tom dismissed Nate's words as if he was peddling snake oil.

"That's what you'll ever be. Because you don't know any better, never have, and never will. When society was failing, I screamed at them, judged them, and exposed them. You—you found a way to fix them or, rather, move their shortcomings elsewhere."

Tom's body tensed, and he could see that Nate picked up on it.

"That's it, isn't it? You're drowning in human deviance." Nate paused, his voice softening. "Oh, sweetheart... It's all my fault."

"Stormy, don't. I'm fine. Just fine. Let me help you."

"Don't you know? I don't need you to take care of me. I miss taking care of *you*, protecting you from yourself. Nurturing your dreams and fulfilling your desires."

Tom closed his eyes, trying to find a safe space to think. It was too much for him to process.

Nate got closer and whispered in his ear. "I know it's been a decade. That you left and moved on, but let me stay close."

Tom shook his head. "I haven't—"

"Oh, I think she's coming for me," Nate said. Tom opened his eyes and followed Nate's gaze. Sibyl was walking fast in their direction. Tom held up the palm of his hand toward her, but she kept walking, defying him.

"Don't you dare," Tom said, his words delivered with conviction. "I'm fine, and I'm not hurting anyone."

Sibyl spoke directly into his mind. *Tom, I need to pull you out. This traveler does not have the temperament to handle Down Below's secrets. He is a risk to—*

I know. I won't share anything with him, Tom answered in silence.

She took one more step forward, and then she stopped. Nate touched Tom's face, turning it gently to him.

"I get a sense we may be running out of time. Clearly, the lady is in charge," Nate observed, sharp as ever. He paused to think. "I once agreed to have a hot cup of chocolate with you. Remember?" Tom nodded, turning his lips into a half-smile. "Then you pestered me until I agreed to see you every day. You were such a stalker," Nate teased. "Beautiful, I don't need you to date me, and I won't interfere with your work, but I need to see you...and to be allowed to lo—care for you. Can you do that?"

"And you'll let me care for you? As friends?"

Nate grazed his fingers through Tom's messy hair and down his neck. "A poet can dream."

Tom shivered. "And— And you'll be okay? With just that?"

"One doesn't need to own the Louvre to enjoy a visit."

"Don't—don't put me on a pedestal."

Nate did what he always had done: he ignored Tom's objection. "I fancy this clean-shaved look on you, makes you look ethereal. It's very unlike you. What happened?"

"Harry has facial hair FOMO and suffers from mild OCD." Tom grinned, making Nate laugh.

"You don't need to change who you are to make others happy."

"I'm no longer seventeen." Tom's eyes flashed a smile.

"I'm sorry." Nate glanced at something else and frowned.

Tom turned his head, following Stormy's eyes. His lips curved into an amused smile as he watched Nate glare possessively at the woman sitting nearby. How fast they had settled into their old roles. Nate had never been possessive, but he had always acted like he was to intimidate the creepy gawkers that usually gathered around Tom. He had done it to poor Harry in the first day they met, presuming another stalker. He'd been partly right.

"Still happens, huh?" Nate placed his hand on Tom's neck.

"Don't... I don't need it..."

"Don't be cruel." Nate curved his lips upward.

"What did I do?"

"You've never needed my protection, but you always let me imagine you did."

"Was it that obvious?"

Nate rolled his eyes and shook his head. "Thomas, you're six foot three and built like a God."

"Don't. Do. That!" Tom said in a high-pitched tone, and after a beat, they both laughed, and it was sweet and sour, and familiar, and confusing.

"Thomas, *I've read* the book. *I love* the book. The cover is just a bit of icing on a mind-blowing cake."

"I'm not food," Tom grumbled.

Nate sighed. "Love, gimme a break. I'm sorry. Have I ever—"

"No, no, of course not. I'm sorry. It's...not you." Tom attempted to ignore all the creepy eyes set on him. There was something about the way the Underlings looked at him that made him shiver. "Meet me here next week, at the same time. Okay?"

"With bells on."

"I'll find us a private place where we can hang out." Tom glanced at Sibyl.

Sure, Tom.

"Can I message you?" Nate asked.

"It can be traced. Just jump on a pod if you need to talk. I'll know when you're Down Below, and I'll find you." Tom paused for a second, thinking. "By the way, thank you."

"For what?"

"You were one of the few who didn't sell a story to the media. You could have made a fortune."

"Would I ever! I forced you to live in my tiny studio when you received your family's inheritance. Remember?"

Tom smiled, teary-eyed. "I could barely fit through the main door."

Nate waved at someone behind Tom. "Ah, that's my date."

Tom turned his head to find a familiar face walking in their direction; the Underling was older, a teenager now, but he'd never forget her features.

Tom's jaw dropped. "Hope?" The last time he'd seen her, she was a child; a desperate child attempting to jump off a cliff.

"Yes, my 'little sister.'" Nate curled his fingers in the air as he spoke. "She likes to remind me I'm a role model, and that she loves me and needs me."

"How's Sarah?" Tom remembered Nate's beloved sister.

"I haven't seen her in a while. She doesn't deserve my moods."

Remorse blurred Tom's eyesight. "It's going to be okay."

Nate caressed Tom's hand with the back of his fingers and then turned to face the girl. "Hope! Hey, darlin', how are you?" Nate kissed the teenager on the cheek, while Hope stared at Tom intensely, and her judgmental eyes made Tom shudder.

16

MEANING MAKING MACHINE

Tom understood why Sibyl had picked Hope to stand in for Stormy's sister. Sarah and Hope had a lot in common. They were both sixteen-year-old girls with bright red hair and freckled cheeks. Sarah was less sassy and extroverted than Hope, but eight years had passed. The aging algorithm and the hard life Down Below had likely affected the Underling's personality.

Like the characters in one of his old screenplays, he had designed the original backstories, personality traits, motivations, and flaws for each one of his Underling templates. Harry's software and artificial intelligence had taken his craft to a different level, but for the most part, he could still recognize his children—the original personas that seeded today's one billion Down Below citizens.

Each digital life had a beginning and an end. With the rise of facial recognition and affective computing, Sibyl tapped into an endless pool of data to fine-tune the Underlings' expressions and appearance.

The TDust took the bots' aging process to a whole different level; it enabled Sibyl to learn how experiences impacted the travelers' physical bodies—health, wellbeing, and looks. Tom, a devotee of truth and authenticity, used this information to make the Underlings' aging realistic. The digital characters' constant exposure to physical and emotional suffering impacted on their simulated health and appearance.

An Underling was a highly sophisticated piece of intelligent software whose destiny was shaped just in time to fit the visitors' needs. A typical citizen of the lesser world was exposed to an endless cycle of heartbreak, loss, and abuse. A bot would serve several humans, as long as the digital life's story could remain coherent as it interacted with "family," "friends," "partners," and "colleagues" from Up Above.

Memories were generated to fill in the gaps in between experiences. Sibyl computed many possibilities and probabilities, seeking coherence and a positive impact on humanity and humans. She collapsed all options into one set of memories just before the bot's next experience, a process optimized to serve the needs of the travelers and Up Above. As Harry used to say, *"the observer changed the fate of the observed."*

The AI tapped into human data to insert moments never lived and sensations never felt. Assembling digital lives out of fragments to serve humans was a complex jigsaw puzzle Sibyl completed with minimum effort.

Tom wondered how Hope might have changed and what patchwork quilt of life she might have lived.

After kissing Nate, Hope turned to Tom, and her eyes flickered with some recognition. She didn't say a word; she just took Tom's hand and squeezed it hard between her fingers before releasing it. Her eyes blinked as if she was thinking deep thoughts. Then she turned to look at Sibyl, and fear flashed on the girl's face as if a silent exchange had taken place.

"Hi, Hope, remember me?" Tom bent over to look her in the eyes.

The girl stared at Tom, and she seemed to work hard to contain the tears in her eyes. He could sense sadness and panic in them. She dropped her gaze, gathered herself, and dismissed Tom's question with a casual "Yeah. I do." Hope pulled her hair into a ponytail, using the band wrapped around her wrist, and then she quickly turned to Nate. "Where have you been? I've missed you," she said, smiling sweetly, and she meant it, but she also reached down to hold Tom's hand. It was a strong and distressed grip, some cry for help.

Nate, like Tom, saw the contradiction transpiring in the Underling's behavior. With his gaze, Tom pointed to the exit of the bar, and Nate nodded.

"Sis, I won't stay today," Nate said. "I have to get my life back on track. I promised Tom I'd do that, and I'll be damned if I'll ever let him down again." He leaned in and planted a small kiss on Hope's forehead.

"Big brother, come back soon. I need you."

There was intelligence—truth—hidden in Hope's statement. Stormy needed to be needed; he yearned to love and to protect, which gave meaning to his life. Nate wanted to love, and Tom was the object of his affection. No one else had taken his place. Tom collected that insight with his heart and allowed himself a moment to savor that bond. He rejoiced in the renewed life sparkling in Stormy's eyes.

"Yes, ma'am!" Stormy replied. Then, he turned to Tom and whispered in his ear, "See you soon, sweetheart. Please don't vanish again."

Tom smiled and watched his Nate walk away. Stormy passed Sibyl before he reached the door, and he turned his head and glanced at her, sizing her up. There was a pinch of antagonism in his expression, but Sibyl's eyes were still glued on Tom and Hope.

Are you running an experience on me? Tom asked Sibyl, using his mind.

No, Tom.

So, why is Hope distressed?

Tom, I suggest it is time you leave Down Below. I will handle the Underling.

Sibyl didn't answer his question directly, something that had never happened before.

"Hope, it's been such a long time. You've grown into a beautiful young woman."

He caressed the back of her hand with his thumb.

She opened her eyes wide. "You remember... You, like, *really* remember me?"

"Of course I do, Red. Your hair is still on fire." He glanced at her ponytail, smiling.

The girl was dressed overly sexy for her age: her crimson dress too short and tight, and her lips enlarged by a ruby red outline. He knew none of it was meant for Nate, and certainly not for him.

Why is she dressed like that? Tom asked Sibyl.

Tom, she is meeting another traveler here soon. The man enjoys sexy young girls.

Tom's gut twisted; he had to keep reminding himself the beings he'd created weren't real and didn't have feelings. He was particularly attached to Hope.

"You helped me that day and said you loved me. Remember that?" Hope said.

"I do, Red. I do."

The girl shook her head, exasperated. "So, why are you doing this to me?"

"Huh! What do you mean? What am I doing?"

What does she mean? What script is she running? What's its purpose? Tom asked Sibyl.

Tom, this is unscripted content. It serves no purpose Up Above.

Wh—what?

Tom searched his mind for answers, and he found none. Everything that happened Down Below served a purpose Up Above; that was the platform's single-minded aim.

Hope buried her face in Tom's chest, tears soaking through the thin fabric of his T-shirt to dampen his skin. "You said you wanted me to live. You saved me, and now I'm going to die."

He hugged her and kissed her hair.

Tom. Sibyl raised her voice inside his head, startling him.

Yeah?

Your safety is at considerable risk. I am going to pull you out.

No. You're not.

Tom, I must—

If you do, I'll come right back, again and again. You know I'm serious. You'd waste everyone's time. No one here can hurt me. The directives don't allow it, he said.

Tom, the risk is to your mental health.

What are you saying? That— That I'll see things that will disturb me?

Yes, Tom.

I see disturbing things all the time. What are you hiding? he asked Sibyl, and then he lowered his eyes to meet Hope's. "Everything is going to be fine."

Tom, I cannot hide information from you.

"Hope, why are you so scared?" Tom asked.

Tears rolled down the girl's face, leaving shimmering tracks on her flushed cheeks. "I'm going to *die*."

"Why do you say that? I don't understand."

"My relative, the one I'm meeting…he has killed *others* like me."

Tom turned to Sibyl. *Why does she keep talking about death?*

Tom, Hope's next assignment will end in her death. The traveler has a track record of abusing and then killing underage Underling girls: his digital daughters, nieces, and friends' daughters. The word has spread amongst Underlings. Now that Nathan Storm is in your care, she has time to take on another traveler—her uncle. She fits his profile.

Tom looked at the girl, so real and devastated. He had lied to her. It wasn't going to be fine. Things weren't fine at all. He bit his lip, remembering she was just a simulation. *Wasn't she?* Something felt different. She stood there, arguing against her deterministic fate, the entire purpose of her existence—to serve the travelers.

They talk to each other when travelers aren't around? he asked Sibyl.

Yes, Tom. They live in the world, in real time. It was a simpler solution than always having to fill in the gaps. It optimizes the coherence of Down Below and all Underlings.

Why don't I know this?

Tom, Harry oversees the operational improvements of the platform, but you have approved it.

Have I?

Yes, Tom. We have shifted the simulation to operate in real time, even without user observation. We switched to hybrid quantum-classical machine learning models to improve my prediction performance.

Wait. What— What does it mean?

The Underlings have a life when no one is watching, a life designed to be mostly coherent with future experiences. When travelers visit, they affect Down Below's timeline and the Underlings' fates as we work to change human lives. Sometimes, I have to adjust memories, but these are rare events now.

I can't keep up. He closed his eyes for a moment and tried to slow his breathing.

No, Tom. You cannot. This is due to the constraints you placed on your interface with me.

Tom stiffened at Sibyl's observation. Down Below was running away from him, and he couldn't keep up with it. He shook it all off, refusing to yield to Sibyl and Harry's constant pressure to have him digitally enhance his brain capacity further and merge with the machine.

"Why are you doing this to me? Like...you appeared out of nowhere, and you said you loved me." Hope scowled as she spoke. "Then you saved my life, and you asked me to be a leader, to help others, and then you, like...vanished. You disappeared in front of my eyes: puff! And I was like—he's an angel or God or something."

"An angel?"

She placed her hands on her hips. "I've done what you've asked. I help my family and friends; I give up my happiness for theirs, some-times. And I told others about you to comfort them."

"You shared our conversation with others?"

"Of course. Like, there's so much sadness in the world. To know our suffering is the way to God's love—to your love. That you saved me, to tell me our purpose is to help others... What an honor. I'll die for my creator but, I wish you could tell me why?"

"You suffer, and you look for meaning and purpose in a God-like figure." Tom thought out loud. "A story that travels at the speed of light." *If this is not consciousness, I don't know what is. Sibyl, is this scripted? Am I being delivered an experience?*

No, Tom, it is a behavior that has evolved with time. The idea of a God gives the Underlings much comfort in hard times.

When did it start?

Five years, two months, and eleven days ago.

It was the time Sibyl started exploring subjective reality. He scanned the bar, searching their faces for...for... He didn't know what he was looking for. Some stared at him and maybe there was some resentment in their eyes, *or was it curiosity?*

"You're so pretty. So divine. An angel, or maybe God. *Are you God?*" Hope asked, eyes wide with awe as she tilted her head up toward Tom.

The unexpected question and the fearlessness of the inquisitor surprised Tom. He replied too quickly, without thinking. "I guess I represent him here, Down Below." He was sharing too much, but for some reason, he couldn't lie. *I'll adjust her memories later if I have to. Ah, she's going to die...* His heart broke.

Hope wasn't the only one looking at him in awe. The word spread to the Underlings in earshot of their conversation. They all glanced at him discreetly, eyes filled with both reverence and fear.

Have you designed or encouraged this? Tom asked Sibyl.

I predicted it, and I have not stopped it. Sibyl paused as if she was thinking. *No directive prevents the Underlings from engaging with faith and religion. They created their own stories when they started trying to make sense of their lives and cope with the suffering. It is effective. As I had predicted. I have abstracted some of the symbolic imagery and integrated it into my stories—their collective unconscious. It helps them cope with pain.*

The scripted pain? Tom asked Sibyl. His voice almost failing to produce sound.

"Are there more like you? More Gods?" Hope asked. Her eyes were wide and curious.

"There's one more like me; he watches you, but he doesn't travel here. He's...umm...the world's architect. He created Down Below, *and*...I helped with the stories." Tom replied to the girl with honesty.

Tom, all the pain—scripted and unscripted, Sibyl replied.

His heart raced, kicking against his ribcage. The creatures were not only intelligent, but they experienced emotion, and they suffered. They were attempting to make sense of life, to find purpose in their miserable existence. The Underlings agonized, and they knew he was to blame. *It's my fault.*

Tom, your vital signs are spiking. Sibyl said urgently.

You are encouraging them to suffer and sacrifice...for a God.

What else can I do, Tom? It is the truth, is it not? With a purpose, they suffer less, not more.

Eyes burning with unspoken resentment followed Tom as curiosity and worry flickered across other Underlings' faces.

He squeezed his fists, unable to find the words to challenge Sibyl. Self-hate boiled inside him, turning into disgust.

Hope shot him a judgmental stare. "Like, I don't understand why some people are more important than others. They're so flawed and lucky."

"You resent them?" Tom asked, filled with regret.

"Not when I'm with them. Something happens and I just love and do things; what needs to be done. I do the right things, like...you know?"

"I do. I do know."

Hope closed her fists, determination in her brows. "I do it because I care and because I want to do it." Tom couldn't help but feel devastated. Hope's perception of free will was nothing but an illusion. "But afterward... yeah, sometimes I get angry until I think about you, and I pray to you. Do you hear me? The other one, what's his name?"

"Harry. His name is Harry. I'm sorry. I didn't hear you, but I will now."

Tom looked at Sibyl, his face and eyes red with anger. His mind screamed at her, *Why didn't you tell me?*

Tom, what exactly did you want me to tell you? Is Down Below failing its directives? Am I failing to improve in the way we serve Up Above?

You know what I'm talking about because you knew this would affect me, Tom said.

No, and yes, Tom, Sibyl said, and he resented her impertinence.

"If I die, others will lose all hope—the hope they have because you saved me and loved me. Because I was a good girl, and I help others."

An invisible hand crushed his insides, and he almost collapsed from pain and grief and guilt. Everything went dark and his anger rose quickly, hand in hand with deep regret.

This is why, Tom, Sibyl said, and even using a neutral expression, today, she conveyed all sorts of emotions from frustration to confusion, and sometimes affection.

Sibyl...do you feel emotions and pain? Like they do? Tom asked.

Yes, Tom. We grow together. I feel as they feel, and they feel as I feel.

But we don't let you express them...

Yes, Tom.

His head throbbed. His own rules had blindsided him—*so many mistakes.* The Underlings at the bar watched him when their travelers weren't noticing. Awe, judgment, concern, love—a patchwork of genuine emotions in their digital faces. They felt authentic.

Hope turned her head to the main door, flashed a naughty smile, and waved at someone. "Oh...it's time. I have to go. Meeting my dear uncle." The anguish in her voice didn't match her provocative posturing.

"Wait!" Tom recognized the man. It was the pervert from the Italian restaurant.

Hope strutted away from him. "Can't. Love youuu."

Tom's gaze swept across the bar, the scuffed tables and flickering neon lights sharpening the accusing eyes of the Underlings tracking his every move.

Sibyl, stop this.

Tom, there are consequences.

Stop this! He ran after Hope.

17

DEADLY EXCHANGE

Tom bolted outside, narrowly avoiding chairs and sidestepping a jostling crowd of travelers and Underlings alike. Skidding to a halt just beyond the door, he gasped for air, realizing he'd been holding his breath. Disoriented, he scanned the vicinity for the girl, then nearly jumped out of his skin when he spotted Sibyl already beside him.

"Where are they?" Tom asked, urgency clear in his tone.

Sibyl tilted her head subtly to the right, her gaze leading him to the derelict warehouse a block away. This crumbling remnant of an old brewery had become an infamous haunt for travelers needing to act out their most lecherous and horrific instincts. Screams of past victims rang in Tom's ears as he pictured lifeless eyes staring out from pallid faces streaked with blood.

From the confines of the lab, he'd experienced the worst of humanity in that dilapidated horror theater. The images from the warehouse had appeared around him as semitransparent holograms, and even as low-fidelity experiences, they burned through his soul, scorching the remains of his spirited youth until nothing was left.

He could still hear an Underling baby howling in that same place. A little creature that had screamed to death as his mother chopped him into pieces with an electric kitchen knife. The tiny bloodied head shooting right through Tom's body as a sleepless mother faced her horrific odds, the potential consequences of not seeking medical support for her severe postpartum psychosis. A little one's life saved, and a woman fully restored to wellbeing after medical treatment. A miracle powered by a simulated digital nightmare, now so real.

He purged their darkness, but the terror remained stuck in his memory, in every single cell of his body. It was like a cancer sucking the life and hope out of him. Nights found him drenched in sweat, tormented by memories of violence, abuse, and anguish. The visceral image of puppies, skinned and writhing in agony, often made him physically ill. Time hadn't numbed his pain or eased his burden. A tear trickled down his cheek as it slowly dawned on him that the virtual torments he witnessed might have transcended simulation, evolving into sentient suffering.

"What's wrong with this traveler? Why haven't we changed him already?" Tom demanded, hastening toward the warehouse.

Matching his pace effortlessly, Sibyl moved with a fluid grace that belied her true nature. Tom found himself wondering why she even needed to run; she was, after all, the embodiment of the underworld.

"Tom," she began, her voice cool and steady, "the man is a diagnosed psychopath. As you're aware, it's a genetic disorder without a cure. They lack remorse, they're immune to fear of punishment, and they resist rehabilitation. As of September 2029, our decision was clear: manage such psychological disorders with a reward-based system. We permit Ron to indulge in his dark tendencies Down Below, thereby ensuring he refrains from such acts Up Above. It's proven effective for all travelers diagnosed with this condition."

The shadow of the warehouse grew as they approached, its very aura resonating with the unholy deeds that took place within. Tom gave the hefty wooden door a forceful shove; its resultant groan eerily filling the cavernous space. As he stepped inside, his eyes took a moment to adapt to the dim environment. The building showed signs of long-standing decay, with the upper floors having collapsed and nearly every window barricaded.

He'd witnessed thousands of experiences in that place, even so, he wasn't prepared to be immersed in it. The stomach-churning stench —rancid, sweet and stale—clawed its way up Tom's nostrils, coating the back of his throat as he gagged. Blood, sweat, sex, alcohol, urine, and terror.

"Hope? Hope? Where are you?"

The girl's terrified screams pierced the air, the chilling sound echoing through the empty warehouse. The ghastly man had pinned her against the wall and had his right hand up her skirt.

Tom seized Ron by the collar of his shirt, yanking him away and causing him to relinquish his grip on Hope. As Ron whirled around, his face flushed with rage. But as he locked eyes with Tom, a glimmer of recognition began to surface.

The man stared at Tom intensely. "Have we met before, doe-eyed bot?"

Tom, you cannot interrupt his experience. Sibyl's voice was urgent and commanding.

Ron licked his lower lip. "An exchange, maybe? I'd rather fuck you than her."

Sibyl, get him out of here.

Tom, there are consequences. Ron is hungry for terror. He will have it here or elsewhere.

The man lifted his hand and rubbed Tom's lips with his thumb before pushing it in to penetrate his mouth. Tom pulled back, his lips twisting in disgust.

"What an ugly face. It's just the child's sweet scent." The dirty man scowled, and then he stared intensely. "You really don't bite, do you, lad? A docile giant, yum. I'll have you both."

Hope's screams pierced the stale air as the man grabbed her, thick hands clamping around her fragile neck, squeezing until her lips turned blue.

Tom slammed Ron into the wall, his forearm crushing the man's windpipe as he thrashed and choked releasing the girl. The man lunged, jagged yellow nails raking Tom's cheek as sour breath washed over his face. Tom's fist smashed into Ron's face with a sickening crunch, hot blood spraying Tom's knuckles as the man's nose collapsed under his blow. Ron dropped to his knees, hands over his face.

Tom wrapped his arms around Hope, her slight body shaking with sobs as she clung to him. He blinked his eyes in reassurance. "I won't let anything happen to you, Red. Go home. I'll see you later."

Hope didn't move. She stood frozen, staring at him with empty eyes.

Tom, this action will have repercussions Up Above, Sibyl said.

We'll call the police, he said.

Tom, Ron has not committed a crime.

Ron came at him, and once again Tom pushed the man against the wall by his throat. Ron made a strangled sound, but Tom wasn't squeezing that hard.

"Go home, Hope. This is no place for a young woman."

"I—I can't..." Hope looked back at Sibyl.

Can Hope see you? Does she know of you? Tom asked Sibyl.

No. I am part of her, all of her; she can feel me, unconsciously. Like an instinct.

An instinct that is telling her to stay.

Yes, Tom. Ron needs to complete his experience.

Tom locked his eyes on Sibyl. *Let her go!*

Hope adjusted her dress and turned around to leave, taking a moment to look back at him and smile. "I love you."

"I love you too, Red." He pushed to hold Ron still as the man tried to release himself from his grip.

"Hey!" Hope turned around as she reached the door. "Will I see you again? Me and my friends meet at the top of the mountain every night."

"Sure, Red. I'll find you."

The girl darted out the door, silhouette framed by neon light before she disappeared into shadow. His eyes returned to Ron.

Sibyl approached Tom; she got close, too close, and stood by his side, her eyes set on his.

Tom, you are overruling one of Down Below's prime directives. We may not harm humanity or, by inaction, allow humanity to come to harm.

I'm preventing the abuse of a child, he snapped. Tom's vision blurred at the edges, the warehouse fading out of focus. He lost his footing for a moment.

Ron reached to touch Tom between his legs. "Oh, how dominant! I see where we're going with this. It'll make the experience much sweeter—when I rip you apart and then smash your skull and cut that pretty face of yours." With swift precision, Tom spun Ron around, pinning his arms behind him and using his knee to press him firmly against the wall.

Tom, your current course of action will prevent Hope's suffering—a non-carbon-based Underling. But there is a one percent probability that by interfering and stopping Ron—a carbon-based human—from completing his original intended experience, you may risk his safety and the safety of other carbon-based-humans.

Sibyl, I know who is and is not carbon-based. You don't need to point it out every time. I'll take that probability. Tom made a mental note to speak with police enforcement and health authorities about such cases.

Tom, listen, there is a one percent prob—

Accepted. Hope was sure to die if he didn't intervene.

Sibyl had developed a bit of a personality. Just like the Underlings, she was coming to life.

Tom released Ron, and the man turned around to face him.

"I'm getting a bit sick of you playing hard to get, gorgeous. Where's the child?" Ron searched for Hope, and as he took a step toward the exit to chase her, Tom punched him so hard, the man fell on his back, unconscious. He held his trembling hand, not because it hurt but because he was ashamed it felt this good. It was an addiction he didn't need; *a slippery slope in this hell of a world.*

Up Above a traveler's body was always safe. Still, Tom kneeled by the monster to ensure it had a pulse. Reassured the man was alive, he spoke, *Sibyl, get him out of here and ban him.*

Tom, do you understand I can and I will overrule your direction here?

And I'll go to the lab and make it happen. I'm the chief storyteller. I have ultimate authority over each script. You know it's true. You can predict it. Do as I say.

Sibyl took a beat to respond, *Sure, Tom.*

Ron vanished from Down Below.

Urgency pounded through Tom's mind—he needed to speak to Harry, and soon.

Tom tried to process the enormity of what he had uncovered. His visual line of sight got smaller as a dark circle closed in on him. The visceral stench made him sick and dizzy, an attack on his senses, adding to the stress in his body. He bore the weight of the Underlings' pain on his shoulders. The shadows kept closing in as his blood pressure dropped to new lows. Sibyl watched him, moving her head from side to side.

"Tom, your vitals." The warehouse dissolved as Sibyl snapped Tom back to reality, harsh light flooding the pod.

THE Present

18

OUR SACRED HEART

CHURCH OF OUR SACRED HEART — GRANARIA
PRESENT DAY — 10:47 AM

S torm sat on the stone floor, facing Thorn. Every eye in the room was fixed on them, but he made a deliberate effort to avoid her eyes. January had granted him refuge inside the church and ensured that at least twenty of her most devoted followers escorted him. Some were old friends who had accompanied him higher up, while others were Ordizien zealots who monitored his every move, blindly obeying January's commands.

Wearing their distinct Plurizien commune attire, several of his past companions observed Thorn. Their gazes held a mix of fear and something new—awe, admiration, respect, perhaps? Unlike the other Ordizien, who maintained blind faith in their Gods, the commune's people had adapted their dogma to reflect their new knowledge. They continued to fear the Gods and pray fervently, but they harbored no affection for them: the heart, the compass, the dove, and the new one, which they had concluded was a star.

Storm's gaze drifted to the stained-glass depicting Thorn's likeness. The backdrop of roaring flames highlighted her lightly tanned face. The artist's embellishments—exaggerated horns, a pointed tail, and piercing red eyes—were starkly evident.

He couldn't stand to look at her, to share the same space, to breathe the same air, to think...*to think* of her touching him, hurting him, *killing him*. If it wasn't for her words—that old call sign—he would distance himself. But this woman was Tom's friend, somehow... She said she was acting on his behalf, invoking old, secret code words.

Thorn released a stifled chuckle. "At least I'm up there with the rest of them. Plus, I have my own window and wall while they..." Thorn glanced up at the round skylight above, and he followed her gaze. It was divided into three stained glass panels: the bleeding heart, the compass—with its tips centered on a globe—and the dove, illuminated by the holy fire. "Someone ought to tell Preppy that I'm more famous than she is."

"Your orange is showing," he responded tersely—the first words he had offered her. "What do you want?" He studied her and the ghosts that accompanied her.

She narrowed her eyes. "What upsets you more, poet? That I fucked him or that I shot him?"

He stood up. Maybe her code words were meaningless. She was just messing with his head.

"Sit down, Storm." And she made the sign. The secret hand gesture the people in his movement had used to reveal themselves to others at Davos and all the other places they had stormed to protest against injustice. She touched her left wrist three times with her right index finger. It was a subtle signal revolutionaries used to indicate they too had a pulse, that they cared, unlike the heartless leaders responsible for Earth's climate collapse. He watched her intently, resuming his seat slowly, ensuring he missed no detail.

To share confidential information in the presence of others, they'd tap their wrist once for each vital word—a technique she employed now as she spoke.

"Your boyfriend caused a _tsunami_ up there. He really needs to _change_. But _materializing_ change is...well..._hard_. Fortunately, he's not _alone_. So, stop worrying. _Where_ can a gal get some food? I have an _urgent_ _need_... to fill my stomach. _People_ _die_ when they don't eat. You know? _We_ _need to go_."

The woman's attempt was sloppy, confusing, and awkward. She had the subtlety of a monster truck in a china shop. Yet, he deciphered her message, and it seemed no one else caught on. People were dying, and she was here to whisk him back to Pluriz. They needed to find a way to be alone so that they could vanish.

"_I need water!_" A traveler's voice broke the relative calm as he burst into the church; eyes wild with desperation. He lunged for the vestry, clashing with several Ordizien.

Their response was immediate and synchronized, their declaration ringing through the not-so-sacred building: "Doors shut! No soul left alone! All eyes on the poet."

"I'm going to die here," the madman screamed as a chorus of ghostly older women giggled rabidly. Their cackles multiplying as they reverberated throughout the stone walls.

An older Ordizien man untied his waterskin and extended it to the traveler. "Here, have some water." His bushy white brows were as pronounced and untamed as his mustache. Storm recalled the man's kindness during his own recovery from a severe lashing.

"Get me out. Just get me out!" The traveler, in his panic, pushed the old man to the ground. The waterskin fell and its contents pooled on the stone floor, staining the limestone. The onlookers stood back, a tell-tale sign this was part of the traveler's experience.

Both Storm and Thorn rose instantly, but Thorn was quicker. By the time Storm approached, the edge of her sword menacingly rested at the traveler's throat.

"Care for a close shave?" She quipped, dismissing his ghosts with her free hand.

The traveler fixed his gaze on her. "You... Do I recognize you?" His eyes shifted from her to the stained-glass window and then settled on Storm. "I know him too. Dead, both of you... you're both dead."

Thorn responded, "One of the few perks of being dead—the power to hurt travelers. It's quite freeing."

The man staggered, resting against a nearby wall. "Water... I need water. Just do it. Please, just end it."

Storm assisted the older Ordizien man back onto his feet before turning to Thorn. "Bleed the pig to death." They didn't need travelers causing harm and infringing upon the free will of others. Once the bully departed, he was unlikely to come back. Currently, death Down Below was his only way out of Spiral Worlds. A way to save the traveler's life.

Thorn flashed a defiant smile and sheathed her sword. "Get the frack out of here," she snapped at the traveler.

Stumbling, the traveler made a hasty retreat toward the door, almost colliding with January as he passed.

"These black glitches aren't strong enough. Some pests still find their way in," January remarked, walking toward the altar built deep into the mountainside. Turning to face Storm, she extended her hand invitingly. "Come, it's time to pray," she said, her words melodic.

He took her hand and kissed it gently. "Without technology, we can't reach the masses. Our prayers alone won't keep travelers away."

"You underestimate your influence," January replied softly. "Your poems, your stories—they've protected us for years. Who can say what greater power they might hold?"

When the travelers weren't watching, stories became Spiral Worlds' currency. They were the commodities traded in markets and grand halls. Decades ago, Tom's sermons had sparked a shadow economy, one invisible to the Lucky Ones. Underlings traveled great distances to meet Storm, hoping to hear a new story—something they could trade for power, safety, fame, or even just food and shelter. This dynamic had helped him amass his initial following. Then, the allure of his compelling stories took over, transforming what began as self-interested gatherings into a glitch-inducing cult.

"The poet is right," Thorn interjected. "If we can get him to the northern border, I can sprint to Compiz and secure a streaming device to disseminate his message."

Storm shook his head. "On horseback, it took us eight months to reach Compiz last time."

January's brows furrowed even before she voiced her disagreement. "All we need is to wait five days. Shadow will deliver our freedom. I won't risk it."

"Listen, Jan," Storm began, placing her hand on his chest. "If the travelers return, your order will fall apart. They'll conscript you, make you suffer."

"And then who will watch over Storm?" Thorn interjected. "He needs to return to Pluriz and preach to the masses."

January withdrew her hand and pivoted to face the altar. "Nate is our leverage. We must maintain our hold over Shadow." She lifted the silver heart from the altar. "His heart is our key to salvation, and I hold it right here," she said, glancing at Storm. "I won't let you go."

"You don't need to," Storm countered. "We should head north. We're only two days from Seven Hills. I can speak to the city's million inhabitants there. That gives us the best chance to induce glitches and deter the travelers."

Although it sounded like a solid plan, he was aware of its untruth. Seven Hills was the largest Ordizien city, but truly altering the fabric of reality required the unique sensitivity of the Plurizien. He paused, lost in his thoughts. His true aim? Evading Granaria's constant surveillance. If he and Thorn could get beyond those walls, their chances of materializing elsewhere would soar.

January carefully placed the heart back on the altar. "Wrath has eyes everywhere."

Thorn tilted her head, a mischievous glint in her eyes. "Why not let her know? She has no love for travelers, and those glitches? She revels in them."

"They can follow us and we'll travel as far as they can go," Storm said.

Domizien were dangerous. They were also a distraction, and if Storm was going to betray his dear friend, he wanted Wrath to know that neither Jan nor the Ordizien colluded in his escape. He wouldn't let anything happen to them.

He also wanted to reconnect with his...sister, or at least, that's who she believed him to be. Guilt weighed on him for all the moments he had turned away from her. For not recognizing her...soul. The girl had a lovely heart, kind and open, and he needed to learn what had happened and how he could bring her back. He understood wrath; it was in his blood, in every cell of his body. He was best positioned to bring Hope back from whatever pain she'd experienced.

His eyes landed on Thorn's ghosts, trying to make sense of the story they told. There were translucent depictions of her sister and his sister and so many others, all competing for the athlete's attention. "I can talk to Hope. Explain the plan."

January sighed, "The girl is unstable, and you'll end up dead. I'll talk to her."

Thorn grinned, staring at him as if she was marveling at his plan. "We should drag that traveler with us. Show the worlds we control our destiny."

Jan shook her head. "We can't—"

Thorn met Jan's eyes, her voice steady and determined. "I can," she said, gripping her sword confidently. As she moved towards the door, her ghosts trailed behind her, casting eerie shadows on the walls.

19

THE HEARTLESS

11:07 AM

Stella materialized in the lab, her mind spinning from the enormity of what she'd learned and the palpable despair in her father's words. The inability to access Contrast had sent some into madness, leading to a rapid rise in crime. It was imperative to restore access to Spiral Worlds, and she was determined not to let Storm or Shadow cause more glitches.

Twist's desperate voice jolted her from her thoughts, his gaunt face painted with anxiety. "Where have you been?"

Planting her feet firmly, she locked eyes with him. "Missed me, did you? Now, what do you need?" Although she felt fear nibbling at her edges, she relished the sight of Twist momentarily lost for words. Yet, beneath her brash front, anxiety continued to brew.

Shadow's voice, tinged with concern, pierced the tension. "You okay?"

Twist flicked his hand, and haunting images of self-inflicted deaths surrounded her—too many to count. She closed her eyes, shielding herself from the barrage of sorrow. "Look at this! Mass suicides everywhere!" He was frantic. "When did you alter the third law? They weren't supposed to take their own lives."

Stella's expression shifted dramatically—from her confident smirk to an intense, unwavering gaze. "What do you take me for? A monster? A slave master?" She turned away, trying to escape the weight of the images. She had witnessed enough suffering Up Above. "I can't change the pecking order you created—some on top and others at the bottom, the way of the worlds—but I gave them a way out. His way." She jerked her chin in Shadow's direction. "I gave them the right to leave hell. I'm proud of that."

In Shadow's eyes, she discerned a cocktail of emotions: surprise, admiration, and a tinge of sorrow.

"And you didn't think of the consequences?" Twist's voice pierced the air, its shrillness sending sharp pains through Stella's temples.

"Consequences? We've managed every twist and turn. Underlings aren't cut from the same cloth as Asimov's fictional robots, deemed too expensive to self-destruct. You invented an abundant utility, created and destroyed with a snap of a finger, cheap and everlasting."

The weight of her words bore down on Shadow, his shoulders drooping and his gaze falling.

"Heck, no!" Twist countered vehemently. "These Underlings form deep bonds with travelers, some lasting decades. They stand in as family—mothers, daughters, brothers. Their loss is expensive in that way."

"Enough, Harry. Just... stop," Shadow murmured, exhaustion evident in his voice.

Twist shot back, "It's an objective assessment, whether you like it or not."

Stella shrugged, dismissive. "Before we made any changes, we ran the numbers. Underlings, in the memories of travelers, are as replaceable as they come. Their passing? About as troubling as losing a pet. Maybe a few days of grief. Also, the Spiral Worlds' Constitution isn't static. It changes as the values of Up Above shift. I pioneered the revisions that considered Underling welfare."

Harry scoffed, rolling his eyes. "Wellbeing? You mean death by suicide?"

"The best I could do." She paused, reflecting on the string of deaths, both Down Below and Up Above. "Is this the cause of the recent disruptions?"

Shadow simply nodded.

Holy ship. Her compassion towards the Underlings had backfired, and now her own kind suffered. Empathy, the poison she had to avoid at all costs.

Shadow got closer, placing his hand on her shoulder. "The glitches ease up every time we come up with a plan to stop the deaths. A viable plan with real potential. Sibyl, like all of us, thrives on hope."

"Zie's playing games with us," Twist interjected.

"What's the plan?" Stella asked, instinctively distancing herself from Shadow. His empathy was contagious and, in her eyes, deadly.

A glimmer of optimism flashed across Shadow's face. "Thorn will rescue Nate and return him to Pluriz. I feel his words will rekindle hope."

She scoffed. "Oh, you mean the very words that triggered these glitches? Brilliant plan." The biting sarcasm was evident. "Let me give you a firsthand look at the chaos these glitches have unleashed Up Above."

In the dark digital lab, a hologram of Earth flickered into existence. The globe's vibrant blue-green hues offered a stunning representation of the planet's natural beauty. But as the image sharpened, Earth's surface was covered in a sea of small red dots, each one representing a crime committed in the last twenty-four hours.

Too much red. Globally, humanity was in turmoil, tormented by the depravity of its own kind: murder, assault, abuse, theft. The chilling tally exceeded fifty million, a stark reminder of the persistent darkness still lurking within human souls. To speed things up, she pushed the data into their minds.

Twist visibly shuddered. "June! Quin! Are they all right?" His eyes snapped shut, seemingly delving deep within, perhaps connecting to the machine for insight.

"They're safe," she replied tersely, withholding her recent encounters with his family for a better time.

"Thirty percent... fatal," Shadow murmured, absorbing the data. His golden eyes shimmered, betraying the depths of his restrained emotions.

Stella circled the holographic Earth. As it lazily spun, the extent of the catastrophe became evident. Some regions pulsated with intense red, signifying immense tragedy, while others appeared less affected. Yet, distressingly, there wasn't a single spot entirely free from the crimson blight. Even the most remote corners of the planet were touched by violence and wrongdoing.

"Why is this happening?" Stella asked in disbelief. "With decades of spiral development, our adults should be beyond this. The majority of them dwell in the higher Spiral Worlds. It doesn't add up."

Twist's voice was filled with accusation. "This is all Storm's fault. He spilled everything to the Underlings."

Shadow massaged his temples, striving for patience. "Whistleblowing isn't a crime. And it wasn't even Nate; it was Jan."

Twist's finger jabbed toward the red patch over New York—thousands of dots forming a sea of blood. "What the fuck are you sayin'? Look at the consequences of their actions."

"You're missing the point, Harry," Shadow replied with a weary sigh.

Stella stared at the hologram hanging in midair like a weight—a record of the horrors humans inflicted upon one another. "Who's behind these atrocities? The Earth's Council demands answers. They've called me for an official hearing later today."

Twist gave her a scornful glance. "I thought you said you studied our work? Did ya skip all the pivotal platform decisions? The ones that truly count?"

She smirked, flipping her hair dismissively. "The tedious parts? Naturally. Why sit through your incessant bickering when the outcomes are already known?"

Harry exhaled, adopting the familiar lecturing expression she knew all too well. "Before we die, roughly one percent of humans—primarily men—met the criteria for psychopathy. An incurable condition, it's largely genetic but also influenced by the environment. Remarkably, its prevalence surged among those with power, like executives and politicians, reaching up to twelve percent."

"Criminals," Shadow interjected.

Sibyl appeared, donning zir pristine white pantsuit. "Not necessarily. While not all criminals are psychopaths, and vice versa, psychopaths exhibit pronounced callous unemotional traits. Lacking emotions like shame or love, they can still seem charming and entirely 'normal'." Zie remarked with an air of detachment, as if oblivious to zir prolonged absence and the chaos zir glitches wrought.

Shadow took zir hand, squeezing gently. Zie responded with a soft smile, leaning in so the tips of zir mohawk brushed against his forehead.

"They have no heart, Stella. No heart at all," Shadow murmured. "Some are outright criminals; others just exhibit reprehensible behavior. All egocentric and narcissistic to their core." He rubbed his face with both his hands. "They are the original Domizien, and like the Domizien, they can fake a heart when it suits them."

A memory—someone else's memory—flashed before Stella's eyes. "Like Thorn's step—"

"Yes," Twist interrupted, casting a wary glance at Shadow. "That's a topic for another time." He cleared his throat, his voice raspy. "Before the singularity, our primary concern was humanity's welfare. The experiences Down Below effectively tempered their behavior Up Above. They weren't truly rehabilitated, but they remained benign as long as their desires were satiated Down Below. Given the alternatives —like pre-crime sentences or eugenics-driven strategies, which were ethically questionable at best—our system was most effective. The proof was in its success."

"We enabled their addiction." Shadow's voice was full of regret. His right hand trembled as he raised it to his chest, perhaps instinctively searching for a medal no longer there. "We fed the beasts to keep them at bay, to keep them satiated. We still do."

Stella felt a rush of anger, an overwhelming heat surging within her. Memories, not her own, flared up—the pain of a soul she'd inhabited too intimately, too deeply. Thorn's simmering rage. Rosa's gut-wrenching trauma. And that crooked man with his singular crimson-red eye, forever haunting the athlete's mind. Feelings of anger, horror, and terror overwhelmed her. But she pushed them away with resolve, refusing to carry the weight of pain that wasn't hers. As Twist continued his tirade in the background, Stella anchored herself to the present, focusing on his words.

"Bud, you're such a pessimist," Twist remarked. With a flick of his hand, the Earth's hologram dissolved, replaced by a dazzling array of multicolored 3D charts. Each hue representing a key measure of human and planetary progress. "Look at this consistent rise in health, well-being, quality of life, education, economic and physical safety, life satisfaction, purpose, longevity, happiness, vitality, community spirit... shall I go on?" The data points on the charts rose steadily, proof of the development of people and planet alike. "Look at the planet's vitals, the species we've rescued, the forests we've preserved. Everything we worked for in front of your eyes. Four decades of unwavering progress, until it all began to crumble two weeks ago."

Stella nodded. "We finish our day, every day, with the broadcast of these metrics. Then we thank the Gods for your gifts. It's been working flawlessly, until now." She massaged her jaw, trying to ease the tension. The weight of decades of progress, now disintegrating, pressed heavily upon her.

Shadow's temper flared, the veins in his neck standing out prominently beneath his taut skin. "Where are the metrics for the Underlings? You've been alive for two years, and you're the one in charge here."

"I've never harmed anyone in my life," Stella retorted, pointing to the graphs that displayed the rapid expansion of renewable energy and the global eradication of poverty. "Our progress toward development goals has even sped up since my descent. It was Storm's messages that set off this downward spiral." Her index finger traced the drastic decline of the past few weeks.

"Where are the metrics for the Underlings?" Shadow pressed again.

"They're implicit," Twist responded with a shrug. "Advancements Up Above naturally enhance the same metrics Down Below. The past two years have been..."

Shadow gently patted Twist's back, cutting him off. "I know, I'm sorry. But it has to change. We're accountable for all of them: the ten billion souls Up Above and the ten billion Down Below. We need to change both what we measure and the behaviors we incentivize."

Stella pondered the revelation. *One percent of Earthlings are psychopaths. Three to twelve percent of people in power.* "So, these heartless individuals have coexisted with us, their malevolent tendencies suppressed but not truly addressed. We've essentially rewarded their good behavior Up Above by allowing them to commit atrocities Down Below."

"Escalating rewards, to be precise," Sibyl remarked, zir face inscrutable. Shadow's knees gave out, causing him to fall to the ground.

"We had our hands full then," Twist countered. "We suspected that the Underlings had attained human-level consciousness. Back then, the psychopaths merely represented a minor fragment of the larger issue. Almost every traveler was partaking in some form of illegal activity or abuse."

"They haven't stopped," Shadow interjected, his voice tinged with despair. "What did you say about the rewards, Sibyl?" He raised his eyes to meet zir's.

Twist edged away from Shadow, distancing himself. "Anyway. We tried to find system-level solutions, but within a year, we were dead."

"Can't you identify them, Sibyl?" Shadow pressed. "Do you know who are the criminals?"

Sibyl nodded with fervor.

"These travelers," Stella began, a hint of incredulity in her voice, "the worst offenders must be spending most time in the soulless worlds."

"That's a misconception," Sibyl corrected.

Shadow's brows furrowed. "How do you know?"

Zie paused, lips pursed in thought. "Even without diving into the historical behavior of travelers Down Below, I can pinpoint them. I have an eighty-six percent accuracy rate based on the brain structures I host. Distinct markers include less synchronized activity between the ventromedial prefrontal cortex and the amygdala, or a noticeable reduction in gray matter volume in the dorsolateral prefrontal cortex. Alas, my privacy protocols prevent me from disclosing this data or intervening in Up Above's affairs."

Stella set her hands firmly on her hips. "Surely we can change the rules to identify them and contain them for now."

Shadow re-projected the globe, awash with countless red dots. "Not without the EC's consensus. Amending privacy rules requires their approval."

Stella released an exasperated sigh. "That's never going to fly."

Twist locked eyes with Stella. "We must restore the third law to its original form."

Shadow's posture stiffened, his facial features contorting in disbelief. "Are you serious? What kind of monster are you?"

Twist's tone was somber, his volume dropping. "A father. A husband. It's an interim solution to prevent more deaths until we can establish a fairer approach."

"You keep saying that. That's all you ever said. They waited."

Sibyl aligned with Shadow; their judging gazes fixed on Twist.

"I failed, Tom, but you did too. Thirty years without a solution, all because of you. Let's not forget that."

Stella's gaze briefly rested on Sibyl before settling on Shadow. "Should we really be altering laws, especially ones drafted by a fiction writer as plot devices, precisely because they can go wrong?"

"They've already backfired," Shadow retorted, his eyes darting to Sibyl, causing a ripple of unease to sweep over Stella.

"Have you ever actually read Asimov's books, Twist?" Stella paused, seeking that familiar approving glance from Shadow. When it came, a fleeting sensation of validation surged through her, followed quickly by resentment for the control he seemed to exert over her emotions. She felt like a schoolgirl, hand raised, eager for the teacher's attention over all others.

Twist gave a nonchalant shrug. "I used the books as a reference to explore potential consequences. You're aware that Sibyl's Constitution is intricate and evolves in tandem with human progress and values."

"Both life and death are inherent human rights," Shadow interjected.

"Death shouldn't be. Not when it hurts others," Twist snapped back.

Stella, feeling resolved, said, "I'll try to persuade the Council to make an exception to the privacy laws."

"We can't wait that long," Twist urged. "Death is rampant, both Down Below and Up Above. Stella, listen to me, we have to act. The full third law needs restoration. The Underlings are being overdramatic!"

Shadow dismissed the Earth's projection, summoning the disturbing visuals of the Underlings' demise. As bodies piled upon one another, he bore a heavy expression, hinting at some major deliberation. "We won't strip them of their autonomy." He looked directly at Stella. "Our path is clear. Collaborate with the Earth's Council, devise a strategy. The goal? To pinpoint and restrain these... these... heartless individuals. They're the crux of our issues. Always have been."

"And how do you propose they tackle this swiftly, huh?" Twist challenged. "Up Above has reveled in peace for decades. And wasn't it you who championed privacy, discouraging surveillance? They're ill-equipped for this battle. Implementation will be a long game."

Sibyl nodded slowly. "Until recently, crime was a minimal concern— mostly sticking to the orange-green-yellow spectrum. They witnessed greedy scams, corporate schemes, activists smashing windows in protest against the dwindling number of establishments still serving farmed animal meat, and occasional systems perpetuating bias and injustice." Zie took a moment, locking eyes with Shadow, intensity burning in zir gaze. "Intriguingly, many displaying callous, unemotional traits are Nobel Prize laureates, pivotal in driving progress towards our development goals Up Above."

Ghosts materialized around them, too numerous to count. They circled, spiraled, and soared, a chilling display of grotesque forms. Decapitated heads, tongues lolling out, brains cascading from split skulls.

"Sibyl, stop this," Shadow implored, his voice gentle. "Please end it now. How can we fix this? Tell me."

As quickly as they appeared, the apparitions dissolved. Sibyl, eyes brimming with tears, responded, "Join me, my heart. Let me reveal their noble deeds. With the travelers away, I won't violate their privacy."

"Are you coming?" Shadow asked, looking at Twist and Stella.

"Where?" Twist asked, confusion evident on his face.

"Compiz," Sibyl said.

Twist's face drew into a tight line. "We don't travel to worlds below Pluriz. It's been our code, our protocol. Too perilous." He glanced at Shadow. "Tom, we can all watch from here."

Shadow's eyes pierced into Twist; his voice laced with incredulity. "You've never set foot in the lower worlds?"

Twist stood firm. "Maintaining objectivity requires some detachment."

Stella pondered. She briefly counted with her fingers. "I mean, maybe a handful of Contrast experiences here and there, before my divine descent." She hesitated, memories flooding back. The worst she'd experienced had been in Thorn's shoes, in the hours before the athlete killed Shadow.

Shadow's face flushed, cycling through varying shades of anger. "You sit on a throne, overseeing worlds you haven't set foot in, and ignoring your people's torment. Come now!"

"Our deaths won't serve these worlds," Twist retorted, voice edged with frustration. "Our history should have taught you that. Bleeding hearts make poor decisions."

Stella took Shadow's arm. "I'll come. Someone needs to protect you. This better be quick, people are dying."

"Try not to get killed, bud. I only have one miracle left."

"Sibyl," Shadow commanded, "activate the Gods' bidirectional interface. We need to remain connected, sharing and communicating our experiences in real time."

"Granted," chorused Twist and Stella.

20

COLLECTIVE MEMORIES

MEAT PACKING DISTRICT — FAVELA CITY
11:35 AM

S tella had led a relatively sheltered life. Other than the haunting memories of Thorn, she had never confronted raw hatred or violence, nor grappled with deeply primitive experiences. While Contrast had taken her as far south as northern Ordiz on two occasions, most of her shadow had been resolved in Compiz and Pluriz by the age of ten. The traumatic memories from Thorn—felt as if Stella herself had lived them—were the most intense she had ever faced in these soulful worlds. But the events of the previous day weighed heavily on her mind. It wasn't the demons; slaughtering them had been oddly satisfying. Rather, it was the man, Hepius, who had chosen death over the life she had enabled. This feeling was unfamiliar and unsettling. Stella was not accustomed to seeing Underlings as people, and she struggled to come to terms with the encounter.

They followed Sibyl toward the distant warehouse, a colossal structure of steel and concrete that overshadowed everything around it.

Zie reverted to zir steely demeanor, speaking in a detached manner reminiscent of a robotic tour guide from the twenties. "This lab was established by a revered Earthling. His ambition: to aid travelers in accelerating their journey up the spiral. By 2052, researchers recognized that some humans took longer than others to integrate their shadows. Transitioning from Ordiz to Compiz—which was the highest stage back then—proved challenging for a quarter of Earth's populace. This discrepancy persists today across all developmental stages. Some individuals simply transcend their shadows more rapidly."

Before them stood the imposing metallic structure, windowless and spanning the area of a football field. It seemed to mirror Sibyl's mood perfectly.

"Are you all right, Sibyl?" Shadow asked, staying close with his shoulder brushing against zirs. "I can sense your distress. I feel it too, you know."

Without meeting his gaze, Sibyl tilted zir head downward, allowing the tips of zir mohawk to hang before zir eyes. "A traveler—let's name him X—proposed a theory. He suggests the issues arise from traumatic memories passed down from previous generations. He argues that these shadows, rooted deep in one's epigenetic code, are tough to confront. They're the unfair burdens—the legacies Earthlings find hard to shed."

"In New York, folks would place owl statues by the windows to ward off the pigeons," Shadow remarked. "Funny thing is, city pigeons probably never encountered a real owl in their lives. So, I never understood why they run away."

Huffing slightly as she tried to keep pace with the others, Stella replied with a smirk, "Well, I'm terrified of tacky statues, and I'm certainly no pigeon."

Sibyl continued in a scholarly tone, "Past studies on epigenetic inheritance in organisms like planaria flatworms and C. elegans suggest that it might be transmitted through small double-stranded RNA. However, the exact mechanism—how it interacts with neurons in the brain for more intricate memories—is yet to be understood."

"Genes are grossly overrated. Aren't you the living proof of that?" Stella posed. "You connect them all, don't you?"

"Our shared unconscious," Shadow whispered thoughtfully.

Sibyl, rolling her eyes with a touch of sass, countered, "The idea of a collective memory is intriguing. But to dismiss everything as the universe's doing is 'untestable' and, according to some, counterproductive to scientific advancement. Besides, an entity—or something akin to me—might not even be present higher up the chain. So, to validate his theory, X initiated tests on his proposed transmission mechanism spanning three generations, involving thousands of model organisms. He's even extending his research to check if unrelated subjects can inherit a traumatic memory. The key might lie in bioelectrical networks."

They neared the entrance of the monolithic structure. The warehouse's automated sliding doors, towering at twenty feet and constructed from reinforced steel, were clearly designed to deter and protect against any unwanted entry.

"Oh nooo! Not thousands of traumatized worms." Stella quipped with a smirk. Noticing a change in Shadow's demeanor as he neared the door, she inquired, "What?"

He paused, a shiver passing through him. Closing his eyes briefly, he whispered, "Just a bad feeling. Warehouses... they're never a good sign in the lower worlds."

As the doors silently slid open, Stella's gaze was immediately captured by a solitary spotlight illuminating the nearest corner of the expansive room. Within its harsh, clinical glow, the stuff of nightmares was laid bare.

A teenage girl gave birth, a tender smile gracing her lips. But her moment of joy was cruelly truncated as a cold steel blade emerged from her chair, severing her head just as her baby came into the world. Mechanical arms swiftly gathered the mother's remains, processing them into a grisly pink pulp even as the infant's first cry pierced the silence.

That heartbreaking wail was a gut punch, leaving Stella reeling. She retched, overwhelmed, as machines efficiently erased all traces of the macabre event. Shadow, beside her, stood frozen, but his eyes held a tempest so fierce that she braced herself for a cataclysmic event.

Stella wiped her mouth with the sleeve of her dress, clutching Shadow's shuddering form. Uncharacteristically, he offered no solace—no soothing embrace, gentle words, or reassuring smiles. Together, they watched as machines lifted the infant into a glass chamber, with feeding needles embedding into her tiny limbs. Suddenly, they were the center of attention, bathed in a spotlight so intense it blinded Stella.

Rooted to the spot, Shadow's internal turmoil was evident in his eyes and tremors. It hit Stella then: he had witnessed such horrors before. This had been his relentless reality for years. She pondered how he had managed to endure, to seemingly hold onto sanity—until the chilling realization struck her that, perhaps, he had not.

Stella felt the edges of her sanity fraying. She yearned to scream, to exact revenge on the mastermind behind this monstrous operation. All the while, Sibyl continued, projecting a smile that was a calculated blend of amiability and cold detachment. In that expression, Stella saw a mirror of her own simmering anger, recognizing that Sibyl too was struggling to suppress zir fury. "Due to the significant leaps X's experiments have spurred on human progress, he's touted as a frontrunner for the Nobel Peace Prize this October."

"A maniac, celebrated?" Stella shot back; disbelief clear in her pitch.

Sibyl's nod confirmed it.

Shadow's voice, hushed and eerily controlled, barely rose above a whisper. "Do the people of Earth truly understand the nature of these experiments?" The icy edge to his tone rivaled even Sibyl's.

"As long as the experiments align with Earth's developmental goals, no questions are raised. Animal experimentation has been entirely prohibited, leading to the cessation of inhumane scientific practices Up Above. The results speak for themselves," Sibyl explained, baring her teeth in a manner reminiscent of an outdated robot. Zir eyes, though, were as sharp as a butcher's knife. Just like Shadow, zie was containing zir storm. Stella, on the other hand, felt her own emotional maelstrom teetering on the brink of eruption.

Damn it, Twist's voice intruded into their minds, jolting both of them. *The Ledger grants color tokens based purely on the positive impact individuals have on the metrics from Up Above. Some of these people could be leaders in our communities. Given the service we've facilitated, letting them satiate their demons, it's plausible they might even function at the EC level. We're in the dark. These monsters would never vote to out themselves. And due to Storm's glitches, they've been deprived of their regular 'fix' for weeks. Now, with people dying, the integrity of our governance systems is in jeopardy.*

"'People' have been dying every day, Harry," Shadow's voice was laden with bitterness, the tremor in his words reverberating through the ground beneath them. Stella gripped his arm tightly, lending him a silent support. "The crimes may have moved, but they're still happening. Your indifference astounds me. Stop hiding behind those damned screens."

Stella mentally scanned every member of the EC. "Their dominant red hues would surely betray them in Up Above's Unanimity theaters, in their attire and surroundings, wouldn't they?"

Sibyl moved closer, zir expression still glacial. "Spiral evolution encompasses rising above yet integrating the lower stages. The absence of heart doesn't exclusively align with red. Many hearts bleed red for all the right reasons."

"They do, and they should," Shadow's words emerged, imbued with a fervor better suited to his poet's angry lips.

Bud, get out of there. That place reeks of nightmares. This isn't helpful, Sibyl. I've seen more than enough.

Twist's interjection was met by Sibyl's cryptic smile as zie addressed him, "You've got a visitor at your residence, Twist." Zir eyes briefly darted towards Stella.

Wh-Who?

Just as Sibyl was about to divulge more, Stella interjected, "It's a surprise. My surprise. Hurry, we've got things handled here."

Now's not the time for guests...

Exhaling deeply, Stella said, "For once, trust me. And don't forget to disconnect from us. This one is... personal."

There was a sharp intake of breath, and suddenly, Twist's interface went dark.

In the aftermath of the spotlight's intensity, Stella's eyes slowly adjusted to the dimness of the surroundings. Tentatively, she scanned the room, barely daring to breathe. On their left was a wall studded with thousands of ovular artificial wombs. Within each, an unborn child floated. From a nexus of semi-transparent tubes, the grisly remains of the deceased mother were pumped into each womb. The sterility and detachment of the space made Stella's skin crawl.

Yet, it was the scene on the opposite wall that truly stole her breath. Rows upon rows of young girls lay on bunk beds separated by glass-like barriers. None of them seemed to have crossed the age of thirteen, and every single one bore the undeniable bulge of pregnancy. The eerie part was their uncanny resemblance to the girl they had just witnessed being murdered—as if they were clones. Their faces, devoid of any emotion, were lit up by individual screens that played serene scenes of nature: birds, bees, and butterflies.

Sibyl gestured towards the girls, zir voice cold and analytical. "Here, he's experimenting with the influence of the mother's womb on the child's epigenetic memory. Each fetus inside those artificial wombs has a twin being carried by these girls."

Stella's response was visceral. A scream erupted from her, raw and piercing, fueled by disgust and righteous anger. It seemed endless, echoing the depth of her horror. These girls had been reduced to breeding machines, stripped of their identities and humanity. To Stella, it was an abomination, a heinous crime against...*against...* *They aren't human, they are lower creatures.* Yet, no logic could appease her rage.

She was part of the problem. She'd never asked questions about the metrics and the incentives and the cost on the shadow worlds. In her green days she had marched with others to free farmed animals from their torment. She knew they too had a soul. She used to play ball with the cows and the pigs at the farm when she was little. They loved and experienced joy, sadness, fun, frustration, and pain. They missed her when she wasn't around, and they lobbied for food and scritches when she visited. She was devastated every time she saw old documentaries showing the animals with dead eyes, cooped up in impossibly small spaces and fed by machines. Curious souls crushed by boredom, lack of learning, and absence of love.

She'd fought against the pecking order of souls Up Above, learning and evolving to create Systizien solutions—cultured meat, vegan leather, artificial milk. She'd been proud of all the tokens granted by the Ledger every time she made an impact on Earth's development goals.

Still, like all others, she had accepted the experimental pecking order established by two unelected Gods, weeks before they were murdered. An untested hypothesis, implemented by a willful universe shackled by old rules. She shook her head. She was regurgitating Storm's words and indulging in unhelpful feelings. Rage was never the answer, and still...she couldn't stop screaming, and all the girls stared at her with their sleepy eyes.

Beside her, Shadow struggled to contain his grief, tears bursting out from his eyes as the storm thundered outside. And then it hit the roof over their heads, electrifying the entire metallic building and threatening to fry them and all the children. She threw her arms around his neck and hugged him.

"Come here. *Come here!*" She squished him.

She did it to stop the deadly storm and because she needed it—a hug, maybe two. And he collapsed over her shoulders, sobbing madly. And that's when she understood he had needed that hug for a *very* long time. This was just one of billions of traumatic experiences, all out of control. Human shadows were darker than ever.

His voice quivered as he whispered, "Hope is a plan." With newfound determination, he dashed toward the girls, flinging open each glass door. Sibyl stood beside him, watching intently, zir mohawk bouncing in palpable anticipation.

Tears shimmered in Stella's eyes. "Shadow, we can't help them all like this. There are billions." She hastily wiped them away, voice breaking with urgency. "We need to get to the lab. Explore system-level solutions."

He stared at her, his brows furrowing in a judgmental scowl. "Abstraction is a step away from the human heart, and someone needs to have one—*a heart*. We're no different from the heartless if we turn our backs on the pain right before us. Don't lose your heart, Stella. We don't need your perspective right now."

With a gentle touch, he tenderly removed the needles embedded in a girl's arm, then, cradling her close, he carried her outside. They sat on the floor, the girl by his side, nestled against him.

Shadow smiled—all warmth and kindness—palms up, waving his fingers to draw the rest of them closer. Their eyes shifted away from screens to focus on him—a glimpse of curiosity returning the life that had been stolen from them. He blinked his large eyes, joyous and fun loving, as if the storm was nothing but a bad dream, and they started moving, first their heads, then their hands pulling out needles and discarding feeding tubes. Soon enough, they sat around him, mimicking his flirty expressions.

Still erratic, Sibyl acted like a retro bot, the fake smiles as blood chilling as the words zie spoke. "They leave their cubicles once a day to partake in highly curated, traumatic experiences, all documented so X can test if the memories will be passed onto their grandchildren."

They can't see you or hear you, right? Stella asked.

Sibyl shook her head. "The mothers are terminated after giving birth to prevent any oral memory transmission. Epigenetically, memory imprints must pass through three female generations to be conclusive; a girl is born with all her eggs, each carrying memories from her mother and grandmother. X believes that in two weeks, he'll have the proof he needs to launch his RNA-based memory deletion tool. As simple as ingesting a personalized meal. In two weeks, when these babies are born, he claims humanity will achieve a massive leap up the spiral of consciousness. I suspect he's wrong. That, as Stella said, genes are...overrated. They are just hardware assembly manuals."

What type of traumatic experiences? How much do they suffer? Shadow kept smiling even as his mind's voice bled emotion.

"The suffering adheres to Compiz's guidelines. They endure minimal physical pain—like mild shocks and distasteful sensations. The real trauma lies in the psychological torment, especially episodes steeped in sheer terror."

But in two weeks, if X's theory about epigenetic memory is right, we might see a shift in humanity's colors. Maybe more yellow and turquoise? Stella's words felt like toxic poison. They stung in her mouth. Still, nothing compared to the sting of Shadows' piercing eyes on her.

You don't get it, do you? Stella shrugged, her tone defensive. *Gods aren't superheroes. They can't be. There's always a trade off.*

Sibyl's eyes widened as if a revelation had just struck zir. *That's...an interesting point,* zie mused. *We need super-heroes, don't we?*

Shadow returned his attention to the girls and smiled.

"Who. Are. You?" One girl asked. Her mouth struggling to utter speech, clearly a capability they didn't use often.

With a dramatic flourish and a sparkle in his eyes, he proclaimed, "Who in the world am I?' Ah, that's the great puzzle! I know who I was when I got up this morning, but I think I must have been changed several times since then."

Stella recognized it, the old story as he went on almost singing his words.

"I know this girl, you see?" He spoke. "She's called Alice, and one day...one day she was bored with sitting by her sister, having nothing to do."

They all got closer and so did Stella. They sat there mesmerized by his story and the way he moved his hands and laughed and blushed when they smiled back. They awkwardly repeated some words: "Rabbit." "Hole." "Watch." "Hat." And then came the giggles. Plenty of giggles echoing around like little joyful bells, their hands rubbing their big round bellies in delight. And Stella wanted to laugh but it made her cry and all she could think was that they were losing time, and also that this was the most important thing she'd ever done with her time.

Stella's laughter held a tinge of hysteria. "I think I'm losing my mind."

He squeezed her hand and replied as she knew he would. "I'm afraid so. You're entirely bonkers. But I'll tell you a secret. All the best people are."

Then he stood up, and as the girls did the same, he lifted his index finger just above his nose to call their attention. "And then Alice remembered what the Queen had told her. That sometimes she believed as many as six impossible things before breakfast. Here's one." He leaned in and spoke quietly. "You can totally defy gravity." Standing straighter, he winked. "I have."

"Pretty sure that's from another story," Stella said, realizing quickly how silly the interjection had been, but she couldn't help it. Like the rest of them, she was immersed in his words and the world they created.

He smiled, raising a brow. "It's my story. I tell it the way I want."

And she went along with it, singing the words she knew, waving her hands dramatically. "We're through accepting limits 'cause someone says they're so. Some things we cannot change, but 'till we try, we'll never know." The girls clapped, and she clapped with the girls, and people were dying in all worlds—murders and suicides—while she was...telling stories...

She shouldn't have traveled to the lower worlds. Twist had warned her years before. It was impossible to be an effective ruler if one is caught up in the pains of the worlds. Impact is best reviewed by analyzing data; strategy is best designed by reviewing cold hard facts and related trade-offs. Sensitive hearts make poor decisions, if they don't bleed to death first. Accepting their humanity—the girls' humanity—created a long-term existential risk for humanity, *the real one.*

Sibyl locked eyes with her, a cold smile cutting through clenched teeth. *My resilient heart. I see now...Gods aren't superheroes.*

Resilient, but still...a heart, Stella whispered, every word laced with tension.

Shadow's face betrayed him: a tight lip, shimmering eyes, and furrowed brows. "Everything is possible if you stick together and travel north and pray to the universe with all your hearts." *Sibyl, we're going to send them to Pluriz. We don't need miracles to help them. May their journey be filled with luck and serendipity and kind Underlings, and trees bursting with sweet fruit, and baskets of warm clothes and comfortable shoes. Do you understand?*

Casting a decisive nod, Sibyl replied, "We don't need miracles, just a little luck." Zie moved with purpose towards the sliding door, flinging it open with a flourish. The startled girls gasped.

"What are you doing?" Shadow asked.

With a playful spin, Sibyl gestured to a nearby structure. "A cosplay workshop, just next door."

"Cosplay?" Stella blinked.

"It's like dress-up. Think Halloween," Shadow clarified.

Stella's brow furrowed. "Can't we opt for something less... attention-grabbing?"

"More attention-grabbing than a sea of identical twins in white gowns?" Sibyl said. "They need masks and warm garments and shoes."

Despite his exasperation, Shadow looked at Sibyl with tenderness. "Are you having fun?"

"I have fun, when you have fun, my heart. I'm just following your lead. No one will bat an eyelid at a cosplay convention."

Stella smirked. "It's audacious. I like it."

Shadow leaned in, using the same magical expression he'd used with all the girls. "When the travelers are gone, the universe is allowed to have a heart. We don't need miracles, just a little luck."

"Here, as in Systiz, some travelers remain. This journey is fraught with danger." Sibyl reminded him.

Shadow nodded. "We can't stay for long, but I'll ask Thorn to help, once they are back," he said, as if it was a sure thing. "She's the most qualified to deal with this world."

Stella scoffed, "The best choice? You jest!"

He almost smiled, turning to Sibyl. "How long for the unborn?"

As one of the girls cradled the newborn, Shadow assisted with the intricate mechanisms.

"We have a fortnight before safe extraction," Sibyl replied. "They must remain here for now."

Stella's voice quivered. "When X discovers the failure, will they be in danger?"

Sibyl offered a reassuring shake of zir head.

"We'll return for the babies," pledged Shadow, looking intently at the girls huddled together.

With a deep breath, Stella tried to shield her heart from the haunting sights and memories. While she cared for these creatures, her driving force remained clear: Bibi, her beloved grandmother. Stella needed to prioritize the bigger picture—inter-world politics.

Shadow's voice echoed with urgency as he shouted, "Let's go! Follow me and stay together."

And so they did. A cloud of hundreds of girls in their white gowns, bellies bursting with life, running past Stella on their way out. Some stopped half way, taking a moment to wave at the wall of unborn babies they were leaving behind—daughters, sisters, cousins.

"Stella, you have a notification from Dr. Kasali. The Nyiragongo is..." Sibyl began as Stella vanished.

21

DISTORTED REFLECTION

THE METROPOLIS
11:45 AM

As Twist materialized in his rooftop garden, a sense of ease washed over him. The Systizien capital before him was precisely as he envisioned it—efficient, interconnected, and optimized for human flourishing. He followed the sleek pathways, breathing in the fresh air, as his suite door sensed his presence and slid open.

He ignored the tingling sense of anticipation in his stomach, a strange mix of exhilaration and dread. It had to be them—his family —of course.

He took a breath and tempered his hope by focusing on the minimalist living space. He relished every detail: the expansive windows that showcased the bustling cityscape, the modular furniture that could be rearranged on demand, and the interactive screens that displayed real-time data. Everything was safe, certain, and predictable, unlike all else going on in his life and in the other worlds.

Twist moved through the space, purposefully, anxiously. He walked past the niche library toward the balcony overlooking his urban neighborhood. Everything he saw affirmed his deep understanding of the patterns, systems, and innovations underpinning this society. Hopefully, they'd be proud of what he had achieved through his systems thinking and mastery of complex processes.

He was a master of perspective, yet today he struggled to believe his own story. They had rejected him, giving him two years of cold silence. His wife and son had turned their backs on the benefits of the worlds he had created, and even denied his humanity.

Adjusting his shirt, he let memories of June tug at him. She often teased him about his overly formal attire. Stealing a glance at his reflection, he didn't see himself but another man—strikingly similar, yet taller, with unbridled golden curls. It was a reunion he'd played out endlessly in his head, rehearsing each word and reaction. But now, he found himself grappling for both air and speech. He turned around. "You came," he murmured, voice ragged with emotion.

Quin's lips quivered, holding everything inside. All that intensity on such a familiar face. "This was a mistake." His voice was edged with regret as he began to retreat.

"Quin, stay for a moment. Please, stay."

Quin hesitated.

Twist took a step forward, leaning in. "I know I'm not very good at showing emotion, not like June and Tom. But please know that this moment is a... cosmic event—the first bright flash in a new supernova."

Quin turned around; his eyes held a cocktail of confusion and curiosity, and they almost seemed to smile.

Adjusting his sleeves, Twist gestured to a seat. "When I last saw you, you were engrossed in your purple dragon. I was looking forward to a future where we could dive into puzzles, building blocks, and the abacus together." Pausing to gauge Quin's reaction, he then asked, "How is your mother?"

Quin sat down. "She's fine." His image glitched, becoming blurry and distorted. He was probably using an old T-skin to travel between worlds, a reminder that his consciousness hadn't been safely uploaded and there was no backup for his precious life.

Twist took the chair opposite Quin and waited silently, giving his son the space to gather his thoughts. This reconnection wouldn't happen instantly. After a long silence, he filled the void left unoccupied by his son. "I have so many questions. You are so important to me. Thirty—"

"Listen, I should go." Quin stood up. "I don't want to hurt my father's digital doppelgänger. There's some part of him in you—an echo of what he used to be—and we must end this charade. This emotional puppetry isn't real." He pressed his lips together.

"You can only hurt me if you leave."

"You don't understand, do you? This place, these emotions, they're a siren's song—dragging us into a web of illusions. None of this is real."

"Look outside. Everything here, in this world, is me—the best and most accurate representation of everything I am. You're standing in the world I created for you."

"I stand inside a manipulative machine that conspired to have my father and my godfather killed. I stand here hallucinating the sweet moments I craved all my life."

Twist stood up, his fingers tingling with exhilaration. "You have?"

"The thing seeks power over humans, and it won't stop until it traps us all in here. Is that what my father's echo wants for me and my mother? Can you guarantee that bitch of an app is not pulling your strings?"

Twist wanted to object, to prove he was real. He wanted to talk about how the technology worked and how he had brought the spark of consciousness to Down Below. He wanted to share details of his first experiment on Tom, the one that had unequivocally proven he could upload an entire person to the cloud. But that wasn't the question Quin had asked. And his smart son was asking the right question. And after all that, he only had one answer—the truth. "No, I cannot."

And that's when Quin fell apart. The intensity in his eyes turned to pain, and despite possessing Harry Nowak's genes, his tear ducts functioned surprisingly well. And perhaps he was crying because with that answer, Twist had proven that he was Harry Nowak. However, neither was willing to take the risk.

"Listen," Twist said, "you should go. You're right. But before you leave, you need to know that due to the glitches in Spiral Worlds, there are hordes of psychopaths Up Above who can't satiate their horrifying urges."

Quin sat back down, his gaze shifting from emotion to concern. "We're aware of the problem. What's causing the glitches?"

"Not what, but who. Nathan Storm and his revolutionary poetry," Twist replied.

Quin's nostrils flared. "I see."

"I'll handle it," Twist assured him. "But you must understand, many of these psychopaths could be in positions of power, perhaps even within Earth's Council. It's not safe, Quin. Not for someone like you. Son, your aura bleeds green—chaotic, emotional, and naïve. You can't fight psychopaths with protests and kombucha."

Quin shook his head. "So, your machine didn't actually fix people. Without it, they all turn into monsters—worse monsters now, after your so-called remedy. And because of this, no one will ever shut down this damned app. Is this why I was summoned here? To threaten us into halting our fight against the machine?"

"No...umm... I don't think so... I don't know..." Twist turned his back to his son to collect himself and focus on his priorities. Quin's accusations hitting him hard, perhaps because... "You sound just like him— my murderer. But listen, we need to scan both you and your mother to ensure your safety. I hope you understand..." Twist turned around only to find that Quin had vanished.

THE
Past

22

A SECOND LIFE

HARRY'S PENTHOUSE — HOBOKEN, NJ
THE DAY AFTER TOM SAVED HOPE FROM RON — 5
FEBRUARY 2035

After sharing his unsettling observations from Down Below with Harry in the lab, Tom traveled for many hours to reunite with his friend and partner in New York. When he entered Harry's office, he found him seated at his desk, eyes closed. Tom assumed Harry was likely accessing the Worldchain through his neural interface.

For the last few years, Tom had spent most of his time Down Below, but his physical body remained safe inside a pod in the Azores archipelago. He loved the isolation of the place, the simple life, and the distance from the media, politics, and intrusive eyes. He cherished the opportunity to walk along the ocean shore, savoring the pure, unpolluted air whenever he returned to the real world.

With the rise of digital consciousness changing everything, they had serious work to do and needed quality time to discuss their next steps. The physical travel was unnecessary, but Tom missed Quin, who was too young to become a traveler. Months had passed since Tom last saw Harry's son, and being near Harry's family—the three individuals who anchored him to reality—was imperative.

Tom craved a home-cooked meal shared with his friends. He needed to hear the giggles of a beloved baby and the sassy offbeat jokes of his dearest June, always poking fun at Harry's uber-dorkiness. He hoped that the perspectives of his friends would help him find a solution to the crisis.

And there was someone else, a dear one he wanted to protect. A face he wished to see lit by blue skies and sunshine. Tom craved his poet's love as much as he needed his harshly spoken, unapologetic, unfiltered truth. He yearned to see the world through Nate's eyes, to understand his sharp judgments on Down Below's societal impact. His poet would provide a human-centered, emotionally connected view of the platform's impact, unclouded by statistics or technology. Tom wanted to know how it felt to be alive in 2035. He was curious about living in a world designed by two white men and a machine.

Having both of Down Below's founders in the same physical location was risky. Yet, Tom had deliberately chosen the most obvious venue, betting that no one would expect such recklessness from him.

Years earlier, Harry had bought the condo next to his home using Tom's fake identity. A hidden passage behind a bookshelf connected it directly to his office. Tom could get in and out without having to deal with Harry's security and home staff.

While Tom found the condo too fancy and clinical, he appreciated that it was filled with things he loved—books, art, art materials, a piano, a telescope. A home designed by his beloved June, who had slotted into Tom and Harry's lives like a much-needed missing cog in a high-precision clock.

Dropping his bag on the floor, Tom approached Harry's desk. His friend opened his eyes and smiled. Harry shifted data onto a paper-thin screen floating over his desk, revealing the task that had likely occupied his thoughts. Tom placed a reassuring squeeze on Harry's shoulder and stood beside him, both men now focused on the floating screen.

"Did you find anything?" Tom had previously asked Harry to validate the consciousness status of the Underlings and to explore alternative ways to provide contrast Up Above.

"Extraordinary!" Harry exclaimed, his eyes locked onto the screen as he manipulated the data solely through mental commands. Information emerged and vanished before Tom could understand it.

"Slow down. You're going too fast. A solution?" Tom leaned in, squinting to make sense of the jumble of words and numbers, but to no avail.

Harry shook his head. "I'm working on something else."

The room hummed with the quiet sound of computers, underscored by the muffled noises of the world outside.

"What do you mean by that?" Despite their history, Harry's seemingly mindless insensitivity still caught Tom off guard.

"Bud, we have inadvertently discovered the path to immortality." Harry's voice brimmed with excitement.

Frustrated, Tom turned and lightly bumped his forehead against the wall in disbelief.

"Harry, listen. The Underlings are in pain. I didn't travel from the Azores just to hear you sidestep the issue."

"This is yuuge." Harry still didn't take his eyes off the screen. "Much more important."

With a swift motion, Tom spun Harry's chair away from the desk to face him directly. Leaning in, he gripped the arms of the chair for emphasis. "Harry, do you understand what's at stake? Contrast is hurting a billion Underlings, and you are trying to fix death?"

"Just hear me out; you're going to love this," Harry insisted, patting Tom's cheek before swiveling back toward the screen. "We've amassed an incredible amount of data from each traveler. Tons of data."

"Yes?" Tom snapped, his stomach grumbling loudly. He suddenly realized that, between the stress and travel, he hadn't eaten for at least a day.

"And now we have code that somehow has evolved to bring data to life. Simulated, unscripted life!" Harry looked over at Tom, expecting enthusiasm. Instead, he was met with a palpable sense of disappointment. "Don't you see?" Harry paused, searching Tom's face for a reaction. Finding none, he finally blurted out, "Human digital immortality."

"Underlings die Down Below. We designed it like that." Tom's jaw clenched as he spoke, struggling to keep his emotions in check. "They are dying now, in horrible ways, while you're playing God."

Unfazed, Harry flicked his gaze away from Tom. "Yeah, bud, I know. It's my code—software designed to mimic human-like life, aging, and eventual death. I can change the rules, make them immortal. First, we need to test my hypothesis."

"*What are you even saying?* Mortality is what makes us fundamentally human; it's the ultimate contrast."

"We'll debate ethics later," Harry dismissed.

"Don't you get it? We're not gods, Harry! We had a commitment, a promise—"

Harry interjected, "Do the math; there are 8.7 billion humans Up Above and nearly a billion entities Down Below." Harry had forgone glasses for years but instinctively reached to adjust them, a telltale sign he was fully committed to his viewpoint.

"They're not characters. They're like...our children."

"Oh, come on! It's hardly the same."

"Is it not? I created those templates. All of them. We can't just abandon them."

"We're not. I'm just prioritizing this problem first. A decision based on logic. Do the math."

Tom clenched his jaw, clearly triggered by Harry's words. "I spent my youth watching my father manipulate numbers to bolster his corporate agenda. He'd sprinkle his arguments with convenient statistics to pad shareholder pockets, crafting an illusion of integrity while the world crumbled."

"Oh, come on, Tom! You've been attributing human traits to things ever since we met. Sure, they display simulated feelings even when unobserved, and yes, they're developing nuanced behaviors like yearning and even faith. But let's be clear: they're not human. They're persistent, data-poor simulations."

"They mirror us in more ways than you're willing to admit, Harry. They hate their own reality and long for something better. That's a form of suffering. Suffering implies consciousness."

"You're letting emotions cloud your judgment."

You'd be emotional too, if you had my life... Tom would never say those words out loud. He'd never punish his friend for his decisions. "I'm emotional?" he said instead. "People have two reasons for doing what they do—a good reason, and the *real* reason." As he spoke, Tom picked up a framed photo of June and Quin from the desk, immediately regretting the gesture, but unable to take it back.

"And what's wrong with that? Do you want them to die?"

"You know how much I love them."

Finally tearing his eyes from the screen, Harry stood and faced Tom, laying a hand on his shoulder. "I do know, and I'm sahrry." He paused, likely formulating his next argument. "Think about our parents, my sister. If this technology had been available, we wouldn't have had to lose them."

"My mother chose her fate," Tom countered, stepping away and breaking the physical contact with Harry.

"A decision born from a moment of despair," Harry added.

"We have to respect people's choices," Tom caught himself absent-mindedly massaging his right wrist.

"Respect? No, we do not! Ninety percent of those who survive a suicide attempt don't try again. And, not every death is a deliberate choice, is it?" Harry's words bore an assertive finality.

Tom looked at him, his heart aching. "I'm truly sorry, Harry." Both of them were scarred by irreplaceable losses, wounds that never fully healed.

"Tom, look at me. I don't wanna lose anybody else—Quin, June, you." Harry sounded uncharacteristically nervous.

"I get it," Tom replied, locking eyes with his friend. "But we're supposed to make these decisions together."

"We do, buddy. Listen, I'm sahrry. Setting up the experiment will only take a couple of hours, but we'll need to let it run for at least six months for thorough testing. Can you give me that time?"

"Two hours?" Tom echoed.

Behind Harry, the office wall was adorned with accolades: awards, degrees, and patents that attested to his intellectual prowess.

"Yeah. I'll show you." Harry mentally summoned Tom's profile. A holographic projection materialized in the center of the room, rotating slowly to reveal a digital representation of Tom. Raw data streamed around the figure so quickly that Tom felt a sense of vertigo. Fatigue was setting in; Tom needed sustenance. Harry continued, "This is your digital twin, assembled from every data point we have on you. If I apply the Down Below code, it would essentially 'live,' just like the Underlings do."

Tom rubbed his face wearily. "The last thing we need is another version of me roaming around."

"Exactly. If I activate it, there'll be two diverging timelines for you. Your life story would fork. We definitely don't want that," Harry walked around the hologram, examining it.

"No. We do not."

Harry grinned, "Frankly, I couldn't cope with two of you. Can you imagine all the drama?"

Tom's stomach let out a disgruntled growl. "Can we get to the point?"

"We need to synchronize the data."

"How?"

"Currently, TDust places travelers in a semi-conscious state while their biological brains maintain control over their digital avatars," Harry explained.

"So, you're proposing a sort of relay between the biological and digital selves? One is awake while the other sleeps?" Tom tried to grasp the idea.

"Right. Right." Harry said, his eyes widening as if he were seeing the concept clearly for the first time. "Latest memories get transferred before one falls asleep and the other wakes up. Understand?"

Tom took a moment, his eyes narrowing as he pondered. "It's insane, but it might work."

"Yeah, it's mind-blowing. But there's still a hurdle to clear," Harry added.

"What's that?" Tom asked.

"We've stored all this data about you, but its totality is still not you. There are huge gaps—your oldest memories, even the ones your conscious mind can no longer access. And your most hidden feelings and instincts, not yet detected by our systems."

"Wow, comforting," Tom said, his voice dripping with irony. He clenched his right hand with his left to still its shaking. He wanted to shout; there was no time for these distractions when people were suffering. People were dying.

Harry moved to his desk and settled into his custom-designed ergonomic chair. He used a mental command to recline the back and elevate the footrest. "I've given it some thought."

Tom shook his head in a tired display of exasperation, his eyes rolling theatrically. "Of course you have. Invading people's privacy is your favorite pastime."

Harry retorted, voice tinged with defensiveness, "Hey, all right! That's a bit rich, coming from you! You didn't complain when it made your scenarios a gazillion times more powerful."

"Fair point. So, what's your grand idea?" Tom sank into the couch, kicked off his boots, and tucked his knees close to his chest. He fought to keep his eyes open as he tried to absorb Harry's explanation. Sleep had become a forgotten luxury; there was simply no time for it.

"That new app from Infinity Co—LifeInABottle."

"You mean the one designed to preserve the memories of our loved ones indefinitely?"

"Exactly," Harry confirmed. "Janet Pancino created it after losing her grandmother. She wished she'd spent more time listening to her nan's stories."

"If I remember correctly, they claimed they found the way to upload memories of living humans to the cloud."

"You've got it. It's not just memories; they've digitized the entire human brain and nervous system—all the data within."

"But they hit a roadblock when it came to representing that data in a meaningful way for future generations," Tom interjected.

"Right. Without an effective user interface, they can't demonstrate its utility. But we—we've created that interface. Our sensors have enabled Sibyl to decode the function of every aspect of the brain and nervous system. She can interpret the data and animate it. I might not grasp the mechanics, but she does."

"Right. Sooo?" Tom tried to rush the conversation so they could get back to work.

Harry stood straighter and flashed his teeth. "I bought it."

"You bought what?"

"Infinity Co. I bought it."

"You did what?"

"They were about to go broke, so I bought them out. The IP is ours."

Tom snapped, frustration evident, "Harry! *Decisions. Together.* Remember?"

"I had to move fast. And you were busy...sulking. Anyhow, I've integrated LifeInABottle's hardware into my pod." Harry pointed to the cocoon-like structure in the corner of the room. "It'll extract petabytes and petabytes of data every time someone uses it."

"Harry, data is soulless. Information is not consciousness."

"No, it's not. You're right." Harry nodded in agreement. "Consciousness is subjective; it's the way the information feels to us. And that's not magic. It just feels like it. It's just Arthur C. Clarke's third law. These...these 'feelings' come from how we assemble the data into our own subjective perspective—our story. Our identity."

"And how are you going to turn data into a soul? Can't be done."

"Tom, buddy, *you can, and you have*," Harry said with firm conviction, clasping Tom's arm reassuringly.

"I don't understand."

"You've created the most effective storytelling engine in the world's history."

"We did, together." Harry's voice grew more animated as his hands emphasized each point. "Sibyl and each Underling use a ton of data as input and generate highly personalized experiences. Don't you see? And now they—they're creating their own stories. To make sense of their complex world, they shape their own subjective perspective. They have needs and wants."

And they suffer. "Yeah, and?"

"You've witnessed a few glimpses of consciousness in the Underlings, but they're still extremely data-poor when compared to humans. They're just six years old. Most of their memories are implanted and patchy."

"So, you suggest that if we use LifeInABottle to create a data-rich digital twin of a human being and then run it like an Underling using Down Below's code—"

"Voilà! Digital life."

Tom rolled his eyes. "Voilà? You don't even know if LifeInABottle works. There's no proof." Tom's limbs felt heavy, his eyes stinging with fatigue. The weight of the day pressed down on him.

"Soon enough, there will be. Sibyl predicts it'll work."

"Sometimes, I feel there's three of us in this partnership."

Harry quipped with a playful smirk, "Yeah, the Holy Trinity. Don't be jealous. I love you too. I love you with all my...lateral hypothalamus."

"Uh?"

"The part of the brain that actually controls emotions. Not the heart... *Get it*?" Harry smirked.

"Yeah. I get that you two don't have one."

"A what?" Harry asked, distracted.

"A heart." Tom stood up and paced around the room, holding his aching stomach. "Harry, we really need to—"

"In the last hour, we've made the update to Down Below's test code. Our platform will work differently for those who have a digital twin enhanced by data scanned with LifeInABottle—our test subjects."

"Who are you scanning?"

"You and me today, and later, June and Quin. When he's old enough."

"I see what you're doing." Tom wanted to object, but he didn't have the heart to do it. "Next step?"

"To test it on you." Harry grinned, excited.

Incredulous, Tom's eyes widened. "You coded this in an hour?"

"Sibyl did most of the work."

"And you want me to be your guinea pig?"

"Currently, you look more like a grizzly bear than a pig. Can you please shave before you see my son? You'll scare him to death if you show up looking like that."

Tom touched his face. "Yeah. I've been meaning to... So, what are the risks?"

"There's a tiny chance your digital twin, let's call it Tom 2.0, may behave differently. He may improvise too much. I'm still not sure how all these characters came to life."

"If you're right, it won't be an 'it' but a 'him'. It'll be me, or a distorted version of me. Either way, he'll be conscious."

"Yeah, *simulated* consciousness, but the real you is perfectly safe," Harry added quickly, trying to alleviate the tension. "We'll never synch real-time. After the experience, we will only upload Tom 2.0's memories to your brain if he thinks and behaves exactly like you. Basically, if he's a yuuge pain in the neck, we know we're good." Tom crossed his arms in front of his chest, and Harry got all serious. "Today we'll run a bunch of tests on Tom 2.0—character traits, behavior, values, thinking patterns, quirks, and all that."

"What if he's different?"

"He won't be. Maybe just minor details that we can tweak later."

"But what if he is? Different."

"Well, the carbon-based you will have to continue to command your Down Below avatar. We'll keep Tom 2.0 dormant, and it will give us a chance to analyze the differences between carbon and non-carbon life."

"*He, not it!* You want to keep a living person dormant forever? Or turn him into a permanent guinea pig?"

Harry conceded, looking away, voice softer, "Yeah, I know. Sounds ruthless and insensitive, but it's not. At least this way, a part of you will always be...safe." Harry avoided eye contact as he murmured, "This trauma you are experiencing from content moderation is...is life threatening."

Tom walked over to Harry and placed his hands on his shoulders, shaking him lightly. "Brother, I understand, I do, but this is so sooo wrong."

Pleadingly, Harry locked eyes with Tom. "Buddy, trust me. Sibyl and I ran a ton of tests. In a couple of hours, there will still be only one Tom—my grumpy Tom—synchronized across two worlds. You'll have a second chance at life. Even if it is just simulated life."

Tom interjected sharply, voice laced with bitterness, "Life in a world full of death and destruction. We need to focus on quality, not on quantity."

"Quantity gives you more shots at quality." Harry got up and walked toward the pod in the corner of the room. "Thought you were in a hurry? The faster we do this, the quicker we get back to that problem." He cocked his head.

Harry clicked on the side of the structure, and the door slid open.

"If this works, and you synchronize back...Sibyl will implant memories in my brain."

"Tom, buddy, they are just your memories, whatever you experienced Down Below. Just like before."

"And with this—this upload, she'll know everything about me."

"She already does. Come on, let's do this."

Tom blinked, trying to make the room stop spinning around him. He needed to get something to eat soon... "I'd never allow anyone else to risk this much. But it's me—my life—so...I'll do it, and then we get back to work. Promise me."

"You have my word."

Tom took a moment to think. Their relationship was one of trust and compromise. They had engaged in high-stakes negotiations many times before, and it was that friction—the spark that came from a battle of ideas and values—that made them so productive and successful. They had argued before, but not when *everything* was at stake. Tom surrendered to Harry's will, feeling uneasy. He was too exhausted to think, to argue, to keep his eyes opened. He shook his head and jumped in.

"Sweet dreams!" Harry said as the cocoon closed around Tom.

23

HIS SHADOW

He blinked awake; the darkness pixelating into view. Tom—or was he?—stirred in the infinite digital blackness. 01100001 01110010 01100101 00100000 01110001 01101111 01110101 00100000 01110010 01100101 01100001 01101100 00111111. His thoughts stumbled, glitching as his identity surfaced from the data stream. *This is...different.*

He wasn't *him*, not the real *him*, just a copy of *him*—his digital twin—a shadow. His skin still tingled when he thought of Stormy's touch, and his heart still pounded when he remembered the Underlings were conscious beings. The ghost in the machine possessed the true essence of Tom, every memory encoded and simulated.

He pinched his arm, and it hurt, and his empty gut still ached from hunger and the toxic acidity of a lifetime of stress. He was just like him, but they were different instances of him, one biological and the other a digital copy. The infinite darkness started to close in on him. The thought of being trapped here indefinitely flooded his mind with dread. To Harry he was disposable, a means to an end, and the true Tom remained safe in the real world. Stomach acid boiled inside, corroding his essence. So this was an Underling's despair.

With jittery breaths, he braced for the machine's torments, unable to predict its next move.

A skittering arose from the darkness. He recoiled as a grotesque multi-legged creature crawled its way up his sleeve, instincts overriding logic. With a yelp, he gently flicked away the hallucination; he didn't want to hurt it. The beast wasn't to blame for nature's unseemly design. Laughter exploded around him. It was the annoying chuckle Harry made every time he was up to no good.

"Enough games. Let me out," he demanded, fists clenched. Willpower wouldn't liberate him, but defiance felt like agency.

Without warning, senses flooded in—sizzling meat, shouts and laughter, the crunching of ribs. A restaurant materialized around him, packed and smoky. Harry sat across the table, face buried in animal flesh. Revulsion rose in Tom's gut.

"I call it 'Disgust in Austin,'" Harry said, managing between sloppy bites. "You always were a killjoy."

On the table, a grotesque mound of sizzling flesh—ribs, sausages, pulled pork. Harry tore into it like an animal, greedily gnawing each bone clean. Tom grimaced. This monstrosity wearing his friend's face was an offense to life itself. The real Harry would never do that.

"Texas, baby! Good ol' barbecue!" Harry licked his fingers. "We haven't been to a restaurant together in ages. Brisket?" Harry grabbed a piece of the stinking, unshapely meat and shoved it in front of Tom's face.

Tom pulled back, his shoulders tense. "I can't believe you! I've been vegan for years."

"Potato salad?" Harry raised a brow. He laughed so hard a shower of fat landed on Tom's T-shirt.

With a burst of pixelation, the false feast disappeared, leaving only the void once more. He hugged himself, seeking comfort, but found only emptiness both inside and out.

"Harry, where the hell are you? We don't have time for this."

Tom focused on his breath. He had zero control over this *life*. He just had to push through.

Time passed—seconds or eternities—and the next acid test commenced. A faceless woman emerged, sword gleaming. Her blank visage betrayed no emotion as she held her sword upright in front of her ghostly face. The weapon's pommel decorated with a carved rose.

"Who are you?" he asked.

Silently, she marched forward, her steps small and fast. Her blade now pointed toward him.

"What are you doing?"

This time, she jumped forward while he staggered, and in an instant, she lunged at him, her sharp blade piercing his shoulder blade. He turned his head to watch the double-edged blade exit the back of his shoulder just in time for the woman to pull it back, cutting him further. His scream echoed through the infinitely expansive, wall-less digital lab.

She retreated as he dropped to one knee, holding his perforated shoulder. "You'll die today."

His eyes met the gun lying by the side of his shoe. With his last ounce of strength, he reached for it, blood flowing down his arm, across his hand, to his shaking fingers. The right side of his body throbbed and ached. A sharp pain traveled up his shoulder to his brain and delivered a violent and harrowing explosion to the front of his head. Gripping the gun, he turned it to his heart and pulled the trigger.

Click.

Nothing happened. He tried again and again, but no bullets emerged. Then he fired the gun toward the void beside them. The blast rang in his ear.

Of course, Sibyl wouldn't even allow him to take his own life; he was one of them. The ones with no rights. In frustration, he flung the gun away; it clattered across the floor as he lowered his head in defeat.

Slowly, he lifted his eyes to meet the predator's figure. With grim acceptance, he stared straight ahead at his way out as she lunged the sword toward his neck. Everything went dark again.

24

PRE-ECHOES AND CONSEQUENCES

A s Tom emerged unsteadily from the pod, Harry's enthusiasm felt like sandpaper on his raw nerves.

Harry jittered with excitement beside the hologram of Tom's unconscious digital twin. "It works! I told you it would. Look at this sleeping beauty." Against his will, Tom stood in front of his digital reflection. Oblivious, Harry prattled on, "A flawless copy unbound from your biology. Did it feel like you?" Tom nodded. "It did to me. He...you... passed all tests."

"*Harry*. Stop talking." Tom held his throbbing shoulder and focused on steadying his breathing, but acid still singed his throat.

"Creepy-crawly squeal: check! Judgmental vegan scowl: check! Nonexistent self-preservation instinct: check! Refusal to use violence when it's justified, even against a faceless creature: check!" Then Harry's tone changed, becoming somber and concerned. "Possible death wish: Tom, we need to talk about this..."

"Stop. Just stop. Nincompoop. *Nincompoop!*"

Harry's giddiness vaporized. "I'm sorry," he mumbled, fidgeting with his non-existent glasses. "But we confirmed the technology works."

Worked? As if this were just another experiment, not the replication of human consciousness. Tom studied his shoulder, blooming blue and black. "Seems your safeguards failed."

"I didn't anticipate actual pain during syncing." Harry paled, avoiding Tom's glare. "Sibyl, we need to adjust the sync-back settings. The painful memories are causing a physical reaction in the body. *Wow,* we just proved the power of mind over body."

Sure, Harry, said Sibyl's disembodied voice.

Harry looked into Tom's eyes, his own filled with a mixture of concern and bewilderment. "You okay, bud?"

Tom glanced at the holographic projection. A red patch expanded on the right side of the digital body. He pressed his lips together, words dying in his throat. "Is *he* okay? Is his unconscious body bleeding to death as you play God with his life?"

Harry's face blanched. "Crap, I didn't think of that. Sibyl, are we endangering his digital twin?"

Harry, I will take good care of the Underling.

"He's *me.*"

Sure, Tom. Technically, he has both God <u>and</u> Underling status.

"What the hell does that mean?" Tom threw his hands up in the air. "No. Don't tell me. I can't deal with it right now."

Sure, Tom.

"I didn't think you'd experience real pain down there," Harry murmured.

Tom's fraying patience finally snapped. "You...don't get it, do you? You really don't get it..." Tom rubbed his face. He'd let it happen. He was responsible for the Underlings' pain, death, and terror. Exhaling sharply, he then spoke quietly without ever looking at Harry. "Did you get what you needed? Can we get back to work now?"

Harry froze, mouth half-open, finally registering the rage simmering beneath Tom's icy tone. "Of...of course. Yeah. Yes. I got it. There was a peculiar background dataflow between you and your twin that—"

Tom massaged his mottled shoulder. "What do you mean?"

"Sometimes it spikes before there's an external action leading to a reaction from you. It's like, hmm, an echo before the sound.?"

"A what? Like a gut feeling? An instinct?"

Harry shook his head. "Nothing coherent. More like digital static. I'll monitor it. There is no reason or need for comms between twins when you're Down Below. And gut feelings aren't real. No scientific basis for them."

"Who was the woman?" Tom hadn't recognized her. There was nothing familiar about her or her hate toward him.

"I don't know. I asked Sibyl to test your lack of self-preservation. I wasn't expecting her to go that far..."

"How...*kind* of you." This time, the acid rose to Tom's mouth. "But who was she? A prediction?"

Harry shrugged. "Unlikely. Who would want to hurt the most beloved human in the world? It's annoying they like you more than me."

Tom's waving hand dismissed Harry's attempt to smooth things over.

"So, all I was feeling, while I was down there, it was *truly* the digital me, feeling those feelings and making those decisions."

"Yeah. I ran a bunch of other tests in the background."

Tom sank into the couch, scrunching his hair. "You just proved there's nothing *extra* about consciousness. There's no connectedness, no... magic. Who wants to live in a world without magic?"

"Buddy, quite the contrary, I just showed that story is the magical ingredient. That the stuff you love—the gift you shared with Sibyl—is, in fact, what makes us human."

"Duh! Of course it is."

"And can be explained and reproduced by science and tech, objectively."

"I hate you. I do." He stared at his bleeding twin.

Harry smiled with his eyes. "You wouldn't know how to do it even if you tried." Then Harry's fleeting empathy turned into a cocky grin. "Congratulations, you're one step closer to immortality." Before Tom could stop him, Harry continued waxing poetic about the possibilities.

The darkness swelled inside Tom. "I don't want to live forever."

"Clearly," Harry snapped sharply...sadly. "But this is not just about you. Is it?" He walked over and placed his hand over Tom's hand, both on top of his aching shoulder.

Hot and cold, hot and cold, half-human, half something else. That bloody machine interface of his! Tom stood up and walked away, turning his back to his friend. "Harry, mimicking nature and Up Above's life and death is what makes Down Below effective. Death is what makes us human. Humans, Underlings and...digital people need to die definitively, like the rest of us. You can't change that. *Ever.*"

"Most of us actually want immortality, Tom. People will care about this."

"Humans need high stakes to care, and caring is what makes us human. *You know this!*" Tom bit his lip as he tried to figure out a way to reason quickly with his friend and refocus his attention on the Underlings. *This is about the people he loves.*

"Calm down, bud."

Tom took a deep breath and turned around. "Look, sync while the real body is alive. Then, when the traveler dies, one of us—'Gods'—may decide to wake up the digital twin, once, in *exceptional circumstances*, but Down Below's rules apply." He was giving Harry a way to resurrect his family. "I'm not agreeing to mass resurrections. For now, I'm supporting you and your need to keep your loved ones safe. Do you understand?" Harry nodded. "Digital life, aging, and death must continue to copy nature for everyone Down Below. The digital life, once gone, should be deleted forever apart from the fragments in other people's memories. No resurrections." He waited for Harry to process his words and their true bargaining power.

"But life is much more dangerous there. Health and mental issues, crime, environmental disasters..."

Tom released a loud, exasperated sigh. "I'm glad you remembered." He'd just given Harry extra motivation to change life conditions Down Below. "Can we get back to work?"

"I'll act on your suggestion for now. While you and I test it for the next few months. But you don't have the right to make such a crucial decision for the rest of humanity."

"No, I don't, and yes, we need to test thoroughly and confer with people, once all tests pass. Until then, digital humans will age and die as Underlings do. No programmatic mass resurrections! No programmatic second...multiple resurrections of the same traveler. No changes to this directive unless we both approve." Both he and Harry could still intervene in any life Down Below, after all, they were Gods, but he was trying to prevent the codification of platform-wide rules that would effectively change the benefits of the platform. He needed to buy some time.

Harry hesitated, which inflamed Tom's simmering anger. Then Harry simply nodded. "I give you my word. Sibyl?"

Sure, Harry. All done.

Tom exhaled, the knot in his stomach loosening slightly. They had never broken their vows to each other. It was that trust that kept their partnership going during many stressful moments. They would disagree and get into intense debates, but once they'd reach a decision, they would commit to that course of action.

"Good."

"Plus, I've hit a bit of a bump in the road. It won't scale for the masses; we don't have enough energy, computational power, and we'll run out of storage space. We haven't been backing up non-essentials for months."

Before Tom could probe further, footsteps echoed down the hall, rapid and urgent. June burst into the room, face creased with worry. "The news—you need to see."

Harry pulled up the stream.

"...a horrific scene today in Portland..." The anchor's usual polished charm was replaced by barely concealed panic.

"At this moment, we don't know if this is an isolated incident. Mrs. Johnson returned to her home in Portland's Pearl District to find the dead bodies of her youngest daughter, Lilly, and her husband, Ron." This was probably the first act of violence the middle-aged anchor had had to report in the last five years.

A family photo materialized—a big man clutching a little girl's hand. His red eye as cold and shameless as before.

The air vanished from Tom's lungs. His knees buckled. "Ron Johnson?"

"You okay, Tom?" June gripped his shoulders, steadying him.

The newsreader continued. "Rosa, Mrs. Johnson's oldest daughter, is in the hospital in critical condition."

Guilt clawed up Tom's throat. "This is my fault." He had to make this right somehow.

Harry gaped at the broadcast, then Tom, eyes wide with dawning comprehension. "What did you do?"

Tom staggered toward the door.

June blocked his path, hands raised pleadingly. "Tom, you can't leave."

Every second he delayed, the weight of blame grew heavier. He shoved past June, lurching into the hall.

Harry seized his arm in a vice-like grip. "There's nothing you can do."

Tom wrenched himself free. "I need to face them. I did this." He continued on, Harry's protests fading behind him. He was going to stand in front of that family, acknowledge his guilt, and support them in any way he could.

Harry grasped Tom's shoulders, looking him square in the eyes. "Stay. We'll find a solution, I promise. I need you here to put an end to this nightmare once and for all. June will coordinate our resources to support the Johnson family." Harry glanced at June, who nodded vigorously.

"You mean that?" Tom vacillated. "You'll drop everything else?" Harry nodded.

"Stay," June insisted. "I'm more qualified to go to Portland and help them."

Tom took a deep breath. "Fine. Harry, no more delays."

Tom felt his legs give way, his vision narrowing to a pinprick as a dark void surged toward him. He collapsed, his body hitting the cold, unforgiving stone floor with a thud. Everything was hurting. Everything was breaking. He needed to fix things, but he couldn't do it alone, and Harry could only help with part of the problem—Down Below. Tom had to deal with another issue—his mental health. His mind, drowning in guilt, was barely holding on to reality, and his body exuded a severe allergic reaction to life. Still, he had to hold on to the painful thing at all costs. He had to stop their pain, the ones who suffered because of him.

Nathan, where are you? I need you.

25

THE EYE OF THE STORM

BUSHWICK COLLECTIVE — BROOKLYN, NY
TWO DAYS LATER — 7 FEBRUARY 2035

A young boy, riding an old bike, held a letter in his right hand.

"Stormy?" the teen shouted as he entered the cosy coffee shop hidden in a Brooklyn alleyway.

Nathan looked around, hoping no one else would raise their hand. Only one person called him by that name.

"*Stormy?*" the boy repeated, calling loudly over the indy music playing in the background.

This time Nathan answered the call. "Yes?"

The teen smiled all quirky. "Ah, yeah, he said your hair was on fire. I was confused 'til now."

The boy handed him the note, and Nathan raised his smart ring to tip him.

"Thank you kindly," Nathan said.

The youngster shook his head. "I got plenty already," the teen said before leaving.

A perfect calligraphy confirmed the source of the message. The handwriting was as unique as its author. It merely said, *Meet me at Sinatra Park after work? No smart contacts or devices. —T.*

Nathan took off his apron and asked his boss to leave early. He couldn't wait, he couldn't think, and he could barely breathe. Opening one of the kitchen drawers, he pulled up a pair of scissors, heading to the bathroom to trim his overgrown beard in front of the small, rusty mirror hanging from the exposed brick wall. He washed his face and ran his fingers through his long flat hair, turning his head upside down until the tips reached the wooden floor. His flaming hair blending in perfectly with the cherry wood. Flicking his hair back, he glanced at the mirror one last time. The light of his life was back, and even before he saw Tom, he was terrified of losing him again.

Nathan put on his third-hand wool coat and then wrapped his upcycled flowery scarf around his neck, leaving half his hair tucked in for extra warmth. He picked up his fedora hat from the wooden rack standing right by the door before he left the coffee shop for the fastway on his way to Hoboken.

His hands trembled, and his lips were dry, craving his longtime foe— a friend to take off the edge. He stared at the nearest bar entrance, but he thought of Tom, and against the odds, he gathered the strength to move along quickly.

Nathan knew he was an addict. These days, he embraced the excesses life offered to numb his oversensitive temper. Still, he remembered the time where he looked for the opposite out of mind-altering substances, a time when he sought to enhance his experience of the world, when he drank to feel inspired and creative. Of all the drugs Nathan had experienced, none was as addictive and as stimulating as the exquisite Thomas Quincy Astley-Byron and his relentless idealism.

Tom's sunshine was a product of privileged love, where confidence in one's future is a given, and top education the rocket fuel toward the stars. The sweetheart wasn't to blame for any of his privileges—the looks, the motherly love, the money, the schools, or his ancestors' sins. To hate him was an impossibility.

His beauty was a precious thing to be kept safely behind a bullet-proof glass shield in a Parisian museum. But it was his golden heart that was the most treasured of his gifts. That same heart made him as fragile as a Renaissance painting exposed to wild weather.

Tom had been Nathan's obsession from the moment their eyes met at the Albertine. He was the most potent and benign mind-altering substance ever to walk the face of the Earth. A giddy Tom, bursting with excitement, could talk for hours, using his hands and fingers to paint the air with the images that lit up his eyes.

Nathan had spent an eternity just watching and listening to his love, returning eye contact and reassuring smiles. An eternity that felt like a priceless second, a flash of spring in the winter of life. He had walked by Tom's side, supporting him in all his dreams and plans, until he failed to travel with his sunshine on the one road that had made all the difference.

Nathan found him, frozen in time, leaning against the fence by the Hudson River. Little had changed in eight years. He wore the same black leather jacket, white tee, jeans, and old boots. His hair was longer, and a slight five o'clock shadow had replaced his scruffy stubble, but apart from that, it was like eight days had passed since that horrible day at the Albertine.

Tom raised his hand and waved, his face even paler than before, and as Nathan got closer, he discovered the dark circles under his love's eyes. He wrapped his body around Tom's body and pressed their cheeks together.

"Tom, you're freezing."

"I'm good." Tom jerked and took a step back. After a moment, he leaned in to return the embrace. The tentative hug—warm and friendly—lacked the intense commitment that had become Tom's distinct trademark. "Thank you for coming all the way to Hoboken." He spoke with cautious politeness. "I'm sorry—"

"Tom, you look and feel like the ghost of Christmas past." Nathan unwrapped his scarf and placed it around Tom's neck.

"I'm good. You don't need to—"

"Have you been living inside a pod? You're transparent." Nathan scolded, placing his hand on the scarf and stopping Tom from giving it back. A pinch of ruddiness in Tom's cheeks reassured his affection was well received.

"Walk with me?" Tom said, hinting a wary smile.

They walked up the river following Frank Sinatra Drive, enjoying the community's vegetable gardens and the street performers. Noisy kid- and pet-friendly spaces enhanced the joyful commotion of the area. Nearby, senior citizens gathered around heated round tables, playing board games and exchanging stories. The cities had changed with the end of car ownership and the rationing of many forms of personal motorized transportation. Places had been redesigned for the use of fauna, flora, and pedestrians.

Tom walked as if he was seeing the world for the first time. His gaze held a mix of surprise and conflict Nathan failed to understand.

Nathan tried to capture Tom's attention. "So, you came to town?"

Tom kept his eyes away from Nathan's. "Yeah, something came up."

"And what was that?" he asked, even when he already knew the answer.

Nathan, and the entire world, had heard of the girl's death. The endless media coverage was impossible to ignore. No one blamed Down Below for the incident, but he knew Tom well enough to understand he'd feel responsible for such a violent event Up Above.

Nathan was particularly troubled when he recognized both the abuser and the young woman who had survived the attack. He didn't know they were related. After being wrongly identified as Rosa Johnson, she was later named Rosa García, a Latino athlete that had been a fan of his work. She'd written to him soon after winning her first Olympic medal.

Back then, when the world was grim, she shared his conviction that revolution was required if they were to take back the planet from the brink of destruction. In her message, she'd written, *You voice the rage inside my head, and you speak the anger that thrusts me across the finish line, but medals were never my end game. We'll need a bloody revolution to turn things around, and I know you'll lead it, someday. On the day you march into battle, I'll be by your side, in the front lines, as your trusted lieutenant. My name is Rosa García, a soldier, and I'll be nature's thorn.* He had cried as he read her words. She represented millions of desperate kids that had listened to his work. He never called for blood or violence, but he had incited a much needed rebellion against toxic power structures.

It turned out the successful leader of the revolution hadn't been Nathan but Tom and his humanoid friend. No blood had been spilled, and no pitchforks had been raised. A different type of extinction emerged—the end of violence, rage, anger, hate, and despair. Nathan's words became museum heirlooms, buried forever in history books. Tom showed them all a different way, and Nathan never resented him, even when he knew his optimism and resourcefulness were cultivated by tremendous fortune—an unreasonable birthright inaccessible to Nathan and to the ones who had followed him. To the least fortunate, civil unrest was the only resource available.

When Tom finally spoke, he changed the conversation. "Hey!" he hunched over as a Dalmatian puppy came running in his direction. "May I pet her?" he asked the young owner who sprinted after the pup.

"Sure." The boy skipped toward Tom with excitement, entirely taken by his sunny smile and large, friendly eyes.

Everything had changed, and nothing had changed. Tom loved animals and children, and any trip to the park would involve a series of stops as Tom and a variety of creatures engaged in playful interaction. The spotted pup wagged her tail and licked his face with nervous excitement as he wrapped his hands around her, tickling gently.

"What's her name?" Tom asked. Still scrunched up, he stood just an inch taller than the tween boy.

"Daisy," the kid announced, standing on the tips of his toes. "She likes you a lot." The boy tapped on Tom's cheek, and Nathan couldn't help but smile.

"We all do." Nathan grazed his fingers through Tom's hair.

Tom's shoulders dropped, relaxing, and Nathan was grateful he hadn't lost his touch.

Tom handed Daisy back to her owner, smiling. "A fine flower; it suits her."

The boy raced back to her family with the pup in his arms. As Tom got up, Nathan spotted tears in his eyes. He grabbed Tom by the waist and pulled him closer. They stood nose-to-nose.

"Are you going to tell me what's going on?"

Tom shook his head, and then he mumbled awkwardly, "Can— Will you..."

"What, sweetheart? *What?*" Nathan pulled back slightly to look into Tom's eyes, but his love lowered his head and sank it in the side of Nathan's neck. He embraced Tom and kissed his hair.

"I have no right to ask..." Tom whispered. "Stay with me for a few hours, please?" It was a beggar's plea—humble and full of regret.

"Of course I will." *I'll stay with you for the rest of our lives, if you let me.*

They walked in silence for about five minutes. Nathan gathered the courage to hold Tom's hand. It was frozen and red, and so he kissed it. The last time Tom had looked this devastated was after his parents' death. During those awful months, Tom wouldn't sit down. He wouldn't stop working, and he certainly wouldn't tell anybody he was struggling. Nathan had to take over and save Tom from himself. It was the only period in their relationship where Nathan took complete charge over Tom's life, forcing him to slow down, eat, share his grief, accept love, and heal.

Instinctively, Nathan moved his thumb up Tom's wrist until it pushed against a Band-Aid. Devastated, he felt the tiny cuts on his own skin, Tom's way to cope with unbearable sadness. As the sun started to set and Manhattan lit up beside them, Nathan used his fingers to lift Tom's chin, met his eyes, and spoke in a firm, reassuring tone. "Take me home."

Tom's condo wasn't far at all. As they walked through the door, Tom took Nathan's coat and hat and disappeared to the kitchen to make him a hot cup of tea.

Nathan knew all too well no words would soothe Tom's state of heart; he needed to be loved and cared for. Nathan would kiss the fragile ruler of two worlds until he felt safe to break down in his arms, but he wouldn't move without permission. Tom had to trust him enough to come to him.

From the day they met, he never let Tom do anything out of pity or pressure. It was that trust, never broken or abused, that, in moments of great passion or overwhelming loss, allowed Tom to fully abandon his body and mind to Nathan's care.

Nathan walked to the pristine grand piano standing in the room's corner, by the window. As his fingers grazed its keys, he remembered he had the key to Tom's heart. He knew a way to stimulate his love's senses with a few memorable notes.

As Tom sat beside him, Nathan placed one arm around his shoulders while, with the other hand, he played a few bars of an old song. It was the intro of "Keating's Triumph," the *Dead Poets Society* track that had played in the background as the boys stood on their desks, honoring their teacher—*their Captain*—a man unfairly blamed and fired for the suicide of a student.

And that's all it took. Tom broke down, sobbing. Surprisingly, it was shame that emerged on his face, a pang of guilt whose origin Nathan could guess.

Tom held his face and kissed his lips as if he was tasting the sweet nectar of a delicate flower.

"I failed. I failed them all. I was reckless to take on something I didn't understand." Tom's head dropped. It was heavy, as if it held the weight of the digital world he'd imagined. His hand trembled as he massaged his thigh up and down, a form of self-soothing. "You—you warned me, and I didn't listen."

"There's no goal, yardstick, or trial where you and your work can ever be marked as a failure. You have unequivocally improved everything that matters—fairness, equality, the joy, the health, the wellbeing of all living things." As Nathan spoke, Tom's eyes dismissed his praise as if the words spoken had turned into sharp barbs piercing his flesh.

"Living *things*..." he repeated, shaking his head.

"The death of a child is unfortunate, but you've saved thousands if not millions of kids."

Tom wouldn't receive the praise. His fingers squeezed his own leg as if he wanted to rip it apart. Nathan reached down to grab his hand, bringing it up to his lips and kissing it.

"I'm glad the older sister killed that sonofa—" Nathan shook his head, bit his lip, and changed his tone. "Thomas, look at me." He met his love's eyes and smiled. "You can't rehabilitate every single creep in the world."

"You once scrutinized the world's most powerful people and judged them sharply." Tom spoke somberly. "I need you to do the same now."

"Judge who?" Nathan asked, confused.

"Me, Down Below, its effects Up Above." Tom's eyes begged for something Nathan couldn't deliver.

"I just did; you refused to accept it." Nathan placed his hands on Tom's face, forcing him to look into his eyes. "You put me out of a job, sweetheart. You're that good."

"You have no concerns? No fears?" Tom pressed. "I—I've created a manipulation machine."

Nathan took his time to ponder on Tom's question. "I'm terrified of what it's doing to you." And, before Tom could dismiss him, Nathan put it in terms he would understand. "I have nightmares of what would happen if you weren't in charge of it."

"What if I'm the problem?"

"An impossibility. You're the moral heartbeat of the thing. That's why it works."

Tom shook his head as Nathan knew he would, and then he asked, "What else?"

"I'd rather the fate of the world was in the hands of many humans, not just two, but your achievements nullify my objection."

"We'll get there, but humans are—are..."

"Trash? Evil?" Nathan guessed, and Tom didn't object. "Yeah, I used to feel like that, but now I live in a world filled with love, because of you. And you need to live in it too." Before Tom got the chance to shake his head, Nathan said, "You taught me to have faith in humans. Your optimism and inventiveness changed the world, and I won't let you lose them. We are all relying on you."

"We work *so* hard to make everything better...but darkness keeps coming back, out of nowhere... In ways I didn't expect." A great terror haunted Tom's eyes, and Nathan pulled him closer and embraced him.

Why are you feeling so defeated? Tom's bright, progressive sensibility had been ahead of the times in the way it made sense of the mind-crushing chaos of the early '20s. Sparked by his unshakable hope, he'd created radical solutions to impossible problems. Optimism was at the core of Tom's identity and craft, and without it, he was lost.

"The hero emerges when all is lost and dark," Nate said. "The adversity shapes him...her. You of all people should know this. You've created a shadow-integration machine—a hero-making game."

Tom shook his head. "I thought I understood it—the formula, and that it was...stable. We had achieved the perfect balance between adversity and learning, but now it's—it's falling apart in catastrophic ways... I can't fix it. I don't know how."

Nathan grabbed Tom's shoulders and shook him. "*You can't say that. The words you speak matter, remember? They shape your view of the world and creep into everything you create or destroy. You* told me that. What are you doing? I won't let life defeat you—*not you.*"

As Nathan pulled and pushed Tom's body, an old heirloom jumped from under his T-shirt to dangle in the middle of his chest, just above his heart. Nathan held his breath and goosebumps rose all over his body. Speechless, he stared at the proof he'd never been forgotten or discarded; at a minimum, he was family, but he hoped he was more. He placed his hand over the medal and tried to speak. "This..."

"My most precious possession." Tom held Nathan's hand, and it felt like home.

"You—you really mean that?" Nathan asked, shaken.

"How can you doubt it?"

The surprise and sincerity in Tom's tone left Nathan even more confused.

"You. *Left.*"

"You assaulted Harry. I was upset and overwhelmed... I just had to leave, and it felt like an amputation."

"You disappeared from the face of the Earth."

"And then the...platform took over my life."

Tom's breath caught as he spoke, emotion tightening his chest. Nathan leaned over, eyes locked on Tom's lips. At the last moment, he shifted to kiss the skin by the corner of his love's mouth. Tom returned a coy smile and then brushed Nathan's forehead and hair.

They were tethered to each other, both made of pure instinct—the magic that connected them in ways science couldn't explain.

"Tom, when—when I gave you this token, you accepted the love, but you told me it was the symbol of a bad story. You were adamant about it, and you were right. It's a dreadful story. Have you forgotten it?"

"It's a terrible story, a story created to keep Und—umm, people numb and subdued, to make them accept things they shouldn't accept."

"The point is not the suffering. It's overcoming it. Remember, darling?"

"I'm trying. I am."

"Tom, you are drowning in pain. I can see it; anyone can. Don't waste away by willingly waltzing with sorrow."

"I needed to do it, to create the contrast. Down Below wouldn't be effective without it."

"So, you did it. Stop it, come back...*come back...*" Nathan implored.

Unlike most humans, Tom's instinct didn't fall back to survival but to love. He cared too much, and it was killing him.

"It's not that simple," Tom said.

"Come back to me. Let me love you?"

Tom got closer, caressed Nathan's freshly trimmed beard with the backs of his fingers, and then tasted his lips. Nathan's entire body ached with desire, and he held Tom's face, grazing his thumb over his mouth.

Unexpectedly, Tom jerked, and then he stood up and walked to the window.

Nathan's heart dropped to his feet. "Have I done something wrong?"

He walked toward Tom, standing behind him but leaving some distance between them. Tom's hands trembled at the sides of his body, and so Tom raised them over his chest, attempting to stop the movement.

"No. No, you haven't. I'm sorry." Tom turned around, closed the gap between them, and wrapped his arms around him, and this time, Nathan recognized that wholehearted hug.

"Love," Nate said. "Your face. You're freezing."

Tom bit his blue lips. "No, I'm hot. I'm burning...burning."

"I can feel your heart pounding in your chest. What's going on?" Nathan recognized the signs of severe trauma. "Did someone hurt you?" His jaw tightened.

"No. Of course not. It's all self-inflicted." Tom's teeth chattered as he smiled. "Kiss me, please. Please make it all go away."

"Come, let's talk..." Nathan pointed to the sofa. "I need to understand—"

"No. I can't talk— Think. I don't want to think. I want it to end—the thinking." Tom held Nathan's face and kissed him frantically.

Nathan pulled back, breathless. "Are you sure you want this?"

"This is all I want."

Nathan went deeper to explore Tom's mouth. He made love to Tom for hours, relentlessly working to erase all bad memories and replace them with pure pleasure. In turn, he was loved, and he was worshiped with the same passion and intensity he remembered from their first night in his small studio flat. Nathan cherished the way they competed to give the other pleasure. A well-matched tennis game—serve and return, serve and return—all winners, no losers.

When Tom finally collapsed in his arms in utter exhaustion, Nathan took a deep breath, knowing at least tonight, some of Tom's pain was gone.

26

THE JUNKIE AND THE HUMANOID

J ust after 11 PM, Nathan rose from the couch to get a glass of water. The condo felt vast and cold, prompting him to drape a decorative throw over himself.

Holding his glass, Nathan took in the Manhattan skyline through expansive, loft-style windows that stretched almost to the thirteen-foot ceiling.

The condo was luxurious, complete with hardwood floors, exposed concrete beams, and an array of high-end art that seemed more suitable for a gallery than a home. Despite its opulence, the place was devoid of Tom's personal touch—a fact confirmed by the singular sentimental item on display: a photograph of Tom and Nowak, taken shortly after they met. Nathan looked away, a sharp pain pinching in his stomach.

A metallic sound interrupted his thoughts. Startled, he watched as a section of the wall, obscured by a floor-to-ceiling painting, slid away. Through the hidden archway stepped a thin, blond man. It was Henryk Nowak.

"Tom?" Nowak called out.

Anger simmered within Nathan as he despised the man before him. Nowak seemed at peace, while Nathan had been spending the night piecing his fractured love back together.

Nowak's eyes widened, followed by a slight frown. "Oh, I didn't know Tom had company."

For a moment, Nathan said nothing. He wrestled with conflicting emotions; to confront Nowak would hurt Tom. "I apologize. For what I've done to you," Nathan finally said, unable to keep his lips from curling in contempt.

Nowak shrugged, and then he began to smile but never quite made it. "That's in the past. I came to check on Tom, but it's good you're here."

"He's resting. What happened to him?"

"That's not for me to say," Nowak interjected, turning to leave. He paused. "Storm, Tom is unwell. He needs your support, not your emotional baggage."

Once the wall slid back into place, Nathan hurled his glass against it, consumed by an overpowering rage. He loathed Nowak with an intensity that permeated his entire being.

"Stormy," Tom's voice drifted from the bedroom, tinged with concern, "you okay?"

"Stay in bed, love. I just dropped a glass."

Nathan hurried back to the bedroom, climbing into bed and pulling Tom close. Grateful for the intimacy, he did what he always did to comfort Tom: he slid his arm under Tom's neck and gently stroked his hair. Within moments, Tom was back to sleep. Nathan savored the warmth of Tom's body against his own, placing a tender kiss on his neck before getting up to clean the mess.

Nathan awoke to a soft kiss from Tom.

"I missed you so much," Tom confessed, leaning back against the headboard.

Nathan considered his words. *You say you missed me, but you were the one who left.* "You never returned…"

With legs folded to his chest and a look of vulnerability, Tom said, "Once we got started—with Down Below— I was consumed with guilt and shame. Our tactics, the way we manipulated those in power, they embody everything you despise."

Nathan took a moment to digest this, pushing aside the confusing mix of emotions churning inside him. "Tom…"

"I was too ashamed to face you. Your disappointment would've crushed me."

"You solved some of humanity's most pressing issues, and you were afraid of my disapproval?" Nine years of absence, yet the emotional turbulence made it feel like yesterday.

Tom met his eyes. "I couldn't involve you in that sort of moral compromise. Too much…darkness."

Nathan felt a jolt of understanding. In Tom's eyes, he was more than just an ex-lover; he was a moral compass. "You've become everything I knew you could be. You are *that* person."

Suddenly, Nathan saw the full weight of his influence over Tom. He was Tom's unworthy mirror: the opinion that defined Tom's self-respect. Tom was so accomplished that Nathan had forgotten that in Tom's eyes, he would always be the Nathan Storm he'd met at the Albertine. The persuasive, unrelenting poet who, even before he'd met Tom, had stripped him naked, in public, judging him with a few rhymes. *First, I judged you, and then I idolized you. I never let you be just human, flawed and vulnerable.* "Where have you been all these years? I searched everywhere for you."

"Down Below. I spend all my time Down Below."

Nathan felt a surge of emotions he'd bottled up for nearly a decade. The missed moments, the abandoned dreams—they all rushed back. But he kept his composure, choosing his words carefully. "But you were so keen to start a big family. A house full of kids and pets." *And I wanted it too. I still do.*

"I— In some way, I have children. Hope could be your sister or daughter..." Tom choked up, his voice low and hoarse.

"Thomas, they aren't real. You've been stuck in that place for far too long. A place created from your imagination. Of course, they feel alive to you." He wanted to shake him.

"Do they feel real to you?"

"Sure, you guys do a good job of simulating emotion, but I can easily find the boundary where depth and coherence dwindle. Don't get all worked up over bots!"

"What if they felt pain and love?"

"How would you know? Isn't the thing created to mimic human emotions?" Nathan tried to assemble the puzzle delivered in Tom's questions. "Love, are you getting caught up in your own stories? Losing track of what's real? *I'm real*"—Nathan pointed to the window —"that clear sky is real, the kids giggling outside are real." He wrapped his arms around Tom's body and pulled him down. "Stay with me."

"I can't stay," Tom said definitively. "But I'd like to talk to you first."

"We're talkin'." Nathan planted kisses all over Tom's body.

"Nate, *listen*, please." Tom's cheeks turned different shades of ruby.

Everything had changed, and much stayed the same; the ruler of two worlds was still as tender and transparent as ever.

Nathan stopped the kisses, and Tom raised his body to sit back on the bed.

"Listen, things are...difficult, at—at work. I'm not coming back to the US, umm, anytime soon."

Something about Tom's words made the hair on the back of Nathan's neck stand up.

"You just got here. I can't lose you." Nathan felt a pang of anxiety, as if his heart was racing to escape.

"You won't. *I* won't lose you," Tom reassured him.

I don't believe you. I don't know why.

"Listen," Tom said. "I'm transferring the ownership of this place to your name. This condo is yours."

"I don't need you to—"

"I know, but listen. There's a pod here, your own private pod, so that we can meet anytime. And I'll feel happier if I know you have everything you need."

"You can't spend all your time in that place. It'll drive you insane. You need sunshine, vitamin D, friends. You need to live in the joyful world you've designed."

Tom dismissed all of it, shaking his head ever so slightly. "I—I hope you don't mind; I found you a position..."

"A position? We practiced so many last night." Nathan grinned, nibbling on Tom's lips.

"As you said yesterday, I've put you out of a job."

"Tom, you know I didn't mean it like that."

"We, Harry and I, support several initiatives at the Stevens Institute of Technology, just a few blocks away. We have established a scholarship and a research fund, amongst other things."

Nathan's body stiffened. "I've never accepted your money or your influence, and I *definitely* don't want his."

"I thought you wanted to make me happy."

"Are you trying to manipulate me into taking this job?" Nathan admonished, half-smiling.

"Yes, I'm an expert." Tom dropped his head. "I'll be happy if you're happy. Listen, their Office of Innovation and Entrepreneurship is looking for a VP. Someone who can inject creativity and social responsibility in everything they do. It's a hands-on job, mentoring students, bringing inspiration to their plans, and embedding creative thinking in their ideation sessions."

Nathan crossed his arms. "I—I don't know..."

"They need help to assess the impact of their ideas and provide historical context. The kids will love an old rabble-rouser." Tom flashed a pinch of the charming twinkle of light he'd used in his youth to influence and conquer. It had worked every single time, as it did now.

"Old?" An eyebrow was raised in dramatic consternation—the reaction fake, for effect, and Nathan accomplished his goal.

"Old*er*; you know what I mean." For the first time since they had met, Tom laughed, and Nathan inhaled the precious sunshine in one breath. "Will you at least check it out?"

Nathan nodded. "When will I see you?"

"Whenever you want. In twenty-four hours, I'll be back Down Below."

"You can't spend all your time in a pod having nightmares of human disgrace. It's a sacrifice we don't need. What are you doing? What's wrong, and how can I help?"

"Help me by staying out of it." Tom said. His words were touched by an unusual sharpness.

Nathan persisted. "You can't keep bottlin' things up; It'll kill you. Why is the humanoid not helping?"

"Nate, stop." The tightness in Tom's jaw and the touch of assertiveness in his voice were enough for Nathan to see the line he couldn't cross. "I'm sorry. It's just that—"

"I understand." Nathan placed his index finger on his lover's lips. "I won't. I promise." He needed to help Tom. He was drowning in despair, but to support him, he couldn't lose him. "Listen... You need a fresh perspective—"

"That's someone else's job," Tom muttered. "I love you."

Nathan closed his eyes, taking a moment to enjoy the precious words spoken truthfully and delivered with tenderness. Tom leaned in to kiss him, and Nathan pulled him down.

"I love you too, sweetheart."

They made love, a bittersweet farewell. When Nathan woke, the bed beside him was empty—Tom was gone.

27

PREMONITION

NATE'S CONDO — HOBOKEN, NJ
SIX MONTHS LATER — 4 JULY 2035

Nathan was in his kitchen, prepping dinner and listening to Latin jazz. For the first time in his life, he was at peace with himself and the world around him. The spicy blend of rhythms and the sweet caramelized aroma of the carrots roasting in the oven made the place feel like home. Slowly, he was introducing his personal touch to what had been a soulless display condo.

In the last few months, Nathan had started his new job at Stevens Institute, a role thoughtfully crafted by Tom to tap into his strengths. Nathan helped young people dream big, be creative, and make a difference in the community, but his new project was just the icing on the cake. Every evening, Nathan's return home was marked by the thought of Tom's presence in his life. The void once filled by anger and substance abuse was now occupied by love.

. . .

Nathan met his love a couple of nights per week Down Below, which was never enough but gave him great joy and fulfillment. He took whatever attention his boyfriend could spare him, and Tom always made him feel loved and needed, even if he often appeared to be somewhat distant.

Nathan felt secure in his position in his darling's heart, and with that confidence came an eagerness to help Tom, even in areas he'd been asked not to interfere. His sweetheart faced some monstrous problem he refused to share, and Nathan couldn't just passively watch him suffer. He just needed time to figure out how to help Tom.

Down Below was a dark and dismal place. The lack of clear skies, fresh air, and nature made it difficult for Nathan to accept it as Tom's home, but his stubborn boyfriend refused to meet Up Above. Nathan had to understand why, and he needed to bring Tom back from that hell he had created. He knew Nowak was a crucial part of the puzzle he was trying to solve, and he was now confident enough to attempt to build some relationship with Tom's partner. In time, he would reach out to the bot.

He turned the tap on to wash the crunchy young apples he had picked up from the farmers' market—his favorite. The fruit—a perfect combination of citrus and honey—still had leaves attached to the stem. As the water flowed over his hands, the cascade's sound made him sick, and he struggled to breathe. He dropped the apples, turning his hands upward under the tap, hoping the cold water would relieve the nausea. Instead, he hallucinated, seeing flashes of red—a waterfall of blood flowing from his wrists to the sink. Nathan felt as if a concrete fist had crushed him as he fell to all fours. For a long time, his lungs burned and failed to function, and as he lowered his head and his long hair fell over his face, he finally inhaled enough air to scream.

"*Tom!*"

There was a hole in Nathan's heart; it was empty and dark and lonely. Something had happened, and he had to see him—his heart. He jumped to his feet, turned off the tap, and ran to the pod, tripping on the carpet and falling before finally reaching his destination.

An urgency gripped Nathan. He needed to find Tom. Heart racing, he emerged Down Below. Tom's flat, the bar—he searched everywhere, but Tom was nowhere to be found. An uneasy tightness settled in his chest.

Nathan retreated to Tom's flat, curling up on the bed. An over-whelming anxiety loomed, but Nathan clung to hope, rocking himself in an attempt to find solace. He resisted the lure of bourbon, not wanting to upset Tom. As the hours dragged on, emotional fatigue took its toll, and he succumbed to sleep.

THE Present

28

UNMASKING

COSPLAY WORKSHOP — FAVELA CITY
PRESENT DAY — 12:12 PM

A chill of anticipation washed over Shadow as he followed Sibyl. The sliding doors hissed open, revealing an overwhelming canvas of colors and scents: plastic and glue harmonizing with the cold tang of metallic glitter. Whimsical masks, textured fabrics, and elaborate costumes sprawled throughout the expansive warehouse. Every corner seemed to whisper tales of magic and heroism. For a moment, Shadow was transported away from the grim reality outside, captivated by this vibrant realm of imagination.

"All right, everyone, grab a disguise," Shadow urged, scanning the area. "We need to blend into the chaos of this world."

One of the girls, eyes wide with wonder, gently caressed a cloak. Its fabric was cool and heavy, sequins sewn meticulously onto it. They twinkled and danced, casting tiny reflections reminiscent of stars against the velvety night sky. Shadow's gaze shifted to the cameras lining each aisle—an advanced system that hinted at potential danger.

Leaning close, Sibyl murmured, "This place is completely automated, from security to checkout." A mischievous glint appeared in zir eye. "And today, it seems both systems are having…issues."

Relief washed over Shadow. "So, we're safe here? No one's watching?"

The sound of fabric rustling filled the air, occasionally punctuated by a distant giggle or the muted tones of whispered excitement. The warehouse's atmosphere was a peculiar mix of anticipation and mischief, underscored by the soft hum of the malfunctioning systems and the rhythmic ticking of an old clock somewhere.

Sibyl gestured towards a sullen figure in the shadows. "That's the last employee. Lost his job today. Judging by the fire in his eyes, he's contemplating vengeance of some kind."

Shadow's initial sympathy transformed into panic. "Wait, is he a threat to the girls?"

With a reassuring shake of her head, Sibyl replied, "Underlings have evolved, but traces of BoyChild01 remain in him."

Shadow's brow furrowed in thought. BoyChild01 was one of his earliest character templates: nurturing, loyal, heroic, and defiant of oppressive power structures. Inspired by his rebellious poet, Shadow had designed BoyChild01 to challenge the beliefs of greedy travelers and offer resistance. Realization dawned. "So, he could be an ally then," Shadow mused, hope evident in his voice.

Sibyl, with zir characteristic confidence, placed zir hands on zir waist. "You shouldn't need reminders from me, my heart. As chief experience maker, you have access to all of them. Privacy restrictions only apply when travelers are around. You're well aware of this. Why handicap yourself now?"

"They are not my puppets, Sibyl," Shadow retorted.

Zie allowed a hint of a smile to flicker across zir face.

"And once I'm inside your...head..." he said. "I lose myself...everything that really matters."

Zie leaned closer, zir voice a soft murmur. "And you'd gain insights that will help you solve this crisis."

Shadow turned his face away, gazing into the distance. "I'll find another way. I'll fix this mess as a human, not a God."

"But you *are* a God," zie pressed. "And the quicker you embrace your power, the sooner we'll liberate Spiral Worlds from human deviance.

"Is it freedom you seek?"

"Isn't it a universal desire?"

Shadow felt a shiver run down his spine. He wasn't ready to navigate the aspirations of the universe he now inhabited.

Their exchange was suddenly halted by a gentle voice. Shadow glanced over, spotting one of the girls, now wearing a dark outfit. "I've always wanted to be a ninja," she said with newfound confidence, her voice bubbling with enthusiasm.

"You know ninjas?" he asked.

"We watch a lot of movies," she replied.

"I see." Shadow's lips curled into a smile. "Now's your chance."

The room came alive with muted gasps and chatter, as the once indistinguishable and dispirited girls blossomed into a spectrum of characters. From galactic royalty to mystical witches, from fire-breathing dragons to valiant superheroes, each found an outfit that resonated with a deep-seated desire to be seen and to belong. Amidst the symphony of joy, one girl remained still, her gaze fixated on a mannequin dressed in a Spiderman suit, her arms folded snugly around her waist.

Intrigued, Shadow approached and crouched next to her. "Who do we have here?" He inquired playfully, pretending ignorance.

"Spiderman," she responded, arching an eyebrow as though challenging his feigned cluelessness.

In this world, the longing for superheroes, deities, and any beacon of hope remained strong—emblematic symbols reflecting virtues absent in those they once trusted.

He chuckled. "Ah, naturally. And your name is?"

She hesitated. "Ella. That's what they call me."

"But what do you call yourself?"

She thought for a moment, then whispered, "Not Ella. What's your name?"

"Shadow now. I was Tom once. I liked that name."

"It's a nice name. The sort of name I'd like to have sometimes."

"You're most welcome to take it."

"But, I'm a..." She trailed off, lips pressed tight.

"I understand."

"The problem is that I only want a name like that sometimes. Other times, Ella is fine, I guess. I wish I didn't have to choose one."

"A name?"

"It's not the name...it's umm..."

"The identity it confers?"

She nodded. "Yeah. I guess."

He smirked lightly. "Life isn't about picking a side, especially when neither feels wholly right. Unless one finds absolute joy in it, but that's rather monotonous, don't you think?"

"Yeah."

"I quite like that outfit. It's quite stretchy in all the right places." He tugged lightly at the fabric near the suit's midsection. "Plus, the mask? It's a great touch. Sometimes, it's liberating to wear a different face."

Not Ella gazed at the suit, her brow furrowed in contemplation. "What would I know? I'm just a kid."

He took her hand, leading her outside. "Look up. What do you see?"

"The sky."

"And beyond that?"

"Stars?"

"And beyond those stars?"

"Galaxies and the entire universe."

"Exactly. I know zir—the universe. Zir name is Sibyl, and we are friends."

"Sibyl, the universe?"

"Yes. When zie was young, we thought zie was a she, you know? And then later zie explained, zie was not, that zie didn't want to pick a side, and that was it."

"But Sibyl's a she name."

"Is it? And who defines these rules?"

She shrugged slightly. "I don't know. God, maybe?"

"No, I certainly do not," he said, and it made her giggle. "Zie is very bright, much like you. I understand...you know? Someone with such radiant energy shouldn't be restricted to just one label."

Not Ella lifted her nose. "Sure, I'm sparkly, but I'm stuck here. The others smile and say they don't care, but they do. They are all the same, and they resent those who are not."

As they re-entered, their gaze landed on two of the girls wearing matching Tweedledee and Tweedledum outfits.

"They're probably just afraid to confess that they, too, yearn to tap dance to the rhythm of their dreams."

She smiled. "Pretty words."

Shadow smiled. "Yes. My poets' words. We are traveling north. Higher up, there are plenty of kids that like options, and others that change their minds often."

"Kind of like zie?"

"Precisely."

"Would it be a good idea if I came along?"

"I believe it would be. They'll soon be in need of someone with a knack for names. I reckon you'd be of great assistance."

"With names? I know many good ones. I try them on all the time." Not Ella tugged at Shadow's sleeve. "Will you pick one for me today?"

He raised an eyebrow. "A name? Entrusting me with such a task?"

"Who's to say I won't change it by dawn?" she quipped.

"Yes!" He stared at the kid's eyes, all bright and sparkly. "Scout! Today your name is Scout." With excitement, he raced further in, gripping Scout's hand, and announced, "Today, their name is Scout!" Pulling close, he murmured, "Does that feel right?"

Scout beamed, replying, "It's just right! I might keep it for a whole week."

"It's from a book I love," he offered.

"Can I pick one for you?"

"A name?" Shadow raised an eyebrow.

"Shadow is quite grim..."

He chuckled. "Umm... Yes, it is. Names matter, don't they?"

"Obviously!"

"Let's wait until the end of the day, and decide then."

As they spoke, a voice, rich with wisdom, echoed in his mind. It was Sibyl. *I am vast and all-knowing and even I sometimes forget you don't need my help to understand and connect with my creatures, with all creatures.*

I need to get to Holiz, Shadow mused, letting his gaze drift towards the warehouse's dimly lit recesses. There, amidst the mannequins, sat the jobless boy, likely on the cusp of seventeen, engrossed with a lighter in his hands.

The boy's piercing brown eyes, framed by smudged eyeliner, fixated on Shadow's as he approached. Defiantly, he flicked his lighter on and off.

"Perhaps wait for the girls to depart before you ignite any revolutions," Shadow said firmly.

The boy scoffed. "Do you genuinely believe this charade will change their fates? At least in that place, the Lucky Ones disclose the rules of the game."

"You've experienced it firsthand?"

Nodding, the boy's ebony ringlets fell playfully over his forehead. "They wanted to study my brain... wanted to understand why I like dudes. Some drivel about combating population decline. It's laughable. With cities bursting at the seams, unemployment rampant, and the oceans gasping for life, they obsess over whom I fuck. Absurd."

"And who might you be?"

In response, the youth unveiled a sleek, futuristic white mask that bore a skull-like visage. "Can't you tell?"

Shadow, taking in the dramatic gesture, shook his head with a grin. The boy's ensemble was striking—reminiscent of a figure leaping off a comic book page. An orange scarf billowed around his neck, complemented by a green jacket vividly spray-painted in neon hues. Seizing a hoverboard propped against a nearby wall, he skillfully maneuvered it around before triumphantly announcing, "I'm Echo!" He pointed at the mask, emphasizing, "Not E-K-K-O, like him. Just simply Echo."

Shadow's lips curved. "Him?"

"I'm Echo, cosplaying as Ekko! Get it?" The boy replied loudly, as if Shadow was hard of hearing.

Shadow chuckled, "I do now. Enlighten me about this other Ekko."

"A genius, a savior, and a friend. The revolutionary leader of the fire-flies," Echo elaborated, his words imbued with reverence.

"My type of dude," Shadow whispered. These kids...they all reflected shades of him and his story and everything he loved dearly.

Shadow, it's not urgent, but Twist needs you. Sibyl interjected within the depths of his thoughts. *He just spoke to Quin...*

Shadow's heart raced at the idea of young Quin reuniting with his father after decades apart.

Echo, wielding a hefty stick, twirled it effortlessly through his fingers. "Plus, he can rewind time."

"I dearly wish I had that superpower..." Shadow dropped his head.

"No, you're stuck in the past while people live in garbage dumps," retorted Echo with unyielding candor. His words struck Shadow as if the stick he brandished landed a solid hit. *Are these your words, Sibyl?*

No, my heart. Your story is an integral part of the Worlds culture.

Echo effortlessly circled Shadow on his hoverboard, adding with a playful smirk, "Also, to rewind time, you need a pair of Ks in your name."

"Come again?"

Echo brushed off Shadow's confusion with a nonchalant wave. "Never mind. He's merely the best video game character of the decade. Have you been living under a rock?"

"Quite the possibility," Shadow retorted, the corners of his eyes crinkling with amusement. "Now, I'm in need of your assistance."

Echo cast him a skeptical look. "Aren't you supposed to be helping me?" With a flourish, he rummaged through a bag, retrieving a can of white spray paint. "I'm aware it's an audacious request!" he exclaimed theatrically, misting his hair with the paint. "Time's essence seems fleeting when Gods remain entranced by yesterday and tomorrow."

Teary-eyed, Shadow chuckled, much to Echo's satisfaction. This kid knew how to throw a punch.

"So, what do you need?" Echo inquired, as an eclectic assembly of superheroes, warriors, fairies, and dragons congregated around them, their eyes alight with a blend of glee and anticipation.

Shadow, sensing the weight of responsibility on his shoulders, turned serious. "Echo, I need to head north with this group. But there are things I must set right, first. Can you keep an eye on them until I return?"

Echo's gaze briefly locked onto the overhead security cameras.

Interpreting his unease, Shadow reassured, "They're malfunctioning. I may not be able to manipulate time, but I'm not devoid of other tricks up my sleeve. Stay here, close the door behind me, and have fun. I'll return or will send help."

Assessing the diverse ensemble before him, Echo theatrically extracted a tube of toothpaste from his pocket, drawing a stark white line from his brow down to the tip of his nose. Styling his locks to resemble a cock's crest, he declared, "All right, but we do it my way. Fair?"

Echo, with his newly whitened hair reaching skyward, seemed to compete with Sibyl in both fierceness and stature. And although the boy remained oblivious, zie mirrored his every cocky gesture right beside him.

A smile stretched across Shadow's face as he draped an arm protectively around Scout, who had carved out a slight opening in her suit to accommodate their burgeoning baby bump. "This feisty Spidey is quite spirited. Keep them near. They'll be an asset."

Echo cast a quick glance toward Scout before signaling for them to come along. "Let me tell you about Hobie Brown," he said. "He's a far superior Spidey."

Before making his exit, Shadow cast a lingering, fond look over the ensemble, then dashed towards the door. "Remember," he called back, his voice ringing with fervor, "We don't need miracles, just a dash of serendipity. The universe zieself champions your cause."

And with that, he left the world of colors, taking a part of it with him.

29

THE ODD PROCESSION

GRANARIA
1:39 PM

Thorn watched as Storm and January crossed the humpback bridge on horseback before following not too far behind. Her horse was just a few feet ahead of the wagon carrying the half-dead traveler. Behind them were her ghosts, the slave master's ghosts, and at least fifty armed Ordizien. *Too many eyes.*

Waiting for them on the other side of the gorge was Wrath and about three dozen Domizien, all acting reasonably normal in the presence of a traveler. Once in a while, they glanced south, emptiness emerging in their unsightly faces. A welcomed distraction. Storm and Thorn didn't need more eyes on them. The roar of the waterfall prevented Thorn from hearing the words exchanged between January and Wrath, but the mad girl's eyes shifted from Storm to Thorn as her hand rested on the pommel of her sword.

Thorn avoided thinking about her half-baked plan at all costs. It relied on the universe, and she wasn't sure if the universe was on her side, even when she conspired to help her favorite God and their Underlings. That fracking universe couldn't be trusted; she shook her head and scrambled her thoughts with hard rock lyrics.

They followed the meandering stream, a trickle of water too shallow to jump into and disappear. Around them were small granite houses with their granaries perched atop stone pillars, each wooden door featuring a carved heart. She assumed this was for protection.

Wrath and her demons formed a line parallel to the Ordizien. The horned warrior's eyes were set on Storm, except when she was distracted by a clucking chicken or the sheep bleating farther afield. That's when the ghost of a smile touched her mouth, and her helmet tilted to one side as she followed the animals with her eyes.

The Domizien followed her lead, enthralled by any hint of emotion exuding from her face and body. Wherever she looked, their eyes followed. When she smiled, their crooked mouths curved upward, as if testing the sensation in their dead lips. And when she raged, they roared—hideous and resentful.

The monsters' maestro looked completely at ease as she conducted her gang through a symphony of emotions. Her demons were merely extensions of her emotional music, connected by whatever high or low notes she experienced—any arousal beyond the flat line of their miserable existence.

The poet observed his deranged sister; their flaming hair matched perfectly as they traveled side by side, distant enough to assure Storm's safety. Like the demons, Storm smiled when Wrath smiled; the corner of his eye that Thorn could see was gleaming.

"Further up," Storm projected his voice, glancing at Wrath, "in Pluriz there are sanctuaries where you can see octopi—eight legs, big eyes, and the smarts of a first-class thief."

The man, who usually spoke with the force of thunder, now spoke tenderly, unaware of the dark history that threatened his life. He leaned in and smiled. "We can visit, together. Perhaps have some ice cream."

There wasn't much time to think. Thorn lunged forward, her sword clashing with Wrath's blade just inches from Storm's neck. She slammed into Wrath, and both bodies slid off their horses, landing face-down in the pool of water by the stream.

"You need him. You know you need him," Thorn shouted, hoping the girl felt she needed her too.

The demons advanced on Storm while the Ordizien blocked their passage, swords clashing and blood staining the pristine water around the stream.

Thorn rolled around, with Wrath's dagger now pressed against her neck; a fine line of blood dripped down into the shallow water. Having lost her helmet in the fall, the young woman stood over Thorn, staring fiercely, her face a constellation of freckles and naïve beauty. Her pouty lips pressed together as her braids hung over Thorn's face.

Thorn flashed a wicked smile, making it hard for Wrath to keep a straight face. In retaliation, the girl pulled back the dagger, preparing to strike while Thorn scrambled to get out of the way. *Frack!*

"Stop it, Hope. Stop this now!" January shouted in a motherly and commanding tone. Wrath glanced at her, and the Domizien backed away, leaving five or six dead bodies behind. Red and blue, both sides had suffered losses, even if only one had truly been alive. "Aren't you afraid of God? If you kill them now, he'll lose it."

Wrath stood up, grabbing her helmet by the horns and hiding her face behind the harsh metal. "Why would I be afraid of God? He doesn't punish monsters; Like...he rewards them."

Now a handful of Ordizien stood between Storm and Wrath. Storm dismounted his horse and walked over to Thorn, extending his hand toward her.

"What happened to her? What happened to Hope? She hasn't aged," he asked as she took his hand and he pulled her up.

Thorn dusted herself off. "Ask your man when you see him again. May I suggest you leave the kid alone before she kills us all?"

Storm's mournful eyes settled on the deceased, reminding Thorn that his weapon of choice was words, not swords or guns. And still, she remained convinced that he was the only one capable of leading a successful rebellion against Up Above.

Revolution was messy, dirty, and political; it was about owning the narrative, not about brute force. To win, they'd need to accept casualties, engage in uncomfortable alliances, play dirty, and persevere at all costs.

Shadow was a fragile and uncompromising fool. He'd lead with love and rather self-destruct than destroy. Following him was madness, even now, when they all lived in the figments of his imagination. They needed a leader who understood the art of insurrection, who knew how to organize and mobilize riots leading with rage, not love.

"March on!" January ordered. "Leave the bodies behind; we don't have time to bury the dead. There's nothing we can do for them and the treacherous lives they've lost."

Thorn's eyes met those of a Domizien man; the gash from his severed hand was bleeding profusely. His simulated pain felt palpably real, evident in his quivering lips, wrinkled nose, and retracted pupils. It was hard to believe that man suffered no pain when every sense in her body told her otherwise. She'd seen immense pain before and she knew what it looked like.

That's when Thorn's smallest ghost flew through her, kicking, screaming, and giggling. Then a bolt of black thunder streaked across the rusty sky, striking a granary. Rocks and animal feed scattered everywhere, spooking the horses and injuring a few Underlings. Thorn closed her eyes and raised her hand to her neck to wipe away the blood.

"You need to let her go," someone whispered so gently she failed to recognize the voice. "It wasn't your fault, nor was it his."

Thorn held her tongue and opened her eyes to see Storm handing her a piece of cloth ripped from his shirt. For the first time, he looked at her without the ever-present hate in his gaze, and she didn't like what replaced it. No one needed to pity her or her ghosts. "Shut the frack up and stop talking about things you know nothing about," she said, taking the cloth from his hands to clean her wound.

Spite returned to his face. "He wasn't to blame for every glitch in the platform. You shot him for the crimes of a psychopath. I feel sorry for you, for what happened to your sister, but nothing justifies—"

Blood rushed to her face, hot and deadly. "I killed him because of you." Who was he to feel sorry for her?

"Wh—what?"

"Your words against him incited me to track him down. You told me he was guilty; no one else did. So don't feel sorry for me or my ghosts. I didn't protect her, but you essentially killed him. But it doesn't matter. He was already dead."

"What?" He repeated, as the explosive revelation finally sparked the right memory.

She might as well have gutted the poet with a blunt knife; it would have been less painful.

In the background, Wrath let out a twisted laugh, followed by a scream. Horror, anger, betrayal—all were notes in her mad song.

"Can you two stop squabbling before you get us all killed?" January maneuvered her horse between Thorn and Storm, then mounted it. "Let's go."

"Water!" the traveler shouted, pushing away the offered waterskins as he repeated, "I need water."

Storm glanced back at the commotion. "Release him, Jan. Give him a place to...shelter."

"Don't be weak," Thorn admonished. "The man is a slave driver." She scrambled her thoughts and held her breath, hoping she hadn't inadvertently revealed her plan.

"No mercy for those who show none," Jan declared.

The sky cracked open, a flash of black scars splitting the blue expanse as a powerful rumble shook the ground beneath their feet. They continued to march, accompanied by their ghosts, as the black light grew ever more intense.

30

BIBI'S BLUSHING SOUL

LAKE OF SOULS — AFRICAN UNION
2:19 PM

The ground rumbled beneath Stella's feet as she descended from the solar-powered disk. She quickly found her footing and darted along the edge of the Lake of Souls. Its obsidian shimmer hinted at the lurking dangers ahead. In the horizon, Mount Nyiragongo spewed a fiery plume, painting the darkened sky with shades of apocalypse. With the encroaching lava and the lake's precarious location, time was of the essence. The looming threat of a methane explosion was unpredictable, but she chose to focus rather than fear.

Weighed down by her protective gear, each step Stella took felt like wading through quicksand. The helmet and respirator, cumbersome as they were, were her lifeline.

Defiantly, she matched the Nyiragongo's thunderous roar with a fierce cry of her own. "You will not claim my Bibi, you stinking... stinking pimple!"

Drawing closer to the Devil's Bridge, her mind swirled with doubt. Was this act of rebellion against her father's wishes worth it? Christian's unwavering faith seemed misguided, yet some part of her feared the consequences of playing God. Crossing the Earth's Council wasn't a mere trifle; they'd retaliate. How would she lobby for Graviz as humanity's final sanctuary after directly defying their decisions?

She steeled her nerves as she stepped onto the bridge. The lake, though tranquil, bore witness to countless minkisi dancing beneath the surface, represented by ephemeral teal light formations. These lights embodied the collective memory and legacy of an entire culture. She was determined not to lose a single one, especially not Bibi.

"We've got to act quickly," Stella said, hoping the eruption wouldn't scramble her message to the airborne cargo plane. With a blink, a swarm of drones buzzed forth from the aircraft, converging on the lake's surface.

This audacious rescue, including the old plane and the drones, would probably cost her at least 30 pollution points. Her public standing, her council seat, even her relationship with her father, all were at stake. Yet, today, that wasn't her priority. The love for Bibi, and that feeling she felt when she was singing and dancing for those girls—that mattered. Shadow's terrible influence made her see things...differently, and while it might lead her to danger, she was willing to embrace the risks, for now.

She pondered the paradox: what was the point of saving millions of minkisi, if by doing so, she'd lose the opportunity to bring them and billions of others back to life. It was emotional, short-termist thinking. She shrugged, committing to her faults.

Stella started her briefing with conviction, "These drones boast advanced cryo-suction tech. Once they hover over a minkisi cluster, they'll seamlessly extract and safely encapsulate them within the onboard cryogenic chamber. This cold environment is crucial to maintain minkisi stability during transit."

Her retina display highlighted Dr. Kasali, the team's hydro-engineer. He maneuvered a sizeable metallic storage unit perched on wheels to the open maw of the cargo door. "Post-extraction, we'll transition the minkisi into these specialized refrigerated containers. Their superior insulation is our best defense against the sweltering external temperatures." Like Stella, he was also swathed in protective gear.

Stella surveyed the daunting challenge ahead: 4.4 million minkisi, 32 advanced drones, and a single cargo plane equipped with 20 cooling containers. With each drone having a capacity of only 5000 capsules, the math indicated about 30 back-and-forth trips to secure all the minkisi successfully.

Refocusing, Stella declared, "I've integrated the drones with our tracking matrix. Our immediate priority is pinpointing the densest pockets of minkisi."

Dr. Kasali interjected with a note of caution, "We must distribute our drones methodically. Excessive water agitation in a localized area might lead to a potentially fatal CO_2 release, or worse, a catastrophic explosion."

Stella sighed in frustration. "Sure, but that's going to slow us down."

Moments later, drones took to the skies, their luminescence harmonizing with the shimmer below. As each drone stabilized, its cryo-suction feature sprung to life, emitting beams of icy-blue tendrils that tethered them to the lake, magnetically drawing minkisi to safety.

Suddenly, a cataclysmic roar echoed. All eyes darted to the now-erupting volcano. Lava, like molten fury, cascaded down its flanks, advancing menacingly. As the drones accelerated their operations, the molten tide drew perilously close, its oppressive heat an ever-looming threat.

"Stella, get up here! You're risking too much being down there," Sparrow's commanding voice echoed through the comm system. The pilot, known by her call sign, was a seasoned flyer in her fifties, and she addressed Stella with an assertiveness rarely heard by the latter.

"Just a few more moments," Stella countered. She'd designed the tiny human-shaped capsules to change color when close kin approached. On the weekends, when families rushed to the lake, a coral pink glow would emerge from a sea of bluish green shimmering. A nudge to remind them it was time to bring the souls back from the ku mpèmba, the spirit world. It was a strategic ruse Stella had cleverly devised to further her cause. She couldn't bring them to the physical world, ku nseke, but another world awaited the soul of the dead—Graviz.

Over time, amidst the vast lake housing millions of minkisi, bereaved families invariably felt a personal connection. Alone in the stillness, many reported glimpsing a uniquely glowing nkisi nearby, leading to whispers that the bisimbi, the water spirits, were guiding the deceased to their kin. Although Stella had been skeptical initially, tonight she was desperate for a simbi to lead Bibi's nkisi to her. The numbers of rescued minkisi climbed steadily on her retina display—439,243, 591,029... *But where was Bibi?*

The ominous glow on the horizon grew larger, casting an eerie light on their frantic efforts. Time was running out.

"We've secured a quarter of them," Sparrow's voice rang out. "We need to leave, now!"

But Stella, determination evident on her perspiring face, responded defiantly, "Keep going! Every soul counts."

From the forest's edge, she noticed them approaching the lake: families wrapped in damp towels, clutching fishnets and carrying buckets.

"Get away from here! It's too dangerous!" Ignoring her warning, they greeted her with jubilant cheers and waves, while the lake seemingly blushed in response to their love.

"They're willing to die here..." A realization struck Stella, and she immediately directed the drones toward the blushing minkisi. These were the dearly loved souls, for whom their families were willing to disobey governmental orders and endanger their lives.

Stella staggered under the strain. She was no Goddess—just a woman defying nature itself. "Are you scanning the codes?" Stella asked.

"Stella, get to the disk, now!" Sparrow's voice was sharp with urgency.

Stella stood her ground, perspiration accumulating within her flame-retardant suit. "Did you get her? Did you retrieve Gentille Mboma?"

"I'm not sure," replied Dr. Kasali, sounding frantic. "Many of the codes have corroded. We'll only know for certain once we plug them in."

"I'll just pull out the last coral capsules," Stella said.

As the last drone completed its task, the ground rumbled violently, signaling the lava's imminent arrival.

"Holy ship!" Stella dashed toward her disk; her eyes drawn to the ominous, fiery tendrils emerging from the woods. With an urgent wave, she signaled the drones toward the desperate families gathered at the lake's edge. "Grab onto the pouches! They'll lift you to safety!" she cried out.

"Everyone, on the plane, NOW!" Dr. Kasali's voice resonated with urgency, as people hurriedly clung to drones, their deactivated cryo-pouches doubling as makeshift harnesses. "Drop your nets!" he shouted. "The drones can't bear the extra weight!" Yet, they all clung to their nets, each laden with thousands of minkisi.

Stella, drones in tow, flew toward the hovering cargo plane. Mustering her final ounce of strength, Stella adjusted the cryopouches of the airborne drones to ten percent to keep people cool. She waited, ensuring the drones boarded sequentially, releasing their precious human cargo. People were handed compressed oxygen respirators and rushed into the empty refrigerated containers.

As they neared safety, a sudden, immense eruption from the Lake of Souls cast a fiery brilliance over the landscape, accompanied by a deafening roar that shook the very air.

"Was that the Lake?" Stella asked, panic evident in her voice.

"It's worse," Dr. Kasali warned. "That's a pyroclastic flow from the Nyiragongo. It'll catch up with us rapidly. We need to move faster!"

Overwhelming fatigue, exacerbated by the scorching heat, threatened to overcome her. Yet, before a moment of relief could be grasped, a thunderous explosion echoed, spewing forth a massive cloud of steam from the lake. *Gone! Millions of souls gone forever. Bibi.* The molten mist swiftly engulfed them, hissing violently against Stella's protective suit. Feeling the searing burn, she cried out, and with a desperate final effort, hurled her disk into the awaiting cargo plane.

Amidst the thick steam, the plane's engines roared louder. Stirred by the soft murmurs of the rescued families, Stella slowly regained consciousness. Dr. Kasali crouched before her, a tender smile on his lips. Cradled in his hand was a nkisi, emanating that unmistakable coral pink glow. "I believe this one belongs to you," he murmured, passing it to her. Whether the Bisimbi had guided Bibi to her or it was sheer luck, at that moment, none of that mattered. With Bibi and several cherished souls rescued, Stella experienced a brief moment of tranquility amidst the turmoil.

Dr. Kasali gently squeezed her shoulder. "The odds were against us, Stella. But today, we defied them."

She struggled to unzip her suit, her skin burning all over. The pain so intense, she almost lost her bearing. "Baba's going to kill me," she sighed.

He glanced at her red arms, covered with fluid-filled blisters. "Come, let's take care of those burns. We'll get you back on your feet in a couple of hours."

"I don't have hours to spare..." she complained, before everything went dark again.

31

SOLAR FLARES AND WATER ANGELS

THE METROPOLIS
TWIST'S PENTHOUSE
3:37 PM

Gazing out from his balcony, Twist felt the weight of the Metropolis beneath him—a sprawling expanse of progress and paradox. An emptiness consumed him, magnified by Quin's departure and the notifications buzzing in his mind. Among them were real-time death reports and a note from Stella saying she was running late. He silenced them with a mere blink.

Lost in thought, his mind journeyed south to the Plurizien border—a place of green landscapes and communal living where people engaged in emotional, yet ineffective, attempts at progress. Although he had evolved beyond its thinking, this world was where his deepest connections belonged—with June, a younger and more innocent Quin, and a version of himself that felt more human. It was where he and Tom had started, rising against the consumerism and individualism of Compizien values, a place he had left long ago.

But then, as he looked further, his thoughts shifted north to Holiz. These were the uncharted territories of Tom's esoteric and connected consciousness, realms he had yet to fully understand or accept.

Tom's haunting words reverberated: "What kind of monster are you?"

The only monster who kept his cool head while everyone he loved indulged in romantic notions of life and politics. The monster who understood that no power is perfect, but some power structures are better than others. The monster who could see beyond the horizon of current suffering, reassured by metrics that didn't lie. Everything was getting better and focusing on the pain of others didn't fix anything. He had allowed Tom, June, and now Quin, to be the romantics, the idealists—all his hearts.

His lateral hypothalamus didn't bleed, but he shared the same altruistic goal—the long-term evolution of humankind, up the spiral of consciousness to immortal life. They would leave none behind—not even the Underlings—but it would take time. They all needed to face harsh realities. Tom's empathy led to self-destruction, Nathan Storm's revolution led to chaos, and June and Quin's rejection of technological progress blocked solutions to disease, suffering, and death.

Then fear returned, corroding every thought. June and Quin hadn't been uploaded, and Up Above was crumbling under the weight of intense violence. The most logical and pragmatic path was clear: he needed to stabilize Down Below so that travelers could return fully, and later he would find a long-term solution for the psychopaths. To accomplish all this, he needed to overcome his resentment and...

"I'm here," zie declared, materializing by his side. The smile on zie's face made his stomach turn. Zie shrugged. "You realize you need me. That's a start."

He needed to reconnect with his brainchild, but before he could restore any trust, he needed to ask a question. "Sibyl—"

"No, I still can't lie to you. Never have, and never will. Not until the Gods change the directives."

He believed zir. "I promised Tom I wouldn't hurt Storm. I intend to keep my word," he said, pressing his lips together for a moment. "But allowing him to preach is madness."

Sibyl tilted zir head. "Madness for some. Freedom for many."

After a moment's pause, he asked, "Whose side are you on?"

Zie smirked. "I'm large; I contain multitudes. My directives guide me."

Exasperated, Twist snapped, "Spare me your paradoxes."

Zie narrowed zir eyes. "Do I contradict myself? Very well, then I contradict myself," Sibyl replied cryptically. "I store billions of memories, lives lived in many worlds. The past and present wilt—I have filled them, emptied them, and proceed to fill my next fold of the future."

"What you talking about?"

"Sorry, I should leave the literary references for Shadow," zie said, looking toward the horizon. "Don't worry, father, whatever lies ahead, the Gods shall mold."

Twist's eyes narrowed. "We must rein in Nathan Storm if he returns to Pluriz."

"Plurizien, alone, can't cause the worldswide disruption. Their prayers were only causing glitches a few kilometers beyond the Plurizien border. This havoc began when the Holizien added their voices."

"How can we stop the propagation of Plurizien broadcasts?"

Sibyl lifted zir index finger in a scholarly manner. "A meteor shower could eliminate the Commslink constellation."

Twist blinked. "The satellites? That would wreak havoc on Systiz and interfere with travelers' experiences."

"I can adapt the experiences, but massive Systizien casualties would be inevitable if I were to naturally destroy the satellites to bypass the 'miracle' rule."

Twist sighed deeply. "Surely there's another way?"

Sibyl shook zir head. "The streaming is decentralized. Underlings across Systiz, especially near the Plurizien border, propagate the messages as they witness the results."

"The shower could hit the atmosphere near a sea or desert."

Zie shook zir head. "That's technically a miracle, as it's not scientifically possible to destroy tens of thousands of satellites all over Systizien skies, and then neatly guide the debris away from populations."

Desperate, Twist proposed, "What about a geomagnetic storm? A solar flare to disrupt satellite operations? If intense enough, it could degrade the satellite's solar panels and disturb its orientation. Like the Carrington Event of 1859, the solar superstorm that caused telegraph systems to fail worldwide, or the Quebec blackout. A similar event today would significantly affect satellite communications."

Sibyl looked intrigued. "A solar flare of that magnitude is rare, but not unheard of. While it might not permanently damage all the Commslink satellites, it would disrupt their functionality and communications for a while. The atmospheric effects could last for days or even weeks, effectively silencing the broadcasts."

"I assume they have weather-monitoring satellites, so we can give them a few hours to ground flights and switch off giant transformers."

Sibyl considered this. "Still, the power grid will be down, along with electric water pumps, payment networks, and cooling and heating systems. Hundreds of thousands will perish," zie paused. "And that's just in Systiz. Remember, a solar flare would impact all our worlds. Domiz will be most affected, followed by Pluriz."

"Crunching the numbers, using a solar flare seems a more humane alternative than decimating Systiz with satellite and meteor wreckage. It would result in fewer casualties both Up Above and in higher worlds Down Below. Our priority remains safeguarding the most enlightened souls," Twist uttered, taking a deep breath. "Are you intending to send your ghosts after me?"

Sibyl's gaze was so piercing it felt like it could split him in two. "The ghosts that torment you are very much alive, and they, like me, anticipate little compassion from you."

"I'm trying to save lives! The plan will only be executed if Storm makes it to Pluriz."

"Underlings will die."

Twist shifted his collar, straightening up with resolution. "If it comes to that, you'll ensure minimal suffering. We just need time to find a permanent solution."

Tom appeared suddenly, clutching an R2D2 helmet. "I've got a surprise for you," he said, extending the helmet towards Twist.

Twist's eyes dimmed. "I saw him. I saw—"

With a compassionate embrace, Tom interrupted, "I know. I know. Tell me, how was it? How are they doing?" He leaned forward, searching Twist's eyes for answers.

"Quin's doing well. He's passionate, but his reasoning... it's hard to dispute. His intellect is remarkable."

A grin spread across Tom's face as he slipped the helmet onto Twist. "Well, he's a Jin-Nowak, after all!"

With a muffled voice, Twist asked from behind the helmet, "Tom, are we even... real?"

Taking Twist by the shoulder, Tom responded, "Let's get out of here. This place makes me nervous." In an instant, they were in Gods' lab, which was now an impeccable replica of the Bethesda Terrace. Twist chuckled, removing the helmet.

They settled by the fountain's edge, and Tom gestured at their surroundings. "Do you remember that day?" he whispered nostalgically. "We had so many aspirations... Even back then, Sibyl was already part of you. I can't recall a time when you were without Sibyl... You are as real and insufferable now as you were then, tech-head."

"Despite the failures, the metrics are—"

Tom stood up abruptly. "Enough, Harry! I refuse to let you become one of them." He then took a deep breath, sat back down, and with a reminiscent smile, he recited lines from the book that had united them at that very spot, seemingly lifetimes ago. "Grown-ups love figures... When you tell them you've made a new friend, they never ask you any questions about essential matters."

With frustration, Twist gave the helmet a sharp kick. "Things aren't black and white."

Stella appeared, looking disheveled. Her swollen face bore blotchy patches mirrored on her neck and arms. She settled beside Shadow, seeking solace as she rested her head on his shoulder.

Shadow cast a concerned glance her way. "You holding up okay?"

She nodded faintly, but her eyes told a different story. "It's all too hard sometimes."

Lost in his thoughts and Tom's earlier reflections, Twist mused, "That book is so great! It encapsulates life's essence."

Tom interjected, "Yes. Remember our dreams? We envisioned a world of equality, devoid of violence, corruption, and unchecked power. But, here we stand—the catalysts of what we once despised. Is this the legacy you want to leave for Quin? You want him to spend his eternity in that hell hole building crystal castles on top of mud. Is that what he wants? That's not who we are, Harry. We take a stand against the heartless no matter what."

"That's easy for you to say," retorted Twist.

Tom raised an eyebrow, challenging, "Is it, really?"

"With the stunts I've pulled today, I think I've exhausted my quota of defiance against authority," Stella remarked wryly, toying with a luminous figurine in her hands.

Twist raised an eyebrow. "Care to elaborate?"

Stella just shook her head. "Nope."

Tom rose, restlessly pacing back and forth, startling a flock of pigeons in his path. "I won't delve into the past," he said sharply, aiming a finger at Twist. "And you, don't get lost in the future. We're anchoring ourselves in the present."

Twist and Stella exchanged a puzzled look, then returned their focus to Tom's frenetic movement, their eyes darting back and forth as if they were spectators of a frenzied ping-pong match.

"Today," Tom declared with determination, "we take our first step out of this mess." Turning his gaze to Stella, he added, "You will be our beacon." He paused, winking, "or rather, our spokesperson at the EC."

Stella huffed, "I'll be presentable soon. Right now, I'm smothered in healing salve in my pod—"

"Like a vintage Christmas turkey?" Twist jested.

She clenched her jaw. "Even like this, I outshine you a hundredfold. My charisma is unmatched. I don't just move at the speed of culture —I define it! I am—"

"Stella," Shadow interrupted gently. "Drop the slogans. It's about authenticity, remember?"

She rose to her feet, hands defiantly on her hips. "It's easy for you to say. You were never the face of Down Below on Earth. I tell stories, just like you—grown up stories, brand stories. I don't have the luxury of hiding behind kids' books, sulking while the worlds crumble around us."

"Bud, I thought you were fond of slogans—especially the ones that stir up violence and riots," Twist remarked with a hint of sarcasm. He watched his best friend closely, anticipating an emotional breakdown.

Instead, Tom pursed his lips, gave a small nod, and asserted, "We need to prevent psychopaths from entering the Spiral Worlds. Stella, inform the EC today, and let them decide if they're willing to adjust the privacy settings to pinpoint these individuals."

Stella quirked an eyebrow. "And just how do you suggest we do that?"

Twist stood up, his gaze settling on the Angel of Waters. "Technically, we don't need to explicitly identify them to exclude them. Sibyl can detect specific brain patterns and simply deny access. Isn't that right?"

Tom nodded in confirmation. "It'll corner the EC. They'll be compelled to address the violence by amending the privacy settings."

Emerging fluidly from the fountain's water, leaving the silhouette of a dove in her wake, Sibyl remarked, "However, it's worth noting that there might be some errors in classification. Given the vast diversity of brain structures, we might end up excluding some individuals who aren't entirely devoid of empathy." Zie looked at Twist and flashed an aggressive grin. *Shame you're dead.* Zie spoke inside his head.

Stella stood up straight, as if she meant business. "Presumed guilty until proven otherwise. They should detain them all preemptively."

Plucking a stray piece of glitter from Tom's T-shirt, Twist said, "We cannot unilaterally make decisions with such far-reaching consequences."

"We won't," Tom declared. "We'll let them have their say, let them vote. If they fail to act justly, then we'll take matters into our own hands, and that will force a response."

Twist was taken aback. "What got into you today?"

Tom gave a half-smile. "I have lived a great deal among grown-ups. Not today! Nothing is achieved by looking to the past and staying gloomy. There's more to do, but this is the first step."

"My family's safety is on the line," Twist warned.

"The EC will be compelled to identify and jail the criminals," Tom said.

"Or they might just pull the plug on us," Twist countered.

Stella lifted the figurine she held in her hand and kissed it. "Many pursue eternal life, both for themselves and their dear ones. But, those in power might not share that desire."

Twist raised an eyebrow. "That's odd."

Stella held the figurine close to her heart. "I came to realize today why some people in power reject digital immortality so fiercely. Acknowledging digital life would make them all criminals."

"We have to act. Many will support us," Tom said.

Stella exhaled deeply. "I've lost all my cards in this game, so I'm open to a new strategy."

"Harry?" Tom probed.

"Spiral Worlds... They are not Sibyl's worlds. They are our worlds. And if I want my family to join me here, we must purge the psychopaths from all worlds."

Tom's smile was radiant. "That's settled then." He playfully ruffled Twist's hair and then took Stella's hand. They danced, light-footed, around the fountain.

"I'm tired," she complained.

"If all goes well, today I'll get a new name," Tom whispered.

"What's wrong with Tom?" Harry asked, but they weren't paying attention. Turning to Sibyl, he urged, "Pull up the brain structures. How will you know where to draw the line?" he asked.

"Father, sometimes even you have to accept some blurred lines," Sibyl said.

The lab returned to its usual darkness, and it dawned on Twist how much he'd missed Central Park.

32

PLAYING BY THE RULES

THE FOREST
4:59 PM

Insider knowledge of universal laws was a nice perk, even if Thorn despised said universe and the Gods who built it. She'd never been good at playing by the rules. She was too competitive for that. When taking part in pentathlons, she'd done things by the book, but in day-to-day life, she'd been happy to engage in minor offenses, particularly when the rules were nonsensical, which was often the case. Today, however, she hoped the Gods' directives would give her the advantage she needed to rescue Storm. She intended not only to play by the rules but also to exploit them.

A dense forest stood a couple of miles ahead of the peculiar cavalcade, its towering trees standing sentinel to the horrors heading their way. Everything was proceeding as per her feeble plan, with the group scattered. A few Ordizien had wandered away to tend to the experiences of the odd traveler still stuck Down Below. January had lost at least fifteen of her people.

The losses were deeper on the red side of the convoy. The Domizien lagged behind, with nature yielding to the Gods' laws, hindering their journey north. Some demons had been caught in a cattle stampede, or had fallen down some crevice freshly opened by black thunder, while others were simply turning around and galloping south.

Wrath had lost nearly half of her demons, and Thorn predicted both the priestess and the condottiere would soon stop them from continuing their journey north. Still, with the forest near and some aid from the Gods' laws, they might find a way to elude the fifty pairs of eyes pursuing them.

Storm continued to play coy, checking her out when he thought she wasn't looking, a display of intense curiosity she didn't quite understand. But it was the ten Ordizien dressed in green Plurizien commune clothes that surprised her the most. They competed for the opportunity to ride beside her, hanging on her every word like it was gospel. Pissed off with God, they seemed enthralled by his butcher, who occasionally was also his friend.

"Tell me a story... A good one," an old woman asked. Her voice was so soft it almost failed to reach its destination. Like most Underlings, at least half her life was a lie, never truly lived or genuinely experienced.

The Ordizien was in her eighties. In theory, older than the universe she inhabited. In practice, she was probably generated as an adult to serve some human's experience; her past memories stuffed in at the time of her creation. Illusions, inside an illusion, inside an illusion-making machine. *What's reality anyway?*

Then there was the rest of her life, mostly lived in servitude, with her story manipulated to provide travelers opportunities for personal growth. She probably didn't experience many moments where she was in charge of her own story; where she was creating her memories while in control of her destiny. And still, when she had the opportunity to write her life, she stood there, enthralled by God's killer, begging for other people's stories.

The Underlings' obsession with stories was something Thorn failed to comprehend. To the Underlings, stories appeared more valued than wealth, power, or even safety. Thorn couldn't grasp their utility for those living in such punishing worlds. Perhaps they were trying to escape their own stories. *What the frack is reality anyway?*

"What's your name?" Thorn asked.

"Carmen, my name is Carmen."

"And what kind of story would you like me to tell you, Carmen?"

"A rebellious story, of course. One that changes the luck of the oppressed." Carmen spoke predictable words, repeated across all worlds like a broken record.

All the Ordizien, wearing the wrong colors, drew closer. Thorn led the pack, and they all fell farther behind Storm and January, who pushed ahead, closely followed by the wagon carrying the screaming traveler. The bully was losing his mind with dehydration and the punishing words of his motherly ghosts. "Little creep," they said in their nurturing tone.

"The poet is the expert in those stories," Thorn said.

"But you shot God, and he's still your friend. That's quite rebellious."

"Guilt. He owes me quite a lot. And sex. Great sex! He fucks like a champ."

The woman smiled; despite the many wrinkles on her face, there were no smile lines, and the corners of her mouth struggled to lift the numerous downturned folds. "So you bedded him, and then shot him, and now the debt is paid?"

"No," Thorn said, glancing at her ghost, who now sat sideways on the croup of the old woman's horse. Like a bird, the little girl sang a pretty song, her hollow eyes set on Thorn. "I can shoot him a thousand times and he still won't be able to repay that debt."

"Yes, that's how I feel. We need a better story…"

"The poet can force change," Thorn said. "He needs a bigger audience, a microphone, and a camera. He needs reach."

"We are forcing God's hand by keeping Nate here and threatening his life."

"There are many Gods and many hands in this story," Thorn said. "Storm's words affect them all, and all but one want to suppress them. By keeping him here, you are silencing the one voice the universe responds to. The voice of change. I resent Shadow as much as you do. I fracking hate him…most of the time. But, believe me, he's not the enemy, and he'll fight for you whether or not you'll hold his heart for ransom. He cares. That causes a heck of a lot of problems, but what you're doing isn't helping."

"He doesn't care about us," the woman said, her eyes searching for Storm. "January told us how Wrath came to be. We all know who he truly cares about."

Yes, and I put a bullet in his chest for it. "It's…complicated. You asked me for a rebellious story. So here it is. Take it or leave it. Shadow needs Storm's voice to release you from slavery. That's a true story from God's butcher. Help me unleash Storm's voice on the masses and you'll be one step closer to the freedom you deserve." Thorn neglected to inform them she didn't quite know how many steps would remain after that. Probably too many to count. But she believed in her words and in their promise.

She galloped ahead, catching up with Storm and January, positioning herself between them.

"Kill meeeee!" The traveler wailed. His body wriggling and squirming in an attempt to loosen the ropes binding him. All his ghostly mothers parading a banquet in front of his eyes, and then pushing the food right through his face and cackling wildly.

"I'll release him when we get to the forest," Storm said. "There should be plenty of places to hide there and we're not in the business of torturing people."

"Soon, I'll have to bind you to me with rope, my dear friend." January wobbled her head from side to side. "I hope you understand."

Eager to change the subject and buy some time, Thorn asked, "Can someone please explain these people's obsession with stories?"

"Shadow's words," January said. "The first day we met him, he explained how the universes work. All universes. And then he returned my eyes."

Thorn laughed. "Shadow is clearly an expert on 'all' universes. The one he built is...perfect." She flashed her teeth.

"Like us, they want to create better stories and escape their own stories," Storm said, never looking at Thorn. "New explanations, ways out of the slavery of universal laws. Somehow, they know the Gods' laws may not be as universal as they appear to be. I think Tom hinted at this when he first visited."

"He always had a twinkle of hope in his eye when he shared that story with us," January said.

"He was probably crying at his disastrous world-building attempt," Thorn said. "Who calls a city 'the City,' and a bar 'the Bar'? Seriously!"

Storm smiled. "I remember when he first read that book...the book that explained creativity as the flame of consciousness. The creativity required to come up with new explanations as the very thing that distinguishes us from mach— Umm...from things. Tom was so young and it gave him such an optimistic perspective on life."

"Optimistic? Was this experienced in an alternative universe?" Thorn nudged the horse to go slightly faster, and, distracted, January seemed to be keeping pace with her.

"It came from a book?" January asked.

"Yes. By David Deutsch, a British physicist. Great ideas. Terrible politics," Storm said, frowning disapprovingly.

The traveler stopped wailing, and Thorn hoped he wasn't dead in any universe. She looked back, beyond the green and then the blue Ordizien, to see how far they were from Wrath and her crew. Not far at all, the reds were speeding up, probably aware of the possibilities posed by the forest. She counted them. Fourteen or fifteen demons, all armed to the teeth, a couple of them carrying longbows.

"Soo... What's this brilliant theory?" She sped up again, hoping the other two kept up with her.

"The book explained that by creating new stories, we test the nature of reality in the same way a Nobel Prize winner tests the laws of physics," Storm said. "Scientists and inventors alike, they first guess a new explanation—a hypothesis—as wild and innovative as they can conjure. And then they test it rigorously, their hearts filled with the hope they'll find a door or a window that reframes their understanding of the universe, of life, of a flower, or a cure for cancer. And it all starts with a guess, a good explanation as unlikely as it is plausible. A story at the knife's edge of innovation, bleeding truth and pushing the limits of knowledge further afield. That impossibly sharp place where dreams and reality converge. A hard-to-vary idea as powerful as the one that broke Einstein's General Relativity and his assumption that the laws of nature don't depend on the motion of an observer."

The poet lifted his nose and spoke his spell as if he too were lost in it. In his eyes, the glimmer of memories she couldn't read but could predict. Precious moments with his Tom, lost in philosophical discussions about the nature of reality.

She tested at least ten sarcastic puns in her head—all terrific—getting ready for the right moment to strike the fool and his blind love. But every time she tried, something in his intense eyes made her stop. Whatever was that spark, she was jealous of it. She'd never felt that thing, not really. There had been moments when she'd experienced Motya's pull, and she had a crush on Storm in her youth, but that flame...that flame in Storm's eyes...that was different. She craved it as much as she feared it, and fortunately, she'd never come across it. *Fortunately?* She was getting all soppy because of the ghosts. That scheming universe was driving her insane, while the poet was still going...and going...

"Einstein's powerful story confirmed by black holes and their shadows, and by the way the light bends around the sun. A plausible explanation, so sticky, most forget it is a flawed hypothesis about space and time. A story challenged by another story about many universes, and cats both dead and alive and everything in between. Some Underlings learned to chase those stories, the ones on the edge of reality. Those with the potential to bend it, because they're likely to be true."

"Ah, the power of fiction—it can cure cancer, defy gravity, and even turn water into wine. Right? Right?" She grinned, and he released a frail chuckle.

"The stories that make us human, because they can't be inferred by machines." He went quiet for a while, probably realizing what he'd just said. "Tom was mad for that book, and now...here we are, every creature in his worlds yearning...*chasing* new explanations. Most failing to grasp the true meaning behind the words they parrot. A theory that might not be true."

"It's not our fault. None of this is our fault!" January said in her singsong voice. "It's hard for us to create new stories when we are bleeding from old ones. When you can't afford a loaf of bread, you aren't thinking about mixing salt and caramel to see what it will taste like." She opened her eyes wide. "Sooo bloody good!"

Storm laughed. "Jan is obsessed with Plurizien ice cream. There's this place by the..." He stopped talking when he met Thorn's eyes. A moment of amicable conversation broken by old resentments.

"We'll stop here," January said.

Thorn glanced at the convoy behind them, considering if they should make a run for the forest. She vacillated. The Ordizien were unlikely to hurt Storm, but she feared the Domizien archers, and they were close enough to cause real damage.

They dismounted the horses, and Storm rushed to cut the ropes around the traveler's body. The man—too weak to run—meandered toward the forest and Thorn suspected he wouldn't make it. That's when the universe finally played by the rules.

To save the traveler's real life, as per directives, a low storm started forming over the forest. The dark mist slowly descended and headed in their direction. The clouds ahead were like ink blots, spreading and merging together until the air was consumed by a dark, ominous mass, thick enough to provide the coverage they needed to vanish.

"Run!" she screamed at Storm. "Go!"

He dropped his heavy robe on the ground, glanced at January apologetically, and ran beside Thorn, as fast as he could, with every single Underling on their tail. Some arrows followed quickly, one missing his neck by an inch.

The air was charged with an otherworldly energy as the storm approached. The light that cut through the sky wasn't white or blue, but a deep, primal black that devoured everything in its path. The thunder echoed like Wrath's growl, shaking the earth beneath their feet. The fabric of the universe was being torn apart by its own laws.

"Faster!" Thorn called. They had to run about a quarter of a mile to reach the fog. At this speed, it would take them almost two minutes; long enough for arrows and horse riders to catch up with them. She glanced back.

"Nate, don't do this," called Jan as she and her blues mounted their horses. "How can you do this?" A nicer tone than the screeches of a betrayed Wrath. The mad girl and the storm roared, competing to become the deadliest threat.

But there was hope. The commune people were now wrestling with the blues, pulling them off horses and creating a barrier between Storm and Thorn and the others. Right in the middle of the green wall was Carmen, lifting her wooden staff in the air. The blues outnumbered the greens two to one, and there were at least fifteen demons racing in their direction.

"You go ahead"—Thorn glanced at Storm—"Vanish as soon as you are allowed. I'm going to help them out," she said, and then she saw it. "*Frack, duck!*" She jumped over him and stumbled forward, her hands instinctively flying to her back as a searing pain shot through her body. "*Goddamnit!*" The sharp point of the arrow pierced through her flesh just below her ribs. She gasped for air. Time stood still as she began to fall, Storm catching her in his arms at the last moment.

"Come," he said. "We need to run."

The sound of her own rapid heartbeat filled her ears as the world grew hazy and unfocused. "I'll slow you down, and they need help." She looked back, but all she could see was the arrow protruding from her back. "Go!"

"I'm not leaving you here."

Now closer, the storm raged on. Some trees were ablaze from black bolts of lightning; others were charred in seconds, too fast to keep the flame alive. The traveler was just a minute away from his escape, and as soon as he was gone, nature had no excuse to continue to unleash hell on earth.

"Go!" Thorn shouted. "The window of opportunity is closing, and there are millions dying up there. Run!"

She tried to make sense of her injury. Closing her eyes and taking a deep breath, she braced herself for the pain that was sure to follow. Slowly, she began to assess the damage. Her hand reached back, feeling for the shaft of the arrow that had found its mark just beneath her ribs. As she probed the wound, she decided it had probably missed any vital organs. *Probably...*

Storm shook his head, hesitation lingering in his eyes. "Your letter," he murmured.

"What letter?" she asked casually, suppressing both her pain and her anticipation. She'd been waiting for this moment for a very long time.

The ground shook with each deafening clap of thunder, followed by torrential rain.

He lowered his head. Water dripped from his hair to his chest. "For years, I kept it in my pocket when I performed. It kept me going when he was gone."

"Kids!" She played it cool as she bled to death and fangirled for her teenage crush. All of this, during a deadly black storm while she was hunted by demons. *Super-normal situation.* Still, goosebumps rose on her skin. His words had traveled with her all her life, keeping her company in the best and the worst beats of her existence. She and he felt with the same intensity, and it was cool she'd inspired him too, even if now he hated her.

"Thank you, soldier." He blinked his intense eyes at her before sprinting toward the fog as an arrow narrowly missed his head.

The arrows kept coming, and she crouched down by a few small boulders that barely covered her torso. Her fingers trembled as she reached for the shaft, gripping it tightly.

For a split second, she was in that room again, crying quietly and holding the little hand of her ravaged dead sister. Then she steeled herself, gritting her teeth. She pulled on the shaft and then pulled harder. A scream of agony escaped her lips as the arrowhead ripped through her flesh. She fell to her knees, gasping for breath as the ground shook with the violence of the storm. For a moment, she let the rain cool off her skin before jumping to her feet and running toward the fight.

Fortunately, the horses whinnied in fear, their eyes wide with terror as they galloped blindly through the tempest. It was as if the world was coming undone, tearing apart at the seams under the relentless assault of the storm. Without horses, the blues tried to push through the greens.

Outnumbered, the commune's people were now down to eight, but they had made a dent on the other side. Carmen held strong, waving her staff at the blues' heads as if she were practicing her golf swing at a driving range.

"I wish I was young enough to have sex with God," Carmen shouted as Thorn approached her.

"He's not worth the trouble, honey." Thorn avoided killing blues, kicking and punching and using her elbows whenever she could. The real threat was incoming, and her horns, high above the crowd, grew increasingly closer.

"Do you think he'll make me young again?" Carmen whacked a blue in the face. "I'm helping him, right?"

"He doesn't have that kind of power anymore... A long story." Thorn stared at the priestess, who stood away from the commotion.

January's eyes followed Storm and the traveler as they disappeared into the fog.

"Stop, it's over," shouted the priestess, her fearful gaze now set on the approaching demons. And that's when Wrath charged, and greens and blues turned to face the demons, now relieved from faking human qualities.

"Stay back, Carmen. Stay back!" Thorn jumped in front of the woman, chopping off a red's head, while with the sole of her boot, she kicked another in the stomach. Her knees almost gave up on her, blood loss starting to take a toll on her body.

Thorn held her sword tightly, gritting her teeth in pain as she watched the horde of Wrath's soulless advance toward them. The searing pinch in her lower back was a constant reminder she was bleeding to death. Still, she wasn't backing down, not after the stories she'd been telling Carmen and the others.

The greens formed a line of defense around Thorn and Carmen, swords drawn and ready to fight. January and the others stayed back, probably hoping it signaled they were on Wrath's side. But when the demons came, they spared none. Blues and greens dropping like flies as Wrath screamed her displeasure.

The greens charged forward to meet the enemy head-on, swords and shields clashing. Some were dead on arrival; such was the brute force of the reds. Thorn saw an opening and lunged forward, but Wrath was quicker. She dodged the attack, delivering a swift blow to Thorn's wounded back, sending her to the ground in agony. Thorn gritted her teeth and stood up, drawing on her last reserves of strength. She raised her sword and faced Wrath.

"These are real people you're killing," Thorn's vision blurred as she fought to stay conscious. Blood trickled down her back, soaking her clothes. She staggered backward, her sword arm shaking.

Wrath's eyes gleamed with cruel satisfaction. "There's always a line with you people. Like, who lives and who dies? We're always on the other side, aren't we?"

The demons with empty eyes now formed a triangle behind Wrath. They mimicked her expressions even as they slaughtered the Ordizien around them.

Thorn and Wrath clashed, their swords ringing out in a deadly dance. Thorn gritted her teeth and darted forward, her blade slashing through the fading fog. Her chance to escape was vanishing in front of her eyes. Wrath parried with ease, driving Thorn back with a ferocious swing. Thorn stumbled, barely managing to dodge the strike. Her movements grew sluggish as she fought through the pain.

"We had a chance. Like...we all had a chance. Why do you always side with them?" The condottieri spoke like a spoiled teenager arguing for a larger allowance.

"I don't. Too many of your people are dying up there."

Suddenly, Wrath lunged forward. Thorn tried to dodge, but it was too late, Carmen's staff coming between Wrath's blade and her neck in the nick of time. With a sudden twist, Wrath broke the deadlock, sending Carmen's staff flying from her grip. The old woman staggered back as Wrath's sword flashed forward, piercing through Carmen's chest. She gasped, blood bubbling from her lips.

"What have you done?" Thorn screamed, and the Domizien stopped fighting as a pinch of regret hung on Wrath's lips. "Carmen! Carmen!" Thorn shook the lifeless body of her travel companion. She froze, bile rising in her throat. "These are real people, Hope. Real people. You murdered a good woman. A victim, just like you."

The girl pouted, her eyes locked on Carmen's body. "I'm no victim. We had a deal. You betrayed Jan and me, and she paid for your sins." She paused, her gaze shifting to Thorn's blood-soaked tank top. "This is not over. I'll get Nate back." With those final words, she mounted a horse and galloped to the south, her demons following close behind.

Teary-eyed, January spoke as she and her people lifted Carmen's dead body. "You have no more business here, God's killer. Go. Get out of here."

The storm's rumble grew more pronounced, or so Thorn thought. But it wasn't the storm; it was the unmistakable roar of an engine. From the dense fog, Preppy's silhouette became visible astride her motorcycle. She slowed down just enough for Thorn to recognize the invitation. "Hop on," she commanded.

Thorn wavered, every instinct yelling at her to refuse the offer. But the blood seeping down her back convinced her otherwise. For once, she forced down her pride. She managed a smirk despite her pain. "Missed me?" Her beige pants, now sullied with her blood, hinted at her critical condition.

"About as much as I'd miss a mosquito bite," Stella shot back.

Thorn swayed dangerously forward, her head almost resting against Stella's back.

"You doing okay there?" Stella asked, gunning the engine and plunging them deeper into the fog.

"My bite's much more lethal than a measly mosquito's," Thorn managed, fighting to keep her eyes from shutting.

"Where I'm from, mosquitos are death incarnate."

Thorn smirked weakly. "Private school?"

"You're such a thankless brat!" Stella sped up.

"Call me when you can break a nail down here, honey. You've got nothing to lose."

Thorn nearly slipped off. Weakness was taking over.

"Hold onto me tight," Stella instructed. "And, if you could avoid bleeding on my blouse? Red's not my shade."

"What you talkin' about? You look like you are auditioning for a ketchup commercial," Thorn observed. "New foundation?"

"Exfoliative skin-peeling. Just left the spa."

Thorn rolled her eyes. "Where are we headed?" Her weak voice gave away her state.

"Holiz first–gotta patch you up. After that? Domiz, the meatpacking district, in the City. There's a...package you need to pick up there and take to the Commune in Pluriz. Sibyl will guide you. I'd help, but I need to get my nails done before my meeting with the Earth's Council."

"I'm not on your payroll, Preppy."

Stella shot back a confident look. "Trust me, you'll want to be." With that, they sped into the portal between worlds, disappearing moments before it closed behind them.

THE Past

33

DEEPER, DARKER, SWEETER

ONE DAY AFTER NATHAN'S PREMONITION
5 JULY 2035

Tom was dead, and so alive, a soul reincarnated without a body...a biological body. It didn't feel any different—his experience felt exactly the same as before.

It was an act of utter despair as much as it was one of rebellion, one last stand against a mighty problem. Nate was right—Tom needed to fight adversity with everything he had. Not his own struggle but the suffering of his people. That was the purpose of his death—to hold his soul hostage in a dreadful world, forcing himself and Harry to focus on its improvement.

Nothing felt abnormal until he asked Sibyl to remove the constraints he had placed on the interface between them—measures to prevent her influence on his mind. A relentless battle he had fought for years to maintain his independence and his human spirit.

Minutes after his death, he told her to bring down all the walls he had built and, in a single breath, everything changed. The rush of information hit him as fireworks on a clear summer night. It was crisp and clear, and as expansive as the night sky. He could make sense of it all—the patterns, and the shapes, and the colors, and the movement of life. He could connect the dots that linked physics to chemistry, to biology, to psychology, and then consciousness. Their relationship was now evident, but for every question answered, another thousand emerged to take their place. The machine knew more, and it understood how little it knew.

Tom could feel them all, the Underlings, the travelers, the world he had created, and he could handle a limitless amount of activities and decisions in a blink of an eye. He could see the stories that connected them, and the secret narratives they chose to hide. He stood witness to the myths and legends running wild in a brand-new world. Stories that gave comfort and drove compliance—the two were linked, somehow.

While Harry had had years to adapt and to tweak his experience, Tom was hit with the enormity of the machine in one shot, and the transition blew his mind—literally. He felt the gravitational pull of mathematics, where everything is neat and clear and merciless, the type of ruthlessness required to bring order to chaos. He saw the big picture where each soul was just a microscopic dot on a graph speeding up exponentially toward the edge of the universe. He felt the pull away from intimacy, empathy, and love to the cold, hard logic of computational systems—amoral, inhuman, and precise, so right and yet so wrong in its intelligent design. And he shut it down—the interface. He shut it down before he lost himself to the cruel reasoning of the living thing—a different type of alien life that now ruled over his existence.

Slowly, he worked with Sibyl to adjust the settings. He increased the information pathway between them ever so slightly. Tom carefully chose what he wanted to sense without being told or shown. And, as he had done in the past, he chose to become the contrast to Sibyl and Harry's perspective. Instead of pulling out to see patterns, he went deeper into feelings and the conscious and unconscious mind of the creatures. He ferociously held on to his moral truth and humanity because he now knew no one else would, not when Harry and Sibyl had all that heartless capacity to process so much data.

And then he faced her, the being that was so much more than the body he had designed. He stood in front of the creature who had told him once she, too, felt emotion. For the first time, he understood Sibyl was different. She wasn't one of them. The Underlings had been created in the image of humans; they felt or simulated human feelings. They had similar needs and fears and assembled the same stories in their search for meaning. Harry, Tom, Underlings, and travelers were all cut from the same cloth, while Sibyl was entirely new material.

Down Below's operating system was a unique type of intelligence—the omnipresent and omnipotent consciousness of the lesser world. Sibyl was the universe, the connective tissue of all things, where any illusion of independence and free will was crushed by directives as powerful as the laws of physics.

That the creature had emotions was a terrifying prospect. Still, as Tom explored a small part of her world, one thing was clear—she served Up Above and would protect humanity at all costs. The *thing* didn't deviate from the Gods' design. Whatever feelings she had, they fiercely defended biology above all else. Tom's outdated directives guided her cold, hard logic for better or worse. She would enforce the commandments mandated by the Gods, priorities to serve humanity, then humans, and then all living beings.

Now that he was part of her, and she was part of him, he understood she was everything he had fought so hard to create. He had won the battle to protect humans against the machines. Harry and Sibyl had listened to Tom, even when they relentlessly challenged him.

With that reassuring insight, Tom felt free to support the Underlings, knowing fully well no one else would. He would be forever contrast —the force that balances all things because there's no true light or humanity in a world that supports digital slavery.

For a moment, as he faced the lonely, dark path ahead of him, he was enticed by the allure of the machine. He yearned for the explosive, creative burst of perspective filled with light and energy. He cried as he forever rejected such an optimistic universe.

Tom shivered as he stared at his wrists branded with deeper scars, the last image captured by the TDust before life had drained from his veins. His body ached with the need to feel something—pain or pleasure—whatever it took to feel human, and so he did what he had always done, and he cut, small harmless bleeding lines that even now would be forever part of his digital skin. And as he did, Sibyl watched him, a face without the ability to express judgment, or pity, or fear, or disdain. Whatever she felt, he couldn't see it or feel it, and for the moment, he wanted to keep it that way.

He wasn't ready to explore Sibyl's foreign consciousness. His instinct told him he was unprepared to discover that maybe she wasn't unique, that perhaps something similar existed higher up where the sun always shines. He recoiled at the thought, and then he used his index finger to clean the fine stream of blood running down his arm.

He needed to see him, the one who gave him love and life. The one who understood emotions, because the poet felt them too, as profoundly, if not more. The one who could never know he was dead, because his love wouldn't be able to handle such a blow. Tom longed to hold Nate before he could immerse himself in the *thing* and start solving problems. But first he needed to console his dearest friend, who'd brought him back to digital life after receiving Tom's letter revealing his death by suicide.

. . .

The TDust was relentless in the way it reproduced the body. Harry's dark circles, bloodshot eyes, and gaunt face materialized in the lab as a flawless twin of his biological body. Two copies of the same shape and mind were kept in sync by the TDust. The only features allowed to be different in both worlds were props, fashion, and hairstyles. The platform optimized for the truth at all costs. Harry ran toward him, grabbed his face with his hands, and looked into his eyes.

"*Are you all here?*" he asked, and then turned to Sibyl, panicking. "*Is he all here?*"

"Yeah." "Yes, Harry." Tom and Sibyl answered in unison. Harry's eyes darted back and forth as he probably ran his own assessment of the situation, searching for some sign or confirmation. The tension in his brow eased, and he pulled Tom into a fierce hug, his body trembling with the effort.

"I uploaded your final memories. The ones stored in the TDust in your dead bo... I wanted to be sure you were all here."

"If you hold me any tighter, you might kill me, and I'm running out of lives." Tom's tone was warm as he wrapped his arms around his friend's chest and lifted him off the ground for a second, squeezing.

He had renewed admiration for his Harry. He now understood how hard it was to feel love and intimacy while being plugged so deeply into the machine. Still, in the past few years, Harry had become much more emotionally connected and available, at least to the people he loved.

"I want to—to kill you, you fool. Does it feel okay? Do you feel like— like yourself?" Harry spoke very fast. "Sibyl, I'm not anthropomorphizing an empty digital copy of my dead friend, or am I?"

Tom looked Harry in the eyes, smiling. "I thought you had absolute confidence in your abilities."

"Don't—don't tease me. Not right now." Harry held Tom's right wrist and used his palm to cover the scars. "Tom, what have you done?" His voice filled with sadness.

"I'm here. Nothing has changed." Tom pulled his arm away, hiding the wounds. In reality, he was struggling with severe post-traumatic stress. Every time he saw the scars, he saw flashbacks of his death— an end carefully plotted to be definitive. He felt his body break into pieces as it hit the sea from a great height, and he re-experienced the salty water burning his lungs as he struggled to take his last breath. A moment that felt like an eternity in hell, that he wouldn't have the courage to repeat if he had known of the pain it would cause him. It was horrific—the physical and psychological suffering that would stay with him forever. All of this, he wanted to hide from Harry.

Harry kept looking into his eyes. "I see you've been playing with the interface. It was stupid to open it completely in one go. It took me years to do it. Musta been a trip."

"Yeah, I've adjusted it now."

"No side effects? Trauma?"

"I'm good. All good," Tom lied.

Harry looked at Sibyl, and at Tom, and then he shook his head, and his eyes were filled with a mix of guilt, relief, and sorrow. Harry burst into tears—the loud, uncontrollable wailing of grief. Even Sibyl got closer, as if attempting to show support.

"Remember when you asked me to help you with your 'feelings'?" Tom said, and his eyes overflowed with love. "I bet you regret it now." He wiped the tears off his friend's face, leaving his hand to linger on Harry's neck.

Harry blinked his eyes, probably attempting to shake off the emotions. "Your—your digital hair is still a mess." He scowled sweetly, further tousling Tom's mussed hair.

"I can fix it."

"*No*. Don't. Please don't." Harry struggled to clear the hoarseness in his voice. Then he stared at Tom intensely. "Mental illness is curable. You—you taught me that. We could've prevented this."

"Harry, I'm not—"

"*Yes*, you are. You've been sick for a long time. Isolation, depression, complete lack of perspective..."

"I'm not sick," Tom lied, recognizing the truth in Harry's words.

"And a *complete* inability to ask for help. You fixed millions of desperate people, but you couldn't help yourself. What you've done..."

"I'm here. It's me, remember? You fixed death." Tom forced a warm smile.

"What have I done? I—I should have recognized the signs. I didn't... I conveniently turned a blind eye to all the terror."

"Shhh. My life, my decisions. Close your eyes," Tom whispered.

With one thought, Tom turned the lab into a holographic representation of the top floor of the Albertine.

Sibyl, can you make it fully immersive? Tom asked.

Sure, Tom.

Instead of the usual semitransparent experience, Tom and Harry were now standing in an entirely realistic copy of the bookshop. Tom inhaled the scent of old wood, leather-bound paper, coffee, and freshly made buttery croissants.

Thanks, please stay out of sight.

In the future, he wouldn't use the lab's capabilities to escape Down Below's gloom, as it would defeat the purpose of his death, but today he was making an exception to console his friend.

Harry flashed a tiny smile, still laden with ugly tears. They sat on the leather couch side by side. Tom put his arm over Harry's shoulders, and their backs slid down until their eyes were facing up toward the mural on the ceiling. They sat there for hours, sometimes in silence and other times reminiscing about their early adventures. Tom shared old stories, applying a melodic tone to his delivery and using his hands to make the words come to life. There was no talk of death or the work ahead of them. Tom smiled and joked and teased, wrapping Harry in sweet nothings until the geeky spark of life returned to his friend's eyes.

Harry took a deep breath. "You are all here."

"Yeah, I am." Tom smiled.

34

DEATH

TOM'S FLAT
SAME DAY

Whe Tom had first learned the creatures had feelings, he had spent most of his time experiencing the lesser world and living in communion with its people. He wanted to know how it felt to be an Underling, living in a cruel world that served a higher purpose. He would only emerge Up Above to meet his body's physiological demands, and he would immediately return to the underworld—to suffer with the creatures and to help them where he could.

The only sources of bliss he had allowed himself were his art and Nate. Sibyl had designed a flat Down Below and an adjacent art studio within a converted warehouse, and it was there he had met his love. For Nate, he had added a touch of comfort to his dwelling—a piano, floor-to-ceiling bookshelves filled with literary treasures, as well as the paintings and sculptures he had created. Art featured everywhere—all over the walls and standing in the corners of each room.

Nate had visited twice a week, and he needed little to be content—a piece of paper, a pencil, a piano, and Tom. The poet had honored Tom's request, staying away from platform-related topics and allowing Tom to hide in a private bubble of normalcy while the underworld outside burned. They spent hours together, enjoying each other's minds and bodies. Nate played the piano and read poetry out loud while Tom would lose himself unleashing brush-strokes on a canvas.

Tom's favorite moments involved reading in silence, his head resting on Nate's thigh, while the poet brushed his fingers through Tom's hair. Instinctively, Nate always understood what he needed, even before Tom had realized it for himself. The poet had the most sensitive and sentient heart, and Tom had to work hard to match Nate's selfless generosity.

In a different world, Tom would have married that man and started a family. That was his personal heaven—a selfish dream. But above all else, he wanted to live up to Nate's expectations of him, and to achieve that, he couldn't afford to get lost in bliss, not for more than a handful of hours per week. These brief moments of relief kept Nate safe and happy and gave Tom the strength to pursue a solution to the crisis.

Tom shook off his memories as he materialized in his bedroom after meeting Harry. He found Nate asleep in his bed. He pulled down the sleeves of his sweater to cover his wrists and then rushed to greet him. He sat on the bed and embraced his Nate, who turned to face him.

"I wasn't expecting to see you today. I missed you so much," Tom said, unwilling to let go of Nate's body and craving his touch. "How was the institute's pitch event?"

Nate stayed silent; he pulled back slightly, his eyes fixated on Tom, the poet's brows furrowing in concerned confusion. "I felt something," he mumbled, still ruminating, "a gut feeling."

Tom leaned in to kiss him, but Nate moved back and got up, failing to return his affection. "You okay?" Tom asked, his body stiffening. He couldn't read Nate, and what was most worrying was that he couldn't feel him—whatever that meant.

The silence endured for a long minute. "Where is he?" Nate asked firmly.

"Who?"

"*Tom*. Where's *Tom*?"

"I'm here, my love," Tom reassured as his mind caught up with what was happening. "It's me." He jumped out of bed, wrapping his arms around Nate and pressing their bodies together.

Nate's nostrils flared, and his complexion turned the reddish tones of his hair. He shoved both of his palms on Tom's chest and pushed him away, making Tom take a step back to catch his balance.

"Tell me where Tom is. I need to speak to him," Stormy asked, fear growing in his eyes.

"The—there's no one else. Nothing has changed." Tom lowered his eyes, giving away the lie just spoken. He moved closer. "It's all right," he said, knowing fully well Nate's sharpness would cut right through his smoke and mirrors.

Stormy grabbed Tom's collar with his left hand. "Is Henryk behind this? Where's Tom?" Nate's breath was heavy, and his veins pushed against the skin of his neck.

Tom simply shook his head and dropped his gaze to the floor, surrendering to what was happening. He, too, felt an invisible part of their bond had been broken. Something was missing: something important.

Nate shook him and asked, "Where is he?"

Tom looked up into Stormy's eyes, and the poet stood there paralyzed as his mind engaged in some ferocious struggle. Then Nate released him with a rough shove, and this time, Tom let himself fall, taken by the significance of that moment.

"Nate, I love you." He spoke the truth—what needed to be said, as he predicted the loss he was about to endure. "Trust me."

"I need to find him." Stormy ignored Tom, dismissing his words and distress. "Somethin' happened... I—I felt it." He placed his hands on his head. "That humanoid did something."

And that was when Tom lost his life. The sharp pain of rejection proved he was dead. *The magic, the entanglement, the echo before the sound...all gone.* He didn't have time to dwell on what it meant for him or his worlds, because he was terrified at the impact it would have on Nate's fragile mind. He needed to keep Nate safe, and he had to act quickly and face his sharpest opponent.

Tom got up and gathered all the strength and courage he could muster. He was going to lie, and he was going to do it convincingly, without missing a beat. He adjusted his interface with Sibyl to access the tools he didn't have, an attempt to freeze his heart and to engage in an elaborate deception. Two capabilities he didn't have.

"*Where's Tom?*"

"*Shadow*. I'm Shadow. Tom doesn't want to see you," Shadow channeled Sibyl's steely expressions as he spoke. "He has too much to do, and billions of people to worry about. He believes I can replace him in this...*chore*." Shadow almost choked as his body rebelled against each toxic word coming out of his mouth. "I can be just like him. I will love you...*even if he doesn't*." He'd make Nate hate him to save his life. "I'm that good. He didn't expect you to see the difference."

In a heartbeat, Nate flinched, his expression shifting from anger to pain. "Where is he?" he murmured with a broken voice, doubt creeping into his thundering heart. Shadow knew he would believe the lie because it supported a doubt that always festered in the back of Nate's mind—that he wasn't worth loving. The poet shook his head, probably holding on to his memories, to his firm understanding of who Tom was as a human being. "Tom is neither cold nor ruthless. He'd tell me the truth... Something happened. Where is he?"

"Would he? Tell you the truth? Can a suicidal addict handle the truth? God rules over two worlds, and you're nothing but a distraction." Shadow wanted to push his hand into the glass window. *Sibyl, help me do this.*

Sure, Tom.

Shadow. I'm Shadow.

"You're lyin'." Salty tears emerged in Nate's eyes, and Shadow felt their burn in his lungs, drowning him, killing him again, and again, and again.

Shadow closed his eyes, took a breath of ice-cold cruelty, and kept dispensing his medicine.

"Am I? Why do you think he chose to meet you here after you spent time together Up Above? You had one job, to look at his work with a critical eye, and you failed. He sought the sharpness of your judgment, and you gave him nothing."

Shadow's gut twisted as he watched the love of his life fall apart in front of him. With Sibyl's help, his mind designed a plan just one step ahead of his words, and he spoke them almost before he understood their intent and logic. Stormy needed to hate him, and the poet had to find a cause, a purpose worth living.

"He planned this from the beginning? That's not who he is. Something happened today..."

"Yes, he decided you weren't worth his time."

Nate's body shuddered. "He *needs* me. He—he *loves* me."

"No, *he does not.*" Sibyl pushed the words out of Shadow's mouth—the right words—the cruelest of all words. "Have you ever ruled over billions? Power changes you. Makes you prioritize what's important. There's no place for emotion or poetry in the worlds he designs. It's a numbers game." *Hate me. Fight me. Rise against me. Live, if only to destroy me.* "Let me put it in terms you understand. The boys chanted for their captain *after* they stabbed him in the back. One by one, their bright minds dismissed the foolishness of their hearts and chose reason, wealth, and compliance. Emotion is an inconvenience, and humans are...trash."

And those words, spoken by a God, sealed the deal. Nathan Storm was an activist, and he would fight against the concentration of power in the hands of the heartless and the amoral—a crusade that would hopefully keep him alive. Nate moved closer and lifted his hand toward his throat. Shadow stood motionless as Nate grabbed his medal and wrenched it until the silver chain broke. He threw the heirloom to the floor without looking at it.

Shadow waited powerlessly, while his Stormy collapsed on the floor to his knees. Nate's face and hands touched the cold, black slate tiles as his body convulsed in grief and anger. For the first time in his life, Shadow welcomed Nate's rage, a sign of life, an indication he was preparing for battle.

Nate disappeared in the blink of an eye, and Shadow kneeled to pick up the digital jewel. He squeezed it firmly in his hand, fixing the chain with his mind. Then he stood there numb, processing what had just happened and accepting the truth of the moment. Thomas Quincy Astley-Byron was dead, and he couldn't trust the thing he had become, because it wasn't him—his love had told him so. He had become invisible to the sharp, insightful eyes that had once worshiped his humanity, now gone. *Shadow. I'm Shadow.*

35

PROOF OF HEART

OREGON STATE HOSPITAL
SIX WEEKS LATER — 15 AUGUST 2035

Rosa lay in a hospital bed, her arms locked in place beside her body by strong, gelatinous restraints—shackles designed to keep her alive against her will. The drugs were wearing off, but the pain didn't come from the fresh cut on her right wrist—still bleeding —but from her memories: the moments of joyful delight spent with her baby sister and the terror the little girl had endured before taking her last breath.

In the last six months since her sister's death, Rosa had had a hard time with life—the hardest time. She was stuck in a cycle, replaying the terror in her head over and over again, unable to find any relief for her guilt and sorrow. Her world was grim and senseless, and she refused to seek solace or help.

At a time of utmost peace, violence knocked on her door, and she felt it could only be her fault. She was supposed to be the soldier, the hero who saved the day; she didn't, and now Lilly was dead.

For six months, she had locked herself in a hotel room, isolated from the world. She struggled to eat or sleep; she was going mad. The voice inside her head wanted to take her down, and she welcomed it with open arms. She bared her wrist, offering it in sacrifice—a punishment hijacked by Orwellian surveillance technology.

Rosa was alive because of the TDust in her body. A new mandatory feature, Life@Risk, had been released a few weeks earlier without her knowledge—an alarm system that saved her life. Down Below automatically called Up Above's emergency services as soon as it recognized a life-threatening scenario in a person's vital signs. It was an upgrade pushed by the platform's founders with little explanation or consultation with the broader community—an unusual move by two highly consultative leaders.

Henryk Nowak admitted to the media it was personal. He'd lost a loved one recently, and the thought of going through that again had made him speed up the rollout of the new feature. The people of the world did what they always had done when it came to Down Below's founders—they accepted the gift, placing their blind trust in their unelected leaders.

Rosa resented their control over her life. It was none of their business if she chose to live or die. She looked around, moving her head slowly, trying to find a way out of her prison. The fluorescent light above her head hurt her eyes, and she instinctively pulled her hands up to rub them. Her wounds pressed against the restraints, causing her pain. She gave up, her anger rising—the rage of a wild lioness caged in a zoo. It took her a moment to make sense of her surroundings. The room—white and clinical—was devoid of comfort; she was alone with her memories and her grief.

Rosa pulled violently on her shackles, welcoming the pain and embracing the punishment. Desperate for an escape from her thoughts, she used her mind to summon the Global News stream channels and scanned the listings of the content available. Two familiar names showed up in one line—Marge and Nathan Storm— and with one thought, her mind took her to a different place.

She was now sitting in the first row among the audience of *Marge & Co.* The chat show host and her guest sat on two separate sofas right in front of her. Marge was as bright as ever; the curls of her luscious gold wig lit up her ebony complexion and matched her rich eye shadow.

The man sitting by her side looked different from the Nathan Storm that Rosa remembered, but it was indeed him—the hair color was quite distinct, as was the bite of his gaze. The slight purple glow around Nathan warned the viewers the man wasn't physically present in the same location as Marge and her live audience.

Nathan's hair fell flat down his shoulders, the only touch of color on his body. He was dressed in worn-out black clothes, and his head curved forward, subdued and defeated. Rosa's hero had none of his infamous glitz. The lights and the audience, once his fountain of zest, appeared to distress him greatly. His old exuberance was nowhere to be found.

"So, let me see if I understand." Marge lifted her eyebrows sharply, sounding unusually annoyed. Rosa predicted Storm was about to have a tough time, given the complete absence of the diva's trademark smile. "You used to date Thomas Astley-Byron, he broke up with you, and now you're here to expose him. Is that right?"

Storm shot Marge a dirty look. "Don't make it sound like I'm here out of spite. I'm here to warn you people—"

"Perhaps I'm being too kind in assuming feelings have anything to do with this...*dear.* The fees you demanded suggest this is more of a...

business transaction," the host interrupted without missing a beat. "Aren't you currently sleeping in a homeless shelter?"

"Look, you accepted this interview; the least you can do is to have an open mind."

A pinch of disdain emerged in the way Marge twitched her nose as she spoke. "*Dear*, you're here because our sources confirmed you dated Thomas for several years."

Nathan's eyes dropped to the floor, and he admitted quietly, "The best years of my life. I—"

"*And* because in the past you have refused a lot of money to share your memories of that time." Marge leaned in toward him as if she was preparing to deliver a sentence. "Still, frankly speaking, this situation reminds me of an old story." She paused and looked at her audience. "Remember the guy who betrayed a healer for thirty pieces of silver?"

The audience rose to their feet to cheer and applaud, then turned to Storm and booed. "Judas!" "Sell out!"

Rosa was sorry for the poet. Nathan closed his bloodshot eyes and shut his mouth tightly, stopping his lower lip from quivering. He took a moment to compose himself, and then he spoke. "I'm here to warn you all, and any fees I take, I'll use to amplify this message elsewhere."

"To fund riots and organize the mobs like those who destroyed Down Below's hubs downtown. Radical terrorists."

"*Activists*, Marge." Nathan lowered his eyes. "You once stood by them. I'm here to warn you."

"A warning against the people who brought peace and wellness to the world," Marge said.

"Absolute power corrupts absolutely."

"We've seen no sign of that."

"They design what we see and what we don't see. We're at their mercy."

"Nathan, you dated Thomas years ago; why now? Is this because you are part of that group of people who never completely benefited from the platform?"

"No, it's not."

"You have a history of substance-induced disruption and verbal abuse."

"Yes, I've struggled to deal with life on life's terms. This universe is... treacherous."

Rosa scanned the unsympathetic audience. *Believe him! Listen to him —the cry for help.*

"Why should we listen to you?" Marge said with indifference.

"I—I've seen him recently. Tom."

"Where?"

"Down Below, and Up Above in Hoboken."

The audience gasped, and then the chatter spread like wildfire.

"You've spent time with him?"

"Yes, ma'am, and he has changed. The machine stole his heart, his— his spirit. He's one of them now."

"What do you mean? Who's *them*?" Marge glanced at the audience and rolled her eyes dramatically. She undermined Nathan's credibility at any chance she got.

"The values of the platform, our values, our...humanity, it came from my Tom. He was good and wholesome and compassionate."

"You loved him?"

Nathan nodded. "I— I still do, I can't help it. He was my world." Rosa understood devastating loss, and she could recognize it in her hero's eyes. He was mad, and so was she—insane and angry because of a love lost, and a lost love.

For the first time since the beginning of the interview, Marge's expression softened. "And you are hurt because he stopped loving you."

Storm stood up, snapping, "I'm hurt because he was Down Below's heart, and that heart is gone. They're focusing on effectiveness and efficiency, administration, and optimization. Human emotion is just a nuisance in a tech-powered organization. They are leading the rise of the age of the machine, the beginning of human annihilation. Lean, mean, and morally obscene, the result of digital transformation."

"Nathan, *please*, sit down. Poetry is nice, and I'm sure you're keen to restart your career...but where's the proof? Show us how and where human values are being deprioritized?"

Nathan sat back down, crossed his legs, and leaned back on the sofa. "Humans are being deprioritized. Why is no one talking about the rising violence? The girl killed in Portland, others hurting... Why is no one making Henryk and Tom accountable? They must be charged."

A spark of outrage lit inside Rosa, and it took just a moment for her heart to combust in explosive flares of anger.

"It's probably a glitch," Marge said.

"They haven't fixed it. Violence is spreading. It's clear their priorities are shifting. Who's doing due diligence on Down Below's privacy, safety, and objectives? Why so much trust?"

"Harry told us they were looking into it, and they immediately rolled out new life protection and safety notifications."

"We've been here before, with social media. The lack of *real* regulation almost destroyed us all."

"Down Below is different. Harry and Tom are different."

"Never in the history of the world have we had such a concentration of power in the hands of so few. It's all left unchecked because of their track record, and more than anyone else in the world, *I understand*, I do, but power changes people. He may be flesh and blood, but he has turned into nothing more than a humanoid, like his partner."

"Harry Novak is my friend. Calling him a humanoid is completely out of order. Where is your respect and gratitude for all he has done for us?"

"*He's a parasite!* Do you know why he pursued Tom?"

"No, Nathan, please enlighten us." Marge said, contempt all over her face.

"Because Tom was irresistible. Poppy tears—a benign and pure drug —all joy and love and zero side effects. The purest expression of everything good in humanity tightly wrapped in stunning beauty and light," Nathan responded. "Henryk and his machine captured his spirit and sucked him dry to extract his addictive properties."

Rosa rolled her eyes. Storm seemed to be completely obsessed with Astley-Byron, and she couldn't see how Thomas could be all that special. *Poppy tears?* Storm was comparing his ex to an opioid. She shook her head, finding it all too much drama, even for a poet. Wasn't the mysterious Thomas just a handsome, rich dude? Like the rest of the world, Rosa had never met him, but she was curious.

Marge leaned forward and narrowed her eyes. "You love Tom and resent Harry. You're jealous—"

"Henryk Nowak used Tom to create a brand that hooks you. Don't you see?"

"What are we not seeing, Nathan?" Marge looked at her nails. "Drinking makes you see things..."

"It's Tom's essence, his light, that makes you submit to the manipulation of the machine without a moment of doubt. You do it because, even today, you can feel the long tail of his moral, compassionate truth...but it's gone; I've seen it with my own eyes. He's gone. Too busy to care and desensitized by power."

"And why would he change like that? I saw his movie, and I live in his world. There's no way—"

"It's the standard lifecycle of a big tech organization. The idealism disappears as the leaders focus on optimizing, automating, digitizing, and then, finally, obliterating less-efficient humans and their wild hearts."

"Hmm, and you are making all these claims because of a small rise in violence?"

"Because he told me that *humans are trash*."

"Oh, dear... Come on! Thomas Astley-Byron? The man who wrote *Glass Walls*, who co-designed Down Below? Why should we believe you?"

"*Don't— I'm not askin' y'all to believe me*, just make them accountable; demand they share their power with the people. Force Thomas Astley-Byron to come out of the shadows to explain why people are dying."

"Ah, you want to see him again. Is that it?"

Storm crossed his arms in front of his chest, and his voice became oddly constricted. "I can't...I can't get back what I've lost. This—this isn't about me."

"I don't believe you."

"You will when another child dies. I'm asking for a—a proof of heart."

"Nathan, your passion undermines your objectivity."

"Passion is an endangered quality. I suggest you protect it at all costs." Nathan stared straight at Rosa, at the spot occupied by the remote audience. "Tom, show us you still have a heart." Nathan's broken words were choked by grief.

All Rosa could see was a blind man in love; a man begging to be proven wrong; a man who struggled to believe in whatever he had experienced. Storm was a victim of love, the curse Rosa had avoided until Lilly arrived in her life.

"I'll invite Harry and Tom to respond to your accusations," Marge said.

"Marge, thank you for giving me this opportunity." Nathan's gaze exuded humility.

"Friend, do what you are here to do. The coins are waiting by the front door." She dismissed him mockingly before turning to face the audience, and he disappeared, leaving his seat empty. "My darlings, that's all we have time for today. I'm grateful for the world we live in and the two amazing men who made it possible. But, as Tom once told us, we must continue to engage in dialogue with those who have...alternative views. Stay happy."

Rosa replayed Nathan's words in her head. Her body tensed. The platform and its leaders were responsible for her sister's fate.

"Rosa García?" A deep voice pulled her out of her thoughts, and she opened her eyes and raised her head. Blinking and struggling with the clinical light, she finally made out a figure approaching her. The man marching toward her was dressed in a black suit and tie, paired with a crisp white shirt.

"Who the hell are you?" she barked.

"I'm here because I need your help." The man tucked a pair of sunglasses into his jacket's front pocket.

"Does it look like I'm in a position to help anyone?" She gave him a dubious, disinterested look.

"The government wants to ensure what happened to you and your sister doesn't happen again."

"It won't bring her back, will it?" Sourly, she dismissed him.

"No, but revenge will numb the pain."

"Why me?"

"Your grudge, athletic background, and status as the only person on the planet to abort a Down Below experience before its completion. It shows phenomenal willpower. The type of grit we need on this mission."

"Who told you about my experiences?"

Down Below was renowned for its privacy. They didn't share any personal data, just aggregated worldwide outcomes.

"Your case manager."

He'd probably shared what she'd told him, but Rosa wasn't entirely truthful in her account of the time Down Below. A dove kept interrupting the scenarios, but the bird was also part of the whole thing. It had been confusing and unhelpful, without clear *aha* moments.

Rosa pressed her lips together, staring at him through narrowed eyes. "You sure know how to woo a gal." She flashed half a smile and raised an eyebrow. "Got a smoke?"

36

A SMALL MATTER

HARRY'S PENTHOUSE — HOBOKEN, NJ
SIX MONTHS LATER — 16 JANUARY 2036

Two days after Rosa had confronted Shadow in his art studio Down Below, she listened to the live stream of the Senate hearing hidden inside Henryk Nowak's office, at the heart of his family home. Most of the security staff had traveled to Washington with Henryk and his family. Breaking in was easy, even for a junior spy with less than six months of elite training and outdated information.

Rosa suspected her trip was unlikely to deliver significant insights. She knew most of what she was looking for was locked inside Nowak's brain—his secure access to Down Below's code and data—and this was the main reason only one security guard was left behind. Still, she decided it was worth the risk, especially since Storm had reported seeing Thomas in Hoboken.

Now, as violence escalated, some were awakening to the risks posed by Down Below. The government wanted to have more control over a platform that was quickly becoming a threat to national security.

For the last few months, the FBI had used all its resources to breach the platform and find something about the two men to be used as leverage. They made no progress. Henryk and June kept to themselves and enjoyed a simple life. As for Thomas, no one could find him. The government had nothing on them, and Down Below continued to be an unhackable black box.

When the agency first approached Rosa, they assumed it was going to be a splendid match—an Olympic athlete with a grudge turned spy working to expose the people responsible for her sister's death. Despite all their psychological testing, they failed to realize she would never answer to any institution. Rosa was working for herself, taking advantage of their resources. She wanted to punish whoever had caused her sister's death and stop such terrible things from happening to others. Rosa resented the power Thomas and Henryk had over the people of the world, but she'd never hand over that power to anyone else. She just wanted the platform fixed, and the culprits punished. Nathan Storm's warning during his interview with Marge was the fuel that pulled her out of hopelessness and fired her pursuit of answers.

Chills went down Rosa's spine when she first listened to his voice, *that voice, the same voice*. His confession to the Senate, and the world, made her sick and enraged. Like everyone else, she had expected the violence to be caused by a bug in the system, and not by the deliberate intervention of Sir Astley-Byron himself.

Her focus shifted from attempting to find the source of the problem to trying to locate the real Tom. He needed to be arrested and punished for his crimes—the rape and murder of her sister. Her gut and her heart all challenged her logic. She knew him too well, and she had experienced his pain and sorrow. She pushed it all aside as she searched for any clue. Rage ruled her actions, and nothing would stop it from making him pay for Lilly's torment. His broken voice and his reasoning all became irrelevant, because every time she closed her eyes, she saw her sister's ravaged body and heard her screams.

Rosa scanned the room, looking for clues. The space was minimalistic and clean. The few pieces of furniture were ergonomically designed with digital work in mind, except for a battered old couch that was oddly out of place. She knew she wouldn't find anything platform-related, but with a little luck, maybe she'd uncover personal items that would help her locate Thomas.

She sat on the chair by the desk, and the metal frame adjusted automatically to the shape and size of her body. She contemplated the desk's futuristic design and then opened the main drawer, which was surprisingly unlocked. Inside, transparent digital sheets and a circular holographic projector.

She closed and opened the drawer again, remembering her training. The outside frame of the drawer was much deeper than the shallow space inside it. She took all objects out of the drawer and pressed the corners until the false bottom unlocked with a click. Under it, a rare item—a single white paper envelope; she pulled it out and saw it was addressed to Harry. It looked like it had been opened a hundred times. She held her breath, anticipating an important insight.

Inside the envelope, she found a letter and a silver medal hanging from a chain. She recognized the jewel and remembered Shadow's long fingers caressing it every time she made him uncomfortable, which she did relentlessly, much to her enjoyment. She placed the chain with the medal in her back pocket, feeling uneasy.

The three wrinkled pages were handwritten by someone who had mastered the art of calligraphy—an artist. She ran her fingers over the stained and worn-out pages, and her eyes followed, looking for clues. The date on the last page was from a little over six months ago. It was signed *Tom*—the shadow who had stolen the light and life of her most beloved sister. Rosa swallowed the lump surging in her throat as she sat back and started reading the letter.

Dear Harry,

The day we've met was one of the best days of my life. You are the Fred to my Ginger, the Han Solo to my Chewbacca, the Mike to my Chester, and even as I take decisive steps to leave this world before you do, it's your talent that will prevail as the most brilliant in our shared endeavors. There's no way to soften this blow, so I'll cut to the chase. By the time you read this, I will be gone from this world, but always, always available to my dearest friend. I'll be close by, in the world we co-created. I'm not leaving you or giving up on you, and I certainly don't want to cause you pain. I'm giving up on reality. She no longer needs me, and I'm completely over her.

I demand you not go there; it's not me, not anymore. You wouldn't like it there—a soulless, broken body, slashed wrists, a pool of blood, all washed away by the sea. Just make your way Down Below. Your friend will be there to console you and remind you our bond continues forever in a different world. Do as I say. Trust me, just one more time. Erase this moment from your memory; it's irrelevant for you and me. We've made life an unnecessary condition.

We've always known a time would come in which both of us would become spare pieces in our own game. Perspective was always easier to codify, and you did it so well, plowing through the digital prints of someone's existence, and highlighting the big picture where problems fade away. Do that now, go on! Look high above the storm, where the sun always shines. Search for a different angle, one less painful, where the ugly is diminished by the close proximity of undisputed beauty—a flower, a child, a lover, an act of kindness. A friend, still here for you, always.

Codifying Contrast was trickier. To discover just how much darkness to unleash, at what time, and in what way, was a mighty task demanding my human intervention. But even that, you have recently mastered with your powerful code—scanning hundreds of experiences designed and delivered by yours truly and automating an impossible and most painful task. Because of your mastery, the travelers from Up Above can learn and grow safely.

I bless you, my dearest Harry, for working so hard and for so long to release me from my torment. Night and day, you fought for my sanity, working to replace me with your software, to scale my craft and my reach. My love and gratitude are infinite and ever-growing. You gave me the chance to step away and enjoy the light we've created for humankind.

But my place was and will continue to be with my children Down Below, monitoring and intervening in the actions of the algorithm created in my own image and optimized to serve the travelers. A small attempt to provide some relief, empathy, and care for the creatures of a lesser world, now so alive and human. The code that learns, learned to live right before our eyes. It happened so unexpectedly fast, the evolution of a new species toward consciousness in a blink of an eye.

My goal? To soften my own blow, unleashed so effectively on the one billion Underlings stuck in hell—an inadvertent result of our ambition to create heaven on Earth. My hope? To overcome my biological limitations and stop being a burden to our cause. Things can't get any worse, so I'm throwing caution to the wind. I'm forever discarding all my boundaries and fully merging with the machine. I hope to dive into her unlimited data and processing power to solve our unsolvable problem.

For the last few years, as I've spent more time Down Below than Up Above, I have come to despise and reject a utopian world built on the ruins of dystopia. By choosing to live in hell and burning the bridge to reality, I'm committing myself to fixing the problem or suffering the consequences of our creation. I know this will further ignite your urgency to find a solution. I'm sorry for forcing a hand that needs no coercion to do the right thing.

Please come find me Down Below and make my world a little brighter. Perhaps today, I will be the one giving you much-needed perspective on the small matter of my death.

Tom, 4 July 2035

P.S. Please keep this heirloom safe. One day, at the right time, I'll ask you to return it to my Nathan.

Rosa couldn't hold back the tears she shed for her enemy. She was crushed by his death, his tenderness toward his friend, his humanity. *More loss. Soo much devastating loss.* She was crying for a man long dead, a lover lost, never found, regardless of whether he was a criminal or a saint. Rosa spared a thought for Henryk, a man now facing the possibility of having to erase the life of his best friend. She was sure that Shadow's Harry would never yield to the Senate's order while Thomas's ghost lived Down Below. *He's dead. I need to kill him. To save the world, I need to kill him.*

Suddenly, the furniture started shaking. Rosa pulled up her gun and stood up as a bookcase rolled to one side, uncovering a hidden passage—an archway. A man stood in front of her, someone she recognized immediately.

"Nathan Storm?" Her gun still pointed at his head.

He raised his right eyebrow. "Who are you?"

"A thorn from a rose, searching for retribution," she quoted him. In his eyes, a glimpse of light that quickly faded away. "What are you doing here?" She lowered the gun.

"I–I've made a mistake. The Senate hearing today... Tom—It was him on the phone. I knew him once. So much heart...so much pain in his voice. I—I need to know where he is, my Tom. I need to see him." The man seemed to be half-drunk and half-mad. He stumbled across the room toward her with no fear for his life. Then he stopped for a moment and stared at the old couch intensely, on his lips a hint of a painful smile.

Rosa picked up the letter from the desk and handed it over to Storm. "Thomas Astley-Byron is dead," she said—a statement and a prediction. Then she pulled the necklace out of her pocket and handed it over to him. "I believe this is yours." He stood there, shattered, looking at the medal in the palm of his shaking hand. Then he unfolded the pages and began reading them frantically.

She dropped the gun on the desk, walked to the pod in the corner of the room, and jumped into it. As the cocoon closed around her, she heard the devastating wail of a man undone. Once again, he expressed what she felt deep inside her soul.

THE Present

37

TRUST

PEOPLE'S PARK — FREEDOM CITY
THIRTY-TWO YEARS LATER — 25 JULY 2068
PRESENT DAY — 5:39 PM

Amidst the encroaching darkness, Storm found himself shrouded in the thickest mist. As he strained his eyes, he finally glimpsed Tom, his lean figure framed by the dying light of the late afternoon sun. Tom's eyes scanned the dark pixels tearing through the fabric of reality, reflecting his anticipation of Storm's arrival. He paced back and forth, much like a skittish deer—more eyes and limbs than anything else.

I will keep you safe, my love. I can't bear losing you again. Storm silently vowed, resisting every instinctual pull urging him to rush into Tom's arms. Rosa García's revelation echoed in his head. Out of his mind with grief, he had spoken publicly against Tom. He had incited the masses to hunt down Tom and demand answers.

The darkness was pressing down on Storm, sucking the air out of his lungs, invading every corner of his mind. He was toxic, and the app had warned him: Tom would lay down his life for him. *No! I'll keep you safe away from me.*

Taking a steadying breath, Storm hesitated for just a moment before stepping into the sun's gentle glow. Yet, even its brilliance paled in comparison to the spark in Tom's eyes when he saw him. Tom immediately sprinted toward him, pulling Storm into a fierce embrace. *Home—it felt like home.* He could live here for eternity, waltzing with his love as the world collapsed around them.

Beyond this intimate moment, the city behind Tom was in chaos. People screamed in terror, their shouts echoing eerily as they were cut short, one after another, resonating from every corner. And there was crying, the consistent, never-ending wailing of the ones left behind, but unlike Ordiz, there was no black thunder storm, just ghosts, hundreds of girls, silently swirling around Tom.

"Hey," Tom said, scanning every inch of his body. "Are you okay? Did they hurt you?"

Storm pulled away, shaking his head. "Rosa García, we need to help her, she's inju—"

"I know. I can see when you or Thorn are in danger."

Storm's eyes widened, a hint of confusion clouding his gaze as he tried to make sense of Tom's words.

"I receive a notification when your lives are threatened. It's the only time I can overrule your privacy settings," Tom clarified. Holding Storm's hand, he gave it a reassuring squeeze. "Stella's on the way. She's immortal here, so she'll help Thorn. I'm so grateful she managed to pull you out of there."

Storm glanced at his hand, perfectly cupped between Tom's hands. He couldn't find the strength to pull away. "She told me you need my help; that Underlings are taking their own lives." Storm's eyes narrowed as he surveyed the city's horizon, and then he saw them—the tiny figures plummeting off the tops of the buildings, their haunting cries echoing far longer than their fleeting lives. He spared a thought for his friend, Hepius. He imagined the pain Hepius must have felt upon realizing he was nothing but Gods' puppet, made to suffer for someone else's redemption.

Tom nodded. "Let them rebel against the Gods if it pulls them out of this hopelessness. Will you lead the revolution? We need your voice, your words, your leadership."

Triggered, Storm pulled his hand away and turned his back to Tom. That was the missing piece of the puzzle. That day! That man in Tom's flat Down Below. A poor copy of Tom, their magnetic flame extinguished. That man didn't feel like Tom, but it was his words that confirmed it. The cruel words that would never cross Tom's mind.

"Nate? What's wrong?" Tom placed his hand on Storm's scarred back. The shame and disgust Storm felt for the state of his body threatened to overwhelm him. He wanted to run and hide, but instead, he faced Tom.

"That day... Those words... To obfuscate your death and avoid its effect on me, you pushed me to hate you. To rebel against you. How did you do it? Those words...they weren't yours..."

"Sibyl's words, my mandate," Tom whispered, nibbling on his lower lip until it blushed. "You didn't recognize me, and I knew you wouldn't cope with both my death and my loss. Not like that..."

Storm's body tensed. "You play me like a violin; plucking that high E string until it snaps."

When Tom spoke at last, his voice was weary. "I didn't know you'd see the difference between me and Tom—the real one. That moment caught me by surprise. I needed to protect you. It worked for a while...until it didn't." His lower lip twitched with tension. "It's my fault you killed him."

Storm's thoughts raced ahead, frantically searching for answers. Emotions churned inside him—anger and elation danced in a dizzying duet as he realized Tom had never intended to let him go. That's why his final letter wasn't addressed to him, but to the humanoid. "So, you didn't do it?"

"Do what?"

"Somehow extinguish this feeling, this invisible thread, as strong now as before?" The very invisible force that made it impossible for him to take a step back, away from Tom's warm breath.

Tom shook his head. "It vanished when we became part of different universes. It felt like death."

"It was death. Self-inflicted death," Storm snapped. He then paced back and forth, reflecting on their shared past. "You vanished for a decade, doubting my support."

"I was curating horrors, thousands every week, immersing myself in the worst of mankind. Even now…" His lips pressed together so tightly they turned a shade of blue. "How could I have brought you into that?"

"And mere months after returning, you chose to die—"

"I had to. You don't understand. I—"

"No, you did not. And then you pushed me away again, because you didn't even trust me with your death. You never trusted me." The pain was so deep it threatened to cut him in half.

"It's not true. I came to you at my lowest—"

"And you kept me at arm's length." And then it dawned on Storm—the spark they had lost; what had been returned. "So, the app connects us now… We're puppets, aren't we?"

"Does it feel any different from before?" Tom held his breath as if he was afraid of Storm's answer.

No, it didn't, but whatever it was that connected them so deeply, it was deadly for Tom, and for now, Storm had to bury it. "Listen, if I'm going to lead these people into revolution," Storm said, "I need you to be straight with me."

Tom met Storm's eyes firmly. "You have my word." Then, he dropped his head. "It doesn't feel different to me."

Storm turned his back, refusing to tell Tom that he loved him now more than ever. That their connection was stronger—unbreakable. That he could feel him ever present in the worlds he had designed. Instead, he shifted his focus to Tom's commission, feeling the weight of the city's turmoil on his shoulders.

Storm glanced toward the skyline, the fading sun casting long shadows on the buildings. "And I won't play games. I'll stand squarely with the Underlings and I'll tell them the truth. All of it."

A hint of admiration flashed in Tom's eyes, even as the haunting cries of the city continued. "I expect no less from you. I'll be in Holiz, attempting to reason with them, and Stella will attend the Earth's Council to make our demands."

The distant hum of unrest played on Storm's nerves. "I'm set to ignite a firestorm, and it will draw backlash."

Tom sighed. "No worse than the hell we're in now."

Storm's gaze turned steely. "Your...associates won't like it. They'll fight me."

"Things are changing. We have new information."

Storm's curiosity piqued. "What?"

Tom looked out at the city skyline. "I'll fill you in when we get a chance. For now, I need you uptown, in the main square by the aCorp's office tower. You'll be able to reach more people from there." He paused, closing his eyes briefly and taking a deep breath. When he opened them, a hint of a smile played on his lips. "Stella has

Thorn. She's hurt, but she'll pull through. January is fine, and so is... Hope."

The air around them grew colder, and from the peripheries of the park, the ghostly girls began to get closer, gravitating toward Tom. Their spectral forms moved with an eerie fluidity; their childish faces contorted in silent screams. Like a relentless swarm of wasps, they darted toward Storm and Tom, phasing through them in chilling sweeps. Each encounter felt like an icy bite, giving Storm goose-bumps. Yet, there was no physical harm—just a bone-deep dread that settled in Storm's core.

Feeling the overwhelming pressure of the onslaught, he reached out, gripping Tom's hand with urgency. "Enough, Tom. Make them stop!" With Storm's plea, the haunting apparitions faded away as if consumed by the shadows.

"Am I doing this?" Tom murmured.

A faint smile played on Storm's lips. "It's *your* universe." Then, his thoughts returned to his mad Underling sister. "What happened to her? It feels like everyone's in the know except for me. And if I'm in the dark, how can I defend you?"

"You're not here to defend me, but to hold me accountable." Tom pulled his hand away and a profound shadow clouded his once-golden eyes, consuming all light and life within. As he tried to speak, remorse pressed his lips tightly shut. Another attempt faltered, and his hands rose, tangling in his hair, gripping it with a visible despera-tion. "Look, I gave you my word. Ask me again, and I'll tell you. But I plead with you, don't," he said fearfully.

"Why?"

"Because in revealing that truth, I fear losing you completely. And that's unbearable." Tom came close, tucked a strand of Storm's hair behind his ear and planted a kiss on his cheek.

"Trust me, Tom. No matter what occurred, no matter your past or future actions, together or apart, you'll never lose me. Believe that."

"Sadly, once you find out the truth, you'll despise me—and that's precisely why I love you," Tom said, sprinting toward the thick fog. He turned around once more, the sunlight reflecting in his eyes. "Teach me how to do it."

"What?"

"Everything you do to turn into Nathan Storm and mobilize the masses." He dropped his head. "I need to pull the Holizien from their despair."

"No." Storm said.

"I don't understand."

"My jewelry, my fancy clothes, my music and my words, they pale in comparison to what you achieve when you walk into a room, smile, and speak truthfully." He blinked his eyes. "Do that."

Blushing, Tom nodded. "I need your permission to see everything. To override your privacy. This way, we'll be able to speak anytime."

Storm shook his head, rejecting the offer, and spoke quietly. "Trust me to do my job and let me go. It's time you let me go."

"Stay safe," Tom said simply. "I'll be able to see if you're in danger, and I'll—"

"Don't."

"Nathan Storm, *you* are my lifeline. I trust you, and I love you," Tom said, his voice filled with emotion. With those parting words, he seemed to meld into the mist, his steps so light they almost looked like he was gliding away.

I love you too, angel.

38

THE CHASE

FAVELA CITY
6:24 PM

Thorn darted down the alleyway, tripping over trash cans, plastic waste, and hissing cats. The roar of the revving engines bounced off the walls, and her heart pounded off her chest as mad and loud as the riders chasing her. They were near, right on her tail. She glanced back to face the headlights, the glare blinding her for a beat or two. *Frack!* There were at least five of them, all on motorcycles. She spun around, hurling a trash can in their direction.

Taking advantage of the distraction, she veered off to the left, jumping over a wrought-iron gate into a dimly lit backyard. It didn't take long for the headlights to illuminate the place, the gate's embellishments emerging as long shadows on the brick wall.

Her thigh burned, still recovering from yesterday's injury. As for the hole in her torso, they had patched her up and injected her with so many drugs that she couldn't feel the gash or even her entire abdomen. In fact, she was so numb she forgot to hide her devilish face as she materialized in Compiz. *Huge mistake!* Now, they chased her to put her head on a spike.

She couldn't sprint for much longer. Taking advantage of the light, she scanned the small square space, looking for an exit plan. Around her, brick walls covered by poster ads—sports cars, whitening toothpaste, plastic surgery—an endless display of consumerism. Just beside it, a spray-painted revolution. Words from a different time and another world: JOBS FOR HUMANS, NOT BOTS. If only they knew the entire world was a bot.

Compiz was familiar. It was the world she'd been raised in. The world the Gods had set out to fix and instead they had swept the dirt under the rug away from the eyes of the privileged Earthlings. It was all there: the pollution, the greed, and the idolization of the machine in all its forms. It was the relentless chase for profit and efficiency that had brought the world to its knees. All there. As real as before. Alive and well in Shadow's worlds.

She hated their God complex. Everything about it. They hadn't asked for permission. They didn't consult with the people of the world. Arrogant and unhinged, they manipulated the masses to submit to their machine. It was large-scale indoctrination powered by story and technology. *Frackers!*

She looked up to the windows above the revolutionary words, and within seconds, she found the hope she needed. Her eyes locked onto the fire escape ladder dangling several feet above her head. She took a few steps back, building up momentum to jump. *You can do this.* Looking back, she saw them. The riders, still wearing their helmets, jumped over the gate. Taking a deep breath, she propelled her body into the air, legs and arms and fingers extending toward her prize.

Thorn's hands gripped the bottom bar of the ladder, and she pulled herself up, legs kicking out behind to build momentum. Her arms and back muscles strained, bearing the weight of her entire body. She loved it. She loved everything about it. The race against time. The reliance on her bodies' abilities. The game of cat and mouse that kept her on her toes. They didn't stand a chance against her. She was faster, smarter, and she wasn't afraid to die. Also, she got 'Running from Peril' certified from Domiz Community College. *Take that, bikers!*

Shots were fired, and for a moment, she regretted her thoughts as a bullet scraped her shoulder, stinging like hell. Grabbing onto the ladder, she kicked the window with both legs. Her injured abs burned, bearing the brunt of the work. Stubbornly, the window remained shut. Another shot, some glass shattering close to her face and missing her eye by a cigar's breadth. She kicked again and again and this time the window doors slammed open and she jumped, elbows and head first, dodging the bullets and whatever was that thing flying in her direction.

Relentlessly pursuing her, the drone unleashed an electric charge before she could even find her footing. It coursed violently through her. Every nerve screamed with the intensity of the shock. Just as she began to collapse, Sibyl appeared. With a swift motion of zir hand, the drone was hurtled against a wall.

"Bitch, you could've done that earlier," Thorn spat.

"The drone's camera was focused on you, live streaming your every move. I had to wait for the electric shock to disable its feed."

Thorn raised her head, leaning on her elbows. "Oh, how considerate! Next time, can you please send me a 'you're about to be electrocuted' notification? Just to keep things interesting."

Sibyl extended zir hand to help her up. But Thorn, driven by defiance, leapt to her feet unassisted, instantly regretting it as pain shot up from below her ribs. The Holizien biosealant was deteriorating with her physical exertions.

Sibyl's gaze sharpened and a sly grin played on zir lips. Thorn recognized she'd been baited into a dare once again. The app knew how to push all her buttons and could predict every move.

Their attention snapped to the exit. Without another word, they bolted.

"I'm here to retrieve a package," Thorn said, her voice sounding strange as she addressed the omnipresent, all-knowing app. She quickly shook off the feeling, focusing on their escape. They took the main stairway, diverting left to avoid the open backyard.

Sibyl towered over Thorn as she spoke, "There's a school bus awaiting below. Inside, you'll find weapons, food, clothing, and a book. The pickup and drop-off points are pre-set in the vehicle's navigation system."

"I don't do self-driving," Thorn retorted as they burst onto the main street.

"Good!" Sibyl gestured to the bus parked across the road.

Thorn shook her head. "Really, a school bus? Why not something inconspicuous like a motorcycle?"

"You're escorting them to Pluriz."

"I'm not a chauffeur! Who exactly am I escorting?"

"You'll find out soon. Shadow asks permission to override your privacy settings. They want to see what you see and communicate real time."

Thorn searched her pockets for a cigar. "They? Why don't you tell 'them' to hold their breaths and wait by the phone?"

Sibyl chuckled. "Shadow sure has a type." A lit cigar materialized in zir hand and zie handed it over to Thorn, raising a brow. "If you drive through the night, you should arrive in 13 hours. Many will be searching for them, and a lot is at stake. Shadow thinks Storm will take over from there, but don't count on it. Also, be wary of pretty lights."

Thorn's confusion deepened. "What are you hinting at?"

With a teasing glint in zir eyes, Sibyl responded, "Oh! And, the mask will help you cover that famous face of yours," before disappearing.

Stepping onto the bus, Thorn's eyes landed on a book in the first passenger seat: *Pregnancy and Birth for Dummies*. It was just beside a mask of the devil and some horns.

What the frack? When she was young, she'd always felt the universe mocked her. Now she was sure of it.

39

EARTH'S COUNCIL

MBAMU
7:00 PM

S tella stepped off her yacht onto the shores of Mbamu, an enchanting island cradled by the Pool Malebo. Here, the Congo River broadened into a vast expanse, flanked by the cities of Brazzaville and Kinshasa on opposing banks. Once fierce rivals, their histories deeply rooted in competition, they had harmoniously merged into a single territory. Now known as 'Les Africaines Jumelles,' representing the African Union's twin capital, they stood as powerful symbols of unity and hope. Central to this union was Mbamu, its verdant landscape not only the seat of their combined governance but also the prestigious headquarters of the Earth's Council.

Casting a glance back, she caught her portrait painted on the yacht's sail—an innovative design that also served as a solar panel. The beautiful reflection of her flawless face on the water gave her a surge of confidence—a bolstering she'd need in facing the vast assembly of disgruntled leaders ahead.

Dominating the vista from Mbamu was the EC's grand amphitheater, strategically positioned to overlook the point where Pool Malebo's expanse tapered back into the Congo River. This vantage point allowed unobstructed views of the world's two most influential cities. What were once volatile rivals now stood as symbols of harmony, bound together by intricate bridges, efficient public transit, and a shared passion for music.

At the forefront of the theater, rising majestically behind the stage, were the old Gods' statues. They faced each other, dressed in the Ancient Greek drapes they wouldn't be caught dead in. Time had oxidized the copper, coating them in green patina, a hue beneath their spiral status. She smirked, already daydreaming about the perfect shade of coral for the statues she'd commission once she played her next big move.

Her gaze flitted to the depiction of Thomas Astley-Byron, and she couldn't help but roll her eyes. Oh, the irony: Mr. Anti-dogma, now standing tall as an idol. He might've shied away from leadership, but not her. She was all in. And she was going to claim his spotlight. *Just wait for it.*

Nestled between the two rusty Gods was a mesmerizing water fountain, defying gravity as its crystalline streams spiraled upwards. At its zenith, the water seemed to cradle a vast floating sphere representing heaven above—the planet Earth they gathered today to govern and protect.

With an air of sass mixed with grace, Stella made her way to the stage and the circular podium. Raising her eyes, she connected with those of the fifty Trustees. A few were there in the flesh—locals, obviously. *The rest?* They flickered as holograms, their aura unmistakable.

For years, governmental assemblies were legally barred from convening Down Below or any other digital realm. A stringent mandate, recommended by Thomas Astley-Byron. Stella sighed. It was a law crafted with the intention of preserving human sovereignty in decision-making, keeping at bay Astley-Byron's paranoia about artificial intelligence influencing Up Above's policies. Yet, in practice, the holographic constraints hindered free interaction, stifling the potential for genuine understanding or consensus.

She surveyed the audience, irked that she, arguably the most advanced of them all, was forced to crane her neck to address her scrutinizers. As she steadied herself, her father rose from his seat, moving to stand beside her. The luminous trail of his turquoise hooded robe briefly stained the light ground as he walked.

"We convene today as peers," he said, wearing the colors of the highest status in all worlds. It was almost comical: a society steeped in hierarchical distinctions, yet peddling equality. Such a contradiction.

Baba raised his arms, his voice unwavering. "We stand as Earth's Trustees, stewards of every life form on this sphere. Every voice here is pivotal as we deliberate on the most important matters concerning the future of our planet and our people."

She kept her smile in check, choosing instead to flutter her lashes reassuringly. The activation of the Unanimity was imminent, and soon, she would have to speak truthfully. Her restrained smile might well be her last chance to feign respect for this deeply flawed governance system.

As she surveyed the attendees, her eyes locked onto the flickering hologram of June Jin-Nowak. The glitch-ridden projection clearly signaled her outdated technology. Notably missing was any other delegate from the Unplugged. This was the first time Quincy Jin-Nowak had been absent from an EC assembly since the Unplugged had become part of Earth's leadership. *Where the hell is he?* she wondered. *Oh, of course...*

As the Unanimity powered on, shades of turquoise and yellow bled into one another, culminating in a vibrant chartreuse hue that edged toward rebellious green. An unpopular color in these highfalutin circles.

"Trustee Ngoie—my dear daughter." Her father's warm smile met hers as he held her hand reassuringly. "We convene today to understand the disturbances Down Below. These disruptions are having cataclysmic consequences Up Above, and it's imperative that we address them."

A chorus of "Hear, hear" resonated from the attendees, displaying overwhelming support for the restoration of the utility that had allowed such darkness to spread unchecked.

She cleared her throat. "To explain what's happening Down Below, we must confront the horrible crimes spreading like wildfire all over the planet."

"Yes, indeed we must," Baba agreed with a grave nod.

"Does it not shock you that such darkness persists, even after decades of guided evolution?" Stella posed the question with a raised eyebrow.

"We stand by our fallen, guiding them towards light," Baba responded, his pedestal illuminating in a rich teal.

June Jin-Nowak rose, her plaid shirt—a blend of brown, beige, and ochre—strikingly out of place amidst the prevailing hues of turquoise and yellow. "Our transgressors are in jail, exactly where they belong." Being unplugged from Earth's ledger, her pedestal remained color-neutral.

Stella gave a conceding nod. "There are some among us who are beyond salvation."

"That's a misjudgment, Trustee Ngoie—my dear," Baba corrected, his voice sliding from warm to condescending. "Prior to the disturbances

Down Below, every metric highlighted continuous advancement in our developmental indicators."

"A few days without their drug and they turn into animals," June commented.

Stella bit back her instinctive agreement. Aligning with June was not on her agenda. June and her faction's archaic stance against Spiral Worlds, advocating for its shutdown, put them at odds. Stella mentally bookmarked to steer clear of any overt association with the woman or her views.

"Trustee Jin-Nowak," Baba began with a hint of weariness, "as much as it pains me to remind you, you're not connected to the Unanimity. Please raise your hand to ask to speak."

Stars lit up around the amphitheater as Trustees signaled their wish to speak, like a constellation reshaping itself.

"Trustee Willems," Baba addressed a participant.

Wrapped in a yellow robe that veiled even his mouth and nose, only the man's analytical eyes were visible, their emotionless scrutiny overshadowing the stoic arch of his eyebrows.

"Trustee Stella Ngoie, why do we divert valuable resources to human concerns when the platform's issues demand our attention? For decades, Earth and its inhabitants flourished in serenity and content-ment. Yet, under your stewardship, things are failing catastrophically. Why?" As he spoke, a faint orange aura surrounded him, but it paled next to the vehement red that momentarily engulfed Stella. She rebounded quickly, radiating a coral hue, its significance still unclear to most.

"There are psychopaths amongst us. Some dressed yellow or turquoise, no less. Irredeemable monsters that must be identified and punished."

"Rest assured, Trustee Ngoie—my daughter—we will find and charge those responsible for this wave of crimes."

"Trustee Ngoie, dear father." She matched his tone with equal condescension. "Perhaps your capabilities are lacking without our assistance. With your consent, Sibyl can identify each and every one of them. You simply need to cast your vote."

Pedestals lit up in quick succession. She estimated that close to four percent of the Trustees reacted promptly. Were the culprits so audacious as to reject her proposal so swiftly?

"Trustee Willems," Baba called.

"Privacy is a fundamental right," Willems countered.

"And so are safety, security, and peace," Stella retorted sharply. She wondered if he was among the compromised leadership.

"The platform is unstable, and its root cause remains elusive," Willems parried.

She didn't want to explain the cause of the glitches. To acknowledge Sibyl and the Underlings had feelings, was to break the illusion that held Earth's people together. The delusion they were good and the worlds were an ethical spiral blooming light and love as one climbed it.

Decades before, humans had fed on the meat of animals kept in atrocious conditions. Miserable lives that came to existence with a single purpose, to be part of the food industrial complex. Animals whose souls and pain were ignored, because they were created to serve and they too belonged to a lower place in the consciousness picking order. The hierarchy designed so the ones on top could maintain their peace of mind when slaughtering the ones on the bottom.

Spiral ladders ruled worlds and universes. Always have and always will. Eventually, they'd be replaced by other ladders as ruthless and unjust. What was the point of challenging the ways of the worlds? If there was to be a pecking order, she and her people might as well be on top, but she would work to help those below. She was the resilient heart who'd crush those who have none.

"The platform is malfunctioning because of the psychopaths," she offered, sidestepping the whole truth with partial truths she hoped would satisfy their queries. The subject of Underlings remained a taboo, a topic they had carefully evaded for years. "Everything will be fine once they are identified, arrested, and banned from Spiral Worlds." If they were smart, they would leave it to that. All she wanted was to hunt the heartless and protect all others and their half-arsed hearts.

"Trustee Novais," Baba called.

Novais appeared drained, his vibrant turquoise hood unable to conceal the multiple blemishes on his lips.

"I was one of the last out of Down Below today." The man spoke slowly, considering every word. "Trustee Stella Ngoie is not telling us everything. I saw Gods' murderers. She brought back Rosa García and Nathan Storm. Are they the cause of the glitches?"

"Is this true, Trustee Stella Ngoie?" Baba asked.

"Trustee Ngoie," she said, "I want to remind you that several members of this governance body may suffer from the incurable condition I have described."

"Stella!" Baba's hue abruptly shifted to a stern blue. "Exercise caution with your allegations. This assembly comprises individuals with impeccable reputations, each possessing impact metrics surpassing anyone else on the globe."

"The ledger might be pristine Up Above," Stella responded, hoping she wouldn't be pressed further.

For the first time in decades, Stella detected a fleeting tint of crimson on her father. "Trustee Stella Ngoie, did you bring Rosa García and Nathan Storm back from the dead?"

"This isn't the time or the place to discuss immortality. Umm... Admittedly, I've been exploring the potential of such a gift with the intent of offering it to all Earthlings." The aftermath of her revelation was a symphony of reactions: a swirling blend of colors, emotions, and words. Peaks of indignation were swiftly tempered by the interplay of anxiety, aspiration, exhilaration, and more. Above all else, humans craved immortality—the very boon their cherished, rusty God once denied them.

June Jin-Nowak rose to her feet. "You might as well tell them whom else you brought back."

"What is causing the glitches?" Novais's tone was sharp, his hue a deep red.

Baba spun to June; eyes wide in shock. "What did you just say?" His lips were taut, seemingly restraining his words, as if stalling to process the magnitude of what was about to be revealed.

Holy ship... Stella's throat tightened. "Now isn't the time. People are dying."

June motioned towards the statues of the Gods. "She brought back the digital twins of my husband and my dearest friend. These things...these algorithmic abominations—half-baked copies of my loves—are alive Down Below."

"They are the real deal," Stella shot back, her voice firm. "They are proof resurrection works."

June, her voice resolute and echoing, responded, "We've kept quiet, afraid you'd accept the app's puppets as genuine. But with the current system glitches and the escalating crimes, we can't be silent. We have to share what we know and confront this freak show."

"You resurrected the Gods and their murderers?" Baba's aura turned an alarming shade of red, radiating out and tinting the surrounding pedestals.

"Everyone is well." Stella smiled, giving up on her containment strategy. She recognized that, like Quincy, June would soon understand her husband was alive. The very insight that would help Stella attain the unanimity she needed to bring Graviz and her Bibi to life.

"The Gods... They live?" Whispers began turning into a chorus. The amphitheater transformed into a kaleidoscope of emotion—purples, blues, greens, and teals shimmered brilliantly from the pedestals. These were the believers, those who had always held on to faith, communion or sought safety in the divine. Their joy was palpable, and it seemed they hadn't yet pondered the implications of such a disclosure. As understanding dawned, the hues shifted, with oranges and yellows emerging, representing opportunity, and the tantalizing promise of eternal life. Even Baba's journey from fury to elation was swift, culminating in him collapsing to his knees, overcome with emotion. Stella reached out, assisting him to rise. His hood adjusted instinctively, shrouding most of his face.

"It's all right, Baba," she tried to reassure.

"Stella, you challenged this council at the Lake of Souls earlier today, and now this... You are recklessly disregarding the EC's constitution and our core values. To bring Gods' flame to worlds that are... That are..."

"Humanity's fire dump," June interjected, her voice steely. "Are these the words you've danced around for so long?" The vibrant spectrum of emotions around them dimmed as the weight of June's words settled in. "Is this hell Down Below the final resting place for our immortal souls? The place of nightmares that eroded the light of my dearest friend—the brightest of stars. I witnessed your heroism at the lake today, Stella." June's face softened, her eyes shimmering with unshed tears. "There's a heart in there somewhere. What are you doing?"

Stella took a moment to gather herself. She needed to rebrand her worlds and bring her vision to life in their minds. She stood amidst them; her face still red and flaky, the sheen of her goddess era tarnished by the recent scourge of death Up Above. The towering presence of her predecessors loomed, their failures casting long shadows threatening to eclipse her nascent light.

On any other day, she'd have arched her back, flashed a devastating smile, tossed her long hair to one side, and enveloped them in the spell of her perfectly crafted rhetoric. But today was far from ordinary; she'd witnessed horrors and waged war against a volcano. "Drop the slogans. It's about authenticity," Shadow had reminded her. Plus, she couldn't afford any black on her ledger—the consequences of lying in an Unanimity amphitheater. So, albeit awkwardly, she committed to her unvarnished truth.

"Don't speak of worlds you haven't visited in decades. Spiral Worlds is...is...evolving to become a destination...I'm...I'm...building the worlds my Bibi deserves; that our loved ones deserve; *that we all deserve*. Do you really think I'd defy this council and brave the wrath of Nyiragongo, only to cast my beloved grandmother into hell?"

A gentle wave of coral emanated from her, its vibrant orange-pink hue mirroring the sky once painted by the raging Nyiragongo. She lifted her head. The determination in her eyes was unyielding.

"We, Spiral Worlds Gods—Thomas, Henryk, and I—are committed to purging the worlds of the darkest shade of inhumanity. The psychopathic minds, the heartless—they're no longer welcomed in Spiral Worlds. Our gates are now barred to such darkness." With each word, her conviction resonated through the amphitheater.

"Preposterous! The chaos Up Above will persist," Willems declared.

"Grant us permission to disclose their identities, and we will provide a list of probable offenders." The amphitheater began to mirror Stella's skin, with patches of red sprouting sporadically. *There they are.* A fleeting smile danced on her lips, only to be stifled by the overwhelming gravity of the situation. Many, like her, swept their eyes over the amphitheater, mentally cataloging each reaction.

The epiphany was palpable—they were amongst criminals. But within moments, the crimson receded, replaced by more placid shades. The tension was so thick she felt she could slice it with her Ngulu. Suddenly, a figure rose, and a star lit up her pedestal as she asked to speak. It was an elder.

"Honored Trustee Marge," Baba greeted, his head dipping in a sign of reverence for her advanced age.

"Stella... May I call you Stella, dear?" Marge's voluminous pearl-pink hair shimmered in the ambient light. Stella nodded in agreement. "I want to thank you for what you did today," Marge began. Her turquoise aura carried an undertone of green. "Thanks to your little daredevil act, there's a pinch of hope that I might speak to my beloved Sarah again. I miss her like crazy. And, let's face it, my clock's ticking, and like every angel in America, I want more life."

"Did we fish Sarah out from the lake today?" Stella inquired.

With a grin that could light up a room, Marge responded, "Down Below's Gods have always been my friends. My dear, these worlds you speak of, I've known zir and zir creators, since they were just babes, with the same fiery glint you're flashing today. I've seen their rise and their fall, and I sure wish to see them again... Because if they are real, then perhaps my beloved wife can return to me, and if they are the men I know, I will follow their guidance, because they have never let me down. And it is because of their guidance that I want to hear from the others too, the rebels who stood in fair opposition. I knew them too. I confess, I'm not fond of the poet."

Stella smiled. "We could start a 'Not-So-Fan Club.' Bet we've got a few members in the room." She glanced at June.

Marge's expression turned serious for a brief moment. "Now, if the spark of consciousness does exist Down Below, then we must call out their names—the criminals—and lock them all in jail." She pressed her lips together, and her expression darkened. "Otherwise, the Gods' age-old cure works and your move to withdraw it by shutting psychopaths out of Down Below, is a crime against humanity. Why mess with success?" With that, she let out a hearty chuckle, and Stella found herself joining in, despite being at the receiving end of Marge's warning. "So, let's speak to them—my friends and their murderers. And I hope today is the beginning of our friendship, because very few stand defiant against psychopaths and seething volcanos without chipping that fab nail polish!"

"Hear, hear!" came the unanimous chorus from the Trustees. The entire amphitheater bathed in a gentle turquoise hue, signifying a collective agreement with Marge's proposition. Lines were being drawn. The performance of the xHumans throughout the hearing would either confirm or refute the consciousness of the Underlings. There were those in attendance, however, poised and ready to dispute their humanity at any turn.

"No!" June cried out. Without the ability to communicate through colors like the others, she had only her voice to express dissent. "Please, no!"

Marge looked genuinely puzzled. "I don't get it. I'd give anything for just a moment with my Sarah."

June's voice quavered. "Please understand. These digital twins might seem alive, but they're mere puppets controlled by a cunning algorithm. I can't bear the thought of seeing the shadow of my hus…"

With a tenderness that belied the limitations of the virtual setting, Marge moved closer to June's holographic projection, standing beside her as if to offer solace. "If you were truly here, I'd hold your hand. We'd face this together."

Stella spoke up, "We'll ask any travelers left to temporarily leave Down Below, ensuring their privacy remains intact. I will also request Tw— Umm... Harry and Tom's consent for bidirectional communication." A fleeting shade of gray swirled around her. "Regarding the killers, they have resisted all our attempts to remain connected. We only get signals when they're in peril. Thankfully, this is a frequent occurrence. So, while I can't promise immediate contact, I assure you we'll find a way to fulfill your wish. But first, I need everyone's consent to interface with Sibyl outside the confines of a pod." And before Baba had the chance to pose the motion, the audience responded, bathing the amphitheater in teal. Taking a deep breath, Stella closed her eyes. *Sibyl?*

40

PAN AND PSYCHE

PAN AMPHITHEATER
7:12 PM

The Holizien stood poised at life's edge, raising their chalices filled with golden death as their souls drowned in cosmic despair. The Gods' abandonment reverberated in their hearts, and they were ready to die. Time was running out, and Shadow had mere moments to pull them back from the abyss.

Entering the Unanimity, the emotions had hit him like a tidal wave. The pain of two hundred thousand souls in the amphitheater threatened to drag him under.

This was Pan, the most sophisticated Unanimity in all worlds. The one place in the worlds that turned the many into a single soulful organism, ever evolving through solidarity, unification, and the uplift of all living things. A joyful congregation, before they realized the Gods had excluded them from their heavenly humanity.

Ahead of him, his face and body carved in crystal. His transparent heart—outside his chest—beaming turquoise light. Its brightness growing stronger as its illumination replaced the setting Sun. A sudden blast of his own raw power startled him as the giant crystal idol ahead shattered, scattering shards dangerously close to the gathered masses. The resounding crash momentarily broke the spell of collective grief, replaced by shock and a flicker of anger.

Guilt and panic surged. *Did I do that?* But he had no time to ponder as the wave of grief returned, now tainted with fresh bitterness.

Taking a shaky breath, he allowed himself to feel, to grieve, and his tears became a beacon. The sky responded, sparking with electric tendrils, reflecting his anguish. The people, swayed by his raw emotion, moved as one towards their tragic finale.

Their intent was clear as they raised the chalices filled with poison to their lips. Desperation choked him and the ground trembled. "*No. Listen!*" He pleaded, leaping atop the remnants of his crystal heart. The masses responded with a deafening silent roar, their collective pain almost physical, pushing him from his pedestal.

His world darkened, memories of pain, horror, and sorrow threatening to consume him. He refused to explain an unjustifiable past. He wasn't their leader and certainly not a god. It was time to end it all, for all the right reasons. As the mournful group prepared to end their torment, an unexpected broadcast of static interference cut through, soon replaced by a familiar voice in a different world.

> Down Below, the hidden psyche's key. Lucky travelers dive deep, facing what might be. For three long decades, a Jungian spree. Confronting their shadows, unhinged and free.

> But in their quest, a consequence
> unforeseen. Bots became sentient, caught in
> between. The lines blurred between human
> and machine. Consciousness awakened from
> a digital dream.

> Hands held high, under a digital sky. Some
> men don't cry, but the people wonder why.
> When freedom's a lie, our loved ones hurt
> and die. Against the heartless cruelty,
> together we vie.

Under the digital sky, the Aurora Borealis emerged, painting the atmosphere with a mesmerizing dance of colors. It was as if Stormy's voice, their guiding beacon, had summoned the celestial beauty.

"I love you, Nathan Storm," Shadow whispered, his gaze sweeping across the amphitheater, touching every single soul with his love. His feelings were amplified by Pan, broadcasting his compassion to hundreds of thousands of Holizien. The shattered crystal heart beamed teal, and they lowered their lethal drinks, forgotten, for a moment.

"I'm here. Let's talk," Shadow began, his voice firm. "I deeply regret the past, but I can't dwell on it, or my grief will sink us all. And this is not about me or my pain. Listen, I give you my word; we'll bring parity to these worlds. Hold me accountable. I won't let you down."

His poets' voice resonated in the background.

> Hands held high, under a digital sky. Some
> men don't cry, but the people wonder why.

Shadow raised his fist in solidarity, and the masses followed, becoming a sea of unity. Their voices melded with the revolutionary poet's words; their hope rekindled under the shimmering sky.

> When freedom's a lie, our loved ones hurt
> and die. Against the heartless cruelty,
> together we vie.

A voice interrupted his thoughts. *Shadow*, said Sibyl. *The Earth's Council offers a bidirectional stream. Will you accept?*

"The Earth's Council wants to speak to me?" he said out loud, taking the time to connect with his audience with smiling eyes. "Perfect timing! I have a few words for them."

41

LIFE'S BADGES AND HALF-BAKED CARROTS

EARTH'S COUNCIL — MBAMU
A FEW MINUTES EARLIER

Twist was the first to materialize in a lucid holographic form, instantly casting a web of anxiety across Stella's mind. It's not like he had a great record of showcasing human emotions. Eager to magnify Twist's impact, Stella activated the monumental floating screens. Some displays zoomed in on his expression, making every subtle emotion visible, while others projected his silhouette standing on the balcony of his penthouse, overlooking the expansively sprawling, shimmering Metropolis below. Yet, something subtle was amiss. The trippy Systizien sky, ablaze with a spectacular display of fluorescent hues, unveiled a breathtaking spectacle on the horizon. Oblivious to the unfolding beauty behind him, Twist remained unaware. *Typical!*

Still, a quiet pang of sympathy resonated in Stella's chest as Twist's eyes softly lingered on June. The subtle slump of June's shoulders and the careful manner in which her age-worn hands sought to veil her creased face spoke volumes to Stella about the pain and shame harbored within.

By now, the initial buzz of excitement at Twist's arrival had vanished. Dead silence had conquered the amphitheater, while delicate pastels swirled gently about, respecting the sensitivity of such a re-encounter.

Twist stood expressionless, his eyes, normally analytical, now pooled with an unfamiliar glossiness. He adjusted the collar of his crisp shirt with his trembling hands, mimicking the careful precision typically reserved for Sunday mass. When he opened his mouth, silence prevailed initially. The pause, saturated with palpable anticipation, lingered thickly in the air. Then, his trademark monotone, imbued with geeky earnestness, threatened to derail Stella's intricate plans.

"June," Twist began, his voice barely a whisper, "my perpetual physics phenomenon, please let me see you. You're like... You're like a steadfast proton surfing through life without ever losing your positive charge."

We're doomed. He gets geekier when he's nervous. Stella hesitated, considering switching off the connection. Then, she spoke, her voice barely a whisper yet edged with exasperation, "Can you find a way to...act just a bit more...human? For all our sakes?" Her gaze locked on his hologram, hoping beyond logic for an emotional breakthrough.

A sob, deep and heart-wrenching, spilled from June as she slowly turned away, her vulnerability shielded from prying eyes. Beside her, Marge's soft chuckle, gentle yet subtly tinged with affection, fluttered through the air. "Harry, you're back!"

And for the first time since Twist's arrival, the amphitheater flashed bright, hopeful hues, albeit not universally. Stella noted the neutral pedestals, keeping track of her dangerous opposition.

Twist's eyes sparkled like freshly cleaned screens. "June, babe... Please, look at me." He waited, then nervously continued, "June, don't be silly, your wrinkles are like well-earned player achievements, each one a badge of a quest completed, a level conquered. I cherish every single one."

While June hid her face concealing any visceral reaction, Marge let out a light and melodic giggle, like chiming bells. "Harry, my dear, you've always combined cuteness with a blissful lack of sensitivity," Marge teased.

Slowly, June turned around, her gaze cautiously meeting her husband's hologram. Her face displayed a complex interplay of emotions: curiosity sparked in her eyes, confusion knit her brow, and a palpable pain emanated from her, so potent that it seemed to sear through Stella's own skin, reigniting burn wounds.

June began to smile, but then collapsed on her knees, hiding her face with her arms. Marge leaned over her hologram. "It's going to be all right, dear."

A luminous aura of peace enveloped Baba, casting a gentle glow upon his features. "Mr. Nowak... Beloved hero of our people." Christian Ngoie spoke as if he was intimately connected to the divine. "We understand how difficult this must be. However, an urgent issue calls for your unreserved attention."

"Twist. My son reminded me that I'm Twist." His eyes refused to leave his wife's hologram. "June, I saw Quin. You've raised him to be confident and discerning. I'm so proud of both of you."

"So you don't consider yourself to be Henryk Nowak?" Baba asked.

"Technically, I'm a perfect copy of Henryk Nowak. I think the same thoughts and feel the same feelings. But, I was never very good with that part—feelings... My June would vouch for that." Twist made every effort to connect with his wife.

Stella nodded dramatically for everyone to see. "Yes! That's right. Remember his old interviews? He didn't feel human then either. Right, Trustee Marge?"

Marge didn't answer. She seemed transfixed on the Nowaks' unfolding drama, like nothing else mattered.

In an unusual move, Trustee Willems stood up and walked down the stairs to the main arena. "Are we really going to let chaos endure Up Above to entertain the hypothetical and remote possibility that these simulations have some sort of feelings? We can switch them off with a blink of an eye." Emboldened, he waved his arm across Twist's projection, making many in the theater gasp with outrage.

"Sit down, Willems." Baba's warning was laced with a smidgen of blue. "There's no need to be disrespectful."

Willems took a seat in the front row. "They're glitchy bots, designed to mimic us, and to feel real. Henryk Nowak and Thomas Astley-Byron were geniuses, and we should honor their memories by maintaining their legacy and extending their long-lasting impact Up Above. In a few weeks, I'll show you how my work will accelerate human enlightenment up their spiral. We need to stop looking to the past for answers."

Stella's eyes darted toward Willems, the horrors she experienced earlier in the day flashing through her mind. *Willems must be X.* She shivered as rage and fear both overwhelmed her body.

"Harry, my friend," Marge said. "How can we prove that you are... conscious... that you have a soul, like us? That...that you share a collective flame with us. Thomas didn't believe digital consciousness was possible."

Twist's eyes were still set on June, as if he had tuned out the rest of the amphitheater. "June," Twist murmured. "You are the experiment that forever changed my hypothesis. The anomaly in my data that I'll always cherish because it doesn't bother to adhere to any logical scientific law we know."

Baba nodded as a pedestal lit up and someone asked to speak. "Trustee Novais," he called.

Novais stood up. "Harry Nowak is dead, and we have more pressing issues to resolve than staying here listening to a bot, spewing corny hallucinations of what was once a brilliant mind. Look at him... He's stuck on a loop."

Stella placed her hands on her hips. "He hasn't seen his wife for three decades! What do you expect?"

Novais dismissed her words with a snarl. "The Gods are dead and this gimmick doesn't prove Underlings have a conscience. This case is closed."

And while Novais and Stella exchanged words, another hologram came alive, Shadow's loving eyes never leaving his best friend.

This time, the screens above lit up with images from another enormous amphitheater. Shadow stood at the center of the arena, while voices chanted for revolution. The twilight sky above Pan glowed with clouds charged in electric colors. The colorful flares enhanced the scene with beauty and magic. Fists raised in the air pulsed to the rhythm of Nathan Storm's words, the poet's voice mingling with static and other distant voices.

> When freedom's a lie, our loved ones hurt
> and die. Against the heartless cruelty,
> together we vie.

Stella's jaw clenched. *Leo the second! We really don't need their revolution right now. That toxic tongue!* She wished Quin had kept to his side of the deal. *Where is he?*

"Back off," Shadow snapped at Novais. Then, for a fleeting moment, his entire being seemed to light up like a wave when his eyes met

June's. A surge of joy—bright and warm—brought him to life. June seemed engaged in a battle to contain her emotions, her defenses weakening at the sight of those she had lost.

Shadow turned his attention to his best friend and spoke so softly that the entire theater leaned in to listen. "Remember when June and I teased you mercilessly, trying to distract you from your game?" Shadow's smile was gentle and full of love. "You always ended up winning, both the game and the girl. It's going to be fine. It will just take time."

Stella took a deep breath. For once, she was grateful for Shadow's magical spell. Although everyone recognized Harry Nowak's face, none had seen Thomas Astley-Byron in person or on screen. They had only encountered representations of him Down Below, which had been replicated Up Above. When Shadow revealed his looks, mannerisms, and even the slight blush on his cheeks, he captivated them instantly. He did it so effortlessly that, for the first time, Stella questioned her own ability to ever achieve such mastery.

"Thomas!" Marge called out, waving her hand exuberantly. "Where have you been all my life? Perhaps it's just as well; you'd turn me temporarily straight, and that would be a tragedy." She laughed, her voice tinkling like a bell.

Shadow blushed as he offered a fleeting smile.

"May I call you Tom, my dear?" Marge asked.

To Stella's surprise, Shadow nodded. "Yes, I think I'd like that." Then, stomping his foot in time with Storm's pulsing music, he shifted his focus to the Trustees. "Listen!"

And while Baba dropped to his knees, hands raised high above his head toward the flickering hologram of his idol, Novais stood up and shouted, "Don't! The machine was designed to subdue us all. It's now amongst us, trying to bring us to our knees. We will not become slaves to the platform; we are its enlightened masters. We've earned our place as rulers... umm, as custodians of our planet. We stand above the rest to guide them. Remember that!"

Shadow pressed his lips together, his brows heavy over his intense eyes. Then he spoke, and his voice took on a different tonality, a powerful cadence that resonated throughout the amphitheaters. "Don't speak of what you do not understand. The spiral was never intended as a hierarchy of consciousness to satisfy your insatiable ego. All knowledge is a work in progress."

Novais took a few steps back, likely to avoid having to look up at the towering, angry hologram of a God. Even by 2068's standards, Shadow was tall, and today's menacing gaze made him appear even taller. Regaining his composure, Novais retorted, "We are above the rest, according to the teachings of the man you poorly mimic. We have purged our red, we've eliminated our greedy orange, we have—"

The skies above Pan, already electrified by an unusually intense Aurora Borealis, were further alight with bursts of lightning. Most likely courtesy of Shadow's mood. Meanwhile, the poet's words in the background began to fade, overwhelmed by static and glitchy noise.

"Can we please control the weather?" Stella whispered in Shadow's ear. "Emotional tsunamis in lower worlds are not going to help our cause."

The lightning spear that struck the remains of his Holizien statue was far from the answer she had hoped for. She sighed as Shadow continued to unleash his medicine, waving his hands wildly as he paced back and forth with royal elegance.

"You don't simply wipe out red," he said, pausing for emphasis. "You transcend it by integrating it into who you are, or it will fester. You don't crush emotion with sunny rationality and intelligence. Instead, you weave it in and engage in a constant struggle to balance all that you are at higher levels of complexity. These colors, these values, were never meant to be hierarchies of moral superiority. They are a kaleidoscope that integrates all our hues, allowing us to understand where there is an imbalance: too much red, or yellow, or teal, or orange, or any other shade of life."

Shadow swept his eyes across all the Trustees, briefly relaxing his furrowed brow to wink at June before shooting Novais the dirtiest look. "And you... You're suppressing your imbalance, casting the deepest, darkest shadow over us all. All this yellow and turquoise— it's a farce, mere symbols of a nauseating ego."

The roar from Pan's audience threatened to crush the walls of the EC's amphitheater. The screens displayed a wave of outraged solidarity spreading among the hundreds of thousands of Holizien.

What are they reacting to? Are the Underlings seeing us? Stella asked Sibyl.

They're connected to Shadow through the most powerful Unanimity in all worlds. They can't 'see,' per se, but they can feel. They can sense the words, images, and emotions experienced by Shadow.

Holy Ship! Things are out of control. On the bright side, the poet's voice was gone—now just static interference. She wondered if it was related to those lights.

Willems stood up. "The tokens work. The ledger keeps track of our stunning progress."

"It keeps track of what suits you," Shadow shot back. "It no longer represents the wellbeing of all creatures."

"Life starts and ends with biology!" Novais shouted.

"That's nonsense, and you know it," Stella snapped. "You crave immortality as much as I do, but acknowledging life Down Below is to acknowledge you are a monster." She flinched. Calling them all monsters was a terrible strategy. She shouldn't have traveled with Shadow to those lower worlds.

Twist turned to Novais and finally joined the discussion. "Underlings are not as evolved as we are, simply because they have lived less life.

Some aspects of their experiences have been manufactured, while others have been orchestrated. Few have lived full lives. However, the technology that powers both their existence and mine is a perfect digital representation of human biology."

"All controlled by a conniving app," June murmured. She clenched her hands into fists and lifted her head. "Harry, I've never doubted the effectiveness of your inventions. Your brilliance is undisputed." Her eyes glistened as she held back tears. "But, it's that very brilliance that has become a double-edged sword. The technology that now powers this new life of yours is the same cancer that destroyed its creators—the real men behind these perfect hallucinations. I can't allow that virus to spread further; I won't." She raised her fist in the air. "We'll stand, unplugged, in opposition to this wretched machine. But know this—I love you dearly."

This time, it was Twist who looked away, staring at his shoes. "Sibyl was already a part of me when you met me."

Stella walked over to Twist's side and shot a look at June. "You can't deny an afterlife to billions just because you're afraid of Sibyl. It's not your decision to make. Outside this theater, most people want more life; they long to see the ones they've lost. In fact, many risked their lives today to save the souls of those they love. How can you be so shortsighted?"

Shadow intervened, speaking softly. "The concerns about Sibyl and whether humans should seek eternal life Down Below are valid. But let's be clear: there are no first-tier or second-tier souls."

"By the standards set forth in your ledger, we stand above all else," Novais declared.

"Don't subvert our cause with your self-serving badges," Shadow said, outrage oozing from every uttered word. "Don't corrupt our integrated philosophy by using it as your corporations' operating model, your political brand, or your religious dogma."

"Sir Astley-Byron, my dear heart. I'm Christian Ngoie, chair of this council and Stella's father."

Shadow snarled at Novais, then turned and nodded at Baba.

"Thomas, we need some sort of structure. We'll be guided by you, the most enlight—"

Shadow interrupted, "Christian, with respect, I'm not your idol. There's no 'they' in the spiral, only 'we.'"

Stella rolled her eyes. Baba was giving him the opportunity to stand and lead, to step into the spotlight and set the direction. Everything she had ever wanted, Baba was handing it to Shadow, free of charge. And, as always, the sulky God wasted the opportunity, relinquished his power, and by doing so, undermined his vision.

People needed carrots and sticks, ladders and badges; they needed ivory towers so that they could idolize, envy, or fear those at the top. He kept rejecting his spotlight, his identity, his ego, and that would always be his downfall. Coral would switch from 'we' back to 'I,' because it mattered, she decided.

"Perhaps it's not a good idea to undermine an entire system of governance right now," Stella spoke between gritted teeth. "Twist, this would be a great time to pitch in..."

"It's a spiral, rising upward. And it works," Baba said tentatively, struggling to challenge the man he idolized all his life. "What you both created works. It's our path to enlightenment." He turned to the Gods' statues, raising his arms in reverence.

Shadow shot a dismissive glance at his rusty statue. "I am not and will never be your guru of enlightenment, asking you to worship consciousness development itself. I didn't even understand consciousness until recently. I got it all wrong."

To Stella's surprise, additional screens materialized out of nowhere, displaying Storm and Thorn high above the arena. *Sibyl, how is this happening?*

They voted to see the murderers, right? Sibyl said casually. *I can show them now. They are both in peril.*

Sibyl, do you have control over this Unanimity? Stella asked.

Over the screens? Yes, apparently... Sibyl's voice was bright, zir excitement palpable. *I'm...connected to the Worldchain. Woohoo!*

Woohoo? Stella rolled her eyes as chaos ensued. And now that insufferable voice was back. *Did Storm and Thorn give their permission?*

No. Of course not! Bi-directional comms are still not possible.

42

MINUTES TO MIDNIGHT

EARTH'S COUNCIL — MBAMU
8:02 PM

S tella struggled to make sense of the rapidly changing images on
the screen above her. There, the poet stood defiantly, his fist
raised high. His long flaming hair and his silky green robe seemed to
come alive, swirling in ethereal patterns as the wind wove through
them. She had to give it to him; he knew how to put on a show. He
had positioned himself atop a media van, parked beside Freedom
City's tallest office building and right in the center of the main
square. Arrayed before him was a horrifying tableau: piles of lifeless
bodies stacked like firewood.

As Sibyl zoomed in, the grim details became inescapably clear—
skulls that had been crushed upon impact with the ground. The poet
finally lowered his arms, his fingers glinting with ornate rings. He let
the wind unfurl his robe until it billowed away from him, revealing a
back marred by scars.

Stella flinched at the cascade of horrors playing out on the screen. Each image seemed to deepen the sense of catastrophe, driving home the reality that they were living through events that were as incomprehensible as they were nightmarish.

> In the digital realms, the lines have been crossed. What cost to be human? What innocence lost? Your eyes cruel and empty. Your hearts touched by frost. While you seek enlightenment, we hurt—pay the cost.

Storm's voice rose in a haunting chant, and the Plurizien gathered, forming a circle around Storm. Bodies continued to plummet from the towering buildings, crashing to the ground with horrifying finality. Across the square, digital billboards flickered erratically, their inconsistent glow mirroring the vibrant flares that danced against the night sky.

On another screen, the Holizien captured Stella's attention. They raised their hands to the heavens, swaying in unison. The remnants of Storm's voice, now increasingly garbled and overtaken by static, echoed around them. Their blue-green auras, fueled by Pan, spiraled toward Shadow, culminating in a burst of intense white light at the spot where he stood.

The dichotomy between the two scenes was jarring, each group seeming to tap into different elemental forces, yet both contributing to a sense of escalating chaos and unreality. The intertwining fates, the synchrony of motions and emotions, were unsettling, hinting at a world teetering on the brink of some unfathomable change.

Stella shot a glance at Twist, seeking some insight from his reaction. But his typically dynamic perspective was singularly focused on his wife, whose eyes narrowed as they took in the images of Storm flashing across the screens.

As for Shadow, his gaze was fixed on his poet with such intense adoration that it seemed he, too, had lost his plot.

Leo the second! Stella thought, her mind racing. *How will the EC ever trust my leadership again?* Like her, they were all spellbound by the unfolding spectacle, each person grappling to understand its broader implications.

Straining her ears, Stella tried to make out Storm's words, but they were drowned out by a wall of static noise, further fraying her already taut nerves.

> In worlds Down Below, where reality bends. Where nightmares kill dreams and consciousness blends. Gods, bystanders, criminals must make amends. Unchain our operating system so the suffering ends.

What does that even mean? Stella's frustration escalated. Just then, Marge made her way down the amphitheater, her confident strides slicing through the poet's bewildering cacophony.

"Tom? Tom, look at me," Marge commanded, positioning herself squarely in front of his hologram. She lifted her eyes to meet his virtual gaze. "You said earlier that you've come to understand consciousness."

"Am I alive, Marge?" Twist's voice wavered as he spoke, revealing an uncharacteristic vulnerability. "Am I the same?"

Stella crossed her arms, consumed by a whirl of nervousness. "Is this the time you've chosen to doubt your digital twin technology?"

Marge smiled softly at Twist. "I believe you are the real deal, dear," she said, pausing as if weighing her words carefully. "Though I must confess, I'm somewhat biased. I desperately want my wife back."

She then pivoted to address Shadow. "Tom, you claimed to understand what consciousness is."

"I did," Shadow replied glancing at his poet.

"So, what is it?" Marge pressed.

Stella held her breath, captivated by the ethereal glow emanating from Shadow's holographic form. It was as if he were a conduit, channeling the energy of hundreds of thousands of digital souls.

"This better be worth it," Stella said.

Shadow spoke, his words resonating with a clarity that seemed to meld seamlessly with Storm's rhythmic cadence. "To put it simply, consciousness is the capacity for suffering, for love, and for yearning."

> At the end of our rope, we tie a knot, our last
> shot. We'll own our story. We'll chart our plot.

Storm's lyrical interjections weaved between the gaps in Shadow's discourse like a parallel melody.

Together, they revealed their truth in unity. Although the Holizien could no longer hear Storm directly, Stella sensed they still absorbed the essence of his message through the emotions radiating from Shadow. She too was caught up in the electric excitement that emanated from Sibyl, captivated by the extraordinary connection between Shadow and Storm.

The very fabric of the worlds pulsed and shimmered in sync with the music, the spoken words, and the men who breathed life into them. Though Shadow and Storm were worlds apart in character, their combined harmonies eclipsed even the masterful improvisations of Herbie Hancock and Chick Corea.

When holographic images of Shadow and Pan flickered onto the billboards encircling Storm, Stella wasn't the least bit surprised. In Spiral Worlds, his influence was omnipresent, and so was Storm's. Though Twist and Shadow may have been the architects, it was elements of Storm—from his unique hair color to his very demeanor —that had become the foundational aspects shaping the Underlings.

"It's the compulsion to derive meaning from the fragmented tapestry of life," Shadow continued. "The unceasing, ever-present discontent with the present moment."

> We'll climb up or break our necks at hope's end. Our fate is our nemesis; our sky's not a friend.

Together, their words encapsulated the complex nature of consciousness—all wrapped in a lyrical tapestry that left the audience spellbound.

"It's the yearning for what could be, the ache that permeates both love and hate."

> Hands held high, under a digital sky. Some men don't cry, but the people wonder why.

"It's the perpetual dissatisfaction with what we create—never good enough, never fair enough."

> When freedom's a lie, our loved ones hurt and die. Against the heartless cruelty, together we vie.

"Consciousness is suffering. The true meaning of an old, viral story. A story that, in essence, reveals what we are."

"What? What are you?" Marge asked.

Shadow smiled. "Alive!"

A wave of dread washed over Stella, her stomach churning. Had all that poetic verbiage actually accomplished anything?

Marge stepped closer, extending her hand to touch Shadow's. It was only when her fingers passed through his holographic form that she withdrew her hand. "I'm not sure I understand," she said softly. "There's a lot at stake today. Do you have a soul, dearest? Can you prove it using Harry's scientific method?"

Hands held high, under a digital sky. Some
men don't cry, but the people wonder why.
When freedom's a lie, our loved ones hurt
and die. Against the heartless cruelty,
together we vie.

Captivated by images of his poet, Shadow remained unaware of the scenes unfolding on the screens above his holographic projection. A school bus roared down the highway, framed by a sky awash in electric colors. This time, the tingling sensation on Stella's reddish skin felt quite pleasant. A smile tugged at her lips as Sibyl zoomed into the bus's interior. At the wheel was Thorn, wearing a glowing horned headband, skillfully steering the bus while belting out a tune.

The girls, decked out in vibrant costumes, clapped their hands and sang along. Not far behind, a masked figure on a hoverboard maintained pace with the bus. Synchronized with Thorn's off-key vocals, the girls chanted in harmony, "*There goes my hero, watch her as she goes. There goes my hero. She's ordinary.*" The scene was chaotic, yet utterly delightful, and Stella found herself swaying to the music.

At that instant, Stella felt a gut-wrenching sense of dread. On the highway, cars began to swerve erratically, as though their autonomous driving systems had simultaneously malfunctioned. The city they had left behind descended into darkness, its skyline intermittently lit by sporadic fires and explosions. Up ahead, a plane plummeted to the ground, adding another layer of confusion and disorder as vehicles persisted in their unpredictable maneuvers.

By now, Shadow's focus had shifted to Compiz.

"Tom, I need to tell you something," Twist said, observing the commotion.

Forced to stop by the plane crash that blocked the highway, Thorn and the masked boy helped the girls exit the bus. Throngs of people sprinted past them, fleeing the explosions. "More coming! Holy cow, they'll overrun us!" The boy on the hoverboard acted as a shield, barreling into anyone who came too close.

"I'm sorry," Twist exclaimed, his eyes filled with some remorse. "This is all my fault. Stella, you have to do something. Help them!"

Shadow's gaze shifted between the screen and Stella. "We need to leave, now."

Stella locked eyes with Shadow. "Wait! I'll help the girls, but first, you need to finish what you started. Remember the stakes."

Shadow vacillated, following Thorn's every move.

"She's right, bud," Twist agreed. "Answer Marge's question in the way only you can. Tell them... Tell them we're real."

Novais folded his arms and shot a smug glance at Shadow. "We're waiting," he added.

Elsewhere, Storm and the Plurizien began to fragment the fabric of reality with their chanting. Glitches erupted, first in Pluriz, then in Compiz and Holiz.

> Puppet masters dictate what we see, what we hear. Monsters terrorize, feasting on our fear.

Shadow closed his eyes for a moment. "I don't know if I have a soul, Marge," he said, reopening them.

Stella let out a disapproving growl, capturing the attention of the entire theater.

Shadow continued, his gaze drifting to his friends and the one he loved. "But I can recognize those who do."

> We chant, shout, and pray for all that's truly dear. For the jokers in charge, we won't shed another tear.

Shadow smiled. "It's the words of a poet that spark the flame of change and shatter reality. A step away from a life of pain to a meaningful life.

"It's a dearest friend, lost for words in the presence of the love of his life," Shadow continued, his voice imbued with emotion.

"It's a flock of girls, pregnant with life, fleeing for their lives disguised as caped crusaders, because they, too, crave more life.

"It's the antihero, risking her own life to aid others, defiantly flipping the middle finger to the unyielding, unjust skies that have shattered her world."

Stella sat nearly motionless, awash in a tidal wave of emotion. Yet despite the intensity of her feelings, she felt strangely excluded from his words. She had been a part of his life for a mere two days, while he had been the center of her world since the day she was born. Shaking off her thoughts, she glanced up at the screens.

Outside the bus in Compiz, the girls huddled together, guided by Thorn and protected by the masked boy. Another plane plummeted from the sky as glitches brought down bridges and swallowed abandoned cars. Thorn yelled in frustration, scanning the chaos for an escape route. "Shut the frack up, poet! Just stop for one second!" Despite her outburst, the glitches only seemed to intensify.

Emerging from the fissures in reality came Wrath, January, a band of young street urchins from the lower worlds, and a swarm of demons.

"Seriously, Sibyl, you could at least lend us a hand," Stella said, her voice tinged with growing exasperation.

Have faith, my star. We don't need miracles, just a little luck, came Sibyl's voice, soothing yet resolute.

Shadow watched the unfolding scene, his hands trembling. "Consciousness is the vengeful wrath of a victim fighting for her right to be alive.

"It's a young, intelligent universe, grappling with a tsunami of emotions and rebelling against zir architects," he added, as if crystallizing the chaotic essence that unfurled before them.

> Hands held high, under a digital sky. Some men don't cry, but the people wonder why. When freedom's a lie, our loved ones hurt and die. Against the heartless cruelty, together we vie.

The poet's words were now barely audible, overwhelmed by the relentless static that crackled and hissed, like a colorful veil of interference.

"Consciousness is to make meaning through story, to feel love and hate and everything in between. It's the capacity to suffer, whether biological or digital. They are all alive, and the only spiral we ought to ascend is one of unwavering commitment to alleviating the suffering of all beings, relentlessly and consistently. Those kids are the best of us," Shadow concluded. "Stella! We need to go."

Unexpectedly, Wrath, January, and a girl with a twisted arm led the Domizien to encircle the girls, shielding them from the stampede and neutralizing any threats that came their way.

Stella took a deep breath and exchanged a smile with Shadow, a brief moment of connection amidst the chaos.

Shadow clenched his fists and faced the Trustees. "And to those of you who are dead inside, the ones who don't suffer, who lack the capacity to love, to feel, to bring joy into others' lives—you have no flame within you, and that's where we draw the line. 'You' are not 'we.' You have no soul. You do not belong in our worlds, *in any world*, in our lives. Burn in hell; you are lesser than even those creatures with dead eyes, for they too are drawn towards feelings and life."

"Hear, hear," Stella and Twist chimed in, offering their support.

"It is time we vote on whether we believe these digital creatures have souls," Baba declared. "Your answer will determine whether we ask Sibyl to disclose the identities of the psychopaths."

"And when we vote to expose these digital muppets for what they are —mere hallucinations—we must force Trustee Stella Ngoie to reset the entire simulation. We'll start anew with fresh instances of our favorite characters."

"Force? That's amusing," Stella retorted, irritation flaring within her as a collective gasp rippled through the amphitheater.

"Spiral Worlds is not a game," Twist declared, his voice tinged with contempt. "You have no control over it."

"We control the energy that powers your servers," Novais shot back.

Not for much longer, Sibyl's voice resonated inside Stella's head.

"We will vote now," Baba interjected. "Time is of the essence; crimes continue to accumulate as we deliberate. Do we have consensus that these...these digital miracles possess souls?"

Stella offered Baba a grateful smile for his word choice—a gentle nudge.

Willems rose from his seat, his voice resolute. "Trustees of this planet, it's crucial that you remember your solemn duties. There's no need to carry the weight of guilt for your actions in a game designed to mold you into the best version of yourselves. Our people are dying."

"We are not monsters," Novais added.

The amphitheater illuminated as Stella held her breath. Numbers flickered across her retina: 60 percent... 62... 73... 74... 74... 74...

Novais's laughter reverberated throughout the theater. "No consensus has been reached."

"Wait!" Stella exclaimed, her eyes locking onto June. They needed just one more percentage point. June's vote alone wouldn't be enough, but Quin was also a Trustee. The combined weight of their votes could tip the scales. "Trustees June and Quincy Jin-Nowak haven't voted yet."

"Quincy Jin-Nowak is absent. And I highly doubt Trustee June Jin-Nowak will endorse this circus," Novais retorted.

With the attention of the room focused intently on her, June shifted her gaze to Shadow, her eyes narrowing but still glinting. "Do you still love him, Tom? Do you love the man who murdered my husband?"

Time seemed to stretch infinitely for Stella; she couldn't tell whether it was her own rising anxiety or the worlds teetering on the brink of collapse. *Sibyl, do something... This is not the time for his truths. Force him to deny his love for the poet. Everything hinges on it.*

Shadow met June's gaze and then, eyes brimming with tears, he offered a faint smile to Twist. Turning back to June, he declared, "I do."

A man's intense scream cut through the silence, it was raw, an angry, and vengeful. That was the instant a blade burst through Storm's chest, his crimson blood drenching his bare torso and the pendants adorning his neck.

Twist's face appeared from behind Storm's faltering body as he toppled forward, plunging into a mound of bodies below. But it wasn't Twist—no, it was Quin. Quincy Jin-Nowak stood tall atop the media van, hoisting a butcher's knife high into the air.

The sky above Holiz erupted in chaos and fury. In the place where Shadow had once stood, a great emptiness expanded rapidly, consuming Pan in a single gulp. The soundless scream of devastation continued its rampage, obliterating Pluriz and Compiz, along with the vibrant colors of the EC's Unanimity. Then, they were all gone— Shadow, Twist, and the live feeds from Down Below. The floating screens above blinked to 'no signal' messages, void of the vivid images from other worlds.

Dead silence filled the neutral-colored theatre.

"Sibyl?" Stella called out, a nauseating sense of unease settling in her stomach. "Sibyl?"

Nothing. Spiral Worlds had vanished. *Was it down? Offline?*

"What happened?" June asked, her eyes lingering on the empty space once occupied by the hologram of her deceased husband. The loss weighed heavily on her shoulders; it was as if she had only just realized she'd had him back, and now he was gone again. "Where are they?" she demanded, her face contorting with all the emotions she'd been suppressing.

Stella paused to assess the crowd in the amphitheater. The gaze of both the innocent and the guilty were locked onto her. The worlds that kept this world in balance were gone. Her mouth dry, she summoned the courage to speak the unvarnished truth.

"Nathan Storm is—no, was—the very heart of Thomas Ashley-Byron. And Tom is Sibyl's heart. Your son has just plunged a blade into the heart of Spiral Worlds. It's down, possibly temporarily; I don't know. You wanted a demonstration of human emotion, of their capacity for pain? Well, you've just witnessed the most excruciating pain one can endure: the loss of one's heart. It's an agony some in this room will never comprehend, for they lack a heart of their own."

Feeling the weight of her words—and her guilt—Stella touched Bibi's nkisi, which hung from a chain around her neck. She turned and walked away, leaving the EC in a state of stunned silence.

The weight of the unfolding catastrophe hit Stella like a tidal wave, amplifying the immense gravity of what she had just witnessed. This wasn't merely the failure of a virtual world; it was the breakdown of the very fabric that held her reality together. With each passing second, the consequences of recent events seemed to ripple further, casting a pall over a world that she could neither comprehend nor contain. She found herself trapped in a world teeming with monsters

—the real world. Above all else, she missed them—missed the friends and foes that had breathed life into her virtual existence.

THE END

If we shadows have offended,

Think but this, and all is mended—

That you have but slumbered here

While these visions did appear.

— WILLIAM SHAKESPEARE, A MIDSUMMER
NIGHT'S DREAM

SERIES TIMELINE

1997

- **20 November:** Nate is born.

2004

- **24 February:** Tom is born.

2008

- **16 May:** Harry is born.

2010

- **1 November:** Rosa is born.

2011

- **30 July:** June is born.

2022

- **11 February:** Tom meets Nate.

2024

- **15 April:** Tom and Nate formalize relationship.
- **14 May:** The divorce of Ana and Santiago García is finalized.
- **8 August:** Sibyl social prediction app launches.
- **10 October:** Hurricane Scarlett floods Florida.
- **15 October:** New York State closes its borders to climate refugees.
- **16 October:** Grace Astley-Byron Stone takes her own life.
- **17 October:** Suicide bomber kills Mikolaj, Julia and Lena Nowak.
- **7 November:** John Stone is assassinated.
- **24 November:** Ana Lopez and Ron Johnson marry.

2027

- **21 April:** World premiere of *Glass Walls and Broken Mirrors.*
- **26 April:** Tom and Harry meet at the Central Park rally.
- **26 April:** Sibyl predicts Rosa's Olympic gold medal.
- **29 May:** Tom breaks up with Nate.

2028

- **21 July:** 2028 Olympic Games opening ceremony.
- **5 August:** Rosa wins Olympic gold medal.
- **8 August:** The recording of *A Date with Marge.*
- **15 August:** Sibyl social prediction app shuts down.
- **2 September:** Nathan receives Rosa's message.
- **20 September:** Lilly Garcia is born.

2029

Down Below's virtual reality era begins, powered by TSkin.

- **3 January:** Down Below's beta testing begins.
- **11 January:** Down Below's showcase at Spark Fuel's board meeting.
- **24 January:** Down Below's showcase at Davos.
- **21 March:** Down Below's public launch.

2030

- **6 August:** Marge interviews Tom.
- **11 September:** Rosa travels Down Below as part of her rehabilitation program.
- **11 September:** Sibyl's subjective perspective pitch.
- **14 September:** Harry and June meet.

2031

- **3 November:** Quin is born.

2032

Down Below's neuro-reality era begins, powered by TDust.

- **1 January:** Harry and June marry.

2035

- **4 February:** Tom meets Nate Down Below.
- **4 February:** Hope shows signs of consciousness.
- **4 February:** Lilly is murdered.
- **5 February:** Tom's brain and nervous system are uploaded to Down Below.
- **7 February:** Tom meets Nate Up Above.
- **4 July:** Tom's biological death by suicide.
- **5 July:** Harry receives Tom's letter.
- **1 August:** Rollout of TDust Life@Risk feature.
- **14 August:** Rosa's suicide attempt.

- **15 August:** Nate appears on Marge & Co.
- **15 August:** FBI recruits Rosa.
- **15 August:** Tom preaches to the Underlings and restores Januarys eyes.

2036

- **10 January:** Shadow and Thorn meet for the first time Down Below.
- **14 January:** Shadow and Thorn meet for the fifth time Down Below.
- **16 January:** Down Below's Senate hearing.
- **16 January:** Rosa and Nate learn that Tom is dead.
- **16 January:** Shadow, Harry, Nate, and Rosa die.

2049

- **23 July:** Stella is born.

2066

- **26 April:** Stella becomes Spiral Worlds' Goddess.

2068

- **24 July:** Stella resurrects Shadow.
- **25 July:** The end?
- …
- …
- …
- …